By the same author:

THE
HANDS
OF THE
EMPEROR

ISBN: 978-1-988908-14-4

First published by Underhill Books in 2019.

Underhill Books

4183 Murray Harbour Road

Grandview, PEI C0A 1A0

www.underhillbooks.com

THE
Hands
OF THE
Emperor

A Novel of the Nine Worlds

VICTORIA GODDARD

Underhill
Books

Grandview, PEI

2018

To all those who work to change the world from within the system, and especially to Anita and Charles, whose dedication to their work is only matched by their hospitality: thank you.

VOLUME ONE

THE MEETING PLACE OF IKI AND ANI

CHAPTER ONE

IT WAS AN INDICATION OF Cliopher Mdang's status in the eyes of his lord that he was given the use of a sky ship for personal business.

Of course, Cliopher mused as he looked up from his reports to see the Vangavaye-ve suddenly there below him, that was being generous. He was from so very far away from Solaara that every other method of getting to Gorjo City was measured in months, not days. It had been many years since he could take six months off at a time.

The ship heeled as it began the spiralling descent. Out of his porthole window Cliopher saw thethe familiar landmarks of the Outer Ring: the narrow Gates of the Sea permitting egress from the Bay of the Waters; the Five Sisters; all the sweep of reefs and islands and volcanic mounts, remnants of the prehistoric supervolcano that had formed the archipelago.

He loved the view down, the bright turquoise of the shallow lagoons, the darker blues of the Bay of the Waters, the green jungle and white beaches. He permitted himself to watch for a few minutes, until the ship brought him round to the full glare of the sun, whereupon he resolutely turned back to the report he was writing about the state of affairs in Nijan, half an ocean away.

He had almost finished when the shouts of the sailors changed in tone and urgency. The movement of the vessel shifted at the same time, righting itself and slowing appreciably. He had packed his luggage earlier, so all he had to do was mark his spot, layer the documents back into their case, set that into the shoulder bag of travelling clothes and presents, and clean and stow away his pens and ink into his writing kit.

All this accomplished, he slung the bag over his shoulder, tucked his writing kit into its familiar spot in the crook of his arm, and gathered the four finished dispatch cases in his free hand. Because it was not one of his usual holidays he had felt obliged to keep up his work until the last minute.

He smiled to himself. He usually did keep working until the Vanga-vaye-ve came into sight. On this occasion his Radiancy's unexpected gift of an extra holiday had come when he had just begun writing up a set of reports about his last brilliant mad start, as the various members of his office called his more unconventional ideas. He preferred to call them his carefully developed plans for the betterment of the world.

He straightened one of the dispatch cases, which was showing a desire to slip out of his hold, and cast one further glance around the cabin to ensure he had not forgotten anything, especially any stray report. Once, when he was much younger, he had imagined that success would involve a reduction in the quantity of reports.

His faint smile widened into a grin, here where no one could see him so openly amused. He had learned better.

He'd also learned just what you could do with all those reports and how they were written and by whom and under what circumstances they were read.

At a sudden falling series of whistles from outside the room, Cliopher straightened his expression to his habitual mildness, exited his cabin decorously, and made his way to the rope and wood bridge two of the sailors had just finished lashing into place.

"Thank you, Captain Diogen," he said as he passed him.

"My pleasure, sir," the captain replied, saluting. "We'll pick you up two weeks from today. The third hour of the morning, that'll be."

"I shall be here," Cliopher assured him, shifting the dispatch cases slight-ly. He took a deep breath, tasting the air, that familiar scent of flowers and greenery and moisture and *home*. "Safe travels."

"Aye, you're my most punctual passenger. Till then, Sayo Mdang."

The captain saluted again, fist to temple. Cliopher bowed slightly—did *not* drop all the dispatch cases—and stepped onto the bridge, resolutely not looking down. Heights did not particularly bother him but he did intensely dislike looking between his feet to see land several hundred feet below.

On one occasion he had been forcibly escorted across the rope bridges of the Southern Grey Mountains, and he had never quite lost the memory of terror and helplessness. He had learned what he must do to cross the rope bridges between ship and Spire, however, and with his gaze trained on the wall before him he did not even need to catch his breath.

He stopped in the Light Minders' office at the top of the Spire. Princess Oriana was in Jilkano visiting her relatives, so only two people were on duty there, one for incoming and one for outgoing messages.

Cliopher's cousin Tya was one of the Light Minders, but she wasn't on duty this morning. "Some sort of family thing," the outgoing message taker said. Cliopher vaguely recognized her as a contemporary of his nephew, a minor wizard of about twenty. She looked at his cases. "Didn't you just get off the ship?"

"I did," he replied, setting the dispatch cases down on the counter. "These need to go to Solaara, please."

"I've always wanted to go on one of those ships," the other Minder said, turning in his chair from the scrying mirror. His brother had been in Cliopher's year at school, but he couldn't quite remember the Minder's name. "Oh, hello, Kip. No one said you were coming this month. Didn't you already have your holiday this year? Ah, well. It's not like the princess takes people for rides, and the only other ships that come in are on government business."

"Which this is," Cliopher said patiently, pushing the cases over. "The address is on the boxes—"

"We always send them to the same place anyway," the outgoing Minder said. "Practically everything either comes from or goes to you, Kip. I swear you're the very definition of the dedicated correspondent."

Cliopher chuckled obediently at this gentle barb and spent another couple of minutes asking questions about the Minders' families and connections to his own. The outgoing Minder finally promised to send his cases off to Solaara at the next turn of the Light, and Cliopher escaped the interrogation with a mild sense of relief.

The Light Minders' office was a small room at the top of a tall tower, next to the equally small room for the sky ship officials, which was empty. If he'd been on duty—but he wasn't, and it wasn't exactly his business whether the princess wished to keep track of visitors by sky ship or not.

There would not be many, in any case. The other princes rarely, if ever, made the long trek across the Wide Seas, which took days even by sky ship. As far as government business went, Cliopher came for his holidays once a year. Parcel deliveries to Princess Oriana would be more frequent, but that was it. Nothing much of world-affecting note ever happened in the Vangavaye-ve.

The upper portion of the tower was wrought iron painted white; the lower was stone, holding various magical devices and supplies for the princess' sky ship. Cliopher went down the tight spiral slowly, feeling his age in the protests from his knees and thighs.

He had not been exercising enough—he had been too busy—and he hoped, guiltily, that he would not need to participate in whatever family event was going on. Events meant feasts, and feasts meant dancing. And dancing, alas, was not quite as much fun as it used to be.

Cliopher dutifully admired the beauty of the provincial palace, halfway up the eastern slope of Mama Ituri's Son. He derived more pleasure from looking at the university grounds below the palace gardens. He had many fond memories of university studies and friends.

Below the university were a few grand houses and parks at the shoreline, meeting the boardwalks and bridges from the outcropping on which the Spire was located. The royal and university marinas took up the space between the two islands and the floating houses of Gorjo City proper.

He could not pick out his family home near the Tahivoa lagoon from this angle, but the network of canals, private pools, and lagoons, housing and business complexes, rooftop gardens and brightly-coloured sailboats, was every step more familiar and more beloved.

By the time he reached the bottom of the Spire he no longer felt like Cliopher Mdang, personal secretary to the Lord of Rising Stars, Secretary in Chief of the Private Offices of the Lords of State, official head of the Imperial Bureaucratic Service, unofficial head of the world's government, the Hands of the Emperor.

He was, instead, merely everyone's Cousin Kip, the one who left.

★★★

CLIOPHER WAS WEARING THE BASIC black and burnt umber linen robes of the upper secretariat, since he was technically on duty until he got off the sky ship but had no desire to muss his finery to no purpose. He had put on a third layer that morning, for the ship's cabin was cool.

Despite the fact that it was still early enough that the sunlight hadn't reached water level, by the time he got down the lower slope of Mama Ituri's Son he was overheating. He stopped at a row of benches by the university marina to take off his over-robe.

After he packed it into his bag, he leaned against the balustrade behind the benches to watch the activity in the marina.

Activity was not perhaps the right word; not even the pelicans were doing more than sitting on the mooring posts. The sunlight glittered on the water, a black cormorant flew low and swiftly across the open lagoon, the various craft bobbed gently. The university marina had a delightful assortment of vessels, ranging from small wooden dories to a half-finished replica of one of the ancient ocean-going ships, made out of balsa wood and banana leaves, in which his ancestors had crossed the Wide Seas.

He regarded the construction with mild interest, but was too far away to see what peculiarities of design might have gone into it. And it was not as if he knew what to look for, or at, not really. His own experience with a similar vessel had been one he'd made himself, and neither he nor his instructor had been particularly expert.

That had been long ago, long before the floating pines of Amboloyo had been discovered and turned into ships, and long, long before he'd warranted a ride in one. Just a few years after the Fall, in fact, when he had been determined to come home, whatever it took.

It had taken a solitary voyage across the Wide Seas in an eighteen-foot boat made by a clumsy, half-mad, uninitiated civil servant under the guidance of an old and crazy historian from the Isolates.

Cliopher watched the wavelets, the light breeze stirring his robes against his legs, remembering small moments of that journey. It was odd that it was the rope bridges that had left most indelible and undeniable impression on him. Perhaps it was because he was a Wide Sea Islander that the years-long voyage through typhoon and doldrum had faded so easily into the past, while that thirty-six-hour traverse of the Grey Mountains still prickled the back of his neck and visited his dreams.

He had been most pleased, a year or so ago, to accompany his Radiancy to the opening of a new stone bridge across the Haren Gap. None of the men, middle-aged and respectable chiefs of their communities, now, had recognized in the Hands of the Emperor the young man they had chased like a rabid dog across the ropes. He had smiled pleasantly at them and wished them well of the modern world and refused the laughing invitation to cross the old bridge before it collapsed completely.

He turned away from the ship. No, he did not need to look more closely to remember that.

A small pleasure yacht a few slips away being readied for a sail. A middle-aged man with his back to him fussed with ropes and sails. It was nice to watch someone else at work.

"Hoi!" the man on the yacht cried, half-turning. "Grab that rope?"

Cliopher hurried over to where he indicated, catching the mooring hawser before it slipped off the dock.

"Kip?"

Cliopher looked up to see his oldest friend. He smiled broadly. "Bertie!"

"Whatever are you doing here? For the *second* time this year! You didn't write to say you were coming."

"My lord gave me an extra holiday as a reward. It was rather last-minute. Where do you want this rope?"

Falbert Kindraa had ferociously bushy eyebrows, which he used to great effect when scowling, as he did indiscriminately on friends, family, students, or visitors to the university museum where he was Curator in Chief. Cliopher always contrasted them with the scowls of Prince Rufus of Amboloyo, which were half as effective and many times as mean.

"Bring it aboard. I'm heading off to fish for the day. Come with me?"

There were few things Cliopher could imagine enjoying more, just that moment, but he had a nagging sense that he should probably see his mother first. "My mama—and the Light Minders said that Cousin Tya was at some sort of family event—"

Bertie snorted explosively. "Are you not a grown man? Your mama isn't expecting you, is she?"

"Unless she saw the sky ship—"

"Which was here and gone so quickly I assumed it was a parcel delivery for the princess. Come, Kip, don't be absurd. Do you want to come?"

He still hesitated, knowing full well that his mother would expect him to see her first, no matter how attractive the thought of spending the day with Bertie was.

Falbert knew this, too, for he shook his head at him. "The family event is the hundred-day feast for your cousin Hillen's newest child. That's why I'm going fishing and why you definitely should come with me. You oughtn't countenance giving consequence to him."

"That's true."

"Not to mention your mama would undoubtedly prefer you come a day later and thus avoid any potential of you saying what you're thinking to your aunt Hilda."

"Oh, I think I could probably hold my tongue if I had to."

His friend made a face, as if Cliopher had said something strange, but then he smiled, and Cliopher shrugged off his own momentary unease with the thought that a hundred-day feast required not only dancing but also traditional finery. He had always kept his efela in Solaara as a reminder of home, and he did not relish trying to squeeze into an old costume that showed no evidence of anything he'd ever done in his life.

Bertie said, "But you've already been home this year, so you've done all the dutiful visits."

"That's also true," said Cliopher, grinning, and he stepped aboard.

***

"WHY DON'T YOU MAKE COFFEE while I get us on our way?" Bertie suggested, pointing him to a doorway at the stern. "You should be able to find everything right enough."

Through the door was a short ship's ladder leading into a bright and surprisingly spacious room. A minuscule galley faced a line of storage compartments with a bench running above them. A table was latched securely into place on the wall between two round portholes. A door at the far end suggested there was a head and further rooms beyond.

Falbert had written to him about this yacht, which he had bought on the occasion of a long sabbatical some years before. Cliopher had hoped he would come all the way to Solaara to visit him—Bertie had always claimed a dream to circumnavigate the world—but nothing had come of it. He had taken the boat on the month-long journey to the Isolates, however, and that meant it had to have space for stores and sleeping.

As Cliopher grew accustomed to the bobbing motion, he investigated cabinets, lowered the table, opened the ingeniously concealed cookstove. It was very similar to the one he had in his own apartments, the heat source an enchanted stone, though the aesthetics differed. He spent a moment figuring out the controls, which were the opposite of the ones on his but, he recalled after a few moments, the same as in his mother's house. Then he started looking for percolator and coffee.

The apparent orderliness of the space was belied by the chaos within the latched cupboards. He had to pull out half the dry goods before he found the bag of coffee grounds, and all of the pots before he found the percolator. He set the water on—the system of cistern and hot and cold pipes, again, up-to-date, as he saw when he peeked into their cupboard to check. Bertie clearly had not stinted himself on outfitting his yacht.

The boat was threading its way down the central canal, he saw as he glanced out the window to see the great buildings of the hotel district sliding past. He regarded his writing kit, which he'd set on the table, and then decided he *was* on holiday.

Bertie came in just as the coffee was ready and Cliopher, having finished organizing all the cupboards, was sitting to his report. Cliopher looked up when the shadow fell on him.

"Coffee's ready."

Bertie grunted and stumped over to the cupboard where the dishes were stowed. He took out a mug, closed the door, frowned, and opened the door again. Cliopher finished writing his sentence, shook the paper gently in the air to dry it, and watched as Bertie proceeded to open all the cabinets.

"Same old Kip," he said at last, pouring his coffee. "We're out of sight of Tahivoa, you can come on deck without fear of a stray cousin seeing you."

Cliopher put all his papers and pens and ink away again and followed him back out. Bertie went to the tiller and unlashed it. "Fair winds and a fair day ahead," he said as Cliopher found a spot against the railing to brace himself. "The unexpected pleasure of your company. Not to mention tidy cabinets."

"You must keep things orderly at the museum?"

Bertie snorted. "I don't bring my work home with me, unlike some people."

Cliopher turned his face to the sun and the breeze. "It's so lovely to be here. What have you been up to?"

Bertie harrumphed as he guided them carefully around two women sitting reading books under a shade umbrella in a small dory anchored to a marker buoy, fishing lines trailing unattended into the water. "The usual run of things. We've got a new exhibit opening up next month, so I've been busy getting everyone together. What about you? What were you writing up?"

"I just finished assessing the state of things in Nijan."

"That won you a holiday?"

He chuckled. "No, my lord gave me the time off because I've spent the last six months persuading the provinces to set up stockpiles of supplies in case of natural disaster, and I finally got the Jilkano princes to do their part."

"Good on you. Ghilly was involved with the stash here. That must have been five or six months ago, come to think of it. It amazes me that Princess Oriana was ahead of anyone."

"Princess Oriana will sign what I put in front of her," Cliopher said, hoping that was a big enough hint.

"She'll go wherever the wind blows strongest. Hold on, Kip, we're about to hit the cross-currents." He made a minute adjustment to the tiller angle.

Cliopher dumped out the remainder of his coffee so he could wrap his arm around the railing. He reminded himself once again that no one within the Ring cared very much about anything that happened outside of it.

The yacht leaped forward. He decided there was nothing else for it, and laughed.

CHAPTER *TWO*

NO ONE IN THE PALACE of Stars would call Cliopher Mdang a jester.

He was generally known (he hoped) to have a sense of humour, and his deputy Kiri roasted him with almost as little mercy as his family, but he did not deflect every incoming emotion with laughter. He took other people's words at face value, and expected them to take his own the same way. Despite the amusement he personally took in discomfiting other people by doing so, it always disconcerted him to come home and find his every statement of fact taken as a kind of elaborate joke.

After they had passed the turbulent cross-currents in the middle of the Bay, the sailing was smooth and exhilarating. Cliopher hung on to his railing and enjoyed watching Bertie at work. He could have managed the boat, but he would not have the grace of long practice his friend displayed.

"Aren't you hot in those dark robes?" Bertie demanded suddenly.

Cliopher was, but had been disregarding the sensation, as it was a frequent experience. "I suppose I am. Why?"

"Don't you have anything to change into?"

"Not really. I have some things at my mother's."

"Don't you spend any time outside? Get yourself to my cabin and find something to put on before you get heatstroke."

Cliopher obeyed. It was nice to have someone order him around brusquely like that. He had good friends at the Palace, primarily the other chief members of his Radiancy's household, but they did not generally treat each other with such easy familiarity. The Vangavaye-ve in party manners was significantly less formal than the most casual occasion at the Palace.

He refrained from doing more than rehanging those of Bertie's clothes that were jumbled into the wardrobe. After some searching he found a sarong in a bright floral print. Bertie was a bigger man than he, and the tunics were all too large.

He touched the one efela necklace he always wore, the one he'd made when he was twelve, but then left it. There would be no questions as to its meaning, not here, and he did not need to fear it showed his vulnerabilities to his enemies. Given the Vangavaye-ve's general disinterest in the wider world, the only people who paid any attention to him were members of his family and close friends, and they already had all the ammunition they needed.

On his way out he found a wide-brimmed straw hat, which he put on.

"You may laugh," he said when he returned to his spot at the railing.

He saw Bertie eye the necklace, then shrug and ignore it. "Wouldn't dream of it."

"Solaara is much hotter than here, but I don't spend a lot of time out in the heat of the day." He shaded his eyes to see where they were, not recognizing any of the landmarks. "Where are we going?"

"Off the east end of Lesuia. Toucan's cousin Maya told me there's a splendid fishing spot there."

"Don't the people on Lesuia mind you fishing in their waters?"

"They're all radical communists and don't believe in property rights."

Cliopher could wish other communities—the Nijani, for instance—had anything like so coherent a political philosophy. At the moment they could not not agree on anything, not even to what extent they despised their duke.

He had always thought that, unwritten and unformulated though it might be, there was an elegant and effective system of governance binding the Wide Seas Islanders together that went back far before the coming of the Empire and had very little to do with the superstructure of princess and bureaucracy that rested upon the traditional powers of elders and chiefs. In his younger and more idealistic days he had devised a new system of government for the Empire based on the Islander tradition.

He smiled at Bertie. "There are worse beliefs to hold."

"Says the government man."

Cliopher snorted involuntarily. At least everybody the whole wide world around could agree on who to blame.

"Hold the tiller for a moment while I reef the foresail. Keep her heading towards Linoroa."

After some further shouted instructions Cliopher recalled which distantly visible peak was Linoroa. He enjoyed the sense of the sea running against the tiller, making the smooth wood thrum in his hands. The yacht moved with a steady, confident motion, correcting course as he shifted the tiller to compensate for Bertie's work with the sails. Obviously Bertie had been intending to sail it by himself, but it was pleasing to feel he could be of service.

He fell into a kind of reverie, the water glittering brilliantly, the wind fresh against his bare shoulders and back, hands steady on the tiller. There were all those metaphors about the ship of state. He was not the captain—that was his Radiancy—but, yes, he was sometimes the man standing watch at the tiller, holding the ship steady.

"South a skosh!"

Cliopher obeyed the shouted instruction and the more pungently expressed corrections that followed. That was all right, too, both in the literal instance and in the wider metaphorical sense. That no one dared, or evidently even desired, to tarnish the official position of the Lord Emperor did not mean people did not have various and strongly-expressed opinions on the workings of the mundial government. Cliopher got to read those reports, too. It was felt they kept him humble.

Bertie did more things with various ropes and sails, then clomped back to him. "You look very happy."

"So do you."

Bertie looked at his yacht with great pleasure. "I love this boat, Kip. I could never live inland like you."

"There's a river in Solaara."

"How often do you go sailing on it? Didn't think so. What do you even do outside?"

"I go hiking in the Grey Mountains sometimes. There's a park called the Liaau."

"You've written about it."

"I walk outside through the gardens in the morning and the evening."

Bertie grunted. He took back the tiller and did some complicated manoeuvres with various ropes. The yacht heeled over, then straightened on another tack. In the distance ahead of them the low peaks of an island were starting to resolve into clarity. "About another hour and a half. Did you finish your report?"

"I beg your pardon?"

"You keep looking back to the cabin."

Cliopher massaged his hands. "It's fine."

Bertie scowled. "I won't get any fun out of you till it's finished. Go ahead. Make some more coffee."

Cliopher emptied the old grounds into the small waste bucket and made a fresh pot. This was the way it always went: the cross-currents of old friendships and current lives, of competing priorities and serious work. To Bertie the report was something keeping Cliopher's (no, *Kip's*) attention from proper topics, and no doubt boring as hell. To Cliopher it was his duty, his responsibility, and something that would eventually change, however minutely, the lives of millions of people.

He took the coffee out to Bertie, who was standing proud at his tiller, then returned indoors to take out his writing kit again.

Nijan was a large island offshore of the continent of Jilkano. It was nominally ruled by a duke, who was enormously unpopular with his people. Many of them had written to Cliopher to tell him this.

They were not—at least those who took the time to write to the government were not, yet—disloyal to the mundial government; neither were they complete anarchists. They were instead trying to create a new form of government, trying out new methods, holding strikes and protests with abandon, splitting into factions, regrouping, breaking up order, restoring it, rebuilding. The Nijani police service, in particular, was central to both keeping order and destroying it.

Every six months or so Cliopher went to Nijan and walked around the capital and at least one of the outlying districts. He talked to people for a few days, trying to ensure he heard from as many layers of society as he could. He looked in on the small manufactories and the workshops, the warehouses and the marketplaces, the shipbuilders and the farmers. Zangoraville was the trade centre of the Wide Seas, bringing together the produce of all the Islands and the manufactured goods of Dair and Jilkano. What happened there would affect every other community and province chafing under the current systems of governance.

He did not blame them for chafing under the current systems. He had spent a lifetime slowly—so slowly—reforming them, but true change would require a complete restructuring of the hierarchy of power. That might happen in one small island duchy: it was almost impossible to imagine it happening across the whole wide world.

Cliopher hoped that his eventual successors would be able to build on the foundations he had created. He could see in his mind's eye what a juster society could be: could see how close Nijan was to grasping it.

He left the visions of a perfectly just society to the philosophers; in his experience they usually required assuming one could simply ignore some fundamental element of human nature. He had spent his lifetime working within an ancient, complex, and corrupt bureaucracy and court. He no longer believed one could legislate out of existence greed, or stupidity, or sheer perversity of will.

It reassured him that neither could one legislate out of existence love, or hope, or the desire for beauty.

He did have ideas for solving more practical problems. The stockpiles of emergency supplies were only one element in his goal to eliminate poverty.

If he could accomplish that ...

Cliopher wrote his report, pen singing across the paper as he adjusted to the motion of the ship. He wrote about the current factions and his projections for their development over the next few months. He wrote about the new lighting system (invented by a local engineer who had decided that she was not the sort of person to get involved in the protests and politics, but that she could do her part to make the city a better place for all its inhabitants) and his proposal that the system should be examined by the College of Wizards and other engineers for suitability, and then instituted by the Ministry of the Common Weal in all the major centres of population. He wrote that the duke was likely to bring his suit to his Radiancy, and that so were the heads of the three major factions, and that the police service was walking a fine line between autocracy and independence.

He vaguely noticed the yacht's motion changing, the angle of the table shifting under his hands. His conscious thought was how lovely it was to work with his oldest friend just on the other side of the door. In the Palace his rooms were at the end of a wing, with a good view of the city but far from his friends, who lived in close proximity to their lord. And outside the Palace was never the Vangavaye-ve, the wonder of the Nine Worlds, home.

When he arose he discovered that they had reached their destination. Bertie had set out the anchor and taken out his fishing lines. There were two seats amidships under a sun umbrella. One for Bertie—and one for him.

Cliopher watched his friend for a few minutes as he drew in a line and cast it out again. "Thank you."

Bertie grunted. He gestured at the bait box beside him, the other line. "Remember how to use it?"

"Just about."

Like steering the yacht, baiting the line came back to his hands after a short hesitation. Cliopher cast out the line, not as smoothly as Bertie, but well enough for someone out of practice. He settled back in his seat. "I should have brought out more coffee."

"There's beer for when we've caught our lunch."

Cliopher glanced sidelong at him. "Isn't it a little early?"

Bertie snorted. "Relax a little, Kip. You're tight as a drum."

"I am relaxed," he protested, then realized Bertie was teasing. "What about you? Aren't you supposed to be at work?"

"I took today off. Anyhow, I'm on half time. Easing into retirement."

There was a tentative tug on his line, but Cliopher missed hooking his fish. "Really?"

"Don't sound so shocked! Surely you've been thinking about it?"

Cliopher cast out his line again, more smoothly this time. "I can't say I have." He frowned at the brilliant aquamarine water, the white sand, the green jungle behind it. Coral-crested cockatoos screamed at one another in the treetops.

"We're getting on, Kip. Faldo's twenty-two this year. Parno's nineteen. Your nephew's twenty-one. It's about time to stop while we can still enjoy life. Let them do the work for a change."

Faldo and Parno were Bertie's sons from his first marriage. Cliopher had never married, had no children, had none of that. He had—

He had a hundred projects that had made the world a better place.

"And it's been longer in Solaara, hasn't it?"

"I suppose so. It never seems like it."

Bertie reeled in his line, examined the hook, put on a piece of baitfish. "Nearly a thousand years, people say."

Cliopher did not like to think too much about the strange jumps in time that had happened in the early days after the Fall. He blinked against the bright water. "That was mostly right after the Fall. It just seems like the days are long and full. ... After my lord finished the Lights that seems to have been sorted, and it's the same amount of time here as there. Before I think everyone wondered how I found the time to write to everyone, but the letters were farther apart for me."

Bertie grunted. "All the more reason, then, for you to retire."

He thought about the Vangavaye-ve, about those letters from his family and his friends that still asked him when he was coming home, albeit less overtly now than they had in the beginning.

Thought of plunging deep into the world where he knew everyone and everyone knew him, where what he had done with his life was a hazy rumour from beyond the Ring. Thought of the pleasure it would give his mother, his sister, his aunts, his uncles, his cousins, his friends—himself. Thought of how satisfied they would be for him finally to take his place where he ought always to have been.

He thought of his lord, pacing in his study, bearing the weight of the world on his shoulders. Thought of how well they worked together, the enmeshing of respect and knowledge and good humour and experience. Thought of leaving his lord to the court. Thought of leaving his friends in Solaara—Conju and Ser Rhodin and Commander Omo—how none of them had families, had lost them in the Fall.

Thought of leaving his work undone. All those projects slowly, delicately, unobtrusively transforming the government according to his vision of what the world could be.

Thought of his lord, never failing to do his duty.

Thought of his lord, with no one to joke with him.

Thought of losing that—he could not call it friendship, could he? That implied a kind of equality, and there was no equality possible between the Sun-on-Earth and anyone else.

But call it a *relationship*, that was permissible.

He suppressed the wish that he dared call his Radiancy his friend.

He said, "I suppose I hadn't thought about it."

"And now you have, the answer is—no?"

"Certainly not this year."

Bertie scowled at his line. "I suppose that is fair enough."

The words were polite. Cliopher ached for the times when they had been able to speak their hearts to each other. It was not as if he did not know what had changed. Or who had been responsible. He had been planning to come home, once. But he had gone; and each time he might have stayed he had left.

"What are your sons planning to do with themselves?" he asked, that seeming a safe enough topic.

"Faldo's going for to apprentice with a glassblower. Parno—" Bertie sighed gustily. "I don't know what to do with the boy. He wants to be a warrior—a warrior! He'll end up one of those fancy men of the princess' if we can't get him to see reason."

"He could try for the Imperial Guard," Cliopher suggested.

Bertie lifted his fishing pole sharply and started to reel in the line. "Not everyone wants to leave their home behind to feed their ambition, Kip."

Cliopher opened his mouth, but this was an old argument. He could persist—but to what end? He would not change Bertie's mind, and it would spoil things. He smiled instead and changed the subject to the much safer one of neighbourhood gossip.

★★★

THE GOSSIP WAS GOOD, THE fishing was better, and the location splendid. Cliopher slowly let himself drift back towards the joking, laughing, enthusiastic Kip Bertie clearly wanted. No doubt the beer helped.

As the sun sank westward Cliopher said, "Aren't we heading back tonight?"

Bertie beetled his brows at him. "Wind's shifted. The currents will be better in the morning."

He had once known how to read the wind and waves and stars as automatically as breathing. "I'll take your word for it. What about supper?"

"We've got a dozen red snappers. Go wild."

Cliopher was not a great cook by any stretch of the imagination—in fact, he took the majority of his meals in the Palace refectories unless dragged out into the city by Ser Rhodin or Conju, who were both much keener on the subject than him—but he could handle pan-frying fresh-caught fish, and had already found lemons and various greens and fruits in the galley cold box. He made a simple salad and brought it all up on deck, where Bertie was still lounging.

"I could get used to having you on board," Bertie rumbled as he accepted his tray. "If you change your mind about retiring."

"It's not—" Cliopher stopped. "Bertie, it's not that. If my lord … I'm not sure that he would like me to leave his service."

"Would he prevent you?"

Cliopher had never gone against the expressed desires, let alone commands, of his lord. He was not quite sure how to say that it would be somewhere in the region of blasphemy, treason, betrayal.

"I would not like to make my lord unhappy," he said at last.

"Never mind," said Bertie. "Pass the salt, would you?"

★★★

THE NEXT MORNING THE WINDS took them around the north cape of Lesuia island. As they rounded a large rocky outcropping, it became clear to Cliopher that Bertie had chosen this route on purpose, for the lagoon on the other side of the reefs from them was perhaps the most beautiful Cliopher had ever seen.

Making it even more perfect, there was a splendid little building on the beach, exquisitely designed and situated.

"What is that?" Cliopher asked.

"The old duke of Ikiano's summer house," Bertie replied. "No one lives there now, though I hear the current owner rents it out."

Cliopher looked at the building as long as he could see it. Thoughts were forming inchoately in his mind. He did not want to make his lord unhappy—that was the pure truth. But he did not like to see his lord unhappy, either, and here, far away from the pomp and splendour of the Palace, he could look back on his recent interactions with his Radiancy and wonder ... well, things that he could not say aloud.

Bertie thought him stretched tight as a drum, when Cliopher felt himself relaxing after the tense negotiations with the Jilkano princes, the taut atmosphere of Nijan. A day of enforced inactivity later, he was starting to feel truly relaxed, and he wondered what else Bertie—who could be insightful—was seeing in him.

He sifted through thoughts of his relationship with his Radiancy, but he kept circling back to the idea that his lord took no vacations, never fully relaxed from his duties. They were not always onerous, those duties, but they were ever-present.

★★★

JUST BEFORE HE LEFT FOR Nijan he had spent the bulk of the day, as usual, in his Radiancy's study.

It was the middle of the long dry season of Eastern Dair, halfway between the high ceremonials of the Solstice and those of Accession Day. The court was in recess, and his Radiancy's afternoons were preoccupied with an intricate work of magic intended to moderate the typhoons in the Wide Seas.

The first quarter of the lord's new year was the period in which the bureaucratic examinations were held, and in the months beforehand most of the Upper Secretariat were engaged in shepherding their favourites through their studies.

Cliopher had a very capable deputy who was ambitious enough to have reached the second rank, but not so ambitious she was not content to wait there. Kiri preferred the day-to-day work of compiling the reports that were passed up to him and his Radiancy to actually waiting upon his Radiancy.

His Radiancy was sober and even sombre, and if Cliopher saw a gleam in his eye on occasion, and perhaps was the recipient of a witticism or a smile, well, his Radiancy was a very quiet man as a rule, and kept most of his thoughts to himself. Kiri ran her department on laughter and high energy, and the serenity and splendour of the Imperial Apartments dampened both.

Cliopher had tried hard not to lose the pleasure that entering the Imperial Apartments (they well warranted the capitals) had awoken in him on his first nervous entry as the next candidate under consideration. It was not so much that the rooms were appointed with the finest furnishings that money could buy; you could go to one of the great museums and see that. No, the private chambers of the Last Emperor of Astandalas were furnished with the finest that anyone, anywhere, had ever created.

He had chosen one object at a time and learned all he could about it: where it came from, who had made it, when it had been presented to the Emperor, what might be the significance of runes or carvings or symbols or materials.

Cliopher wondered sometimes whether his Radiancy saw the splendour, or if his life as the second heir and then Emperor had meant that he had always been surrounded by perfection, had never seen shoddy workmanship, perhaps did not even truly comprehend that there was such a thing.

That particular afternoon Cliopher finished the final drafts of the day's work. He set them on his Radiancy's desk, ready for signing, and then, seeing that there was a good quarter hour before his Radiancy would emerge from his private study, decided to tour the rooms.

He went first, as always, to a vase made by the Voonran ceramicist Liän do Eza, in a technique that had taken her ten thousand pots to master, and then another ten thousand before she had one perfect one to present to her emperor.

The result was a three-foot porcelain vase ranging from translucent cream through the richest iridescent peacock-blue, the colour of a Glorious Imperial bird-of-paradise. Its asymmetrical curve was so endlessly satisfying that seven poets and three composers had written their masterpieces in response to a glimpse of it when his Radiancy had permitted an exhibition of his familiar treasures.

Cliopher had set his chair so that when he looked up from his papers he could see that fall of colour, that curve, and in the privacy of his own chambers had tried his own halting response on the oboe. The Vangavaye-ve was the homeland of song, and his family were all musicians; he had the love, though not the talent.

A jewelled nightingale that sang on what had been, in old Astandalas, the longest night of the year, and spent the rest of the year golden and brilliant in its golden cage. That was a gift to a former emperor. The mechanical bird had legends woven around it. Cliopher touched the cage with one gentle finger; it made a soft chiming noise.

A table made from sandalwood, whose supports were so intricately carved they appeared of copper filigree. A portrait of his Radiancy on his first accession to the Imperial Throne. Artorin Damara had been just past thirty when he became Emperor.

The painted face was idealized, benevolent, serene, handsome. His eyes were the traditional gold leaf used for representations of the Emperor, one of whose titles was the Lion-Eyed. They were descendants of the Sun, and tradition was that their eyes, even these many generations on, showed that inheritance of power, authority, and divinity.

You could not tell from the portraits which among the Emperors had actually inherited the colour, if any of them had save the last. In the days of the Empire it had been taboo to look directly in the Emperor's eyes.

It was no longer taboo: magic no longer blinded the fool who dared, even though, if anything, the Emperor was far more revered now than in those days when the magic of five worlds had hedged him about with glory.

Cliopher knew he was fortunate to have entered the Last Emperor's personal service after the Fall, when some of those stricter taboos had been relaxed. He had met an old woman, once, who had been blinded in her childhood for her presumption in looking too fully upon her Emperor. Cliopher had not lasted a full hour before looking his in the eye.

He had stuttered his apologies and his Radiancy had returned to his usual imperturbable self, and Cliopher had gone home that night and written to his cousin Basil that he feared he might be disgraced or worse for his presumption. In the days of the Empire he would have been executed as well as blinded. But the next morning he had been told his Radiancy had chosen him as his new personal secretary.

Cliopher often wondered if that portrait of his youthful self ever bothered his Radiancy. He might be a great mage, and the strange magic since the Fall of Astandalas might have made time topsy-turvy for him as for everyone, and he might live the life of uttermost luxury, but he was no longer young. He walked straight and tall, and thanks to his moderate appetites his physique remained reasonably slim, but there were fine wrinkles at the corners of his eyes and an ineffable sense of sadness at time's passage in his bearing.

And people were beginning to wonder.

No one said anything; but they were.

Cliopher stopped at length before an embroidered map of the five worlds of the Empire at its broadest extent which hung on the wall along from his Radiancy's private study. The backing was silk, the threads studded with gemstones for cities. Cliopher had never looked at it closely, and he grew quickly absorbed in trying to name the places depicted.

When the door beside him opened suddenly, he jumped back and exclaimed aloud.

His Radiancy frowned at him. "Did you call me?"

Cliopher willed his heart to stop thundering. "I beg your pardon, my lord?"

"Did you call me just now?"

"No, my lord."

His Radiancy frowned at the room, which was empty apart from them and the two honour guards standing motionless by the outer door, and closed his door firmly behind him. Cliopher thought irrepressibly that it was the only door he had ever seen his Radiancy open or shut himself.

"No one else was here?"

"No, my lord."

"And the guards didn't speak?"

"No, my lord."

"I could have sworn I heard someone call my name ..."

Cliopher did not voice the thought that he could not name a single person who would dare address his Radiancy by name, but his Radiancy clearly was thinking the same, and smiled wryly. "No, I suppose you did not. What are you looking at, Cliopher?"

"The map," he said, gesturing guiltily at it. Not that there was anything to feel guilty about. "It is a superb piece of work."

"Made by the Dezarno fishwives," his Radiancy said, surprising him again. Cliopher briefly met his gaze; his Radiancy smiled and walked over to stand near him. Not too close: the prohibition against touching was the strongest of all.

That taboo had not been lifted after the Fall. Cliopher was no wizard and did not know why it had not broken with the rest of the magical bindings, but he had never been tempted to test it. There were too many stories about people who had in the past dared lay hands on the person of the Emperor without the proper rituals of purification.

His Radiancy passed his hand across the islands of Colhélhé until he could point to a small scattering of tiny pearls sewn into a greeny-gold thread. "There they are, the Dezarno Archipelago. The fishwives made the thread out of the beards of mussels and other shellfish. The pearls came from Uguliaan."

He traced out a few sweeps of blue and grey thread, his finger black as a shadow, nail lacquered gold, until he touched on the tiny stitches around a cluster of four atolls made of soft pink pearls. "The gems from all over. The silk from Ulstin-le-Grand."

Nothing in his voice suggested he knew the infamous story of the Red Company and the Customs House on Ulstin-le-Grand. Cliopher kept his smile to himself as his Radiancy touched other islands, murmuring of silver gulls and sea folk, places where they harvested the scent of rain and others where the nautilus had shells where each new chamber was rimmed with gold. A few snatches of poetry, and then his Radiancy's hand rested on the Long Isle of Colhélhé, the edge of that world. There were no pearls or gemstones on its narrow length, though it must have stretched thousands of miles, a raised lip to the endless oceans.

"Are there no habitations on the Long Isle?" Cliopher asked.

His Radiancy touched a small archipelago, itself a lonely outpost far from either the Long Isle or the nearest other islands. "The Nelosi are the closest. Shepherds and knitters; the only ones who leave are musicians, and not many of them." Then his hand strayed again to the Long Isle, to a point a bit north of the Nelosi, at the furthest curve. He tapped a point right on the edge, where a tiny diamond glittered when his finger moved the fabric. "There's something here."

"Indeed, my lord?"

"One of the anchors for the Empire's magic. There were five." He walked down the length of the map, touching other remote islands so that other tiny gems glittered. "Outside the Vale of Astandalas on Ysthar. Here in far northern Voonra. Out past the Outer Reaches of Alinor. Somewhere past the Isolates there was one."

He paused, hand on the islet way down in the southern portion of the vast expanse of the Wide Seas, far even from the Vangavaye-ve. Looked down the length of his empire back at Cliopher standing near the opposite end. "I was exiled there. Before I became Emperor. That was where I lived."

"It must have been a lonely isle," he ventured, when his Radiancy said nothing more.

"I suppose it was," his Radiancy said softly, his eyes far away.

"My lord ..." But Cliopher did not know what else he could say.

His Radiancy moved abruptly. "Come now, Cliopher. You have done very well indeed with the Jilkano princes."

Cliopher ducked his head down, a little embarrassed by the praise. "It took me far longer than I had hoped, my lord."

"Tchah. You succeeded. I think—yes—you have more than earned a holiday. Go see your family and celebrate making my underling princes bow to reason for once."

"My lord—"

"Take three weeks," his Radiancy said, smiling, and left to dress for evening court.

Cliopher stared at the map. The Vangavaye-ve was so far from everywhere, two worlds away from Astandalas, on the other side of Zunidh from Solaara.

And yet his Radiancy had been exiled to a more lonely spot, an island full of magic and mystery, and lived there until one morning he woke to inherit an empire.

★★★

AFTER HE AND BERTIE RETURNED to Gorjo City, Cliopher spent the rest of his visit thoroughly engrossed in his family's affairs. His nephew Gaudy asked him a few shy questions about life in the Service. Cliopher answered them patiently, trying not to be too eager, trying not to overwhelm his nephew with his enthusiasm.

It was difficult. Cliopher so rarely was asked for details of his life's work … but his mother and his sister were watching and listening.

He thought, again and again, of all those letters begging him to come home, and again and again he sighed inwardly and outwardly put on his polite court smile, and he answered the questions as disinterestedly as he could manage.

The troubling question of retirement ran like an undertow through all his conversations, all his thoughts, all his wanderings with sister and cousins and friends along the familiar canals and streets. Every time he thought about leaving his Radiancy's service his mind turned inexorably to his Radiancy—to the man who was no longer young, whose face was serene and benevolent and hid—what?

He was ten or a dozen years older than Cliopher, and if Cliopher worked long hours because the work was important and challenging and he was relied upon—

—And because there was no one waiting for him in his chambers to complain that he was late. No one to ask him about his day. No one to notice if he was up at dawn and still working when the bells chimed midnight—

Cliopher had woken on Bertie's boat, cradled by the gentle movement of the Bay of the Waters. For a moment he lay there trying to remember what he had to do that morning, unsure why he felt so unsure. Then he remembered that he was on holiday, that he was on Bertie's yacht, that he was home.

He sat up and looked out the window. He was facing the land, away from the sunrise. The light caught the tops of Lesuia island, and he watched as the sunlight slid down to the beach, catching the dawn flights of bats back home and birds out on their journeys.

This could be yours, a voice said in his heart.

It could be. He knew his Radiancy would not prevent him from retiring if he asked. He knew that. He knew …

In the quiet splash of the waves on the hull of the yacht, in the calls of birds to each other, in the soft whisper of the dawn wind, the image of his lord came before his mind's eye. Standing there before that map of his fallen Empire, pointing out those utterly lonely outposts of magic, to one of which the Emperor had exiled his second heir, who had not been supposed to inherit.

But inherit he had. He had been brought to the Palace of Stars, placed upon the golden throne, crowned the Serene and Glorious One, the Sun-on-Earth, the Lord of Rising Stars, the Lord of Five Thousand Lands and Ten Thousand Titles.

No one to look on his face. No one to say his name. No one to touch him. No one to be his own, and no one else's. No one for whom he could be himself.

Cliopher had been ambitious as a young man; Bertie was not wrong there. He had dreamed of serving the Empire, dreamed that his fate was entwined with the Emperor of the Lion Eyes. He had forced the governor of the Province of the Wide Seas to send him the examination texts, to send him the examiner—and when he failed, to do it again the next year, and the next, and the next, until after five tries Cliopher had finally passed.

His family thought it ambition that kept him where he was. He got up, padded silently on bare feet past Bertie's cabin, through the galley, up on deck. He looked to the east, closing his eyes against the sunrise, feeling tears starting with the brightness, the tugs of competing and opposing desires.

All this could be his. He could come *home*—

His lord would let him go. Conju and Ser Rhodin and Commander

Omo would bid him farewell, and perhaps they would come visit once or twice, but after a lifetime of service together there would be a sense of … difference. For none of them had families, and Cliopher did. None of them had homes to go to, and Cliopher did. And none of them would ever leave his Radiancy's household, for why would they?

He made coffee eventually. Bertie was still asleep, so he took his cup onto the deck to sit in his borrowed sarong under the umbrella. He went through his writing kit for his diary of events, and created a calendar of all the things that would be done over the next year by himself and his Radiancy.

By some accident of bureaucratic cycles, almost nothing at all was happening over the six weeks of the Little Session.

Despite its name, it was the gap between official court sessions. After the birthing pains of the annual budget, the monthly Helma Council took its annual recess then. Most years Cliopher used the period to conduct reviews of various portions of the Secretariat and to do in-depth research and development of new projects, while his Radiancy did major works of magic.

His Radiancy was nearly finished with his current project, an enormously complicated effort to moderate the vicious typhoons that had plagued the Wide Seas since the Fall.

Bertie came up on deck at this point of his meditations, just as Cliopher was examining a terrifying idea in his mind and shying away from articulating it even to himself. There were certain lines one did not cross, even in one's thoughts, if one was—as Bertie had said—a government man. And Cliopher was.

Oh, how he was.

Then they went past that glorious little summer palace, and the idea crystallized. The more he examined it—all the way back across the Bay of the Waters, through the next ten days of his visit home—the more he attacked it from every angle, the way he attacked any new idea—the more he examined it, the more precious and important it seemed.

He asked a few questions, scattering them among relatives and across days to ensure no one was likely to put them together. No one cared much, delighted as they were he was asking them anything at all about the gossip of the Ring. Usually he did not ask; did not need to, in point of fact, for observation and attention revealed more than the direct answers would have told him.

It was a lesson he had learned from his great-uncle as a boy, when he had spent a year learning the ways of the ancestors out on Loaloa of the Western

Ring. Buru Tovo had pounded *Listen first! questions later!* into his head until Cliopher had finally managed to rein in his unruly tongue. It was not until he had started to take a position at court that he had realized just how useful a lesson that had been.

On his last day home, he divested himself of company. He went first to buy a strand of efela shells to mark his triumph with the stockpiles. (The situation in Nijan, he acknowledged wryly to himself, would take years before he could justify celebrating it with an efela necklace, if ever he could in his lifetime.) He could be proud of the stockpiles. No one would go hungry again in a disaster: not as they had after the Fall, when he had seen exactly what happened when a government collapsed.

Outside the shop he looked at the strand of tortoiseshell cowries he had acquired. The deep brown shells were glossy, cool in his fingers, familiar and beloved as the buildings and people all around him. He ran his thumb over the underside, enjoying the curve of the opening, the texture of the ridges against his thumbnail. The spots were beige and pale gold, catching the sun.

He tucked the shells into his writing kit. There they would remain, a tangible piece of home, until he returned to the Palace and could put them away with the rest. He did not like displaying them, even in the privacy of his quarters; it made him feel too much like one of the officials who returned from far-flung outposts of the Empire and displayed artefacts from the natives.

He was not accustomed to dithering so much once a decision had been made.

Finally he made his way to the lawyer who acted as agent for the summer palace on Lesuia. The Mdang family was enormous and well-known, and so although Cliopher—or rather Kip—himself was not, the lawyer had no difficulty about him signing a lease for the period of the Little Session.

His hand was trembling as he signed his name across the document.

Fortunately the lawyer did not actually know that he was in fact the head of the Service, and merely murmured something patronizing about using the scribal pens when one was unaccustomed to them.

Surely it was only *petty* treason.

CHAPTER THREE

THE DAY AFTER HE RETURNED to the Palace, Kiri came to breakfast with Cliopher and give her reports of her time with his Radiancy. Nothing unusual had happened. She was glad to be returning to her proper position; she found it excruciatingly intimidating to be in the Presence. Her parents, she said in a burst of candour, were priests of the Imperial cult.

Cliopher readied himself to attend his Radiancy. On entering the Imperial Apartments he was struck anew by the Presence, as Kiri had put it. The Palace was a temple and his Radiancy was its god.

Cliopher bowed formally, head to the ground, when his Radiancy entered.

"Did you have a good holiday?" his Radiancy asked, and belatedly gestured him to his usual seat. Cliopher obeyed. His Radiancy appeared inclined to pace while they spoke. According to the stricter of the etiquette books he ought to remain with his forehead to the ground, even in the Imperial Apartments. Especially in the Imperial Apartments. But his Radiancy always paced, and—

"Yes, my lord," said Cliopher. "Thank you."

His Radiancy paced up to the vase and across to the window, where he stood, looking out across the city. The windows had deep eaves, a necessity in equatorial Solaara but built in the days when the Emperor was considered of such sacred presence that neither Sun nor Moon were permitted to touch his skin directly.

One of the first things his Radiancy had done on awakening after the Fall of Astandalas and discovering his Empire had been destroyed in a magical cataclysm had been to have a small terrace off the Apartments built so that in the cool mornings he might sit over his coffee in the open air.

"Tell us about it," said his Radiancy, and so Cliopher did.

"It sounds lovely," said his Radiancy, when Cliopher took care to describe the little summer house in detail, its beauty, its setting, its privacy.

The words were polite, and his Radiancy's expression was serene, but there was the barest note of something else in his voice, and although Cliopher would never have dared to ask aloud whether it was *wistfulness* or *envy*, it gave him the courage to say the words that changed things.

For he had never, ever, *ever* initiated such a thing. No one had. His Radiancy was the mover, and they—all of them, all the people of Zunidh, perhaps even now all the people of the five worlds of the old Empire—were the moved.

"My lord," he said, "I thought it a place of such unutterable beauty that I could not help but think immediately that it would please your lordship."

"A compliment indeed."

Cliopher bowed. "My lord," he said again, "I was informed that the palace was available to be leased as a private retreat."

"Will you go there for your next holidays, then?"

Cliopher wished his Radiancy would not stand right before the window, where he was a silhouette. In the days of the Empire he had been literally radiant, had glowed with the magic of the Empire, but that was no longer the case and with his black skin when he stood in shadow his expression was even more inscrutable than normal. Cliopher swallowed. "No, my lord. I thought ... I had the very great presumption to think ... that perhaps your Radiancy might like to do so."

There was a long pause. His Radiancy touched the tassel hanging from the long white curtains beside him. Cliopher waited, heart thundering with nerves. He should not have said *Radiancy*. That was the Emperor's title, and it pleased his Radiancy not to be addressed by it, but rather by the slightly lesser *Saavel*, Lord of a world's magic as he merely was now.

Finally his Radiancy said, his voice very neutral, "Did you?"

Cliopher stood up from his desk, came around to the centre of the room, and at the prescribed distance performed the formal obeisance. His Radiancy watched this departure from Cliopher's usual practice in silence. Cliopher had never been very good at formal etiquette. His early near misses with the executioner were the stuff of legend in the Service.

"I did, my lord. And moreover ..."

Cliopher swallowed, but he *did* think his Radiancy looked tired, he *did* think he needed a vacation, he did think that beneath all the trappings of divinity there was a man, and so he went on: "Moreover, I considered your schedule and bethought myself that when you have finished the work on the typhoons it may be that you would enjoy a vacation—"

He dared not say *need*, no one ever implied that his Radiancy might *need* something, officially he was the source of the world's blessings—he finished in a rush: "And therefore, my lord, I took the very great liberty of hoping you would not be displeased, and rented the place for the period of the Little Session."

He set his forehead down to the cool marble floor and waited.

His Radiancy said nothing for quite a long time. Cliopher felt the cold seeping into his bones, for he was not young, and he had spent his life working for his Radiancy and never once had he been so presumptuous.

Never once, he thought, had he gone further than the accidental meeting of eyes or witticism. Any further intimacy—a meal, a game of chess or draughts, a conversation about art—was always initiated by his Radiancy. Always. *Always.*

Finally his Radiancy said, "You rented this place for *me*?"

Cliopher could not quite decipher his tone; but it was not the formal plural, and that—"I know it was exceedingly presumptuous of me, my lord."

"Oh, get up. I wish to see your face."

Cliopher stood up slowly, trying not to creak. His Radiancy came out from the window, frowning at him. Cliopher's heart sank.

"You saw this beautiful place, and you thought I would like it, and that I might enjoy a—a vacation after finishing up my present project, so you rented it for a month in my name, am I correct?"

Cliopher swallowed. But his Radiancy said *I*, not *we*. He held to that. "I did not presume so far, my lord. It is in my name."

His Radiancy continued to frown silently for several moments longer. And then he said: "Thank you, Cliopher."

When Cliopher glanced up in surprise, for his Radiancy's tone had changed utterly, he saw that his Radiancy was smiling and there was even, oh just perhaps, the suspicion of moisture in his Radiancy's eyes, and Cliopher sank back to the ground in sheer relief and wonder and also a kind of pain, for he had seen that kind of surprised pleasure before in the faces of people receiving entirely unexpected but welcome gifts.

And it occurred to him, somewhat later, after they had settled into their usual work, that if he, who was the chief member of his Radiancy's household, had never before dared offer a gift to his Radiancy beyond the tithes and service expected of him, then apart from his Radiancy's sister, who barely wrote and even more rarely came to court, there was no one else to do so.

★★★

FOUR NIGHTS BEFORE THE LEASE began, and three months since his Radiancy had last mentioned it, his Radiancy did not go to evening court. Instead he summoned Cliopher.

Cliopher had been playing his oboe, somewhat despondently. He was disappointed that his Radiancy had not once made any indication that he even remembered the conversation. He would, of course; his Radiancy had a prodigious memory. But he did not mention it, and so Cliopher had with regret let it go. He had almost written a time or two to cancel the reservation, but he had not been ordered to, and ... he hoped.

His Radiancy was sitting in the comfortable little nook where they occasionally played at board games. Cliopher was a touch surprised that his Radiancy had not held court, but when he had left him that afternoon he had been focused intently on the typhoons.

Cliopher made his bows and, since his Radiancy made no other gesture, stood waiting.

His Radiancy drummed his fingers on the table.

His Radiancy had spent more than a lifetime on full public display: his face was unemotional as any of the state portraits. Drumming fingers was an unusual departure for him. There had been a time when that indication of displeasure would have chilled Cliopher's soul.

Now ... he wondered.

Finally his Radiancy said, "We have finished the work on the typhoons."

"Congratulations, my lord."

"We did not require the relocation of the Tina'a."

The final few stages of the magic working had seemed to require the relocation of a small Islander community from one of the archipelagoes southwest of Nijan. His Radiancy had asked Cliopher about it off-handedly, mind clearly on the wider implications of power and magic. Cliopher was no wizard and such subtleties were not for him. But he understood what one's island meant to a Wide Sea Islander.

He had perhaps been more passionate than usual. His Radiancy had stopped pacing, that day, staring at his secretary until Cliopher stumbled to an embarrassed halt in the middle of an explanation about the anchorage of the soul. His Radiancy had said nothing further, and Cliopher had resolutely turned to practical matters of where the Tina'a could go and what he could do to help them with such a transition so that they did not end up with a group of disaffected and despairing people who had once been a thriving community.

"Thank you, my lord," he said quietly.

His Radiancy smiled very faintly. "We shall go to this house of yours tomorrow."

Cliopher bowed to hide his whirling thoughts. They had made no preparations—absolutely none. He straightened to find that faint gleam in his lord's eyes, the one he had not seen often enough of late, the one so few—no one else?—even imagined might be there.

"*We* being Conju, yourself, Ser Rhodin, and Commander Omo. Presumably they have kitchen staff."

Cliopher bowed again. He didn't trust himself to speak. His Radiancy looked as imperturbable as ever.

Something Ser Rhodin had said, when he had mentioned his suggestion to his friends, made him say, "Perhaps a few other guards? It would be hard on Ser Rhodin and Commander Omo otherwise, my lord."

The lion gaze met his, and Cliopher felt power thicken the air around him. He tried not to gasp.

Finally his Radiancy nodded. "Very well. Six. Commander Omo will know whom we prefer. You may go prepare."

Cliopher dropped down to one knee as his Radiancy stood and went to the door to his private study. He waited there when his Radiancy paused, not looking at the two honour guards (no doubt as utterly agog as he), telling himself that surely everyone knew his Radiancy was not *erratic* and although it *was* very short notice it was the Little Session starting tomorrow, and then he did blink in surprise when his Radiancy added: "Tell no one where we are going."

CHAPTER ＦOUR

FIRST HE WENT TO THE outer antechamber of the Imperial Apartments, where four pages sat waiting. Cliopher sent two to find Ser Rhodin and Captain Omo, sent the third to find Kiri, who lived out of the Palace, and then he turned to the fourth, who was looking disappointed to be fourth, and bade her find replacements and then wait on his pleasure. The young woman's eyes gleamed with interest as she streaked off.

The guards standing on the inside of that door held their eyes straight ahead and their bodies in perfect attention, but Cliopher could sense their curiosity and eager interest. He said: "His Radiancy may summon others tonight. He has just finished a great work of magic and he may have orders."

The guard on the left nodded very slightly. Cliopher opened the door and gave the same message to the guards who stood on that side. Then he returned to the lord's study to consider his desk and what might be needed for a month's travel. A month's vacation, he corrected himself, and all of a sudden he sat down in his chair, staring at the splendid vase across from him.

"Are you unwell, Sayo Mdang?" one of the honour guards called from his post by the outer door of the study. His Radiancy was still in his private study, then; this particular pair of guards, or their fellows, were the ones who stood at the inner side of the door of any room his Radiancy was within, with the sole exception of the private study. There had been an Emperor long ago murdered in his toilet.

When Cliopher did not answer, panic washing over him, the guard strode across the room to touch Cliopher's forehead with a cool hand. "Sayo Mdang, can you speak?"

"I am fine," Cliopher gasped finally. The guard took three steps over to the tray of refreshments and passed him a glass of water. Cliopher took it and sipped gratefully. "Thank you."

After a moment he looked at the glass, this time in more practical concern that he had broken one of the great taboos (*no one* used the same utensils as his Radiancy). The guard chuckled. "I have not stood guard these many years without knowing which is yours, Sayo Mdang."

"It's Pikabe, isn't it?" Cliopher said, standing and brushing down his robes. Now that the initial burst of panic was over, he could not help but think of all the things that he needed to do—and it had occurred to him that Conju still didn't know.

"Yes, sir," said the guard, saluting.

"You shouldn't leave your post," he scolded.

Pikabe chuckled again as he went back to his stance next to the door. "His Radiancy would not thank me to let you fall."

Cliopher did not answer that, but he did wonder, suddenly, what the guards made of his interactions with his Radiancy. His Radiancy was certainly benevolent towards him, but how much further it went than that, he dared not imagine. That way lay ... well. But he was smiling as he crossed to Conju's portion of the Imperial Apartments.

Cliopher had been as far as his Radiancy's morning room, where he took breakfast. From Conju's conversations he had gathered a fair idea of what lay on the other side of the ivory-panelled door with its carvings of scenes from the Courtship of the Sun and Moon.

Along with sundry rooms for clothes and servants and other necessities, there was, of course, the imperial bedchamber itself, a large room with an Alinorel-style curtained bed. It was apparently a huge room, since in the old days the Waking of the Sun Ceremony was performed right there as the Emperor awoke.

The little closet with an outside door where the choir had sung the morning hymn was now closed off, that having been one of the first of the old rituals his Radiancy had dropped after the Fall. Conju had said that the Waking of the Sun had involved seven courtiers and four priest-wizards as well as the twelve-person choir and nine servants, so although Cliopher thought the idea of waking to music rather nice, he could quite see why his Radiancy might prefer otherwise.

The Imperial Bath was one of the rumoured wonders of the Nine Worlds. Conju said that it surpassed all imagination, which Cliopher, thinking of the splendour of his lord's study or (yet more) the throne room of the Palace of Stars itself, had taken as a challenge. But he had never before had occasion even to knock.

Conju's first underling answered the ivory door. Lady Ylette was a petite Voonran who was responsible for his Radiancy's clothing. That he was always impeccably turned out in perfectly fitting clothing was her doing, a feat (Conju said) all the more impressive given that she had never even come close to breaking the taboo against touching. She nodded at Cliopher. He bowed. "May I speak with Conju, please?"

She considered this request with raised eyebrows, then nodded and stood aside. Cliopher entered the private apartments with unexpected trepidation.

The private chambers were, if anything, more impressive than the lord's study. At Lady Ylette's gesture Cliopher walked through a waiting room for the Emperor's attendants (as Lord of Zunidh his Radiancy had far fewer), down a short hallway filled with coloured light from painted-glass windows on either side, showing the sun in glory of Astandalas flanked by lions, and finally he came to the splendid antechamber and then the chamber itself.

The bed was everything Conju had said and more. Cliopher halted to stare at its magnificence. He had gone to Alinor a few times in Astandalan days, to visit his cousin Basil's wife's substantial country inn, so he had seen wooden-framed beds, but this was to even the grandest of those as the vase in the lord's study was to the ewer of water Cliopher kept on his own side table.

The frame was ebony and rosewood and ivory with gold accents. It was as finely carved as the sandalwood desk, the pillars meeting in a four-way pointed arch, with nested ivory globes set on its point. The bedclothes themselves were white with gold embroidery, as were the opaque privacy panels.

The curtains were foamwork, the Vangavaye-ve's most exquisite export.

One of Cliopher's aunts was a foamwork master. He knew that each square inch of fabric took something like three months to make, and that was after the thread had been prepared by arcane and complicated methods.

The bed was perhaps nine feet to a side. The foamwork curtains were gathered at the top and fell in glorious profusion on all four sides.

It was one thing to know that the Last Emperor received the tithes of the best work in the Nine Worlds—even to be the person who read over the lists of those tithes—and another to see it represented so casually. He knew how much work went into an inch of foamwork. He did not know what fabrics went into the coverlet or what skill into the carved wood of the frame, but he could guess.

He thought of the pretty little summer house on Lesuia island, and his heart quailed.

Conju was not in the bedchamber, but a door stood ajar on the far side of the room. Cliopher genuflected self-consciously at his Radiancy's bed, as if it were a holy altar, before he tapped on the door. There was still no answer, so he pushed it open.

This was Conju's domain, he saw instantly: a comfortable room, set up for the waiting that his Radiancy's groom of the chamber must spend much of his time doing, with all the domestic necessities to hand. Three clothes racks stood against one wall, with his Radiancy's morning costume arranged on two and a simpler white robe that was presumably his night-dress on the third. A fourth stood empty, awaiting the discarded garments. The gold dressing wands sat gleaming and newly-polished in their rack, ready for the evening's undressing. That had once been a ceremony every bit as solemn and as well-attended as the Waking of the Sun.

Another door stood open. Cliopher went to it, and halted openmouthed.

The Imperial Bath had been built for his Radiancy's grandmother, the Empress Anyoë, called the Short-Lived; she had been Empress for seven years. She was considered the most absolutely extravagant of all the hundred emperors of Astandalas, and she had stinted nothing when it came to her private bath.

Like most things in the Imperial Apartments it was primarily gold, white, and black, the colours of Astandalas. The Empress had liked peacocks, and so there were touches of those colours, in the form of emeralds and sapphires and glazed tiles of equal perfection to the carved jewels. Facing Cliopher was an enormous sun-in-glory flanked by lions and peacocks. A stream of water fell from the lions' mouths into basins and thence into the pool. The water and the stone were tuned, so that a faint harmony thrummed in the air.

The bath itself was the central glory of the room. It was huge, a dozen strides or more long and the same wide, with broad steps leading down into the beckoning waters. Cliopher guessed there was some enormously significant math behind its proportions, but he had never paid much attention to the geomancers and numerologists even back in the days when their arts held the five worlds of the Empire together.

After a stunned moment of appreciation Cliopher saw that Conju was walking around the perimeter of the bath sprinkling flowers on the water. Rose petals, Cliopher identified after a moment, when the fragrance started to waft upwards. Roses did not grow on Zunidh; he recalled the scent from Astandalas. That there were fresh rose petals to be sprinkled on his Radiancy's bathwater was … incredible.

He could not help recalling the lines in the budget devoted to his Radiancy's household use. This was not a special occasion. This was … normal.

That basket of petals cost as much as Cliopher's monthly salary.

Conju came around and saw him standing in the doorway. After he finished strewing his blossoms, he walked up to his friend, smiling, "Your first sight of the bath, eh?"

Cliopher tore his gaze from the room with great difficulty. "I can see why it is said to be a wonder of the Nine Worlds."

Conju looked around with an air of satisfaction. This was his domain, Cliopher saw, as much as the dressing room. He was the one privileged to assist his Radiancy with bathing and with dressing, the most intimate servant of the Presence. "Yes," he said simply. Then he cocked his head at him. "To what do I owe this pleasure? It must be important. Come to the dressing room."

Cliopher recollected himself as they returned to what seemed, in comparison, a very homely sort of room. He said, "His Radiancy summoned me this evening."

"He did not go to evening court," Conju agreed. "He said he continued to work on the typhoons."

"He has finished."

"It is a very great work of magic."

It was years of solid work, Cliopher thought, along with all the other ordinary activities—the meetings and correspondence and court and magic and judgments and tithing-moots and all the rest—no wonder his Radiancy was looking a little tired. He swallowed.

"Yes. His Radiancy did me the honour of remembering my suggestion of a vacation."

Conju set down his basket sharply. "He did?"

Cliopher met his glance soberly. "We are leaving tomorrow."

★★★

WHILE CONJU BEGAN PACKING FOR a trip assuredly unlike any they had ever taken before, Cliopher collected his writing kit and the last of the original pages (now joined by four new ones looking sleepily excited about this unusual activity) and made his way to the considerably less grand wing of the Palace where his own rooms were. On the way he thought about the logistics of the journey itself, and his Radiancy's strange insistence that they not tell anyone where they were going.

If they took the flagship of the sky fleet, everyone would know his Radiancy was on board: it sailed only for his Radiancy or a visiting seigneur of another world. They must take one of the lesser ships, in that case, and once that was decided it was obvious from his own voyages which it would be.

Cliopher had met four of the sky captains, but trusted only one of them to keep his mouth shut about his Imperial guest. Moreover, Diogen was from the Wide Seas and as a *wontok* with Cliopher would do everything he could to assist.

He sent the page to summon Diogen and send coffee and cakes, and with his mind racing entered his apartments to find Commander Omo and Ser Rhodin there and looking curious.

"It's a bit late for coffee, surely?" Ser Rhodin said, as Cliopher poured for them all and blessed the page for having sent for the refreshments before seeking the captain. The Palace bells were chiming the third hour before midnight.

"We will be up all night," Cliopher replied, sighing. "We are leaving for the Vangavaye-ve tomorrow."

"We?" Commander Omo said, eyebrows rising.

"You two, me, Conju, six discreet guards to be chosen by Commander Omo, and ... his Radiancy."

Ser Rhodin coughed into his cup. Commander Omo blinked.

Ser Rhodin was the one to voice their thoughts: "You cannot possibly be serious. Has something gone amiss?"

"His Radiancy has finished his project on typhoons and has decided that he does after all wish to take a vacation. I rented a house, if you remember—" At their nods he continued. "His Radiancy has done us the honour of accepting. We are not to tell anyone where we are going."

"Six guards. That's it?"

"It was nearly just you and Commander Omo."

"What about other staff?"

"His Radiancy presumes the rental house will have some."

There was a short, stunned silence, and then Ser Rhodin said, "Well, this should certainly be interesting."

They were still talking about the logistics when the page returned with Captain Diogen, who had, it appeared, been in the Palace barracks with his crew. He was on the inebriated side, but Commander Omo stared hard at him and pronounced him sober enough for their purposes.

Cliopher liked that Captain Diogen saluted Ludvic Omo, who was technically the highest-ranking military officer, there being no current Commander-General of the Imperial Armies (and indeed, no longer much in the way of an Imperial Army). The sky captain then turned to him. "I do hope that this hasty summons does not mean there is illness in your family, Sayo Mdang."

"No," he said slowly, "though if anyone asks perhaps that is the best thing to say. We need you to prepare your ship to sail for the Vangavaye-ve tomorrow."

"That's the Toromandel Light," Diogen said. "We can sail at either the second hour after dawn or the fourth after noon."

Cliopher frowned. Commander Omo shrugged. "Be prepared for the second, but it may be the fourth."

"Very good." Diogen paused. "May I ask how many passengers I should expect?"

"Eleven." Cliopher paused in turn. "You should prepare the Sun Cabin."

The Sun Cabin was put on every ship built for Imperial business, just in case it was necessary in some emergency for the Presence to board. Just as in every town hall and courtroom and university high table and public assembly there was a token throne. Diogen opened his mouth and then closed it again. "I beg your pardon?"

"Prepare the Sun Cabin, and rooms for ten others. Six guardsmen, Ser Rhodin and Commander Omo, myself and Lord Conju."

Diogen was no fool, and he knew enough of the court to know that the four highest-ranking members of the Imperial household, including both of the chief officers of the Guards, would not travel together unless the Sun-on-Earth was going too. He swallowed. "I am to tell no one?"

"One of the principal members of the court is going to the Vangavaye-ve. The reasons why, the personage in question, and the exact destination are not to be discussed. You may tell your crew that I am visiting my relations again."

Diogen bowed, slightly shakily. "I am honoured by your condescension."

★★★

CLIOPHER SENT A NOTE TO Conju with the proposed sailing times and then packed his own belongings. Kiri eventually showed up, dressed nearly in court finery.

"I was at Kilian's wedding," she said.

"I am sorry to draw you from such an important event," Cliopher said, feeling a stab of regret he had done so. Kilian was the one of Kiri's twin daughters who was not in the Offices of State.

Kiri shrugged. "The ceremony was long since finished. The party, not so much. Has something dreadful happened? I'm not quite sober, I can take it."

He smiled a little stiffly. "You will be acting head of government for the Little Session. His Radiancy has decided to take a vacation and is taking me with him. Tomorrow."

Kiri poured herself a cup of cold coffee with shaking hands. "Tomorrow? Where are you going?"

"His Radiancy bade me to tell no one."

"Including me?"

Cliopher shrugged apologetically. "He did not specifically mention your name, and I was in such a whirl I did not think to. I know where we are going. We will be able to communicate with you should it prove necessary, though it may take several days for messages to come through, even using the Lights, and we won't be checking from our end unless there's an emergency."

Kiri digested this and then grinned. "You must be in a right tizzy, Sayo Mdang. But I am glad for his Radiancy's sake."

There it was again, Cliopher thought: the sense that something was not quite as it always had been with his Radiancy.

They spent several hours going through the matters that Cliopher had been planning to do during the Little Session. He knew he left them in the best of hands, but his mind was racing wildly as he tried to think what else needed to be done. To have the three chief ministers of the government all away incommunicado together for an indefinite length of time ... Well, he thought phlegmatically somewhere around midnight, here was a chance to see how well his surreptitious preparations for potential disasters held up. He could wish he had gotten further in his efforts to decentralize the government, but that was one of the stages in his reforms that would have to wait for some future reformer less bound by the leftover traditions and power structures of the Empire.

They were interrupted only by a page bearing a note from Conju stating that it was his Radiancy's pleasure that they leave at the second hour. Cliopher sent word to Commander Omo and Captain Diogen, then sat watching Kiri in her finery read through papers. They finished three hours after midnight, and Cliopher sat down, exhausted, on his sleeping mat.

He woke with a start an hour later. He scrambled stiffly to his feet, thinking that an Alinorel-style bed would be easier to clamber out of, and hastily did his ablutions and dressed in fresh clothing. His eye fell on the two neat bags he had packed, and then on the small shelf of books he kept for pleasure reading. He wondered abruptly if his Radiancy would think to bring any books with him.

Next to the books he packed the oboe, though when he would practice and where he could not imagine. He was barely a good amateur; he could not play in his Radiancy's hearing and offend that ear. But the Vangavaye-ve was the home of music, and if he went there without his oboe ... well, he did not like to think what his family would think that symbolized.

It did not occur to him until later that he immediately assumed they would find out.

CHAPTER *F*IVE

A REMARKABLY SMALL PILE OF baggage was in the process of being loaded when Cliopher arrived at the top of the Spire. Ser Rhodin and five other guards were already there, including Pikabe and his partner, Ato. They nodded at Cliopher as he looked over the ship.

The *Eastern Wonder* was her name. With a fine flaring keel made of one single trunk of an Amboloyan flying pine, the wooden sides curved up and outward to a gilded rail. The sails were white with golden stripes, indicating Imperial business but not that his Radiancy was on board. Captain Diogen used the same when taking Cliopher to the Vangavaye-ve. Unlike those voyages, the only sailor visible was the captain himself, who stood nervously next to the gangway. He brightened when he saw Cliopher.

"I have my sailors below. Told them a ceremonial taboo. They won't peek."

"Good thinking," Cliopher said, meaning it. The sun was barely over the horizon, the air still cool. He was glad he had thought to put on the heavier robe he wore in Amboloyo.

Diogen looked reassured. "It is precious hard, sir."

"Look sharp," Ser Rhodin said in a quiet voice, and all the guards present leapt to full attention. They were wearing their ordinary uniform, a white kilt and golden belt, not the full glory of leopard skins and ostrich plumes and precious stones and gold that they wore when attending his Radiancy, nor even the lesser panoply for when they were in attendance on lesser royalty. Cliopher wondered if Commander Omo had ordered them to bring their panoply. Conju had sent Cliopher notes to insist he bring court finery, just in case.

Cliopher had packed his court costume and wondered if he should bring his Islander finery as well. In the end he did not, for it was not his holiday, and he went in his capacity as his Radiancy's secretary, not as Kip Mdang. If there came an unexpected need for finery, it would be court wear that was called for. The Islander finery he had at the Palace was too old, anyway, and might not even fit; he had never worn it there.

Commander Omo and another guardsman came processing behind Conju and a man in the hooded silvery-grey mantle of a priest-wizard. It took Cliopher a moment to realize it was his Radiancy under the hood, and marvelled at Conju's presence of mind in suggesting the minor costume. Of course, his Radiancy was a priest-wizard; or rather was the high priest and lord magus. It was just that Cliopher could not remember ever seeing him wear a colour other than white, black, gold, or Imperial yellow.

Cliopher walked over to join them, bowing deeply to one knee but not performing the formal full prostration. His Radiancy nodded an absent approval, his gaze on the ship's captain. "Good morning, Cliopher," he said in a quiet voice. "What is the captain's name?"

"Captain Diogen, my lord. The ship is the *Eastern Wonder*. The crew are below; they understand there is a ceremonial taboo at work."

His Radiancy nodded again. His face was serene, his eyes thoughtful and distant. His voice was distant, too, when he spoke, in a lower tone. "So many ceremonies and taboos."

Cliopher and Conju looked at each other, and said nothing. His Radiancy nodded once, sharply, the gleam coming back into his eye, and proceeded to where Captain Diogen waited on bent knee. "Captain Diogen."

Captain Diogen looked as if he wanted to throw himself down on his face, but heroically resisted. He did not lift his gaze past his Radiancy's foot. "The ship awaits your lordship's pleasure."

"Then let us be off. Conju?"

"My lord." Conju hastened ahead of his Radiancy to the Sun Cabin. Ludvic and Rhodin followed. Cliopher gave a hand to the captain, who thanked him gruffly. "Not many I kneel to. Stiff old joints. Now, as for the rest of you—I will show you your cabins. Sayo Mdang, I know you like to watch us take flight, but given the haste—"

Cliopher stifled a yawn. "Thank you, but all I really want is a bed."

★★★

HE WOKE MIDMORNING. THE SHIP had passed over the Grey Mountains and was already halfway out across the Mgunai Plain towards the Wide Seas. His cabin was in the prow of the ship, with windows facing port. The prow lookout was above him in the carved point of the keel log, with the captain's cabin across from his and the galley below. Behind them stretched the open deck, until the back poop under which were the Sun Cabin and the two lesser guest rooms flanking it. Port was given to Ludvic and Ser Rhodin, Conju had a bed tucked into a nook of the Sun Cabin, and the other guards shared starboard.

Cliopher always gained his sea legs quickly and found the sky ships little different from water-borne vessels save that they were much smoother in motion. He walked down the mid-deck to the aft cabins, passing the hatches leading down as he went. Though there were sailors aloft in the sails and the high decks, the rear of the ship was eerily empty.

He entered the short hallway leading to the Sun Cabin and smiled at the two guards on duty, Elish and—and Zerafin, that was it. He'd seen the roster Ser Rhodin had drawn up. "Has his Radiancy awoken?" he asked softly.

Elish saluted. "Lord Conju called for refreshments ten minutes ago."

Cliopher nodded and tapped on the door. It opened after a few moments. "His Radiancy is on the balcony," Conju said, gesturing for him to go through the cabin.

Cliopher found his Radiancy with a cup of coffee and a spread of familiar gold-bound dispatch cases, none of which were open as his Radiancy was gazing out at the spectacular view before him. Conju (who disliked heights intensely) hovered in the doorway. Cliopher bowed.

"Sit down, Cliopher. Conju—" Conju did his best not to look terrified; his Radiancy smiled. "More coffee for Cliopher."

"Very good, my lord." Conju made his escape, leaving Cliopher to sit next to the Presence, who said nothing. There was a faint, relaxing sound, thrumming around them as the ship cleaved the still, limpid air and the continent unspooled below and behind them. After a long moment, Cliopher realized his Radiancy was humming.

Humming; and smiling, face upturned to the sunlight and eyes closed; humming and smiling and looking by far the most relaxed Cliopher had ever seen him.

A feeling of indescribable fondness welled up in him as he regarded his lord. It was only strengthened when his Radiancy said quietly, without opening his eyes, "Is Conju afraid of heights?"

Cliopher briefly considered prevaricating, but that seemed unfair. "Petrified, my lord."

"I thought so," his Radiancy said softly, and when Conju came out again with the tray of coffee and warm biscuits, dismissed him to his own amusements. And then they had breakfast, and talked about the world below them, and worked through the dispatch cases, just as if it were any other morning, and Cliopher hoped desperately that he had made the right decision.

★★★

THE PROVINCE OF THE VANGAVAYE-VE included the wide scattering of atolls and volcanic islands in the middle of the Wide Seas, as far away from anywhere else as it was possible to be on Zunidh. The Vangavaye-ve itself consisted of the Outer Ring and all within its embrace. It was Gorjo City, however, floating on the waves below Mama Ituri's peak, that was what everyone thought of as the wonder of the Nine Worlds.

Mama Ituri was the live volcano and mother goddess of the Vangavaye-ve. She loomed over the city, stark and spectacular, her flanks clothed in jungle and her head wreathed with the fumes she occasionally emitted. She was considered the perfect exemplar of a mountain; there were paintings by intrepid artists in the Palace collection of her in all her moods.

Or most of them. The last princess of the Vangavaye-ve but one had decided to spite Mama Ituri, ordering a platform to be built at the mountain's summit so that she and her court could have a picnic there and watch an eruption, should there be one.

There had been.

Cliopher glanced at the long black scar cutting through the jungle, and remembered well when the news arrived. His Radiancy had said, first: "There has been an eruption in the Vangavaye-ve," and second: "It did not hit the city," and third, when he finished reading the report: "That serves them right."

He had sent Cliopher off to bring order to the province while the clerks of the court figured out who was next in line for the princess' seat, without saying it but (Cliopher well knew) so that he could go and see with his own eyes that his family was safe.

There had been no need for him to go. The Vangavaye-ve was not Nijan or Amboloyo: its people were not restless, and tended to look on the princes who came and went as a necessary but not particularly important consequence of being part of the world. Without a prince they had continued to live in exactly the same fashion of self-governance as they had for all of their oral history.

It was true that, as in the days of isolation after the Fall, they had not engaged in any ambitious building programmes; nor had they sent tithes anywhere. Their golden pearls, ahalo cloth, and foamwork had instead gone to adorn the most respected elders and artists, as had been the ancient custom.

There had been no famine, no pestilence, no violence, no more crime than usual.

There had been no external need for him to go, but his Radiancy had sent him nonetheless.

It was things like that that made Cliopher stand nervously on the edge of the sky ship dock, waiting for his Radiancy to emerge. His nerves were jangling not only because of the sheer unconventionality of things, the difference between this visit and all earlier ones, all the ways in which they were breaking protocol and custom and coming perilously near to breaking some of the great taboos.

If his Radiancy had been merely a god, this would not be happening.

If his Radiancy were merely a god, Cliopher thought, staring out into the pre-dawn mist (for they had arrived late in the evening and stayed on board while he went to ascertain that the vessel would be ready to take them out to the little palace across the bay in the morning), he, Cliopher, would not be nervous. Gods were eternal, unchanging in their essence, understandable in their sheer otherness. Men, on the other hand, were tricky.

He wanted his Radiancy to *enjoy* this vacation.

He swallowed hard as he felt the gangway next to him vibrate, but it was Captain Diogen.

"Sayo Mdang," he said softly, glancing back up the rope bridge with a nervous roll to his eyes that Cliopher knew was due entirely to the person in the Sun Cabin, and all that he represented. "What are our instructions?"

"You are to await our coming. It may be some weeks."

"Sir?"

That was all the question he dared voice. Cliopher took pity on him, knowing that there would be questions, that his sailors were silent and fearful even if they did not know, exactly, who it was in the cabin that could not be looked upon. Many of them would guess.

"We are here for a vacation," Cliopher murmured. Captain Diogen stared at him in perplexity. "How long we stay depends on many things. We will certainly be returning for the resumption of court after the Little Session, but whether we stay a week or the whole period does not depend on me."

"I understand. I will see to it that my sailors do not speculate."

Cliopher did not ask him how he planned to ensure this, for the gangway started to vibrate again and both he and the captain turned to watch the little procession descend.

Ser Rhodin and Commander Omo came first, in their ordinary uniform but holding themselves with their customary pride. His Radiancy came next, dressed again in the silvery hooded mantle of the court priest-wizards, looking as if he had been formed out of the mist and darkness. Cliopher caught himself from staring when he realized that Captain Diogen was trying desperately hard not to prostrate himself. Every child of the Empire had had it ingrained in him to fall before the Presence.

Cliopher went down on one knee, rising again at the flick of his Radiancy's hand. His Radiancy then turned to the captain, who had sunk down gratefully as soon as Cliopher had, but had not risen. "Captain Diogen," his Radiancy said, his rich, deep voice soft. "That was a smooth flight. Well done to you and your men."

"It was the greatest honour of my life," the captain said, sounding entirely sincere. Cliopher could see the strain in the man's shoulders as he pressed himself into his knee, the desire to prostrate himself warring with the orders. His Radiancy turned to Cliopher. "Lead on."

Cliopher bowed and started down the familiar tight spiral in the unfamiliar grouping. Out of the corner of his eye he saw Conju give the captain what looked like a pouch of money, and was glad that small suggestion had been well received. The captain would probably have been perfectly happy to wait for four weeks for the honour of conveying his Radiancy back to Solaara, and certainly would have done his duty regardless of his sentiments, but extra money for him and his crew to spend in Gorjo City would never come in amiss.

Behind Conju Pikabe and Ato stood guard, while the other four guards carried the baggage. It did not seem enough to get his Radiancy through one day, let alone his Radiancy and ten others. Still, it wasn't as if they were going to hold court.

By the Emperor, Cliopher thought, glancing at his Radiancy; *what have we done?*

★★★

PRINCESS ORIANA WAS AWAY AGAIN, so the only ship was theirs. They had come in so late, and were leaving so early in the morning, that there were few gawkers waiting to see who disembarked. They saw a man in court garb, walking with a grave expression, and they saw behind him half a dozen imperial guards clustered close around two men, and they carefully turned their eyes away.

No one among those gathered at the bottom of the Spire prostrated himself, nor (astonishingly enough) were there any relations to hail Cliopher, so they were able to reach the docks unmolested. He had arranged for the boat to pick them up at the closest docks, those associated with the princess' use, rather than the main city marina or even the university's.

It had been easier to persuade the princess's servants of his need than the boat's captain, who was one of the breed of independent and independent-minded sailors that plied the great Bay of the Waters. He had strenuously resisted coming into royal territory, until Cliopher had finally given him a third again the wages that should have been acceptable. Enough to keep his mouth shut, he devoutly hoped.

At the lower docks the captain stood waiting, his two assistants doing useful-looking tasks on board the small ship. It was a pleasure yacht, the finest Cliopher had been able to find that was not obviously on royal or imperial service, recommended to him by numerous friends on various occasions as being the best, fastest, nicest, and generally most impressive vessel of its kind. Even Bertie had had good things to say about it.

When he saw the boat his Radiancy checked his step slightly. Cliopher looked at him anxiously, but he was staring at it, and the captain, with the blank expression that meant he was thinking hard about something and did not wish to be questioned.

"Captain Achillon, my lord," he said, when his Radiancy nodded at him.

Captain Achillon bowed politely to the priest-wizard and nodded to Cliopher, looked askance at the eight imperial guards, and then said, "Welcome to the *Aōtelēlana*, my lords. Decker will show you where to put your luggage, if you will follow me?"

He led them to seats set in the prow of the ship and left them after another bow. It was deep enough, but somewhat hesitant, for Cliopher had been tired last night when he explained that every courtesy was to be extended to the priest-wizard. *Why?* the captain had growled, and Cliopher had said, *Please, for the love of the Emperor, extend him every courtesy. All hail the Sun-on-Earth*, Captain Achillon had replied with no discernible irony, and Cliopher had left it at that.

He had already had to deal with the officers at the sky ship dock (for once actually on duty), who had not been overly keen on his explanations and had wanted the passenger manifest he would not give them, and he was annoyed that it was only the fact that his cousin Cedric was a respected member of the department that had made them relent in the end.

At least the Light Minders on duty had minded their own business.

His Radiancy regarded the seats, which were finely enough made that Cliopher would have been happy to have them in his own home, had he had one, but which were nevertheless (he sighed) many degrees of quality and comfort down from the Imperial Apartments. The rest of them waited on his command, as ever. Finally his Radiancy seated himself at the side of the boat, where he could look over the side, and gestured to them to choose their positions.

Just before Conju quite sank down his Radiancy said thoughtfully, "Perhaps you should find a bucket, Conju."

Conju nearly gaped at him. "My lord?"

His Radiancy looked out across the sweep of the Bay of Waters, at the gentle swells rocking the boat, and he smiled with a wry edge. "I have a strong tendency to seasickness."

★★★

A LONG FIVE HOURS AND forty-five minutes later, Cliopher heaved a great sigh of relief as they finally finished negotiating the breakers on the inner reef and crossed into the flat water of the lagoon. His Radiancy pushed himself upright, accepted the damp cloth Conju held out for him, and wiped his face while they carefully looked away. His Radiancy had not been jesting, though it was only when they crossed the central currents of the Bay that he had actually begun to be ill. Conju and Cliopher had alternated sitting in front of him with the bucket.

When it had been Cliopher's turn for a respite, he had gone to the middle of the yacht where the guards were sitting. Ser Rhodin and Commander Omo were playing cards; it was actually a very smooth crossing. They dealt Cliopher in and he sat playing with them for a few minutes, trying not to turn around to look at the miserable figure sitting hunched over the bucket.

"The captain said it is an extraordinarily good crossing," Ser Rhodin said cautiously. "I would have thought I'd feel it myself, but ..."

Cliopher looked out at the water, which was as close to perfectly still as he had ever seen. "I suspect the local magic is smoothing the way."

"Not that it seems to be helping," Ser Rhodin murmured, wincing as a stray gust brought an unpleasantly intelligible sound back to them. "I had no idea."

"Neither did I," Cliopher replied glumly. In the days of the Empire this would almost certainly have cost him his head. Not necessarily because of the Emperor himself, mind, but because all the mechanisms of power and glory would have required it. Cliopher had spent a lifetime picking apart those mechanisms of power. This was not exactly how he had thought to test his work.

"What does Ayotaylay—whatsit mean?"

Cliopher was glad for Ser Rhodin's change of subject. "The name of the boat? *Aōtelēlona* means 'The Dances of Those Who Tie the Sails' in the old language. The captain must be related to the Nevans from Epalo. That's the name of their dances."

Ser Rhodin dealt him another hand. "What do you mean?"

"Each of the families has traditional dances and songs, from the old days when we travelled the Wide Seas. The public songs are in the *Lays of the Wide Seas*. There are private ones, too, songs only known to certain people in certain families. The dances are done for special occasions—weddings, funerals, the hundred-day feast after the birth of a child, the coming into adulthood, for some traditional cultural positions, too."

He paused a moment, realizing he had instinctively crossed his feet to hide the tell-tale scars of his own learning. He cleared his throat. "It's a bit odd to name a boat after the dance, but perhaps the captain is *lonà*. That is, the One Who Ties the Sails—the person who is responsible for the knowledge of the dance and the song. It is a rare and special thing, to be the repository of the traditional knowledge. You must keep it perfect, and find someone to pass it along to before you die, so the knowledge is not lost."

Ser Rhodin looked at him curiously. "Does your family have a dance?"

Cliopher was embarrassed at the question. He had a few pieces of Islander art in his rooms, and when he could make the time he practiced the dances for exercise, but otherwise only his colouring and the lingering traces of his accent marked him as an Islander.

It was not that he was *ashamed* of his family or his culture, but that they were so foreign to Palace life he guarded them preciously. He did not want to put them on display the way artefacts brought back by governors or other central-province visitors were displayed in the Imperial Museum of Comparative Anthropology down in the city. He kept them private. They were *his*.

But Ser Rhodin and Commander Omo were his friends. He said quietly, "The Mdang dances are called *Aōtetētana*, the Dances of Those Who Tend the Fire."

He had a sudden vivid memory of his great-uncle teaching him the fire dance, when he was a young boy, before he had gone to Astandalas. He still had the burn scars on his feet to show where he had made mistakes learning the steps. He uncrossed his feet. He was wearing Solaaran-style sandals. Their straps hid those old scars, which would be meaningless to Ser Rhodin and Commander Omo in any case. In Solaara, as in Astandalas before it, the fire dances of the Wayfinders were only the barest legend, unconnected with present day Wide Sea Islanders.

After a moment Commander Omo said, "Thank you for giving us the name."

When the captain at last anchored the boat and lowered the gangplank to the low wooden dock on Lesuia island, his Radiancy gripped the railing and made his way to the shore with a fair show of dignity. Conju and Commander Omo both hovered next to him in case he should fall, but they kept their hands to themselves.

He did not stumble.

Cliopher thanked Captain Achillon while the guards solemnly retrieved the luggage. The captain shrugged, watching as his Radiancy planted his feet firmly on the sand and took several deep breaths. Cliopher watched, too, as his Radiancy's attention moved from what was surely a blessed relief to take in their surrounds.

It was, he was embarrassingly grateful to see, as beautiful as he remembered.

Captain Achillon was talking, and Cliopher hastily returned his attention to him. "I beg your pardon?"

"When you want to go back, send a message with Balgo from the village and I'll come fetch you. He goes to the city a couple of times a fortnight."

"Thank you."

"It's not usually that calm on the Bay. Look you, the wind's picking up again already."

Cliopher sighed, though he also was fairly certain that the Bay would be equally as calm for the return journey, whenever it was and regardless of prevailing weather. "I know, captain."

Satisfied, the captain saluted, cast one lingering look at the dark figure on the beach and his circle of guards, shook his head at some thought, and called up to his two men to raise the sails. Cliopher was certain they would have a much faster return across the Bay. Even as he watched the wind filled the jib sail.

He straightened his back and told himself that his Radiancy was not the sort of man who would punish them for their ignorance of his tendency to seasickness. No matter how stern he looked.

Cliopher approached, bowed, and waited for his Radiancy's response. There was nothing for a moment, and then his Radiancy said, in a tone so neutral Cliopher's heart contracted, "Well?"

"This way, my lord," said Cliopher, and away they went to the exquisite little house.

His Radiancy cast a severe eye over the building, apparently dismissed comment, and strode inside. Conju had rushed ahead and was waiting outside the selected bedchamber. His Radiancy walked through the beautiful rooms without a word and at the doorway made an abrupt gesture of dismissal to the rest of them. Elish and Commander Omo went within, leaving Ser Rhodin and the other guards and Cliopher to take a deep breath and let it out again.

CHAPTER SIX

HIS RADIANCY, CONJU REPORTED SOMEWHAT later, had bathed and lain down and did not wish to be disturbed nor to eat anything. Cliopher and Conju ate with Ser Rhodin, the guard rotation was drawn up and rooms allotted, and then Cliopher went to his own room and unpacked his three little bags and sat down on his sleeping pad thinking that he was next door to the Lord of Rising Stars, who was surely not at all pleased at having had five hours of sea-sickness as the beginning of his first vacation in—well, in Cliopher's memory.

But his bed, as he found after a lazu afternoon on the verandah spent drafting a proposal for what he hoped would eventually become the foundation of a universal income, was the most comfortable he had ever experienced, and he slept very well. He woke in the morning feeling greatly refreshed, and lay in the cool fine linen sheets with a blissful sense of peace.

He had not paid much attention to the room the night before, save to see that it was larger than his bedchamber in the Palace, and that the bed was a soft mattress on a low frame with bespelled mosquito netting draped around a graceful metalwork canopy. He moved aside the netting and looked at the space.

The floors were made of smooth dark stone, cool and welcoming to his bare feet; the walls were whitewashed, with reflected light striping them from the deep-set windows on two sides of the room. A small wardrobe held the clothes he had brought with him; there was a low table pushed near one of the windows, with shelves next to it where he had placed his books and oboe case.

Another low table held an ewer and basin, but as he had neglected to fill the ewer the night before it was empty. He looked at that for a few moments, laughing at himself for his surprise; though no high lord of the court he, too, was accustomed to the silent service of the Palace of Stars.

He dressed in the clothing that he wore for formal family functions that did not require traditional costume. It was grander than his ordinary clothes, but nowhere near court finery, either: an under-robe of white cotton, with a sleeveless over-robe of good linen dyed blue, embroidered in silk with family patterns.

Blue was not a colour he wore on official business. The uniform of the Imperial Secretariat was burnt umber, and as his Radiancy's private secretary red and black.

The privy was in a small outbuilding, as was usual in the Outer Ring, set among flowering vines at the end of a stone-flagged path. The basins for washing one's hands were made of stone, with bamboo pipes providing both a constant stream of cool water and a pleasantly noisy fountain. Towels hung off a trellis covered with jasmine; some little magic kept insects away from the cloth.

The bathing room was similarly set away from the main house, but on the opposite side of the building, with trellises providing privacy but also framing views of the lagoon. Towels had been left in a draughty place. He was very glad to find they smelled fresh and floral.

When he returned to the house he found Commander Omo standing alone in the main living space. The house was built as a long ell, with the bedrooms along one arm, the kitchen and serving rooms on the other, and a large open room where the two arms joined. A dining room on the serving wing side served as a vestibule between the two portions of the house.

Low couches and tables were arranged around a brazier clearly intended for ambience rather than warmth. The inner corner faced the lagoon, opening on to a wide covered verandah; louvred glass doors along the whole front provided access. The materials were all beautiful and beautifully constructed, and if they were not of the quality of the Palace of Stars, they were nevertheless unexceptionable.

And from every window either gardens or that spectacular vista: the white sand, the aquamarine lagoon, the white surf over the reef, the darker blue of the Bay of the Waters, and in the distance the peaks of Mama Ituri and her Son and the buildings of Gorjo City just visible as a pale smudge on the water.

Home.

Commander Omo was looking out at this view. He turned when Cliopher entered. "What a beautiful place."

Cliopher walked up to stand beside him, looking across to the city, thinking that Commander Omo was a very quiet man, a soldier's soldier, every inch a man of the sword and spear: and yet he smiled with simple pleasure in this beauty.

"I hope it pleases his Radiancy," Cliopher said, touching the long gauzy curtains before him, and recalling vividly as he did so his Radiancy touching the tassel on the curtains in the Imperial Apartments.

"It does," said a familiar voice behind them, and both he and Commander Omo whirled to perform their standard greetings to his Radiancy: Commander Omo saluted, and Cliopher knelt.

"We shall not hold you to court standards," his Radiancy said, the words somewhat at odds with the formal plural. He gestured them to their ease, and as Cliopher rose he added: "You have gone to some trouble for us to come incognito; let us continue."

"Very good, my lord."

His Radiancy clapped his hands lightly. Cliopher tried not to jump. "Now," said his Radiancy, "it is time for breakfast. Come join me, the both of you."

Conju was hovering behind his Radiancy. He shook his head in amazement, which was nothing to the look his face briefly held when his Radiancy said, "You, too, Conju—and fetch Rhodin as well."

Conju hastened off, working to make his face impassive, and Cliopher and Commander Omo trailed after his Radiancy to the room where the house servants had laid out a light meal on a low table surrounded by woven mats in the local variant of Eastern Ring style. There was a small fuss while Conju placed a cushion for his Radiancy in the place of honour, then the four of them took their seats, trying not to look at each other.

It was curious what a difference context made, Cliopher thought. The four of them took meals together on occasion, but never had they all been seated in the Presence. Cliopher was not certain that either Ser Rhodin or Conju had ever been invited to eat with his Radiancy before. Commander Omo, the longest-serving member of his Radiancy's household, was occasionally invited to breakfast, and Cliopher to lunch.

They waited expectantly for his Radiancy to salute the morning, which he did with an abbreviated prayer to the Sun and Moon. After his Radiancy accepted the golden eating sticks Conju presented to him, he gestured at them to take their own food. It took Cliopher a moment to realize that his Radiancy would not speak the second half of the prayer, which was to the living god, the Last Emperor, still the Sun of his people.

The lack of that usual benediction was deeply disconcerting, and the

meal continued entirely silent because his Radiancy did not initiate any conversation. Afterwards they all retired to the main room and hovered uncomfortably while his Radiancy decided what to do.

Pikabe and Ato, who were the honour guards on duty, placed themselves
on either side of the door leading to the servants' wing, from which position
they could see the room and most of the forecourt and verandah. Ser Rhodin saluted and went to the guard's quarters, Conju bowed and disappeared
down the hall behind him, presumably to see to his Radiancy's room, leaving
Commander Omo, Cliopher, and his Radiancy.

His Radiancy's expression was serene as ever, but his body betrayed some
inner tension: he walked—no, prowled—around the room, looking at the
furnishings and various pieces of art. Commander Omo planted himself beside the verandah doors, where he could keep an eye on both his lord and
the view, and Cliopher stood waiting, neither acknowledged nor dismissed.

After a long few minutes his Radiancy stopped before him. "Have you
no book to read, Cliopher?"

His tone was sharp. Cliopher bowed, keeping his face impassive. "I do,
my lord. Would your lordship like me to fetch a selection?"

His Radiancy made a gesture Cliopher interpreted as a 'yes', so he bowed
again and hastened to his room. There he hesitated uncomfortably at the
small library he had brought before choosing the history of Ysthar since the
Fall he had been reading, a book of Voonran poetry, and a new translation of
an Old Shaian epic.

His Radiancy picked up the epic. "*The Deeds of Olor.*"

His voice held a strange note in it. Cliopher swallowed. "It is a new translation of an old poem, my lord."

"Yes; it was my favourite when I was a boy." His Radiancy turned the
book in his hands. "I have not read it in many years."

Cliopher made an encouraging noise, which he hoped a moment later
his Radiancy would ignore (which he did, though with an alarming flicker
of his eyebrows). His Radiancy looked around, but before he chose a seat
Commander Omo said suddenly, "There is a swinging chair set upon the
verandah, my lord."

His Radiancy spun on one foot. The commander opened the door in-
vitingly.

"Thank you, Ludvic," his Radiancy said, and strode out. Commander
Omo made a gesture at the two honour guards, who swept through the room
in unison to take their positions on the other side of the door. The guard

captain closed it behind them and came to stand next to Cliopher, who said, "That was an inspired idea."

Commander Omo shrugged. "His Radiancy has often been pleased to sit in the open air."

Which Cliopher had seen, but never quite articulated to himself.

He picked up the Ystharian history and sat down, and quickly became absorbed in its accounts of unbelievable inventions and even more unbelievable political experiments.

But he was not so absorbed that he did not notice when his Radiancy stood up and started pacing.

He held himself ready to be summoned, but no sound came through the louvred windows, and neither Pikabe nor Ato opened the door to call him.

Commander Omo saw him grow alert. "It has been just over an hour," he said.

"What do you mean?"

Commander Omo looked at the dark figure pacing up and down the verandah, book closed and set aside. His face was impassive, though he kept his voice very quiet. "His Radiancy has never had longer than an hour to himself."

★★★

HIS RADIANCY PACED ALL THAT day, interrupted only by Conju bringing out refreshments. Each meal his Radiancy asked them to join him, and at each meal they said nothing. After the meals he read, each time again for an hour, before the book was closed and he stood and paced along the verandah. The guards changed out; he watched them perform the small rituals of transferal with serene face; and then he paced.

The second day was a repeat of the first, save only that at the midday meal his Radiancy asked Conju whether everything was to his satisfaction. Conju replied that the house, though of course nothing to the Palace, held staff of sufficient skill that he dared hope his Radiancy was not displeased.

"We are not," his Radiancy said; but still he paced.

★★★

CONJU ADMITTED TO CLIOPHER THE next morning that the household staff, though few in number, were indeed well-trained. Despite the fact that by birth he was the highest-ranking of them all (for his father had been a high lord of Ysthar in Imperial days), his position as chief attendant meant that the house servants looked first to him. He added, "They think our lord a man of great eccentricity."

"How so?" asked Cliopher, watching his Radiancy pace, a dozen strides up, a dozen strides down.

"The number of guards. They cannot imagine why anyone would need so many, and think that perhaps he is a prisoner of great rank. I made certain they did not repeat that suggestion," he added primly.

A dozen strides up; a dozen strides down. At one end the black figure silhouetted against the white sand and aqua sea; at the other against a stand of green and purple taro edging a small pond in the garden.

"He is not moving so quickly today," Conju said, his voice tentative.

Cliopher wondered what that meant. That his Radiancy was physically tired? That whatever tension filled him was finally ebbing? That he was growing bored?

His Radiancy stopped and stood leaning on the railing, staring out to sea. They watched him for several minutes; he did not stir.

"I will take him coffee," Cliopher said at last, "if you will make it, Conju?"

Conju brought biscuits with the coffee, as close to the Alinorel-style ginger cookies that were his Radiancy's favourite as he had been able to persuade the house cook into producing. Cliopher set the tray next to the book on the table beside the tall swinging chair his Radiancy had once again abandoned.

He waited until his Radiancy's hand flicked an acknowledgement.

"My lord," he said quietly, "I have brought you coffee."

His Radiancy nodded. Cliopher poured a measure into his Radiancy's porcelain cup (thinking as he did that that cup, brought from the Palace by Conju, was probably worth all the furniture and the house as well) and brought it over.

"My lord," he said again.

His Radiancy accepted the cup, but rested the saucer on the railing while he stared out at the brilliant sea. Cliopher hesitated, knowing that if it had been Conju, or his cousins or friends, or Ser Rhodin, or even Commander Omo, he would have put a hand on the other's shoulder and asked what was wrong.

It was taboo to touch his Radiancy, and he had never initiated a personal conversation (and very rarely was the recipient of one), so he stood there, trying to offer his sympathy without speech or insult. His Radiancy stared out to sea. After a while he said, "I used to know who I was beyond my duties."

Cliopher was shocked, and found no words to say. His Radiancy smiled mirthlessly. "I suppose you didn't know me then."

Cliopher had no idea what to say to that. He tried a few words in his mind, rejecting all of them as nonsensical or insulting or simply stupid, but the silence ticked on and he knew he ought to say something, and so at last he said: "Is there nothing your Radiancy would *like* to do?"

He bit his lip. He should not have said *your Radiancy*.

His Radiancy noticed the slip, of course, but apart from a slight compression of his lips his face did not change. He kept looking at the sea, at the waves breaking on the reef, the water still and brilliant in the lagoon. "I think I should like to go swimming," he said finally.

Cliopher felt he was on safe grounds there. "Then, my lord, I shall tell Conju to bring your robes."

★★★

IT WAS NOT QUITE SO easy as that, of course. First Ser Rhodin and Commander Omo had to determine which among the guards could swim—only Ato, Oginu, and Zerafin, the rest of them all being from inland regions—and then Commander Omo had to decide whether it was necessary for them to be in the water with his Radiancy, or if it would be acceptable for them to remain on shore. After it was finally decided they might remain ashore, Conju, who had come out with the robes and towels he felt suitable, asked somewhat fearfully whether there was danger of sharks.

Cliopher was about to explain for the third time that the reefs prevented sharks, jellyfish, and barracudas alike from coming within the lagoon, when his Radiancy (who had been observing their preparations with some amusement) said abruptly: "We are the Lord of Zunidh. There are no natural predators that will threaten us."

The plural meant he was in no mood for banter. He turned to approach the water. Cliopher stood beside Conju, holding a small table for the dry garments. It occurred to him then to ask, "I suppose his Radiancy does know how to swim?"

Conju gave him a reproving glance. "His Radiancy swims each morning in the Imperial Bath."

Cliopher had often wondered what his Radiancy did for exercise, and so was relieved to learn this. He was, however, surprised when his Radiancy reached the water's line and simply discarded all his clothing before walking fully naked into the sea.

Conju smirked at him before going to retrieve the abandoned clothes. "His Radiancy has no privacy," he said, and when Cliopher still stared at him in perplexity, gestured at Oginu and Zerafin standing watchfully at the edge of the water. "These are the guards of his household, and I am his Groom of the Chamber."

And Cliopher remembered that the guards stood within every room his Radiancy inhabited except for that private study in which he never spent more than an hour alone.

★★★

HIS RADIANCY SWAM FOR HALF an hour, going farther out than Conju liked, but not so far that Cliopher felt any alarm. They sat on the sand watching, enjoying the warmth of the sun. His Radiancy swam with an elegant breaststroke, long even motions that kept his head above water. Cliopher wondered idly where he had become so practiced a swimmer.

After a while Commander Omo came to join them. He stood watching the swimmer, then squatted beside them. "What did his Radiancy say to you earlier, Cliopher, that you looked so perturbed?"

The plaintive statement had been echoing through his mind all morning. *I used to know who I was beyond my duties.* He thought of his Radiancy's life, the careful schedules of rituals and ceremonies and duties, the work that began at dawn and lasted through the end of evening court. Sixteen hours a day, day in and day out, every activity and nearly every motion prescribed by tradition and strict custom.

Three days of pacing even to begin to undo that conditioning.

"Oh," said Cliopher, not wanting to betray what seemed a great confidence, knowing also that they were the closest thing his Radiancy had to friends or family.

And if it were himself?

He would want them to ask, he thought. If it were him. He would want them to know.

He swallowed. "His Radiancy said … that he felt he used to know who he was beyond his duties."

They looked as shocked as he must have.

Conju said, "But his Radiancy is the heart of Zunidh."

"When I go home to my family," Cliopher said slowly, "they do not scrape and bow and ask me for favours. They barely know I have a position in the Secretariat."

Conju smiled. "When I first met your mother, she asked me what I did, and when I said I was the Groom of the Lord's Chamber she asked me whether I ever saw his Radiancy. I was not offended because it was so lovely to be ..." he faltered.

"To be treated as a person," Commander Omo said, nodding.

They turned as one to look at the swimmer, who appeared to be coming back towards shore. "But there are all the customary duties ..." Conju said.

"His Radiancy has expressed a desire to continue incognito," Cliopher said hesitantly.

They exchanged glances. Then after a moment, Commander Omo said, "When has he ever given us reason to think he would punish us for impudence?"

"We have never been impudent," Conju said sharply.

"Have you never seen his face when Cliopher makes a jest and he returns it?" Commander Omo said. "I have."

And Cliopher remembered again that he had been offered his position after he had broken one of the great customs and met his Radiancy's eyes.

Conju made a harrumphing noise and stood to shake out the robes and towels. He walked forward to meet his Radiancy, who was coming out of the water, looking (to Cliopher) like some story of Creation as the water streaming off his dark shoulders caught the light and the three men stood awaiting his coming.

"What is the worst that could happen?" Commander Omo said.

Cliopher raised his eyebrows at him.

"Come now, Sayo Mdang, surely your years of loyal service warrant some optimism."

His Radiancy swept up towards them, looking far happier than he had before that swim. "Come!" he said. "Surely it is nearly time for lunch."

And this time when they were seated there silently after the benediction, Commander Omo (to Cliopher's mild shame) turned to his Radiancy and said, "My lord, did you enjoy your swim?"

His Radiancy was lifting a morsel, and paused momentarily in evident surprise at being addressed. Then he smiled, and Cliopher felt burning tears at the expression, which briefly commingled pleasure and relief and wonder and amazement and wry humour before the habitual serenity replaced it.

"Yes, I did," his Radiancy said. "There were many fish and bright corals and things. Do you know what they are, Cliopher?"

"I would know some of them, my lord," Cliopher said, and, when

Commander Omo gave him a speaking glance, added, "In the western Van-gavaye-ve the pearl divers make a kind of goggles with Iveline rubber so they can see better under water."

"If one's face is below, how does one breathe?" Commander Omo asked.

It had been too long since he last went snorkelling. "They use a bamboo pipe, fashioned so it bends and rises above one's head. The reefs are full of many wonders, and often artists go to observe."

"How marvellous," Conju said manfully.

"This sounds delightful," his Radiancy said. "Would it be possible to acquire such a mask?"

"They would sell them in Gorjo City," Cliopher replied, a bit helplessly, but Ser Rhodin (who had been sitting in silent amazement at this near-nat-ural conversation with his Radiancy) spoke up suddenly. "Perhaps there is something in storage here."

"A capital idea," his Radiancy said, and this time when they stood from the meal, he did not go to the verandah to either read his book or pace, but instead rubbed his hands and said to Conju, "Let us explore the rooms."

Conju looked most astonished and as if he wanted to protest the irreg-ularity, but he swallowed his protests and instead led the little party—for Cliopher was too curious not to follow, and the two guards trailed behind, of course—down the hall to where a few storage closets were set between and in the bedrooms.

The first door they came to was his Radiancy's. Conju, who appeared to have resigned himself to this whim, looked enquiringly at his Radiancy.

"There aren't any closets or cupboards to look into," he said. "Next door."

The next door belonged to a small closet that held neat stacks of linens. His Radiancy contemplated these, nodded absently, and gestured at the door to Cliopher's room.

Cliopher was glad he had remembered to make up his bed that morning. His Radiancy gestured at the shelf. "What instrument is that, Cliopher?"

"An oboe, my lord."

"We shall have to have you play for us one night."

"I am no great musician, my lord."

"Not enough time to practice, I expect. Your tastes run to narrative po-etry and history, I see."

"Yes, my lord."

Too many years of habit forestalled any easy continuation of the conver-sation when it had nothing to do with work. He felt a sharp pang of sympa-thy for his Radiancy.

"Was there anything in the wardrobe?"

"Camphor, my lord."

His Radiancy smiled appreciatively, examined the view out of each window, and chivvied Conju to the next door.

They made their way around the three rooms taken by the guards, severely startling those off-duty with what was taken as an impromptu inspection (and to which they responded, stammering, that they were playing dice and backgammon, or snoozing or reading, as the mood took them; Pikabe, who had been the one snoozing, looked flamingly mortified to have been caught asleep by his Radiancy). They discovered a few closets and cupboards that yielded nothing more exciting than spare blankets, extra vases, miscellaneous household items, and a complete set of formal Central Astandalan-style tableware. Coming back towards the main room, his Radiancy abruptly stopped.

"What is it, my lord?" Conju asked anxiously.

His Radiancy held up his hand. His expression was one Cliopher had seen on other men's faces, but it took a moment for him to recognize it on his Radiancy's: a distant, thoughtful, probing look.

"I had a dream about this place. Long ago. Long before I became Emperor, in fact."

He looked at each of them, with alert, wondering eyes, then tilted his head and looked at the hallway walls more intently. Cliopher thought he had never seen his Radiancy look so very alive as in that moment.

"I have always been grateful not to be afflicted with prophetic dreams," his Radiancy said, going to the inner wall and running his hands along its surface. The walls here were sheathed with stone panels, with a geometric carving every few feet. They watched him silently, not sure what to say. Conju looked as if he were fretting about dust or dirt sullying his Radiancy's hands. (His Radiancy, Cliopher noted, did not himself seem at all concerned.) "But I think many have these moments where they walk into the memory of a dream."

"I had thought that a trick of the mind," Cliopher said, following the resolve to foster conversations.

"Quite likely," his Radiancy agreed. "But there is certainly evidence enough that some do dream truly of future events. Often utterly banal ones, I grant, but still ..." He pressed one of the carved rosettes. Something clicked and he stood back as the panel turned smoothly on a pivot and revealed hidden shelves. His Radiancy smiled. "Sometimes they are more interesting."

The bottom three shelves were empty; the middle held a small stack of what appeared to be notebooks. The next held a dusty harp with broken strings and a small cloth pouch, both of which his Radiancy took out, thereby smudging his outfit with all the dust that Conju had been at pains to avoid. He tilted his head back to look at the upper shelf, then looked at Cliopher, Conju, and the current guards, all of whom were his height or shorter.

Cliopher would have gone to fetch a stool, or, more likely, asked Conju if he knew where one were to be found. His Radiancy turned and cried, "Varro!"

There was a thump from the back room, followed by Varro at a dead run. His Radiancy ignored his consternation. "Varro, you're the tallest. See if there is anything on the top shelf, would you?"

"My, my lord," said the hapless Varro, saluting. He was a Plainsman from south of Solaara, with mahogany-brown skin and reddish hair that he teased out in a cloud, and like most of his countrymen was tall and lean and built for running. He was also the youngest and newest of the Imperial Guards seconded to his Radiancy's private honour guard. Cliopher had only learned his name on the voyage. He suspected Varro had not imagined that his Radiancy knew it.

His efforts with the top shelf yielded a thick book. He scrubbed ineffectually at the dust on it before presenting it to his Radiancy, which was an irregularity that made Conju bite back a groan. His Radiancy smiled. "Thank you, Varro."

Varro saluted smartly. "Is there anything else I can do for you, my lord?"

"No, that will be all for now."

Varro saluted again—he really was very tall, well over six and a half feet—and loped off back down the hallway, no doubt to regale the others with an account of his Radiancy's strange new behaviour.

His Radiancy brushed more dust off the cover with fastidious fingers. "Now, let us see … *A Further Volume of Pious Tales for Young Children* … It seems unlikely one would trouble to hide that in a secret cupboard … Aha!"

Cliopher's curiosity got the better of him. "What is it, my lord?"

His Radiancy turned the opened book so he could see the interior title page.

It said, *Aurora, or the Peacock; being a grand tale of romance, courtesy, and derring-do, by the one and only Fitzroy Angursell.*

After a long moment his Radiancy grinned—actually *grinned*. "I wonder if it is still worthy of being banned?"

CHAPTER SEVEN

THESE TWO DISCOVERIES APPEARED TO assuage his Radiancy's interest in the house's cupboards, for he made no motion to go seeking snorkelling equipment down the servants' hall and instead bore off his prizes to the main room. Conju tried to take the harp away from him, murmuring something about it being broken and unclean.

"I am not entirely incapable of using my hands," his Radiancy said sharply. "You may go fetch me some cloths."

He did not relinquish *Aurora*, either, but there Cliopher could not blame him.

And it was true, he thought, as he sat ostensibly reading his book but actually watching his Radiancy, that the distant serene reserve that usually cloaked any hint of personality was gone, and in its place was an alert, amused, *interested* expression.

He looked, in short, like a man seized with an enthusiasm.

He was nearly unrecognizable.

When Conju returned with a basket of soft rags, his Radiancy said, "Thank you," and sat down on the seat across from Cliopher. He set the book on the floor, then examined the harp with careful fingers. He wiped away the dust and grime, until the wood gleamed golden and the strings shone silver. He was not quick about it; to be sure Conju would have cleaned the harp in a third the time it took his Radiancy. But his Radiancy was smiling, and after a while Cliopher realized he was humming, and then that his Radiancy was *happy*.

When he had cleaned the instrument to his satisfaction he poured a slithering coil of extra strings from the little pouch. "Ah," he murmured, touching something in the curved top piece.

"My lord?" Cliopher asked, unable to stop himself.

"It is not that there were no strings, but that some of the tuning pegs have snapped."

"That sounds difficult to fix."

"Not really, if one whittles."

Cliopher swallowed against his first instinct to say, *But the Sun-on-Earth does not hold edged blades.*

His Radiancy looked at him with a gleam in his eye and answered the unspoken thought. "Very true; but then, I do not need that skill."

His thoughtful glance landed on Commander Omo, who was once again standing by the verandah door. Cliopher had not yet seen the guard captain with a book, or indeed sitting down; but then his job involved vast amounts of standing around, and perhaps he enjoyed thinking. Or observing. Cliopher was finding his own observations far more interesting than he had expected.

He was not expecting what his Radiancy said next.

"Ludvic, you come from a family of woodcarvers. Could you whittle me some pegs, do you think?"

They all stared at the commander, whose face was very blank as he saluted his Radiancy. "If we can find a carving knife and some wood, of course, my lord."

His Radiancy extracted one of the whole pegs from the harp before beckoning Commander Omo over. "What kind of wood would you use? Mahogany?"

"Ebony would probably be better, my lord, if we can get it."

"I believe ebony is grown in the Vangavaye-ve," his Radiancy said, glancing at Cliopher, who nodded uncertainly. "Hmm. Ah! Let us go ask the cook."

And off he swept towards the servant wing.

"My lord," Conju said as his Radiancy reached the closed door to the wing and looked at it as if he expected it to open for him. (As, indeed, most doors did.)

"Well?"

Conju set his hand on the door. "They do not know who your lordship is."

His Radiancy lifted his eyebrows. "All the better."

"My lord, they will not know how to behave."

Most likely he meant, *Your Radiancy will not know how to behave.* But that was not something any of them would ever say.

His Radiancy smiled serenely. "I will not hold their ignorance against them."

Conju released his breath and bowed shortly before opening the door. "Very good, my lord."

His Radiancy swept through the door, followed by Cliopher, Commander Omo, Conju (with a pained expression), and trailing along behind them Ser Rhodin and Elish.

The kitchen was, Cliopher was glad to see, scrupulously clean. The cook-housekeeper sat on a stool at the main table, stuffing dumplings, while her underlings did various tasks at oven and fire and sink and counter. They all stopped in amazement at the small crowd fanning out around his Radiancy.

His Radiancy was dressed in a white tunic with a simple grey mantle over it, and looked a great lord but not—quite—the greatest man in the nine worlds. The cook blinked several times and then rose slowly to her feet at this invasion of her kitchen.

"Mistress Cook," said his Radiancy before anyone else could break the silence, with a smile of such frank charm Cliopher blinked in disbelief. "We have not yet had the opportunity to compliment you on your fine cooking."

The cook thawed visibly. "Your honour is too kind."

"It is only truth," his Radiancy said, and took a step forward so he was not quite so obviously framed by the guards. "What delicacy are you making for us this evening?"

"Ituran dumplings and my special sweet biscuits." She cast an arch glance at Conju. "I hear your honour has a sweet tooth and a partiality for ginger."

"Your ginger cookies were much appreciated."

"You will like my special biscuits," she said.

"How could we not?" His Radiancy smiled again at the room. "Your helpers are to be commended, as well. There are not so many of them to serve all of us."

"You do bring a lot of guards with you," she said.

"A hazard of the position," his Radiancy replied lightly. "They're mostly for appearances, you know. Speaking of which, we were admiring the reef when Sayo Mdang here mentioned that the pearl hunters of the western Vangavaye-ve use some sort of masks to see underwater ..."

"Snorkel masks," she said, nodding, then frowned at him. "I hope you don't swim over the edge of the reef, your honour. There are sharks out in the Bay, you know."

"So we have been warned. Do you know anywhere we might acquire snorkel masks from? We should like to try the art."

She pursed her lips. One of the underlings, a cheerful-looking young woman who was staring with unabashed admiration at Commander Omo, said, "The Delanis might have some, your honour. Jiano married a westerner, and she's brought all sorts of things back with her."

"Thank you," his Radiancy said politely. "One more thing before we leave you to your work: do you know where we might find a small piece of ebony and a carving knife? There is a harp with broken pegs to be fixed."

"Eldoshi is the village carver," the underling replied. "He would have some for certain."

"He's a hard man," the cook added. "Anyone else would let you have scraps and borrow a knife, but he don't like strangers and he don't like lords and he don't much like helping nobody."

"Valuable information," his Radiancy said. "Ah—how far is the village?"

The helpful underling replied. "It's about half an hour's walk. Go south along the beach to the rocks, then take the path that starts at the red bougainvillea. You can't miss it, sir."

"Thank you," he said, and they all obediently melted out of the way so that his Radiancy could stride down the hall to the main room.

When he got there, he stopped and looked them over critically. Commander Omo said, "Would you like me to go to the village, my lord?"

"That's probably a good idea, as you will know best what kind of wood to choose. Conju, what sort of walking sandals did you bring for me?"

There was a brief, ringing silence, before Conju managed to control his initial splutters and say, "The jet and leather ones would be most appropriate, my lord ... if your lordship intends to go himself?"

"Yes, I think so," his Radiancy replied, with a glint in his eye of deep humour at their consternation.

Cliopher cleared his throat. "Shall we come as well?"

"As you like," his Radiancy replied carelessly. "Any who wishes may join us."

★★★

IT WAS QUITE POSSIBLE, CLIOPHER reflected as they left the beach for the path into the jungle, that his Radiancy had never once in his life before walked for half an hour out-of-doors in a straight line. Certainly it took longer to proceed from the Imperial Apartments to the Throne Room of the Palace of Stars, but that was not at all the same sort of experience as the walk down a white sand beach under the afternoon sun, the turn into the sudden humid dimness of tropical jungle.

When they entered the jungle his Radiancy stopped and took a deep breath, tilting his head back to look up at the liana-clad trees rising above them. A bird flitted across, calling a warning at their presence; the noise of various insects blended into a shrill buzz; and all was layer upon layer of green. It was moist, cool after the beach, richly scented.

They stood waiting, the honour guards (changed over to Varro and Zerafin) looking into the undergrowth, Commander Omo and Cliopher watching his Radiancy, his Radiancy standing quite perfectly still as he absorbed the feeling of the jungle. Neither Conju nor Ser Rhodin had decided to join them.

When his Radiancy dropped his head Cliopher saw the brightness of unshed tears. But his Radiancy started walking, and Cliopher did not dare venture so far into pretence of equality. They trailed along behind him until they came around a corner and came across a red parrot pecking at something in the path.

"What kind of bird is that?" his Radiancy asked, looking at Cliopher.

"It is a parrot, my lord."

His Radiancy gave him a somewhat withering glance. "Yes; what *kind* of parrot?"

"A red one—I mean," he added hastily, "it is called a red parrot, my lord. On account of it being red. As you see."

"Yes. Do you know the name of that tree?" His Radiancy pointed at a narrow-trunked specimen draped in rattan vines.

"I am sorry, my lord, I do not."

"You're from the Vangavaye-ve," his Radiancy said, not quite accusingly.

"My family live in the city," he replied apologetically, wishing he had ever paid more attention to the names.

(Their various *uses* were coming back, but his Buru Tovo had told him the names in the Islander tongue, and Cliopher had never quite learned the Shaian. 'We are not Poyë,' his great-uncle had said. 'We are Mdang. We hold the fire, not the seeds. Now, go on and catch something for supper.')

He said lamely, "I haven't been much in the jungle since I was a young man."

His Radiancy looked at Commander Omo, who shrugged as if to say that the trees of wherever he was from were quite different, and then at the two guards, who had turned their attention to this conversation. To Cliopher's surprise, Zerafin cleared his throat and said, with bashful pride, "I know some of them, my lord."

"Do you?" said his Radiancy. "Are you not from Jilkano?"

Zerafin fumbled a nervous salute. "I am, my lord, but my mother's people are from the Isolates, if you please."

"I should imagine they are from there irrespective of whether it gives me pleasure or not," was the wry rejoinder, to which poor Zerafin could only nod helplessly. Then his Radiancy said, "Very well: walk with me, and tell me which ones you know."

Cliopher could see Zerafin's Adam's apple bobbing as he obeyed this command. "That one is a Domungli plum, my lord. With a rattan vine climbing up it."

"Rattan?"

"It is much used for furniture, my lord."

"Ah, yes, it is the principal export of Urgalend. And this one?"

"I believe that is a kind of curtain fig, my lord."

And so it went on, plant by plant and bird by bird. Zerafin proved a good resource. Cliopher and Commander Omo walked a few steps behind, listening to the conversation—for conversation it was, Zerafin getting over his shyness as his Radiancy continued to ask enthusiastic questions.

"He must have been bored half out of his mind," Commander Omo murmured very quietly.

"Do you think so?"

Commander Omo shrugged. They ambled along behind his Radiancy, who was not setting a fast pace, being too engaged in looking at various flora and fauna as they came to them. Cliopher watched, and thought again of the intricate schedule of the Palace—that same schedule whose rhythms he, who was free to leave it if he chose, enjoyed—sometimes even loved—and the man at the centre who could neither touch nor be touched, whose life was entirely bound, who no longer knew who he was when those bindings were relaxed.

Bored? he wondered: and then he saw his Radiancy turn his head to follow the flight of a brilliant blue butterfly, with such obvious pleasure that Cliopher's heart nearly stopped with pity.

"I think you may be right," he murmured back.

Commander Omo merely nodded, his face bland and blank as it ever was when he stood guard. He was a large man, his muscles perfectly developed, his features wide and uncompromising: stern, fearsomely moral, utterly loyal, not particularly intellectual, a warrior through and through. Of the four primary members of his Radiancy's household, he had served the longest.

"I didn't know your family were woodcarvers," said Cliopher, who had always thought the commander came from one of the warrior clans of the Dairen mountains.

"I come from humble folk," he replied. "Not something to boast of."

★★★

THEY REACHED THE VILLAGE RATHER more than half an hour later. His Radiancy did not appear to have exhausted either his interest or Zerafin's knowledge of the local jungle life, and had managed to impress Cliopher with his ability to identify products and producers of anything that was created out of bush material in the whole of Zunidh.

Or the whole of the old Empire, he realized, when Zerafin said something about mahogany and his Radiancy said, "The best mahogany used to come from Colhélhé: the Austrivans harvested it, at least until they got into some sort of imbroglio with the Otrese Archipelago in the Emperor Eritanyr's day."

"Is that so, my lord?" Zerafin said deferentially, and then the path opened up into a wide clearing filled with garden plots, and he added: "Shall I return to my post, my lord?"

His Radiancy looked momentarily disappointed. "Of course. On our next visit we shall learn about the garden plants. Now, Ludvic, we wanted ebony?"

Commander Omo stood forward. "Yes, my lord."

"Cliopher, you will look for the Delanis family and see about their snorkelling masks."

"As you wish, my lord."

"We shall find this Eldoshi the woodcarver."

"Very good, my lord," said Commander Omo, saluting.

It was a small village, with perhaps a dozen houses in a cluster around a school and a spirit house. Cliopher supposed that there were a few more houses out of sight in the jungle. He could see no sign of a chief's house; by far the most elaborately carved and painted buildings were the school, the spirit house, and a yam house placed pointedly between the two.

They attracted attention, of course, but no one approached until they had come to the open space before the yam house. Zerafin and Varro squared their shoulders and looked sternly magnificent. The plain white kilt and gold-mounted spears proclaimed their status as Imperial Guards to those who knew the uniform, but it was fairly clear to Cliopher that the villagers were not among that number.

A dozen children appeared out of nowhere, followed by a half a dozen wary adults. His Radiancy smiled, again with frank charm, and most of the adults relaxed easily into welcome. "Good afternoon!" his Radiancy said, in the voice that did not sound more than conversational but which could carry to the far corners of a room—or through the open space of an Islander village.

"Good afternoon," one of the younger men said, glancing at his compatriots and then standing forward. He bowed over folded hands, the gesture of respect to elders; hardly the deep bow that anyone would give a lord. "Welcome to our village, *perioi.*"

Perioi was an old Islander word that meant *strangers*, with the connotation of *guests* rather than *enemies* or *foreigners*. Cliopher's eyebrows rose despite himself. His Radiancy was so *obviously* an aristocrat.

"Thank you," his Radiancy said, nodding politely. "We are staying at the house on the beach." He gestured vaguely back to the path by which they had come.

"Yes, we know," the speaker replied pleasantly. "Navikiani. This is Ikialo village."

All of this was so far from the sort of behaviour that his Radiancy normally commanded that Cliopher was not really surprised to observe that his Radiancy didn't seem to find it objectionable. His Radiancy appeared to have set himself to *not being offended by ignorance*, and since he was himself ignorant of all the variations of behaviour below that due himself, Cliopher supposed that anything short of obvious insolence would be met with serenity.

And it was not as if the speaker was being insolent, exactly. He was merely very politely acting as if he were the equal of any stranger to his village. Up to and including the Last Emperor of Astandalas.

There incognito, he reminded himself.

His Radiancy clasped his hands together. "It looks a lovely village. Are you the headman?"

Several people smiled; one woman laughed outright. The speaker was one of the ones who smiled, as he shook his head. "No, *perio*. We do not hold with chiefs. Lesuia island is home to the communes. I am Ikialo Speaker, when it is necessary, but in general we make our decisions together."

"In council?"

"If a council can be made of the whole community, then yes."

That explained the positioning of the yam house, Cliopher thought, to show it was held by and for the whole village, not one person as chief over the rest.

"How fascinating. We shall have to speak further on your system of government, Ikialo Speaker."

"I should be delighted," said Ikialo Speaker, "but if you did not already know, surely you did not come for that purpose?"

"Ah, yes, we came for two things. Well, three; we were interested in seeing the way of life here. We were told that the Delanis might be able to help us with snorkelling masks, and that we should talk to someone named Eldoshi about wood."

The Speaker exchanged a look with a woman in her early thirties or so. She stepped forward and bowed over her hands. She was pretty, her skin a richer brown than most of the Ikialo villagers'. She wore her hair in a high pouf caught with carved shell combs, a style Cliopher recognized as coming from the western Vangavaye-ve, as had the bright floral print of her sarong. "I am Aya inDovo Delanis," she said. "To whom shall I speak?"

Her voice was lightly accented, sounding to Cliopher's ears much like his beloved grandmother's. His Radiancy made a gesture, and he stood forward, bowing slightly in the Islander fashion, palm over fist.

"I am Cliopher Mdang. Of Gorjo City," he added, though that was probably unnecessary; Gorjo City was full of Mdangs. He had not given the traditional introduction, but then again she had not asked the traditional question. He sighed inwardly, face outwardly court-polite, as she regarded him solemnly.

His skin was much the same colour as hers, and his features proclaimed his ancestry. Yet he wore his hair cropped close in the ancient tradition of the Imperial Secretariat's inner hierarchies, and his accent was Solaaran overlaying Gorjo City.

Give him a three-tiered parasol and red-ochre robes and the right hat (as he wore on formal occasions), and he could have walked into any illustration of the Private Secretary of the past two thousand years.

Except none of them showed a Wide Sea Islander.

And he ought to have said—well, even in the Outer Ring one did not always use the forms out of the old stories. People had indulged him when he was a boy and full of the *Lays*, but those traditions were kept for traditional feasts nowadays.

Aya inDovo Delanis smiled brightly. "You honour our village. Come with me and we shall see what we can do for you."

Cliopher half-bowed to his Radiancy, who appeared to approve, and followed the woman out of the open area and past the spirit house.

As she led him to a substantial house on the edge of the village, she said, "You have been here for three days, have you not? We have been wondering when we might be seeing those who had rented Navikiani. We were thinking perhaps you were of a different tradition, and that we should come to you first, but of course, Sayo Cliopher, you are *wontok*, you know our customs. What is your relation to Aurenia inDaina of Loaloa?"

"My grandmother," he said, and mentally kicked himself for forgetting the Outer Ring custom of the stranger approaching the locals first. Three days was nearly at the outside edge of discourtesy.

"I thought you must be! She was my great-grandmother's sister. You are twice welcome to our village."

"Thank you," he said, bemused.

"When you come again we must be sure to share our family's doings. Now, you were wanting some snorkelling equipment?"

"I mentioned to ... my lord ... that people of the Western Vangavaye-ve use them, and when we asked the cook whether she knew of anywhere we could obtain them she said the Delanis might, as their son had married a westerner."

"Which would be me," Aya said, laughing and going to a stout basket set under the overhang of her house. "I have two sets of masks and fins, which you are welcome to borrow, *hani*."

"Thank you," he replied formally. *Hani* was kinsman, and more than kinsman; it was an expression that they did not only speak the same language, come of the same people (that was *wontok*), but that they shared the same blood. If he had great need, he could call on her; and if she had great need, she could call on him.

He felt a little dizzy with the sudden thrust into familial affiliations and alliances. It was as shifting and occasionally treacherous a sea as the court, but he had spent his lifetime in those waters, not these. This was the stuff his relatives wrote to him about. He suppressed a smile at the thought. Totally uninterested in his work they might be, but his cousins and aunts and more cousins and uncles and even more cousins (the joke went that there was *always* another Mdang) never failed to tell him all the gossip.

Aya passed him the basket. He peeked inside to see bundles of bamboo and glass and rubber. "This is much appreciated. We did not come entirely prepared for so retired a spot."

"You would not be the first one to make that mistake," she said, laughing again. "I like it now, but I was a bit taken-aback when I first came with my Jiano, let me tell you. I kept going to Gorjo City for books and things."

"And now?"

"Now I write my own, and send them back to be published!"

"I should like to read them," he said, being polite but meaning it. Aya had such an infectiously merry laugh that his heart was lifting, and he was sure any books she wrote would be as delightful and delighted as she.

"I will bring you some when Balgo comes back with the new shipment," she promised. "He went to Gorjo City yesterday for the trading market, he will be back in a few days or a week."

"A very relaxed pace of life," he observed, hefting the basket, which was bulky but not very heavy.

"I used to work in the provincial treasury. That took some getting used to—then I came here and was thrown back into people saying, 'Oh, tomorrow,' when they mean, 'Whenever I feel like it.' But it has to be said life is more fun."

He chuckled, but he was thinking of his Radiancy pacing up and down the verandah.

They turned to go back to the centre of the village. Cliopher could see a small crowd gathered around his Radiancy; Varro and Zerafin's spears stood up gleaming out of the throng. Aya touched him lightly on the sleeve before they came quite within earshot.

"*Hani*," she said, "does he have a name we may know?"

Cliopher did not need to ask whom she meant. "It is better we do not say it."

She bit her lip, looking displeased.

"Hanë," he added, surprising himself with his own earnestness, "he is a high one of the court, looking for some time away from the bells, and to forget who he is for a while. Will you let him?"

"It is not as if we would know anyone from so far away."

Cliopher did not say that there was one name they would know, no matter how remote a village it was. He shrugged apologetically. "I am bidden not to say. Perhaps he will tell you later."

Aya frowned a moment longer, then accepted the prevarication with a shrug. "Come, *hani*, we will go around to see what nonsense Eldoshi is spinning now. He's a troublemaker, that one."

A troublemaker he might be, and obviously someone who thought himself a hard bargainer. Cliopher only had to watch for a couple of moments before he saw what was going on: Commander Omo had made some sort of blunt and reasonable request for a few scrap pieces of ebony and a carving knife, and the carver was acting as if the foreigner were trying to winkle his life savings out of him. Commander Omo did not appear to have the experience necessary for the sort of haggling that was going on, and was starting to look exasperated.

Cliopher tried to catch what the sticking point was, but before he felt he had enough of a handle on things to intervene—for *understanding* was not the same as *successfully undertaking*—his Radiancy stepped forward.

Eldoshi was sitting on the raised platform his house was built on, industriously pretending to be busy. He was a scrawny man with a big belly, evidence of too much beer and not enough exercise or good food. The carvings on the poles of his house and on the various unfinished pieces set behind him were of fine quality, no doubt what gave him the confidence and the arrogance to look so insolently at the foreigners.

"What kind of business do you think I am running, that I should just give you, a foreigner no less, the materials to set up as my rival?"

Commander Omo opened his mouth, then glanced at his Radiancy, who had made a gesture Cliopher couldn't quite see, and subsided.

"I think you are exaggerating, woodcarver."

"Exaggerating? Me?" Eldoshi banged his chest. "This is my blood, my sweat, my livelihood!"

His Radiancy raised one eyebrow. "Ludvic has asked you for a few scraps and a carving knife. If you think he could set up as your rival with that, well, perhaps you should rethink your business model."

Someone in the crowd snickered. Eldoshi himself gaped, before sitting up more straightly. "What do you mean, my lord?"

His Radiancy ignored the sarcasm. "Now, Ludvic's grandfather did win the Iliorno Prize for Shaping, and his great-grandfather was among those who carved the Prince of Southern Dair's great decorated palace roof, and his great-great-grandfather was responsible for the famous Tower of the Birds, but since he went for the guards instead of the family business, I do not think you need concern yourself overmuch over what he might do with a few pieces of ebony such as those by your right foot."

Eldoshi put his hand on them as if to shove them away. His Radiancy smiled very sardonically, and the woodcarver froze.

"However," said his Radiancy, as if the thought had just come to him, "it *is* your livelihood we are speaking of, and it is not right that we should presume upon your kindness to such an extent. Let me see … yes. It appears to me you have no shaman or wizard of the village, is that correct?"

He looked to Ikialo Speaker, who was grimacing ferociously but did manage to nod.

"I am a wizard. I will perform such small magics as your village requires in return for the wood and the knife that my—guard requires."

Cliopher wondered if he was the only one who caught that hesitation, and what his Radiancy had almost said instead.

Eldoshi swallowed hard, obviously seeing how he was outmanoeuvred but also unsure about what to do. Cliopher almost felt sorry for him. The mockery and debt he would incur to his fellow villagers would not fade quickly.

"It is only a few scrap pieces, and I have many knives. I cannot possibly accept your terms, my lord."

"No, no, I am afraid I must insist. It is your livelihood we trespass upon, and I should not like anyone to say that we did not give a fair price for aught."

Eldoshi winced visibly. "It is possible I was overzealous …"

"It is important to guard one's dignity," his Radiancy said with such blandness that Cliopher had to look at him twice to make sure his face was as serene as ever it was in court. "Thank you, Eldoshi; we shall, I am sure, remember this for a long time. Now, Ikialo Speaker … what might I do for your village?"

CHAPTER EIGHT

THEY LEFT IKIALO VILLAGE WITH the basket of snorkelling equipment, a string bag of wood chunks, another bag of fruit for the cook, and a rather satisfied Serene and Radiant Holiness, who had spent half an hour performing the most basic of minor charms with an utterly straight face.

It was probably quite useful for the village to have the spring deemed clean and clear, the houses protected against fire, the garden plots encouraged into healthful bounty, and the spirit house returned to its full potency. There was, Cliopher had noted, a small shrine to his Radiancy tucked in the corner of the spirit house. He was reassured that despite the communist principles it was well-tended, the flowers and offerings fresh and plentiful.

"Do you know why our house is called Navikiani, Cliopher?" his Radiancy asked as they left the gardens for the cool jungles again.

Cliopher brought to mind the old stories his great-uncle had taught him. "*Nava* is a meeting-place. It can be both a place where meetings are held, like where we met the villagers in front of the yam house, or it can commemorate a place where a famous meeting occurred. *Navikiani* would be the 'Meeting-Place of Iki and Ani'."

He thought for a moment. "I'm not sure who Iki is—a local name. Perhaps it is their name for Vou'a. Ani is the Mother of Islands—all the islands of the Wide Seas. She is the ancestor of all the Islanders. Her son was Vonou'a, the first of the seafarers, the Wayfinders. It's said that when he first set sail over the horizon, her heart broke in two. She set the two pieces in the sky to show him the way home, the Sun and the Moon. The lament she sang for his going was the first song."

He looked ahead to the shafts of sun spotting the path here and there ahead of them. "Her song was so powerful that Vou'a, that is, the god of mystery, lifted the earth from the sea and gave her a place to stand on. She didn't know who this god was, so she walked along the sands until she found the place where he was waiting for her."

He realized he had slowed his steps to match his words, the cadences jarring with the passages from the *Lays* he ought to have been singing. He cleared his throat awkwardly.

"She sang all her dreams of her son's far-away adventures, singing her grief for his going and her hope for his return. She came walking down the shore of this new land, the first of the islands, and found the place where Vou'a was waiting for her. It was the most beautiful place of all."

He wished he could tell the story the way Buru Tovo told it. It had been so long since he had been home for the Singing of the Waters, when the *Lays* were sung in their entirety. It was not at all the same to read them over in his rooms at the Palace.

"It was sunrise when she came to the beach where he was waiting. She sang her lament again, and Vou'a called to her, said to her that he had gone to the underworld and brought it to the surface of the sea, to show to her that her son was still alive, that Vonou'a had not perished on the far side of the horizon. And when she listened to him she looked far over the sea, against the rising sun, and she saw the sail of her son's ship coming home."

"It is a lovely story," his Radiancy observed.

He made a rueful grimace. "My mother sang the lament when I left for Astandalas."

"Is there no song of homecoming?"

"In the stories," he said, looking after some small bird flashing iridescent-black across the path to hide his face.

★★★

THE RETURN JOURNEY TOOK THEM much closer to the promised half an hour. When they arrived at the beach, his Radiancy paused a moment while their eyes adjusted to the bright sunlight to survey the view.

They stood at one horn of the crescent. The beach swept off to their left towards Navikiani, from here a pleasingly asymmetrical conglomeration of shapes tucked into its gardens and the edge of the jungle. Straight ahead of them the beach curved back to another point, edged by the great figs and a fringe of coconut palms and Tolouan pines. At the very tip of the other horn was a dark spot, which Cliopher, thinking back to the view from Bertie's yacht, remembered was a large stone outcropping.

His Radiancy regarded this for some time, expression impenetrably serene as ever, and then he said: "It could well be the most beautiful place in creation, where Vou'a waited for Ani."

His brisk stride faltered slightly when he turned onto the softer dry sand, as if he'd not realized there would be a change of texture underfoot.

And perhaps he hadn't, Cliopher thought, watching as Conju pushed open the verandah door to meet them, and his Radiancy stepped onto the stairs and stamped his feet to brush off the sand. He had to keep reminding himself how very *limited* his Radiancy's experience outside of Palace life was.

"We did, thank you," his Radiancy said in reply to something Conju had said. "It is always most satisfying to thwart self-important fools."

★★★

THE GUARDS CHANGED OVER TO Pikabe and Ato. Ser Rhodin came out into the main room, glancing often between Commander Omo and his Radiancy as he did so, as if concerned either of them might send him back to the other guards. He was not challenged; indeed, his Radiancy gestured him over to where he was seated across the brazier from Cliopher.

"What did you do while we were gone?"

Ser Rhodin tried visibly not to gape. If they never asked his Radiancy personal questions, well, rarely did his Radiancy ask any of them. He saluted. "I led the other guards in our exercises, my lord."

"Is there a suitable yard to the back of the house?"

Ser Rhodin glanced at Commander Omo, once more standing impassively at the verandah door. "We took the opportunity of your lordship's absence to do so on the beach, my lord."

"I do not object to observing my guards at their work," said his Radiancy, with a slight smile. "Pray continue to exercise wherever is most convenient."

"Thank you, my lord."

His Radiancy nodded decisively. "What book did you bring, Ser Rhodin?"

Ser Rhodin gripped his book as if he were afraid it would move. "An account of the Conquest of Colhélhé, my lord."

"Helarkin, Ngo, or Issemboise?"

"Issemboise, my lord."

Cliopher told himself he really should not be surprised that his Radiancy knew the major scholarly works on various elements of Astandalan history and culture; but he was.

"Are you enjoying it?"

"Yes, my lord." Cliopher could see Ser Rhodin make the decision to go that unaccustomed step further. "My family is of an old lineage, my lord, but

we had little money for education and my father spent it on fencing masters, not tutors. My fencing master was an excellent teacher of many lessons,
however, and he always emphasized the importance of continuing to learn,
especially from the great ones of the past."

His Radiancy gazed at him levelly for a moment, in which Ser Rhodin
tried not to look nervous, before he smiled wryly. "That is a lesson sadly easy
to forget," he said.

Ser Rhodin looked almost astonished at his own daring. "Learning from
the past, my lord?"

"That, too. Even more, the importance of continuing to learn. One
reaches a certain level in one's profession, and it becomes perilously easy to
settle there."

Ser Rhodin settled for, "Yes, my lord," as a safe answer, though Cliopher,
who was once again thinking of his Radiancy interrogating Zerafin on plant
names, guessed that it was a far better blow than intended.

★★★

DURING SUPPER HIS RADIANCY QUIZZED him on what Aya had said about
snorkelling, out of no evident purpose besides curiosity. As they settled into
the main room afterwards, his Radiancy said, "Your accent has grown noticeably stronger over the course of the day, Cliopher."

He hastily put his thoughts back into courtly mode. "My apologies,
my—"

"No, do not mistake me. Pray speak as your heart moves you."

Cliopher swallowed. "Thank you, my lord."

It was cooler that evening, so that Commander Omo shut the verandah
doors, and after a few minutes of sitting there with his book (still, Cliopher
noted, the *Deeds of Olor*, not the banned *Aurora* in its false cover), his Radiancy said: "Perhaps we might light the brazier?"

They all looked at Conju, who dropped his embroidery to jump to his
feet in consternation. "My lord, I will go ask the kitchen staff for a taper."

His Radiancy gave him a puzzled glance. "Why?"

"I do not have matches or a firestarting charm, my lord," Conju said,
every line in his body protesting the lack of proper amenities in this barbaric
house. He gestured at the empty table and the magical lights that illuminated
the room.

"Ah," said his Radiancy. "They are in that third closet. But no matter."
In exactly the same tone of voice he said a word Cliopher did not recognize.

With a soft *puff* the wood caught.

His Radiancy sat back in his chair with the *Deeds of Olor*, smiling at his fire. Cliopher looked down at his Ystharian history, but he was thinking that he had thought his Radiancy entirely a great mage, entirely concerned with huge sweeps of magic: the typhoons, the Lights, the network of floating castles along the Galagar coast that had finally caught the broken magic after the Fall of Astandalas and allowed the world to begin properly to heal. He had never seen him do small magics.

He had never seen him speak to small *people*, either, but he had done that today, too: cook and underling, village speaker and woodcarver, and whoever else had spoken unwittingly to the Sun-on-Earth, the Lion-Eyed, the Lord of Rising Stars, the Last Emperor of Astandalas and Lord of Zunidh.

Conju went off to compose himself. He returned with both a box of matches and a basket of wood to keep the fire going. He knelt beside the brazier to arrange the wood, his posture somehow indicating extreme aggravation that his Radiancy had had to light the fire himself.

"I do not mind," his Radiancy said, when Conju finally sat back on his heels to examine his spiral stack.

"I beg your pardon, my lord?"

People were always earnest in saying that to his Radiancy. It was almost never the empty polite mouthing of common discourse.

"It gives me pleasure to do the small magics," his Radiancy said mildly. "It does not all need to be grand gestures."

"Your lordship should not have had to," Conju said mulishly.

"We are not in the Palace. We do not expect Palace service."

Which was just as well, Cliopher thought, for hard on the heels of those words Pikabe and Ato abruptly sprang into action, spears angled aggressively at the doorway they guarded. Commander Omo and Ser Rhodin both leapt to their feet, Ser Rhodin to stand over his Radiancy, Commander Omo to take charge of the room.

Cliopher's heart caught in a painful seizure. He looked, dry-mouthed, at his Radiancy, who was sitting with perfect composure despite the sudden flashing spears and knives around him. Conju was crouched, panic and determination on his face, a piece of wood gripped in his hand like a club. Ser Rhodin was holding a knife, expression grim.

"I d-didn't mean to interrupt," a woman's voice said quaveringly from the other side of the guards. "I thought p-perhaps you m-might like some wine."

At his Radiancy's nod, Commander Omo said, "Stand down," and with exaggerated precision Pikabe and Ato resumed their former positions.

The cook's helpful underling stood in the doorway, gripping a tray so that the vessels clattered. She was staring wide-eyed, her attention skittering from one guard to the other in near panic. Then her eyes focused on something past Cliopher, and her face calmed.

"That was kindly thought of you, my dear," his Radiancy said, his voice smooth as melted chocolate. "We did not mean to startle you. Come in, please."

She edged past Pikabe and Ato, with sidelong glances at their spears, which looked wickedly sharp in the flickering light of the fire, and which must have stopped very close to her throat from the way she swallowed repeatedly. She set the tray down on the table next to Cliopher without looking at him, all her attention on his Radiancy, who was still seated. He gestured at Ser Rhodin to step back, and smiled at the young woman.

"What is your name, miss?"

"Beila, sir."

"Are you from the village—Ikialo, that is, Beila?"

"Not Ikialo—Ikiava village. Over on the other side of the headland. My father's family is from Ikialo."

"We thank you for your work, Beila."

"Thank you, sir."

"We do not wish to dissuade your initiative, but perhaps it would be kinder to our guards to knock first next time."

Beila gulped back a nervous giggle. "Yes, sir. My hands were full, and there are so many rules for situations, I never can keep track ..."

"We are from Solaara, and no doubt we keep many different customs to the Vangavaye-ve. We hope you are not too distressed?"

"No, sir, just surprised. We knew there were the guards, but, uh." She grinned suddenly. "I suppose I wasn't thinking they were actually here for a purpose."

They thought his Radiancy was a prisoner, Cliopher thought, as his Radiancy asked her a few more questions and got her to pour the wine. When she went back out through the door she smiled brightly at Pikabe and Ato, who were standing at rigidly disapproving attention.

"Well done," said his Radiancy quietly when she had gone, and Pikabe and Ato saluted with great crispness.

Later that evening Cliopher asked Commander Omo how many times someone had ever tried to gain untoward access to the Presence, at least to the extent of causing the innermost guards to react.

"Four times," said Commander Omo. "This was the fifth."

His Radiancy, Cliopher saw, had put on his court face, sipped his wine, and returned to his book.

A log snapped in the brazier. Cliopher jumped; Pikabe and Ato stood reflexively at greater attention; Conju nearly dropped his embroidery; Ser Rhodin's hand clenched on his book. But Commander Omo did not move from his place by the verandah, where he stood whittling a piece of ebony; and his Radiancy's serenity did not falter.

CHAPTER NINE

THE NEXT MORNING IT WAS raining.

Cliopher came out of his room early, yawning after a night of troubled dreams (for what *would* he do, what would *anyone* do, if his Radiancy were to perish?), to find his Radiancy standing at the verandah door staring raptly out at the hidden sun slowly lightening the dimness into silvery grey.

Varro and Zerafin stood at the servant wing door, their alert bearing indicating that they were prepared to sweep out after his Radiancy as soon as he stepped across the threshold.

His Radiancy glanced at Cliopher. The expression in his eyes was ambiguous. In another man Cliopher might have read the glint as mockery, but he had never felt his Radiancy's humour ran that direction.

"Good morning, my lord," he said quietly, coming to stand beside him. He could not think what his Radiancy was so fascinated by; even the reef's breakers were hidden in the thick cloak of precipitation.

"It's raining," his Radiancy said, returning his attention to the outside.

Cliopher did not usually speak with his Radiancy first thing. He did not usually speak with anyone first thing. He stifled another yawn. "It happens."

He lifted a hand to his face in horror, and stumbled over formulating apologies, the words crowding themselves behind his teeth.

His Radiancy said, "I have not seen rain since I became Emperor."

Cliopher opened his mouth and shut it again.

"It is very pretty."

Cliopher bowed and backed away and went in search of coffee.

★★★

HIS RADIANCY ASKED CLIOPHER AT breakfast whether the rain meant it was imprudent to go swimming.

"Ah," Cliopher replied. He did not feel himself the expert on the subject they all seemed to think him. "I believe your lordship is thinking of the dangers of swimming during thundery weather. Certainly it is imprudent to do so when there is lightning abroad."

His Radiancy stared at him for several moments, his eyes bright-gold and the strength in them so intense it made Cliopher's own eyes water. Yet he knew his Radiancy was holding back, and indeed, he realized his Radiancy had not even been focused on him when his Radiancy suddenly did focus, giving Cliopher an instant splitting headache from the wash of power.

"There is no threat of lightning."

He managed to smile, trying not to gasp. "Then there is no danger, my lord."

His Radiancy went out happily into the rain, Conju and the guards following behind him. Cliopher raised himself from his bow to press palms to his eyes.

"Is it very bad?"

Cliopher lowered his hands to see Commander Omo squatting beside him. He smiled painfully. "I forget there were reasons for the taboos."

Commander Omo set something down on the table before lifting Cliopher's chin with a firm but gentle hand. He peered into Cliopher's eyes, then nodded.

"I have some drops that will help," he said. "There are wizards who do that on purpose. Go lie down, and we will see to things."

Cliopher went gratefully enough, more grateful for the drops than he quite wanted to say, and grateful to lie in his bed listening to the rain. It was very soothing.

As Emperor, his Radiancy had not been permitted to go outside except under the most elaborate circumstances for fear the Sun or the Moon would come and take their beloved away.

(Which had happened precisely once, in all the long history of the Empire of Astandalas, back in the ancient days when legends were still being spun, in the days when the Emperor Aurelius Magnus had come to the Vangavaye-ve to make alliance with the Islanders, when those rumours of the fire dances of the Wayfinders had made their way into Astandalan tales.)

One hundred years he had lain asleep upon a bier in the Great Hall of the Palace of Stars, when no one knew what had happened or what would happen or whether he would wake sane, or the same man, or at all.

And—somehow, impossibly—near nine hundred years as Lord of Zunidh, working high magics, in a Palace whose weather was as perfect as ever the Schooled magic of the Empire had wrought.

Cliopher did not remember the nine hundred years, or even the hundred years before them, as more than long days thoroughly occupied with work, dry seasons turning to wet, unremarkable and unremarked. In the Vanga-vaye-ve it had been twenty-odd years since the Fall.

His family probably thought he had no work to do at all, since he wrote home so often.

Cliopher fell asleep wishing inchoately that when he was another decade or dozen decades older that he would find something ordinary as new and pleasing as his Radiancy found the rain.

★★★

HE CAME OUT FOR LUNCHEON feeling much better. The others had already eaten, but a plate of steamed buns and greens had been left for him. They were still pleasantly hot; it was only when he was nearly finished that Conju came in and said quietly, "His Radiancy hopes the food stayed warm?"

It took Cliopher a moment to realize what Conju meant. "Did his Radiancy ..."

"Yes."

Cliopher looked down at his plate. "That was uncommonly thoughtful of him."

By which he meant both *very* and *unexpectedly*.

"His Radiancy was very sorry to realize he had weighed down on you so far."

"Weighed down?"

"His words." Conju paused. "*Are* you feeling better?"

"Yes, thank you. Commander Omo had some eyedrops that helped."

Conju did not look convinced, but when Cliopher stood to go out into the main room, he said merely: "His Radiancy is tuning the harp."

He said it with audible disapproval. Cliopher stopped before opening the door. "I believe his Radiancy feels the constraints of custom more nearly than we do."

"They are there to honour him."

"He does himself no dishonour to relax court formality."

"He cannot do himself dishonour," Conju replied, with absolute conviction, if convoluted logic. "He is the living heart of magic and tradition: what he does is for the good of all."

"But what of his own heart? His own good?"

Conju opened his mouth to protest. Cliopher lifted his hand to stop him, continued earnestly. "You agreed with me that his Radiancy needed a change."

"Might enjoy a change."

"Needed," said Cliopher recklessly. "He took me up on my offer. What service do we do if we do not, then, allow him to do what he wishes for once?"

"There is no one in all the world who would stop him from doing as he wishes."

"No one: but every custom, every tradition, every ritual keeps him to his place as much as us to ours."

"You are speaking of *his Radiancy!*"

"I do not forget it!" The force of the words shook him. He took a deep breath, forced himself to speak more temperately. "We are also speaking of a man whom we both love for his own sake, a man who, it is conceivable, might sometimes wish to do things with his own hands, for his own pleasure, simply because he is a man and it is an ordinary human joy to do such things."

Conju looked as if he wanted to keep protesting. Cliopher wondered what else he could say. If Conju did not *see* the man enveloped in the Presence, there did not seem to be much he could do to show him. But then Conju said, slowly, "I do not like to shirk my duties."

"I know it is your duty to make all the business of living as smooth and unnoticed as possible, just as mine is to make certain the government works as it should and the right problems come to his Radiancy's attention, and not all the dross and folly that could. That he seems to wish for a bit more ... texture ... while we are away from the Palace is no slight upon you. He cannot wish to read *more* reports, even if I had them with me."

"I had not considered it in that manner."

Cliopher tried to be encouraging and not condescending. He did understand how hard Conju worked to make his Radiancy's life as pleasant and easy as possible (and when one had the tithes and tributes of a world to hand, it was quite remarkable what was possible). "When we went on the canoe trip that time you quite enjoyed the experience of roughing it."

"This is true," Conju said, then added hastily: "His Radiancy surely cannot wish to rough it in that fashion."

Cliopher was not at all certain that his Radiancy did not wish to, but he was quite certain that his Radiancy could have no idea—none at all—of what was involved in truly *roughing it*. Conju barely did, and they had gone camping on the Epalos that particular holiday. (They had brought supplies with them, though every day Cliopher had imagined his Buru Tovo laughing at him for being so soft and citified a fancy-man he could not feed and shelter himself with only what the islands and sea gave him.)

"I expect not," he agreed therefore, "but I think if his Radiancy continues to express desires to do unaccustomed tasks and activities, no matter how far from the usual they are, then it behoves us to facilitate them to the best of our abilities."

"That is, we should continue to do our jobs," said Conju dryly.

"Yes, even if it pains us to let his Radiancy do what we are accustomed to do for him."

"Not just accustomed," muttered Conju, but he did not pursue the matter further, and Cliopher felt he had achieved a small victory.

When he went out into the main room everyone was so thoroughly engrossed in what they were doing—his Radiancy bent over the harp, Ser Rhodin in his book, the guards in their watchfulness, Commander Omo with another piece of ebony and the knife over by the verandah door—that Cliopher had an uneasy moment of wondering if they had heard what he and Conju had been speaking about.

The uneasiness passed, for although his doubts persisted, his Radiancy was smiling.

★★★

THE HARP HAD IN EXCESS of twenty strings, and it took his Radiancy some time to tune it to his satisfaction. After a while his Radiancy, glancing up to see him staring, said, "Do you know much about harps, Cliopher?"

"No, my lord. They are not an instrument much played here."

"All the more remarkable to find one in a hidden closet, then. This is an adherin, from the Outer Reaches of Northwest Oriole in Alinor. It makes one curious indeed about how it came to be here. It is not something one would expect to find as a trade good."

"Is it from before the Fall, my lord?"

"Very likely from considerably before." His Radiancy stroked his hand down the curved neck of the instrument, to which he had been fastening the strings with the assistance of the ebony tuning pegs. "It is a lovely instrument. Not fancy: it is not inlaid with gems or precious metal, as the Outer Reaches harpsmiths did for the courtly market. There is one in the Treasury all encrusted with pearls and gold and amethysts."

"It must be beautiful," Cliopher said, who liked this harp's plain elegance.

"It is somewhat rococo, I fear, and does not have a particularly good sound. This one, on the other hand ..." His Radiancy struck his hand down the strings.

Everyone looked up at the waterfall of notes.

His hands were deft; his face, not coolly serene as usual, was warmly content. He played a piece Cliopher had never heard before, in a style he had never even imagined: it rose and fell like a rainstorm, each note separate and yet liquid, running together like birdsong, complex and yet somehow exquisitely simple.

When he finished they all stared at him in unflattering astonishment.

His Radiancy laughed.

Cliopher realized that in twenty (or a hundred or five hundred) years as his Radiancy's personal secretary, he had never once even imagined his Radiancy knew how to laugh like that.

The next song was familiar, a song the court minstrels played often at supper. Translated into harp music from zither it was elevated, with witty little riffs here and there. Those were his Radiancy's addition, Cliopher realized, reeling from one astonishment to another. They made him want to laugh. Instead he smiled, watching his Radiancy play, the bright strings flashing under the dark fingers, the winking brilliance of his Radiancy's signet ring coming in and out of the light, the sure mastery of the instrument.

When he finished that song he paused, hands resting on the strings.

There was a silence, which Cliopher did not want to break. His Radiancy said, "When I was a boy my greatest ambition was to be a Bard like the Bards of old." He played a few notes, picking out what seemed, from its simplicity, to be some sort of folk ballad. Still playing, he said, "The servants used to sing these plaintive songs about doomed heroes—I thought it all very romantic and fine."

He began to sing.

His voice was a rich baritone. A bit rusty at first, by the end of the second verse it sounded out as clear and clean as the harp notes. To Cliopher's half-knowledgeable ear it was evident his Radiancy had been very well taught at some point, even if the occasional hiccoughs due to mistimed breathings suggested he was greatly out of practice.

He had not seen rain since before he became Emperor; and perhaps he had not sung since that lonely exile, either.

The thought that his Radiancy might spend his precious hour alone each day singing and playing to himself was not much better. It was clear from everyone's faces—even Commander Omo's—that none of them had known he played, and his guards would have, had he ever done so outside his private study.

Cliopher listened breathlessly, amazed not simply at the fact of the performance, but that his Radiancy was actually very good. Even superb. Even superlative. Could have performed without disgrace at his own court, given a few months of proper practice.

How? he wondered, thinking of all those days of rigidly proscribed behaviour, of state and ceremony, magic and taboos and the old Imperial fiction that the Emperor was divine become, in the dark days after the Fall, a vital religion.

And then, though he was not quite certain why he was reminded, he remembered that island of exile, and the man who had never been supposed to inherit.

His Radiancy drew to a close and reached for the water glass on the table next to him. He smiled at their reactions, clearly pleased to surprise them.

"Do you write your own music, my lord?" Cliopher asked diffidently.

His Radiancy's face went very still and serene. "Not for a long time."

They all carefully looked away, back to their own activities, and just like that the thin fiction of friendship dissolved.

★★★

THE NEXT DAY AT BREAKFAST his Radiancy said, "Cliopher, will you show us how the snorkelling masks work?"

"With pleasure, my lord," he replied, and after they had finished went to fetch the box Aya inDovo Delanis had given him. He brought it out to where his Radiancy waited on the verandah. Conju came out to assist. He was trying not to look disapproving.

Cliopher demonstrated how the latches on the fins worked, the rubber mask. The breathing pipe was about a foot long, made of inch-wide bamboo hollowed out and varnished to be waterproof. One end had been steam-bent and jointed to a mouthpiece made of wood and rubber.

"Very clever indeed," said his Radiancy, picking up the one nearest himself and examining it thoroughly. "These have, I presume, been cleaned?"

"Yes," said Conju, glaring at Cliopher (who had not, actually, thought to do so), "though I fear they are not ritually cleansed, my lord."

His Radiancy paused, rubbing the bamboo pipe with one thumb as he looked out at the lagoon. "I do not believe that snorkelling masks are mentioned in the lists."

"They do enter the mouth, my lord," Conju said quietly.

"So they do." His Radiancy sighed and pinched the bridge of his nose. "I will perform the abbreviated ceremony, since they are not mentioned by name." He smiled at Cliopher. "We shall try tomorrow. Come, Conju, let us find all the accoutrements."

★★★

THE ABBREVIATED CEREMONY OF PURIFICATION took four hours.

It began with a fire and ended with a final dowsing in sanctified water. It required several sacred herbs, which either Conju or his Radiancy had brought with them, and chants and diagrams and complicated gestures and all sorts of other magic.

Cliopher, thinking of the lines in the Palace budget devoted to His Radiancy's Ceremonies, wondered what would happen if the rituals were simply not done one day.

Then he recalled the woman who had gone blind from looking upon the Emperor Eritanyr, though she had been a healer and the Emperor deathly ill—and instead of wishing he could have that budget line for something more useful, Cliopher wondered what it was like to know that your glance could blind, your touch burn, that your name was sworn by in all sincerity.

"You do realize," Conju said as they watched his Radiancy work his way through the ceremony on the beach in front of the White House, "that we cannot give the purified objects back to your kinswoman?"

Cliopher probably should have. "I will explain matters to her."

His Radiancy looked tired when he had finished the ceremony. Conju presented him with a large piece of silk, into which his Radiancy deposited the snorkelling equipment, and then proceeded silently to clean up. His Radiancy left him to it, and joined Cliopher on the verandah in the shade.

"I don't usually do that myself," his Radiancy commented after a moment, sitting down in the swinging chair to drink the cold water Cliopher offered him. "Iprenna and Bavezh can have it, as far as I'm concerned."

Iprenna and Bavezh were the chief priest-wizards of the court. Cliopher knew that they were responsible for the ritual purity of things appertaining to his Radiancy, but had never watched them at their work. "How long is the full ceremony, my lord?" he asked, the question having frequently come to mind over the hours of the abbreviated one.

His Radiancy stretched out his legs. "It depends on the object and the level of purification required. Some things are naturally purer than others—water, for instance—and fire purifies, so food does not need to be further purified after cooking. It is convention that all methods of cooking count under 'fire', so long as heat is applied."

"But uncooked food must be purified?"

His Radiancy made a quick grimace. "Living things, including seeds and nuts, require the full ceremony. Which, to answer your question, is eighty-one days. It is a rare piece of fruit that makes it. I used to make them try oranges, simply because I missed fresh fruit so much, but ..." He shrugged. "It's much easier to accept that one can only eat cooked food."

Cliopher bit back all his questions.

"There are various degrees of ceremony between the four hours and the ones for people, which take one hundred and twenty days. That is, attendants and so forth. A consort or one who would ... touch ... is yet longer again."

Which perhaps explained why his Radiancy had no concubines or lovers, though for all Cliopher knew he had the normal appetites.

His Radiancy was speaking again, musingly. "There are lists drawn up about what falls under which category. It used to be more stringent, of course, when I was Emperor. The requirements for things I touched then were much more strict, and the purification was not just religious but also magical. That was why I was so taken by sea-sickness."

"My lord?"

"You know that each person is connected magically to the place of his birth? That a mage such as I—by which I do not mean a great mage, but rather one who specializes in natural magic—can tell whether someone is from another world because of the magic around them, and I can usually tell where within the Empire someone is from."

"Yes, my lord?" It was not something he'd ever spent much time thinking about.

"When I became Emperor, I was ritually and magically detached from that connection. The Emperor does—did not belong to any one land, any one world. He was instead to be considered as belonging to all—or rather, as all five belonging to him. Magically as well as legally."

His Radiancy rubbed one hand across his scalp, an old gesture Cliopher had not seen him do for years. "It was quite remarkably disorienting. I felt always at a remove from things, as if there was a barrier between me and real life." He smiled wryly. "I suppose there was. The sandals I wore were specially enchanted. When I woke after the Fall, and I went outside for the first time—

when I walked on the ground, wearing just ordinary sandals, I ... Zunidh claimed me as her own again."

Cliopher shivered, wondering what that had felt like. "It must have been very disconcerting, my lord."

"That would be one way of putting it. Yes. My magic is naturally attuned to fire and air. Although I was mildly prone to seasickness before I became Emperor because of that natural antipathy, after the Fall I found it much exacerbated. Crossing an area of such strong and varied sea magic as the Bay of Waters creates a strong counter-reaction, as you saw."

"What of when you were Emperor, my lord?"

"I don't believe I ever went on a small boat during that period. When we went on the formal procession through the five worlds we were on a great barge, and I was involved in such great anchoring magics that the smaller discomforts were not particularly evident."

"Becoming Emperor must have been a great change, my lord," Cliopher ventured.

His Radiancy rubbed his scalp again. "It was at that." He fell silent for a few moments, watching Conju direct Pikabe and Ato in raking the sand smooth. "My thoughts keep turning to then, to before I became Emperor. You have taken me out of my routine, and that was the last time I was anywhere near so free to choose what I might do with my day. It is a dangerously heady sensation."

"I am only sorry we had not thought of it before."

"I'm not sure I am," his Radiancy replied thoughtfully. "In many ways, it is as painful to wake up one's heart after long slumber as a limb that has fallen asleep. And going back, knowing that things do not and cannot change ... that would be a hard thought. Whereas now ... You may regret what you have awoken, Cliopher."

Cliopher felt he should know what his Radiancy meant, but he did not, and given the remarkable openness of the conversation, he felt audacious enough to ask. "I do not understand, my lord."

His Radiancy was looking vaguely out into the distance. He started, smiled crookedly. "Do you not? But yet all the court is murmuring of it. No one has dared raise the question to my face, so far, but it is surely only a matter of time before my underling princes do so."

"The succession, my lord?"

"Indeed."

"Does your lordship ... that is ..."

"That is," his Radiancy said, "do I have a plan?"

"I would not presume to ask such a question, my lord."

His Radiancy smiled with such sharp humour it was nearly a grin. "No? And you the chief minister of my realm?"

Cliopher flushed: for of course he did have contingency plans. He remembered the bleak uncertainty after the Fall too well not to have made plans. They ranged from the simple transference of rule to his Radiancy's sister to an elaborate and highly impractical rearrangement of Zunidh's political structure to a radically decentralized democracy. All of them faltered on the problem of what the source of legitimacy was when the Last Emperor of Astandalas finally passed on to his rest.

Well, on that and on the insoluble difficulty that there was no magus of sufficient power and skill to take his Radiancy's place in any meaningful capacity.

His Radiancy raised one eyebrow in amusement. "Well then. The answer is yes and no. That is, I am forming a plan, but it is not yet settled. It would perhaps have been easier had I had children, but ... That would have been no guarantee. The lordship of Zunidh is not hereditary."

There was a pause.

"My lord," Commander Omo said deferentially from behind them, "The sunset is very fine this evening."

His Radiancy turned around to raise his eyebrows at him.

"If your lordship would perhaps like to go for a walk to the western end of the beach?"

His Radiancy blinked, and then smiled slowly, and off they went.

It occurred to Cliopher that the gossip and the half-voiced comments at court rarely made the distinction his Radiancy just had between the Lord of Zunidh and the Last Emperor's differing requirements for heirs.

CHAPTER TEN

HIS RADIANCY CAME BACK IN the twilight. They were not worried, of course, for his Radiancy's safety—not with Commander Omo and Oginu accompanying him—but Conju hovered on the balcony looking off towards the palms and the pines and the dark rocks as if he wished his Radiancy would not be so long about it.

"He will be fine," said Cliopher for the third time.

"I'm not worried," Conju retorted.

"You're pacing."

Conju made a wry face and came to stand next to where Cliopher leaned on the verandah balcony watching the stars come out. "I feel as if something is about to happen."

"Good or bad?"

"I can't tell." Conju rubbed his face. "I believe his Radiancy is enjoying his time here. He is a very good musician, is he not?"

"Yes."

"You haven't played your oboe yet."

Cliopher shrugged, smiling ruefully. "No."

★★★

THAT EVENING HIS RADIANCY PLAYED the harp on the verandah for most of an hour. Beila came in with wine, knocking loudly this time, and stopped for a few minutes to listen to the music. Not even Conju had the heart to tell her to go, not when she stood with shining face and open-hearted wonder. When his Radiancy stopped playing, whether between songs or to rest his hands Cliopher couldn't tell, she shook her head and said aloud, "I've never heard music like that, sir."

"His lordship is playing the harp," he replied. "It's an Alinorel instrument."

"Alinorel ... from Alinor, do you mean?" Her eyes went even wider with amazement. "Oh, how utterly marvellous." She suddenly recollected herself and made to leave. "Thank you, sir, thank you."

★★★

THE NEXT MORNING HIS RADIANCY was up early and ate a sparing meal. Near the end of this, he turned to Cliopher and said casually, "Would you like to come snorkelling with me?"

"I would be honoured, my lord," Cliopher replied automatically, before the invitation quite penetrated. But he was honoured, and pleased; nor did he miss Conju's relief.

What followed was one of the most perfectly splendid mornings Cliopher had ever spent. With the fins both could swim farther than otherwise, and the lagoon was full of splendid things to see. They went out to the inner reefs, where they floated over brilliantly coloured corals and fish and all the other wondrous creatures who inhabited them. They could not talk with the snorkels in their mouths, but occasionally one would catch the other's eye and point to something particularly astonishing.

In the midst of the reef there was a small sand bar. They happened upon it at a time when Cliopher, at least, was ready for a break, and clambered out of the water to sit on the warm sand and shake out their masks.

"This is marvellous!" his Radiancy said, smiling brilliantly and looking around them.

Before he could stop himself Cliopher laughed.

"What is it?" his Radiancy asked, not harshly but with evident curiosity.

"Oh, nothing, my lord."

"You are smiling at a joke. Please share it."

Cliopher grimaced in embarrassment. "Last night that servant girl came in with wine again."

"Beila."

"Yes, my lord. Beila came in, while you were on the verandah playing. She said 'How marvellous!' in much the same tone you just did, my lord."

His Radiancy laughed. "I'm not sure I'd call my playing a wonder of the world."

Cliopher didn't know what to say to that, and so said nothing. He looked out at the water, the sea birds crying around them, and far off across the lagoon the two vertical figures of Ato and Pikabe on guard.

"Do you know," his Radiancy said, following the line of his gaze, "this is the farthest I have been from my guards since I became Emperor."

He fell silent again. After a few meditative minutes, Cliopher thought to himself that this was the closest he had ever been to his Radiancy.

Within touching distance, if the taboos had not been strong as a wall between them.

(If he had not remembered that blind woman.)

The sun was hot, but not too hot, and the water was bright. "This feels like my childhood," he said, watching a frigate bird sail past, its long tail feathers white against the blue sky. "Sitting by the water after swimming, the sun like this, the birds crying, the breeze. We just need my cousins shouting at us from the next sandbar."

"You had a happy childhood?"

"Oh, yes, my lord. We lived in a huge ramshackle old house near the Tahivoa lagoon. My aunts and grandmother and numerous cousins and a few other distant relatives all lived with us, and we raised merry hell, my sisters and my cousins and I. We had good schools and good food and good friends, and just about enough money to go round, and yes, we were happy."

"Your cousins—that would be Basil who has the inn on Alinor, and Dimiter the explorer? Your sisters—how many sisters have you? There is one who is a musician, no? And an architect?"

"Those were two of my closest cousins, yes, my lord, though there are a fair number of others."

His lips twitched involuntarily at the gross understatement. The fifty-nine Mdang cousins of his generation were legendary. By this point of his life he was related by blood and marriage to nearly a quarter of the population of Gorjo City.

"My niece Leona is the one training to be an architect. My elder sister Vinyë is the director of the Gorjo City Symphony. We had another sister who was a nurse, but she contracted a virulent strain of yellow fever and passed away."

"My sympathies," his Radiancy said. "I did not know that."

His voice was distressed. Cliopher realized that his Radiancy had remembered about his cousins and his sisters—and had remembered that Zerafin was from Jilkano, and had known Varro's name, and only he knew what else was tucked away in there with the law codes and the magic and the inscrutable thoughts of the Last Emperor.

"It was before I came into your service, my lord," he hastened to assure him. "She encouraged me to persist in the examinations. My sister—Navalia was her name—Navalia was always my champion. I was the youngest of the three, you see, and I never felt myself so brave or so fierce as my cousins. When she died, I felt I had to honour her faith in me, and I sat the examinations."

"Which you passed."

"On the *fifth* try," he admitted, laughing at that long-ago humiliation. "The examiners had all given up on me. My family was urging me to try something less competitive—anything—they thought I was chasing a viau, and worried I wouldn't be able to take the disappointment."

"Yet here you are," his Radiancy said, smiling at him.

"Yes, I am here," said Cliopher, his heart singing.

His Radiancy sat quietly again. He was digging his fingers into the sand, pressing down hard. After a while, he said, "I always wanted a family like that."

Cliopher did not know what to say, did not know whether he meant in his childhood or as a father. He decided he must have meant the latter, ventured tentatively: "You never married, my lord."

His Radiancy looked sharply at him, then away at the distant guards on shore, his face carefully blank. "No. But I would not have had that, regardless. No touching. No running. Precious little laughter."

A pause. Cliopher held his breath.

"I remember reading about families like yours, when I was a boy myself. I thought they were pure fiction. I was ... devastated, when I learned that people did have families full of ... love. I loved my tutor," he added more softly, "but he was the only person I was given to love, and in the end they destroyed him."

"They ..."

"The Emperor—Eritanyr, that was, his heir, their advisors. I read the reports after I acceded to the throne. They had very deliberately broken his mind. For the security of the Empire, they said; he knew too much about the Marwn. They were terrified someone would spearhead a coup, you see, and place me on the throne instead of my cousin."

"But the law!"

"Shallyr Silvertongue was criminally insane," his Radiancy said calmly.

Cliopher began to say something about that, but then bit his tongue, and instead said: "You have a sister, though, my lord."

"I did not meet her until after I became Emperor. I was raised by my tutor, who was under exceedingly strict instructions. In books I read of families. I learned from the reports that my uncle the Emperor had commanded my father never to speak to me. He ordered his sister, my mother, not to love me. It is no surprise they never came but when they were obliged to.

"No," he added more quietly, "I did not have a happy childhood."

"But *why*?" Cliopher whispered, shocked more than he could articulate even to himself.

"Why? Because the Imperial Heir showed signs from an early age of his insanity and his criminal inclinations. Because I was born to the Imperial Princess and the Grand Duke of Damara, descendant of ninety-eight Emperors, and I had the lion eyes of the ancient Emperors. Because the Grand Duke of Damara was almost as powerful and far more popular than the Emperor Eritanyr, and they wished to break him. I was a pawn, nothing more."

Cliopher understood politics. He could not have reached his position if he did not understand compromise.

He could not express why this felt so very wrong.

"And yet you became Emperor."

"Hundredth and last," his Radiancy agreed, with a mocking twist of a smile. "Someone decided in the end that whatever I might turn out to be—whatever the unknown, exiled, enchanted, possibly entirely uneducated Marwn was—would be better than Shallyr Silvertongue."

"You do not mean ... I have never heard ..."

"Shallyr Silvertongue fell off a balcony in front of his betrothed, my sister Melissa; the Lords Magi of Ysthar, Voonra, and Colhélhé; sundry servants and guards; and the Commander of the Imperial Guard. They all swore he just stood up and walked off the balcony, which was the one atop the cliff at the Damaran Summer Palace. There was never any evidence otherwise."

"But yet, my lord?"

"But yet he died within twelve hours of his father, and I was the first of all the Marwns of the Empire ever to become Emperor."

"I am sorry, my lord," he said, the words inadequate.

His Radiancy smiled crookedly again. "You have brought me far out of my accustomed self, haven't you, Cliopher? I have never spoken of this to anyone. I suppose it's because I am thinking about what is coming ..."

"The succession, my lord?" he replied, surer this time, and sure half a moment later that that was not quite what his Radiancy had meant.

"Indeed." His Radiancy wiped sand off his fingers. "It is getting hot. Shall we swim back towards the house?"

★★★

THAT AFTERNOON THEY WERE SITTING in the shade of the verandah when his Radiancy said, "It appears we have guests approaching. Pikabe, call Conju and get someone to fetch two more seats."

Cliopher looked up to see Ikialo Speaker and Aya inDovo Delanis walking down the beach towards them. Pikabe saluted and looked within the house to call Conju, who hastened out, and hastened back in again when his Radiancy asked for refreshments for everyone. Commander Omo followed him out, heard the order for seats, and exchanged places with the guard so that Pikabe could go fetch them.

Cliopher watched him make these arrangements, as if the villagers were visiting princes, and though the court-trained part of him was scandalized most of him was delighted.

"Welcome," said his Radiancy when the two villagers arrived and stood hesitantly at the bottom of the stairs, looking at the two guards. "Please, join us on the verandah."

"Thank you, *ivani*," Ikialo Speaker said, bowing over his clasped hands.

Aya inDovo Delanis echoed the motion, her eyes gleaming with interest as she took in the guards, Cliopher, his Radiancy, the book and the harp set next to the swinging chair, Pikabe returning with the two extra stools. They sat down with vague murmurs of thanks and the honour done to them.

Cliopher thought that they had absolutely no idea of what degree of honour was being done to them. In the days of the Empire no one sat in the Presence. Nowadays the princes might, and visiting lords magi, and favoured courtiers or servants such as Cliopher in the course of his duty.

"What does *ivani* mean?" his Radiancy asked, smiling at them.

"'Revered elder,'" Aya replied, smiling back. "We were all much impressed by your cunning with Eldoshi the carver, and Cliopher is my *hani*, so as a comrade in his household what else ought we call you?"

My lord? thought Cliopher. *Your Radiancy, your Holiness, Serenity, Glorious and Illustrious One ...*

His Radiancy continued to smile even as Conju, accompanied by Beila, appeared with trays of coffee and ginger cookies. Conju's expression was one Cliopher would treasure. Beila smiled awkwardly. "Good afternoon, Jiano, Aya."

Aya smiled back. "Good afternoon, Beila. How is your mother?"

"Very well, thank you. Very pleased I am working here." Beila cast an adoring look on his Radiancy. "As am I."

"We are glad to hear it," his Radiancy said. "Thank Saya Loven for the cookies, Beila."

Cliopher realized he had not, himself, learned the cook's name. Another marker of his Radiancy's remarkable—humility, he supposed was the word. He murmured thanks to Conju for pouring the coffee. Three elegant ceramic cups; one porcelain rimmed with gold of a different order altogether.

"Is your name Jiano, Speaker?" his Radiancy said, taking his. "We did not hear it when we were in the village the other day."

"It is, *ivani.*" Jiano paused hopefully, but his Radiancy did not reply with his own name, and the Speaker let the matter go gracefully. "We hope the ebony was what you needed?"

His Radiancy gestured at the harp. "It was. The snorkelling equipment is also appreciated."

"I am glad to hear it," Aya said. "It is always good to share one's wealth with others."

"They will think us radicals," Jiano said, laughing.

"Aren't we?" Aya grinned. "*Ivani, hani,* we came to tell you that it is the monthly market-day in Ikiava village tomorrow. We thought perhaps you might enjoy coming to see it. It is a humble affair, but it is picturesque. People come in all their finery, and of course there are all the usual things."

"That sounds wonderful," his Radiancy said enthusiastically.

Jiano nodded. "We can pass by here, if you wish, and accompany you. It is about an hour's walk to Ikiava from here. Will just after dawn be convenient?"

"He means the second hour after dawn," Aya said to Cliopher. "I lived in the city, I will make certain we arrive on time."

"I am not always late," Jiano protested.

"You are a Outer Ring villager, love," she said fondly. "You have no conception of structure."

His Radiancy sighed with something Cliopher might just about have dared to name to himself as envy. Aya smiled impishly. "*Ivani,* we must outrage you tremendously with our informality."

"Not at all," his Radiancy said blandly, "though I cannot speak for my attendants."

★★★

AFTER THE VILLAGERS HAD FINISHED their coffee and cookies and finally left, blithely cheerful about seeing them the next morning, his Radiancy said, "I daresay it's always disconcerting to find you have been promoted to the ranks of *honoured elder.*"

Cliopher tried very hard not to look as if he were thinking his Radiancy had joined those ranks long before.

His Radiancy sighed. "Such is life, I suppose. Though perhaps I should work on my disreputability. It is somewhat tedious to be *revered* all the time."

"No one would believe it, my lord," Commander Omo said.

"No?" His Radiancy arched his eyebrows. "Possibly not. Come along, boys," he added to Varro and Zerafin, and disappeared into the house.

Cliopher smiled ruefully at Commander Omo. "And they have no idea at all what any member of the court would do for half an hour of his Radiancy's attention."

"Perhaps the courtiers should try good humour and pleasant fellowship," Commander Omo said.

Cliopher looked at his completely straight face, and then they both started to laugh.

"Cliopher!" came the familiar voice down the hallway.

Cliopher jumped to attention and hastened into the main room. "Yes, my lord?"

His Radiancy swept in from the back hall, robes flying and eyes gleaming. "I need a pen and ink."

"And paper, my lord?"

"No, I have a notebook. Hurry now."

But what the hurry was, Cliopher did not understand at first, for upon his hasty return with fountain pen and inkwell, his Radiancy seated himself by the brazier and stared into space for a good half hour before beginning to write.

★★★

HIS RADIANCY HAD INFORMED COMMANDER Omo that any of the guards who desired might come with them for the market, which all of them did, so it was a large party that assembled to greet Aya and Jiano at the second hour after dawn the next morning.

The villagers were more or less on time. His Radiancy, who had never been late for a meeting to Cliopher's knowledge except on a few very deliberate occasions, was sitting on the verandah with his coffee, watching a flock of parrots chasing each other through a small grove of trees in the garden, and obviously trying not to look annoyed.

"There they come," Cliopher said in relief, seeing the figures turn onto the beach by the red bougainvillaea. They seemed to be wearing elaborate costumes; when they neared, he saw that Aya inDovo Delanis was in the swaying grass skirt and layered efela necklaces of a Western Vangavayen, her cloud of hair twisted up with great abalone-shell combs. From the eight or ten bands of cowries she was a wealthy and accomplished woman as the

Outer Ring villagers reckoned such things; from the gold beads between the shells she had not done so ill with her writing in the city, either.

Jiano wore a two-foot-high feather-and-shell headdress, and looked fierce and dramatic with his entire body in yellow and blue patterns outlined in red and white and black. They were accompanied by two other young people, the young man in similar garb to Jiano and the young woman with elaborate white spirals marked out with yellow, blue, and red. She was wearing a splendid necklace made of an opalescent shell in the shape of a half-moon.

"Reana and Dozo, *ivani*," Jiano introduced them. "Reana has the kula necklace this year, until after the lunar eclipse later this month."

Reana and Dozo each bowed over their hands to his Radiancy, to Cliopher, and to Commander Omo and Ser Rhodin. Conju had insisted they wear a slightly higher level of clothing for the market (taking into consideration Cliopher's explanation, at supper the evening before, of what 'finery' meant in the Outer Ring), and their bright silks and fine linens looked foreign and rich against the villagers' finery.

His Radiancy was in silver and white again, Cliopher in red and blue, Conju (who had decided to join them) in orange and yellow, and the guards in their lesser panoply, such as they would wear for duty with an underling prince. The jewels and leopard pelts were not in evidence, but the gold belts and brilliant white kilts were joined with ostrich-feather headdresses bedecked with pearls, and the spears carried by the two on duty were ebony banded in gold.

Cliopher was not really regretting his own traditional finery—the Mdangs of the city only wore it for very special occasions—but he did feel torn between his two lives, court and family. It was so strange to be at home, but with his Radiancy's household, not his family; to be in the midst of those in finery, and not wearing his.

They walked at a leisurely pace through the woods, the guards arranged behind them in pairs. Commander Omo and Ser Rhodin had decided to be his Radiancy's guards for the visit to the market. Cliopher and Conju walked with Aya. His Radiancy beckoned Jiano to walk beside him at the forefront of the group, and after a few minor pleasantries started to quiz him on the political structure of Lesuia island.

"He has found the way to my Jiano's heart," Aya said when one of the questions ("If this is a commune, as you say, how then do you decide on conflicts between villages?") floated back to them. "Jiano can speak about politics for hours and hours."

"So can his—lordship," Cliopher said, barely catching himself.

"He seems a most amiable man. Have you known him long?"

Conju and Cliopher exchanged glances. "We have had that honour, yes," Conju replied with great dignity.

"And that pleasure," Cliopher said firmly. "It is the height of our ambition to attend him."

"Your branch of the family was always reckoned as the more ambitious," Aya said, and the conversation turned to their shared relatives, leaving the solitary Conju to listen somewhat wistfully.

Cliopher knew his friend liked to hear about his family, so he did not worry overmuch; but he was glad his Radiancy was still quizzing Jiano Speaker, even if he did not articulate to himself what questions or emotions he was afraid of raising.

CHAPTER ELEVEN

THE VILLAGE OF IKIAVA WAS somewhat larger than Ikialo, and to Cliopher's eye had a slightly different set of decorations in use, but otherwise was very similar, being made of bush materials and focused on school and spirit-house. It sat a few hundred yards away from the sea, here facing the outside edge of the Ring. The market was held on the stretch of land between the houses and the sea, shaded by coconut palms and a huge fig.

"It's named for the fig," Jiano said as they approached. "Ikiava is an old name for the tree."

"What does Ikialo mean?" his Radiancy asked.

"It is the name of our spring. It means 'Iki's water', as this is 'Iki's tree'. Iki is the Son of Laughter."

"That is another name for Vou'a," said Cliopher, pleased to determine this.

Jiano laughed. "Oh, you westerners!"

Aya winked, knowing as well as Cliopher did that Vou'a was the name used in the *Lays*.

The market-goers, drawn from the villages of Lesuia and its neighbouring islets, were all dressed in customary finery, with feathers and paint and shells much in evidence. The arrival of his Radiancy's party in their foreign dress occasioned a great deal of murmuring and interested glances.

Cliopher kept being surprised by the feel of cloth against his legs. Was it so easy, then, to leave behind a lifetime of learned behaviours? He had been a teenager the last time he had gone around in a grass skirt. He found himself touching his single efela necklace, safely hidden below his tunic, to make sure it was still there. The pearls and obsidian pendant were warm against his skin and tucked invisible into the hollow of his neck and collarbone.

Accompanied by the Ikialo villagers as they were, there seemed to be no difficulty about their arrival. Three men and two women emerged out of the crowd, and Jiano effected introductions with the Speakers of Ikiava, Lesinte, Lesante, Wailo, and Grandstone villages. He introduced Cliopher as Aya's *hani*, and his Radiancy as "a lord wizard of Solaara, come on holiday, with his guards." Everyone bowed over their hands with great politeness to them. Cliopher bowed back in the same manner; Conju bowed in the courtly style; his Radiancy nodded regally.

"Grandstone. A newer habitation, from the name?"

"By the Emperor, no, we are the oldest," the older woman who was Grandstone Speaker said, grinning. "The name comes from a great battle that was fought there long ago between the Seven Masters of the Toala Guild."

"Of course! As immortalized in *The Lay of Fo Wakailunte*," his Radiancy said, and when they looked astonished at him, won the immediate respect of Grandstone Speaker by reciting a dozen lines of the poem.

He smiled self-deprecatingly afterwards and turned to the off-duty guards, who were trying not to let their attention be drawn away by the market and its denizens. "Enjoy the market, boys."

"Pikabe and Ato, attend in two hours," Commander Omo added sternly, and everyone saluted and dispersed. There were quite a few admiring glances being cast by young women (and a few young men) of the villages at the sculpted muscles and exotic uniforms of the guards.

Cliopher wandered along behind his Radiancy, more to keep Conju from being overly solicitous than because he himself was concerned. Conju, however, was quickly distracted by the fruit and vegetables on offer, and started asking questions about cooking styles of the vendors. Cliopher watched his Radiancy speaking to Grandstone and Ikiava Speakers, watched Commander Omo and Ser Rhodin look magnificent and keep people from approaching too near the Presence, watched the guards flirting, and when Aya came up to him, a string bag in her hand, he started.

"Did you have a bag?" she asked, offering him a traditional string bilum woven, he was amused to see, with a Western Ring pattern. "I don't know if you wanted to get anything …"

"I'm not sure anyone brought any money," Cliopher admitted.

"It's mostly bartering this far into the Outer Ring. People would accept coin—it's always useful if you want to get anything in the city—but it's more efela, or things in kind—but you would know that."

"Unless anyone wants a letter written in chancery script, I don't have many skills to trade."

"I'm not sure I believe you, *hani*. I've been remembering stories of Cousin Kip, the one who left to join the Service."

"I shudder at the thought."

She laughed. "Oh, mostly stories of how you used to raise the ire and admiration of everyone by your willingness to tell them exactly what they were doing wrong and how they should fix it."

"I'm better at keeping my thoughts to myself now," he said, though he could feel himself flush. "I'm not sure anyone admired my obnoxiousness!"

"I think they admired your ideas, actually, as well as your forthrightness."

They walked down one of the side aisles, between vendors of plantains and betel-nut and smoked fish, and beyond them turned to those who had shells. Aya was stopped by someone, and Cliopher walked on a few paces by himself, examining the shells.

One vendor had long strands of cowries. He turned over the shells with great pleasure in their plump curves and glossy shine and varied colours. Cream and tan and dark tortoiseshell. There was one strand of stunning shells, their size small but their colouring exquisite, deep amber with a ring of gold around the curve as if it held reflected sunlight. He ran his fingers over them in deep admiration.

"Eya," the vendor said, eyes lighting. "Your hands know what you're touching."

"My great-uncle," Cliopher said deprecatingly. "You know how it is, you learn these things as a boy."

He turned the strand of shells over in his hands. They were truly stunning. In Gorjo City a string of amber cowries of this quality—without the golden ring, which reminded him of fultoni cowries except that the amber was a much more beautiful base colour than the usual washy tan or even the darker tortoiseshell of a grand fultoni—would be worth something like a thousand valiants. Such a strand would be given as a marker of intent for a major ceremony: a wedding, the birth of a first child, a new chief.

If they were available for sale anywhere else, which was doubtful—they more likely would be given as tithes and disappear into a palace treasury somewhere—they would be double or triple or even fivefold that. An efela necklace such as this would never make it intact to Solaara: he had searched all the markets and stores enough times to know it was hard to find more than a dozen matched shells in any given set. This had thirty or more.

"Where are you from, then? I thought you a *velion* from your appearance?"

Cliopher let his accent thicken, opened his hand in the gestures he had had to train himself out of using. "I was born in Gorjo City, but I've spent my time out along the Ring. Where do these come from? I don't remember ever seeing this kind before."

The vendor was an older man, perhaps in his seventies. He was dressed in a grass skirt whose design Cliopher did not recognize but which seemed very old from its simplicity and its use of only natural colours. Even his Buru Tovo made use of the magical dyes that permitted the weave to hold many layers of colours.

The vendor looked at him through narrow eyes. "What is your name, what is your island, and what is your dance?"

The questions shocked him through to the core.

It took him a moment to pull up the traditional answers. "I am Cliopher Mdang of Tahivoa in Gorjo City. My island is Loaloa." He paused a moment, before the desire for it to be true overcame the fear that he overreached himself in the claim. His third answer came, as a result, much more quietly. "My dance is *Aōteketētana*."

"Where have you danced the fire?"

These were the questions out of the *Lays of the Wide Seas*. Cliopher had been expecting to haggle over price, not his identity. He took a breath. No one was listening to him but the vendor.

"I learned the steps on Loaloa from the direction of the *tanà*, my great-uncle Tovo. My feet bear the scars of my learning."

He gestured down, though the old burns on the sides of his feet, where he had brushed up against the coals, were hidden by his Solaaran-style sandals.

"And I danced the fire across the Wide Seas when I sailed down the river of time in a ship of my own hands' shaping."

He had never made that claim aloud. It was a line from the *Lays*, sung every year when the people of the Vangavaye-ve renewed their vows to the Emperor from over the sea. He was never home for the Singing of the Waters, had not been home for it since he left, since that festival coincided with one of the great sessions of the court. And since he did not live at home, did not work there, it had seemed improper—or perhaps *arrogant* was the word—to suggest he had any right to make the claim.

But here he was on the Outer Ring, where all of his titles from Solaara were of even less importance to his status than they were in Gorjo City, and that claim, that line, was the slender thread on which they would expect him to build all his sense of self.

"I have heard of three brothers who left," said the vendor. "One went as far as he could to see what there was to see. One went searching after his heart. And one went to sit at the feet of the Sun."

That was from another part of the *Lays*. Cliopher, realizing his hands were clenching around the cowries, very consciously loosened them.

He and his cousin Basil and Basil's twin brother Dimiter had laughed, one day in Astandalas when the twins had come to see him (alone out of all his family, they had come to see him), that they were like the three brothers, the sons of Vonou'a.

Dimiter the explorer had perished doing what he loved best, looking for a land where no one had ever stepped before him. Basil had fallen in love with a woman on Alinor and Cliopher had not heard from or of him since the Fall. And Cliopher …

Cliopher smiled, a little ruefully, as he placed himself into the poem. "I sit at the feet of the Sun."

"What will you bring home?"

In the *Lays* that question was *What* have *you brought home?*

Cliopher's heart was beating loudly in his ears. What was worth a whole string of priceless gold-ringed amber cowries? What was worth this revelation of his heart to a total stranger demanding the ancient tokens of a life well lived? What *did* he bring home, what *would* he bring home, if ever he answered the question Bertie had asked him, that everyone in his family always asked him, with a *yes*?

The third son of Vonou'a brought home the gift of fire from the house of the Sun.

What was his career, all told, when he asked himself what he did, what he was worth, what it all was worth?

He was not married. He did not have children. He had none of that.

He had a hundred projects that had made the world a better place, had slowly, carefully, almost imperceptibly transformed the structure of society into something that little bit juster, that little bit richer, that little bit more systematically *good*.

He had for many years made himself rest content with that slow progress.

He had told himself that it was impossible to expect one ordinary man (even given the gift of innumerable imperceptible years in which to work) to completely transform the whole society of the world.

As a young man he had had those ambitions. He had even developed that ridiculous plan for how he could do it.

In those innumerable imperceptible years he had laid the groundwork,

thinking that future generations would take those basics—a reformed bureaucracy, effective worldwide transport and communication, a stable currency, peace—and realize out of them the grand vision of a world where beauty
and prosperity and happiness and health in all their different forms were the
rule, not the exception.

He had taught himself to be content with the idea that future generations would do what he dared not.

He had been willing to reach only for the idea of a new fire, fearing the
flame itself would burn him if he tried to take it.

He looked down at the gold-ringed amber cowries, their beauty worthy
of a tithe-offering to the Lord of Rising Stars, or even to the silent gods beyond the gods whose names were spoken.

He had always prided himself he had never compromised his principles.
He had been willing, though, to compromise his dreams, if that was what it
took to survive.

He could do better.

He looked straight in the eyes of the vendor.

"My name is Cliopher Mdang of Tahivoa. My island is Loaloa. My dance
is *Aōteketētana*. From the feet of the Sun I will bring home the fire."

The vendor did not smile. He had shadowy eyes, old and wise and
deep-seeing. Cliopher wondered briefly what dance he would claim was his,
if Cliopher asked him the questions in turn. Not that he would: he remembered that from the stories.

Listen first. Observe first. Questions later.

"And what is this fire that you bring?"

In the *Lays* it was the gift of civilization.

Cliopher opened his hands again, not in an Islander gesture this time,
but in the gesture he used for making official pronouncements in his role as
the Hands of the Emperor. The gesture meant nothing to the vendor, who
gazed at him curiously, as if he were a bird or a butterfly whose motions
meant nothing in human language. He turned the motion into one that he
remembered his great-uncle showing him, the one that meant a solemn and
binding oath. At this the vendor's eyes narrowed.

"I will bring home the hearth-fire of a new life for the world."

He had said that too loudly: everyone around him, including his Radiancy on the other side of the row of stalls, turned to look at him. After a
moment they went back to their own affairs, as if Cliopher's announcement
were meaningless, part of a joke.

The vendor laughed. His laugh was distinctive, high and rattling, like the sound of a kookaburra. "You say that as if you mean it."

Even though he felt he had walked into a story, and knew what such promises meant in such stories, before he could stop himself he said, "I do."

There was a long silence.

Then the vendor laughed again. "I suppose I will have to believe you."

Even as he walked away with the string of cowries in their woven wrapper, Cliopher was thinking how it had been a long time since he had been so thoroughly bested in a negotiation.

★★★

ON THE OTHER SIDE OF the shells were a series of people selling baskets woven in a dozen minutely different styles. His Radiancy stood examining one carefully, but even as he approached (and even as Cliopher was beginning to formulate the thought that it was a *basket*, and it would look as much out of place in the Imperial Apartments as one of the smoked fish) the vendor popped up from where she had been mending a basket bigger than she was and said, "Are you interested, *ivani*?"

Her voice was very shrill, and she was very small—and about ten years old, Cliopher surmised.

His Radiancy smiled down at her. "It's a beautiful basket. Did you make it, child?"

"My grandmother," she said, looking him up and down with critical appreciation. "They're saying you're a wizard, sir."

"I am," he replied easily.

She wore her hair done up in braids gathered in bunches over her ears, and tugged on them now. She was skinny, not very pretty, but with sharp eyes and an adorable smile when she suddenly grinned. "Can you do illusions? I'll trade you the basket for one. The wizards in my book do illusions."

"What book are you reading?"

She glanced sidelong at a woman who stood a few feet away, watching carefully; the woman shook her head in amused resignation. The little girl tugged a battered book from beneath one of her baskets and passed it up to his Radiancy defiantly.

"No touching," Commander Omo warned, stepping forward.

The little girl said, "I wasn't! Are you sacred, sir, like the hermit?"

"Something like that," his Radiancy replied, giving Commander Omo a quelling glance and flipping through the book. After a moment he began to laugh. "*Tikla Dor*! I had no idea people were still reading this. This was one of my favourite books when I was a boy," he added to the girl. "First the *Deeds of Olor*, now *Tikla Dor* ... oh, this takes me back. Let's see, now, Sayina Basketer ... hmm ... what does Ufin the Tremendous do?—Stand back, now," he said to the onlookers, which by this point comprised half the market.

No one did much more than pretend to step back. Commander Omo looked at his Radiancy, as if to ask whether he should force them, but his Radiancy shook his head slightly. He made a great show of arranging the folds of his silver mantle better, and while everyone was watching him avidly a horse suddenly leaped over the stall to the side and thundered into the small space in front of him.

The crowd gasped and a few people shrieked in surprise. Cliopher stared in astonishment. The horse was dapple-grey and huge, with white feathers over its hooves and a dark intelligent eye. It tossed its head, ears flickering around, and neighed at the little girl, who was gazing with wide eyes up at it. For a moment Cliopher thought he smelled a strange warm animal smell, and his breath caught at the sheer strength of the illusion.

Then a path opened up in the market crowd, and the excited murmurs turned to little cries of alarm, as a tiger bounded towards the horse. The horse reared, bugled some sort of alarm call, jumped the basket stall, and disappeared.

Ooh, went the crowd. The tiger stalked restlessly around the suddenly much-larger space before his Radiancy. His Radiancy was smiling lazily, hands in his sleeves, looking as if he were watching an entertainment put on for his benefit and not at all as if he were the one doing the work. His brilliant eyes were hooded.

The tiger's tail was twitching, and he paced as if in a cage. Then from above came a whistle of wings, and a black eagle dropped down. The tiger jumped away from its arrival, following the horse over the stall, and the eagle swooped around the crowd, nearly touching a few people, until it soared off.

Next came a pair of white cranes, which performed a splendid dance before the crowd. While everyone's attention was riveted on the cranes and their elegant slow movements, his Radiancy removed his hands from his sleeves and made a single gesture.

Off in the distance came a great trumpeting sound, and the crowd parted again to see a huge grey elephant come pacing ceremoniously down from the village. It was caparisoned in red and purple, its ivory tusks tipped with gold, and it bore a pavilion on its back. The pavilion was draped with crimson and orange and gold, and inside the pavilion reclined a young woman of unconventional but truly spell-binding beauty. Silk-haired and copper-skinned, eyes dark, wearing dark robes with a bright blue sash, a sword at her side, she smiled crookedly down at his Radiancy.

Cliopher looked hastily at his lord, who was looking up at his creation with a very bland expression indeed.

The elephant paced down the crowd to the beach and swam out to sea, fading as it went.

The crowd clapped enthusiastically, and his Radiancy made a half-bow of acknowledgement that shocked Cliopher deeply.

His Radiancy laughed at his expression. "Well, Sayina Basketer? Was that worth your grandmother's basket?"

"Yes, I think so," the little girl said solemnly, "but as you did more than the ones from the story, I must give you an additional gift. This basket is one I made all by myself. It was the first one my grandmother said I could sell."

"Then it is doubly special."

The basket-maker's first basket was slightly lopsided, but his Radiancy set it within the larger with great care.

"Now," he said pleasantly, "if it is acceptable, let us see the rest of the market."

The rest of the market appeared to find this very acceptable indeed.

★★★

CLIOPHER COULD ONLY WONDER AT the ease with which his Radiancy charmed the assembled villagers of Lesuia island. When he ventured to express his wonderment to Conju, that gentleman said, "But of course they find him amiable; how could they not?"

Which was quite true, Cliopher thought, but he also thought that it was not very likely that it was merely some sort of innate response to their visiting lord magus on the part of the villagers. He did not share Conju's Astandalan-gentry prejudices about hinterland village life.

But whatever the cause, whether some subtle magic or the yet more subtle workings of personality and charisma, his Radiancy was hailed with joy and frank pleasure by nearly all the market-goers. Eldoshi the Carver was a notable exception, treating his Radiancy with an oily obsequiousness no less despicable for its familiarity. His Radiancy's serenity remained unbroken.

In the early afternoon Jiano and Aya found Cliopher. They were accompanied by the Speaker of Ikiava village, who bowed over his hands to Cliopher and invited him solemnly to join them for the midday feast.

"We have a pig roast and a *mumu*," he said. To Cliopher's relief he did not underline Cliopher's foreign associations by explaining what he meant by the latter. (Cliopher had spent enough of his childhood gathering rocks to heat in the fire, digging the pits, and collecting banana leaves sufficient to wrap all the feast-foods to know what a *mumu* was, thank you.) "You and your ... lord ... will be most welcome."

Cliopher looked around for his Radiancy, seeing Commander Omo first. He hailed the guard. "Have you seen his—" He stumbled over the title.

"His lordship?" Commander Omo said, looking stern. "He is looking at the books."

Aya burst out laughing. "You are too polite to say it, eh? There are two brothers who bring second-hand books from the city. We are not wholly lacking in culture, you know."

"You are not lacking in culture at all, but it is not traditionally given to literature."

"I am not the only writer on Lesuia," she said, somewhat mysteriously.

His Radiancy was thoroughly absorbed in examining the books on offer. Pikabe and Ato stood a punctilious four feet away, using their spears to keep anyone else from encroaching. The brother merchants did not seem as upset about this as Cliopher might have expected, probably because Conju was standing next to his Radiancy holding a foot-high stack of books.

After several minutes of them watching while he methodically went through yet another set of books, his Radiancy looked up to see them standing there. "Well?" he said, weighing the book in his hand before placing it on Conju's pile.

Cliopher did not know what to say to that, but fortunately Aya took it upon herself. "The pig roast will begin shortly, *ivani*, if you would like to join us."

"Then I suppose I should, ah, pay for my choices," his Radiancy said agreeably, ignoring Conju's horrified expression. "What do I owe you, gentlemen?"

The two brothers looked across at each other at this address, then at the pile of books, then at the guards, and at Conju, Cliopher, Aya, and the wider circle of interested market-goers beyond them. After a moment one brother said, "I reckon I've always wanted to see a dragon."

"A dragon?" said his Radiancy, smiling faintly.

"A dragon," the man said firmly.

"A red one," added his brother. "A red fire-breathing dragon."

"Ah," said his Radiancy, and then someone in the crowd gasped, and suddenly there were cries and hands pointing and general amazement.

Cliopher looked up at the edge of the stall opposite the brothers, which was draped with cloth banners in once-bright colours. The bamboo ridge pole was growing red and rough, and then the thatching started to heave and move, the colours shifting from dun and dull green to a deep dark scarlet, and then the dragon began to unfurl itself.

It took a long time before the final wing shuddered free of the thatch. The great monster stretched, first one leg and then the next, and then one wing and the other, and curled its tail and straightened its tail, and yawned and licked its lips, and then at last it stretched one wing up and the other wing up and stepped down off the stall so it could peer at the two brothers with its fire-brilliant eyes.

Its ears flapped and it blinked lazily, then turned its head so that it could rub one horn up and down the carved post of the booksellers' stall. Thin trickles of smoke came from its nostrils, and it smelled like a furnace smelting gold.

The crowd was utterly silent. The illusion was so complete Cliopher clearly saw a leaf hit the wing and fall to the ground. He held his breath as the dragon finished its rubbing and turned its head to his Radiancy. He held out his hand, and the dragon rubbed its muzzle hard against his palm. His nails made a soft scratching noise against its scales. Each tooth was the length of one of his fingers.

Cliopher lifted his gaze briefly to his Radiancy's face. He was looking down at his hand as if he didn't quite know what was happening to it.

A flock of coral-crested cockatoos started screeching above them. The dragon lifted its head with sudden alertness, ears pricked and horns sweeping left and right like scythes as it searched the sky. Then, with a sudden powerful thrust and a clatter of scales it jumped up, wings flicking open. When it reached the cockatoos—now screaming bloody murder at this scarlet intruder—it let out a burst of flame, which enveloped it and the birds and the treetops in blinding brilliance.

When the dazzle cleared the dragon was gone. It took much longer for the cockatoos to stop screaming; and Cliopher thought that the villagers of Lesuia island would be talking about it until the return of the Red Company.

★★★

THE PIG ROAST AND MUMU was held on the beach. His Radiancy was giv-
en the seat of honour, at the centre between all the village Speakers. To his
embarrassment, Cliopher was seated beside him, quite as if they were equals.
Jiano was to his right, with Conju to his Radiancy's left.

"Your friend is very fierce," Jiano said, indicating Conju. "Very protective
of your ... lord."

There was that pause again, Cliopher thought irritably. "It is his responsibility to ensure all the customary requirements are met."

"There appear to be a great many of them."

"There are," he said absently.

Conju had brought his Radiancy's eating sticks, but not, it appeared, a
plate, and was having an intense conversation with the man in charge of the
fire pit. Finally he accepted a fresh piece of banana leaf as a dish, presumably
because it could be destroyed after the meal. Cliopher realized uneasily that
this was extremely close to breaking a taboo. He could almost feel the weight
of it pressing against him.

Once everyone was settled, the speaker of Ikiava village stood up.
"Friends, we have honoured guests with us this market-day. What say you we
ask the *perion ivani* to speak the invocation?"

General acclamation met this point. Ikiava Speaker took a great carved
shell from somewhere, filled it with an oily-looking liquid, and handed it to
his Radiancy, who accepted it regally.

"It is my pleasure to invoke the Sun and the Moon and the high lords
of the heavens to bless this gathering and this food," he said, holding up the
shell. "May their light shine ever on their people, may the rains come in their
season and the warmth and the dry in theirs, may the fruits wax with the
Moon and the shadows wane with her."

He stopped there, and Cliopher, along with everyone else, stared at him.

His Radiancy stared back at Cliopher, his expression blankly innocent. If
it had been anyone else at all Cliopher might have nudged him, but he could
not do that and he was too far to whisper. He made do with meaningful
nods for his Radiancy to keep going.

The silence grew almost humorous. People were starting to look at each
other in amazement and wonder, hiding their scandalized snickers behind
their hands.

His Radiancy stared at him a moment longer, every line of his body
proclaiming his ignorance of the problem, until finally he handed Cliopher
the shell.

Cliopher spoke very firmly, very clearly, and very loudly. "We invoke also our Lord of the Rising Stars, the Sun-on-Earth, the joy of his people, the wellspring of all benefits, the hope of the hopeless and the help of the helpless, the Glorious and Radiant One, the Lord of Zunidh and Last Emperor of Astandalas, that he too many rain down his blessings and his good will upon this gathering and this food."

The *amen* that followed was notably enthusiastic. His Radiancy closed his lips and eyes in an obvious attempt not to laugh.

An old man on Cliopher's other side leaned across him and said to his Radiancy, "So you're a radical, are you?"

His Radiancy said, "Only in the most literal sense, I'm afraid. And you?"

CHAPTER *T*WELVE

Walking back with the Ikialo villagers later that afternoon no one spoke much. When they came to a certain fork in the path Jiano stopped. "If you take this path," he said, indicating the branch, "It will bring you out at the western end of your beach. It is about ten minutes' further walk. If we continue this path, we can cut half an hour from our journey."

"Of course," said his Radiancy, ignoring the slightly concerned looks of Conju and Ser Rhodin. The Ikialo villagers set off after a few further courtesies, and his Radiancy launched himself into the new path.

"My lord, we do not know these jungles," said Ser Rhodin bravely. "What if there is another fork in the path? We could become lost very easily."

His Radiancy had been walking with a serene expression, evidently thinking of something else, for it took him a moment to reply. "Ser Rhodin," he said at last, "You are from the plains south of Astandalas, I know, and used to wide vistas."

"Yes, my lord."

"It is understandable that being enclosed in the trees makes you somewhat nervous."

Ser Rhodin looked as if he did not like his concern being characterized as nerves. What he said, however, was: "Yes, my lord."

"You have a certain small skill at magic, do you not? Enough to boil water, as they say?"

"Yes, my lord."

"You do not have a strong magical sense of direction, however."

"No, my lord."

There was a silence, and then Ser Rhodin saluted. "Very good, my lord." His Radiancy nodded once, and continued on.

After ten minutes—with no forks and barely any twists—the path debouched them onto the beach, only a few hundred yards away from Navikiani. Cliopher felt relieved despite himself.

*** ★★★

THE WEEK FOLLOWING THE MARKET settled into a pleasant routine. In the morning his Radiancy would swim or snorkel—often inviting Cliopher to join him for the latter, though never for the swimming alone—and then he would sit on the verandah and read, or write, or play his harp. After lunch he often napped, emerging to swim again and read and sometimes think of playing chess with Cliopher.

Cliopher finally got a look at the books on the fourth day: they were almost all poetry.

One day at lunch Conju suddenly said, "My lord, I had no idea you could do illusions of the sort you did at the market."

His Radiancy smiled. "Did you not? As it happens, there are quite a few things I can do that my usual life has no room for. Illusions are in the main one of them."

"In the main?" Ser Rhodin asked curiously.

"Do you remember when the embassy of the Lord of Ysthar came, oh, a dozen years ago, and all of them were dressed in lacquered armour and with the most remarkable accents?"

They all stared at him in total shock. Ser Rhodin found his voice first. "You cannot—my lord, do you mean—"

His Radiancy looked solemnly at them all, then abruptly his calm evaporated and he broke into robust laughter. "No, but that was *entirely* worth it. I don't think I could maintain a complex illusion that long, not with multiple independent parts. Not and do anything else. My life may be largely routine, but it does require some attention. Cliopher, you are not eating. Are you feeling unwell?"

Cliopher was disconcerted by the sudden change of topic—and reeling from the joke. How could you know someone for so long—work so closely with them for so long—and still be utterly surprised by their sense of humour?

"Oh," he said belatedly. "No, I am well, my lord. I am perhaps tired. I spent too long sitting in the sun today. I should know better."

★★★

CLIOPHER ROSE EARLY THE NEXT morning. He was not really sick. He was feeling some of Conju's promised change, something sweeping towards them, a pressure of the future reaching back. No one was in the main room when he entered after bathing; it was barely after dawn.

After a moment he decided to go to the kitchen to ask for coffee. He opened the door in the middle of a yawn, and stopped in surprise to see his Radiancy sitting on a high stool and chatting merrily with the cook. Zerafin and Oginu stood guard on the door, wary and alert and relieved when Cliopher entered. Beila grinned from across the room, where she was pounding something in a mortar.

His Radiancy turned, saw that Cliopher had entered, and broke off his conversation. "Thank you, Saya Loven," he said, smiling charmingly at her.

"Oh, you're—you're welcome, sir." She was not a pretty woman, her face pocked with old acne scars and with a narrow nose to boot, but the true pleasure in her face as she looked up at his Radiancy loaned her loveliness and grace.

"And no one is to say anything," his Radiancy said to the room, looking meaningfully at the two guards, who both saluted. "Cliopher, I suppose you are hoping for coffee? Beila, my dear, will you make us some of your delicious brew?"

"Of course, sir," she said, winking at Cliopher, who followed his Radiancy out of the room with his head in no less of a whirl than the day before.

"What was that about, my lord?" he ventured once they were half down the hall.

"What was what about?" his Radiancy replied blandly, as Zerafin reached forward to open the door to the main room. "Ah, good morning, Ludvic."

"My lord."

★★★

SUPPER THAT EVENING WAS MORE than usually delicious, and ran to much spicier food than the cook had so far made for them. Commander Omo, Cliopher noted, seemed particularly taken with the meal, and complimented numerous dishes extravagantly. Cliopher and Conju, who did not routinely eat such spicy food, both drank a great deal of water.

Towards the end of the meal his Radiancy gestured at Pikabe, who produced a small parcel and deposited it on the table beside him.

"Now," said his Radiancy, when they all tried not to look curious, "it is a special occasion today. It is, as it happens, Commander Omo's birthday."

Commander Omo said, "My lord!"

"Now, now, Ludvic," his Radiancy said. "You have refused all honours and titles I have offered you over the years. I have not embarrassed you with earldoms or duchies or what-have-you, richly though you have earned them."

"I am not of noble blood," he growled.

"That could be remedied, but I know you would prefer to remain a commoner. If one can be said to be common when one's family contains such artists of genius as does yours."

"My lord," he said, though the protest was fainter, and Cliopher remembered the proud litany of carvers.

"I had intended this to be a gift on some anniversary of your service with me—never mind which one, for it has taken me much longer than I anticipated to finish. It was some time ago. Nevertheless, it is at last done, and I thought your birthday a proper occasion for the gift."

His Radiancy paused, hand on the parcel, which was small and rectangular—a book, Cliopher guessed—and wrapped untidily in yellow silk. Commander Omo was staring with vivid embarrassment at the table.

His Radiancy said, "You have served me the longest of any of my household. You were the one who told me what had happened in the Palace and among the people after the Fall and during my—my period asleep. I am most grateful for your loyalty and your skill. You will not let me give you riches or titles or lands or any of the other honours it is usual for a lord to give his loyal servants, so instead I offer you this as your friend."

He set the parcel down before the guardsman, who hesitated a long moment before reaching out to undo the silk.

The book thus revealed was bound in tooled leather and consisted of a thick sheaf of paper. Commander Omo opened the book at random, revealing long slanting lines of handwritten poetry, and then he frowned, and flipped to the front of the volume. He lifted his head and stared at his Radiancy.

His Radiancy said, "No one will ever pay me to copy out texts, I'm afraid, but every poet should see his work in book form at least once. It is good for the soul."

There was a perfect silence. Commander Omo looked as if he could not believe his eyes. Cliopher wasn't sure he could believe his ears. Had his Radiancy really just said he *personally* had copied out some poem of Commander Omo's *by hand*?

"I do hope Volume Two is nearly ready," his Radiancy added. "I for one am most interested in knowing what happens to Edriana and the Cavalier next."

★★★

"WHAT KIND OF POEM IS it?" Ser Rhodin asked Commander Omo, who was standing in his usual place holding the book.

"Foolishness," replied Commander Omo, broad face stern.

"His Radiancy doesn't think so."

Commander Omo could hardly say that his Radiancy was a fool, so he settled for glowering at them instead.

"His Radiancy bought a stack of poetry books at the market," Cliopher said, coming to join them. His Radiancy had gone for a walk down the beach, just himself and his guards, saying that the Moon was very beautiful and he felt like thinking. "I would imagine he has a perfectly sound knowledge of poetry."

"It's a romantic epic," Commander Omo said eventually. "I recited it to his Radiancy one day when he was feeling ill, and I ... I suppose he remembered and wrote it down."

"In his own hand."

"It seems so," said Commander Omo, looking at the book. There was a long pause as they each considered the incredible honour this revealed—far more impressive than lands or titles or wealth, Cliopher thought, suppressing a brief flash of envy—and then Commander Omo said wretchedly, "What can I possibly do in return?"

"I don't believe you're supposed to *do* anything," Ser Rhodin said in amusement. "I believe you're to accept it with great gratitude."

"He called me his *friend*."

"Then you must continue to act in the office of friendship," Cliopher said firmly.

Commander Omo looked at him, eyes a little wild. Then some idea seemed to come to him, for he swallowed resolutely and went back to appearing stolid and stern and unintellectual and not at all as if romantic epics blossomed in his heart.

★★★

THE NEXT DAY IT WAS raining again, this time in a thunderstorm that precluded swimming. His Radiancy lit the brazier without waiting for Conju, and sat there with coffee and a pile of books. He looked quite tremendously relaxed. Cliopher sat next to him with his history of Ysthar, trying to reconcile the new kingdoms and tribes with the old continents he had learned in school, and finding he had to turn to the maps supplied in the end papers with embarrassing frequency.

Midmorning Beila came in with drinking chocolate, and his Radiancy stretched out his arms and then sat there staring calmly into the brazier ignoring his books and his harp and the rest of them.

After about half an hour of this Commander Omo announced, "My lord, I have been wondering."

His Radiancy continued to regard the brazier. "Have you indeed, Ludvic? And what have you been wondering about?"

"I have been wondering, my lord, whether it had occurred to you to retire."

There was a pause.

His Radiancy looked up at Commander Omo, standing solid as ever by the verandah doors, and then over at Cliopher, who was torn between shock and admiration.

"I, retire?" his Radiancy said, in a peculiar tone of voice.

Commander Omo spoke placidly. "Yes, my lord. You seem to be enjoying your holiday, and it occurred to me that no one would consider it anything but fully deserved if you were to step down as Lord of Zunidh."

There was an even more aghast silence. Ser Rhodin and Elish stood at mute attention; Conju, coming from the bedrooms in time to hear this, stopped dead, face a study in disbelief; and Cliopher had to work hard to maintain his composure.

His Radiancy said, "I must confess the thought had never occurred to me."

"I had wondered, my lord," said Commander Omo.

"I had forgotten that while being Emperor is necessarily for life—mine or, as it happened, my empire's—being the lord magus of a world is not."

"Just so, my lord."

There was another pause. His Radiancy stared at the brazier. "We will be celebrating the Jubilee of my reign in a few years."

"Even so, my lord."

Another pause. No one else said anything. They were all still staring in shock.

"Well then," said his Radiancy, "I suppose I ought not go haring off without giving some thought to the succession. Conju! Fetch me a notebook. We must decide on a plan."

Conju said, "My lord!"

"Well?" His Radiancy looked sharply at them, at Commander Omo's placidity, Cliopher and Conju's pitiful attempts to appear calm, Ser Rhodin fighting for equanimity, Elish with his eyes wide. His Radiancy's hands were resting on his thighs; while Cliopher watched, he folded them into fists. "Do I move with unseemly haste, Conju?"

"My lord," said Conju, obviously wanting to say yes, but bowing instead. "My lord, I am merely surprised. You do not have to explain yourself to me."

His Radiancy smiled crookedly. "Do I not? You are surprised to hear me say I had never thought of retirement, and within three sentences decide exactly when, is that it?"

Conju lifted his chin. "Yes, my lord, I am surprised to hear you say it."

His Radiancy looked down at his fists. Spread out his fingers. The signet ring gleamed in the firelight. "My life is bounded in a box. It is a very comfortable and well-appointed one, but a box nonetheless. A *small* box."

"You are the Lord of Zunidh and Last Emperor of Astandalas, my lord!"

"You are remarkably good at keeping me within my box, I must say. No, that is unfair. Let us try this another way. Do you know the difference between wild magic and Schooled magic? Rhodin?"

Ser Rhodin said, "Schooled magic is governed by law and reason, my lord. It is rational, reliable, and civilized. Wild magic is untamed, unreliable, and full of impossibilities and the most grievous dangers."

"And what is the difference, then, between a wild mage and a Schooled wizard?"

Conju spoke, a thread of agony in his voice, "A wild mage cannot use Schooled magic, my lord. He may be broken, or he may go mad, but it is counter to the grain of his soul. A Schooled wizard cannot touch wild magic any more than I can touch fire."

"You sound as if that comes from experience," his Radiancy said, in a gentler voice.

Conju's face worked. "I had a, a friend, long ago, my lord, who was a wild mage. He tried. He was a loyal son of the Empire. We wanted nothing more than—he wanted nothing more than to serve—but—he could not learn to govern his magic that way. He tried, my lord. He tried."

"What happened to him?"

Conju lifted his hand to his face, looking out into the distance. Cliopher had heard him refer to this story twice, both times when Conju was very drunk, but had never learned the details. "He left. One night, without telling me—telling anyone. He fled the Empire's magic so he would not go mad."

"That was, unfortunately, not an option given the Emperor," his Radiancy said softly.

Conju looked searchingly at him. "My lord?"

"I spent the time of my exile studying poetry and wild magic. I was an anchor of the Empire's magic, but I was left to my own devices from three days after my sixteenth birthday, when I woke in my place of exile, until the third day after my uncle's and my cousin's deaths, when the Emperor's Dogs came to fetch me to Astandalas."

There was a long silence. His Radiancy had been thirty when he became Emperor.

"Your love of the Empire must have been very great," Conju ventured at last.

His Radiancy laughed harshly. "Love? Do not think my love was so much greater than your friend's, Conju, that I succeeded where he failed. I spent the night before my coronation praying for the Red Company to come take me away. They did not come: and so I became Emperor. I was the *embodiment* of Schooled magic. Every ritual, every ceremony, every *gesture* was part of the magic holding the Empire together. I was subsumed in it, and there was no escape but to fit myself into the box it made around me."

"My lord," Cliopher said, although he did not know what further words to say, or even whether he was protesting or comforting or simply denying the bright, brittle words.

"I worked no magic of my own while Emperor. I wrote no poetry, played no music, wrought no art. *Nothing*. I learned how to govern myself and my Empire, and resigned myself that I would be crippled until at last I died. Then came the Fall, and I thought I *had* died. When I woke ... I was no longer Emperor."

He looked across at Commander Omo, who had been standing guard at his bier, that afternoon when the Last Emperor awoke at last. "Lady Jivane immediately gave over her responsibilities to me, and I ... felt obliged to accept, for it was true that I could do what she asked of me. Everyone was very surprised when I announced I was a wizard."

"Do you still feel ... crippled?" Cliopher asked, not sure how he dared.

His Radiancy rose to his feet and walked over to stand near the verandah windows, a little over from Commander Omo. He spoke quietly to the glass. "It is remarkable how little we ever know one another, is it not?"

"My lord," Cliopher said, again not knowing what he wanted to say.

"My lord," said Commander Omo, "what do you wish of us?"

Conju said, "My lord, what have we not done for you?"

His Radiancy turned around swiftly. "I am the Lord of Zunidh and Last

Emperor of Astandalas. What could I *possibly* want for?"

His voice was light, his posture elegant, his face serene. Only his eyes betrayed emotion: but even without the formal taboo Cliopher was one of the very few who looked.

"What indeed? What is the sum of human happiness, if not power and wealth and luxury and fame and adoration? Who would not want to be worshipped as a god? Who would not want the world at his feet? Who would not give his soul for my position?"

Cliopher's first impulse was to protest that *he* would not, his first thought that he had never envied his Radiancy for the work and the responsibility and the weight of his glory—and then he realized that that was precisely what his Radiancy meant, that he spoke with bitter sarcasm.

"My lord," Conju said, "you are distraught."

"Distraught," his Radiancy replied, with great precision. "Am I, Conju? Shall I close my mouth and accept your suggestion of a bath and supper and tea and a quiet evening? Shall we go back to Solaara and with the greatest solemnity and ceremony institute a competition to the various unattached great or would-be great magi of the nine worlds for the next Lord of Zunidh?"

"My lord—" said Conju.

"And once I have found a suitable heir shall I retire to some palace somewhere, until I finally die and can be buried in the grand mausoleum that my people will surely build for me, in that gap in the Imperial Necropolis looking on Solaara so eminently suitable for the Last Emperor of Astandalas? Shall I let you all pretend that this outburst has not happened, that I am as ever His Serene and Radiant Holiness, benevolent and disinterested and, yes, serene?"

His voice was eerily calm and reasonable, sounding as he did any day, any moment of any day, whether they were discussing lunch or typhoons or laws or some diplomatic squabble former lieges had written to him to solve.

Or sounding as he had every day until they had found the harp in the secret closet and gone to the village, and his Radiancy had found enthusiasm and delight and become almost unrecognizably alive.

Conju responded to the tone and the construction. "Certainly, my lord, if that is what you wish."

"You would make it so easy," his Radiancy said, still in the same light, calm, disinterestedly thoughtful tone. "It would make my people very happy to see me take an active interest in my succession, and I am sure everyone from my underling princes to the lords magi of the former Empire would fall over themselves offering me places to retire. Is that what you meant, Ludvic?" he added, swinging suddenly to Commander Omo.

"It is one path, my lord," replied the guardsman. "It might be that you would prefer a monastery, where you can read and meditate and be undisturbed by the cares of the world."

Conju nodded eagerly at the thought, obviously agreeing that it would be the best option.

"What do you think, Cliopher?"

Cliopher thought that there was something very wrong, but he could not figure out what it was. He said cautiously, "My lord, I believe everyone would agree that retiring to a monastery would be most appropriate. A pleasant monastery, that is."

"So that I can pretend to contemplate the eternal but in reality continue to live in utmost luxury?"

"No one would desire you to suffer any discomfort."

"Except me," said his Radiancy, starting to laugh, though there was little humour in the sound. "Except me. Do none of you realize that I would go mad in a monastery? How do you think I could go from a metaphorical to a real cell with any equanimity? Do you really believe I have all the emotional range of a *statue*?—You do, don't you?" he added, staring around at them, his face no longer serene but full of burning emotion. "You truly believe I am as serene as all the ritual words suggest."

"You have never before given us cause to think otherwise, my lord," Cliopher said unwillingly when the silence seemed too long.

His Radiancy laughed again. "Have I not? No, I suppose usually I am able to retreat into privacy before I quite lose my temper or my sobriety. And it has been a long time since I let myself be so moved. The trouble with pretending to have no emotions beyond a vague benevolence is that after a while you start to believe your lies. But that I do not display my emotions does not mean I do not have them. Oh, no," he added a little more softly, "it does not indeed. Benevolent I think I can generally claim to be, but calm, disinterested, and serene I am *not*."

His eyes were blazing gold, and Cliopher thought that the Lion Emperors of old were said to have been passionate beyond measure, thrusting the Empire out into uncharted territories, across the borders between worlds, under the sea of Colhélhé and even into the outer reaches of Faerie. All those rituals and ceremonies intended to bind that disparate Empire together—and to bind the power and passion of the Emperor?

"No. I do not want to retire to a monastery, to a palace, to some quiet life of luxury. What would I do all day? I cannot sit and read and play my harp all day for much longer. Already here I am starting to feel restless. That is a fortnight, and there have been excitements. What would it be after a month? Six months? A *year?*"

"You are not obliged to retire," Cliopher said uneasily.

"I told you to beware what you were waking! We cannot go back now. I have seen the door of freedom. There is no one who can prevent me from taking it, though I must lose everything to open it."

"My lord!" said Conju.

His Radiancy made an abbreviated motion away from the door, coming to rest on the balls of his feet, hands fisted, eyes brilliant gold. His motion made the light gauzy curtains billow—no, that was a breeze coming in through open louvres.

"What is it, Conju?" he cried. "What do I have to say for you to understand? What do I have to do for you to realize that I am a man? That all this time I have thought there was no escape but death, and since the only thing more pathetic than the Emperor with no Empire is the man who cannot stop butting his head against an immovable object, I have resigned myself to my role and played it to the best of my ability. Have you honestly never *wondered* what I was thinking?"

Conju didn't speak, but the expression on his face said it all.

"I am a human being, Conju! I have emotions and desires and frustrations and hopes and dreams and nightmares as much as anyone else. I have things I love and things I hate, things I prefer and things I abhor, and none of it *matters.*"

"How can you say that, my lord?" Conju returned, his face working. "You have never indicated any of this!"

His Radiancy laughed bitterly. "No? That I no longer walk into the walls of my cell is not because I have forgotten they exist."

"My lord," Cliopher whispered.

"You are not a prisoner! What can you want that we do not give you?" Conju cried, and then dropped to his knees in shock at his own impertinence.

His Radiancy looked down at where his chief attendant knelt, and his face twisted with such pain that Cliopher found his heart in mouth and his tongue unable to form words.

"I have the power to change the lives of billions," his Radiancy said quietly. "I have the power to change the magic and weather patterns of worlds. I have the power to decide whether men live or die and in what manner and with what dignity. I can begin wars and end them."

Conju looked up at him.

His Radiancy spoke with the same controlled calm. "You *still* do not know what I mean, do you? You kneel to me because you dared raise your voice to me. When have I ever given you cause to think I would punish you for speaking your mind?"

Conju said, "I know what is due your Radiancy's honour."

"Can you not *see* me?" he cried, his voice breaking.

All the drapes blew wildly, the louvres clattering, wind suddenly erupting around the house.

"Can you not understand that the walls between us are not of my making? That I do not want to be behind them? Can you not look at me and see not the Radiancy but the *man*? Is it so very hard to understand why I snatch at freedom as a drowning man snatches at a spar? My heart was nearly dead when you invited me here. Another few months and I probably would have said no, because the worst thing, the very worst thing, is that I nearly believed it myself."

He stopped, hands raised in fists, chest heaving with emotion, the drapes around him and eyes such a brilliant burning gold that Cliopher wondered how nothing caught fire from his intensity.

"It was so hard to keep fighting that I had nearly stopped. I had myself nearly convinced that it was merely the responsible thing to be so—so—"

His face worked for a moment as he searched for the word, and Cliopher shuddered with the strain and the hurt and the pain and the fear—and then his Radiancy cried, "So dull!" and the word was so anticlimactic Cliopher had to stifle a laugh.

Conju did not laugh. "My lord, you cannot be *dull*!"

His Radiancy threw his hands above his head in exasperation. "If I made a simulacrum of myself you would probably only notice when it came to magic. You don't need me, you just need some vessel to dress and make the right motions. It is a terrible thing to feel so completely unnecessary and yet be somehow the centre of attention. My life is tedious, routine, monochromatic, and boring.—Yes, boring, Conju!"

"My lord—"

"I do the same things over and over again and there is no meaning to any of it, and the necessity is entirely external, and nobody cares except in the way that people care about customs, which is to say *it must be done* and it must be done *the way it always has been done* or else!—and woe betide the one who tries to say the customs are unnecessary, though he be Emperor of worlds.

"I fought for years to sit outside and to have one hour of privacy a day. I should have kept fighting—but it is much more comfortable not to."

His voice dropped. "I never thought I would be the person who chose what is *comfortable*."

His tone made it a curse, and somehow that penetrated Conju's devotion in a way nothing else had. He looked up with deep reproach. "My lord, I have had no thought except your comfort and dignity in the fulfilment of my duties. I have done my best to make your life one befitting your position. I do not understand why you have never expressed your displeasure with my service if you are unhappy with it."

His Radiancy stared at him. "It has nothing to do with your service!"

Conju responded with the full formal prostration.

His Radiancy looked down at the back of his head with naked hurt, hesitated, turned on his heel, and stalked out of the house into what was becoming a full-blown storm.

Ser Rhodin and Elish swept out behind him, though by the time they reached the bottom of the verandah stairs his Radiancy was already several yards away. They picked up their pace to follow him—Cliopher was watching, mouth still feeling slack with shock—when his Radiancy suddenly spun around and shouted something at his guards, right hand up in an unmistakable gesture.

The two men halted abruptly, sand spraying out from their heels, and there was a long tense moment while his Radiancy stared at them and they stared back. Then Ser Rhodin saluted, Elish hastily followed suit, and the two guards stood at attention while his Radiancy walked off alone.

A moment later the rain came down like a wall.

CHAPTER THIRTEEN

CLIOPHER LET OUT HIS BREATH and went over to help Conju up. Conju was bewildered and hurt and angry, and said, "I don't understand."

Cliopher was only partially sure he understood, and could not quite articulate his thoughts. He looked across at Commander Omo, who was frowning out the window. "Will you not call Ser Rhodin and Elish out of the rain?"

Ludvic turned his head and raised his eyebrows at him. "They would not come. He gave them a direct order to stay there. They will obey."

They might stand there, but movement from the other direction caught Cliopher's attention. He turned to see Jiano and Aya come running through the rain to the door, and hastily let them in.

"Thank you!" they cried in ragged unison, stopping to drip on the mat near the door. Jiano grimaced, wringing out the hem of his sarong. "This is not the season for weather like that."

"Must be the coming eclipse," Aya said. "Is your lord around? We came with a question for him."

Conju made a jerky movement. Commander Omo looked at Cliopher and nodded, as if to say he could come with a story, and turned to look steadily out past the two sodden honour guards to the invisible ocean beyond.

"His lordship went out just as the rain came."

Aya looked at the two of them, then out the window. Her eyes widened when she saw Ser Rhodin and Elish standing at perfect attention in the deluge. "Are those not his guards?"

Cliopher swallowed. "He did not wish for company."

"So he is truly not a prisoner, then?" Aya blurted, then flushed and covered her mouth. "I am sorry. You all look very unhappy and clearly we should not be intruding."

"I told you he was not, Aya, and that we should believe what he said."

"Did you ask him if he were a prisoner?" Cliopher said, knowing he sounded both outraged and amused.

Jiano looked very fierce despite his bedragglement and the glare he was receiving from Conju. "Yes. When we made a turn at the market and his guards seemed not to be listening. You treat him like a prisoner."

"We do not!" cried Conju, so vehemently both Jiano and Aya recoiled slightly.

"You do," Jiano repeated. "I mean you no disrespect, but when a mature man of evident character and intelligence is followed around at close proximity by numerous guards, and when his attendants refuse to disclose who he is and he just smiles meaningfully and refuses to answer, and then when it is obvious he is a wild mage and a radical to boot, what would you think? The house attendants say that he is charming and delightful and not at all high in the instep, and yet you guard him with the greatest care. At least two of you at all times, on short watches so that you are always alert and aware."

"And when I asked you who he was, *hani*," Aya said, "you were very sorrowful and definite about telling us we should not ask. We drew the conclusion he must be a political prisoner of great renown. He does not have the look of any other sort of criminal," she added thoughtfully, "although he is charming enough to be a rogue."

Commander Omo and Conju both looked as if they might have called her out for the suggestion. Cliopher said, "Why did you ask him? Were you just curious?"

Jiano shook his head. "We are an island of radicals and misfits, my friend, and we like him. A great lord of such good humour and such joy in conversation would surely get into trouble for democratic sentiments or anarchy— and we wouldn't mind that here."

"But he merely thanked us for the thought and assured us that he was only occasionally and mostly metaphorically anarchical."

Cliopher closed his eyes and then he could not help himself and started to laugh.

When he recovered his poise Conju frowned at him and said severely, "I will fetch coffee."

He went out, with a suspicious glance at Cliopher, as if he were in league with his Radiancy—which, Cliopher thought defiantly, he was. He would do everything in his power to help his Radiancy find the freedom he so clearly sought. He liked Jiano and Aya even more for being willing to assist a possible revolutionary.

"We would have known he had disappeared around here somewhere," he pointed out.

"There are many hiding places that strangers do not know about," Jiano replied easily. "May we ask you what he has done, then, to require such constant surveillance? If he is not a prisoner, is he prone to erratic or dangerous behaviour?"

"No!"

"He cannot be mad—unless he has a monomania? That is entirely harmless and usually unnoticeable unless triggered."

"My mother's cousin has a monomania," Aya said thoughtfully. "She is a perfectly wonderful woman unless you get her on the subject of the Fall of Astandalas, at which point she will talk for days about how it was all a conspiracy of chickens enchanted by the Red Company. She has this incredibly well-worked out explanation of how all chickens are in league with each other."

"Aunt Moula," Cliopher said, drawn into a smile despite himself. "Oh, she is a wild card. But as you say, wonderful except on that subject."

"His Ra—his lordship does not have a monomania," Commander Omo said severely. "He is a man worthy of the very highest respect. We are his guards of honour."

There was a pause, and then Jiano said, "Well, I'm glad I was born on the wrong side of that blanket. I couldn't bear to be hovered over—or to do the hovering, for that matter."

Cliopher raised his eyebrows. "What is your lineage, then?"

"Doesn't matter," Jiano said, smiling at his wife. "My father was well-known for his wandering ways, and my mother was paid handsomely for the privilege of bearing his bastard."

"My love," Aya said with mild reproof.

Cliopher cast around and realized suddenly who Jiano reminded him of. "Not the Poz? You are surely not old enough?"

Jiano gave him an arrested second glance. "I'd forgotten you are from Gorjo City. Yes, you are correct. I understand my mother was his last flame. I never met him, and never wanted to, although my mother said he was nice enough for a high aristo."

The Poz had been the Prince of the Vangavaye-ve during Cliopher's adolescence. His sole legitimate child was the princess whose picnic had been offensive to the volcano, and she had left no heirs of her own. "Hmm," he said, thinking of how the principality had gone to a very distant cadet branch of the family from Jilkano, who had not much wanted it.

"Don't say 'hmm' like that," Jiano said firmly. "I should not have said anything. I am fully committed to my egalitarian political principles. Besides, only the Sun-on-Earth could make that happen, and apart from the fact I would never ask the Glorious One, I don't think I possibly could. I don't think I would be able to speak in the presence of divinity."

"What of your egalitarian political principles?" Cliopher could not resist asking.

Jiano smirked. "That is all very well for mortals, but when it comes to a living god it is a different matter. I worship and adore the Sun-on-Earth, I do not invite the Glorious One to—" he made a vague gesture.

"To come to our village's lunar eclipse party," Aya said, laughing. "We were going to ask even if your lord were a political prisoner, but now we need not feel we need to plan an escape for him, so this is easier. We would like to invite you all to the feast, and as we understand he is a very fine musician, we were hoping he might be willing to play for us. We have no real musicians in our village, since Balgo is still in Gorjo City."

"Probably playing in bars and getting drunk and spending all his earnings," Jiano said with a sigh.

"We can promise the drinking, at any rate, if that's of interest."

"I cannot speak for my lord," Cliopher said, "but I expect he will be most pleased to come."

"Wonderful. Beila says his music is truly special, but what else would one expect from a man who can work a crowd as he did at the market? He is clearly not one of the idle aristos," she added teasingly.

"No, he is not," Cliopher replied quietly.

Beila came in then with a tray of coffee, and the conversation shifted to the local festivals and the music and foods associated with them, with Conju and Cliopher both making a determined effort to participate, and not to keep looking out the window for the Sun-on-Earth as the rain kept thundering down.

★★★

HE CAME BACK JUST BEFORE dusk. The rain had eventually stopped and the clouds cleared, though the winds were still very high. Jiano and Aya had gone on their way, leaving a deflated and anxious atmosphere behind them.

Conju was compulsively tidying things, face set into a mask of miserable propriety. Cliopher had given up pretending to read and was sitting next to the brazier staring at the ashes.

Commander Omo stood watching the beach. His only movement had been to tell Pikabe and Ato, who had come to take their places as guards, to stay inside and that they were to relieve Ser Rhodin and Elish once his Radiancy returned.

They had looked out at the two guards steaming in the sun, with no sign of his Radiancy even out swimming, and bit their tongues and saluted.

His Radiancy walked up to Ser Rhodin and Elish and spoke briefly to them. They saluted and fell into place behind him. Commander Omo opened the verandah door. Cliopher jumped up at the sound, then hovered awkwardly, and Conju set down the ornament he was dusting for the tenth time with a loud click.

His Radiancy nodded at Ser Rhodin and Elish. "Go refresh yourselves."

This time there was no hesitation; they saluted in unison and exited the room. Both were trying hard to look unmoved, and Cliopher wondered what his Radiancy had said to them on the beach.

He spoke in his usual voice, calm and controlled, his face benevolent and serene, eyes hooded and tawny. He was not wet. He walked into the middle of the room and regarded the three of them solemnly. They felt the armour of formality closing in around them, and after a moment first Conju, then Cliopher, sank into the formal prostration. Cliopher felt rather than heard Pikabe and Ato enter to take their places at the serving wing door.

"You may stand," said his Radiancy, and Cliopher, breathing slightly more easily, levered himself to his feet. Then he saw that Conju remained prostrate, face to the floor.

His Radiancy said, "Conju."

He did not lift his head. "I am ashamed. I must offer my resignation from your service, my lord."

His voice broke there, and his shoulders shook slightly.

"Conju," his Radiancy said again.

Conju spoke still to the floor. "My lord, I must insist. I have failed in the performance of my office."

His Radiancy stood still, gazing down at him with that inscrutable expression, and then he did what Cliopher had never once seen him do: he knelt down.

"Conju," he said, quietly.

The changed location of voice did what the indirect command had not, and made Conju lift his head. When he saw his Radiancy's position, he went grey and flung himself down again.

"Sit up, please, Conju."

Every line in his body showing protest, Conju raised himself to sit back on his knees. His Radiancy did not himself rise to his feet, but stayed kneeling before him. Cliopher noted with a strange detachment that his Radiancy was perched awkwardly on his kneecaps, which surely were going to hurt almost immediately, and that his garments—meant always for standing or sitting on wide thrones, not ever for kneeling—were bunching around his thighs and ankles, since he had not made the gestures to rearrange them that were automatic for everyone else.

His Radiancy took a deep breath. "I should not have spoken to you the way I did, Conju. You have always been an exemplary attendant. More than exemplary." He smiled briefly. "I went through three or four grooms of the chamber each year before you landed on the position, and finally I had found someone neither sycophantic nor a fool, but enormously competent and with a quiet sense of humour, whom I could both respect and love."

A pause, as if he had not intended to speak quite so openly, though that was only a guess; nothing about expression or tone of voice had changed..

"I suppose we always hope that those closest to us can see into our hearts—but unless we invite them, or show them in words or deeds, how can they? Conju, if you insist on resigning I will not force you to stay. But I will be very sorry indeed to see you go—and sorrier than I can say to have made you feel unworthy and a failure."

Conju spoke with visible and audible distress. "My lord, you do not need to explain yourself to me."

His Radiancy's smile was a grimace drawn from that inner, private man. He took a breath before he spoke, possibly to ensure the evenness of his words. "Yes, I do, Conju, because although by all the etiquette books and customs there is an unbridgeable gap between us, both the metaphorical one of social rank and that more literal one which our respective care never to touch has made more powerful than any wall, nevertheless you are a man of dignity and pride and I have injured you. For this I am sorry, and I apologize most heartily."

"My lord!" said Conju, in tones of shock, but Cliopher saw the rising joy in his eyes.

"Will you give some thought to staying in my service?"

"O my lord, I could never leave you unless I failed you. Oh, my lord, please get up. I cannot bear to see you kneeling."

"And it will ruin my robes, won't it?" he said, with a flash of that other man, one which turned thoughtful as he looked around and saw a complete lack of any means whereby to lift himself up. Pikabe, standing by the door saucer-eyed at the sight of his Radiancy kneeling to Conju, ran up and offered his ceremonial spear.

"Thank you," said his Radiancy, and hauled himself upright.

"Now," he added, once he had brushed his hands down his robes and glared smartly around the room until everyone pretended they were not staring and simply had something, dust no doubt, in their eyes, "I reckon it must be close to supper time."

CHAPTER FOURTEEN

ALTHOUGH THERE WAS A VERY definite sense that things had changed between his Radiancy and his household, Cliopher could not exactly determine what was the appropriate way to respond. The level of intimacy was always set by the higher-ranking party: but what level did that incredible and unprecedented emotional outburst set?

(And what had his Radiancy meant, he kept wondering, by telling Jiano and Aya that he was *only occasionally and mostly metaphorically* anarchical?)

After a few silent minutes of unenthusiastic eating, Cliopher decided that his Radiancy's response to their formal greeting indicated that the level of desired formality was exceedingly low, and so he cleared his throat. "My lord."

Everyone looked at him, his friends with veiled wonder and his Radiancy with emotion not so much veiled as buried. "Yes, Cliopher?"

"Jiano Ikialo Speaker and his wife Aya came by this afternoon to invite us to their lunar eclipse party."

"That was kindly thought of them. Did you accept?"

The words were the sort Cliopher might have heard in his mother's drawing room, mild and not earth-shattering as anyone who knew who was the speaker would take them. He swallowed. "We said we could not speak for you, but we thought it likely. They also wished to know if you would play your harp at the party."

His Radiancy finished chewing his mouthful, took a sip of his wine, and when he evidently felt he had controlled his expression, said coolly, "Did they? It would be a pity to disappoint them, when they have been so friendly."

But they could all see how delighted he was.

Cliopher wondered to himself if he dared, and then decided that he did. He wanted to see the bright smiling man within the shell of his Radiancy again. He wanted to *know* that man, he realized abruptly: it was someone he thought he could be friends with.

He summoned his courage. "They were quite relieved to see you had gone off without your guards, my lord, for they felt it confirmation that you were not actually our prisoner. They were fully prepared to spirit you away at their party, if need be."

His Radiancy met his gaze for a startled moment. "They are not very good conspirators."

"But very good neighbours," Ser Rhodin said.

"Oh, true," his Radiancy said. "It is just as well Jiano is not in the line of inheritance, for he would find court a deadly game."

"You know, my lord?" Cliopher spoke in surprise. "That he is the Poz's bastard?"

His Radiancy frowned briefly at him. "The Poz? Oh—Prince Auyre-poz—yes, he looks very like his father as a young man." Then, with evident fascination, "People really called him the Poz?"

"*Everyone* called him the Poz," Cliopher said. "Even my grandmother, and she wasn't given to flouting courtesy. He used to call *himself* the Poz when he gave speeches. He often spoke in third person—well, he was often drunk. He would get up on the Prince's Balcony and ramble on about how the Poz was going to do this or that."

"He was always lamentably sober when he met with me."

Ser Rhodin tried hard not to snicker, but even Conju was smiling.

"Did you have a nickname? Or I suppose, *do* you, Cliopher?"

"Everyone's always called me Kip, my lord," he admitted, disturbed to realize it was an admission; and that only Conju (who had come with him once or twice on holiday) knew that was his family name.

"Kip? Where did that come from?"

"My family likes to carry names across generations. My second-eldest uncle is Cliopher plain and simple. All those in my generation have different nicknames—Whitey, Clia, Ferry, Pico—and I'm Kip."

"No one went for Clio? Too obvious?"

He smiled. "Clia was Clio originally, but she changed her name when she was of age to declare herself a woman."

His Radiancy nodded. "Kip. Hmm. I can see why you prefer Cliopher professionally."

Cliopher made a gesture of wry acknowledgement. "And … you, my lord?"

"I should think you could tell me better than I whether I have a nick-name," his Radiancy said dryly. "People do not call me it to my face."

Cliopher had never heard anyone call his Radiancy anything other than one of his titles or "Emperor Artorin." Jesters tended to add titles, not take them away. He looked at Commander Omo and Ser Rhodin, who was trying to be sober rather than grinning. "Not that I know of, my lord."

"Pity. I've always thought 'Tor' would be a good nickname. Short, easy to say, a small steep-sided hill."

Ser Rhodin stifled his laugh. "Is that what your family called you, my lord?"

Ser Rhodin had not been there that morning snorkelling, Cliopher reminded himself, when his Radiancy had spoken about his childhood.

His Radiancy smiled sardonically. "No, my mother made do with the informal 'boy' on the exceedingly rare occasions she resorted to direct address. Mind you, I have no idea if my parents actually knew what my name was. It is unclear in the records. It is quite possible only my uncle knew my name."

He paused, while Cliopher watched the others try not to stare in horror. Then he continued lightly, "No, someone else must have known, because the High Priests named me on my coronation, and I know they had my true name. I would not have been bound properly had they not."

Ser Rhodin frowned at the way he had phrased that. "Did you not know anyway, my lord?"

"Oh, no, I found out my name that morning."

Conju said suddenly, "But did you not *want* a name, my lord?"

His Radiancy shook his head, smiling. "I was the Marwn. It did not occur to me until my late teens that I ought to have a name that was more than the title. As I studied more magic I discovered the importance of what we name ourselves. I wished to be more than the Marwn—to myself, at least." He glanced at Cliopher. "Like your cousin, marking her transition from outwardly male to outwardly female by changing her name to reflect the inner reality. So after some thought, that was what I did. A name that was all my own."

He stopped there to eat a few mouthfuls. Finally Cliopher asked, "May we know your chosen name?" He realized afterwards he had not said *my lord*, but increasingly doubted his Radiancy cared.

His Radiancy smiled at him. "I think one day I will tell you, but for now it will remain private."

Cliopher tried not to feel hurt.

Conju looked up from where he had been moodily rearranging his dumplings. "My lord, the villagers said you were *obviously* a wild mage."

"Did they?" He sounded slightly pleased. "It was the illusions; they were not the sort a Schooled wizard would do. No chanting or gestures or herbs or mystical objects, you see."

Conju frowned. Commander Omo said, "You do not usually use such things in your magic-working, my lord."

His Radiancy smiled sardonically again. "Well, no."

Conju continued to frown ferociously at his plate. Beila—who appeared to have taken over all of the kitchen jobs that required interacting with them, though whether this was due to her own adoration or the other staff's antipathy Cliopher did not know—came out to take away the plates and bring a cold steamed pudding for dessert. After she had gone, his Radiancy said gently, "Conju, will you tell us about your friend who was a wild mage?"

"There is not so much to tell, my lord."

"What was his name?"

"Terec of Lund, my lord."

"Lund ... in the Duchy of Forgellen on Ysthar? That was next door to Vilius, was it not?"

"Yes, my lord. Our families were neighbours, our mothers very close friends. They had always hoped there might be intermarriage. That we ... well, it was not quite what they had hoped, but they were glad. We were both younger sons, so that was not a difficulty."

Conju sighed. "The magic was. Terec tried so hard to master Schooled wizardry, but he never could. His native powers seemed to get stronger and less controlled the longer he tried to learn the other sort. He ... We had hoped to go travelling together, perhaps to see if we could find a great lord to serve together, but no matter what he or anyone else tried he was a wild mage, and he could not be tamed."

He traced out the line of decorative syrup on his plate with his spoon. "One week I went to Forgellenburg to spend a few days with my sister. When I came back Terec had gone. They all thought he had come to see me, but then I got the letter. There was only ever the one letter. He said he could not bear the strain any longer, and he was afraid his magic would get completely out of control, and so he was going to leave the Empire. He apologized for not saying good-bye."

There was a short, charged silence. Then his Radiancy said, "Why do you think he did that?"

"Wrote that, my lord?"

"No: why did he not tell you in person, before he left?"

"He did not want to force me to choose between the Empire and him."

This time the silence was more meditative. His Radiancy did not ask which Conju would have chosen, given the chance, which for a moment Cliopher was afraid he might. After a few moments, his Radiancy said: "I could write to the Lord of Ysthar and ask him if he has ever come across him. There were not many people who survived the Fall on Ysthar, but it is possible he has returned there since. Did he have any distinguishing features, if he should have changed his name?"

Conju stared at him, as if this had simply never occurred to him. "My lord, I do not think he could have survived."

"We did," was the wry and incontrovertible response, "and one never knows."

"He had a very long nose." Conju smiled suddenly, looking not like any devil-may-care youth but like an earnest and devoted lover. "We all used to call him *Aghrib*, Sharp-Nose, in Old Shaian. He was quite a big man, and he had light brown skin and rather startling green eyes. His mother was only half-Shaian, and the green eyes came from her."

"Green eyes, light brown skin, and a very long nose, plus wild magic. Do you know what element he was most connected with? What sort of things happened around his magic?"

"Oh ... fire, usually."

"No wonder we get along," his Radiancy said, smiling at him. "You are so *very* grounded, and yet you seem to have spent most of your life around fire mages. I am fire and air—not water, as you well know. I will write to the Lord of Ysthar when we return to Solaara and see what he has to say."

"You do not need to, my lord."

"I know," he replied lightly, and the talk turned to inconsequential things.

★★★

THE FOLLOWING TWO DAYS WERE remarkably uneventful. While his Radiancy did not seem to regret his outburst, he did not push the conversation into such personal areas again. He practised his harp and read his poetry, and occasionally wrote in his notebooks, and swam and snorkelled and went for walks along the beach, and all was idyllic and beautiful and seething with undercurrents.

Cliopher was relieved when it finally was the night of the eclipse. They all got dressed up again, his Radiancy in white and silver, and set off just before sunset. It was already rather dark in the woods. His Radiancy (whether accurately or not Cliopher did not know) seemed to feel Ser Rhodin was nervous about the jungle, and after a few moments he made a werelight to illuminate their path.

"Thank you, my lord," Cliopher said.

"It is a benefit of having a mage in your party."

Again the magic had been a mere word, no spells or cantrips required. Cliopher wondered how he had never noticed before how rarely his Radiancy performed actual spells. He recalled the four-hour ritual of purification over the snorkelling equipment, and how that had tired his Radiancy as the illusions had not.

"My lord," he said, "when you were working on the typhoons, what kind of magic was that?"

His Radiancy glanced at him enquiringly.

"Was it Schooled or wild magic, I mean, my lord."

"Ah. All the magic on Zunidh is hybrid compared to what it was before the Fall. When I began my work, I was both unwilling and unable to return it to the pure form. It was, as Conju said, against the grain of my own magic, and although I had forced myself to submit, I could not force myself to recreate something so alien to my nature. The great works I have done—the Solamen Fens, the Lights, the sea trains, the floating castles of the Galagar Coast—those are all mixed. Schooled wizards can use their spells to access the magic, but the heart of those works is not the sort of bindings that held the Empire together."

"And it is the same with the typhoons."

"Yes," his Radiancy replied, not seeming to notice the lack of *my lord* on that comment. "I suppose it would be difficult for me to return to a fully unstructured style of magic. *Will* be difficult," he corrected himself. "I shall look forward to experimenting."

"You will not continue with the hybrid style, my lord?"

(Cliopher found he could not, even in his thoughts, call him by anything other than 'his Radiancy', even if his Radiancy had very nearly given permission to use Tor. There just seemed no way to go from 'the Sun-on-Earth' to 'Tor'.)

"No! If I had realized retirement was an option, I should have done so when I finished the Lights. Everything since then has been make-work, one form or another. It is time for someone else with new ideas to take over. And though I do what I must, I do not actually *enjoy* the hybrid style. I find satisfaction in working complex magic, to be sure, but I think I will be quite happy to stick to small magics."

This from the Last Emperor of Astandalas, now a god in truth to many of his people?

This from the man who lit the brazier, talked the cook into making special food for Commander Omo's birthday, who touched the sand as if it were a new creation.

His Radiancy went on, "The present Lord of Ysthar has a theory that great magi are most akin to hedgewizards in the nature of their magic, though obviously not in terms of power. If he is correct, as I suspect he is, then turning to the proper sort of magic will be much more satisfying to me on a personal level than the great works."

"They are an impressive legacy, my lord," Cliopher said quietly.

"And I am very good at politics," his Radiancy said with a sudden flashing smile, "but I will be glad enough to do something else."

"Aya was much impressed at your skill with the crowd at the market, my lord," Commander Omo said.

"Managing an audience is much the same whether it is a hall full of courtiers or a market full of villagers. People are always people, and respond to the same sort of stimuli—surprise and excellence and timing always being a necessity of any actor in the public eye."

They arrived at the village outskirts then, and there was no time for anything more of this remarkable look at the court down from the daïs.

Several children materialized out of the shadows, giggling and pointing excitedly at the harp, which Commander Omo was carrying. They were followed by Jiano, who greeted them politely and led them through the village to the beach. The view was, if anything, even more spectacular than that from Navikiani. Perhaps Cliopher was biased: he loved any glimpse of his home, and from here he could see the lights of Gorjo City floating between the deep waters and the great sky. Mama Ituri caught the sunset on her peak.

"We have made a stage for you," Jiano said to his Radiancy, leading their group over to a two-foot-high platform made of wood and woven palm fronds. It was positioned in front of a large fire over which an entire pig was roasting on a spit. The drip of fat to coals filled the air with succulent odours. "Aya says this is what musicians in the cities do, play from a raised stage. We are very grateful for your willingness," he added awkwardly. "None of us has heard a harp played before."

"I confess most of my songs will be old ones," his Radiancy said. "I don't get out very often."

Cliopher had to suppress the urge to snort. Aya came up, smiling brightly and with slight mischief at them.

"We will be entirely pleased by what you play for us, *ivani*," she promised. "Now … we thought we would begin with drinks, then if you do not mind, perhaps you could play for us. The eclipse is due at two hours before midnight, so once you are tired of playing we will have the feast. The pig will be ready in an hour or so."

"Are there any particular customs around the eclipse?" Conju asked. "I know some places have quite elaborate ceremonies."

"We take it as an opportunity to give particular honour to the Moon," Jiano replied. "It is also a tradition here on Lesuia to give some sort of small offering to the Moon—a shell or a stone or the like—with a prayer. It is acceptable—even encouraged—for it to be a petition. It is the tradition that sometimes during an eclipse she will come to her petitioner and grant his heart's desire."

"We might so pray," said his Radiancy, putting on his serene face and turning resolutely to the platform. "I believe I will need a chair if I am to sit and play for so long, Conju."

"Very good, my lord," said that gentleman, though where a chair was going to be found in the village of Ikialo Cliopher had no idea. Conju looked around and beckoned Aya to confer, quickly expanding to involve Ser Rhodin as well.

Ser Rhodin in turn beckoned over Varro, who listened for a moment, nodded, and set off at a lope back to the village. Conju returned to their group and said, "Varro has gone to fetch a chair from the house, my lord."

"Thank you, Conju. Now …"

"Now it's time for a drink and the invocation of the gods, though not in that order," said Aya. Cliopher saw that the rest of the village had been collecting around the fire, murmuring greetings to his Radiancy as they passed. He appeared to have learned a great many names.

(*How?* he thought; and *when?* and *why?*—except *why* was obvious from what he had said before, that the walls between him and the rest of mankind were not of his making.)

He certainly was smiling with a more relaxed happiness than Cliopher had ever seen him display within the Palace of Stars.

They offered him a conch shell filled with ceremonial wine with which to perform the invocation. "To the Sun in his majesty," he said in a grand voice, "we offer our thanksgiving and our prayers, that always he may shine upon us and give all things that grow his light. To the Moon in her glory also we give our thanks and our prayers, that she may rule the night and the shadows with her benevolence, granting dreams and art and speaking to the tides below the surfaces of all things.

"On this night of her eclipse, when she stands within the shadow we cast, we ask her to hear us, to listen to our prayers, and to come to us with her bounty if she should so choose. All these things we do in the name of the One Above who set the Sun and Moon and stars in their places in the beginning."

He turned to pass Cliopher the conch, not waiting this time for the speculative glances to begin, but Cliopher was still reeling from the invocation of the One Above—the god of gods, who was never mentioned except by one of the highest priests.

Or by one of the lesser gods, he thought.

He took the conch with shaking hands. Then he looked at his lord, the man called a god, and invoked the Sun-on-Earth, the Lord of Rising Stars, the Glorious and Radiant One, that he might look kindly as the Sun and Moon on these his people gathered there.

The Sun-on-Earth winked at him and accepted the cup of palm wine offered by Conju.

The night had just come down when Varro came loping back, one of the wicker-work chairs on his back. He set it down on the platform, where Conju carefully laid a cushion on it, then, with no sign of any embarrassment at the glances being cast his way, his Radiancy sat down, took his harp from Commander Omo, and addressed his audience.

"I am very pleased to play for you tonight," he said. "I thank you for the invitation. I do not know many songs of the Vangavaye-ve, nor even very many modern ones—most of mine are from long ago in the days of the Emperor Eritanyr, or lays of the elder days. If any of you know any of them, you are welcome to sing along. This instrument, for those of you who have not seen one before, is a harp of Alinor."

He laid his hands on the strings, paused a moment, and then he began to play.

He played for an hour to a rapt audience, his rich baritone voice evoking ancient battles and lovers, cities long gone and people long forgotten. They heard the entire *Lay of Fo Wakailunte*, which told the story of the great battle of the Seven Masters.

They heard of the Conquest of Colhélhé, of the making of the Ivory

Door of the Palace of Stars, of Harbut Zalarin whose son was the first Emperor, of the Wizard-Emperor Aurelius Magnus who had been stolen away by the Sun and the Moon out of jealousy for his power among mortals, but who before then had invited the Wayfinders of the Vangavaye-ve to make alliance with the nascent Empire.

At last he played a humorous song of the Feast of the Birds, which left them all laughing and hungry. He finished with a flurry of brilliant improvisation while they were all still laughing, and then called in a clear voice the old traditional words out of *Fo Wakailunte*: "Surely that roast pig must be eaten before the gods get too hungry?"

"I think it must be," one of the older women of the village replied, cackling.

"I have never heard such music as that," Aya said quietly to Cliopher. "I can see why Beila was so entranced. Is he a musician at the court? Surely even the Sun-on-Earth cannot hear such music often."

"Not as often as he ought, no," his Radiancy said, standing up to stretch his hands and arms. "Thank you, Aya, for inviting me to play. I suspect it was your doing, was it not?"

"I do not miss many things of the city, but I do miss the music, *ivani*. The Vangavaye-ve is the home of music, but some islands are more blessed by the Mother of Song than others."

"Perhaps you will be able to tempt a radical minstrel to settle here," he said, and ambled off to the ocean.

Conju came up to the chair with a bowl of lemon water for Cliopher and the others to wash their hands with. They watched his Radiancy wander along the glowing water's edge with Oginu and Commander Omo four steps behind him. He stopped outside the circle of firelight, where he was an anonymous dark shape against the luminous water, and then he bent and picked something up from the ground and came back towards them with it hidden in his hand.

CHAPTER ℱIFTEEN

AFTER THE FEAST HIS RADIANCY said, "I am happy to play some more, if you would like." His words were tentative, but there was no hesitation in his motions as he picked up his harp and sat down on the chair again. Cliopher conceded that his Radiancy did indeed know how to manage a crowd of hinterland villagers quite as well as he did his court.

This time the music was all about the Moon. The songs must have come from all sorts of places and cultures, for no two seemed to be of the same style. Some were funny, some startlingly lovely, some disturbing. Each seemed to bring a new face of the Moon to Cliopher's mind, from the lover of poets to the patroness of lunatics.

The only story that was not in evidence was the one about the Red Company and the Moon.

Cliopher watched his Radiancy's face in the fire- and torchlight flickering across it. His expression was focused and full of longing, full of deep desire and deeper constraints. Cliopher could not tell if he longed for the Moon or something else that she represented to him: freedom, change, the shadow side of the world. In the mythologies of Astandalas the Sun had courted the Moon; perhaps the Sun-on-Earth felt more than a ceremonial connection with his mythical ancestor.

He played until the full Moon sailed high above them, his last song one of the endless longing of a poet who had fallen in love with the Moon. When he stopped there was silence, and Cliopher looked around to see tears on many faces.

"It is nearly the eclipse," his Radiancy said in a quiet voice, and Cliopher realized that he probably knew its coming far more intimately than any of them. He set his harp beside the chair and reached down for a small white stone beside his foot.

Jiano bowed over his hands to him. "We toss our offerings into the fire once the eclipse proper begins. As we have no shaman, we take turns doing

169

our duty to the spirits. In a celebration such as this we each pray aloud before we make our silent prayer with our offering. We begin with the children and proceed to the elders. As our guests you will go at the end, with you last, *ivani*."

The smallest child was a toddler, carefully coached to speak her very short prayer and throw a handful of sand into the fire. She did this with glee matched only by the next child, who had a shell.

After the children first the youth and then the adults of the village spoke their pieces, some with ritual words and others with what seemed extempore prayers. They threw their offerings on the fire with silent concentration, some with shy glances at others, and Cliopher remembered that this was the season for heart's desires.

When it came to his turn he spoke a short prayer he remembered from his own childhood, and he cast the tiny white cowrie he had found in the sand with the silent prayer for his Radiancy to find the happiness he seemed never to have known.

He was not quite ready to articulate his own heart's desire, even to himself.

He was the second-last; his Radiancy was the last.

High above them the Moon was blood-red but for the finest line of silver on the leading side of the eclipse.

His Radiancy spoke with a slow and quiet majesty.

"Once more I invoke the Moon, that she look with favour upon all those under her shadow tonight, that we who cast our voices with our shadows upon her glory may be heard by her.

"Hear our wishes and our dreams and our desires.

"Hear our hearts laid open to you.

"Hear *me*, O Moon Lady!" he cried at last, tossing his stone so that it arced up through the sparks towards the heart of the fire, his eyes blazing in the light, his face impassioned.

A white hand caught it.

A woman stepped out of the fire. She was perfectly white—not pale-skinned like someone from northern Amboloyo, but *white*, bone-white, shell-white—

Moon-white, said something inside Cliopher that could not believe what he was seeing.

"I hear you," she said, looking straight at his Radiancy.

"Moon Lady," he said, golden eyes wide.

And then he slipped out of his chair and knelt down into the formal bow he had never done for anyone else at all, and Cliopher realized this was no illusion.

Everyone else followed him hastily into the bow, then stayed down on their knees, though of course they all raised their heads to watch what was going on. The Moon Lady seemed entirely focused on the man before her. His Radiancy rose, hands behind him on the chair, and pushed himself back into his seat as if it were his throne in the Palace of Stars.

The Moon tossed the white stone of his heart's desire up in the air and caught it again. "It has been a very long time, Beloved."

There was an even more astonished silence.

"Yes, it has," said his Radiancy.

She took a step closer to him. Her hair was long and shining and smooth silver, her eyes black. She was wearing a thigh-length garment of shining white, sleeveless and bound at each shoulder with a silver clasp, a silver cord around her waist. She had silver sandals laced up her calves in a fashion Cliopher had only seen in half-remembered illustrations from *The Atlas of Imperial Peoples*. Her skin was white as bleached coral. She was glowing softly. She was quite unutterably beautiful.

"You have been hidden from my gaze for so long. I have heard your prayers, but always they have been for others, always the ceremonial words, always as if you had forgotten me."

"Never," said his Radiancy huskily.

Cliopher tried to process the reality of all those ceremonies in which his Radiancy invoked the Moon to look down upon his people, but without notable success. He gave up and simply watched open-mouthed like everyone else as the Moon spoke to the Sun-on-Earth.

She stepped lightly along the sand until she came to the edge of the platform. It was not particularly high, and when she stopped to look at him he was just barely above her.

"You have prayed for yourself tonight."

Gold eyes met night-black. "I have."

Her lips curved into a smile. She tossed the stone up and caught it again. "Are you certain this is your heart's desire?"

"I lost my heart a long time ago, but with all that remains to me, yes."

"I offer you immortality, Beloved," she said, mounting the platform with a graceful motion, ending up on her knees so her head was at a height with his.

He watched without moving as she reached out one white hand. Even his eyes were still, fixed on hers. Her right hand caressed his face, her left took his right hand. He looked like a sculpture.

Do you really believe I have all the emotional range of a statue?

Her voice was low and resonant. "I offer you the youth you have lost. I offer you the extent of my dominion. I offer you the evening star as your palace and the morning star as your vessel."

With each offer she moved forward, until on vessel she knelt over him, drawing his hand up to her mouth for a kiss. When his hand touched her lips he closed his eyes.

"I offer you poetry, and passion, and all the halls of heaven as your own."

Cliopher held his breath as his Radiancy opened his eyes. They were burning-brilliant, but when he met the Moon's he said softly, "That is not what I wished for."

There was a strange noise around the fire, almost a hiss of astonishment.

The Moon tilted her head almost quizzically, as if his words were nonsensical, and then she smiled and wrapped both hands around his neck in an embrace. "Is it not?"

He closed his eyes again as she kissed his face, his earlobe, the crook where neck met shoulder. For an utterly astonished moment Cliopher wondered if she were going to consummate the seduction right there in front of them all, but when she moved her hands from his neck to slide under his robes his Radiancy managed to sit up and say, "My lady the Moon, you forget the place."

The Moon lifted her head, one hand on his shoulder pressing him back against the chair, the other between his thighs. She smiled very slowly. "It is true that I may not outrun my shadow," she said throatily, and Cliopher saw that her eyes were changing from black to a burning silver. "I have been watching you, Beloved, these past weeks, and my desire has been inflamed."

"I am very honoured," he said with difficulty, for her hands had not stopped moving, "but you know my heart's desire, my lady the Moon."

"Best-beloved, you are importunate. Once you opened your heart to me without thought of return."

Cliopher wondered if that had been a literal or a metaphorical action. From his Radiancy's expression, quite possibly it meant he had written that beautifully moody song about the young man yearning for the Moon in all sorts of layers of delicate poetic conceits that had nothing to do with the Moon Lady actually responding with anything except inspiration.

Or then again perhaps in that lonely exile in the middle of nowhere, other sorts of wild magic had taken place.

His Radiancy spoke with his voice catching. "Inspiration of mortals, light of the darkness, mother of the morning, you know my heart's desire."

Overhead the ruddy shadow of the eclipse was nearly gone. The Moon leaned back slightly, pushing him against the chair. She smiled again.

"You have learned to be strong-minded, Best-beloved," she murmured, lifting her hand to trace down the line of his jaw again. She looked like quicksilver against his black skin. He was breathing hard. "You always were stubborn. Very well, I shall let you seek your heart's desire, and we shall see if it brings you to my country in the end."

"My lady the Moon, will you aid me?"

She paused in the act of moving off him, lower hand still resting on his thigh. She looked intently at him through eyes now nearly all silver, and this time when she smiled it was brilliant and cold and fire-bright all at the same time.

"Perhaps you have not entirely lost your heart. I will set you on a quest, and we shall see if that does not make my offer more attractive to you. You will wish for your youth again, Best-beloved."

"But I have more experience now."

She tilted her head quizzically at him again. "I will give you a dream, and something to remember," she said, her voice dropping down an octave again, "and half a hundred poems for you to write to me."

"I hear and obey," he said.

"You never did," she said, with something like amusement. "Your tides are your own, Beloved. You have changed indeed if you will obey me now."

She settled herself down over him again, knees between his legs, and held his head with her white hands dazzling against his skin. She looked into his face from a very close distance. High above the shadow had shrunk to a re-versed crescent; there on earth her glow was starting to blaze.

She spoke unsmilingly. "The poems are locked in your heart. The dream is of what is left when hope is gone. And to remember, Best-beloved—"

She leaned forward and kissed him full on the lips.

He had been passive until that moment. Now his hands came up to wrap themselves in her hair, and Cliopher could see—they all could see—how her power woke some answering leap of passion in him, and the shock of that kiss was nearly blinding.

And then it *was* dazzling, as for one brief moment the Moon shone full in front of them, kissing the Last Emperor of Astandalas, and then the last sliver of the earth's shadow passed from the face of the moon, and she was gone.

CHAPTER SIXTEEN

CLIOPHER WAS NEVER QUITE SURE what exactly anyone did in the first minutes after. The air felt like the air had in the Palace of Stars when his Radiancy awoke from his century-long sleep. It felt effervescent, luminous as the water, rich, strange.

After a while he realized the silence was actually everyone talking madly. Or everyone except him, his lord, Commander Omo.

After a few minutes his Radiancy ran his hands over his face, and then he pushed himself upright and with obvious discomposure descended from the platform. "Excuse us," he said abruptly to Jiano and Aya, and "Come," to his household, and set off at a very brisk pace. They fell into position behind him as he strode through the village towards the path.

The moonlight was very bright, Cliopher could not help noticing, lighting the path clearly. The light seemed to linger on his Radiancy, as if he were dipped in silver, even when they were deep under the trees.

He said nothing, merely walked faster and faster, nearly breaking into a run when they reached their beach. They hurried up behind him to the verandah, where he stopped while Commander Omo opened the door. When he lit the magelights it was obvious his Radiancy was shaking with agitation.

"My lord," Conju said quietly.

His Radiancy made a convulsive movement, half-covering his face with his hands. "I am sorry," he said, gulping air. "I ... I ... No one has touched me since before I became Emperor. I ... I am most discomposed."

"Go for a swim, my lord," Ser Rhodin said abruptly.

His Radiancy dropped his hands, revealing brilliant gold eyes and a desperate urgency. "Swim?"

"Vigorous exercise helps, my lord."

Without a further word his Radiancy plunged back out the door, which Cliopher automatically held open, and actually *ran* for the ocean, shedding clothes as he went. Pikabe and Ato followed more slowly to stand at the water's edge.

"Oh," said Cliopher belatedly.

"That would discompose anyone," Ser Rhodin said.

Conju looked hesitantly after his Radiancy, who had foregone the digni-fied breaststroke for a much more vigorous front crawl, and went down the steps to pick up his clothing.

"Yes," said Cliopher, the silver hands on the black skin flashing through his mind. "Yes, I suppose it would."

The moonlight shone silver on the ocean, black ripples around the swimmer, whose black shoulders were silver. Conju came back to the house slowly, looking up at the sky several times as he went.

"I had no idea," he said, depositing the clothes on the nearest chair, "that the stories about Aurelius Magnus being stolen away by the Sun and the Moon were so *literal.*"

"He said no," Cliopher said.

"She offered him immortality and eternal youth and a goddess' passion-ate embrace and he said no," said Ser Rhodin, shaking his head. "What on earth does he *want*?"

They watched the Moon shine down as his Radiancy swam away his arousal and his agitation and the divine.

"Weren't you listening?" Cliopher said. "He wants to be human."

★★★

CLIOPHER NEVER KNEW HOW LONG his Radiancy spent swimming, that astonishing night. He himself went eventually to bed, but tossed restlessly in strange dreams where the Moon Lady turned her black gaze on him. He woke sweaty and aching with unaccustomed desire, and very much in sym-pathy with his Radiancy. He at least had privacy in which to relieve himself; and it had not been a lifetime since someone had last touched him, either.

It was just before dawn when he finally decided lying in bed would do nothing further. He tied his dressing robe around himself and went to the bath-house, which he found empty but showing the signs of recent use. He scraped himself clean and made himself presentable, and hoped very much for a period alone to settle his whirling thoughts.

When he entered the house his Radiancy was sitting in the front room with his coffee and an expression plainly showing that Cliopher was not the only one to feel unsettled.

"Good morning, my lord," he said, bowing.

His Radiancy looked up from his coffee cup. "Good morning, Cliopher."

His voice was rough, and Cliopher's heart creaked with sympathy. "Would you like to be alone, my lord?"

His Radiancy glanced over his shoulder at where Varro and Zerafin stood guard. He sighed. "No. Fetch yourself some coffee, if you will, and join me."

Cliopher did so. His Radiancy did not appear to have moved, hands still grasping the cup as if it anchored him to the world. At his Radiancy's vague nod he sat down in his usual chair, feeling anxious.

"Tell me a story," his Radiancy said abruptly. "One from here."

Cliopher's thoughts immediately went to that other Emperor of Astandalas whom the Moon was said to have loved. He folded his hands together and paraphrased the story as he knew it from the *Lays*. This was not a time to sing.

"In the days of the Emperor Aurelius Magnus, there came a time when war seemed to press on all sides without respite. The Emperor fought in person in those days. On this occasion he was hard-pressed by many enemies. One by one his guards and companions fell. At last there was only the Emperor, with his back to the sea and his face to darkness and despair."

He paused, wondering if this was, after all, a good story to tell.

"Go on."

"Sorrowing for his lost comrades, despairing of the enemies before him, which seemed to pour out darkness across all the lands under his care, the Emperor prayed for succour, for someone to light his steps and show him the way to victory, or if not victory, at least the chance to be reunited with his brother and the rest of the armies of Astandalas."

He drank a few mouthfuls of his coffee. His Radiancy's face was intent, as if this story were new to him, though it would not be, of course. Most of it was in the histories of Astandalas.

"Whether it was a vision or a dream or a memory I do not know, but there at dawn the Emperor Aurelius Magnus remembered that he had heard tell of great sailors who lived far across the sea, people who, it was said, always knew their way and were afraid of no stranger sea."

Cliopher had been afraid of stranger seas, whether the ones to the west of the Vangavaye-ve when he had left to go to Astandalas on a trading ship, or those to the east when he had crossed them in that small boat of his own hands' making.

He had wept for how poor a son of his ancestors he was. They had crossed the Wide Seas with joy in the adventure, naming the winds and the currents and the islands, the stars and the fish and all the many gifts of the sea. Whereas he ...

Whereas he had found himself forgetting the tally of the Sixteen Bright Guides, and they were the simplest of the stars to find.

But he had an older and grander story to tell.

"Using his magic, the Emperor made himself a boat, and keeping to the path of the sun he sailed westward across the great vastness of the Wide Seas. At last he came to the Gate of the Vangavaye-ve, between Pau'lo'en'lai where the ancestors are and the Brothers of Morning.

"He entered the Ring of the Vangavaye-ve and found himself drawn to the flank of Mama Ituri and her Son. Gorjo City was not yet more than a collection of wharves and docks for the market, where they held the Festival of the Ships, when the Wayfinders recalled their great voyages and made merry."

That festival had, over time, been incorporated into the Singing of the Waters, after this encounter had started to show its ramifications.

"The Emperor came at the time of the Festival and asked to see the king. Now in those days the Wayfinders had no kings, for each ship looked to its chief, but as they had at need during the great voyages of settlement, so in this encounter did they choose among themselves one of their number to be Paramount Chief and Speaker for the Islands to this Emperor who came over the sea."

It was with great effort that Cliopher did not start singing the account as it was given in the *Lays*: the challenge-song and its reply, the debates amongst the people, the long explanations of how they made their decisions and why. On another occasion his Radiancy might well be interested in where Cliopher had acquired the foundation of his philosophy of government, but that was not the point of today's telling.

"They chose for Speaker and Paramount Chief a man named Elonoa'a, who was Kindraa, one of Those Who Know the Wind. He was wise and generous and great-hearted, and when he had heard the Emperor's request for aid, the promise of alliance in the Empire, and the certainty of adventure, he conferred with his people in what became known as the Last Conference of the Ships: for it was after this that the Wayfinders began to think of their Islands, and not their ships, as their heart-homes, and choose other ways of being part of the world.

"Elonoa'a became great friends with the Emperor, and guided him into every sea he needed to go. And it is said in the *Lays of the Wide Seas* that when Aurelius Magnus was taken by the Sun and Moon Elonoa'a sailed after him, until he crossed the boundary between this world and the realms of the gods. You can still see the light of his ship in the night sky, for his star goes counter to all the rest as he seeks out his friend."

His Radiancy was the lineal descendant of Aurelius Magnus' brother, who had come to the throne when the Emperor disappeared so suddenly that myth was the only way to make sense of it.

Or so Cliopher had always thought, until the Moon came down to earth.

"Are there Paramount Chiefs now?" his Radiancy asked quietly.

Cliopher shook his head. "No, my lord, for although the next Emperor had to honour the agreements Aurelius Magnus had made with the Wayfinders, he was a more practical man and a more cunning politician, and so he sent the first of the princes to be governor here."

"And so an alliance between equals and friends became subordinate colony and imperial protectorate."

"Indeed, my lord," Cliopher said, a lifetime of practice keeping any hint of bitterness from his voice.

★★★

HIS RADIANCY PACED ALONG THE verandah for hours that morning. When he came in at last for the midday meal, he announced that they would be returning to Solaara as soon as possible.

Cliopher tried to turn his thoughts back to his usual practical self. "We are supposed to send word to Captain Achillon with Balgo from the village, but he has not yet returned at all. Shall I send someone to ask who else has a boat that can cross the Bay?"

His Radiancy frowned thoughtfully. A flock of parrots were squabbling noisily in the gardens outside the dining room. He watched them for a moment absently, then his face cleared. "We will send a message another way. Conju, fetch me paper and pen and some string. Rhodin, open the window."

Ser Rhodin jumped up to do as he was bid, looking baffled. His Radiancy accepted the paper Conju brought and wrote a note in his slanting hand, then rolled it tightly and tied it off with a piece of raffia Conju passed him without comment. He handed it to Cliopher, who took it without knowing what he was supposed to do.

His Radiancy looked intently out the window, his eyes going the burnished gold of his magic-working. After a moment one of the parrots landed on the window, peered with equal intensity out of each eye at the room, and then hopped in to land on the table in front of his Radiancy.

"Tie the message on its leg," he ordered.

Bemused, Cliopher used the rest of the raffia to do so, trying not to pinch the bird's leg but also to make certain the message was not going to fall off. His Radiancy murmured something to the bird and passed his hands in the air around it. Cliopher felt the magic moving, which he did not usually, in a fine shimmer of gold.

"There," his Radiancy said at last, sitting back. "Fly quickly, little one."

The parrot took off with a noisy squawk.

They all stared at his Radiancy.

He smiled sardonically again. "I told you I had hidden talents. Cliopher, let us go to the village and make our farewells."

★★★

CAPTAIN ACHILLON SHOWED UP THE next day, the parrot sitting on his shoulder and looking as pleased with itself as a bird could look. The captain himself appeared resigned to his passenger.

"I had been wondering what you would do, seeing as that Balgo has been drunk for a fortnight," he said without bothering with any greeting more formal than a slight bow. "M'lord, will you be right? The wind is fresher today."

"I may take the bucket again, Captain," replied his Radiancy, smiling faintly.

For whatever reason—quite possibly, Cliopher thought, the fact that he had been doing wild magic all this time and not the hybrid Schooled magic he did as a rule—his Radiancy was merely queasy for most of the journey. He clutched at the bucket as they crossed the central currents, but managed to contain his retches. He looked quite pleased to be on the putative dry land of Gorjo City, however, and let Cliopher do most of the talking with the captain.

It was mid-afternoon when they arrived—at the city marina, not the princess'. His Radiancy frowned at the long walk along the harbour to Mama Ituri's Son, and the even longer climb to the Spire. Captain Achillon shouted at his assistant to cast off and the yacht moved back out into the bay.

His Radiancy said, "Cliopher, it occurs to me you might like to see your family before we leave."

"That would be wonderful," he said, unsurprised but nonetheless pleased.

"We should also give Captain Diogen some warning so that he may corral his crew." He looked around the city, at Conju and Cliopher, at the eight guards, and the small pile of luggage sitting on the wharf. There were a few people further down the quay, but no one was paying particular attention to them. "It occurs to me that I have never seen the famous fish market of Gorjo City."

Cliopher decided that nothing his Radiancy said or did should surprise him at this point. He was surprised at the words which came out of his own mouth, however: "There is a fine old inn farther along the harbour, my lord, not far from here. It is an admirable location from which to see the principal sites of the city."

Ser Rhodin and Commander Omo both looked at him. Cliopher shrugged, his Radiancy having already turned to walk down the wharf towards the quay, Pikabe and Ato close behind him. "Well, what would you?" he asked them in a low voice.

"It is a different matter here than in a backwater village," Ser Rhodin hissed.

"He has shown himself perfectly capable of speaking with all sorts of people," Cliopher pointed out. "And *I* barely recognized him in grey. If he were dressed in another colour and wearing a hat probably no one else would."

They managed to get to the Dolphin Hotel without anyone seeming to recognize the Sun-on-Earth. When they arrived, there was a slight awkwardness about the fact that his Radiancy declined to give his name, and the hotel manager was looking doubtfully on the guards' weapons.

Cliopher had been delayed by a large party exiting the hotel, and it was only when he pushed himself forward, ready to invoke his own rank, that he discovered to his surprise that the hotel manager was none other than one of his cousins. "Cousin Maius!" he said.

"Cousin Kip! Whatever are you doing here? Are you with the sky ship that came last month?"

"Yes. I am in attendance to my lord." He gestured discreetly at his Radiancy, who was smiling more sardonically than benevolently and thus did not look *exactly* like the state portrait hanging directly behind him.

Cliopher went on hastily, trying to distract Maius from looking from the one to the other. "We have been in the Outer Ring. My lord has decided to spend a few days in Gorjo City before returning to Solaara, and I thought of the Dolphin, though I did not know you were manager here now."

Maius looked very pleased. "It is a recent promotion," he said, slightly pompously. He was rather younger than Cliopher, in his early forties, and had always seemed to find Cliopher's lack of courtly gossip a sign of his lack of success. "You and your friends are very welcome to stay here. Must they all be armed, though? It doesn't do well for the image of the hotel."

Cliopher tried very hard not to laugh, glad Commander Omo and Ser Rhodin had drawn his Radiancy to a chair out of earshot. "My lord is a very important personage of the court, Maius," he said gravely. "He will need your best suite of rooms."

"Oh, very well, Kip. I do not want to spoil your social climbing. The mystery will be good for business, anyhow. Fortunately the ducal suite has just been cleaned."

He took keys from a cupboard, bustled over to his Radiancy, bowed deeply. "My lord, you are very welcome to the Dolphin. I am sure you will be delighted with the ducal suite."

"Why is it called that?" his Radiancy asked curiously as they were led up the grand sweep of the central stairs and along a hallway towards the back of the hotel.

"The Duke of Ikiano frequently stayed here," Maius said proudly, opening the double doors to the suite with a flourish.

It was nearly as lovely as Navikiani, Cliopher thought, and let out his breath.

"Ikiano hasn't been a duchy since the Fall," his Radiancy said thoughtfully. "Thank you, Maius. We will want refreshments sent up."

"Of course, my lord," Maius said with another bow and a wink for Cliopher, and then he took himself off.

"This will do," his Radiancy said, barely looking around the rooms. "I am going to lie down. Cliopher, you have my leave to go visit your family or friends here. Attend me tomorrow afternoon."

★★★

OF COURSE, FIRST CLIOPHER HAD to write a message for Captain Diogen, and then persuade Maius to send a messenger up to the sky ship with it. Then he changed into his less-fancy robes, was bidden by Conju to give his regards to his mother, assured Commander Omo that the fish market was every morning from dawn until eight o'clock (they did not use the Palace clock here), was assured by Ser Rhodin that they all had sufficient money for what they needed, and at last he ventured out.

It was a beautiful day, so Cliopher threaded his way along the canals, enjoying the familiar sights and smells of home. He thought of the tidy sum he had saved away, for his Radiancy was generous with his salaries, and Cliopher had few vices to spend it on. Enough to buy a modest house in the old quarter, or something rather nicer farther away, and have more than enough to live well on besides. Perhaps on his next holidays he would start looking.

If his Radiancy was going to retire, that changed everything.

He arrived at the family house after about forty-five minutes. It was quite possible his mother would be out visiting, but somebody would be there. Somebody always was there in his experience, however unexpected his arrival.

He rang the bell-pull sharply.

His sister answered almost immediately. She was dressed up, in a long red gown and a feathered headdress, and stood there in astonishment. "Kip!"

"Vinyë," he replied, stepping forward to embrace her. "You look wonderful, my dear."

"I was just going out," she said in confusion, retreating backwards into the hall. "But I will take you up to see Mama first. Whatever are you doing here? We didn't see another ship come in. No, wait, Mama will want to hear as well. Look who is here! For the *third* time this year!" she said as they entered the sitting room.

His mother sat with two of her sisters and her grandchildren, all of them working on various projects: his mother with some kind of knitting, his aunt Moula (she of the infamous chicken monomania) with a sketchbook, his aunt Oura (who was a natural philosopher) with some collection of specimens, his niece Leona with a model of something she was building out of balsa wood, and his nephew Gaudenius with the set books, Cliopher recognized with a curious shock, of the Imperial Bureaucratic Examinations.

"Kip!" they all cried, and it was a cheerful babble for several minutes before they sorted themselves out again and demanded explanations.

"I was on the sky ship," he explained. "I am attending my lord."

"*Your* lord?" Gaudenius asked eagerly. "The one whose secretary you are?"

"Yes," he said, then wondered if he had broken his Radiancy's command of secrecy, but his family had never grasped his position, and even Gaudenius' studies did not yet appear to have cracked the riddle of what "Secretary in Chief of the Private Offices of the Lords of State" actually meant.

On the one hand, perhaps the governing structure of the Service should be made clearer in the books ... but on the other, he was glad enough for his comparative anonymity outside of the Palace. And it was quite possible his family had forgotten everything past 'secretary in chief'.

Or even past 'secretary'. That would explain quite a lot.

"But that came in weeks ago," his mother said. "Where have you been?"

"Lesuia," he said, chuckling at their amazement. "My lord is taking a holiday. He has decided to spend a few days here in Gorjo City before we head back to Solaara, and gave me leave to visit you today."

"How marvellous," Leona said. "You will be able to answer Gaudy's questions about the exam and save us all from excruciating boredom."

"You forget it took him five tries," Vinyë said slyly.

"It's not a high bar," Cliopher said, not sure how he was supposed to take this.

"How long can you stay today?" his mother asked. "When must you return to your lord?"

"Tomorrow noon."

"Oh, splendid. Will you be leaving then?"

"I don't know. He is not expected back until the end of the Little Session, which is not for a while yet."

"Splendid," Vinyë said briskly. "I needn't abandon my symphony so I can spend time with my little brother. I'll see you at supper, Kip."

She gave him a quick, casual kiss on the top of his head, smiled at everyone else, and swept out of the room. Cliopher sat back at a question from Gaudenius about the logic puzzle portion of the exams, and thought to himself that this was what his Radiancy wanted and had never had, from the causal kiss to the earnest nephew.

But he had discovered the door to freedom, he reminded himself, and vowed that he would do everything in his power to help his Radiancy walk through it.

CHAPTER SEVENTEEN

IT WAS A QUITE MARVELLOUS afternoon and evening, simply happy and with only one awkward moment, when Cousin Louya came thrusting in after supper, eager to tell Cliopher all about her newest crusade. His response to her initial sallies were a little sharper than he meant, for he had thought he had made it clear that he would not abuse his position, and was disappointed to have to tell her, again, not to ask him to.

"It's different this time," Louya said. "This time—"

"It's always different," Cliopher said, resigning himself. "Louya, if you disagree with Princess Oriana's policies the proper thing to do is write to the Lord Emperor."

"Oh, as if! Kip, all I'm asking you to do is look at this—"

"What do you think I can do with it, besides take it to the Lord Emperor?" He caught his voice before it rose into exasperation. "Put it through the proper channels, Louya. They exist for a reason. And when it comes up before—"

"As if it would," she muttered darkly. "Everyone knows only the rich and the noble have the ear of the government. We little people get ignored all the time."

"I don't ignore you," he said plaintively. He fielded letters from or about Louya nearly every month. "I always write back."

"You're in the thick of it! You always say no!"

Cliopher sighed. Vinyë winked at him and took their cousin by the arm. "Louya, dear, you know Kip's very busy and it's not as if he can bring up every fancy of yours before the Lord Emperor—"

"There's a conspiracy to *hide* the *truth* from the Lord Emperor!"

Cliopher's temper rose. He made himself speak very, very mildly. "I assure you, Louya, I do nothing of the sort."

"You don't understand," she said, and launched into her theory of government conspiracy, which was almost as well-thought-through as Aunt Moula's chickens, and which Cliopher had read in numerous iterations. He was able to set his staff to dealing with the majority of the crank letters that came into the Private Offices, but Cousin Louya's, alas, came to him as private mail.

When Louya finally left, still ranting—and still without him having the least idea of her current passion—he told his mother about seeing Aya in Dovo Delanis and being claimed as a kinsman. He discovered that Aya had been one of the under-directors in the provincial treasury and considered a strong contender for the next opening as director, but had gone off on a solitary sail around the Outer Ring and met Jiano, and now wrote funny mysteries set in exotic locales.

The next morning Gaudy suggested they go to the bookstore to look for Aya's books and to get ice cream on the way back. It was something Cliopher tried to do with him at least once every time he was home (Leona, not being as bookish as Gaudy, usually wanted to go fishing). He was not expecting Gaudy to have an ulterior motive.

They found half a dozen of Aya's novels, acquired their ice cream, and began ambling back. Gaudy directed them the long way, along the edge of the Tahivoa lagoon. Cliopher paced along, trying to ensure he didn't walk too fast, and wondered if he could ask about the exam books.

"Uncle Kip," Gaudy said abruptly, voice strained. "You haven't—you haven't said anything about—I'm studying for the Service exams!"

"Yes, I saw," Cliopher said, forcing his voice to stay calm, so as not to overwhelm his nephew with his joy, his concern, his—gratitude.

"You looked—when you saw the books—you were so *polite*, Uncle Kip! Are you upset with me? Do you think I'm unworthy—I've done everything you said—do you think I can't do it?"

"Slow down!" Cliopher glanced around to see who was in earshot. No one just at the moment, though there was a cluster of fishermen ahead, outside The Palm Tree, that almost certainly included an uncle or two. He slowed his steps still more.

Gaudy was taut and trembling beside him, vibrating with pent-up emotion.

"How can you possibly think I would be anything other than thrilled to know you're applying for the Service?"

"You didn't seem interested—"

Cliopher stopped, forcing his nephew to look at him. "Gaudy, I have spent my entire adult life being chastised by my family for leaving the Van-gavaye-ve. What do you think your mother would do if I encouraged you to leave?"

"It was her idea!"

This seemed incredible. Cliopher stared at him. "Really?"

Gaudy scuffed his feet along the wooden boardwalk. A gull perched a few posts ahead of them turned one yellow eye on them, then hunched its shoulders. Cliopher sympathized.

"Uncle Kip, last year when I was all worried about what I was going to do after university, I wrote to you for your advice."

"I remember."

"You said to go through all the things I liked to do, look hard at what I do with my free time, what makes me feel challenged and excited and creative, and how I want to participate in my community—and when I told Mama what you'd written, she looked at me and said, 'Oh, Gaudy, look at the Service.'"

It still seemed incredible. Cliopher remembered writing that letter—was it only last year?—the inverse of what he looked for when hiring or assessing people, when he tried to match skills and interests and talents and desires with the work that needed to be done. He cleared his throat, looked up at his nephew, who had inherited his mother's height. "What do you like to do, Gaudy?"

Gaudy scuffed at the boardwalk some more. "Mama always says that my favourite hobby is reading your letters. I love how you do all sorts of things— you go all sorts of places—working to make the world a better place. Uncle Kip, I read all the history books I can. You can see—I mean, of course there are all those warriors and generals and things—I remember, in one of your letters you said that armies and lords are all very exciting but it's the people who do the slow and steady work of government that change the world—I want to do *that*—I want to make the world a better place!"

Cliopher cleared his throat again, this time against a lump of wonder. "Not here?"

Gaudy gestured wildly at the Tahivoa lagoon, the brightly-coloured houses facing the water, the old men fishing outside the café. "I want to see the places that you've written about, Uncle Kip. I want to see the floating castles of the Galagar Coast—I want to see the Palace of Stars—I want to see the Lord Emperor! I want to see the thunder lizards of the Yenga. I want— oh, Uncle Kip, I don't know what the world needs—but I think I have—I think I can—I know I have something to share! I don't know what it is, but I'm sure—I read your letters and each time I think, oh, if only I was there working beside you …"

He turned his head away from Cliopher, the taut energy draining out of him. "Sorry, Uncle Kip," he muttered. "I didn't mean to … that is, I know it's different in Solaara—it's not like apprenticing as an architect or something—I know you can't—"

"Gaudy," Cliopher said, gripping his upper arms and turning him to face him. "Gaudy. I would be honoured and pleased beyond measure to see you enter the Service. You are everything I want to see in new aspirants—smart, enthusiastic, engaged, willing to learn, willing to *do*, willing to stand up for what you believe in. The only reason I haven't bored you stiff with stories is because I didn't think … I didn't want to make your mother sad that I was encouraging you to leave."

"It's not like it was when you went to Astandalas. There's the sea train now—I remember you didn't use to be able to come home very often, now it's every year. Twice this year! Or *three* times now. We were so disappointed you weren't going to be able to come to Mama's concert tonight, we didn't even write to ask you, and then you showed up after all."

"You won't get to use the sky ship as a new aspirant, you know," Cliopher said, smiling, as they started to walk again. "I am fairly senior now."

They had just reached the fishermen as he said this. Cliopher's Uncle Lazo was one of them. He tilted his head so he could look at Cliopher from under the brim of his hat. "Hark at my nephew," he said to no one in particular. "Sounding like he's reached retirement."

"These young'uns," another old man said, not turning his regard from the line running into the water. "No staying power."

"Who is it?" said the oldest, squinting at them. This was Cliopher's great-uncle, Buru Tovo, who was from the Western Ring and disdained modern fashions in clothing—'modern', in his case, including any style developed after the ascension of the Empress Anyoë the Short-Lived and any material that couldn't be acquired by wandering into the jungle with a stone knife. He was rather deaf and rather blind and occasionally his memory jumped in time, but in the difficult year after Cliopher's father's death, he had taken the young Kip off to the Western Ring to learn the ways of the ancestors.

Cliopher had never told anyone in the Palace that he could, if pressed, provide a fully legitimate Outer Ring Vangavayen tribal costume. And the dances that went with them.

Come to think of it, he wasn't sure if he'd ever told anyone in Gorjo City, either.

"It's Kip and Gaudy," Uncle Lazo said loudly.

"Good morning, Buru," Cliopher said politely, the honorific for a revered ancestor feeling so much more real and anchored than the noble titles he spent his life saying.

"Eh? What did he say?"

"He said, 'Good morning, Buru'!" Uncle Lazo said.

"What's that? Come closer, you," Buru Tovo said, beckoning wildly in their general direction. "Only Kip ever remembers to call me that."

"It is Kip, Buru," Cliopher said, the nickname feeling odd on his tongue. He squatted before his great-uncle, grasped his upper arms gently, touched forehead to forehead. "I'm home for a visit."

His great-uncle held him close, peering intently into his face. His breath smelled of stale coffee and dried fish, a combination that took Cliopher back immediately to his childhood. "Not to stay?"

"Not this time, Buru."

Buru Tovo snorted. "No children yet?"

"No, Buru."

"Bah. Do you at least have a woman to bring you to sense?"

Cliopher sat back on his heels. He smiled, a bit sadly. "No, Buru."

"What do you do without a woman to keep you hopping?"

There was his Radiancy, who managed to keep him hopping—Cliopher snorted, turned it into a chuckle. "Oh, I find work enough."

"Bah," Tovo said again, turning back to his line, the glittering water of the lagoon, the breeze coming off the Bay carrying the scent of the flowers of the Western Ring. "I thought I taught you better than that."

CHAPTER EIGHTEEN

"DO INVITE YOUR LORD TO come as well," his mother said as he got ready to leave. "I am very sorry Conju could not join you last night. I hope your lord will let him off."

"He is the only attendant," Cliopher explained again, glossing over the eight guards. "But I will certainly tell them both."

"I do hope you'll be able to come to the assembly," his mother said again.

"I will try my best," he replied patiently.

It appeared that he had come at exactly the right moment to come to an assembly being held to support the Gorjo City Symphony. This was obviously important to his sister, but (as his mother, his niece, his nephew, and various aunts and cousins both separately and together had informed him) there was a surprise element insofar as the members of the symphony had planned to honour the ten-year anniversary of her tenure as director.

"It's at eight o'clock tonight, in the Town Hall. Four doors down from the Dolphin."

"I do love you all," he said, and embraced his family closely.

He enjoyed the walk back, the warm sun and the lambent air. Gorjo City always seemed to be the perfect temperature, neither too hot nor too cold. Cool enough to make fires enjoyable in the evening, warm enough to make them essentially unnecessary. He found Solaara rather too hot in the summer, though the Palace itself was always cool.

Maius was on the front desk again, listening sympathetically to a woman complain about something. He interrupted her complaint to beckon Cliopher over.

"Your lord left me this message for you," he said, handing him an envelope.

Cliopher unfolded the note. In his Radiancy's hand it said, "We have gone to see the Aquarium. Conju has made arrangements for lunch at Potlatch for 1:00; join us there."

He had signed it with a sun-in-glory. Cliopher smiled, went upstairs to dress in an outfit suitable for the best fish restaurant in the city, and walked down the splendid sweep of the harbour towards Mama Ituri's Son, wondering as he went whether anyone had recognized their lord magus.

★★★

THE MASTER OF THE HOUSE at Potlatch was another one of Cliopher's cousins, who looked at him and cried "Cousin Kip!" when he arrived.

His Radiancy, Conju, and Commander Omo and Ser Rhodin had evidently just arrived themselves, for they were only a few steps within, and stopped to look back at the salutation.

"Of course it's you," Galen said, grasping him by both upper arms in the old Astandalan greeting. "I was trying to think why on earth Uncle Cliopher would make a reservation for the best table through the front desk. You didn't tell your friends to ask for me or Enya?"

"Is Enya here?" Cliopher asked in surprise, bowing to his Radiancy but cutting it short about two feet higher than usual when he saw his lord shake his head slightly. He coughed at Conju's expression. "I thought she was at Gaspar's?"

"She moved last Emperor Day," Galen replied cheerfully.

"Somebody's fallen down in their gossip-spreading. I didn't know Maius was at the Dolphin, either."

"Aunt Oura's obsessed with her monograph, that's what it is. Your mama's never been the best gossip among the aunts. Yes, Enya's the chef here now. Your friends will be very pleased, I'm sure." He shook his head severely at one of his underlings, who had been trying to guide the party over to the table. "No, Nando, no menus. Enya will want to do something special for her favourite cousin in the Imperial Service."

"Aren't I her only cousin in the Imperial Service?" Cliopher asked, smiling, then caught Conju's expression as they started to move through the room. "Ah—Galen—"

He pulled his cousin back as his Radiancy suffered Nando to lead them across to the seat in the window embrasure, where they had one of the great views of Mama Ituri and Gorjo City and the palace above its reflective pool.

"My lord has some, er, dietary restrictions. No raw food, primarily." He looked at Conju, who was trying to govern his face as Commander Omo decided where everyone would be sitting. "Conju, what else does the chef need to know for his—his lordship's meal?"

"Oh, is this your lord?" Galen said, looking delighted but not fall-on-his-face awestruck. "How exciting! My lord," he added to his Radiancy, who had turned from the admittedly stunning view to regard them, "we are honoured by your presence in our humble restaurant. Kip has always spoken of you with the greatest respect and fondness."

Cliopher tried not to wince at *fondness*.

His Radiancy said, "I am very pleased to hear it."

Galen rubbed his hands together. "Oh, if only we had known Kip was bringing you … My lord," he added abruptly, "what delights you? Your secretary's cousin is chef here, and she will set before you a meal worthy of the Lord of Rising Stars himself."

"I'm sure," his Radiancy said politely. "From my brief glance at your board, it appears you specialize in Jilkanese food?"

"Chef Enya went all the way to the City of Emeralds to apprentice with the great Rosvau himself, great lord. He cooked for the state visit of the Queen of Voonra to the Palace of Stars."

"I recall the occasion. Something of that tradition will be most acceptable to myself and Ludvic here … though perhaps the others might prefer something a little less spicy."

"Cousin Kip has never been known for biting the nose of the dragon," Galen said, laughing. "Now, we would usually accompany Jilkanese dishes with cooling salads and creams, but Kip mentioned that there are some dietary restrictions?"

"*All* food for his lordship must have had heat applied," Conju said firmly. "Even the garnishes. And it must all be of reasonable size to be eaten with eating sticks." He pointed at the golden pair laid neatly on the table before his Radiancy.

Galen looked very intrigued. "I have not come across that requirement. From your appearance you must be from old Ysthar, or perhaps western Kavanduru, my lord?"

"Damara, as it happens."

Galen looked briefly as if was trying to connect two pieces of thought together. Cliopher watched in horrified fascination to see if the connection of "Damara" with "my lord" would bring him to—but his cousin's thoughts had gone elsewhere. "Damaran food is very spicy indeed. Hmm. Now, so we are clear, must your food be hot when served?"

"No, that is unnecessary, so long as it has been cooked."

"Splendid. I will tell Enya. What of beverages?"

"They are not under the same restrictions, except no juice."

"Oh, I am sorry, my lord," Galen said mournfully. "But you may have wine? Water? Coffee? Chocolate? Tea?"

"Do you trade so far? I should be delighted with tea."

"*Wonderful.* You will not be disappointed, my lord, I assure you. Kip, I am delighted to see you. For the *third* time this year! No one can believe it. It's so exciting to meet your lord at last. Remind me to speak to you before you leave, Louya's got a viau in her net again. Nando, bring tea for my cousin's lord, and water for my cousin and his friends, and we will see what Enya chooses and bring the wine accordingly."

He bustled off, leaving Cliopher somewhat in a daze of embarrassment and relief. He sat down in the last open seat, between his Radiancy and Ser Rhodin. He blinked at this arrangement, realizing only then that there was no sign of the other honour guards or the usual spears.

"It seemed rather conspicuous to go abroad in full glory when we are trying to remain unrecognized," his Radiancy said placidly, picking up the vase in the centre of the table to admire the orange and scarlet blossoms within it. "How is your family, Cliopher? Or Kip, should I say?"

"As you prefer, my lord," Cliopher said. "They are all very well, thank you. I am grateful that you gave me the opportunity to visit them."

"They must have been pleased to see you."

"And surprised indeed, my lord, but pleased especially as my sister is being honoured at a symphony concert tonight. They have all invited us to go."

"Us?"

"You were certainly not forgotten, my lord, and of course they have met Conju."

"Mm." His Radiancy seemed about to say something further, but was interrupted by a party of four who were coming through from the deck and had caught sight of Cliopher.

"Kip!" cried a chorus of happy voices belonging to the old friends who had cheered him through his seemingly-endless examination attempts. At his Radiancy's somewhat sardonic gesture of permission, Cliopher stood up to greet the group.

Falbert grasped his arms and then held him out to look at him severely. "What are you doing here again? Is this your third holiday in a year? I don't believe it! You're looking well, by the way, much better than last time. I don't think you've ever actually met Irela? She always seems to be out on inspections when you come on holiday. Irrie, my dear, this is the infamous Kip

Mdang who took so long with the Imperial Bureaucratic Examinations he's been too embarrassed to show his head in the city again."

Irela was Bertie's second wife; Cliopher had known Cora, the first one, quite well, and he had always faintly regretted their separation. He did not quite like how Bertie wrote about Irela, nor the fact that she was always out on inspections when he came home. At some point, surely, this had become deliberate.

Cliopher had missed their wedding (which had been extremely hastily organized, for reasons he did not know) because of a diplomatic mission to Voonra, but that did not seem a good reason for her antipathy. It was one of the small frictions of life at home that had never seemed worth dealing with when he had only three or four weeks to spend there.

She raised her eyebrows. "I'm sure the only cause he'd have for embarrassment is because you all keep reminding him. Kip, I'm pleased to meet you at last. Bertie has such stories about you."

All of which was perfectly normal and polite. He smiled equally politely in return.

"I never made the mistake of trying out for the Emperor's service," Falbert said genially. "I left that prize for Kip to run at. And at. And at. And—"

"We're celebrating his retirement," interrupted Toucan—whose real name Cliopher had never actually learned, his nose being so prominent a feature that everyone from the Chief Justice, whose clerk he was, down to his little grandchildren called him by it. "Can you believe it? Bertie, retiring! What will the good folk of the museum do without him to order them around?"

"You're next," Falbert said loftily, while their wives laughed. "Toucan and Ghilly are finishing out their year and then they're going to come fishing with me."

"Fishing?"

"Bertie can fish," Toucan said. "I'm going to paint. We're going to take his yacht around the Outer Ring, maybe go all the way to the Isolates again. What about you, Kip? Will you come and torment us with your oboe?"

Cliopher did not dare glance at his Radiancy. He had promised the shell-collector of Lesuia that he would bring home the fire ... but that meant he had promised also to come home. And his Radiancy had decided to retire ...

He smiled. "I'm five years behind you, remember."

Bertie's eyebrows beetled fiercely in surprise, but he said nothing.

Toucan laughed. "Is that a promise? Can we expect you to show up in five years with a—I don't know, what do they give long-standing civil servants in Solaara?"

"Isn't it a watch?" Ghilly said brightly. She'd been the one who Cliopher had hoped might be *the* one ... but he was not Toucan. And Cliopher was too ambitious, she'd said once, one quiet evening long ago, aiming at a star far removed from the one she followed. He smiled at her. Toucan had made her much happier than he ever would have; and he would not have achieved what he had if she had said yes to him.

Bertie harrumphed. "Oh, surely Kip's moved past the watch level. Surely he's earned at least a clock."

Toucan shook his head. "He works for the Lord Emperor—an orrery would be more appropriate."

"Or a sundial," Ghilly said, as they all laughed. "Oh, Kip, it's so lovely to see you. We haven't seen you more than once in a year since—since you left. Are you in town long?"

"Or may we start making plans for five years hence?" Toucan struck a pose. "With the warning, perhaps you'll be able to play that oboe properly."

Cliopher shook his head, smiling, and saw behind Ghilly his Radiancy. His blood ran cold.

Three weeks ago he would never have forgotten for the least moment that he stood in the Presence.

"I, er, I think that may be up to my lord to decide," he said, looking straight into the lion eyes. For a moment he wondered if he should not prostrate himself; but his Radiancy was smiling from the inner man, and so he bowed. Not down to one knee, but with the greatest courtesy he could muster in the less-formal gesture.

The lion eyes held his for a moment, then moved deliberately away. "Will you introduce your friends to me, Cliopher? Are these more cousins?"

"No, my lord," he replied, taking a deep breath, as his friends turned curiously. "They are friends of my youth. Falbert Kindraa, who as you heard has just retired from his position as Head Curator at the Museum of the Vangavaye-ve; his wife Irela Nossian, who is an investigator of environmental health for the province; Ghillian Poyë, who is with the Provincial Ministry of Agriculture, and her husband, Toucan Nevan, who is chief clerk of the Provincial Court of Justice."

They all made deep bows over their hands, as befitted one of the great lords of the court—Vangavayen style.

"We are delighted," Ghilly proclaimed, not looking at all serious or worried—though possibly slightly puzzled that Cliopher did not name any of his party. "Kip never writes of you but in the greatest terms of affection, my lord. I do hope you will forgive our impudence on his behalf. It is a long way from Solaara to the Vangavaye-ve and we do not see him nearly so often as we would like, and we let ourselves get carried away. Of course we should have realized he was here with work, he has already had his holiday this year—and a second one by your favour, I understand."

Affection was almost as bad as *fondness*, Cliopher thought, schooling his expression as best he could.

His Radiancy said, "If I give him a sundial when he retires, will you hold him to it?"

They all laughed robustly. "No, no," said Toucan grandly. "This is the Vangavaye-ve: this is where the Sun comes on his holidays."

Cliopher hoped they missed the way his Radiancy's party all tried hard not to react to this statement.

Ghilly went on blithely. "And where the Moon meets her lover." She pointed out the window at the Bay of the Waters. "Did you see the eclipse the other day? My brother is an astronomer at the university, we were watching from his telescope. There was the most extraordinary phenomenon to the east, it looked like the Moon had come to earth. It lit up the whole Outer Ring from the Five Sisters to Pau'lo'en'lai. My brother said he had never heard of its like and has burrowed himself in his books to find out what caused it. I reckon he should be asking the mythologers, but what can I say, he's a scientist."

"So are you, Ghilly," Cliopher couldn't resist pointing out.

"I study fertility," she said, laughing again. "It is all about the mythology. We can say the soil needs more iron and less magnesium, but what we really mean is that the blood of the giants is growing weak. That's a much better story, do you not think, my lord?"

"I am a poet," his Radiancy said solemnly, "a wild mage, and a principal actor in one of the great plays of the Nine Worlds. Of course."

"Oh, I can see why our Kip loves you so," she said impulsively. "Once he started talking about working for you we knew we'd never get him back."

Falbert grinned. "Cheeks burning, eh, Kip? He also likes wearing all the old costumes. That is a nice one, Kip, very grand indeed. It's not the right colour for the Upper Secretariat, though—shouldn't you be in burnt umber?"

"As my personal secretary he is permitted to wear red," his Radiancy said.

Falbert narrowed his eyes, evidently trying to place that uniform. His efforts were interrupted by his Radiancy, who added with mild curiosity, "What was the element of the examinations that kept giving you such trouble, Kip?"

Cliopher took a deep and rueful breath. "Etiquette, my lord."

Everyone laughed, even Conju, who tried to muffle it in his hand. His Radiancy's merry laugh carried above the rest.

"Oh look," Cliopher said gratefully, "here comes our food."

"We shall never stand between a man and his food," Falbert said grandly. "Let us know when you're getting your sundial, Kip, and we'll sail my boat to Solaara to come pick you up. Yes, I know it's inland," he added testily to Toucan, "but there's a river running through it."

"I think you need to work on your geography."

Cliopher bade them farewell, then turned back to where yet another waiter was reverently placing a large dish in front of his Radiancy. Once the man had gone, he bowed. "I am sorry, my lord."

"You do not need to apologize for your friends, Cliopher. Sit down."

Cliopher sat. The other three men were carefully looking at their plates, though Cliopher could see out of the corner of his eye that Ser Rhodin was trying not to smirk.

Conju was frowning at the large bowl, obviously meant to be shared between them all, of fried squid in a fiery batter accompanied by what Galen, whipping by on his way back to the front desk to pour them all sparkling white wine, said was a chilled baked savoury custard. After a pause Conju said, "My lord, if I may serve some onto your plate … or if you prefer we will take some and leave the rest …"

His Radiancy nodded assent to the first option, leaving the rest of them to share the bowl. He ate more heartily than Cliopher could manage, although the squid was superbly cooked and the smooth richness of the chilled baked savoury custard was a perfect accompaniment to the hot and spicy batter. After they had finished, his Radiancy cocked his head at Cliopher, who felt the squid congealing instantly in his stomach.

"I have received the distinct impression, Cliopher, that none of your friends or family has any idea who your lord is."

Cliopher thought for a moment, and then said simply, "No, my lord."

"And why is that?"

The question hung there, interrupted by Galen whirling up again, this time to proudly present a platter of seared bluefin tuna squares accompanied by a "medley of lightly stir-fried vegetables," running primarily to a variety of colours of long beans.

"Here we have one of our most requested dishes," he said, describing it lovingly. "I hope you enjoyed the squid? Wonderful. We shall take away the sparkling wine and bring instead the chilled white. Is that nose satisfactory, my lord? It comes of northern Amboloyo, from the vineyards of the Monks of Lezar, of course. Kip, Cousin Louya wants—oh, I'll be back in a moment. Enjoy the tuna, gentlemen."

Cliopher girded his loins. "It seemed to be boasting, my lord. I told them my title but did not explain it, thinking that surely they would learn what it was, but as you have seen ..." He shrugged. "People in the Vangavaye-ve believe the Sun and Moon circle around Mama Ituri, my lord. They did not ask for details, and when I had not given them the first time, it was easier the next ..."

"They have never asked for your lord's name?"

"Oh, well, on occasion they'll enquire, out of politeness, but they do not press."

His Radiancy shook his head. "How different from the court, where your allegiances and alliances are of paramount importance. What sort of sundial would you like?"

"My lord, I will not be retiring before you."

His Radiancy smiled and turned to the tuna.

★★★

COUSIN ENYA, CLIOPHER CONCEDED TOWARDS the end of the meal, had pulled out all the stops for him and his lord. Galen swirled round as he managed the room, delivering them wines to match their courses and tidbits about the origins of the foodstuffs, but did not find a moment to finish telling him about Cousin Louya until they got to the final course.

Dessert in the Vangavaye-ve ran largely to fresh fruit and frozen ices; neither of which, of course, his Radiancy could eat. Cliopher wondered what Cousin Enya would do with his Radiancy's dietary restriction—everything else having been superb, and only the tuna seeming to have been cut into bite-sized pieces from its more usual size.

She came out with the dessert, directing the waiters to place the platter upon the table with the utmost care. Cliopher looked at the platter: it bore a beautiful pattern of fresh fruit sprinkled with sugar and smelling pleasantly of the finest rum.

"Say nothing, Kip," Enya said, smiling at him. "I have not forgotten. Nando, place that bowl there—just so. This is your lord, Kip? I am honoured to meet you at last, sir. I hope you have enjoyed your meal?"

"It was fit for the Emperor's table, Chef Enya."

She blushed charmingly. "You gave me a challenge, sir, and like any artist, my joy is to find the beauty within the constraints given me. I studied under Chef Rosvau, who always told me that the finish of the meal is the moment in which glory ought be made most manifest." She paused theatrically, then said to Galen: "The taper."

Galen passed her a lit taper. His Radiancy started to smile.

"And the pitcher, Galen."

Galen poured a thin stream of warmed rum over the fruit, starfruit and oranges and three types of banana, and Enya lit it with a little flourish of her wrist. "Caramelized fruit with rum sauce, with vanilla ice cream—from a cooked custard base, sir—to accompany it," she said grandly. "If at some point you wish to grant us knowledge of your name, my lord, we shall call it after you."

"Thank you," said his Radiancy, watching the blue flames dance over the fruit, the sugar bubbling and the aromas releasing into the air. He looked as if he could barely wait, his eating sticks already in his hand. "And this is a dish that has not been seen on the Emperor's table, for reasons that escape me. I hope you are taking notes, Conju."

Enya looked thrilled with this accolade, as well she might, thought Cliopher, yearning to tell her just who her guest was and why that was not at all hyperbolic praise. Galen brought them coffee and another pot of tea for his Radiancy, and then pulled up a chair from the table next over and sat beside Cliopher.

He moved so quickly that Cliopher could not ask anything of his Radiancy, who was at any rate focused on his caramelized fruit and ice cream to the exclusion of all other concerns. Ser Rhodin shrugged, as if to say all the customary behaviour was so far removed from what they were doing that it might as well be a dream.

"Cousin Louya," Galen said, looking intently at Cliopher, "is worked up about this fish farm project Earl Baljan is trying to ram down everyone's throat. Now, Louya is always chasing viaus, but this time it's more serious. She's dead set against the project, and she's got a lot of people, including most of the university scientists, on her side. The problem is, the Earl doesn't listen to anyone but the aristos, and he's a rising star in the Princess' court."

"Mm," said Cliopher, watching his Radiancy look regretfully at the remaining bits of ice cream in his bowl and then carefully set down his eating sticks.

"Everyone knows you don't play games with your position," Galen said, glancing around the table, accidentally catching his Radiancy's now-interested eye, and shifting position to include him in his conversation. "And of course, for anything to go anywhere, you would have to be persuaded of the matter's importance, and then you would have to persuade your lord ..."

He nodded awkwardly at his Radiancy, who nodded blandly back.

"Who might, being from the far side of the world, not be at all interested in doings in the Vangavaye-ve except if you were to beg him to take an interest. And even then he would have to go to his prince, or I suppose it would be the Grand Duchess for Old Damara, and persuade her to take the matter to the Glorious One."

The Glorious One, Cliopher thought, and prayed he was right in so thinking, looked slightly amused at this reading of his rank.

"We all know you wouldn't—that you haven't—been willing to do that, and we respect your impartiality, though I can think of some things that ... well, no matter now. It is different outside the Ring, we know that. But Louya is determined to stop this project if she has to go to the Palace of Stars and present her case before the Glorious One herself. She has been talking to the wider family, and I think she has a lot of support, about writing collectively to you. I don't think she's spoken to your mother or sister yet, but ..."

"She came by last night," Cliopher admitted. "I didn't let her get as far as the fish farm."

Galen snorted. "Naturally not. But I thought I should warn you to expect the family to get behind Louya." He winced. "I can't believe I'm saying that. But this time—"

He looked at his Radiancy. "My lord, my cousin your servant delights in his work in Solaara. He also has a large family here who love him dearly. The Vangavaye-ve is a long way from the Palace of Stars but I hope your visit here has shown you how special it is, and that you will hold it in your mind if there should come a petition your way. I do not ask for myself. I merely warn you that it is likely to come."

"Thank you," said Cliopher, since something needed to be said.

"I assure you," said his Radiancy, "that I always listen very carefully when Cliopher asks me something."

CHAPTER NINETEEN

THEY WALKED BACK ALONG THE edge of the water, the glittering harbour on their right, and beyond it the nearest of the Outer Ring cliffs, black basalt speckled with innumerable white seabirds. Ahead of them three people were having an intense argument in the middle of the walk. All three glared fiercely at their party when they approached, then one of the two women said, "Why, it's Orlo's cousin Kip!" and he recognized her as one of Ghilly's colleagues.

"You work in the department of agriculture, don't you?" he asked, racking his memory for some long-ago party where they'd been introduced. "I know we've met before, but I'm afraid I don't recall your name."

"Maya Nevan. I'm Toucan's cousin. This is Naura Foronto, one of my colleagues, and this is Yoros Sayo Ilfariz."

Yoros was a *velio*, from outside the Ring; with his milky-brown colouring and tight spiralled black-brown braids probably from Jilkano. He frowned at his Radiancy, but did not seem to recognize him, for he transferred his frown to Cliopher in short order. "Who is this?"

Maya spoke with air of pulling a surprise out of a basket. "This is Kip Mdang."

Yoros evidently did not appreciate this. "Another Mdang?"

Naura snickered. "You haven't been here long enough. There is *always* another Mdang. Anyhow, Kip, Yoros—"

"Sayo Ilfariz!"

Maya rolled her eyes. "Honestly, anyone would think you were someone important. Kip, Sayo Yoros here was brought by Earl Baljan to tell us all how we should be doing fish farming—"

"Aquaculture!"

Cliopher checked to make sure his face was as resolutely bland as for a Council of Princes meeting. His Radiancy was nearly vibrating with suppressed laughter beside him. "Yes, Maya?"

"We as a department are being pressured to accept his findings—"

"Always unpleasant," he murmured.

Her eyes flashed with amusement. He realized that he had unconsciously thickened his accent in obedience to her baiting.

Yoros was white-lipped with fury. "Just because the earl is aware of nuances beyond your pathetic excuse for scientific rigour—"

Naura interjected conversationally, "Sayo Yoros finds our, ah, casual approach a bit off-putting."

"I don't, as a rule, think it a bad idea to bring in scientists from other provinces to exchange ideas and knowledge, but Sayo Yoros—"

"Ilfariz!"

"Sayo Ilfariz—you prefer that, really?—isn't actually a scientist, he's a 'project manager' from Nijan or somewhere." Maya dropped the jargon as if it were something she had found under a rock.

Yoros burst out, "Jilkano!"

"Oh?" Cliopher said encouragingly, wondering where this was going but much diverted.

"The princess is trying to make us say that this stupid fish farm of Earl Baljan's is a good idea instead of something that will pollute half the Eastern Ring. I'm not saying aquaculture is impossible—someone just got a grant to see if they could raise falao on ropes, like mussels, over in South Epalo—but nothing about this project deals with the fact that the currents in the Bay of the Waters are nothing like the mouth of a river in Jilkano."

"Nijan," muttered Yoros, but a little more quietly.

Cliopher had visited the fish farm at the mouth of the Nikao River both before and after it had been taken over by the workers. On the whole he thought they were doing a much better job running it than the petty aristocrat who had hitherto used it as his own personal tax break. He could guess whose project manager Earl Baljan had hired.

"Oh?" he said encouragingly again.

"So we were wondering who we go complain to. Then we saw you!"

He blinked. "I beg your pardon?"

Maya grinned. "How should we complain about Princess Oriana? She's far overstepping herself."

Cliopher blinked again. He was saved from an immediate response by Yoros bursting out again. "You should be ashamed of yourselves, you, you, you unnatural women!"

"Unnatural, really?" Naura said.

"Speaking of your princess that way! Ruling her people is her glorious and sacred responsibility! It is your duty to obey and respect her!"

Naura and Maya exchanged glances, met Cliopher's desperately-maintained straight face, and then burst into whoops of laughter. It was good healthy laughter, belly-shaking, side-splitting laughter, the sort one never heard in the Palace. Naura snorted through the middle of it, gasping for breath. Yoros gaped. Cliopher stole a glance at his Radiancy, whose face was impenetrably serene.

Yoros said, "That's—that's—that's treason—" He glanced around as if looking for the police or informers.

Maya whooped some more. Finally she stuttered to a wheezing halt, wiping her face of tears of merriment. Naura stuck her fist in her mouth to silence her own eruptions of giggles.

Maya said, "Oh, we shouldn't be so unfair. Princess Oriana's no worse than Princess Aralia was, really—so long as she keeps to playing dress-up in her palace."

Even his Radiancy stifled a snort at that.

Naura hiccoughed, then managed: "I wouldn't mind if she came down and talked to us, but she won't come past the marina."

"She's afraid of water," Maya added. "Can you imagine? Anyway, Kip, I think this has gone far enough. It's one thing for her just to be mediocre at her job—"

"Even princesses need to eat," Naura interjected piously.

"Especially princesses, or so I am informed. But really, she can't go round telling everyone what to do!"

Cliopher cleared his throat, fighting for equanimity. "The, ah, protocol is to write to the Lord Emperor."

"And it will get to him?" Maya said, a bit doubtfully.

"I can nearly guarantee it."

Yoros snorted magnificently. "The Imperial Bureaucracy is efficient and orderly and effective."

Maya and Naura swung round to look at him with identical expressions of arch surprise. Maya made a show of recovering first. "Oh, are you still here, Yoros?"

"—Sayo Ilfariz!"

"We assumed you'd've gone already to report back to the earl."

Naura grinned. "It's good to know the bureaucracy is efficient and effective and, er, whatever else you just said."

"It's not run by Islanders," he said viciously.

"You only need one," Maya said, winking at Cliopher. "Thanks, Kip! We'll see you around, no doubt."

And there you had it. He wished he knew what to say to make his family and dearest friends so insouciantly accepting of his life's work.

"Are there often letters complaining about the ruling princes?" his Radiancy asked as they continued on.

Cliopher sighed. "Just from Nijan, my lord."

"And I do get those."

"Of course, my lord."

"And is there truly only one Islander in the Service?"

"Yes, my lord." He paused a moment, and then added shyly, "My nephew, Gaudenius, is studying to take the examinations this year."

His Radiancy glanced at him. "You must be pleased."

Pleased was not the right word. "Yes, my lord."

They came abreast of the merchant warehouses. Cliopher looked for his cousin Quintus' ship, the *Gold Pearl*, but was unable to see it amongst the half-dozen oceangoing vessels in the Palaoa Lagoon.

Outside the Ahalo Clothmakers' Cooperative two older women in excellently cut clothes stood, confidence and easy authority in their bearing. A few snatches of their discussion floated on the wind to them, full of arcane jargon about whether *tillovëa* was more *entoffled* than *rellovyë*, and even if it were, was Farza the Rellovyëna-lo really going to be able to supply three dozen *inajao* in the requisite colours by the time the tradewinds began.

Cliopher was still trying to disentangle this when they reached the pair. One woman said, "Oh, hello, Kip! I didn't realize you were home. Didn't I hear you were here already this year?"

"Good afternoon, Clia," he replied, smiling. "I am attending my lord."

Clia regarded his Radiancy with a thorough and appreciative glance. "Your tailors are superb, sir. I'm Kip's cousin Clia, assessor for the Co-op."

"Charmed, I'm sure," replied his Radiancy, eyes twinkling.

The other woman said, "There's Penyë now, so we can start whenever you're ready."

Clia nodded. "I'll be right there. Oh, hello, Conju, isn't it? We met when you came on holiday with Kip that time. I seem to remember you were quite interested in how we made ahalo cloth—would you like to come see how we assess its quality? You and your, er, lord, are welcome too, Kip, of course."

Cliopher looked at his Radiancy for direction. His Radiancy regarded him thoughtfully, then turned to Conju, whose expression was wistful.

"Why don't you, if you'd like, Conju?" his Radiancy said. "If—Kip—doesn't mind, we shall walk out along that breakwater there to the lighthouse."

"Thank you, my lord," said Conju, and followed Clia inside eagerly. Cliopher fell in beside his Radiancy, directing their steps towards the long breakwater—actually part of the docking arrangements for the sea train—that formed the outer rim of Palaoa Lagoon.

They walked in silence for a few minutes. Cliopher was reviewing his family and friends' interactions with his Radiancy, uncertain whether he felt pride in their candour and independence or embarrassment at their ignorance, and whether their reciprocal exasperated fondness was love.

They turned onto the breakwater, the stone suddenly firm underfoot after the subtle vibrations of the city docks.

"You did not, I hope, have any strong desire to see the assessors at their work?"

"I am always pleased to learn new things, investigate people's specialties, but I have been within the ahalo warehouses before, my lord."

His Radiancy nodded. They were walking on smoothly fitted stone, black basalt from the farther side of Mama Ituri's Son. Here and there in the cracks were tufts of grass and flowering herbs. A light breeze played over them, and the water glittered. Commander Omo and Ser Rhodin paced along silently behind them.

At length his Radiancy said, "Your friends spoke of retirement."

"Yes, my lord."

A little ahead of them four pelicans sunning themselves lifted huge wings and flapped ponderously to the water.

"You have not mentioned the subject to me."

Cliopher watched a bright blue lizard freeze at their approach, then dart into a crack like a shadow.

"Bertie asked me when I was home last. I told him I had not thought about it, as was true."

"Then. And since then?"

"I have come to no conclusions, my lord, save that if you choose to retire yourself, that ..." He trailed off, not sure how to speak his feelings. The water to their left, on the city side, was brilliant turquoise, wavelets glittering white until bisected by the shadows of the city. The water to their right was deep blue, transparent where their own shadows touched it. Silver fish darted in and out of sight.

He tried again. "My lord, I have not yet resolved the matter in my mind."

"It seems to me that the conflict is in your heart, not your mind."

"My lord?"

His Radiancy glanced ahead to where the lighthouse gleamed, then back at the guards. "Stay here," he said to them, and, "Come," to Cliopher, who followed, curious and a little nervous.

They said nothing until they reached the lighthouse. It was a squat cone with arched windows for the glowing crystal to shine through. A stone balustrade ran along the base of the cone, with a wide rail to act as a seat; it was a popular destination for a walk. It was a bit surprising no one else was there, actually.

His Radiancy sat down facing the city and gestured for him to do likewise. Then, as his Radiancy was doing, Cliopher gazed at Gorjo City. Home.

The warehouses were to their left now, followed by the opera house with its unexpected dome. Then the three grand hotels, the Dolphin in the middle, and the sweep of buildings running through theatre and business districts towards Mama Ituri and her Son. Palace and university were both visible, their grounds brilliant strokes of green, and above them the deeper green of the Reserve at the top of the Son.

His Radiancy said, "I want to ask you a charged question. I wish you to answer me honestly, without fear of offence or hurt or disappointment—or any reprisal. But first—Cliopher, Kip, do you *wish* to retire?"

Cliopher could not help himself. He laughed. "My lord, that is not the charged question?"

"No, or not the one I was thinking." His Radiancy smiled wryly. "Cliopher, Kip, I have never seen you in your own country before, among your family, at home. I had not realized how much you missed them, how great a sacrifice it is for you to live so far away."

"My lord, my vocation is to serve."

"I have been showing you another aspect of myself this journey. I did not realize until just now that you have been showing me another aspect of yourself as well."

Cliopher didn't know what to say. They watched the city. A flock of parrots wheeled up into the sky, green and purple in the sunlight before they disappeared again.

"I am seeing Kip," his Radiancy said softly, eyes on the water, the city. "Not only quiet, competent, articulate Cliopher, not only my chief diplomat and incomparable secretary, not only the fierce defender of all the goods, big and small, in the world.—Perhaps that last is Kip, too. I have not been enough in his company to know. I have seen that Kip is beloved and desperately missed, that his absence has never become fully accepted, that his sacrifice is ongoing."

The parrots wheeled up again. Their raucous cries came faintly over the water.

"Kip, I have seen the door of freedom, and I will do whatever it takes to go through it. You ... For you the door is always open. You desire what lies beyond as deeply, as desperately, as I, and yet ... You stay."

A little shoreline bird, black and white with a bright-orange beak, darted along the stones of the breakwater, winkling its beak into the crannies as the waves slapped gently.

"I love my family," Cliopher said at last. "I love my work. There seems no way to have both. And ... I believe I have done good work for you, my lord, for the world as a whole. And for the Vangavaye-ve, little though they realize it. I know you would not force me to stay if I asked leave to go."

"No," his Radiancy said very quietly.

"My family ... sometimes I wonder if they have never desired two conflicting things at once in their lives. Surely I am not the only one whose heart says 'go' as loudly as it says 'stay'? Who must therefore choose which longing is to be fulfilled, which to be deferred or denied?"

"You have a home here."

"I have meaningful work in the Palace, my lord. And I still have dreams of what I might yet accomplish."

They watched the sunlight on the sea, the darting shoreline bird, the people passing by in the distance, the upright punctuation of Commander Omo and Ser Rhodin. Cliopher swallowed. "Also, my lord ... I have not been able—that is, Conju and Ser Rhodin and Commander Omo, there is the difference that I have a family, I have a home, and they do not, beyond your household."

He winced at his awkwardness. His Radiancy watched a line of cormorants fly low across the water before them, left to right like an augury.

"Cliopher, I intend to abdicate. I must find a successor and appoint her. I must do some magical preparations for that successor. I must also—I am the Last Emperor of Astandalas. Your friends, your family, our friends on Lesuia, they did not know who I am, they spoke of me as the 'Lord Emperor'."

"Most do, my lord," he admitted.

"My successor will not be the Emperor, will in no way inherit that role, that power—those responsibilities. But yet they will inherit a government whose structure is based on the Lord of Zunidh being also the Last Emperor of Astandalas."

"This is true, my lord."

"Now for what I had thought the more difficult and charged question. Cliopher—and I repeat, you may certainly say no. I have a better understanding now of what I am asking you to give up—to sacrifice—a while longer."

Another line of cormorants went past them, right to left this time.

"My lord?"

His Radiancy kept his gaze firmly on the water, the city skyline, the light. His face in profile was serene, benevolent, at repose; like the profile used on coins, the old Astandalan sunburst, the Zuni valiant, most of Alinor's, most of Voonra's, most of Colhélhé's.

"Let me propose it in the form of an agreement, a bargain," he murmured at last, causing Cliopher to wonder immediately how dire—and in what way—this proposal could be. It was highly unlike his Radiancy to have such difficulty.

"My lord?"

"Seven years from now is the Jubilee."

"Yes, my lord."

"I have decided to retire—abdicate my position, resign my title—however you wish to present it—on that occasion."

"Yes, my lord," Cliopher said patiently.

"I have not yet decided what form that retirement might take, save that it will not be to any sort of monastery or remote palace. I do not know if I—it may be that I will travel, see the lands whose Emperor once I was with my own eyes, see the lands beyond those borders."

Cliopher watched the light rippling on the waves. The sun was sinking noticeably westward, the colour deepening towards yellow.

"This, then, is my proposition: over those same seven years, will you undertake to revise and redesign and recreate the mundial government of Zunidh, shape it into the best form you can devise, restructure it so that is no longer dependent on the Astandalan hierarchy, so that when I hand over my throne to my successor she may look upon Zunidh from a seat firmly founded?"

Cliopher did not have to think very hard about this. "My lord, I would be honoured. It would be the crown of my life's service—"

His Radiancy smiled. "Wait until you have heard the downside, which for many would be the reward."

It did not take more than a handful of seconds for Cliopher to imagine what might be some of the conceivable downsides of *actually* recreating the world's government.

"We would have to ennoble you to start with, give you real and enforced authority. You would have to step down as my personal secretary, for there will be far too much work—even for you! We have already spoken about the ceremony and ... painful conformity to ritual and etiquette of my position. As Lord Chancellor—Cliopher, you would be required to fulfil many of the courtly, ah, performances you have managed to evade thus far."

Cliopher found he was not, after all, without ambition. It was even, perhaps, the same ambition that had taken him to Astandalas in the first place.

In those days serving the Emperor personally had been as much of a daydream as adventuring with the Red Company. But he had persevered, always persevered, because he believed that the government affected everything about life—and because he believed it was possible for the government to be good.

He watched a fishing boat of ancient design cant across the lagoon from the university marina, aiming at the channel on the other side of the lighthouse. One of the sailors waved at them as the boat passed. Cliopher waved back.

He could have this.

Or he could—

Well, what could he do for the Vangavaye-ve, for the whole world, in a position where he was *officially* in charge of the government?

I will bring home the hearth-fire of a new life for the world.

He looked sidelong at his Radiancy, who was regarding him steadily. Met the lion eyes. They were veiled, but Cliopher knew his lord's moods and minute indicators of emotion, could see that he was anxious and genuinely unsure of the answer.

Yet there could only be one.

For however much that the Vangavaye-ve called to Kip to come home, it was nevertheless the case that Cliopher Mdang was not yet ready to listen.

CHAPTER TWENTY

HIS RADIANCY GAVE CLIOPHER LEAVE to go to his sister's assembly, but asked Conju to attend him. Cliopher shrugged philosophically, put on his best outfit, and walked down the four buildings to the Town Hall just as the bells were striking eight. He was, of course, nearly the first person to arrive.

"Dear Kip, you look wonderful," his mother said, beaming, when she arrived, and took him on her arm to show off to all her cronies. He had not hitherto worn his court finery in Gorjo City, and he attracted much more attention than usual.

After a great deal of internal debate he had left the amber cowries packed away. The thought of wearing them with his court finery, where the difference in style would stand out so sharply, seemed distastefully close to boasting. He was not, really, as wealthy or as important as the gold-ringed amber cowries suggested.

And he squirmed at the thought of explaining just what he had claimed, out there on the Outer Ring, that the shell-collector had given *that* efela to him in response. He was no longer fifteen and oblivious to what people thought of his grander dreams.

"Conju couldn't come?"

"Alas, our lord required his attendance. I gave your invitation to them, but it is his—my lord's decision."

"It's not really the sort of occasion a great lord comes to," his sister said, sweeping up to them in a magnificent purple dress and the amethyst necklace—a kind of courtly efela, in his mind—that Cliopher had given her when she first became director. "I'm so pleased you're here, Kip. What a splendid outfit that is! Come meet my symphony."

He went over happily enough to the group of men and women milling around the far end of the room. They were setting up chairs and music stands—there was to be a concert, his sister explained—and greeted him warmly. He noticed that a few people frowned at his outfit, evidently trying to place the antiquated richness of the cut and material—and the red and black that was not the usual burnt umber of the Upper Secretariat.

Vinyë was called to solve some problem with the drums, leaving him in the company of the trumpet player, a cadaverous man of about his own age by the name of Hugon, who seemed to have some north-Amboloyo blood by the sharpness of his features and the grey of his eyes. "You belong to the Service, then, Sayo Kip?" he asked politely, gesturing at his outfit, his accent identifying him as Amboloyan indeed. "What is your department?"

"The Private Office," he said absently, watching his niece flirting with a violinist with Islander features and bony wrists.

Hugon raised his eyebrows. "I had not realized you were so highly placed." At Cliopher's sharp glance he added, "My elder brother was in the Ministry of Culture in Amboloyo for many years."

"What is his name? I may know him."

"He retired a few years ago, when I got the position here, but his name is Paulin Oldis."

"He was a great civil servant," Cliopher said with respect. "I had the honour of working with him over the Littleridge treaty."

Hugon's eyes sharpened. "Did you now?"

Cliopher smiled ruefully, realizing he had probably said too much, but Vinyë came floating back across to them. "Oh, are you trading stories? Kip, Hugon's brother was in the Service, too. They're from Amboloyo. Is Paulin here tonight, Hugon?"

"Yes, if I can just see him—ah! There he is, speaking with Thalia. She's the other trumpeter," he added to Cliopher.

"Probably explaining how it is utterly imperative she be *at all times* prepared to play the Imperial Salute," Vinyë said, chuckling.

"Oh?"

Hugon shook his head, amusement in his eyes but not his lean face. "Probably not. There was one occasion, when I was much younger, when I told Paulin I didn't need to learn it because there was no chance whatsoever I would ever be called upon to play it, and he read me such a lecture on the duties of the citizen I have never forgotten it. We still joke over it. Now that he's retired from the Service, I told him I would make myself forget the fanfare."

"But not really," Vinyë said.

"No, not really. You never do know."

No, you never did, Cliopher thought, as Vinyë waved Paulin over. Hugon murmured something about his trumpet and wandered off.

"Paulin, this is my brother Kip. Kip, we've been terribly disappointed that Paulin can't tell us any stories about you."

Paulin bowed formally in the court style, but when he rose his eyes were twinkling with amusement. "Vinyë, you've never mentioned your brother's full name! Of course I know Cliopher Sayo Mdang. The whole Service knows him, by reputation at least."

She half-frowned, half-laughed. "Surely you realized it was the same last name? You're not pronouncing it properly—it's Md*ang*, not M*a*don."

"The court accent finds the *a* difficult to pronounce," Cliopher murmured.

"I knew you were from the Islands," Paulin said to Cliopher, "but I didn't—I presumed you were not a close relative of the Gorjo City Mdangs—they do not boast enough about you, sir!"

Cliopher tried not to look as if he agreed. "Surely you've been in the Vangavaye-ve long enough to realize that what happens outside the Ring does not weigh heavily within it."

"Kip!"

Paulin gave Vinyë a thoughtful glance, but did not follow up. They chatted of mutual acquaintances for several minutes, interrupted by various more-distant relatives and family friends who wanted to greet Cliopher. Not a single one of them asked him anything about his work, though several mentioned his outfit; Paulin's eyebrows worked as he obviously restrained comment.

Hugon came back with his trumpet in hand, looking fatigued but in a desultory sort of way, as if it were a chronic condition he preferred to ignore. He accepted a glass of the champagne that servers had begun circulating.

Gaudenius showed up to bow very respectfully to Paulin. "Thank you for your advice, sir," he said. "My uncle gave me much the same opinion earlier today. When we spoke about the nature of the Service."

Paulin chuckled dryly. "Now that I know who your uncle is, I can tell you just to ignore me and listen to anything he has to say. There's no better player of the game than him."

"Not really," Cliopher demurred. "I do my best to stay out of the intrigues."

"What does he mean?" Gaudenius asked, eyes narrowing. "Aren't you just a secretary?"

Paulin choked. Cliopher sighed. "I'll explain later, Gaudy."

"Uncle Kip—"

But Cliopher's attention had been taken by the entrance of Conju. He went very still as Conju, enthusiastically met by Cliopher's mother, followed her across the room to where they were standing. Paulin said, "Surely that's not—"

"The Cavalier an Vilius, yes," Cliopher said quietly. "Good evening, Conju. I thought you were attending our lord?"

"I am," Conju said solemnly. "He sent me ahead to let you know he has decided to accept your mother's kind invitation."

Cliopher's mother looked delighted. "Isn't this wonderful? It will be so wonderful to meet your lord at last, Kip. He's very closemouthed about his work," she added to Paulin and Hugon.

Paulin looked as if his eyes were about to stand out from their sockets. "*Your* lord is coming *here*?"

Vinyë looked at them, frowned, and made her way over.

"It would appear so," said Cliopher, watching as Conju walked unhurriedly and without fuss to the golden throne set on a low daïs in the centre of the room—for it was the Town Hall, and every public meeting-house in the whole wide Empire held a token throne—and used a cloth to wipe down the seat. Only a few people noticed this at first, but that was enough.

"Just who *is* your lord, Uncle Kip?" Gaudy asked uncertainly, as the assembled crowd focused intently on the stranger at the throne.

Vinyë said, slowly, "He always jokes he works for the Lord Emperor ..."

Conju gave a satisfied nod and stepped off the dais to rejoin them. Cliopher swallowed against his dry mouth. "Well," he began, and faltered.

Paulin shook his head in amazement. "You are *remarkably* closemouthed, Sayo Mdang. Hugon, I do hope you've not forgotten the Imperial Salute."

"Paulin," Hugon protested, "this is hardly the time to make that joke."

"He's not," Cliopher said unsteadily, as the hall's double doors opened. Pikabe and Ato marched in and took positions on either side of the doors. They were wearing their full panoply, jewels and ostrich feathers and leopard skins and ebony-and-gold spears and all, and in the familiar room looked astoundingly magnificent.

When he was satisfied the room's attention was held, Pikabe struck the butt of his spear on the floor and cried out, "His Serene and Radiant Holiness, the Sun-on-Earth, the Lord of Rising Stars, the Last Emperor of Astandalas and Lord of Zunidh!"

Paulin poked his brother, who lifted his trumpet in a daze and played the familiar fanfare of the Imperial Salute. Cliopher's mother looked at her son with astonishment, and his nephew at his uncle with something approaching fury, but Cliopher's attention was on the door and on the figure who swept in, Commander Omo and Ser Rhodin behind him, wearing what was not full court costume but was exceedingly impressive nonetheless.

Everyone in the room went down into the full prostration. His Radiancy stepped through the doors, which Pikabe and Ato closed quietly behind him, and then said: "Rise."

Everyone rose. They watched in dead silence as his Radiancy paced ceremoniously down the centre of the room to where Cliopher stood with his mother, his sister, his nephew, and the two Oldis brothers. When his Radiancy reached the correct distance, Cliopher went down to one knee.

"Cliopher."

"My lord."

He was much surer now than he would have been a month ago of the amusement in his Radiancy's eyes. His Radiancy looked around the small grouping. "Will you present your companions, Cliopher? This lady must be your mother."

Cliopher smiled as his mother tried not to react with visible shock. "Of course, my lord. Eidora Saya Mdang, my mother. Paulin Sayo Oldis, formerly of the Ministry of Culture in Amboloyo. He was the chief attaché to the Prince of Amboloyo during the Littleridge treaty negotiations. My sister, Vinyë el Vawen Saya Mdang, the Director of the Gorjo City Symphony. Paulin's brother, Hugon, lead trumpeter of the symphony. Vinyë's son, my nephew Gaudenius."

"Ah yes," said his Radiancy, looking down on the young man. "You are the one who has contemplated following your uncle into the Service."

Gaudy swallowed hard, then realized he was supposed to bow when addressed by the Presence, and then realized he was supposed to answer. "I am, my—my lord."

"And what is your ambition?"

Gaudy straightened his shoulders and lifted his chin in unconscious bravery. "I would enter into your service, Glorious One, and surpass even my uncle's position."

His Radiancy smiled. "It is a worthy ambition. We wish you well in the examinations."

"Thank you, my lord."

"Though perhaps we should tell you, as it appears that he has not, that it would be difficult to surpass your uncle's position."

Gaudy gaped at him. Cliopher tried hard not to show the mixed emotions he was feeling.

His Radiancy spoke in a clear, carrying voice, which did not sound loud to those he was ostensibly addressing but which would be heard in every corner of the room, Cliopher well knew. "It has always been something of an idiosyncrasy that the highest position of the civil service should be called the Secretary in Chief of the Private Office of the Lords of State. It is both a mouthful and deeply uninformative, is it not? Yet it is the title given to the effectual head of our government."

His Radiancy paused, as if an idea had just now struck him, but Cliopher could see the glint in his eye and knew, just knew, it had to do with the question, and the answer, given at the Palaoa lighthouse.

"My lord," Cliopher said, unable to stop himself.

His Radiancy smiled benevolently at him, then turned and stepped onto the daïs so he could seat himself upon the throne. Pikabe and Ato swept out in unison to flank him on either side. "Come here, Cliopher."

Cliopher obeyed, of course. He knelt at the proper distance from the throne, looking up at his lord. The room was very silent.

"It has occurred to us," his Radiancy said in his court voice, "that we have been remiss in honouring the chief member of our personal household and the principal official of our government of Zunidh. While we are given to understand that this is an evening devoted to honouring the Symphony Orchestra of this city and its director, we wish to take this moment to speak forth those honours to an audience containing so many of his friends and family."

Who were going to *kill* him.

"While we might enumerate his many excellences and achievements at great length, we think it best simply to state that we are most grateful for his many years of loyalty and service, we consider him our friend, and we take this opportunity to bestow upon him the title of Lord Chancellor of Zunidh, which position he has fulfilled for many years without formal acknowledgment. You may rise, Lord Mdang."

INTERLUDE ONE

$\mathcal{A}$ $\mathcal{L}$ ETTER

MY DEAR BASIL—

It is the middle of the night, so if this letter is somewhat incoherent, I do apologize. It has been a long day.

I write you from the Dolphin Hotel—yes, our Dolphin Hotel!—at which Cousin Maius is now the manager. I think you are probably better at your innkeepering than he is, but then you are far less officious than he. He did nearly manage to refuse admittance to my lord today, which gave me much more pleasure than it probably should have.

I am writing in the middle of the night from the Dolphin because I wanted to talk to someone, and though I am, for once, in Gorjo City with my family scattered across the city around me, and indeed my closest friends from Solaara also here (a concentration—a collocation?—a *collision* of worlds that I am finding, to be honest, a bit of a challenge), I miss you.

It has been a long time, hasn't it, since we got run out of the Dolphin for not being dressed up enough for the dining room. I can't even remember why we were wearing grass skirts—I suppose you always did, and I'd just come back from that year with Buru Tovo out in the Western Ring and was almost as wild as you.

Come to think of it, I can't remember why we wanted to go *into* the dining room at the Dolphin. It's not as if either of us had any money or desire to eat at one of the big hotels.

I am meandering. I suppose that's my prerogative. I have not had a letter back from you since the Fall of Astandalas. I keep writing them, and every time the Alinorel ambassador goes home or someone new goes to the Zuni embassy there, I put my bundle of letters together in a package and give it to them with the plea that they see it sent from Nên Corovel to what they tell me is now the end of the road.

Often I fear that the reason you have never written back is the most likely one, that you did not survive the Fall. The Alinorel ambassadors I have spoken to say that nothing very much ever happens in your part of the province that they hear about. They say it has been increasingly difficult to get your honey, and so I fear ... oh, the obvious. I remember when we first came to the gate between Ysthar and Alinor, back when your road led to the capital, and we heard that incredible thrumming sound blowing down the wind towards us, that turned out to be the bees. I have never forgotten it.

I cannot quite make myself believe that these letters are unknown to you.

They disappear into the diplomats' luggage, and disappear with them across the Border between worlds, and I receive back ... silence.

Mind you, not all of the diplomats I have asked to be my courier liked me. I can think of at least two, perhaps even three, who might have ceremoniously burned my letters as soon as they got outside of the Palace simply to spite me. I'm afraid I still sometimes let my tongue get the better of me. Though I have gotten much better at that! I no longer *immediately* tell people what they're doing wrong and what they could do instead. Sometimes I am even able to not tell them directly at all, and everyone congratulates me on my splendid tact.

Oh, gods, I was so horribly obnoxious.

Basil, I miss you. Do the letters sit somewhere because someone has stopped sending them on? Do they gather dust in a post office? Are they ashes in the wind? Are you?

After the Fall I wrote letter after letter home to Gorjo City. When I finally followed them I discovered out of dozens—scores—even a hundred?—one had made it. One.

And so I keep writing you, in case.

I am possibly a little drunk.

That doesn't happen very often, either. I don't particularly like being drunk, and I have so many state secrets to keep to myself. (Does that make me sound like I am bragging? I am sorry. I don't mean to. I know I used to be able to tell you exactly what I was thinking, knowing you would understand when I wanted to share a triumph, when I wanted to share an embarrassment, when I simply needed to say that my family—our family—is utterly infuriating ...)

Basil, I am sitting in a bedroom in the ducal suite at the Dolphin Hotel, across the city from my own bed in my mother's house, looking out at the moonlight over the Bay of the Waters.

Last week there was an eclipse of the Moon and I saw a wonder I do not even know how to begin to describe. And then ... and then ... I wish I could be sure no one was reading this! I was less worried when there was an

Imperial Department of Censorship. I used to have the office next to them; we sometimes ate lunch together. I have never met anyone who did less work than they did, and I have spent my entire career reforming the Imperial Bureaucratic Service.

You will laugh and, if you receive this, if you have received any of these, if you can write back—do write back, care of the Ambassador of Zunidh in Nên Corovel, who is presently Lady Hnila, who may hate me with an abiding passion—I'm not totally sure of that, but I might have made an enemy of her when I proposed that Haion City, whose prince is her cousin, be dissolved as an administrative province and folded in with the rest of the Jilkano principalities (dear lord, I was angry that day)—and I have lost track of my sentence. And my thought, apparently.

Oh, Basil, I miss you. Vinyë had a concert to honour her being director. Gaudy wants to apply for the Service. My mama has only asked twice this holiday (which is not actually a holiday of mine; I am attending my lord) when I will be coming home.

Last holiday Bertie asked me when I was going to retire—and this time I told him I was five years behind him.

I have many more things to tell you but I am not sure I can, yet, for some that haven't been officially announced, and a few points are too close to my heart to set down, even to you. If I knew for certain you were not reading them, and this was nothing more than an elaborate kind of personal diary—

No. I would still be worried about snoops opening it. I have always wished for that little gift at magic you had … not that it ever helped us much when we ran wild through the city playing at our ancestors!

That's right—we wanted the conch shell on the wall of the Dolphin's dining room—why on earth did we think we could just walk in and take it? Two boys in grass skirts and feathers singing the *Lays of the Wide Seas*, wanting to pretend to be the Paramount Chief greeting Aurelius Magnus when the Emperor came out of the sunrise asking the Islanders to join with him—

Oh, that was long ago.

I still know the dances. I have not forgotten all of who I am, far away from home as I am. I hope you have taught them to your children, children of Alinor though they are. They are descendants of the Wayfinders who crossed the Wide Seas, too, and as I have written in other letters you may or may not have received, you never know when those songs will be the ones to cheer your heart through the dark times and guide you through the stormy seas.

I should probably go to sleep. I don't know what time it is … I am so accustomed to the Palace bells, it seems so strange not to hear them chiming through the night.

I am going back to the Palace tomorrow. But this time, for the first time, there is an end date. Five years. Or maybe it's six. Seven to the Jubilee, anyway.

There is so much more I should like to write to you, but … not tonight. Tonight is for me to say, Basil, I wish you were here so I could tell you all these things in person. I would have liked you to have been there to meet my lord today when Bertie and Ghilly and Toucan did. Though you will probably be glad to know they teased me enough about the exams almost to make up for you.

—Kip

—Oh. The reason I am sitting drunk in the ducal suite of the Dolphin Hotel is that I was made the Lord Chancellor of Zunidh today—yesterday. My mother is never going to forgive me.

Volume Two

THE NOBODY
FROM THE ISLANDS

CHAPTER TWENTY-ONE

"BUT WHY DID YOU NEVER *tell* us?" his mother asked, not for the first time.

It was the next morning. He was only now beginning to grasp what his Radiancy had done. The rest of the assembly had passed in something of a blur, with endless congratulations and belatedly the concert and honour given Vinyë. His Radiancy had finally decided to leave at eleven o'clock, and Cliopher had gone with him, not at all sure what to say and guessing that his Radiancy knew perfectly well what was going through his mind.

His Radiancy had granted his permission for the filial visit this morning with a bright gleam in his eye. When Cliopher descended, head aching from the wine he had foolishly decided would be a good idea, Maius had waved from across the hotel lobby, but made no effort to come over. Cliopher was grimly certain that would change by the time he returned that afternoon.

"I'm so sorry to have upstaged your evening," he said to Vinyë, who sat beside him. "I can only assure you it was not my intention."

"Oh, Kip, we never get to see what people from your work think of you. There will be other anniversaries for me. There will never be another time when the Sun-on-Earth decides to make you his Lord Chancellor."

Cliopher set his coffee cup down again. "I don't know what he was thinking."

Though of course he *did*. He had just not thought through what 'you will have to be ennobled' *meant*.

There was a knock on the front door, which Leona went to answer. She came back up a little doubtfully. "It's Paulin and Hugon, Grandmama," she announced. "Shall I tell them to go?"

"No, let them come," his mother said. "Vinyë will want to see Hugon."

Vinyë grinned at Cliopher. "And Mama will want to hear what Paulin has to say. Kip, you brute, you're not getting away so easily. Gaudy, fetch more cups."

Paulin and Hugon came up. They bowed to Eidora—and to Cliopher. "Lord Mdang," Paulin said gravely, using the correct pronunciation. "Permit me to offer my congratulations again."

Cliopher sighed. "Thank you, Sayo Oldis."

"Come sit down, Paulin, and tell us all about our Kip's actual job. It seemed so straightforward and so boring, because all he would do was joke about it, but obviously he has been misleading us about a few things."

"I've never lied to you," Cliopher retorted, hurt.

"You just never sat down and explained that you're the head of the Imperial Service?" Paulin said, chuckling and accepting a cup of coffee from Gaudenius, who appeared torn between fury and awe at his uncle. "Lord Mdang—"

"Cliopher," said Cliopher, vehemently.

Paulin bowed in his seat with a suspicious twinkle in his eyes. "I am honoured by your condescension. Your son Cliopher, ma'am, has aroused the entire Palace's admiration for his unbending probity combined with his great bravery in being his Radiancy's personal secretary. He bears the brunt in both directions, you know: everything gets passed *up* to him from below, and he must be the one passing his Radiancy's decrees *down* to everyone. It is not always an enviable position."

"It's not quite like that," Cliopher said, but no one was listening to him.

"He is the most important man in the government below his Radiancy himself, you know."

He tried not to grind his teeth. "His Radiancy has said so."

"And so it must be true. It is: you are the final arbiter of all that goes before his Radiancy. If you decide not to pass something to him, he does not see it. If that is not power, I do not know what is."

Cliopher set his cup down with sudden fury. "I would *never*—"

Paulin held up his hand hastily. "No one has ever suggested it! Indeed, all the Palace knows you cannot be bribed, and mourns the fact that his Radiancy found an incorruptible secretary at last. Your predecessors were nowhere near as honourable ... which is probably why you have been Secretary in Chief for as long as you have, and why, indeed, the government of the world is in as good a state as it is. He oversaw the overhauling of the examination system," he added to Gaudy, who appeared to be less furious and more awestruck now.

"You said it was a different department," Vinyë said.

"It is."

"The heads of each ministry report to the Private Office," Paulin explained. "I was only a department head, so I did not report directly to him, but I remember the howls when he discovered the bribery scandal in the Department of Examinations. He fired the entire Upper Secretariat that year."

His family were all staring at him as if he had grown another head. Cliopher sighed again.

Paulin grinned. "And then there was the time when that conspiracy to fix the election results in Kavanduru was discovered, and his Radiancy sent him to apprehend the conspirators. People still talk about how he told the Prince of Kavanduru that he was a disgrace to his name, his rank, and his people, and that unless he begged with the most extreme remorse he would be facing the executioner."

Cliopher winced. "I was merely repeating the words I was given to say."

"Which you did with the greatest aplomb, I have been told, and struck a terror into the hearts of anyone who had ever tried to do you wrong. Everyone knows you have the ear of the Radiancy."

"I beg your—"

"Probably because you do not misuse that honour," Paulin went on affably. "Don't look at me like that, sir. His Radiancy does not shower titles and responsibilities without reason."

"Oh, there's a knock," Leona said, and jumped up to get it. She paused in the doorway. "You won't say anything interesting while I'm gone, will you?"

"We'll try not to," Cliopher said dourly.

She returned very quickly with a man Cliopher was delighted, if surprised, to see. "Quintus!" he said, getting up to greet this cousin, who ran a large shipping company. "I have not seen you this age. I didn't see your ship yesterday?"

Quintus embraced him. "Your holidays always seem to coincide with my outbound voyages." He greeted the rest of the room, evidently already acquainted with Paulin and Hugon. "I arrived this morning and might have missed you this time, except that the town is abuzz with rumours about you. Is it really true that the Lord Emperor is here and made you his Lord Chancellor last night? No one can believe it. They all think it must have been a dream."

"One which we all are sharing," Cliopher's mother said, smiling at Cliopher to show he was forgiven. More or less. The door-bell clanked loudly. "Oh, Leona, go and get the door again, will you?"

"Must I? Really you won't talk about anything interesting?"

"We're just going over the same points again and again," Cliopher said. "Yes, Quintus, his Radiancy has done me that honour."

"Well!" declared Quintus, and sat staring at him. Everyone else started talking again, trying to fill him in on how Cliopher only ever joked about his position, which reproaches Cliopher told himself ruefully he deserved.

Except—they never *did* ask him for details.

Leona's shriek cut through the babble. They all looked at Cliopher, as if this were his fault, or at least something he should understand. Then Leona's voice came shrilly up the stairs and through the open door: "I am so sorry, my lord, er, your Majesty, please come upstairs, sire."

"'My lord' is quite sufficient," came the familiar amused voice, followed by the sound of numerous feet on the stairs.

This time when everyone looked at him Cliopher said, "It appears the Lord of Rising Stars has deigned to honour this house."

"Kip!" cried his mother, and everyone hastily stood up as Leona entered, eyes round and staring, followed by Zerafin and Varro to stand at the door, followed by Ser Rhodin and Commander Omo, followed at last by the Sun-on-Earth, who was smiling.

Everyone did as deep an obeisance as the furniture permitted.

"You may rise," his Radiancy said, still smiling genially. He walked several steps over to Eidora, who gazed up at him in consternation. "Forgive us this unexpected intrusion, ma'am," he said, with the same blazing charm he had shown the various villagers at and around Navikiani on Lesuia. "I wished to speak with you at greater length and with less formality than last evening permitted."

"My house is your house, my Emperor," Eidora said promptly, although Cliopher noted that his mother's eyes were not exactly warm. "Will you have coffee, sire?"

"Thank you," his Radiancy said, and sat down in the chair beside her. Cliopher looked automatically for Conju, to see him enter quietly, take a deep breath, and then release it again without saying anything. Cliopher felt for him. His Radiancy could very easily and with far more propriety have summoned Eidora to the hotel.

For a moment no one said anything, all staring at his Radiancy breathlessly instead, then Aunt Oura's granddaughter Dora came wandering in, wiping her eyes sleepily and dragging a blanket behind her. She looked curiously up (and up) at Varro by the door, then marched determinedly over to Cliopher. "Cousin Kip!" she said, embracing his knees fiercely. He picked her up automatically and set her so she could see the room, at which point she noticed his Radiancy.

"My cousin Dora, my lord," he said, and then closed his eyes at the gaffe. It was not, alas, the first time he had flubbed an introduction.

"You do have a remarkable number of cousins," his Radiancy murmured.

Dora was staring at his Radiancy. "You look like the man on the money."

His Radiancy smiled. "I am."

"What's your name?"

"*Dora*," Aunt Oura whispered.

His Radiancy was still smiling. "My name is Artorin Damara."

"That's a long name," she said, evidently approving of this fact. "Where are you from?"

"Originally from Damara," he replied solemnly, "but I have lived most of my life in Solaara."

"Do you work with Cousin Kip?"

Cliopher closed his eyes briefly, trying not to clutch Dora into silence. He opened his eyes again to see the lion gaze trained severely on his five-year-old cousin. "I do indeed. What of you? Where do you work?"

She giggled. "I'm too little to work, silly."

It was almost certain, Cliopher thought, that no one had ever, ever, *ever* called his Radiancy that before.

His Radiancy chuckled. "My mistake! You must be a big enough girl to be going to school, though?"

"I start next month," she said. "Cousin Kip says that when I'm big enough I can come visit him in Solaara and see the Palace."

"What a good idea!" His Radiancy glanced around the room, taking in the faces staring owl-eyed at him. "Cliopher will be very busy over the coming few years as we prepare for the transition of government, and it would be good if his family were to come visit him. None of you have, I believe? Certainly he has never asked for time off to show you the sights."

There was a very definitely embarrassed silence. Cliopher wondered if his Radiancy had any idea of how long, or how expensive, the journey from Gorjo City to Solaara was when one was not given the use of an imperial sky ship. He wasn't sure how he could frame that comment without being totally boorish, however, and he tried not to sigh at the embarrassment and hurt in his family's eyes. He did not *blame* them for not coming.

"Can we go on a flying ship?" Dora asked excitedly.

"Oh, I expect that could be arranged," said his Radiancy casually.

Dora beamed. "That would be brilliant. Cousin Kip, did you hear what he said?"

"Yes, I did," said Cliopher. "Thank you, my lord."

After that, of course, it was hard to be quite so formal, and after perhaps a further three minutes of edge-of-the-seat behaviour his Radiancy managed to draw Quintus and Oura into a conversation about just how many Mdangs there were, and Dora wriggled off to go sit with Leona, and Cliopher sighed in relief and went to introduce Commander Omo and Ser Rhodin to Vinyë and Hugon. His mother, he noticed a few minutes later, was sitting watching his Radiancy with a determinedly blank expression on her face.

Cliopher was just about to go over to her when footsteps on the stair heralded yet another arrival. From his position he could see out the open door to the stairs, and saw yet another cousin bounding merrily up. Cliopher nodded reassuringly to Varro and Zerafin, who accordingly did not thrust their spears into Zemius' face when he flung himself through the door.

"Good gracious, Kip!" he cried, striding up to give him a fierce embrace. "They are saying the most remarkable things about you in town today. I came down from the university and every third person was talking about you. The general consensus is that there must have been a collective hallucination at the Town Hall last night, unless His Serene and Radiant Holiness the Last Emperor really did make you the Lord Chancellor of Zunidh last night? What on earth happened to start that rumour?"

His tone was light and teasing, and he grinned at Cliopher without any fear at all that this rumour might be true.

"Well," began Cliopher, for what felt like the fifteenth time, but before he got any further Zemius looked past his shoulder to share the joke with the rest of the room, and his gaze fell on His Serene and Radiant Holiness the Last Emperor.

"The Emperor," he said weakly, and fainted.

CHAPTER TWENTY-TWO

"REALLY, ZEM," CLIOPHER SAID A few minutes later, when his cousin had come round and was trying not to die of mortification, "what possessed you to faint?"

They were in the next room over, whither his Radiancy had suggested Cliopher take Zemius in order to revive him. Cliopher dreaded what conversation his Radiancy wanted to have without him present, but there was an order couched in the suggestion, and so he obeyed.

"Don't even, Kip. What possessed you to bring the *Lord Emperor* here?"

"I didn't, his Radiancy showed up on his own."

Zemius opened his eyes to glare at him. "That is entirely absurd. What is he doing here?"

"His Radiancy came to talk to my mother, as best as I can make out."

"Did he really make you the Lord Chancellor last night?"

"He did."

"You sound very glum for a person who has just been ennobled."

Cliopher winced. "We should go back in so I can present you."

Zemius shook his head in wonder mixed with chagrin. "I have never imagined outside of my wildest pipe-dreams that I would one day be presented to the Glorious One."

And whose fault was that?

"And then to *faint* ..."

"You always were a lightweight, Zem."

"Kip, Aunt Moula sacrifices pigeons to him."

They went back in so that Zemius could make his obeisance before the Presence. "My cousin Zemius Dominus Mdang, my lord," Cliopher announced. "Zemius is a professor of Zuni history at the University of the Vangavaye-ve."

"Is he indeed?" his Radiancy said. "Rise, Domine. What is your special field?"

For a brief moment Zemius looked as if he had entered the realm of terror and had entirely forgotten his life's work. Then he managed, "The history of the lords magi, Glorious One."

His Radiancy looked at Cliopher with an inscrutable expression. Cliopher bowed slightly, not having any idea what his Radiancy meant by the look. His Radiancy smiled slightly and began to quiz the hapless Zemius on his research.

Cliopher circled around to where his mother stood next to the coffee cups. "Mama," he said quietly, putting his arm around her. "Are you all right?"

She looked at him with narrowed eyes. "He is the lord you have written of all these years?"

He swallowed and nodded.

"And you never insisted. Not once. No matter how much we teased you about your job."

He did not quite understand her tone. *Should* he have insisted?

He remembered too many scolds for getting a swollen head to think that was what she meant.

He thought of all the letters telling him to give up and come home. The comments that he had missed this or that or the other important celebration or festival or moment in his family's lives. He had come for as many of his family's great events as possible—weddings and significant appointments and other triumphs—but none of that made up, he had always known, for all the daily interactions that held together a family, a community, a culture.

No matter that they were descendants of the Wayfinders who had crossed and re-crossed the Wide Seas; his ancestors had taken their families with them on their voyages.

He smiled at her, the polite courtly smile that he knew said nothing, because if he spoke just then he would erupt with twenty years of suppressed resentment that nothing he accomplished—no, not though he became Lord Chancellor of the world!—ever made up for the fact that he had left.

Quintus spent ten months of the year sailing his ship to Nijan and half the southern islands, but his house was in Tahivoa. For all Cliopher knew his cousin had paramours (or even wives) in every port; but that did not stop anyone from considering him a full and respected part of the Mdang family. That extra month and the house made all the difference, apparently.

His mother lifted her chin to gesture across the room. "Should we go rescue Zemius?"

Cliopher collected himself, as if he were in some committee room with an unknown dynamic among its members. He spoke calmly. "One does not interrupt his Radiancy, Mama."

She cast him a startled glance. Cliopher shrugged. He did wander over closer to where his Radiancy was still grilling Zemius on his research. Cliopher listened desultorily for a moment, then realized what they were talking about and why.

"Your Radiancy's attainment to the lordship of Zunidh was unusual, indeed, but not entirely unprecedented."

"How not? No other Emperors of Astandalas took upon themselves the lesser mantle."

"The Emperor Aurelius Magnus did briefly take upon himself the crown of Ysthar after the death of the Lord Mirshave, my lord, during the wars with the Tanteyr," Zemius replied, warming to the subject. "However, that was not what I meant, Glorious One. In the old tradition, when it came time for the Lord of Zunidh to consider his succession, there was a certain series of spells to be performed that were intended to draw him to that likely successor, and then he went questing to find him. On two occasions, of which your Radiancy's accession was of course one, the successor was present in the very near vicinity of the sitting lord magus, and therefore the physical portion of the quest was unnecessary."

Cliopher met Conju's eyes. He wondered what his own expression revealed, and tried hard to govern it.

His Radiancy frowned. "Did Lady Jivane perform this spell?"

"She did, Glorious One," Zemius said, "in the dark days of your Radiancy's, er, indisposition."

His Radiancy turned to frown at Ludvic Omo, who said, "I am sorry, my lord, but I was a very junior guard at the time."

"Yes, given the unenviable duty of standing watch over my bier," his Radiancy replied dryly. "I wonder if that spell is what woke me ... I have wondered. Have you written on this topic, domine? I should like to read further on it."

Zemius bowed deeply. "I have written a monograph, *The Succession of the Lords Magi of Zunidh from Ialo to*, er, *Artorin Damara*, which was published out of the Universities of the Wide Sea Press three years ago, Glorious One."

"Splendid. There will be a copy I can get from the Imperial Library, in that case."

"That's not a lending library," Zemius said automatically, then looked deeply mortified when his Radiancy raised his eyebrows at him. "Of course that does not apply to your Radiancy, Glorious One."

"No, it does not."

"I believe I have a copy here, my lord," Aunt Oura volunteered, into the strained silence. "I'll go fetch it, shall I?"

"Thank you," said his Radiancy. He glanced amiably around the fascinated room as Aunt Oura extricated herself from the corner. She let go of Dora as she did so, who came bounding over to stand next to his Radiancy.

"Will you pick me up?"

"I'm sorry," he said, still amiably, "but that's not allowed."

She frowned, but it must have been as clear to her as everyone else that that was a definite *no*. Varro and Zerafin were standing very alert, though obviously unwilling to harm a child. Commander Omo extricated himself from his conversational group to stand next to his Radiancy.

"Why not?"

His Radiancy looked down at her. "It's the custom, child."

"Like for the statues in the temple?"

"Very like that, indeed."

Dora brightened with ghoulish interest. "Would I be hit by lightning if I tried to touch you? That happened to someone who tried to steal the statue from the Sea Temple. He was all smoke afterwards. It smelled like a pig roast."

His Radiancy visibly tried not to flinch. "I should hope not," he said after a moment, "but it's probably better not to tempt matters."

It was painfully obvious when Dora decided on another tack, that of looking winsome. "Is it Sayo Dam—Dam—"

"Damara," his Radiancy supplied, as various people in the room tried not to exclaim in horror. "No, it's—it's—it's Lord Artorin."

Cliopher noted the hesitation, and wondered with a small internal shock whether his Radiancy had ever introduced himself before.

"Lord Artorin," she said, nodding with a gesture very like her grandmother's. "I like your outfit, sir. What kind of yellow is that?"

"It's called Imperial Yellow," his Radiancy replied, brushing his hand down his silk outer robe. The yellow was familiar to Cliopher after so long in his service, but it was a remarkable colour, a clear rich yellow at heart with shimmering falls to gold and bronze and white shot through it. It was so familiar he had not even noticed that his Radiancy was wearing it rather than the silver of a priest-wizard.

"It's very pretty," Dora said, peering at it. She glared at Commander Omo when he frowned sternly down at her. She put her hands ostentatiously behind her back. "I've never seen it before."

"You wouldn't have. I'm the only one allowed to wear it."

"Where does it come from?"

"It's made to a very old recipe that requires ingredients from all the worlds of the old Empire. It represents the symbolic union under the Emperor."

"What does symbolic mean?"

"It's one thing that represents something else. Like a letter represents a sound."

Dora gazed at him owlishly. "Is it your favourite colour?"

There was a pause. Cliopher could see his Radiancy adjusting. Then his Radiancy smiled. "No, I like red better."

"What kind of red?"

"Scarlet," he replied promptly. "What's your favourite colour?"

"Blue. Kivi blue."

"Kivi blue? And what is that?"

She stared at him in such astonishment that several people could not quite hide their smiles. "Kivi! Kivi and the Koala Kids! Don't you have them in Solaara? Cousin Kip, you must have them in Solaara!"

"I believe they're a toy, my lord," Cliopher supplied, looking across at his mother, who nodded.

"Ah! Alas, Sayina Dora, I'm afraid I don't have any."

Dora made what was, for her, a grand gesture of generosity. "You can come see mine, if you like, Lord Artorin. I have *nearly* the whole collection. I'm just missing two. Which Grandma says I might get when I start school, if I'm a good girl. But I have more than Mindi *and* Zaia."

"Oh, well, one ought hardly reject the honour of an invitation to see a connoisseur's collection, ought one?" his Radiancy said, smiling, and stood up. "Shall we, then, Sayina Dora?"

"Come this way!" she cried, and ran out of the room, followed more slowly by his Radiancy. Varro and Zerafin swept out after him, leaving the rest of the roomful of people to stare at each other in consternation and amazement.

The silence was broken by Aunt Oura's return, holding Zemius' book triumphantly. "I'm sorry that took me so long to find, my lord," she began, and then faltered when she discovered the noticeable lack of Emperor in the room. "Where did ..."

"His Radiancy has gone to look at Dora's Koala Kids collection," Cliopher said blandly, catching Conju's furious eye as he did. "Don't look like that, Conju. Think of what we will be doing when we get back to the Palace."

"Not looking at children's toys."

"Most likely not, no."

"This is all your fault," Conju said with a sudden access of annoyance to Commander Omo. "Suggesting his Radiancy retire, indeed!"

Commander Omo nodded phlegmatically. "His Radiancy has devoted his considerably long life to his Empire and to Zunidh."

"And now he knows there is a traditional, if apparently lapsed, method for the lord magus of Zunidh to find his heir," Cliopher said, taking Zemius' book from Aunt Oura. "Tell us, Zem, is there anything we should know about this method?"

"You don't mean to say that the Glorious One will be following it, do you?" Zemius asked in disbelief. "I thought he was merely being polite. No one but me thinks that Lady Jivane actually followed it—generally people think that it was chance or politics that led the lords magi to their successors."

"I am sure he was interested in your studies, but yes, I expect that his Radiancy will probably be quite happy to modify his original plans to make use of these. He is very aware of the importance of custom and tradition."

Zemius swallowed. "If there is no heir in the immediate vicinity of the sitting lord magus, the tradition was that the lord go questing. Alone. The custom seems to descend from the old vision quests of the Eilmanius shamans, which of course is where the first Lady of Zunidh was from. The ancient custom was that the lord magus perform the ritual spell and then set out on his quest with only the barest minimum of equipment. The lists and references are in the appendix," he added dolefully. "I have done extensive research, Kip, that is the custom. I didn't make it up."

"His Radiancy has always fulfilled all expected customary requirements," Cliopher said with a sigh, all too able to imagine the work that would land on his shoulders as a result of this discovery. He was equally able to imagine his Radiancy's joy at the prospect of setting off on a quest—a quest, of all things!—out of a book of fables. He twitched his mouth into his court expression so as not to give away either his amusement at the thought or the stab of envy that he would not get to accompany him on it. "I'm sure he will feel it incumbent on himself to do this one as well."

Conju glared at him. "Cliopher!"

"We shall just have to do our best to make sure his—"

"Look sharp," Ser Rhodin said from the door. Cliopher shut his mouth and rose to bow again as his Radiancy re-entered. Dora was prattling eagerly about the Koala Kids.

"They certainly sound very entertaining," his Radiancy said. "Thank you for showing me your collection. Now run along, child."

Dora grinned and went over to be picked up by her uncle Quintus, who gazed from her to his Radiancy in wonder.

"My aunt Oura has brought the book, my lord," Cliopher said as his Radiancy sat down next to his mother again and looked expectantly at him.

"Very good. Now, Domine Zemius, it is our intention to retire at the coming Grand Jubilee. We had been developing our plans accordingly, but the addition of your information, though most welcome, will naturally require a modification of those plans. We shall therefore read your book during our return voyage to Solaara, after which we will no doubt have some questions."

His Radiancy paused there. Zemius said nervously, "I am entirely at your Radiancy's disposal."

"We are gratified to hear it. Lord Mdang, at which point will it be most useful to have your cousin's advice?"

Cliopher blinked at the new address, and tried to move his thoughts back to life in the Palace. "My lord, there remain yet two weeks of the Little Session before the resumption of court."

His Radiancy nodded. "At which point we shall be making our formal announcements, and then you will be fully occupied in developing the plan for the transition of government to our successor."

"Very good my lord," said Cliopher, as there was nothing else to say. He bowed for good measure. The glint of humour in his Radiancy's eye was rather terrifying, he realized, when combined with the unexpected resumption of the formal plural.

"We shall send the sky ship for you immediately on our return," his Radiancy declared to Zemius. "Lord Mdang will arrange matters."

"I hear and obey," said Zemius, who also had nothing else to say, but who did go down to his knees at the honour given him.

His Radiancy nodded decisively. "We have heard from Captain Diogen. The *Eastern Wonder* will be sailing at sunset. We shall therefore bid you farewell, madam, and look to see you in perhaps two years' time. By then our new Lord Chancellor should have his preparations well in hand."

His Radiancy stood up, followed hastily by everyone else, who then shuffled around awkwardly before Cliopher could make a gesture at Zemius, who gratefully sank down into the full obeisance again. Everyone else followed

suit, his Radiancy gave them a formal blessing, and in very short order Cliopher found himself standing outside the house of his family with his mind in
a considerable whirl.

"There is a bookstore just down the way," his Radiancy said; "we saw it
on our arrival. While Elish and Oginu go for the litter we shall wait there, and
you may return and make your proper farewells to your family."

"Thank you, my lord."

"Will half an hour be sufficient?"

Cliopher bowed in agreement and returned inside, where his family were
all jostling for room at the window. He stopped in the doorway to watch
them for a moment, feeling all the surreality of the experience, listening to
them murmur excitably about the impossibilities of what had just happened.

Gaudenius saw him first, ducking away from the window to dash tears
from his eyes. "Uncle Kip!" he said.

Cliopher was immediately surrounded and half-suffocated with love and
questions and the repeated exclamations of how extraordinary, in all senses of
the word, was the Glorious One. Zemius rather quaveringly asked what he
should bring with him.

"Whatever notes you need to explain your research about the succession
of the lords magi," Cliopher said. "Your best formal robes."

"We're not very formal here, you know," Zemius said anxiously.

"I do know," Cliopher said dryly, and everyone laughed as the tension
broke. "Zem, bring your best, and when you come to the Palace I'll make
sure you have appropriate clothing made up. I'm not sure if his Radiancy
intends for you to be presented at court, so you may not need full finery, just
what is appropriate to a private audience."

"The Glorious One is not nearly so distant as I had imagined."

"That was the least formal I have ever seen his Radiancy," Cliopher said,
although that was not quite true. "It will be quite different in the Palace. But
do not work yourself into a fret—you have been invited by his Radiancy
himself, and he is not capricious."

Zemius gulped. "When will the ship come back?"

"It is three days' journey from here to Solaara. I'm not sure if there needs
to be a break or not—so be prepared for either the sixth or the seventh day.
Captain Diogen is a good man, he will treat you well."

"And you are his Radiancy's private secretary." Zemius shook his head. "I
still cannot believe you let us think you were joking the whole time!"

"Believe me, I am reaping the consequences," Cliopher replied.

Everyone laughed again. His mother said, "His Radiancy took great pains to tell us why he honours your modesty, Kip, but I think he was slightly miffed."

Cliopher knew his Radiancy was not the only one. He opened his mouth, but was forestalled by Quintus' chuckle.

"Let his Radiancy be miffed with everyone, if it means he hands out titles. Good heavens, Kip, you're the Lord Chancellor of Zunidh now! How will we know you?"

He smiled lightly, cheerfully. "By the hat."

"But we must bow and scrape and say 'my lord' now, no?"

"I think not."

They talked a few minutes longer before Cliopher realized reluctantly his half-hour was nearly up. "I must go," he said at last. "His Radiancy has done me—done us all—great honour today, and I must not keep him waiting."

That started off another round of fond farewells, weeping, embraces, kisses, and general admonitions ranging from "don't forget to write now" to "don't forget to practice your oboe." At the end, Cliopher found his sleeve tugged by his nephew. He turned aside from his aunts to speak more privately with him in the corner.

"Uncle Kip, will this change things for me? I don't want …"

"You don't want to get in on my account, do you?" Cliopher supplied when Gaudy trailed off. "Of course you don't. Fortunately you have a different surname from me; no one needs to know we are so closely related until we choose to tell them."

"You won't tell anyone?"

Cliopher laughed. "The internal hierarchy of the Imperial Service is complicated, and I'm not sure what my new title will do for it. I am officially the head of the Service, though as I do act as his Radiancy's personal secretary my deputy, Kiri Kalikiri, is primarily responsible for the daily activities of the Offices of State. She is the one most reports go through first. I only deal directly with the most egregious problems."

"Like widespread bribery, corruption, and insider trading," Gaudy said. At Cliopher's raised eyebrows, he added, "Paulin told me some more stories."

Cliopher coughed. "Well, yes, that sort of thing requires official attention. Anyhow, my portfolio is focused on what comes before his Radiancy. I rarely even speak to civil servants outside the State Departments unless something has gone awry. If I were to suggest you be hired by someone, that would be one thing, but as it is no one is very likely to connect you with me."

Paulin, attention caught by his name, snorted softly. "Once you're out of the pages, you have to be very high up in the Service before you even *see* Sayo Mdang, dear boy. Lord Mdang, my apologies."

"That's because I go to court as little as possible." He sighed. "I'll be going more often now, I suspect. Gaudy, do your best on the examinations. Once you're in, as I told you, all the new-passed civil servants come before his Radiancy to swear their oaths of loyalty and service."

"Before you, you mean," Paulin said. "You're the Hands of the Emperor."

Cliopher frowned at him. "After that there'll be a year or so as a page. I'll write you, Gaudy—I really must go now—I must attend my lord."

His mother shook her head. "How many times you have said that in your letters, Kip."

But Vinyë, as she escorted him down to the front door, said softly: "You always read in Ystharian novels about the loyal servants who devote their lives to their noble masters. But it's always from the perspective of the masters. You forget that the loyal and devoted servants must have come from somewhere …"

He clasped her hands tightly in his. "Seven more years, Vinyë. That's all."

She smiled sadly, eyes brilliant. "Take care of yourself, Kip. We want you to come home."

"Seven years," he repeated, but she shook her head and withdrew her hand, and, once again, he left.

CHAPTER TWENTY-THREE

THE JOURNEY UP TO THE sky ship was slow. His Radiancy had acquired a litter, from the town storehouse as best Cliopher could gather, which four of the guards carried, leaving Commander Omo, Ser Rhodin, Varro, and Pikabe—the latter two on account of their being the tallest and shortest of the guards—to stand at each of the four corners. Conju and Cliopher walked behind, watching the way people turned, saw the Imperial Guards in full panoply, the black-skinned man in Imperial Yellow within the litter, and dropped down into the formal obeisance.

Before them, the regular noise of the city; behind them, cheering; and around them the wave of silent obeisances as the litter passed. His Radiancy had retreated into his formal posture and expression, smiling benevolently and making gestures of blessing upon his people. He looked exactly like the state portrait commonly used in Vangavayen schools, undoubtedly to everyone's great gratification.

They reached the sky ship without any incident beyond adoration. Captain Diogen waited at the foot of the dock, openly relieved that he did not need to pretend his passenger was anything other than what he was. He went down on his face as soon as the litter approached.

"My ship is yours, Glorious One," he said.

His Radiancy said all the courteous phrases that the captain could hold in his heart ever after. The baggage had been sent ahead from the hotel and was, it appeared, already loaded, and so they went in to take their places. His Radiancy gave them leave to spend the hour remaining privately. Cliopher sat in his cabin looking at the pile of dispatch cases the captain had brought him and wondered how long he could go before the dream dissipated and real life began again.

His Radiancy sent Pikabe to summon Cliopher to the Sun Cabin just before the ship sailed. He was sitting on the balcony, looking out over the city and the Bay of the Waters and the curve of the Outer Ring beyond, and appeared slightly melancholy. Conju brought in coffee and then departed on silent feet, no doubt to sit with his back to the porthole in the main cabin and pretend firmly they were not heading several thousand feet up into the sky.

"This has been quite the holiday," his Radiancy said, not taking his eyes from the view.

"Yes, my lord."

Far distant came the cries of the ship's crew as they unfurled the sails and readied the ship. She rocked slightly and began to tug at her lines as the Light came into full influence. The network of Lights, providing near-immediate communication and letter-sending and the anchoring routes of the sky ships and who knew what other arcane influences, was one of his Radiancy's great works of magic.

The last of his real projects, his Radiancy had described them, Cliopher remembered suddenly. *If I had realized I could retire, I should have done so after the Lights. Everything since then has been make-work, one way or another.*

"I hope you are not aggrieved that I gave you your title so soon. I am not certain if you are happy that I did so in front of your family, or angry."

"My lord, I could never be angry with you."

"You speak with a courtier's tongue, Cliopher."

There was a soft thump as the lines were cast off, and then with only the faintest jar the sails turned to the wind and the ship was aloft. They watched the land fall away behind them. As Gorjo City disappeared behind the Outer Ring mountains Cliopher said, "My lord, may I speak very frankly?"

His Radiancy turned the lion gaze on him, holding his eyes for a long moment. Cliopher felt his power like a huge reservoir behind the dam of his will.

"Yes."

Cliopher took a deep breath. They were almost as alone as they had been sitting on that sandbar, the honour guards having been set at the cabin door. He gathered his words together carefully, knowing that the opportunity thus presented him would never come again if he did not take it now.

"My lord, I have no brothers and my father died when I was very young. I had my cousins—many cousins, as you know—my sisters, my mother, my aunts, my uncles, my friends. I always dreamed of serving the Emperor. I had only the vaguest conception of what that meant, what form it could take, and if the Vangavaye-ve is still very far from Solaara, in those days it was even farther away from Astandalas. Hardly anyone ever thought to try for the Imperial Service or even the Navy, and certainly everyone thought me a fool for dreaming so high as Palace service. When it took me so long, everyone thought it was a sign that I was chasing a viau and a fool many times over.

"When my sister died I was ready to give up ... but her last words to me were to ignore the naysayers and listen to my own heart. I tried one last time, and succeeded, and found my heart's desire laid within my hand."

"And once it was in your hand, did you find it what you had hoped?"

Cliopher had not thought of those first days in the Service for a long time. He licked his dry lips. "I was deeply lonely and extremely homesick at first, my lord, and I found the ways of court poisonous. I was both middle-class and from the infamously remote Vangavaye-ve, and it was not good at first. But I persevered, and found a place for myself in the Lower Secretariat, and my family were able to boast of their son in the Palace. Then came the Fall ..."

He was silent for a moment, thinking of all that had been lost.

"I became then an under-secretary to Princess Indrogan, who spearheaded the reformation, and learned much under her."

"She was a great loss. She was one of the best ministers I ever had."

"She was a great woman," Cliopher agreed carefully; she had been extremely hard to work under. "When you awoke and took upon yourself the crown of Zunidh, the interim arrangements were formalized, and I found myself out of my appointment—for I had been secretary to the central committee shaping the new Service bureaucracy—and in somewhat of an awkward state, for I had a powerful patron in Princess Indrogan but had made enemies in the rearrangement."

"I see my choice of you to shape the next transition *is* as inspired as my courtiers will no doubt inform me it is."

Cliopher smiled reluctantly. "My lord is very kind."

His Radiancy snorted softly. "You were in an awkward place, lacking position, losing patronage, making enemies. What did you do?"

"I resigned."

His Radiancy looked at him, arrested. "To come home?"

He nodded, tracing out an incoherent pattern on the wall beside him. "We had heard nothing of the Vangavaye-ve—nothing of all the Wide Seas west of Jilkano. I was in charge of synthesizing the reports. Nothing. When I got home, I found ... it was not what I expected. Nothing had changed here, except ..."

He shied away from plumbing the depths of that homecoming. All those letters saying, *come home, come home, come home,* and when at last he had ...

His Radiancy said gently, "Many were hurt by the Fall in secret ways."

Cliopher had not thought about it that way. He shrugged, smiled pain-fully. "I returned to Solaara. When I came back Princess Indrogan was willing to give my name to the Master of Offices, no more. He kept sending me to all sorts of important courtiers he knew I would not do well with. It was a difficult period."

"How did you then end up in my study?"

"You know formal etiquette is not my strength. The Master of Offices was sure I would trip afoul of some arcane rule relating to the Radiancy, and that would be the end of my career in the Imperial Service."

"Did that happen to all the secretaries whom I rejected? There were about eight of them that year. Obsequious incompetent fools, the lot of them. I was becoming seriously displeased with the Master of Offices, but he kept protesting the Service was not yet fully staffed. He wished to oust Princess Indrogan as chief minister, I take it?"

"That was what I came to believe. At the time I was much more con-cerned for my own career, as I had no friends of influence left at court. He sent me to trial for your Radiancy, and ..." He swallowed hard at the mem-ory of that terrible night. "I made a joke, my lord, and while I was waiting to be dismissed you capped it. I was so surprised I looked directly at you."

"I remember."

"I went to my room and wrote to my cousin Basil that I thought I would be going home. I did not tell him I expected to be executed the next morn-ing for my impertinence. I was shocked I had not been blinded."

There was a brief silence. His Radiancy looked out across the great sweep of ocean glittering behind them, a few fluffy clouds near the horizon catching golden-white. "You were not the first person to make a joke in my presence after I became Emperor, but you were the first one to look at me as if I were a human being instead of a god."

"That was treason, my lord," Cliopher said quietly.

There was another silence. "I hate my life at times, Kip."

Cliopher looked at his lord, his heart breaking. "My lord, I—I did not know. I suspected, but was never sure until this voyage, of the inner man. The whole of the Palace is designed to make everyone *know* without any doubt at all that the god in its centre is you."

His Radiancy sighed. "And so I will not ask you to call me 'Tor'. What do you call me, when you and Conju speak about me to yourselves? Do you call me 'his lordship'?"

"We call you 'his Radiancy', my lord."

"Hence the occasional slips. I can't say I am very surprised. Conju finds it even harder than you ... but then you have a livelier sense of humour than he does. Cliopher, your friends spoke very freely to your lord. None seemed to think I would be alarming in the least. I had thought myself a very hard master, given how difficult it was to find you and Conju. But they seemed certain of my good nature and good humour."

Cliopher reached down into the quiet, secret well of his emotional life, which apparently came through far-too-clearly in his letters home. He swallowed. "In my letters home, I write of you stripped of all titles. *My lord*, I write."

"And in the common script the difference between *saavel* and *savel* is as small as in spoken speech."

"Just so, my lord. I am not a member of the upper court, not a gossiper by nature, and I cannot write about the particulars of my work, for much of the time I deal in state secrets. So I write about my day and my lord."

His Radiancy narrowed his eyes. "But I don't *do* anything. If you exclude all the customary and ritual activities, there is not much left of me."

Cliopher thought sharply of the three days of pacing on the verandah of Navikiani of Lesuia. How much had changed since then. He swallowed again.

"My lord, I write of the shape of our relationship. I write that you have been working long hours on a certain work of magic—I do not name the typhoons, or the Lights, or whatever—I write that you called me to play chess one evening, or invited me to lunch, or that we spoke about the opera or the new exhibition in the Imperial Gallery or the pieces in the competition for the Emperor's Prize or what-have-you. And out of those letters, my lord, my friends and my family have seen the truth, which is ..."

He wished very much he might take the hands of the man before him, but he contented himself with trying hard to meet the brilliant eyes. "My lord, I would have been honoured to serve you in any part of the Service. I would have been delighted with any position that brought me into your Presence, even once. All my yearnings to serve the Emperor, to serve the Empire, to serve Zunidh, have been fulfilled.

"I never expected, when I tried so hard and so long to pass the examinations, that one day I might sit across a table from the Lord of Rising Stars, never imagined in my wildest pipe-dreams that I might one day become friends with the Sun-on-Earth. I hoped, in those dark and lonely days when I first arrived in Astandalas, that I might find in that morass of a court a master I could admire and respect. I have been fortunate beyond the lot of many men that not only can I, do I, admire and respect my lord and my master, but that I could, that I do, also love him."

His Radiancy was very still.

Cliopher took a deep breath, met the lion eyes once more, and a feeling of wild abandon to the unknown, pushed over the edge.

"I may not touch you. I may not kiss you or embrace you or grasp your arms or your knees or your feet as I can all my cousins and aunts and uncles and friends. I may not lay my hand on your shoulder when you are sad or clasp your hands with you when you are jubilant. I am not the Moon Lady to be above those strictures. I do not know what history lies behind her naming you her Best-Beloved, but my lord, my ... Tor ... if you were my brother or my cousin I could not love you more."

His Radiancy stared at him with a face utterly drained of expression. It occurred to Cliopher then that it was possible no one had ever said that to him, to the inner man, before.

His Radiancy lifted his hand, the signet ring catching the light, and then he let it fall again and curl around his cup and keep that wall unbroken between them, and Cliopher remembered the brief flash of horror and uncertainty on his face when Dora asked him if she would be struck by lightning for touching.

He watched the motion, feeling in the abbreviated gesture a benediction worth far more than any title or public honour that could ever be bestowed. He felt a strong compulsion to say something more. He let his heart open, imagined the words welling spontaneously, and without quite consciously planning it, said: "When you are no longer sitting on the Lion Throne, I would like to know the man behind the Serenity. As a friend."

His Radiancy stared at him blankly a moment longer, and then he smiled, a smile that lit up the shadowy recesses of his irises, crinkled the corners of his eyes, as if Cliopher had just made the greatest joke in all of time.

"One day, Kip, I will tell you my secret name, the name I named myself. You will know then why I do not name myself today."

And Cliopher, hearing a whole universe of unspoken thoughts and mysteries in that simple statement, said with perfect honesty, "I will be deeply honoured."

"And I am not to say you are speaking as a courtier, am I? Your set-down was masterly. I am quite overcome."

"My lord," Cliopher replied, laughing, "the sundial should be quite magnificent."

CHAPTER TWENTY-FOUR

THREE DAYS WAS REALLY NOWHERE near long enough to get through the dispatch cases that had been piling up at the Toromandel Light.

★★★

THEY ARRIVED IN THE LATE morning. His Radiancy sent Cliopher off to spend the rest of the day catching himself up and to attend him in the morning as usual. Cliopher parted from the Radiancy's party at the second hallway to make his way down other stairs and other halls. As he walked he found a strange sense of quiet, almost of sleepiness, almost of emptiness.

The route took him past the main offices of Kiri's department, so he ducked in. A handful of pages waited for messages by the door, looking sleepy; a dozen secretaries and officials sat at their desks, reading reports and summarizing them; behind them the door to the upper office stood half-open. No one paid him much attention as he walked through the room.

Kiri's office—once his—was a large room full of bookcases containing assorted files and regulations, with a huge desk on which she composed the reports that were sent to him to review before passing on to his Radiancy. There were dispatch cases stacked up to the ceiling next to the door. He looked at them in some dismay.

"Is that really what we go through in four weeks?" he asked.

Kiri jumped up with a hastily-swallowed oath of astonishment. "Sayo Mdang! You've returned!" She glanced at his civilian outfit. "Just returned?"

"This hour," he replied.

"You should not come here first," she chided, but she smiled with relief. "You are looking very good, sir. Did his Radiancy enjoy his ..."

Cliopher closed the door. Her face went very still.

"Is anything wrong, Sayo Mdang?"

"There have as of yet been no official pronouncements made," he began, "but I will warn you of very major changes shortly to come."

"You worry me."

Cliopher took a deep breath. "First of all: his Radiancy has determined he will retire upon the occasion of the Grand Jubilee. He has therefore decided—take your time, Kiri."

Kiri had taken a breath wrong and started to cough violently. He fetched her a glass of water from the carafe on a side table, and waited solicitously while she swallowed down her astonishment and recovered her composure. "Sayo Mdang, you cannot possibly be serious. His Radiancy, retire? What about the succession?"

"Indeed! It turns out that there is some spell that was traditionally performed by the lords magi of Zunidh when it came time to ensure their succession."

"A spell!" said Kiri, her face lightening. "That is good news ... or isn't it?"

"It depends on whether there is a suitable heir nearby or not. It appears that if there is no one nearby, the sitting lord magus goes off on a quest to find him."

Kiri opened and shut her mouth several times, obviously trying to imagine His Serene and Radiant Holiness doing anything of the sort, and failing miserably.

"Moreover," Cliopher said resolutely, "his Radiancy has made the determination that we will need to rearrange the structure of government for his successor, who will not, of course, be also the Emperor of Astandalas."

"Hell. Who gets the joy of that?"

"I believe I am to be given that honour. To which end his Radiancy has given me the title of Lord Chancellor. I am not sure whether his Radiancy means that my other duties will change. He presented it as if it were merely the acknowledgement of a *de facto* position."

"Which it entirely is," Kiri said, with an expression on her face that made Cliopher stop in the middle of protesting.

"Do you think so?" he asked doubtfully. "I really am not sure ..."

"Oh, Sayo—or did you say *Lord* Chancellor? Are you then *Lord* Mdang now?"

Cliopher tried not to shudder.

Kiri snorted. "You have been running this government for years, you know that. Everyone knows that. His Radiancy is truly just acknowledging what is already so. And," she added more thoughtfully, "by giving you that title it will be much easier for you to deal with the aristocracy, especially the upper princes."

"They won't be happy dealing with a jumped-up commoner from the Islands."

"They've never been happy dealing with a jumped-up commoner from the Islands, but they'll be much more inclined to speak pretty to the Lord Chancellor of Zunidh. Huh."

He looked at the dispatch cases again. "Is that really what we usually go through in four weeks?"

Kiri looked over at him, raising her eyebrows. "Oh, not at all. That's *this* week's. Now, Lord Mdang—don't hunch your shoulders like that, sir, it makes you look like an errant schoolboy."

"I shall try to remember that people will be watching me more carefully now."

"Oh, they've always watched the Hands of the Emperor very carefully. Now ... before I send you off to your rooms to recover yourself before things start tomorrow, I'll take the opportunity to ask you if there's anyone from last year's crop of aspirants you fancy bringing on? You're going to need some secretarial assistance if you're really to start overhauling the government."

"Let us see what his Radiancy pronounces before we begin," he said dryly; though of course he was itching to look at those so-very-idealistic notes he had carefully put away—and equally carefully saved. "I can't say any of the pages has caught my eye this year. They all seem much of a muchness. Polite and political."

"True. It was a small crop, with hardly anyone from the hinterlands."

"Does that make such a difference?"

Kiri laughed. "Does it ever! I am from Solaara, as you know, and it had not occurred to me until I came under your department what a difference it makes to be from the hinterlands."

Cliopher felt stung on behalf of his home. "Despite what some of the lords of state say, I am not actually from a barbaric nation."

"No, but it is very far away, Sayo—Lord Mdang. I mean no disrespect—quite the opposite! Haven't you ever noticed how many of our department are from outside the Dairen cities? More than half are from the hinterlands."

"I think I must be tired, for I'm not sure I follow."

"Look, sir," Kiri said patiently. "When I wished to apply for the Service, I merely had to ask my family for their connections, and I had half a dozen dinner invitations within two weeks with civil servants ranging from my cousin's best friend in his second year to my uncle's oldest friend's sister-in-law, the Deputy Minister of Interprovincial Trade, not to mention advice from all corners, a short walk to gather the set books from Clarke's, all the tutors my family could afford, and the opportunity to sit any or all of the three examination times."

Kiri, Cliopher reflected, came from a higher level of society than he had quite realized.

"Whereas someone from the hinterlands who conceives the ambition to join the Service—well, sir, you know better than I the determination and resolve and courage it takes to win a place as an aspirant, and then leave all behind to reach here. The ones who make it want it. That's not to say no one from Solaara or Csiven or New Dair or the like is unworthy, but that they rarely have the hunger that drives someone from the hinterlands to reach the Palace."

Cliopher was about to protest, but then he thought of himself, of the five tries it had taken him, of the mockery of his friends and family for that ambition, of the long and lonely journey from Gorjo City to Astandalas, and the cold welcome he had found once finally there.

"I mislike favouritism," was what he said.

Kiri laughed at him. "No wonder you have such a wasp in your ear about his Radiancy's gifts to you."

"At any rate," Cliopher said, "no, I have not particularly noticed any of the aspirants this year as an individual, more's the pity. Let's hope this coming crop is better. Pick one or two of the best and we'll see if they shine better in closer proximity. I doubt I'll have much more than the usual to do for a while, anyhow. His Radiancy will have much to consider before he begins to move."

"He's not hasty, no," Kiri agreed.

Cliopher cast another look at the dispatch cases, but she shooed him off with the words that they would still be there tomorrow, and he made his way without further detours to his comfortable apartments. He could, however, feel how the Palace was starting to wake up: for his Radiancy was home.

★★★

THE NEXT MORNING HE PRESENTED himself before his Radiancy, only to be told that his first duty was to move.

"I beg your pardon, my lord?" he said, nearly falling over as he stood up from his genuflection.

The lion eyes were sparkling with mischief. "We have been considering," he said grandly, gesturing Cliopher to his seat while he himself paced across the middle of the room. "Your rooms are too far away."

"I beg your pardon, my lord?"

"I asked Conju as we were coming yesterday where exactly your rooms were. I had not realized they were all the way at the far end of the Alinorel wing. It will not do, my dear Kip, it will not do at all."

Cliopher eased himself back on his seat. Pikabe and Ato were on guard. Ato was a stolid man of very few words (and, unlike Commander Omo, did not appear to cherish romantic poetry in his breast; but Cliopher had learned to mistrust his assumptions about what the guards were thinking). Pikabe, of livelier wit and intelligence, was trying hard not to smirk.

But—*my dear Kip*?

Cliopher decided that "My lord?" was always acceptable, and accordingly said it.

"Now that you are my Lord Chancellor." His Radiancy said the words lovingly, bestowing a blazing smile on him. "One, we must increase your consequence; two, we shall be of greater and more frequent need of your company; three—the Alinorel wing is dull."

"I'm a career bureaucrat, my lord, not a—"

"You," said his Radiancy with precision, "are not dull. Stop acting like it."

Pikabe made a noise that sounded like he was trying to swallow laughter.

Cliopher remembered abruptly that his Radiancy's greatest castigation of himself, that astonishing evening in Navikiani when he had lost his temper, had been that his life was dull and he had settled for *comfortable*. Neither word was one he had ever associated with his Radiancy, though the Imperial Apartments *were* deeply comfortable, or actually, well beyond comfortable in their luxuriousness and beauty and, indeed—

"Very good, my lord," Cliopher said, not sure whether he had just been complimented or insulted. "I will go seek out, er, more satisfactory—"

"No, no, it is all taken care of. Conju thought of the solution, most happily. As I occupy the Imperial Apartments, those traditionally given over to the use of the Lord of Zunidh stand empty, so you may have them."

Cliopher's mouth dropped open. "My lord, I cannot presume so far!"

His Radiancy looked very seriously at him. "Cliopher, I would not so abuse your sensibilities or your loyalty or your capability if I did not feel it necessary to the future of Zunidh and if it were not that I can see how necessary it is that you be seen to have the authority which I am granting you."

"My lord …"

"I am intending to disrupt the thousand-year government of Zunidh and destroy what remaining hopes there may be that I restore the Empire. Unless there is some chambermaid or new aspirant to the Service who is secretly a great mage of intelligence, experience, and ambition, I am going to have to leave the Palace for an unknown length of time to find my successor. I require at my side someone whom I can trust absolutely to choose always for the good of the whole, not his own ambition or partiality, as we rearrange the entire governance system of the world."

His Radiancy paused there, looking hard at him.

Cliopher swallowed. "You do not need to elevate me to have me at your side, my lord."

His Radiancy smiled coolly. "No, I do not: but you are my hands in a work that will make many powerful people very unhappy. And when I leave on my quest, I wish to be certain that everyone knows beyond the slightest shadow of a doubt that you are my chosen minister and have all my authority behind you. I wish it to be clear long before then that you have my complete confidence."

"I am honoured, my lord," Cliopher said after a moment.

"I wish for people to grow accustomed to thinking of you as not simply my personal secretary and titular head of the Service, but as a man of very real power. You will see the difference soon."

"Very good, my lord," he said, for there was nothing else to say.

★★★

IT WAS A DISPIRITING DAY all round, Cliopher found. The regretfulness of returning to work after a holiday was compounded by the news that his new title meant a great deal more than the simple confirmation of a de facto state of affairs—and by the fact that by the time he and his Radiancy had finished for the day, he discovered that the efficient Palace servants had finished cleaning his new apartments and all of his belongings had been removed there.

Or all of them but a few ancient and beloved pieces of furniture he had to spend forty-five frustrating minutes persuading a footman to bring over.

The Palace of Stars was a large and rambling building, made coherent by the brilliance of its original architect. A central block rose ever upwards from the great buttressed cellars honeycombing the old volcanic plug on which it was built (and which had, mysteriously, come along with the Palace when the Fall removed it from Astandalas of Ysthar to Solaara of Zunidh), from the central Starry Court itself to the high tower which his Radiancy's apartments occupied. The rooms directly below his Radiancy's were devoted to the guards and servants on the most intimate duties. The practical rooms which served the Palace functions were largely in the cellars and lowest floors.

Extending out in a starburst—or sun-in-glory—pattern were the five great wings, each named after one of the worlds of the Empire. These held various rooms for various functions, but their grandest floors—the ones linking with the central block at the heights near to (though not, of course, *the same as*) the Imperial Apartments—were where dwelled the nobility, once of the Empire and now of Zunidh, in strict order of rank from the primary suite devoted to the lord magus of each world all the way out to where Cliopher Mdang, Secretary in Chief of the Private Offices of the Lords of State, had been accustomed to live.

His new apartments were two floors down and three hallways over from the Imperial Apartments.

He was still wandering around helplessly staring at things when Conju and Ser Rhodin came to see him. He heard the knock, but by the time he had realized what the sound was, a footman had appeared out of nowhere, let them in, led them to where Cliopher was trying to recover his poise, and announced sonorously, "The Cavalier an Vilius and Ser Rhodin an Gaiange, Lord Mdang. Shall I bring refreshments, sir?"

"Er, yes, please," said Cliopher, trying to sound less panicked than he felt.

The footman disappeared through a panel Cliopher hadn't realized contained a hidden door. He stared at it, not at all sure what to make of this. "Who is he, I wonder?" he said at last. "And where did he come from?"

"He's an under-footman of the house of Damara desirous of advancement," Conju supplied, "and I sent him here to audition as your majordomo."

"Oh yes?" said Cliopher, turning to him. "I understand I have you to thank for this—this preposterousness!"

"They're very nice rooms," Ser Rhodin said mildly, strolling over to examine a map of the world hung on the wall.

"They should be, as they're intended for the Lord of Zunidh! I cannot believe this is happening! There was nothing wrong with my rooms!"

"Except his Radiancy decided they were too far away," Ser Rhodin said with a gurgle of laughter. "And that the Alinorel wing was too dull."

"Do you mind?"

"Now that we have met all ninety-nine of your cousins—"

"Fifty-nine."

"That's really not any better, Cliopher. His Radiancy was much taken with your family."

"That doesn't answer for why he's decided I need to jump half the Palace above my station!"

Conju said, "Sit down and have a cup of tea. Thank you, Franzel. Did you put Lord Mdang's personal belongings in the Gold Tree chamber?"

The under-footman, who'd reappeared as silently as he'd gone, laid out a silver tea tray reverently in front of Conju. "Lord Conju, I have done so, though I am not certain Sir will not prefer the Rose rooms, which are the most magnificent ..."

"If he does, they can be switched out in the morning. I think that will be everything tonight, Franzel. Thank you."

"Thank you, sir," said the under-footman, with a look of ardent gratitude at Conju and a bow of excessive depth to Cliopher.

"I don't warrant that depth of bow," Cliopher protested.

"Yes, you do," said Ser Rhodin, while Conju hummed over the teapot. "You are the Lord Chancellor now, the head of the pillar of the Service. Your voice is equal to that of the Council of Princes," he added, when Cliopher stared at him in total consternation.

"Dear lord."

"Always," said Conju, passing him a teacup. "Shall I tell Franzel to be your majordomo, Cliopher? You'll never manage on your own."

"I don't need—I'll need a new court costume, won't I?"

"Oh, more than one."

"Hell," said Cliopher, "that's what this is. Hell."

"Just think how beautiful your sundial will be when you retire," Ser Rhodin said, eyes gleaming with unholy amusement. "Come, come, sir, you can bear this for a few years. Not more than seven. Why, you may find you like being a Power."

"I sincerely doubt it."

"You do like dressing up," Conju said coaxingly.

"And dressing down fools."

Cliopher chuckled reluctantly. "You'll not abandon me to this—this absurd suite, will you?"

"Certainly not!" Ser Rhodin said.

"Especially as it's so much more convenient for us," Conju added, with a sly glance and a sweet biscuit. "That forty-minute walk to the end of the Alinorel wing made it hard to visit when I only had an hour or two, but I do, you know, very often have an hour or two in the evenings when his Radiancy is at dinner or at court."

"And the barracks are a mere ten minutes down from here, when I'm not on duty in the Tower."

"I hadn't thought of that," Cliopher admitted, somewhat mollified.

"Though I expect his Radiancy will call you whenever he's not holding court," Conju said practically. "He was very pleased at thinking you so close. Do reassure him you're not too angry, will you?"

"I? Reassure his Radiancy? Conju, will you listen to yourself?"

Conju met his glance soberly. "His Radiancy is distressed that he is forcing you to a position you neither expected nor want. He does not wish to lose you as secretary, either."

"He could elevate someone else to his Lord Chancellorship," Cliopher said acidly.

Ser Rhodin grinned and refilled his teacup. "But who else would you want to reorganize the government?"

"I—" Cliopher stopped, then frowned at them, then sighed. "No one, of course. But what *will* everyone think?"

Ser Rhodin laughed. "Is that the best you can do? I had never received the impression you cared."

CHAPTER TWENTY-FIVE

THE NEXT MORNING HE WAS woken by the solicitous Franzel, who assured him that he need not bestir himself about anything to do with organizing the household, and that a bath had been drawn for him, his clothes for the morning laid out (though, sniffed the majordomo-cum-valet, they were not quite as he would desire for Sir, except that Sir was very new to his title and no doubt better clothing would come with time), and his letters set beside his breakfast-tray in the Waterlily Room.

It took Cliopher three tries to find the Waterlily Room, and although he tried, he couldn't quite shake the feeling that this was all a horrible nightmare shortly to turn into sharks, or snakes, or some sort of monstrous giant lizard from the Yenga.

It got worse when he finally found his way out of his apartments (how *many* rooms were there? he expostulated to himself on discovering yet another beautifully constructed, superbly elegant, perishingly old-fashioned, and nearly empty parlour when opening what he was certain was the outer door), for it was clear that the rumour mill had begun its work. About half the people he encountered nodded distantly or frowned; a further quarter bowed slightly; the remainder bowed deeply. Since he knew precisely four of these people well enough to greet, he was not much pleased.

He was in a bad temper when he reached the Offices of State. This time when he entered the pages jumped to attention and the other secretaries jumped up to offer their congratulations and commiserations. He felt slightly ashamed of his ill temper, and grateful for the lightness with which most of them were treating his elevation.

He felt better after throwing himself at the dispatch boxes and getting caught up by Kiri with all the things that had been happening while his Radiancy was on holiday. He had quite forgotten both his new position and his ill humour when a knock on Kiri's office door was followed by her chief assistant, the respectful Aioru. At least, he was mostly respectful; he was also trying not to laugh.

"Beg pardon to interrupt," he said, "but there's someone here for Sayo—sorry, Lord Mdang."

Cliopher felt an ominous chill at these words. "Who is it?"

"Lady Ylette, sir."

Of all the people who might have sought out his person that day, Lady Ylette was quite possibly the last one Cliopher would have thought of. He went out in great puzzlement, followed by the curious Kiri, to see what his Radiancy's costumier wanted.

Lady Ylette was standing in front of the pages. She was dressed in a cherry-blossom-pink and white north Voonran-style kimono, her silky black hair done up in elaborate braids held in place with long sticks, gold with pink diamond drops to show her rank. She looked like a delicate flower in front of the sand-coloured uniforms of the pages. Despite her long service with his Radiancy, Cliopher had barely crossed paths with her; he was not sure he had ever actually heard her speak.

"Ah," said she, looking him over head to toe with a practiced and very critical eye. "Yes. Yes."

"Yes what?" Cliopher said, then caught himself and managed to smile. "What can I do for you, Lady Ylette?"

"It is not what you can do for me, but what I can do for you," she said, giving him the closest thing to a smile he had ever seen from her. Her voice was lightly accented and quite high-pitched. "Come, there is not a moment to lose."

"Come where? And for what? I do not mean to be disobliging, ma'am, but we have been away and I am trying to catch up on the affairs of state."

"Oh, pish," she said, waving her hand at him. "The affairs of state will wait until tomorrow. *I* cannot."

"But what have I to do with you?" he said, still feeling bewildered.

"Your court dress," she said impatiently. "Come now, you are no fool, sir."

"*You* are going to make me a court dress? Did his Radiancy bid you?"

"His Radiancy has given me leave," she said, walking over to circle him with a predatory air. He tried not to back away. "When Lord Conju mentioned your new rank, it came to me that you would of course need new clothing, and there was nothing for it but to ask his Radiancy for the permission to dress you."

"Surely my usual tailor is quite sufficient—" he said desperately.

She stopped circling and stood to look up at him, her hands on hips. "Lord Mdang, you are a man of good figure, and what is more, you have countenance and dignity and elegance of taste. Your clothing, however, is barely passable for the Secretary in Chief. It is certainly unacceptable for the Lord Chancellor of Zunidh. I told his Radiancy so, and he was in *perfect* agreement and told me his new court dress could wait while I dressed you to perfection. So!" She clapped her hands. "There is no time to lose."

Cliopher opened his mouth and shut it again. He could see the barely-hidden grins of his department members and the failing attempts on the part of the pages to pretend they were paying no attention.

Everyone could, he was sure, see him capitulate. He sighed. "Very well, then."

"We'll see you when your new duties permit," Kiri said, with a brave effort at a straight face.

Lady Ylette nodded decisively. "When I am done with you, sir, you will be *magnificent*."

★★★

LADY YLETTE, TOGETHER WITH FOUR of her underlings, took what felt like several hours to measure every possible proportion of his body. The underlings did the actual work; Lady Ylette made records with what Cliopher eventually realized was Voonran mnemonic knotwork rather than macramé. Accustomed as they were to working for his Radiancy, the underlings did this wearing close-fitting silk gloves and using various tools that looked as if they belonged in a dentist's office but were, it appeared, intended to move delicate clothing without nearing the skin. Cliopher tried to be appreciative of their delicacy rather than fume, but it was hard going.

Lady Ylette's collection of knotted strings had grown extensive and her notebook full of arcane scribbles when at last her underlings started packing up their equipment. Cliopher could not restrain himself and heaved a great sigh of relief, only to find Lady Ylette regarding him with a sinister smile. "What is it now?" he asked apprehensively.

"Now we must consider fabrics," she replied demurely. "We have laid them out in the Yellow Lotus Room."

The Yellow Lotus Room was, apparently, a different room from the Waterlily Room, though to the uneducated eye of its new inhabitant, it looked nearly identical, being a white-walled room with a coloured tile floor mostly hidden by a large carpet. Most of the carpet was in turn hidden by a waist-high table which was covered in white silk and on which was laid out swaths of fabrics Cliopher could not even begin to name. He felt panic rising along his spine as he looked at them. He was fairly certain the swatches alone were worth his entire life's savings.

"Ah," said Lady Ylette in satisfaction, looking behind his back. When Cliopher spun around to see what she was looking at, he realized to his total shock that the doors to the Yellow Lotus Room had opened on his Radiancy, with Ser Rhodin and Elish coming in behind him.

This was rather too much for him. He went straight down to the formal prostration without even looking at his lord's face, and without desiring in any way to lift his head up again. Perhaps, he thought, he could just *stay* down there.

"Come now, Kip, you need stand on no such formality," his Radiancy said, with what sounded like as much suppressed laughter as Conju and Ser Rhodin the night before (traitors! Cliopher thought balefully, not having realized Conju had it in him). "Or lie down, as the case may be. Lady Ylette requires your decisions."

He got up reluctantly, to find a Sun-on-Earth looking serene—except for that damnable glint in his eye. "My lord, I did not expect you to call."

"It occurred to us that perhaps you would appreciate some assistance in choosing your new clothing." His Radiancy looked him up and down with nearly as critical an eye as his costumier. "You were quite correct, Ylette. It is elegant, but a certain want of ... flair. But you will soon fix that."

She nodded briskly. "Now, m'lord, what say you to the sarcenet?"

"Not in hyacinth, surely," his Radiancy said, walking over to the table to consider the length of brilliant purple cloth Lady Ylette was holding up for inspection. "It will clash with his robes of office. It is possible, however, for an informal outfit."

"It's very purple," said Cliopher, but they ignored him.

"Very true, m'lord. There is also this."

"Apricot is acceptable. What is that, gold thread? Yes, he does warrant that now—or will—Set it to one side. What is that black? No, not the silk— oh, no, that satin will never do. Satin, Ylette!"

"Not everyone mislikes it as much as you do, m'lord."

"Cliopher will not wear satin."

Since Cliopher had never worn satin, was not entirely sure what it was made out of, and certainly distrusted the slithery material on sight, he felt no reason to contest his Radiancy's flat pronouncement. When his Radiancy

demonstrated equal disapproval of a linen in a subdued green, he did, however, venture to register a protest.

Both his Radiancy and Lady Ylette looked at him in surprise that he had
spoken. "If you please, my lord," he added.

"Not with your skin tone, Cliopher," his Radiancy said after a moment.
"Olive green is *not* your colour."

Lady Ylette shuddered expressively.

Cliopher decided to let them have it, and wandered over to stand next to
Ser Rhodin and Elish at the door.

"Are you permitted to speak with me when you're on duty?" he asked
Ser Rhodin diffidently.

Ser Rhodin gave him a judicious nod. "Since his Radiancy is occupied,
we are within your private apartments, and there are other guards between
here and the door, certainly."

Cliopher did not, as it happened, have very much to say. He stood watching the rigorous selection of fabrics for what seemed an endless number of
garments. Finally he said, "Where am I going to wear all those?"

"Court?" Ser Rhodin suggested.

Cliopher groaned a little too loudly, for his Radiancy turned around and
raised his eyebrow at him.

★★★

BY THE END OF THE DAY, Cliopher had not only a headache but also the
threat of more fittings to come, as well as some underling of Lady Ylette's
who would be responsible for his clothing.

He had, seeing a piece of rare aquamarine silk go by, experienced a
sharp pang of homesickness for the Bay of the Waters, followed by a rueful
acknowledgment to himself that Gorjo City would not be a restful place to
be until the news of his elevation had died down, followed by a vague hope
that Gaudenius passed the exams on his first try, followed (after a series of
dispiriting reflections that his nephew was determined not to be aided by his
uncle in any way and that therefore Cliopher could not really look forward
to his company) by the sudden recollection that his cousin Zemius would be
coming to the Palace in the near future.

When the deliberations over five seemingly-identical pieces of white
linen had landed on two as being most suitable (for what? he had no idea,
any longer), he cleared his throat and ventured to remind his Radiancy of his
cousin Zemius.

"Yes, what of him?" said his Radiancy, examining now a spread of seven slightly different shades of dark blue silk.

"As you know, my lord, Gorjo City is much more casual than the Palace, and my cousin does not have wear suitable even for an informal audience with your lordship. If you desire him to be presented at court ..."

"Do you?"

Cliopher stared helplessly at his Radiancy's back. "Um, not particularly."

His Radiancy's back quivered slightly. Cliopher felt he should perhaps explain. "Zem gets very tongue-tied in public. He'd much prefer to stay out of notice. If you do wish to notice him, my lord, it would best to do it at the *end* of his visit, because I should imagine that seeing you in full regalia would make him quite unable to answer your questions satisfactorily, which would be a shame."

He trailed off, feeling uneasy at the way his Radiancy was standing silently, no longer turning over fabrics, but simply leaning on the table with his face hidden.

"He's not a very *important* scholar," he added at last.

There was another pause, and then his Radiancy started to laugh. "Oh, Kip," he said, "you will never change, will you?"

CHAPTER TWENTY-SIX

BY THE TIME HIS COUSIN ZEMIUS arrived, Cliopher had acquired a footman, a costumier, and three servants of the chamber, as well as Franzel, who seemed to consider himself his gentleman's gentleman. All of these were Conju's choices, drawn (it appeared) from his Radiancy's staff. Cliopher assumed at first they were not quite up to scratch and accordingly demoted to serve him, but Franzel disabused him of this notion when Féonie came with the first costume out of Lady Ylette's workshop.

"What a gift it is that you brought her into your household, Sir."

After a week of bewildering changes to his life, Cliopher had resigned himself both to having a household and to being called Sir in portentous tones by its members. His new proximity to his closest friends (including, said a quiet voice, his Radiancy, who had graced him with no fewer than three unexpected visits) was doing much to counterbalance the less pleasant elements, as were the determined good-humour and teasing of Kiri combined with the focused work that stack of dispatch cases required.

"She is a delight to watch at work," Cliopher responded carefully. Féonie was very beautiful and very young and very serious about her craft, and he could see that Franzel was half in love with her.

"This is a great opportunity for her. As for all of us," Franzel added conscientiously.

"Is it? Do you not reckon it a—a demotion to be removed from his Radiancy's staff?"

Franzel laughed indulgently. "Oh, no, Sir! While the honour of serving in the Tower is exceedingly great, we were very junior members of The Household. We have been vastly increased in consequence in being chosen to serve you as principal attendants. You can believe the competition was fierce when his Radiancy bade Lord Conju choose some of our number to attend you, Sir. It would be many years indeed before Féonie or I could come to the notice of his Radiancy in the Tower."

Cliopher made note to ask Conju for confirmation of this, which that gentleman did with a quiet laugh when he came to visit Cliopher that evening and Franzel had disappeared after leaving them wine. True to his word, Conju had come nearly every evening, usually for less than an hour, such as he had never been able to do before.

"Were you thinking I'd foist off my incompetents on you? For shame, Cliopher! I hope you know me better than that."

"I can't imagine you have any incompetents under your command, any more than I keep them in my office, but there are certainly always those promising ones who, er, do not fulfil their promise."

"They get sent off to his Radiancy's princes. I chose the best of the junior household for you, my friend. It was the least I could do. Let me see your new clothes?"

"Haven't you already seen them?"

"Ylette is jealous of her creations."

By this time Cliopher could nearly always find the four rooms in which he spent most of his time, and not lose his way from bedchamber to sitting room to front door, but the costume-room nearly defeated him.

"These apartments have more rooms than my mother's house," he told Conju, closing the door on Waterlily and Lotus Rooms and trying a third, which led eventually to the Lion Room, which Féonie had taken as her domain. He sighed with relief and indicated the three outfits hanging in the wardrobe.

"Oh, these are lovely," said Conju, examining the fabric with gentle hands. "I see three sets of working robes so far. Of course, the court costume will take longer. His Radiancy is quite delighted with the whole thing and eagerly looks forward to seeing you in your court costume next week, I heard him tell Ylette so."

Cliopher tried hard not to sigh.

The next day he made a determined effort to finish the dispatch cases and clear his Radiancy's desk by lunch. "My cousin arrives this afternoon, my lord," he told his Radiancy. "When would you like to see him?"

"Come the usual time with him tomorrow."

"Which audience chamber have you selected, my lord?"

"Oh, here, I think."

Cliopher tried hard not to stare. His Radiancy *never* held audience in the Imperial Apartments.

His Radiancy smiled fleetingly at him and ignored the unspoken question. "After that your cousin will have leisure to see the sights before you are formally inducted at the resumption of court. I have informed Ylette that he will need robes sufficient to the audience. It is good for one member of your family at least to witness the ceremony."

"Thank you, my lord."

His Radiancy regarded him for several moments. "You are adapting well, Kip."

He laughed ruefully. "I am afraid I must seem very ungrateful, my lord. I have always been most satisfied with my position, and never sought such a change."

"I know it. I have every confidence in your ability to rise to the occasion and your position."

"Thank you, my lord."

"You may have the two days before the resumption of court off to show your cousin around the city. After the installation things will no doubt be somewhat hectic for you."

"Thank you, my lord."

"It is I who must thank you. Off you go now to the Spire to meet the ship."

Thus dismissed, Cliopher did so, climbing up the long spiral with a sense of weariness and a definite complaint from his knees. He had not been exercising enough, overwhelmed with everything and shy about dancing in front of his new servants.

He reached the top in good enough time to see the ship break through sunlit clouds as it came over the Grey Mountains to the Solamen plain. After exchanging greetings with the keepers of the Light, he went outside to stand on the parapet with the wind blowing in his face.

He realized he had not been outside since his return to the Palace, and resolved to find whatever was the nearest garden to his new rooms. His old rooms had been only a staircase away from one of the great gardens of the Palace, and he had usually made the trip home out-of-doors rather than through the halls. The lack of exercise and fresh air, he thought, was probably contributing to his sense of malaise.

He had a full twenty minutes to stand in the fresh air, and he relished every moment of it.

He watched the ship heeling in the sky, its gold-striped sails belling majestically, the white-garbed sailors bright dots moving about the decks and rigging, and felt quite on top of the world.

Zemius was escorted down the gangway by Captain Diogen, who did not appear to have much faith he would not fall off. Cliopher brushed his hands down his robes and walked over to greet him.

"Cousin Kip!" Zemius said gratefully on reaching the stone parapet. "You're here to meet me!"

"I am! Thank you, captain. I trust the journey went well?"

"Aye, though we went through a storm over the Yenga and lost a sail. Your cousin's a good sailor, mind, didn't lose his head and start screaming like some."

Cliopher forbore making excuses for Conju, who had nearly refused ever to set foot on a sky ship again after their second trip together to the Vangavaye-ve had taken them through the edge of a typhoon. "No harm done, Zem?"

"N-no."

He would not have thought to bring his footman, but Franzel had sternly ordered the young man to go with Sir to carry his cousin's bags, so Cliopher was able to say to Captain Diogen, "Havor will fetch my cousin's bags, captain. Thank you."

"Any time, Lord Mdang."

"I'm not sure I'll ever quite get used to that," Cliopher told his cousin as they started down the staircase. "I hope you are well, Zemius? Everyone at home?"

"It's only been a week, Kip," Zemius said, laughing. "They were still hashing over every detail of your visit when I left—they hadn't even moved on to missing you yet."

"It feels so much longer." They passed a page sent up to the Light minders, who glanced politely at them, saw it was Cliopher, and bowed hastily. Cliopher nodded, having found this much the easiest response, and went on to his cousin, "I've been assigned different rooms, and, well, everything is much changed since we came back. The bowing, for instance, is new."

They came out into the main hall, and Cliopher paused so that his cousin could take in his first sight of the interior of the Palace of Stars.

"Oh," Zemius said.

The Palace was made out of many different kinds of stone, on this floor a creamy limestone. The walls were shaped with bas-relief geometric carvings of great fineness of detail and superb beauty of form. It was lit partly by windows (whose pale-gold alabaster grilles were carved in the same manner as the walls) and partly by mage-lanterns in pearlescent glass globes, suspended

on golden chains every dozen yards or so. It was, however, the superb proportions that never failed to impress.

Cliopher drew his arm through his cousin's. "Isn't it wonderful? Wait
until you see the Imperial apartments."

Zemius looked at him in astonishment. "I beg your pardon?"

Cliopher realized he had made a misstep, and guessed that if he explained
his Radiancy's plan he would have a cousin prostrate with nervous anxiety
all evening instead of one understandably nervous but mostly in control of
himself. He smiled reassuringly. "I shouldn't gabble on, when you've been
travelling for three days. Let's go have some coffee and I can tell you the general plan. His Radiancy has granted me the time off to show you the sights
before court resumes."

"That is uncommonly kind of him."

"It is, isn't it? Well, not uncommonly, but certainly kind."

"He seemed to be distressed that no one had come to visit."

"I hope you've not been dwelling on that? I understand, even if his
Radiancy does not, how long and how expensive a journey it is from the
Vangavaye-ve!"

"Yes, but Kip—"

Zemius fell silent as several gorgeously-arrayed persons broke apart a
conversation to observe their progress down the hall. When they reached
them with the party still watching, Cliopher bowed deeply to the Prince of
Western Dair, dragging his cousin down with him.

"Sir," said the Prince of Western Dair, with a gracious half-bow in re-
turn. The three lesser nobles, regarding this as a remarkable distinction to his
Radiancy's commoner secretary, all made haste to make very elegant bows to
Cliopher. He decided to err on the side of courtesy, and bowed back.

"I understand that you will be heading a new committee," said the
Prince, surveying Cliopher's new outfit appreciatively and Zemius's neat but
plain scholar's robes with something like marvel.

This was the first Cliopher had heard of it, but he assumed that rearranging the government would involve a great many new committees, and that
he would certainly be heading some of them, and that it was quite possible
that his Radiancy had been telling his underling princes of his plans, so he
smiled deferentially. "That may well be so, your highness."

"Good, good," said the Prince, rubbing his hands. "Do you remember
me when his Radiancy populates it."

Cliopher had not received such a blatant request for preferment since he had cleaned out the upper bureaucracy in the wake of the great Examination Scandal, and certainly never from one of the aristocracy—let alone from one of the highest noblemen in the world. He decided that, just as for his Radiancy, a bow could hardly offend, and so he bowed respectfully and said, "Your servant, your highness," and towed his wordless cousin around the next corner.

Zemius ventured, "Who was that, Kip?"

"The Prince of Western Dair," Cliopher said absently, revolving in his mind what possible committee his Radiancy might be thinking of that such a personage would like to be on, together with the astonishing evidence that his new rank was, as Ser Rhodin said, equal to the princes'.

Zemius said, "Oh," rather faintly, a response that did not seem to be helped by their stupendously beautiful surroundings.

It had to be admitted that the apartments intended for the Lord of Zunidh were off a glorious corridor that would not have been unworthy of being a lesser palace's central hall or throne room; that the doors, which were carved and painted and gilded with the tiger insignia of Zunidh (rarely used, since that of Astandalas superseded it in most things pertaining to his Radiancy), were magnificent; and that the two footmen in midnight blue and orange livery stationed on either side of them were altogether superb.

Cliopher halted in front of what he could not quite bring himself to think of as his door, and stared at the two footmen. "Where did you come from?" he demanded finally.

"Old Damara, sir!" The footman on the right made a respectful gesture, fist over heart, which Cliopher vaguely recognized as being a Damaran custom.

"Yes, I see, but why are you *here*?"

"We are assigned to your household, sir," the footman on the left said helpfully.

Cliopher felt his headache rapidly returning. "Whose livery is that?"

"Yours, sir!"

He had nearly forgotten Zemius' presence when he felt a tremor running through his arm, which he still held. He looked across to see his cousin desperately trying to maintain his composure, and his sense of humour, which had been noticeably absent for most of the week, suddenly asserted itself.

"Of course it is," he said, once he could speak. "Of course it is. What are your names?"

"Baion and Ewan, sir."

"Very good. No doubt Franzel has sorted you out?"

"Certainly, sir. Will you go in now?"

He nodded, unable to bring himself to speak, and the one on the right—Ewan—opened the door for him. Zemius waited until the door was closed before dissolving into laughter. "Kip! Livery! Your face!"

"There are many elements of my new position I find bewildering, Zem," Cliopher said, opening the next door and finding himself not in the Secondary Receiving Room but in a parlour decorated with orange flowers he couldn't name. "For instance," he added, closing that door and opening the next one along, which also wasn't the Secondary Receiving Room, but was instead a privy decorated all in pink, and finally finding the room he sought on the third try, "these apartments have far too many rooms."

"Is that the right one?"

"It is." Cliopher frowned at it gloomily. "Let us see if I can find your bedroom."

"Oh, am I staying with you?"

"Assuming we ever manage to find our way to the private rooms—oh!" he said, opening a door on Féonie, who was carefully unpacking what looked very much like a bird-of-paradise flower from a large quantity of tissue paper.

"Oh indeed," said Zemius appreciatively, though whether of the splendid Féonie or the even more splendid court costume Cliopher had no idea.

"It is not yet finished," Féonie said firmly, coming over to turn Cliopher forcibly around and out of the room. "What have you been doing to your robes, sir? You have dust all down the front."

Cliopher looked down at himself in embarrassment. "I was leaning up against the parapet of the Spire watching the ship come in."

"That will not do for your dignity, sir. Is this your cousin? You did not mention he was so much taller than you!"

"Only a couple of inches—"

"Only! Only! Perfection is what we aim after, perfection. Only. Pah." She stabbed Zemius in the chest. He stopped smirking abruptly. "I shall bring your robes for fitting."

"He's just arrived from a long journey—"

"He will not go before his Radiancy looking like that," Féonie said flatly. "My honour is at stake. Go, bathe, while I consider."

"As you can see," Cliopher said when he had found the next doorway and Féonie, muttering to herself, had gone back to her work, "I have suddenly acquired a household, including a tyrannical costumier. I am sorry things are so topsy-turvy, I don't know where I am half the time."

"It does seem like having a rope to guide you would be of assistance."

Cliopher found his sense of humour returning again. "That would probably help! I daresay I'll learn my way around in time. I managed with the Palace, you wouldn't think a single apartment would be anywhere as hard, would it? Ah, here we are at last! This is—well, I don't know what it's called, really, but it's my favourite room."

"It is the Deer Room, Sir," Franzel said serenely, coming in from one of the hidden servant doors with a tray full of refreshments. "You must be Professor Mdang, sir."

"This is Franzel," Cliopher said. "What room is my cousin in? Did Havor get here with his bags? When did the new footmen come?"

"The White Lotus Room, Sir. Yes, certainly. Lord Conju sent them over with his compliments this afternoon."

"Conju is taking far too much pleasure in this," Cliopher said, but he smiled as Franzel left again, and sagged down on the comfortable old couch. In the gracious elegance of the sitting room it looked like a battered old bear, but along with his few artworks (for he had always chosen to save for the best he could afford) and other mementos, it made it feel just a little bit more like home.

"I'm astonished you remembered about my robes, Kip," Zemius said quietly. "Thank you."

Cliopher smiled wryly. "Fool that I am, I thought the title wouldn't change anything. Coffee? Or it appears that Franzel has brought tea." He stared at the pot. "I don't know who is paying for all this. I certainly didn't order *tea.*"

"I've never had tea," said Zemius in wonder, so Cliopher poured him some of the fragrant golden brew, imported at vast expense and trouble from Ysthar. People had tried for centuries to get tea to grow on the other worlds, but like roses the plant was temperamental and refused all but Ysthar of the Magic's soil. After they had drunk it, and Zemius had decided the faintly floral astringency was certainly very interesting, Cliopher managed to get his cousin to the White Lotus Room after only two false doors.

"It has its own bath chamber and privy," he said, pointing out the door, then having second thoughts and opening it to demonstrate to both of them that it was, in fact, the bathing facilities.

"You have sub-apartments?" Zemius said in wonder.

"This was designed for a lord magus' household," Cliopher said wearily. "I am like a pea in a rattle in it."

Zemius assured him that it was absolutely lovely to stay with him and that he would be delighted to have a bath. Cliopher decided this was as good an idea as any, and accordingly went to his own room (after only one mistake) and had one himself, whereupon he felt in significantly better charity with the world.

After about an hour or so one of the chamber attendants escorted Zemius back into the sitting room, which meant that Cliopher could set down the reports he was reading and pretend he did not need to know all of the details of who was moving where within the Service hierarchy in the Lord's New Year. Franzel brought in red wine from Amboloyo, and he left his desk for the couch and a sense of surreal pleasure in finally having one of his family sitting there with him.

"Your costumier came in," Zemius said, shaking his head. "She seemed truly offended that you hadn't told her of the two inches in height difference between us, but I mollified her with fulsome apologies and many compliments."

Cliopher snorted. "Tell me about your trip," he said, so Zemius did, enthusing about the glorious vistas, the kindness of Captain Diogen (who had had him to dine at his own table), the splendid feeling of flying, so that he quite forgot to be nervous in his wonder.

"I confess," he said, when the first bottle was nearly finished, "that I am growing much more nervous again now that I am here. It didn't seem real until I saw all those people bowing to you, Kip."

"That made it real?" Cliopher replied, laughing. "I find it utterly surreal. I am used to being unknown outside the Service, you know. Finding that half the Palace knows what I look like is most disconcerting. I can hardly imagine what it will be like after the official announcement is made. At the moment this is all running on gossip."

"Just gossip?"

"Well, that and my move up here, and I can't imagine the pages have been quiet about the news—they never are."

"Lord Conju and Ser Rhodin," said Franzel at this moment, opening the outer door of the room to let them in.

"We've come to dine with you," Ser Rhodin said, smiling at Zemius. "We've not met formally, sir. I am Ser Rhodin, the Deputy Commander of the Imperial Guard. I will be on duty tomorrow morning when you meet with his Radiancy, and I thought perhaps you would like to know another person in the room."

"And I am pleased to meet you again," Conju added, as Zemius made an awkward bow to them. "I'm sorry we didn't get the chance to speak when we were in Gorjo City."

"I didn't know you were a lord," Zemius said, with a sideways glance at Cliopher.

Conju smiled. "Oh, I'm just a younger son. My father was a marquis on Ysthar before the Fall, but he and my older brother were great gamblers and ran through the whole estate, so I went into service. Not being inclined towards the priesthood or the army, which everyone said was such a pity since my title is actually 'the Cavalier Conju enazo Argellevian an Villius', and they thought it just made for the army."

"You'd have been a good priest, Conju," Ser Rhodin said judiciously, helping himself to a glass of the new bottle of wine Franzel had brought.

"I was too much of a fashionable atheist as a young man. You wouldn't guess it now, but I was a great fool."

Zemius relaxed as Cliopher and Ser Rhodin both laughed and abused this notion, and the conversation moved lightly to questions of fashion and literature and Ser Rhodin's overabundance of potential new guardsmen who had to be winnowed down to a mere dozen. When at last the Palace bells chimed the second hour after sunset, Zemius was laughing and talking with as much ease as if they'd all known each other for years.

"Now," said Cliopher as they went into the next room out and he surveyed the five doors on offer, "let's see if I can find the dining room without mishap."

Conju cast him a bemused glance and walked across to fling open a door and reveal the dining room. "Are you having difficulties finding your way around?"

"I should think so! These apartments seem to be deliberately designed to be as confusing as possible. I can just about find the front door, but not with any assurance anything else."

Ser Rhodin and Conju exchanged glances, and then Conju said delicately, "Did you not know to follow the door tiles?"

Cliopher stared at him. "What do you mean?"

Conju came back to the doorway from where he had been ushering Zemius to the table. "Look," he said, pointing at the frieze of decorated tiles running around the doorframe. "Each room has its name—"

"I had gathered that."

"And its symbol. The one in the centre is the next room out, so in this case, the tiger. Next over shows whether it leads towards the front hall, which is the sun, naturally, or to the private rooms, so the moon. As this next room out leads to both, you have sun to the right and moon to the left."

Cliopher took a deep breath and then decided not to say anything for just a moment, and instead walked out of the room to look at the other five doors. The one to the left showed a deer in the centre with the moon flanking it on both sides; the next one, the lotus; the one to the right, the sun flanking pink flowers.

He followed the sun through seven rooms out to the main hall, where Ewan and Baion gave him their hand-over-heart greeting again and did not seem at all bemused by his looking at the front door, shaking his head, and going back in, following the moon back to the tiger room, and then he went into the one to his left, which was marked with a tortoise.

They all fell about laughing when he came in. "I'm sorry," Conju gasped presently, "I had no idea you didn't know about the door tiles. That's how all the great apartments are laid out. No wonder you've been in such a bad temper this week!"

"It's not solely to do with my inability to find my way through my new rooms."

"No, but it can't have helped," Ser Rhodin said, grinning. "Professor Mdang—"

"Oh, please call me Zemius. Not even my students call me Professor Mdang."

"Things are much more casual in the Vangavaye-ve," Conju said seriously. "Why, I remember when Cliopher first—"

"Don't you have to go back to his Radiancy?" Cliopher interrupted. "I'm sure you must."

Conju laughed. "You will get to know my evening schedule much more completely now that you are up here. His Radiancy has been dining with his princes as they come to the Palace. Court resumes three days from now, Zemius, and since the rumour-mongers are going mad what with all the honours being showered on your cousin, all the princes are making sure to sound out his Radiancy."

"The Prince of Western Dair greeted me in the hall today and asked me to remember him for some committee I am evidently going to be chairing. His toadies were utterly shocked at his condescension."

"Everyone can see which way the wind is blowing."

Zemius turned shocked eyes on him. Cliopher tried his hardest not to growl.

"You do have a wasp in your ear," Ser Rhodin added. "Calm down. Now, what I was going to say before we got sidetracked, Zemius, is that I am off-duty at noon tomorrow, and if Cliopher continues closeted with his Radiancy as usual into the afternoon after your appointment with him, I would be pleased to take you around the Palace. I gather Cliopher has the days following off to take you into the city?"

"It's such a long way to come for just a couple of hours," Zemius said doubtfully.

All three of them laughed. Ser Rhodin finally said, "I don't think you have any idea what trouble people go to to have ten minutes in the Presence. His Radiancy has cleared his whole morning for you."

"Probably because Cliopher said you wouldn't want to be presented at court. Is that true?" Conju added anxiously. "His Radiancy particularly asked me to determine if you would like to be formally presented."

Zemius' expression of horror was enough to set them all off laughing again.

"I wasn't projecting my own disinclination onto him," Cliopher said indignantly.

Ser Rhodin smiled. "He made his Radiancy laugh outright by saying he had no interest in having you presented. Everyone else spends all their time jockeying for position and trying to get their relatives noticed by the Sun-on-Earth, and Cliopher firmly declines the invitation with thanks. You're going to go to court to see Cliopher formally inducted as Lord Chancellor, however, his Radiancy has said so."

"I'll stand with you," Conju offered bracingly, no doubt seeing Zemius' still-horrified expression.

"What, you're coming?" Cliopher said in astonishment. "You never go to court."

"Of course I'll come see you inducted! What kind of friend would I be if I didn't?"

"His Radiancy hasn't decided if Commander Omo and I will be his honour guard for the occasion, or if he would prefer us to have it off so we can come as courtiers. I think we'll likely be there as the guard, but if not, we'll come stand with you. I wouldn't miss this commencement for the world. Besides, we might be necessary to keep you from running away. Or fainting."

Zemius looked mortified. "That was the only time I've ever fainted!"

"Not you—Kip."

CHAPTER TWENTY-SEVEN

THE NEXT MORNING CLIOPHER PUT on one of his new outfits and, delighting in his newfound ability to find his way through the rooms, went to knock on his cousin's door. Zemius came out looking nervous and anxious.

"You look wonderful," Cliopher said in what he hoped were reassuring tones.

"I've never worn anything this grand, not even for Senate or graduations." Zemius ran his hands down his white linen tunic, then touched the black linen robe which went over, and finally adjusted the over-mantle of aquamarine silk. "It is truly splendid. You look wonderful, too."

Cliopher smiled deprecatingly, but he did have to admit his new outfits were quite astonishingly pleasant to wear and looked very elegant—with a little something else he supposed was what Lady Ylette and his Radiancy had called 'flair'. This morning he wore two layers of robes, the under pale golden linen, the upper a rich bronze silk, with the black and white tasselled belt of his office as secretary. "Can you eat something?"

"I'm not sure," Zemius admitted. "I'm really to have an audience with the Glorious One?"

"You are. I'll be there, though. I'm still his Radiancy's secretary until court resumes, and I'm sure he will want me to take notes."

They ate a light meal of herbed flatbread and the soft cheese that was a specialty of the plains around Solaara, and at the three-quarter chime Cliopher and his cousin washed their hands and faces and set off to the Imperial Apartments. Cliopher gave his cousin the advice to address his Radiancy as "my lord," to bow deeply, and to try not to be too nervous.

"Easy enough for you to say!" Zemius said, but he managed to force out a laugh.

They arrived at the Imperial Apartments. Two guards whom Cliopher knew by sight but not by name stood on either side of the great sun-in-glory double doors and gave them the ritual challenge. "My cousin, Zemius Do-minus Mdang, to see his Radiancy," Cliopher said to them.

The guards stamped their spears and the doors opened behind them.

Cliopher and his cousin passed through the first room, where four pages sat on benches awaiting messages and facing another two guards, and so on through the six layers of rooms it took to reach the lord's study. Zemius grew visibly more nervous as the rooms increased in magnificence and the guards in majesty.

"These rooms used to be full of courtiers in Astandalan days," Cliopher murmured as they paused in the sixth waiting room so that his cousin could adjust his handful of books and papers. Cliopher suspected he should proba-bly have found a page to carry those for his cousin, but he guessed that Ze-mius would have been overcome by that extra degree of courtliness. "Let me take those," he added, watching them nearly slip out of his cousin's shaking hands. "I'm more accustomed to making my bows holding things than you."

Zemius relinquished them with a mixture of gratitude and reluctance. He rubbed his hands down his robes again, re-adjusted the overmantle for only the fourth time, took several deep breaths, and finally, under the watch-ful and not unamused eyes of the outer guard, nodded decisively. "I'm ready, Cousin Kip."

"Very good," said Cliopher, nodding at the guards, who turned as one to open the doors and announce: "Lord Mdang and Zemius Dominus Mdang of the University of the Vangavaye-ve!"

Zemius got four feet into the room before he sank down into the full prostration.

Cliopher, meeting his Radiancy's amused eyes, stepped to one side, made his own genuflection, and at the usual subtle gesture rose again and deposited his cousin's books on his desk.

"Rise, domine," said his Radiancy. Zemius seemed to take this as an optional suggestion, for he rose to his knees and stayed firmly planted, eyes well down.

Cliopher met his Radiancy's glance again and shrugged. His Radiancy was standing in the middle of the room, dressed in what Cliopher knew was one of the least intimidating outfits he possessed, something he would wear within his own apartments and never outside their walls. He looked down at Zemius and for a moment no one did anything. Finally his Radiancy ges-tured him to his seat and said, "Take notes, Cliopher."

Cliopher sat down at his desk, nodding to Ser Rhodin and Elish as he did so. He arranged his papers carefully, set out his pens, and stacked his cousin's notes neatly on the farther side of the desk. His Radiancy watched this; Zemius stared at the floor; and finally, when Cliopher had indicated himself prepared, his Radiancy said: "We have read your book, domine."

He paused, and after a moment Zemius said, nearly inaudibly, "I am honoured beyond measure, Glorious One."

His Radiancy stared down at him for a moment, then lifted his eyebrow at Cliopher. Cliopher, not quite sure what he was to make of this (except that Zemius surely could manage to put two words together? He was reckoned a most engaging and delightful professor, he knew that), shrugged again.

He could see his Radiancy suppress a sigh. "What brought you to this topic, domine? How did you come to be so interested in the history of the lords magi?"

Zemius said, "I have always been interested in history, my lord. I had just completed a second degree and was considering going to Alinor for a third when the Fall took place."

"You have a cousin there, do you not?"

"Yes, my lord."

"And so, the Fall?"

"In the Vangavaye-ve we were not so ill-used by the Fall, my lord, but for the complete lack of communication with the rest of the world. We didn't even know that the rest of the Empire had been lost. I started looking into the succession of the lords magi because it seemed such a topical subject. Not that I presumed I would be sought out by Lady Jivane or anyone else, my lord, but I was interested and we—we didn't know what had happened."

Cliopher diligently took notes so he didn't have to look at his Radiancy. It occurred to him he'd never asked Zemius what had led him to his subject; his cousin had always been fascinated by history and magic, and it hadn't seemed a particular stretch for him to focus on a topic that combined both.

His Radiancy had started pacing; now he stopped to regard the scholar again. "Your cousin Kip was in Astandalas when the Empire Fell. What did you know of him?"

Zemius looked up in surprise, looking across to Cliopher (who tried not to glare at him for so forgetting etiquette as to pay attention to anyone other than his Radiancy), then back to his Radiancy. "My lord, we had no news of him for many years. No one could get past the Outer Ring reefs because of the storms. Finally someone from the navy made it in, on a ship that grounded on a reef on its passage into the Bay of Waters. The captain and crew were saved, and most of their things, including a letter from Kip."

"How many letters did you send, Kip?" his Radiancy asked him.

Cliopher swallowed. He'd lost count somewhere above fifty. "Many, my lord. That particular one had come back to me six or seven times."

"Yes, you kept adding postscripts explaining what you were doing then. You had broken an arm; the broken arm had healed, the city was being rebuilt, the Emperor was still asleep … but we couldn't write back to you because the ship had been wrecked." Zemius trailed off and bowed again. "I am sorry, Glorious One, I did not mean to stray from my topic."

"You must have been worried, Kip," his Radiancy said, ignoring this.

"I was, my lord. As I have told you, at length I resigned my position and made my way westward. But my family were alive, and it was well worth it."

"I should imagine so. I am almost amazed you returned to Solaara afterwards."

Cliopher could not quite meet his glance. He had intended to stay in the Vangavaye-ve, until it had been made very clear to him that the man who had come home was not the one they had wanted. And Ghilly had not wanted to come second—

His Radiancy turned his head. "Please be seated, Professor Mdang, you have brought notes and references with you and I expect you will need them."

Zemius got awkwardly to his feet (not being at all accustomed to spending ten minutes kneeling on a stone floor, Cliopher thought) and took the seat across from Cliopher to which his Radiancy pointed him. His Radiancy did not sit down, but paced with his robes swirling about him. Zemius pulled his papers towards himself and seemed to take some comfort from their presence.

His Radiancy didn't let him have enough time to grow nervous again, Cliopher saw with appreciation. "You have evidently done a great deal of research into this matter of the succession of the lords magi of Zunidh. It is convenient we met you in Gorjo City: though of course Lord Mdang would have found what books treat this topic in the Imperial Library had we not. To our questions: how did you come to learn about the spell?"

"It is mentioned in some of the older chronicles, my lord, in *The Book of the First Ones* and *The Wars of Yr the Conqueror*. It first came to my notice, however, in an old poem, the *Saga of the Sons of Morning*, when the Lady sets out to find the Tiger."

His Radiancy, frowning, spoke out a few lines in sonorous Old Shaian.

"Exactly, my lord," said Zemius, growing slightly enthusiastic. "*Seeking the Tiger of the Western Gate, the Lady of the Peacock Throne cast the yarrow and rang the bronze hammers before she proceeded along the road of the waters to the city of heavenly repose* ... To give a rough translation, my lord, which is obviously unnecessary, and I apologize, Glorious One, I did not know you knew Old Shaian, let alone knew such an old——"

"It has been long since I read the old sagas, but I learned many by heart when I was young. So the Lady of the Peacock Throne cast the yarrow and rang the bronze hammers ... how do you gloss that?"

"The *Saga* treats the history of Zunidh before the emergence of Yr the Conqueror. It is most famous for the account of the Courting of the Sun and Moon, of course. The Lady of the Peacock Throne is Laiala, the third lord magus, and the Tiger of the Western Gate is Nwo Ya, the fourth, whom she was seeking. The casting of the yarrow and the ringing of the bronze hammers are what led me to suspect there was a spell, my lord, because in *The Book of the First Ones* there is another reference to 'casting yarrow' when Nwo Ya, despairing of maintaining independence in the face of the Conquest, wished to retire and sought a younger heir. The bronze hammers are mentioned in *The Wars of Yr the Conqueror* in another description of the same moment of despair."

"I do not recall mention of bronze hammers in that passage," his Radiancy said, frowning. "Does it not describe Nwo Ya throwing down the gates of the city of Viren before the army of Yr?"

"That is the text that is usually published, my lord, but when you go back to the original scrolls, you will see that certain scribal errors have crept into the text. The original is *kidor ngai zivelliaran na Viren*——"

"'He took the bronze hammers from out of the city of Viren.'"

"Just so, my lord. *Zivelliaran* is an unusual word, however, already antiquated when the text was first composed, and it is little surprise that the scribe corrected the partial abbreviation *zivellrn* to *zivaran*."

"'Cast down.'"

"Exactly!" Zemius favoured him with a smile that indicated why he was a beloved teacher, before he abruptly remembered to whom he was speaking. He tried to bow into the table; his Radiancy made an impatient gesture. "And then, my lord, once it was 'He cast down the bronze hammers from out of the city of Viren,' it was not so long before *kidor* was read as a corruption of *kithar*, and it became——"

"'He cast down the bronze doors of the city of Viren.' And so I read it in the histories. How do you know that is not the correct reading, domine?"

"One of the basic principles of textual criticism, my lord, is that the more difficult reading is usually the more correct, because people tend to simplify complex matters over time."

"How true." His Radiancy paced back and forth a few steps. "I accept the role of the bronze hammers. The casting of the yarrow—I presume that is to do with some form of divination? Casting yarrow is still practiced for such by the Mother of the Mountains in Kavanduru."

"Is it, my lord? Oh, how marvellous. That was something I have found much more difficult to find analogues for. What manner of plant yarrow is, for instance. It clearly has a long straight stalk, for there is much made of the direction of roots versus flower heads, but the word seems to refer to several different plants."

"It is a kind of roadside weed in certain temperate parts of the nine worlds," his Radiancy said, then smiled briefly when Cliopher forgot himself enough to look curious. "As a boy my tutor was Alinorel and his special interest was temperate-climate wildflowers. It is quite pretty, and I believe has some medicinal properties as well as its magical ones. Very well. What of these bronze hammers, which the Tiger of the Western Gate removed from Viren before its destruction by Yr? Have you had better luck finding them out?"

"It took me much searching, my lord, but eventually I discovered that they were part of the tribute brought by Lady Injeda to Empress Zangora the Fifth, when the last independent city of Zunidh fell to the Astandalan Army. They were incorporated into the building of the Palace of Stars, and form part of the superstructure of the bell-tower, my lord."

His Radiancy turned back from the window to regard him silently. Zemius, obviously not certain of the etiquette, cast a nervous sideways glance at Cliopher, who smiled reassuringly, being as aware as his Radiancy of the time.

Into the silence fell the sweet resonant chimes of the hour-bell ringing the fourth hour of the morning.

"Now," his Radiancy said, once they had finished, "we have the bells and the yarrow. What am I to do with them?"

"Appendix three gives the spell, my lord, as best as I was able to recreate it with the assistance of some of my colleagues in the Department of Magic."

"It is incomplete," his Radiancy replied firmly. "It cannot be performed as it stands."

"Oh, no, my lord! Megana did say she was afraid there were elements missing, because of something to do with the way the ritual went, but she couldn't figure out what they could be, and thought that perhaps it was different for a great magus than it is for regular wizards."

"It is clearly a variant on Harbut Zalarin's famous Seeking Spell. There are certainly some differences in how the matter is intended to go ... but of course it may be that there are papers in the Archives or the Imperial Library that may shed light on the missing elements."

"How wise you are, my lord," Zemius said, with nothing but genuine admiration in his voice. His Radiancy accepted the compliment at face value with nothing more than another speaking look over at Cliopher, as if they were two friends set together as a unit against the rest of the world.

It occurred to Cliopher, as his Radiancy turned with another flare of his robes to pace around the room some more, that the Lord Chancellor of Zunidh was someone with whom the Lord of Rising Stars might conceivably condescend to associate in a way entirely prohibited to the Secretary in Chief of the Private Offices of the Lords of State, be he never so much the same person.

He earnestly regarded his notes to hide his smile.

His Radiancy said, "Very well, we shall leave the completion of the spell to some researches in the archives. Let us go to the second portion of the succession: the discovery of the heir once the spell has been cast. What, precisely, do you suppose the purpose of the spell is? As a variant on the Seeking Spell the divinatory elements of yarrow, combined with the bronze hammers, which it seems are part of the pre-Astandalan regalia of Zunidh, are clear enough in terms of divining someone who will be appropriate to the world's needs. You mention shamanistic rituals?"

"Just so, my lord. It is my considered belief that the ceremony was developed by Lady Ialo herself, who was one of the Eilmanius shamans. There is little to be found of the Eilmanii, since they were not a literate people and are now extinct, but many of their religious practices were incorporated into the rites that became the early structure of the Schooled magic of Astandalas, and so there are some few details to be gleaned from the early records, though many are still classified and unavailable to scholarship."

"Are they?" His Radiancy glanced at Cliopher. "You have not brought this to my attention."

Cliopher blinked. "It had not come to mine, my lord. The Prince of Amboloyo is chair of the Ceremonial Conclave. Nothing has been brought before me on the subject."

"I see," his Radiancy said, his serene countenance unmoving. "You will write us a proclamation that credentialed scholars may have full access to the Astandalan Archives, Lord Mdang. There are only a few sections that must remain inaccessible at this late date, which we shall detail later."

"Very good, my lord."

His Radiancy turned back to Zemius. "Since you are the expert in the matter, we shall give you the task of filling in what gaps in your research you can from the Imperial Archives before you return to Gorjo City."

"Your Radiancy is very kind," said Zemius, lighting up. "I would be honoured and delighted to render you every assistance in my power, my lord."

Not to mention to have full access to the Imperial Archives, Cliopher thought.

His Radiancy gazed at him for a moment. "Continue, domine, with your account."

Zemius nodded anxiously. "Yes, my lord. The ceremonies associated with the spell are connected, as best I could determine, to the vision quest rituals of the Eilmanii. Usually the vision quest is the beginning of a person's career—in many cultures it is what gives direction to one's life and marks the passage from child to adult—but among the Eilmanii there was a tradition of a second quest that marked the passage from adult to elder.

"It may be that I will be able to find confirmation of it in the Archives, my lord, but I have long thought there a strong likelihood that the Eilmanii tradition always involved the quest to determine the worthiest successor, and that Lady Ialo was following her cultural traditions in this instance. It is not altogether dissimilar from our—that is, Islander—practice. Later lords magi then added further elements to the spell as the needs of Zunidh changed and the Empire and its magic developed."

"Did Lady Jivane alter the spell?"

Zemius shrugged apologetically. "That may also be in the Archives, my lord, if she left any written account of her actions. As far as I have been able to determine, no."

"She was not the most inventive of magi," his Radiancy said thoughtfully. "One reason why she was chosen for the position, I had always thought. She was very willing to bow to the Emperor. Indeed, when I awoke after the Fall, she was immediately concerned with handing her responsibilities back to me."

"She was the viceroy of the Emperor on Zunidh, Glorious One," Zemius said. "Surely that was her duty."

"In some ways," his Radiancy agreed. "In others … well, it is long since done and gone into the past. We should be very certain, however, that the spell does not incorporate any additions intended to make our successor ... biddable. But that will be our concern rather than yours. Continue, domine."

"The order of events is fairly clear, my lord," Zemius said, with a slightly puzzled air. "The lord magus performs a full ritual of cleansing—although that likely began with an Eilmanii ritual, over the centuries it developed into the full Astandalan rite, of which I give an abbreviated account in Appendix Five. You will be able to find details of the full rite, my lord, I am sure."

"We are familiar with the Astandalan rite of purification," his Radiancy said flatly. Cliopher thought of the eighty-one days it took to purify an orange, and winced.

"Oh ... of course, my lord. Um, after the purification, the lord magus then performed the spell."

"Is there a particular time at which the spell ought to be cast?"

"That is something I hope to find further data on in the Archives, my lord, because Astandalan spells invariably changed with the seasons and movements of the celestial bodies, and I cannot believe this one was fully independent of the temporal element so noteworthy in Schooled magic. However, there is very little indication that there was a set time or conjunction or the like in this case. Which I find puzzling, but my colleague Megana, who is our university's scholar of Astandalan magic, said that there were some spells that were thus unconnected, and that a seeking spell would be as likely as any to be able to be cast at any time."

"This is Megana Courtenay?"

Zemius nodded very deeply, almost bowing into the table again. "She will be deeply honoured that you know her name, my lord."

"We have read some of her articles. She appears to have a good understanding of Schooled magic. Very well. We shall see if you come across anything further in the Archives on this subject. Harbut Zalarin's magic was not part of Astandalan Schooled wizardry, though many of his spells were incorporated into it. I wonder, however, about the *Saga of the Sons of Morning*. It comes to my mind that before the Lady of the Peacock Throne casts the yarrow, she notices that it is *orgellian zo enphantassai*, which is to say, 'the time of the rising stars'. How do you gloss that?"

"It is usually understood to mean sunset, my lord."

"But the stars rise at all times as the world turns through day and night," his Radiancy said, his expression inscrutable. "Hence our title as Lord of the Rising Stars: the sun never set on nor the stars ever failed to illuminate our demesne."

Zemius swallowed. "Perhaps it has meaning to do with the growing might of Astandalas, my lord."

"Perhaps it does. We shall ask our Master of Ceremonies to determine when that title was adopted."

Cliopher made a note in the margin to this effect. He wasn't sure why his Radiancy was going back and forth between formal and informal pronouns. It made him slightly uneasy.

"To return to your account: the lord magus performs the full Astandalan rite of purification, followed by the casting of the spell proper. And then?"

"And then, my lord, if there is no successor nearby, he undertakes the quest."

"Does this spell then provide such clear knowledge of the successor's location and identity?"

"It is unclear, my lord. Some of the passages seem to indicate the heir was known to the sitting lord magus on sight, others suggest that although the spell found the heir quickly, the sitting lord magus took the person as companion in the quest rather than its object. The Lady of the Peacock Throne, for instance, was going to see the Tiger of the Western Gate for advice, and they travelled together for an extended period of time before she handed over the crown of Zunidh to him."

His Radiancy started to pace again, his face perfectly inscrutable. "We did not know, when we awoke to find our Empire destroyed, what Lady Jivane had in mind." He turned abruptly to his guards. "Summon Commander Omo here."

Ser Rhodin saluted and opened the door to relay this order to the guards on the other side.

His Radiancy strode over to the great woven map on the wall and stood looking at it for a few moments before raising his hand to touch first the very centre, where Astandalas the Golden was marked by a great glittering yellow diamond. After a meditative pause he walked over the dozen feet to the farthest edge to touch the tiny stone on the Long Edge of Colhélhé he had said was one of the anchors of Schooled magic. Then he walked back along the length of the map to touch his hand to the small white pearl representing Solaara, then a remote village notable only for its proximity to the Necropolis of the Emperors and for being the hometown of Yr the Conqueror.

His Radiancy looked at the map some while longer, then turned and said: "Lord Mdang, you were in the Palace when I awoke after the Fall. Describe the events of the day as you recall them."

"As you wish, my lord," said Cliopher, who then couldn't remember anything at all.

"Domine Mdang, take notes, please."

Zemius murmured something polite and took one of Cliopher's pens. Thus freed from the necessity of writing while he was remembering, Cliopher closed his eyes and thought himself back to that strange day at the end of the Dark Century when the Last Emperor had been a silent, sleeping presence in the heart of a palace that did not know what to do either with or without him.

"At the time I was on Princess Indrogan's team for the restoration of government," he said, keeping his eyes closed. "Our offices were over in the Ystharian wing, on the second floor but close to the Central Block, directly below the princess' own apartments. I was in a room with about a dozen other people, and ... yes, that's right, we were talking about how the outlying regions were raising armies for themselves and setting up as independent countries, and what with the famines and unsettled weather everywhere we could see that there was going to be a hard time of things going forward, and we should be fortunate if the whole world didn't dissolve into outright war."

Who had been in that room with him? He'd known them all well, once. Most of them were long since dead, as they'd been much older. He'd been young then, and pleased with his position. Even if it was tremendously difficult to work under Princess Indrogan, who was an abrasive woman utterly sure of her own brilliance, he was well aware of the assistance her patronage was to him, that he was accepted as he had not been before she had promoted him. And every once in a while he could contribute an idea to the complex program of restoration.

"Princess Indrogan had just said something about the hope of a trading route re-opening along the Eastern Sea when all the Palace bells started to ring." Cliopher smiled involuntarily. "I've never heard them like that. They all rang, at first we thought the hour—it was just around noon—but they kept on ringing, as if they were going to break the Palace with their thunder. They went on and on, almost—almost cascading—as if each time one rang the next did, and the next, and we all sat there staring at each other as the room almost shook with the sound.

"When it stopped, we all stared at each other some more, but the whole Palace was dead silent except for some strange whispery echoes. Finally the princess sent someone—not me—out to find out what had happened. It must have been over an hour before he came back to tell us the Emperor had woken up. Then, of course, no one got any work done, the whole city and Palace and everything just dissolved into a party."

He opened his eyes to see that his Radiancy was looking peculiarly at him. Zemius had written a page of notes in the common script. Cliopher swallowed and pulled his own notebook and pen towards himself.

"Commander Omo," said Ser Rhodin.

His Radiancy turned to gaze sternly at his chief guard. "We have been discussing the succession," he said. "We would have you describe the events of our awakening after the Fall in detail. Describe also as many of the *emotional* reactions you recall."

If he were surprised, Commander Omo gave little indication of it. He saluted and at his Radiancy's gesture came to stand easily in the centre of the room.

"I was a junior member of the Imperial Guard at the time, my lord. I had been given the honour of standing guard in the throne room several times. It was a position of very great honour, but many disliked it because it was very strange to stand guard over someone who seemed neither dead nor alive."

"Describe the room."

Commander Omo saluted. "It was the throne room, my lord. The—the bier had been set upon the lower dais, below the throne. There were four candles always lit, and four guards to stand. The—your Radiancy had been placed there, on your back, arms folded, with white linen and cloth-of-gold hangings. Under your head was the Sun Banner, and in your hands were the staves and the sceptre. You had been dressed in the Greater Jewels, and sometimes the flickering of the candles made it seem as if you were moving. But apart from breathing you were utterly still. We guards stood facing out, in our full panoply. It was always very quiet. You cannot hear anything from outside the room but for the four bells of the day, even when there was no court within."

The four bells of the day: dawn, noon, sunset, midnight, rung—as Cliopher now knew—by the bronze hammers of ancient Zunidh. In equatorial Solaara the days did not shift length, were twelve hours long the year round.

"After six months on the night watch—sunset to dawn—I had been promoted to the day watch. It was the end of my first week, and I was still finding it hard to shift from being awake nights to being awake days, though I thought the throne room very beautiful in the daytime, with the sun shining through the coloured windows. I found the nights very peaceful—my people stand guard over our dead, my lord, we do not fear the spirits coming—and you were not dead. Others did not like it so well. Even in the day."

Cliopher tried to imagine standing watch over someone who had slept for a hundred years without moving, and shivered slightly.

"I came on duty that day at dawn, and I remember the noon bell rang. I was facing the northwest corner on that occasion, so I could not see the hall but I had before me the wall listing the hundred Emperors of Astandalas and the windows representing Ysthar in my line of sight. I watched the coloured light cast on the floor move with the sun, and remember there was a spray of pink from the roses that nearly touched my feet at noon. At noon and midnight we made a formal salute to the Emperor. The noon bell rang, sounding much louder and more prolonged than usual, as we turned to make our salute, and just as we did so—you sat up."

Cliopher looked at his Radiancy, who was looking serene, and Commander Omo, who looked blank as ever, and addressed himself back to his paper. He had never heard Commander Omo speak so much before.

"We were, of course, very surprised. I do not know why it was I was not shocked as my fellow guards were. We saluted, and your Radiancy sat up and started to cough, and I remember thinking that of course you would need something to drink, who wouldn't be thirsty after so long asleep? But when I looked Tiko had fainted and Issakar was sobbing, and Diego had cried out and was standing with his eyes like saucers. So I sent him to fetch water."

Some guards, Cliopher thought, unable to recall who had been Commander in those days. He or she had probably not put the best on duty for the silent vigil; even Ludvic had been young and untried.

"Your Radiancy stopped coughing and said: 'Where am I?' And I saluted and replied, 'In the throne room of the Palace of Stars, Glorious One.' 'But this is not Ysthar,' you said, 'it is Zunidh. And the Empire is no more.' It did not occur to me to wonder how it was your Radiancy knew these things, because of course it had been so long since the Fall. I said, 'You have been asleep for a hundred years.' And Diego came running back with the water, and your Radiancy drank it and looked around and finally said, 'Who is in charge, then?' And I said Lady Jivane, and your Radiancy asked if she were in the Palace and I said I thought so."

He stopped there for a moment. His Radiancy said, "Continue."

"Your Radiancy came down from the bier and took the cloth-of-gold as a mantle—I remember I had not realized it was one, I had thought it a burial-shroud—and still in the full jewels. Our duty was to protect the person of the Emperor, so we formed up behind your Radiancy—by this point

Issakar and Tiko had recovered—and we went out of the throne room and Diego found a page to ask about the Lady, and we were told she was in her apartments, where she usually held court in those days."

Those were now *his* apartments, Cliopher thought.

"We saw people as we went, and all of them could see that the Emperor had awoken as we had all been longing for. I was so proud that I had the privilege of accompanying your Radiancy on this journey. I knew I would not be granted so high an honour once the Commander of the Guards knew the Emperor had awoken, because I was too junior. But I was so very proud and happy to walk from the throne room to the Lady's chamber. We arrived, and were shown in to the receiving room, where Lady Jivane sat with her council."

"Describe the room," his Radiancy said gently.

"It was the First Receiving Room, the White Tiger Room. Lady Jivane had her chair in the centre of the back wall, and there were perhaps seven or ten others with her. They had evidently been arguing, or at least conversing vigorously, for the room felt tense and full of unspoken matters. We came into the door and I announced your Radiancy, and Lady Jivane stood up from her chair and fell to her knees before your Radiancy and said, 'O Serene and Glorious One, you come in answer to our prayers and supplications. I hand over Zunidh to you.'"

He paused there, and Cliopher had time to think that if he had been his Radiancy, waking up after a hundred years asleep, his Empire fallen and all its magic out-of-sorts, and he had walked from the throne room to the current ruler to find out what had happened, he, too, would be somewhat annoyed at her precipitousness.

"Thank you, Ludvic," said his Radiancy. "Professor Mdang, have you any questions?"

Zemius looked as if he had enough questions to last him the rest of his life, but none appeared to be for Commander Omo, for he shook his head.

"Very good."

"Is there anything else, my lord?"

"No, thank you. You may return to your other duties."

Commander Omo saluted and exited. His Radiancy watched him go, then turned expectantly to Zemius. "I think that makes the sequence of events somewhat clearer. I do not recall what date exactly it was on which I awoke, but it is certainly in the records. It is clear that the Palace bells rang before I woke, not after, and I think it is most likely that it was indeed the spell that woke me. There may, of course, be some other explanation, but that is simplest. Yes, Cliopher?"

Cliopher bit his lip that his expression had revealed him so easily. "Is it not certain that you woke in response, my lord?"

"It is a matter of wild magic. Coincidence and serendipity are to be expected. As the coincidence of your cousin studying this topic and coming in just at that moment."

"A cousin for every occasion," Zemius murmured; it was one of the family jokes.

His Radiancy's eyes glittered with amusement. Cliopher wished he would say what he was thinking.

He realized, with some perturbation, that at some point in the past six weeks his Radiancy had ceased to be the inviolate god and become a person to him. The perturbation, he then discovered in an unexpected flash of intuition, was for how very easily the transformation had occurred.

No matter how he had tried, he never had managed to internalize court etiquette.

"Now: we will be able to determine the date with comparative ease, and we have seen that the ceremony was timed so the bronze hammers were sounded at noon. It remains to consider the fulfilment of the spell ... Lady Jivane, it would appear, recognized in me immediately her successor, though I am not sure why she thought I had any gift at magic ... there was nothing to have said it in my time as Emperor."

He pondered a moment, while Cliopher watched Zemius try not to ask why that would have been the case. His Radiancy went on after a while, "Lady Jivane was an intimate of my sister. Possibly she had heard of my gift of magic from her or our mother." His tone suggested this was highly unlikely. "Tell me, domine, what has happened in the past regarding the quest."

"Glorious one, as I said, it was an Eilmanii-style vision quest. The sitting lord magus performed the ritual spell, and then set off—as the *Saga* has it—'alone along the road of the waters to the city of heavenly repose'."

"By ship?"

"The Eilmanii were a seafaring people, my lord."

"And the City of Heavenly Repose?"

"I believe that is glossed as the city of Aurden, which was lost in the Conquest. However, there have been several studies of the Eilmanii vision quests—none recently, but there were several notable Alinorel Scholars in Astandalan days interested in the subject. The most noteworthy is *Vision*

Quests of the Ancient Days of Zunidh, by Eduardes Desindago of Morrowlea, which was published in the days of the Empress Anyoë. You will see my summaries of his findings in Appendix Three. He has much fuller accounts in *Vision Quests*, my lord. It did not occur to me that it would be necessary to go into such detail in my account, as I was concerned more with establishing the fact of the spell and its consequences than with explaining the Eilmanii."

"Very good. I presume there is a copy of this work in the Imperial Library, as it was published within the Empire."

His Radiancy frowned at the floor for a moment. Zemius watched him warily. After a moment, his Radiancy spun on one foot (his robes really did flare superbly, Cliopher could not help noticing; they seemed almost designed for the purpose) and went to his own carved-sandalwood desk. He dipped his brush in the ink-pot and briskly wrote out a note, signed and sealed with the gold-and-rose-petal-infused wax that he alone used. He passed this note to Cliopher, who looked down at the words in bemusement:

> *Zemius professor Mdang of the University of the Vangavaye-ve has our permission to access any of the holdings of the Imperial Library and Archives and make what notes he requires for his research.*

"That will give you access to the Library and Archives until our coming proclamation goes into effect," his Radiancy said. "You will, of course, stay for your cousin's induction as Lord Chancellor of Zunidh, and you may stay as long as is required for your research. It is our hope you will amplify your knowledge of this matter of the succession for our use. If anything comes to mind that you would we learn, you may relay it through your cousin."

"Thank you, my lord," Zemius said, and then, obviously feeling something else was required, he got up and performed the deep obeisance again.

His Radiancy raised his eyebrows at Cliopher, who smiled ruefully at his cousin's obliviousness of his dismissal.

"With your permission, my lord," he said, "I will escort my cousin to the pages and ensure they see him safely back to my rooms."

"Of course," his Radiancy murmured. "Return after. We have much to discuss."

★★★

THE REST OF THE DAY passed in a blur of conversations circling around when his Radiancy ought think about preparing his spell. Cliopher managed, subtly he hoped, to convince his Radiancy that he needed to wait for the results of Zemius' researches in the Archives before he made his final decision.

His Radiancy appeared to take his hesitation for concern over his own new role as Lord Chancellor, and finally chuckled abruptly and said, "You'll have plenty of time to get your people in hand before I leave, Kip. It'll be at least a year, in any regards."

"My lord?"

"The full ritual of purification for me will take even more than the eighty-one days, alas."

"Oh?" he ventured. But his Radiancy smiled and said that they had done enough to ensure the succession that day, and he was to enjoy his brief holiday with his cousin, and shooed him off.

CHAPTER TWENTY-EIGHT

IT WAS, CLIOPHER CONCEDED TO himself, the most stunning clothing he had ever seen on anyone not actually his Radiancy.

He was standing in front of the great wall-length mirror in his dressing room as Féonie and Franzel poked and pulled to get his new court costume perfectly arranged. It was in several layers of midnight blue and rich orange and gold and white and aquamarine—the blue and orange what marked him out as peculiarly Zuni, the gold an indication of his new rank, the aquamarine that he was of the Vangavaye-ve.

It was the princely heraldic colour, not any true Islander decoration, but it was more than he had ever been able to show before. And Féonie and Franzel had made no demur when he had said that he would be wearing the efela necklace. It was not visible, true, but then again it never was.

His feet were in sandals, cork soles gilded, the straps made of intricately woven bands joined by gold and electrum fasteners liberally decorated with amber and aquamarine. He wore three layers of silk, the bottom white embroidered with orange and black tigers, the middle midnight blue, the topmost the rich orange, nearly umber, whose golden embroidery glinted as he breathed. Little sparks of aquamarine in the form of gems and the intricately knotted and braided silk ropes of his various positions within the Service added a touch of relief.

"Is there no hat?" he asked after a long moment of silence. "I thought there was a hat."

Féonie gave him a possessive smile. "His Radiancy will give you the hat at the installation."

"It is nearly time, Sir," Franzel added, beaming at him.

"I really don't know what to say," Cliopher said, then was emboldened enough to add: "It is the finest clothing I have ever seen but what his Radiancy wears."

"It should be, as Lady Ylette makes both," Féonie replied tartly, but he could see that his faltering gratitude pleased her.

"Thank you," he said. "I don't know what time this will be over ..."

But then one of his new footmen was there. "Ewan, isn't it?" he asked desperately.

"Very good, Sir. The guards are without."

And Cliopher swallowed down his dry throat and let Ewan lead him through the maze of his apartments to the front receiving room, where Sir Rhodin and Commander Omo waited.

"You're not—not with his Radiancy tonight?" he asked.

"We are not," Ser Rhodin said, eyes glimmering with humour.

"We wished to stand with you," Commander Omo said, and added, with a rare smile, "Though we had to argue with the other honour guards for the privilege of who would be guarding his Radiancy tonight to watch! Pikabe and Ato won the toss in the end. Zerafin was mighty disappointed, let me tell you, so we let him come as one of the wall guards."

Cliopher swallowed again, and forced himself not to clutch at any of the delicate silk he was wearing. "Thank you, my friends."

"Conju has your cousin under his wing," Ser Rhodin went on, chuckling. "His Radiancy did ask! And he is waiting."

"We must not keep him."

"No."

But Cliopher stood there, palms sweating, for a long moment, before he swallowed again, nodded decisively, and forced himself to get moving.

"Good lad," said Ser Rhodin. "It'll be over in an hour."

★★★

IT WAS, OF COURSE, MUCH closer to five; few were the court events that took less than three hours.

It was the first court of the Lord's New Year, which meant that his Radiancy had to perform lengthy ceremonies to anchor the year's beginning and ensure auspicious harvests in those portions of the world that were shifting seasons.

It was the first court after the Little Session, meaning that it was when new appointments were made and new titles given.

Everyone was waiting to hear what exactly had prompted his Radiancy's secretary's move to the Lord of Zunidh's apartments. Cliopher could not pretend to himself that this was anything but the most intriguing appointment of the year—perhaps the decade—perhaps the century. When he arrived, flanked by Commander Omo and Ser Rhodin in their lesser panoply, the herald at the door smiled at him and gestured at the man beside him.

"The Master of Ceremonies awaits you, sir."

The Master of Ceremonies had naturally been told what was toward; he bowed deeply at this introduction. Cliopher bowed back as he had ever been accustomed to, aware as he did so of the Master's mild censure. He told himself firmly that there was no need to feel embarrassed, and that until the announcement was made, it behoved him to continue as he had.

He was not imagining the buzz of commentary that started to ripple out from the door when he entered. The Master of Ceremonies was dressed in a startling green robe much embroidered with silver, overlaying a white tunic, with knots of twisted silk and tassels to show his rank. He and Cliopher had spent many an hour together working through visits of state made and received, and although they had never become friends, they respected each other. At the moment Lord Lior was puffed full of consequence and as much pride as if it were he himself being granted the honour.

As he had not for anyone besides visiting heads of state or those being given the very highest military or artistic honours, the Master of Ceremonies led him personally through the throngs of brilliantly garbed courtiers to the knee wall below the daïs on which was placed the great throne of Astandalas. Out of the corner of his eye Cliopher saw his cousin and Conju standing in a place of honour.

The throne room of the Palace of Stars was one of the glories of the nine worlds. The floor was laid with an intricate mosaic of all nine worlds, each tile made of a precious stone set in gold or silver, so that as the courtiers shifted position they stood on rubies and opals and sapphires, on Alinor and Arvath and Ysthar, on amethysts and tourmalines and Voonra and Eahh and Colhélhé, on emeralds and topazes and Zunidh and Kaphyrn and Daun. The spaces in between the oceans were taken up by the Sea of Stars, jet set in silver studded with diamonds.

In contrast to the floor the walls were elegant simplicity itself. Made of the creamy limestone that composed much of the Palace, which had some sort of element in its composition that caught the light with subtle glitters, they soared up to the high vaulted ceiling. Clusters of pillars supported the ribs of the vaulting, each seeming far too slender to hold the weight of the roof, whose underside was a mosaic made of sapphires graded from clear cerulean at the edges to the deepest midnight at the zenith.

The sapphires were interspersed with diamonds, these set into the constellations of the River of Stars, which was supposed to be the path left by the tears of the Wizard-Emperor Aurelius Magnus for his bereft Empire when he was stolen away by the Sun and the Moon.

White hands on black skin flashed into his mind. He made himself concentrate on the room again.

Neither the Sun nor the Moon were represented on the ceiling; even they were symbolically subordinated to the throne.

Each of the two long walls of the throne room were lined with windows that reached from head-height to the top of the walls, so that the walls were more glass than stone. These were stained and painted with the images of the first lords magi of each of the nine worlds and the emblems and symbols of their worlds, with Eahh closest to the door and Ysthar closest to the throne.

In the band of stone running below the windows were listed the names of the lords magi of each world. Every time Cliopher entered the throne room he always looked sidelong at the last name under the Zunidh windows, taking some obscure comfort from seeing *Artorin Damara* named there.

The band of stone was the height of the lower daïs, which swept out a good twenty feet into the room. Two flights of steps, one on each side, led up in graceful curves to the lower daïs. The space in between, directly below the feet of the Emperor, was given over to a listing of the vanquished enemies of the Emperor. A bas-relief running below the stone lip—directly at eye-level to the average person—showed tribute being brought from a hundred lands.

Every person, every horse and bull and elephant and slave, every eye and every gesture and every line was directed towards to the centre, where a figure in the garb of a priest held lifted above his head in his hands the orb of the world.

The top names on the lists below the Emperor's feet were the members of the Red Company, who had disappeared shortly after the accession of the hundredth Emperor of Astandalas, who would prove to be the last.

The huge doors facing the throne were made of ivory and gold and ebony and rarer woods and metals. They were intricately carved with scenes depicting the life of Yr the Conqueror, the First Emperor, from his miraculous birth through the building of the monolithic tomb in what became the Necropolis of the Emperors.

The double doors were never opened except for the coronations and funerals of Emperors, though Cliopher knew the hinges were oiled punctiliously; ordinary courtiers entered and exited by the smaller doors set to each side of the greater. High above the lintel was the great round window of brilliant glass and stone fretwork, oriented so that the Sun would shine directly through and the circle of coloured light land on the throne only on very specific days and times in old Astandalas, for particularly significant events in the ritual calendar.

After the Fall and the removal to Solaara, the Palace's orientation had changed, and the light did not fall as it had; but Cliopher knew, again, that astronomers and wizards had spent much time working out the calculations on when the Sun or Moon might shine through that window. Probably the Jubilee ceremonies would centre on one such date.

But it was rare for anyone on his first visit—or even his second or third or fifth—to look at anything but what every line of the room was focused on.

Above the knee wall with its litany of victories, above the lip of the lower daïs where the highest lords of the nine worlds might be permitted to stand, above the heads of every person in the room howsoever tall—on a second raised daïs of five steps sat the great golden throne.

It was very simple. It was a beautiful chair, with a curved back and a slight curve to the seat, all of it fully covered in brilliantly polished gold leaf. The seat was cushioned, and Cliopher knew that that cushion (made of the highest grade of silk and stuffed with the finest down) was changed every single day, that his Radiancy might never know the least discomfort.

Above the throne the creamy limestone rose up, unbroken but for two things. In the centre, the great hanging that had been the tribute of the Queen of the Fairies to the Hundredth Emperor, of merriweather cloth (of which it was said that there were no more than four pieces in all the mortal worlds) wrought in the colours of the Standard of Astandalas: black to the left, white to the right, and the great sun-in-glory in gold directly centred above the throne.

And on the left and the right, the names of the hundred emperors of Astandalas.

And the centre of every gaze and every mind and every subtle line, that hundredth and last Emperor of Astandalas whom Cliopher loved.

Cliopher walked down the whole length of the court, mind buzzing incoherently, eyes fixed on his lord.

He kept thinking how every once in a while he set aside a fortnight in which to go through all the records pertaining to the practical management of the Palace, and how fully one-tenth of its operating budget went to the maintenance of the throne room.

There was a glint in his Radiancy's eyes.

Cliopher was mortally certain he was the only one in all that room looking into them.

CHAPTER TWENTY-NINE

THINGS EVENTUALLY SETTLED DOWN INTO a new routine, and if Cliopher had frequent cause to think back with nostalgia and regret to when he was merely doing two jobs, as his Radiancy's secretary and unofficial head of government, well, his new rank did bring with it some few consolations.

He had far more work to do and concomitantly far less time to himself: but since he no longer had that forty-minute walk to and from his chambers to his work, he did manage to squeeze in enough quiet time not to feel completely frazzled; and he was closer to his friends. He and Conju took to walking in the gardens in the cool of the evening, when the great lunar moths came out to suck nectar. Occasionally Ludvic Omo or Ser Rhodin would join them, as their duties permitted, and in those quiet, pleasant conversations about nothing much in particular Cliopher found his old friendships deepening and enriched.

And then there was his Radiancy. No longer his secretary, Cliopher found his position evolving into something like his confidant. Not that his Radiancy ever spoke of such private and personal matters as he had in Navikiani on holiday, but there were many more witticisms, smiles, even laughter.

Those were good things.

Then there were the other parts of the job. The endless committees. The endless toadying. Admittedly he did his best to put his foot down on that, to the extreme surprise and displeasure of a number of courtiers who had thought him a dazzled commoner.

What position, he asked Conju acidly one evening, did they think he had held all these years that he would be dazzled *now*? Too late did he realize that his Radiancy had paid him one of his infrequent unexpected visits and had heard this. But that was an evening when that delicate seedling friendship put down another few roots, for his Radiancy laughed and agreed and told the two of them—and the omnipresent guards—that the courtiers were like a menagerie where the exhibits and audience were one and the same.

The work was endless. Although he no longer had the direct secretarial work for his Radiancy, he spent many hours each day in the Presence, going over all the matters that still had to go through the Secretary in Chief—and all the new ones that the Service appeared to have been just waiting to hand over to the Lord Chancellor. He had decided to begin his duties with a thorough review of the governance of Zunidh, and if he had thought his reports endless before, well!

But even so, things eventually settled down, and after two months Cliopher felt he had found his feet and was able to begin accomplishing things rather than simply responding to the various crises that landed before him. His day began with the first bell, his work with the second. He read the reports passed up from Kiri and took the important ones to his Radiancy; they discussed anything requiring immediate attention; then he would return to his office and work through the rest of the day in blocks of time devoted to the review of current practice, the various committees he sat on, and the decisions and judgments on current affairs.

The Lord Chancellor was, he discovered, the recipient of all sorts of problems and queries and requests which had not been judged quite serious enough to warrant an application to his Radiancy, but were too important to go before a mere secretary. These judgments had all been made by the applicants themselves, and it amused him quite frequently that the addition of a title made all the noble houses of Zunidh that much more willing to treat with him.

Late one afternoon he was coming back from a meeting with the various ministers of public works and infrastructure—Roads and Terrestrial Transport, Marine and Aerial Transport, Civic Waterways, Wild Waterways, the tiny but very vocal ministry of Intermundial Trade—when he turned into the Offices of State to see what had happened and to request another secretarial assistant, since the one he had been given was proving unable to withstand the pressure of the Lord Chancellor's requirements.

Kiri shook her head and sighed. "You are getting near as bad as his Radiancy, Lord Mdang. That's your third; he's on his fifth."

"I suppose I had noticed that there kept being different people in his study."

She laughed. "He keeps sending pages down with notes to the effect that you are, it appears, irreplaceable, but unfortunately he finds you such in your new position as well as your old, so please can I find someone with a better grasp of diplomatic history? Or economic theory? Or political prudence? Or—"

Cliopher felt obscurely pleased. "Well, I don't need someone with those skills, but I do need someone who isn't going to start panicking when I ask him where the reports from last week were filed."

"No, did Bedro really?" She shook her head and made a note on a pad of paper. "I'll put him into a less stressful position. He's really very good at figures and analysis, that's why I thought he would suit. Perhaps he'll do better under Aioru. I'll see who I can send you tomorrow—possibly Ashendra—anyway. While we're on the topic, the examination results have come in."

Cliopher had nearly forgotten about that yearly ritual. "Oh?"

Kiri grinned at him. "It appears that your elevation has spurred an extraordinary surge in the number of successful aspirants from the hinterlands. I expect there will be even more next year. We have people from every province and territory, including both the Vangavaye-ve and the Azilint, and to top it all off, for the first time ever in the recorded history of the Imperial Service, we have a Tkinele tribesman."

She said this with an air of impishness, as well she might, for the Tkinele were an anomaly among the Zunidh tribes. While his Radiancy encouraged the maintenance and ongoing development of traditional customs, and indeed gave practical assistance in the form of grants and awards and the like for such in the face of trade and other cultural pressures, he also insisted on universal education, tithing, and thoroughly ritualized conflicts. All of these had been part of Astandalan law, but few emperors before him had been as interested in the hinterlands of Zunidh.

The Tkinele, however, occupied a special position. They were not under any of the seventeen princes; their island archipelago and the tribes therein lived in a kind of traditional anarchy which they defended vigorously and violently against all incursions. There was one trading post on one of the outlying islands, which few merchants visited, for the Tkinele produced nothing anyone else wanted, and wanted very little from the rest of the world. They claimed that Astandalas had never conquered them, and in the records of the Empire Cliopher knew the ancient Emperors had made a treaty with the Tkinê Islands to the effect that they would leave each other alone but for that one trading post and its little attached school-cum-hospital-cum-government office.

It was a highly unusual, nearly unique treaty, arisen out of the fact that the Tkinê Islands were of no strategic or economic importance whatsoever, the people there were fierce, warlike, and would have died before submission—and because they were the closest living tribe to the Imperial lineages of Astandalas. Harbut Zalarin, the greatest wizard of pre-Astandalan Zunidh and father of Yr the Conqueror, was Tkinele, and Yr the Conqueror's first Empress-Consort, Ailissa, had been a Tkinele warrior princess.

The Tkinele considered Harbut Zalarin (the son, in the stories, of the Sun and the Paramount Chief of the Tkinele, who were fully matriarchal) as one of their own, far-travelling as he was. He had begotten three sons of the Moon, then settled down in the tiny village of Solaara with his human wife Orinara to raise them, whence in turn Yr the Conqueror and his brother Damar the Bold set their sights on glory. Cliopher had often wondered about that human wife and her semi-divine family.

"Well," said Cliopher, reflecting on all this, "I suppose there is always someone who gets restless. Even in Tkinê. Are the letters of invitation ready for me to sign?"

"Yes, as are the envelopes."

"Bedro can handle this," Cliopher said. "I'll try out Ashendra in the morning."

When they were back in his own office, Cliopher told Bedro that he thought the young man might do better in a less intense position and that Kiri had agreed to trial him under Aioru in the Offices of State. Bedro's reaction of rueful acknowledgement and relief relieved him in turn, and they sat down amicably to the signing of the hundred and fifty-odd successful aspirants of that year's crop.

Cliopher scanned each letter hastily to make certain no one had accidentally or unscrupulously slipped another form or letter into the pile, signed his name, and passed each over to Bedro to slip into the addressed envelopes. Kiri had organized the names by region, so that he could see that the proportions were, indeed, unusual: nearly equal thirds between the Dairen cities, the aristocracy (who often sent their younger children for a period in the Service), and the hinterlands. Usually the Dairen cities supplied more than half the yearly crop.

Down at the bottom were the handful of names from the more obscure parts of the world: two from the Azilint; one from the Yenga; the promised Tkinele; and, right at the bottom, the sole successful aspirant from the Vangavaye-ve, Gaudenius Vawen.

Cliopher cast a quick glance at Bedro, who was yawning and slightly behind in his envelope-stuffing and not looking at the letters except to see that the right name went with the right envelope, and he took a moment to read over that last letter just to savour it.

> Gaudenius Vawen of Gorjo City of the Vangavaye-ve has successfully passed the Imperial Bureaucratic Examination. He is invited to present himself before the Lord Emperor to take his oath of loyalty and enter the Service. A list of instructions is enclosed.
>
> With congratulations, Cliopher Mdang, Lord Chancellor of Zunidh and Secretary in Chief of the Private Offices of the Lords of State.

Cliopher saw that Bedro was still totally abstracted, and below his signature he scrawled a note in his private hand: *Well done, Gaudy!*

He waited until Bedro had just about finished the rest of the letters and was trying to suppress another yawn, and said, "Here's the last—Gaudenius Vawen of the Vangavaye-ve."

"Thank you, your excellency," said Bedro, folding the letter and putting it into its envelope without looking at it. While Cliopher started to tidy up his desk, Bedro stacked the envelopes back into their regional piles, looked up at him, hesitated, and then said, "Lord Mdang?"

Cliopher closed his writing kit. "Yes, Bedro?"

"I am very sorry I cannot—that I am not—that I cannot be your secretary. But sir, I have learned so much from you even in this last fortnight, and I … I thank you."

Cliopher felt somewhat nonplussed. "I thank you for your service," he said, "and I know it is not willingness or accomplishment but temperament that makes it better for you to have another position within the Offices of State."

Bedro swallowed and looked close to tears, and alarmed Cliopher considerably by wanting to kiss his hand as they parted; though he realized, as he went home to his apartments, that that was a custom from South Dair.

★★★

HE CORRESPONDED REGULARLY WITH HIS mother and his sister, a bit more infrequently with his closest cousins and friends. Falbert and Toucan had each written a month or so after his return to Solaara, both teasing him about how very magnificent his sundial would be now that they knew who his lord was, and expressing their awe and amazement at his lord's condescension and graciousness.

They still, Cliopher noted distantly, had not actually congratulated him.

He supposed he should be grateful that they had not turned into toadies (the thought of Bertie attempting to do so gave him a much-needed lift of spirits during one particularly awful Council of Princes meeting), and that Toucan had enthusiastically continued on their correspondence about how the traditional structure of Islander society could be codified.

He was more grateful than not that they wrote to him as they always had, he decided. He would have felt entirely alienated from himself had they dropped more than teasing hints that he was too grand for them now.

The evening after the examination results were announced, Cliopher wrapped himself in a light robe and sat in his battered old chair with a lap desk and wrote a letter to his sister.

Then he sat watching the light glisten on the ink as it dried, thoughts roaming through his experience of the Service, picking out moments here and there, circling back to his own difficult early years, trying to gather together all the half-heard comments from the younger members in halls and offices, the reports and occasional complaints that came up to him from the officials in charge of aspirants and pages. He wrote a letter, then, to Gaudy, giving him odd pieces of practical advice, not knowing how to say what he felt in any other way.

He steepled his fingers and sat there, looking at the comfortable clutter of the room, at the art he had so carefully saved up for and chosen over the years, at his books and the small gifts that had come from his family and friends.

He wanted, he realized slowly, to celebrate his nephew's accomplishment. He wanted to share the news with all the world that he, Cliopher, had a nephew who was coming into the Service after him, that he who had no son to follow after him did, at least, have that.

But he had promised Gaudy not to tell anyone, and he knew that it would change Gaudy's reception considerably if it were known that his uncle was the Lord Chancellor.

He was still sitting there staring into space some time later when there came a light knock on the door.

"Come in," he said, assuming it was Conju or Ser Rhodin or Ludvic Omo and brightening at the reflection that he could share his news with any of them.

It was Conju, but behind him came Pikabe and Ato and with them, of course, his Radiancy.

"My lord!" said Cliopher, hastily getting up and knocking his writing kit and the pages of his letter everywhere. He began his bow but was gestured to stop, and stood up in some consternation.

His Radiancy had visited him in his new apartments a handful of times, but had not come into this back room, which was done entirely to Cliopher's taste and was, therefore, considerably cozier and more informal than any of the other rooms in the apartments.

He said now, looking at his flustered Lord Chancellor (for he was, indeed, flustered), "Authro, my newest secretary, mentioned to me that the examination results were in, and I wanted to know whether your nephew had succeeded."

Cliopher stared at him. Conju murmured something, set down the basket he was carrying, and started to pick up the pages of the letter. Pikabe and Ato had stationed themselves by the door, leaving his Radiancy and Cliopher to stand in the middle of the room.

After a moment Cliopher said, "He did, my lord, thank you."

"I thought he must," his Radiancy said, "so I brought something with which to celebrate. Conju, have you done with those?"

"Yes, my lord." Conju passed Cliopher the papers and went back to his basket. Cliopher, feeling the pressure of much older manners than the palace etiquette learned so hard, said, "My lord, will you sit?"

His Radiancy smiled brilliantly at him and chose the couch, which was another battered old bear of a piece of furniture but very comfortable.

Conju poured out some sort of sparkling wine into superb fluted glasses, and his Radiancy made a toast to all the new aspirants, and Cliopher said that there were people from all sorts of places including the Tkinê Islands, and then the sparkling wine started to course through him and his Radiancy laughed and asked him questions, and he told stories about his nephew and his family, and all in all, two hours passed before Cliopher quite knew what had happened.

CHAPTER *T*HIRTY

"IT'S THE SORT OF THING you can expect from a nobody from the Islands," Prince Rufus of Amboloyo said, shoving his copy of what Cliopher had come to think of as Part One of The Plan violently enough that it knocked his wine glass onto the floor, where the glass shattered. "Certainly what we all know to expect from Lord Mdang. Idealistic, expensive, and benefiting no one of consequence."

A murmur of agreement rippled through the assembled Council of Princes, the rulers of the seventeen provinces of Zunidh.

Cliopher watched as a servant silently entered, silently replaced the glass with a new one, silently knelt before the Prince of Amboloyo, silently picked up the pieces, silently placed them on a lacquered tray, silently exited. The only other person who looked directly at her was the Lord of Rising Stars, the Last Emperor of Astandalas, the Sun-on-Earth; she didn't look up at him.

The Council of Princes met in a square room of elegant proportions and cool grandeur. Maps of the world hung on the walls, along with significant works of art, carefully lit by mage-lanterns and exquisitely positioned windows. The tables were arranged as three sides of a square, with his Radiancy's throne in the centre. Cliopher's desk was positioned in the opening of the square, facing his Radiancy, where he could see the expressions of the princes to include as necessary in his records.

As Lord Chancellor he was technically no longer the recording secretary, but no one else had yet to be appointed to that position, so Cliopher continued to perform the familiar task, with a few small additions drawn from his Radiancy's role as Chair. He appreciated his Radiancy's purpose in this, for it meant that the princes often forgot his new position and authority even as he increasingly controlled the shape of their meetings.

At his Radiancy's nod, Cliopher rose from his desk to stand in the centre of the square. He put himself in his battle position: back straight, head up, shoulders square, abdomen tight, hands loose at his sides, weight even on his feet, expression nearly as blandly calm as the benevolent serenity of the Sun-on-Earth before him.

For a very brief moment he met his Radiancy's eyes. He could see that they were glinting with anticipation, though he was far enough away not to feel the weight of magic his Radiancy could bring to bear. He took another deep breath. He was ready for this. He had his Radiancy's support. They had agreed how he was going to present his argument, and after seven hours of doing so, now it came to the final frank discussion before the vote.

I will bring a new hearth-fire to the world …

"Glorious One, your highnesses, I am ready to answer any further questions you have."

"We shall conduct this as an open question period," his Radiancy said. "You may begin, Prince Rufus, if you desire."

"Start with the expense, then," the prince replied, jabbing at the papers before him. "You seriously propose to provide an annual salary to every person in the world? How, pray, do you intend to pay for this?"

Cliopher nearly smiled that Prince Rufus had begun with this of all possible questions.

He set the mundial government's annual budget: no one knew better than he the balance of income and expense.

Also he had asked the Lady Felicia, a noted mathematician and, not incidentally, Prince Rufus' wife, to go over his numbers for him.

He did not bother to mention that he had already gone over all this with them some six hours ago.

"If you will turn to the third section, beginning on page forty-nine, you will see the summary of expenses, followed by the detailed analysis of the projected income and expenses. You will note that I expect the first three years to involve a deficit in the annual budget while the annual stipend becomes established and the current taxation and tithe system is adjusted. After that initial period, the government will gain, rather than lose, in each subsequent year."

"Oh, yes, gain," Prince Rufus said, lifting his lip slightly. He was a short, pugnacious man, pale-skinned from his Ystharian ancestors, and he had ferocious red eyebrows, heavy freckling, and glittering pale blue eyes. Cliopher secretly admired those freckles. "Lord Mdang, you seem to believe that you can simply make all the problems of poverty disappear by this plan of yours. Even granted the finances are correct, how long do you expect the world to continue to function when the people no longer have to work?"

It was at that point that Cliopher was sure, at last, that he would succeed, with this plan he had never dared believe could be implemented in his lifetime. He was nearly dizzy with the hope of what he might do from this foundation in the years to come. He shifted his feet slightly so that they were more properly centred in his sandals, took another deep breath, and focused on the task at hand. It would not do to blurt out his real plan before he had convinced them of this essential first step.

"Your highness, you bemuse me. Do you seriously think that no one will work simply because their basic needs are accounted for?"

"Do you seriously think that people will continue to work when they don't have to?"

"You do."

Prince Rufus choked. Several other princes snickered or giggled. Princess Oriana of the Vangavaye-ve tittered delicately. She looked like a dream of young Islander royalty in her pearls and her gown of ahalo cloth, the foamwork trim six inches deep, but Cliopher knew at a glance that though the materials might reflect the Vangavaye-ve's three exports, the design owed everything to the princess' upbringing in Jilkano.

He was almost certain his Radiancy was trying to hide amusement; he was sure it was not directed at him.

"None of you need work," Cliopher said, gesturing at those before him. "You do so to fulfil your responsibilities, your duties, your sacred oaths—your own desires, your ambitions, your enjoyments. What do your kin do, who are not ruling princes? Some of them are lazy, taking rather than giving, but most of them are not. They are artists and wizards, scholars and athletes, scientists and courtiers. They find much to occupy their days and to offer to the world. You do not know, your highnesses, what cost there is to the world that we lose so many to the depredations of poverty."

"Giving the poor money will not stop them from being poor," the Prince of Jilkano-Lozoi said. "It is a state of mind."

Cliopher stopped himself from rolling his eyes. "That may be, your highness, but the fact of the matter is, dire poverty is good for no one. It is obviously detrimental to the people trapped within it, but less obvious are the costs to everyone else—including to you yourselves, the ruling princes, and to the Glorious One most of all. Do you not wish your provinces to be full of beauty, of art, of industry, of happiness? Do you not desire your people to be healthy in body and mind and spirit and soul?"

"Idealistic *and* expensive," Prince Rufus muttered. "Lord Mdang, we all know your fondness for small goods. No one is arguing that we *prefer* our people to live in dire poverty—"

"We are glad to hear it," interjected his Radiancy, in a perfectly indifferent tone of voice.

"Harrumph, yes, of course, Glorious One. What I mean to say is—what of the jobs no one wants to do? Who is going to, er, pick up garbage if they don't need to? What of my mines—Xiputl's plantations—the farms and factories of Dair and Jilkano—what of all that, Lord Mdang?"

"Do you mean that the conditions in your mines are so terrible that only those in direst poverty will work in them?"

Behind his Radiancy his two honour guards stood in their full panoply of fine white linen kilts, ebony spears with razor-sharp heads tipped in gold, ostrich-feather headdresses, leopard pelts, gold, jewels. Ser Rhodin was on the right. He winked.

Prince Rufus glared at Cliopher. "You twist my words, Lord Mdang. I mean to say, who would go underground if they didn't have to?"

Cliopher had spent a great deal of time talking to people in all walks of life, from those who had been beggars in the great cities of Dair to the merchant princes of Jilkano to, yes, the plantation workers and miners of Xiputl and Amboloyo. He decided to come at the matter obliquely. He turned to the Prince of Western Dair, who was dressed in a confection of magenta and orange silk that made him look like a particularly eye-blinding sunset.

"Prince Belu, have you found your factories lacking in workers since the institution of the Indrogan estates in Csiven and New Dair?"

Prince Belu glanced nervously across to Prince Rufus, whose eyebrows had drawn fiercely together. The Prince of Western Dair cleared his throat several times. "Er, of course not, Lord Mdang. As you know, my tithes are up considerably since ... I don't have that endless drain of all those people with nowhere to go or ..."

"Princess Anastasiya, I have not noticed any slackening of production in rubber, coffee, or even the deep jungle medicinal products which are so dangerous to harvest. Have you found any detrimental effects to the Indrogan estate recently completed in Zachuotl?"

The Princess of Xiputl was his Radiancy's great-aunt. She was noted for her unflinching devotion to duty and for believing that everyone, possibly including the Sun-on-Earth (whose accession to the throne of Astandalas had been unexpected), was of lower birth and consequence than herself. Cliopher had never caught her smiling, and the deep lines on her face (for magic and cosmetics only went so far) suggested she never had.

But he admired her devotion to her duty.

Her voice was thin and sharp as a spear-head, her eyes as hard, but not entirely disapproving. "Lord Mdang, I am quite certain you know from your reports that I have not."

Cliopher turned next to the Princess of Mgunai, but Prince Rufus jumped in before he could speak.

"Yes, yes, we get the point that your bloody estates are all that is good and splendid. Getting beggars off the streets is one thing—that can only be a good. But what of all the people in the middle? Who is going to pick up the garbage, I ask you? Answer me that."

Cliopher smiled. "Prince Rufus, the Indrogan estates—bear with me, please—were developed in order to alleviate the worst conditions of poverty in the world's largest cities. At first we intended—"

"Don't be disingenuous, man. *You* intended."

His Radiancy steepled his hands before him and regarded them intently.

"My lord requested me to come up with a remedy for the slums of Csiven. My solution, the Indrogan Estates, required many trained professionals of a multitude of occupations: physicians, teachers, engineers, architects, wizards, entrepreneurs, artists. When I set out the terms of my contract, which in return for a reasonable amount of work would give housing, leisure, and enough money to live on with some luxuries left over, I had an overwhelming number of applicants for each position. When I spoke to those applicants, asking why they wished to leave what were often higher-paying positions to work in what had been former slums, I was told over and over again that they were drawn by the idea of having time for their own projects without fear of financial disaster."

He glanced at Princess Oriana, who was twirling one long strand of pearls hanging down from her headdress and staring off into space. That was how things worked in the Vangavaye-ve, to her oft-expressed disapproval: there was always time for the important things, for food and family and music and conversation, and no one much cared for money or status except insofar as it related to the traditional hierarchies of community and communal responsibility.

"So much for the middle and upper classes," he said. "The annual stipend will provide them with the foundation to follow their passions, to fulfil their dreams—of new businesses or public engagement, of art or athletics, of scholarship or service for its own sake. Each province, each region of Zunidh has its own culture or cultures, each with its own emphases. Some places it is dancing; others, music; still others, fabrication; and in others it is mining or smelting or farming."

Prince Rufus slopped down his glass again, hitting the edge of the silver charger in front of him with a ringing noise. "But who will work on a smeltery or a farm if they can avoid it?"

On one notable occasion Prince Rufus had lost his temper and told Cliopher that he was the only person not of noble rank that the prince had ever spoken with. He did, naturally, speak *to* servants, but he did not expect them to reply.

Cliopher had been so shocked by this admission he had not known how to respond, but he had never forgotten it, and tried to remember that Prince Rufus had a very limited experience of human nature.

The Lord Chancellor kept his voice steady. "It is true that there are always some, in any occupation, who do the barest minimum possible."

He carefully did not look at Princess Oriana, though he noted that Prince Rufus' eyes flicked in her direction. "They will do as little as they can regardless of their situation. We cannot change their natures, only give them every opportunity and support to do so. Whether they are vermin- and illness-ridden beggars on the streets of a city or healthy idlers watching other people work is something we can affect, however. If they have a pleasant place to live in a thriving community and there is food on the table and hope in the air, your highness, and the infrastructure to help in cases of illness or despair, I think you will be happily surprised to find how few of them remain idlers."

He looked around, holding the room silent, until he had met each prince's eyes in turn. "The vast majority of people wish to have meaningful lives. They wish to live well—to do meaningful things. If we give them all the opportunities to do so, and take away the fear that they will have nowhere to go, nothing to eat, nothing to support themselves with—the world will change."

"But who," said Prince Rufus, stabbing his finger in the air at him, "who is going to clean up?"

Cliopher did chuckle at that, making the prince flush angrily so his freckles stood out lividly. "Forgive my laughter. Prince Rufus, human beings live in communities. We are able to grasp that there are jobs that must be done for the benefit of all. I am, as you say, a nobody from the Islands: I am a Mdang of Gorjo City. My family's name is not listed in any book of heraldry or peerage. Yet we have our pride, our traditions, our own measures of worth."

He did not let them vocalize their ideas of what those measures of worth might be. He had heard all their views and more in every possible form from open assertions to sly editorials. He swept on.

"When I was growing up, we had no servants, and few of us were household wizards. We had the usual charms, but in the Vangavaye-ve there were none of the amenities of the central provinces of the Empire. Yet we did not live in squalour or filth. We all pitched in, to cook, to clean, to wash the windows or the floors, to scour the bathing facilities, to paint the house. And under the guidance of the elders we pitched in to make the community at large the way we wished it to be."

"Are you suggesting that wishful thinking will make communities 'pitch in' to do the nasty jobs that make things run?"

"I am suggesting that as a leader it is your responsibility to shape the culture of your communities, to encourage them to beauty and resilience and prosperity, to make them thrive. Prince Rufus, all you princes, the annual stipend I have here proposed is enough to live on if you have no great expenses. For those who have no residence at all, it is a place for them to stand: a home, whether in the Indrogan estates or in other public housing, with all the infrastructure of community, whether physical, magical, spiritual, or economic and cultural. Most people wish for more than the bare minimum—and most people take pride in doing worthwhile work well."

He looked directly at Prince Rufus. "If it is not work intrinsically worth doing, you will struggle indeed to find people to do it. You will have to make it worth their while in other ways—by offering more money, for instance. It may be that some of the tedious or disagreeable aspects of civilized life fall into that category. However, I have spoken to many people across the world, in all walks of life, and even now, under the current conditions, there are those who take great pride in making our cities the envy of the Nine Worlds. I have met street cleaners and sewer mechanics who take satisfaction in their work. If they did not have to work so often or so hard, and had much to look forward to in the rest of their lives, they might take more."

"But," Prince Rufus began. He did not finish his objection.

"Do you find the service or the cleanliness in the Palace of Stars objectionable?"

Prince Rufus looked utterly appalled at the question. "Of course not! The glory of this building reflects the glory of the Lord Emperor."

Cliopher nodded. "It has been over a year since I gave each and every member of the housekeeping staff of the Palace the stipend. There was no requirement that they stay in order to keep it. Perhaps twenty-five percent chose to leave; we had many applications for their places. I shall be interested to see if the proportion holds over time and across the world."

Privately he expected that more than a quarter of the world's population were dissatisfied with their careers, but this was perhaps not the ideal time to mention that.

And he did have plans for all the contingencies he could imagine—including simultaneous wholesale strikes of necessary industries and positions. He did not want to have to deal with a situation where every law officer, medical practitioner, farmer, and civil servant in the world decided not to come into work, but he had a plan for it.

He would still come into work, and his Radiancy, and at least the central core of the Imperial Guard, and between them and the stockpiles and the approximately twenty percent of any given population who would always side with established authority, he could deal with it.

There was a prolonged silence. Most of the princes were looking down at the table before them, at the thick document sitting demurely on the silver chargers before each seat, at the glasses of wine or water or coffee or tea.

They knew it was the fulfilment of Cliopher's life's work: or they thought they did. Many years ago Cliopher had made a list of what he thought the world could be like, if only. If only there were peace; if only there were no poverty; if only …

He was looking forward to their reactions when they discovered that alleviating poverty was only the beginning.

His Radiancy met Cliopher's gaze with serene, shuttered, imperturbable dignity. "My lord princes," he said in a low, carrying voice, "do you have any further questions for Lord Mdang?"

He waited. Several people shifted in their seats, trying to catch their allies' attention or avoid it. They had all gone through iterations of the many small stages of this proposal over the years Cliopher had been developing it, though none of them had realized all those parts did fit together into a whole until he had presented it to them as such. They had experienced for themselves the effects of the Indrogan estates on their provinces, had listened to him carefully explaining every page of the thick report before them. It was a good plan. If he did nothing else with his life, this was something to be proud of indeed.

Cliopher met his Radiancy's gaze again, and decided it was time to push. He straightened his shoulders again, lifted his chin. He had not had the emphatic lessons in posture and etiquette that the princes before him had. He had been taught other lessons by his family.

"Princes of Zunidh," he said, trying to match his Radiancy's imperturbable dignity, his calm strength, aware that his emotional conviction came forth in his intensity, his words, even his accent. He realized he had not been breathing enough, and took a deep breath. The mingled perfumes of the room tickled at the back of his throat. "The true question before you is whether you rule by fear—or not."

That caused a reaction, as an unexpected wasp does, modified for the audience, which lived for subtleties: raised eyebrows, exchanged glances, sudden hand movements. Cliopher liked that Prince Rufus scowled unashamedly. His Radiancy's expression did not change.

Ser Rhodin winked at him again.

"Glorious One, you have always sought to govern by wisdom, not rule by fear. You do not use fear of violence, whether physical or magical, to rule. There are more subtle forms of fear, and it is one of these this proposal seeks to address—economic control. My question for you, princes of Zunidh, is whether you are so weak as rulers that to give your people freedom from that fear will ruin you?"

"Lord Mdang, you speak very strong words."

The Prince of Amboloyo did not add the rest of his thought, though it was there for them all to read in his posture, his expression, the placement of his hands on the table; in all the conventions of the court, in all the left-over conventions of Astandalan days, where Cliopher, saying what he had just said—even before this same Radiancy!—would have been dead by morning. He was not of noble blood, so it would not have been a duel; it would have been a knife or a garrotte in the dark, or the executioner's block as the sun rose. The Empire of Astandalas had not agreed with Cliopher Mdang's philosophy of government.

But Astandalas had fallen, and though Zunidh had inherited much from the old empire, much also had changed.

Cliopher looked Prince Rufus right in the eyes. "Your highness, I do not think you are weak or fearful. Neither are your people. Let them surprise you."

The pale eyes glittered furiously, like the ice on the mountains of north Kavanduru. Cliopher was inured to staring contests from long familiarity with his Radiancy, who often forgot how searing the gaze of a great mage could be.

He was also inured to contests of perseverance and patience, from long familiarity with the workings of government, from being one of a large and boisterous family who loved to argue almost as much as they loved each other.

And the prince could not have been paying much attention over the years if he had not noticed that Cliopher never backed down from a matter of principle.

He saw the moment Prince Rufus gave in, and with its spokesman, all opposition to The Plan.

"I shall hold you *personally* responsible for the cleanliness of Boloyo City, Lord Mdang."

The Sun-on-Earth winked.

Cliopher smiled and said, "Of course."

CHAPTER ᘔHIRTY-ᘀNE

PART OF THE RESPONSIBILITIES OF the Secretary in Chief of the Offices of the Lord of State was to act quite literally as the hands of the Emperor in the oath-taking ceremony for the new aspirants. The cumbersome title for the head of the Service had not, as it turned out, been dropped when 'Lord Chancellor' was added on. ("Titles are cumulative, not reductive," said his Radiancy at one point when Cliopher ventured a small protest about this. "Why, I am still Lord of Ten Thousand Titles, only about fifteen of which I could name off for you.") On the whole, Cliopher liked the fact that he had not lost that role.

He dressed in the finest of his new court costumes, the one that looked like a Glorious Imperial bird-of-paradise, and took up his position on the lower daïs. The throne room was full, not with true courtiers but with many who did not usually attend court: the ministers and upper secretariat of each department in their official garb, along with a smattering of local families there to see their sons and daughters take the Oath of the Service.

There were a few proud outposts of the aristocracy among these, their brilliant court costumes and satellite attendants providing knots of colour and glitter among the soberer reds, blacks, browns, and oranges of the Service. The Prince of Amboloyo was the most prominent in every regard, his sky-blue mantle an invigorating splash of colour.

Looking out from the lower daïs Cliopher could see the range of ethnicities and cultural traditions in the room. Only the closer families could come—though more this year than ever before, thanks to the first three months of the annual stipend—but he could see Plainsmen from around Solaara, Mgunaivë in saris ranging from cheap cotton to fine silk, two proud Azilinti parents holding intricately carved wooden staffs, and many different embroidery patterns for the people from Southern Dair, Western Dair, and Jilkano. Skin tones ranged from pale cream (the Prince of Amboloyo) down to deep dark-brown (the Azilinti couple).

At a signal from his Radiancy, passed by Cliopher to the guards at the door, the trumpets began, and the side door to the throne room opened with a flourish. First came the two trumpeters, dressed in white tunics with yellow silk sashes. A herald in antique costume followed them, his scarlet robes almost hallucinatory in brilliance. Behind him came an official in the dark orange of the Offices of State—Kiri, looking solemnly exalted, as she did on occasions that took her into the Presence—followed in turn by the single file of new aspirants in sand-coloured robes.

As they passed each of the windows, the trumpeters blew a fanfare and everyone in the line performed the full formal obeisance to his Radiancy.

Cliopher waited patiently, trying not to search the line for his nephew—who would, of course, be near the end of the line both alphabetically and by province. He wondered idly why the aspirants' robes were always described as sand-coloured: they were sort of a pale tan colour, nothing like the white sand of the beaches of the Vangavaye-ve.

At last the trumpeters reached the front of the room. They blew an extended fanfare as they smoothly moved to positions on either side of the sweeping double staircase leading to the lower daïs.

The aspirants filed up in two lines, with a wide band of jewelled floor visible between them. Cliopher, trying once again not to look as if he was doing anything other than waiting patiently to fulfil his duties, looked down the lines. The map of Ysthar was closest to the throne, with Zunidh the next out. The throne was no longer oriented to true east (as it had been in Astandalas), but as it had been designed so, the hemisphere representing the Wide Seas was displayed before Cliopher like the patterns of the fire dance he had learned from his great-uncle as a young man. He wondered what the spaces in the pattern would reveal if he laid them out across the jewelled floor.

The trumpeters made a magnificent sound as they ended their fanfare with the obligatory and familiar Imperial Salute. Everyone went down into the obeisance.

On this, and only this occasion, the aspirants would mount the stairs to the lower daïs, that they might come as near as anyone outside his household could to the Presence to whom they were dedicating their life. For the occasion there was the full complement of thirty-two guards, one at each corner of the throne, twelve along the back wall of the daïs, and sixteen lining the stairs up and down. Each was dressed in the full panoply of the Imperial Guard, leopard furs brushed glossy, chests oiled to gleam in the light, jewels glittering and spears dipped in gold.

Everyone except for the guards, the trumpeters, and Cliopher himself stayed down in the obeisance after the Imperial Salute fell into silence. In this role he was the Hands of the Emperor, and by ancient custom he was to keep his back to the Throne and pretend he was not himself but only the channel for that power behind and above him. He did not speak, did not smile, was not really to be looked at.

The first time he had performed the office he had been severely disconcerted by the feeling that he really was nothing more than a channel, by the almost mystic feeling of power surging through him as the oaths were given and received.

At a signal from his Radiancy that Cliopher could not see, the herald rose. The trumpeters blew another fanfare, this one the Salute to the New, and the rest of the assembled court arose, leaving the river of sandy-robed aspirants running down the length of the throne room still prone.

The herald cried, "Elia Imboten Aata of New Dair!" and the first aspirant, a tall young woman with the mahogany-coloured skin and reddish hair of a Plainsman, rose from her obeisance to climb up the stairs on her right, Cliopher's left. She knelt before Cliopher, who took her hands in his own, and then from behind him came the calm melodious voice asking the ritual words:

"Elia Imboten Aata of New Dair, will you enter our Service and swear to serve us and our people?"

"So do I swear, Glorious One," Elia replied. Her hands in Cliopher's trembled, but her voice was clear, and her eyes looking over his shoulder blazed with triumph and wonder. "I swear by the Sun and the Moon that I will serve you and this world of Zunidh to the best of myself."

"Enter then our Service and be welcome."

The words were ritual, ceremonious, punctuated by trumpets, but each one of them was truly spoken, from above him, from before him. Cliopher fell into a kind of meditative trance, the conduit for the remarkable ceremony, not sure if there was magic at work, or any magic besides the power of will and word.

Young men and women—and a few older, a few younger, for after the reformation of the exams there had been no limits set on who might sit them—came before him, their names sonorously declaimed by the herald, spoken by the Sun-on-Earth.

It was, perhaps, the only time their names would ever be spoken by the Glorious One, the only time they would ever be within a dozen feet of the

Presence, the only time they might hope to be looked on by the lion eyes. It was special.

The last four were the interesting ones. First came Eldo Vardes of Amboloyo, the reason for the Prince of Amboloyo's presence at the Oathtaking. Eldo Vardes was a pale-skinned young man with rather hot grey eyes and his father's red hair. He was, Cliopher knew, the third son; the eldest was fostered with one of the Dairen princes to learn the ways of governance, the second was a scholarly wizard, and the third and youngest, it appeared, had entered the Service.

It was a pattern one could have found in dozens of noble families in Astandalan days, with either the Service or the Army being likely options depending on family tradition. It was, however, most interesting to Cliopher that Amboloyo's son should have entered the Service under him.

Eldo spoke his oath clearly and genuinely. Cliopher glanced very briefly at the Prince of Amboloyo, and caught on his face a fleeting expression of exultant pride before the usual cool arrogance smoothed over that human emotion. Cliopher did not have much time to think about that, but he did register to himself a very clear, *Huh*.

Third-to-last was Tulliantha nai Vasiaan of the Yenga, who provoked some curious interest by virtue of being from a continent inhabited mostly by thunder lizards and the scientists and park wardens who studied them. She was a striking-looking young woman, her skin a beautiful honey-brown, her hair hidden by an elaborate headdress of indigo and white batik.

But Cliopher was not attending to Tulliantha nai Vasiaan, because Gaudenius Vawen of Gorjo City was next.

Very few people ever remembered that Cliopher was from the Vangavaye-ve proper—they always decried him as being an 'Islander', as if there were not hundreds of islands in the Wide Seas. He did not fuss; he had long ago learned to pick his battles, and when it came to his culture he had decided that the substance—the way he knew the world and his place in it—was much more important than the form of what he wore or how he spoke or how people said his name. There was, therefore, no great buzz comparable to hearing 'Vardes', just a slight hum of interest for someone coming from so far.

Alone of all the aspirants, Gaudenius looked into Cliopher's eyes before turning his attention to the Glorious One. Cliopher dared not smile and show favouritism, dared not do anything out of the ceremony, but he did, as Gaudenius spoke his oath, squeeze his nephew's hands tightly. Gaudy looked shocked with amazement, but he returned the pressure before he got to his feet and went down the other stair and into his new life.

Any slight irregularity was more than covered by the response to 'Zaoul of the Tkinele'.

★★★

IT WAS ONE OF CLIOPHER's longstanding practices to address each year's crop of new aspirants to the Service the day after they had taken their oaths, first in a general assembly and then in necessarily brief individual interviews. After so many years doing so, he was ordinarily not particularly nervous about giving the address, and was somewhat bemused to discover in himself, this year, a certain attack of concern. For this year, of course, *Gaudy* was listening.

He usually gave the same speech, much to the amusement of those of the secretariat who were responsible for the aspirants. This year, the first since his elevation to the Lord Chancellorship, he added a brief comment about what that meant.

He looked out over the rows of politely attending aspirants as he came to the end of his prepared speech. There was a certain rustle from the officials in preparation, but he silenced them with a sharp glance. He set down his notes.

"Young men and women of Zunidh, you are aspirants to the Imperial Service. Yesterday you gave your oaths to Artorin Damara, last Emperor of Astandalas and our beloved Lord of Zunidh. Over the course of this coming year you will learn what it is you have vowed, first as a page and through your training in the duties of the junior secretariat. Some of you will rise speedily; some will decide this career, this vocation, is not for you; some of you will find your place quickly, and others will struggle to find their home in the Service. These are all honourable paths.

"This past summer his Radiancy made me his Lord Chancellor, a new position in his government. The reason for this is that his Radiancy is coming to the end of his reign. You, and those who are your new contemporaries in the Service, will be the ones who will help us in our work to prepare the government of Zunidh for the Lord Emperor's successor.

"There has not been such opportunity, or such possibility of upheaval, since the days after the Fall. Work hard, my friends, for not only will you serve the world as it is, but you will shape the world to come. That is our task over the next few years. Within the decade you will be swearing to serve a new Lord Magus. It is our duty to present the world in its best state to her."

"That woke everyone up," Kiri said, as he exited a slightly stunned room. "What prompted it?"

Cliopher didn't want to say, the sight of his nephew sitting there looking up at him with wonder and challenge, so he shrugged. "Sometimes I have these little inspirations."

She laughed. "Not usually when you're speaking in public, sir! Interviews are in the blue room as usual."

"Very good." He arranged himself on the raised platform, a design owing much to old Ystharian ideas about energy movements in rooms. Cliopher was much more accustomed to chairs, which his Radiancy preferred, but he spent enough time in some of the older department rooms to have the posture and just about enough flexibility to manage the cushions.

He spent five or six minutes with each aspirant, asking a few polite questions about their backgrounds, answering the tentative questions offered him. He had long felt a universal uncle to the Service, something which must have come out in his bearing, for the shy questions were the sort that no one had wanted to ask the more immediately intimidating officials in charge of the pages.

By the time his actual nephew arrived, way down at the bottom of the alphabet again, he had answered scores of variations on 'What do I need to do to succeed?' and 'Is it true you came through the Service the way we are?'

Tulliantha nai Vasiaan of the Yenga had one different question. "Your excellency," she said in a quiet, self-confident voice, "what are the rules about contacting our families?"

"I beg your pardon?"

"My family is in the Yenga. It is a long way away."

"Ah, I think I see. As a page you have the ordinary holidays and days off of the lower secretariat—you should have been given that information along with your letter of welcome."

"Yes, your excellency."

"The longer holidays are kept to the spur weeks. If you have any major personal concerns requiring a visit home at another time—an important religious or cultural celebration, a wedding or funeral—then you may ask me for leave." He smiled as she looked as if she wanted to protest that she was not already thinking of leaving when she had just arrived. "I am from far away from Solaara, and I know how difficult it is. As for letters, as a member of the Service you are permitted to make use of the Lights for your personal correspondence. You will learn how to submit letters during the course of your orientation."

"Thank you, your excellency. I am not looking to leave when I have just arrived, sir."

"I know." He paused then, looking thoughtfully at her. There was something about her face he found appealing and likeable, a quick intelligence in her eyes, an engaging firmness to her mouth, a kind of determination to her bearing. "There is a young man of the Tkinele who has joined the Service this year."

"I have noticed him," she said hesitantly.

Cliopher was quite certain everyone had noticed Zaoul of the Tkinele. The young man had skin has dark as his Radiancy's, but instead of the shaven head of the upper aristocracy, he had waist-length hair plaited into many braids much adorned with beads and carved charms and colourful cloth wraps. He also had ritual scarification on shoulders, upper arms, and face, and when he had given his oath to the Sun-on-Earth Cliopher had noticed he had sharpened eye teeth.

He was not sure if he had ever heard rumours that the Tkinele were cannibals before, but the palace was awash with them now.

"He is the first Tkinele ever to join the Service. You are also the only person from your principality to come to Solaara, and I expect you understand the loneliness that comes with being the only one to do something. The Tkinele are an isolated culture and rarely interact with the outer world. Perhaps you might do your best to help Zaoul answer any questions he might have—discreetly, you understand."

Tulliantha gave him a curious glance. "Are you asking me to befriend him, your excellency?"

"You may find you do not like each other," Cliopher could not help pointing out. "But that doesn't mean you cannot assist each other to negotiate the sometimes-murky world of the Imperial Service. You seem like a sensible person, and I know you are determined and intelligent, for you have made it here."

"Thank you, sir," she said quietly. She hesitated a moment longer, then said: "The young man after me is also the only one from his province. We met on the sea train across the Wide Sea. I think he might be a good person to help Zaoul, too. His name's Gaudenius Vawen."

Cliopher pretended to think. "Thank you, Saya nai Vasiaan."

She got up a bit awkwardly, a bit lanky, looking as if she had still to grow into herself. Cliopher thought of that shy declaration, and was looking carefully when Gaudy passed her coming through the door. But Gaudy's smile did not flicker as he entered the room until he saw his uncle sitting there alone.

He made a proper bow, however, and knelt on the mat before his platform. "Lord Mdang," he murmured, with only a slight hesitancy.

But he said it the correct way, not with the court pronunciation, and
Cliopher's felt the shock of it like a blow to his heart.

Cliopher waited until the door was closed all the way by the official on
the other side, and then he stood up from his careful posture and, as Gaudy
followed him upright with surprised alacrity, fiercely embraced his nephew.
"Oh, Gaudy," he whispered, "I am so proud of you."

He felt immediately embarrassed by this display of emotion, and returned
to his seat with a bit of awkward clearing of his throat. Gaudy sank down,
looking nearly as embarrassed and more astonished. "Your excellency—"

"They can't hear us if we speak quietly," Cliopher said, chuckling. "No
one wants to listen to me having nearly the same conversation with a hundred and fifty new aspirants. They were all laughing that I varied my speech
this afternoon. Is everything going well, Gaudy? The sea train was all right? I
know that there can be some jostling as people make friends and try to figure
out who their competitors are. Not that it's supposed to be a competition,
exactly, but that's how people are, alas."

Gaudy smiled. "Your letter has been so helpful, uncle. I am—I feel all
over the place, seeing all these things, experiencing all these things, you've
written about—seeing you—I've dreamed so long of coming here—I—I
don't know what to say. Am I supposed to ask you questions?"

"If you have any. I have a couple of things to say to you before I forget,
however: one is, the Light minders know the name of my family. When you
write to your mother, write to her as Saya el Vawen, and enclose letters to
your sister or grandmother or the other cousins in it, for if you write to the
Mdangs, everyone will know very shortly. No one else knows how common
a name it is in Gorjo City—and of course, it's not as if we *weren't* actually
related."

"Please don't—sir, I don't want to be like that Eldo Vardes—*Lord* Eldo,
sorry."

"Don't cast me in the role of a Prince," Cliopher said. "One more thing,
Gaudy: have you met Zaoul of the Tkinele yet?"

"He has the room beside mine. Why?"

"He's a long way from home. The Tkinê islands are very isolated—even
more than the Outer Ring—there will be many things about life in the Palace that are strange to you, but they will be even stranger to him simply by
virtue of where he's from. He will also face snobbery and ignorance—so will

you, I'm afraid—and having an ally makes a great difference in that sort of thing. If you can at all like him, please be that ally for him."

"I like him quite a bit already."

"Good, then." Cliopher paused, hungry for connection, but knowing that it would be many months or years of hard work on Gaudy's part before there could be any hint of comradeship between uncle and nephew, between Lord Chancellor and new aspirant.

He said: "Gaudy, I have every confidence in you. When you want to acknowledge our relationship, I will not hesitate. Until then, I will not let anyone in the Service know. My closest friends know—they were with me in the Vangavaye-ve when we saw you—but they are not going to gossip. They are members of the Imperial Household, they are discreet."

"Thank you, Uncle Kip."

"Now go and send in Zaoul."

"One more interview before you can stop working."

Cliopher laughed. "Oh, this is not by any means the end of my day. You'll learn."

CHAPTER 𝒯HIRTY-𝒯WO

AFTER EIGHT MONTHS AS THE Lord Chancellor of Zunidh, Cliopher felt he had mastered his new job. That, of course, was when his Radiancy began to add to it.

At first this took the form of suggestions to sit on this or that committee in his Radiancy's place, for one or other once-only reason. The fourth consecutive time his Radiancy made an excuse for why Cliopher should take his place in the Helma Council, which semimonthly committee oversaw the financial activities of the government, however, he challenged him on it.

"My lord, I have gone alone to the past three Helma Council meetings."

They were in his Radiancy's office, his Radiancy pacing, Cliopher at his accustomed desk. For one reason or another his Radiancy rarely had his new secretaries stay when Cliopher was there, so it was just the two of them and the ever-present guards.

His Radiancy stopped next to the great tapestry map. "Have you? Something about your voice seems to indicate you think this excessive."

"It was my thought, my lord, that you might wish to personally oversee the deliberations on the new budget."

His Radiancy turned and regarded him steadily for quite some time. Then he said thoughtfully: "Do you know, Cliopher, I have read your reports of the past three Helma Council meetings. What struck me most about them was how the meetings appear to have been significantly more efficient under your chairmanship."

This was an unfair comment: for how could he agree; or disagree? Cliopher coughed. "There are many courteous ceremonies that it would be inappropriate to follow when you are not present, my lord."

His Radiancy laughed richly. "I am sure that accounts for some of it, but my dear Kip, the fact of it is that you are much better at numbers than I am. When you deal with all those accountants and treasurers and so on, they know you understand, and they do not need to explain in layman's terms."

"My lord, you are no layman."

His Radiancy laughed again. "Only by virtue of the fact that I have run major governments for a lifetime. If I never had to look at a budget again I would be well content. I will come to the Helma Council with you this time and make you my proxy."

And so Cliopher found himself *officially* the Chair of the Helma Council, to the moderately expressed but clearly strongly felt approbation of the Treasurer and other members of the Council. And it was true, he admitted to himself, that he was much better with figures than his Radiancy.

Little by little his Radiancy first silently and then explicitly granted him new and (to his mind) extraordinary powers, until a year or so in he woke up to the fact that he was making the majority of decisions for the entire executive arm of government. This came to a head the day he brought a tall stack of reports to his Radiancy's study, intending to go over them with his Radiancy as ever he had.

His Radiancy was pacing again. Watching him, Cliopher suddenly wondered when was the last time he had seen his Radiancy sitting quietly in a chair when not actually holding court or sitting on the Throne of Judgment. Every time they met the Sun-on-Earth was pacing, up and down the beautiful study, robes swirling, lion eyes gazing into a distance unbounded by creamy stone walls and the intricate edifice of ceremony, ritual, and magic.

"If we may begin with this report from the auditors on the Ministry of Culture—"

"Is there anything untoward about it?"

Cliopher stopped with his hand half-on the dispatch case. "I beg your pardon, my lord?"

"Is there anything untoward about this report? Anything important?"

"No, my lord, just that—"

"I have a major project to begin," his Radiancy said, swinging back around again. "When I leave on my quest, I wish for the magic of Zunidh to be perfectly in order. I will be occupied with that. I desire you to make the decisions on everything that does not utterly depend on me."

"My lord, everything depends ultimately on you."

"Utterly, I said, not ultimately. I am well aware of the structure of power. You have settled into your new position's basic work: now is the time for others to know that you have authority. Take it."

"My lord!"

"I am granting it to you! It is time for you to take the responsibility for the decisions you have always made."

And that, of course, was that, though Cliopher was feeling a little mutinous as he left the Imperial Apartments and went to the Offices of State to inform Kiri of these new developments. Doing his old work was usually soothing: but on this occasion, he entered the Offices to discover half-a-dozen new faces sitting at the desks of the junior secretaries. One of them belonged to Gaudy, who glanced up at his entrance, then with ferocious concentration back down at his work.

Kiri had been regarding them with a benevolent eye, but she broke off this activity to usher Cliopher into the back office. "What do you think of my little additions?" she asked with impish delight.

"Isn't it a little early in the year to be selecting them out?" Cliopher asked, his tone more astringent than he intended.

Kiri raised her eyebrows at him. "It's the middle of the Little Session, sir. Oh, I know, sir, it's a month or so early, but there are some superb aspirants this year and I didn't want anyone else to snatch them up. I think this year might be the best since—oh, I don't know when. All these wonderful bright young things from the hinterlands! And one surprisingly brilliant lordling."

"That would be Eldo Vardes of Amboloyo?"

"Yes. He's thriving under the competition, which is fairly remarkable as he's probably never had a thwarting word in his life before."

Having had ample interactions with the Prince of Amboloyo, Cliopher felt that this was highly unlikely, but he forbore such gossip. He wondered how he could bring up the presence of Gaudy without entirely giving everything away, but even as he deliberated, Kiri added: "There's quite the cluster of potentials from the bottom of the alphabet, actually. There must be something in being the only one to come from your province—not that Eldo Vardes is the only one from Amboloyo, of course, but he's of so greatly superior a social class to everyone else he might as well be from the Outer Ring like Gaudy Vawen."

Gaudy was *not* from—well, Kiri wouldn't know.

"He's from the Vangavaye-ve," Cliopher said, turning to regard the stack of outgoing dispatches to hide his face. "Are you sure ..."

"Am I sure of what?"

Unable to express any of what he was thinking, he shrugged. Kiri regarded him narrowly for a long moment, irresistibly reminding him of his Radiancy doing the same thing half an hour previously.

"Sir, there is no way I am going to refuse to promote one of the most

promising young secretaries it has ever been my pleasure to work with because he happens to be from the same province as you. Besides, unless you
want to get exceedingly heavy-handed, you're not running this department
any longer. If you want to busy yourself with busywork, well, there are plenty
of other things to do."

"I don't wish anyone to think we are promoting anyone due to their
origin rather than their skill."

"We have Eldo Vardes of Amboloyo, Tulliantha nai Vasiaan of the Yenga,
Zaoul of the Tkinele, Gaudenius Vawen of the Vangavaye-ve, and a pair of
identical twins, Iri and Iro, from Csiven in Western Dair, whose family has
been involved in the Ministry of Fabrication for seven generations. I will
rotate them all under you and you will see shortly how brilliant they are."

"I stand rebuked," Cliopher said, and added on a lower note, "His Radiancy is undertaking a major project."

"Ah," said Kiri, and turned immediately to the files containing the lists
of positions and responsibilities for everyone in the Upper Secretariat so they
could make sure that everything was taken care of by people who could, and
would, do the work.

★★★

AFTER THE FIRST FEW HOURS, Cliopher lost his sense of awkwardness in
pretending Gaudy was a stranger—possibly because the nature of Kiri's department was such that its members quickly ceased to be strangers to each
other. The work was hard and the hours long, and they were dealing with the
highest matters of government.

"We have our fingers in every pie," Kiri was saying the first afternoon
he came to spend with them. "One day you will find out all sorts of intimate
details about the inner workings of an incorporated town in Jilkano, and another day you will spend the time in the library researching what the laws on
cattle branding were in old Astandalas. Then the next you will be writing fair
copies of a treaty with Alinor or a judgment on a trial of treason. You must
be prepared to shift your focus quickly, but also to keep your mind alert for
any strange links or repetitions or discrepancies. It is our office to ensure that
the government works properly—and it is the Lord Chancellor's to see that
we are doing our job. Lord Mdang, I give you the newest members of the
department."

He smiled. "You sound so delighted, Kiri. Well, everyone, as Kiri has
hopefully explained, one of my projects is to examine the current function-

ing of every ministry of the government to see what improvements we can muster. We are beginning with the Ministry of Finance, as without financial stability everything else tends to fall apart. Who has been researching what department?"

They answered: Tithes—Taxes—the Mint—the Budget—the Palace— and so on. Cliopher nodded briskly and started to question them, getting them to paint him the picture of the ministry, where the moneys were coming from and where they were going, which departments had enough people and which too few and which too many, and that all-important sense of the health of the culture of the place.

At the end of the second hour the six young secretaries were visibly wilting, stumbling over their responses and starting to repeat themselves.

"Very well," Cliopher said, deciding they had reached the end of useful conversation. "Write me up a summary of your reports, then we shall move on to the various ministries of trade, beginning with Land Transport. Stick with the equivalent sub-departments as far as possible to begin with. I want to know if you start to see any patterns forming. Is everyone clear on what they are to do?"

He surveyed them with a decidedly avuncular feeling oddly poised between complacency and exhilaration. How excellent they all were! And how well they worked together despite their disparate origins and temperaments.

They chorused agreement, but Cliopher's attention was caught by the hesitation before Gaudy said, "Yes, Lord Mdang," a heartbeat after the others.

The hesitation, Cliopher saw with a stab of insight, had nothing to do with either the assignment or the title, but the pronunciation of 'Mdang'. Gaudy's wavered between the true Vangavayen *āng* and the Solaaran *on*.

Cliopher held his nephew's gaze for a moment. Every other time someone had mispronounced his name he had not corrected them. He introduced himself with that hard nasal *a* the court (indeed, most of the rest of the world) found so difficult, but he never made a fuss. There had always seemed—there had always *been*—so much more important battles to fight.

But—

The silence, the stare, had gone on far too long. Gaudy was flushing, and the other secretaries in the room were glancing at each other in puzzlement over what could possibly have caused the Lord Chancellor's arrest and sharp attention.

And—

Things were different now than when Cliopher had been the young secretary learning (eventually) how to pick which battles to fight. He had learned, for one thing, just how important the little stands of principle were.

Once upon a time he would have said something clever and scathing and, no doubt, humiliated Gaudy. (Possible words came crowding to mind: *I had not expected you to require constant assurance in order to do what you know is right*.) No one would have forgotten the lesson; but he would have caused hurt unnecessarily and possibly even created an enemy.

Learning to hold his tongue had been a hard, hard battle to win.

He said, mildly, "As one of the few people in this Palace or indeed on this continent who can pronounce my name correctly, Sayo Vawen, I would prefer it if you were to continue to do so."

Gaudy dropped his eyes in visible mortification. He did (to Cliopher's great satisfaction) lift them again a moment later in query and intense *demand* and say, "I had wondered, your excellency, since I hear it always said 'Madon'."

"The pressure of general opinion can be exceedingly great." He smiled slightly and went on to articulate a principle he had long since formed out of his experience and observation but never really put into words. "Indeed, the strength of social pressure is one of the greatest forces in the world. The only force that is stronger is the individual will."

"But—" said someone; and "What do you mean?" said another. Gaudy regarded him solemnly, embarrassment fading and leaving the inward struggle writ large in the tension of his face and shoulders and hands.

Cliopher said, to his nephew and to all of them: "The correct pronunciation of my name is a small matter, nearly frivolous. You may notice, Sayo Vawen, that I always introduce myself as Cliopher Mdang." He gave that *a* its full value. "I do not insist on how others then say it. I decided long ago that it was not a battle I would fight."

He looked around the room, meeting eyes with as much gravitas as he could muster. "Make no mistake: it was, and is, a battle. It is a very small thing, nearly frivolous. But. But. It is by taking stands in small matters that we change the world. Sometimes in small ways. Sometimes in much larger ones."

He looked again at Gaudy. "I am not trying to pick on you, but this is an occasion for certain things to become clear. One is that I do, in fact, enjoy hearing my name said correctly. The other is more serious, and is of concern to all of you.

"Sayo Vawen, you know what the correct pronunciation is—what is, in this instance, right. You feel the weight of social opinion against you. It seems clearly opposed to you in everything you observe, in everything you hear, in everything both official and casual. And so you begin to doubt. You wonder how much it matters to let this one small thing go."

Gaudy nodded slowly, frowning as he tried to pick out what Cliopher's real point was. Cliopher would normally have left him to it (Buru Tovo's voice in his ear: *Listen first! Look first! Questions later*), but he did want to make the moral lines clear. And not everyone had had the benefits of a catankerous relative beating the need to learn to think for oneself into their heads at a young age.

Cliopher sighed. "It is so much harder to stand up for a small, nearly frivolous thing. It is far easier, at least in imagination, to stand up for the great things." He smiled wryly at the room. "One thing I have learned is how rarely we get to stand up for the great things. Or rather: how rarely we *know* we are standing up for the great things.

"When I came to Astandalas, joined the Service, everyone pronounced 'Vangavaye-ve' as 'Vonyabi'. Everyone."

Aioru said, "I've never heard that."

Cliopher inclined his head to him. "No. I let people mispronounce my name. I consciously decided that one day. There is, alas, only so much energy one has, and at the time there were other battles I chose over that one. But I fought for the Vangavaye-ve. I *always* corrected it. Four and a half worlds of the Empire said otherwise: but they were wrong. I was right. I persevered."

He stopped for a moment. He was much better with the written word. He had once been a splendid debater, sharp-witted and sharp-tongued, but he had learned through many harsh lessons how treacherous a weapon a sharp tongue with a sharp wit behind it could be.

"Public opinion is like the sea. It seems vast, primordial, unstoppable, immutable. In some ways it is. But the individual is a stone."

Gaudy nodded more decisively, obviously recalling the passage from the *Lays* where this particular analogy was made. Cliopher smiled gently and continued on for the sake of the rest, who did not have that particular store of wisdom in their keeping.

"A stone can be tumbled to and fro, buffeted, broken, polished by the sea rubbing it against all the rest, turned into a round pebble like all the rest."

It occurred to him then, for the first time, that that was how his family thought of him: that their anger and disappointment was because he had (to all appearances) thrown himself into the sea of public opinion and turned himself into a highly polished round pebble indistinguishable except by accidents of colour from all the rest.

Sometimes he feared they were right. But ... but ...

Cliopher had to stop himself from lifting his hand to the efela necklace tucked beneath his tunic, wanting to touch the many-faceted piece of obsidian set amongst the golden pearls. How many months of work it had taken to turn the sharp-edged volcanic glass into something he could wear against his skin, knowing that at any moment of great need he could strike the stone and from the pieces have all the tools he needed to build a boat or a house or a life.

"Or," he went on, "that stone can stand firm, and then—who knows? Around a firmly set stone the sea breaks and parts and changes currents. Around a firm stone a reef might form, or an island. Upon a firm stone a shipwrecked person might find a place to stand; a weary bird a place to rest; a piece of magic to be anchored or a train or a dock or a city to be built.

"An individual person, taking a stand, attracts laughter and opposition and opprobrium—and assistance. For every person who speaks there are many more who stay silent."

He looked around the room again. "Extremely few people from Solaara have ever been to the Vangavaye-ve. Even fewer from the Vangavaye-ve have ever come here. But you all do pronounce it correctly.

"It is a small thing, yes, but on small things hinge the turning of the world. Very rarely does the opportunity come to stand up against torture and evildoing—or for justice and equality—in the grand gestures most of us dream of."

He smiled at the stir, the embarrassed smirks and half-smiles of those who would never admit aloud that they had ever spent any time imagining themselves heroes.

He spoke more softly. "On the other hand, the opportunity to stand up against a small injustice, or for a small truth or a small good, comes nearly every day."

He made a wide gesture. "The pronunciation of my name doesn't really matter—or perhaps I should say, it *hasn't* really mattered. I chose, very consciously, to fight for other things, things I considered more important to who I am. I have fought, and do fight, and will continue to fight, for other small, seemingly unimportant, even frivolous goods.

"But."

He stopped there, meeting Gaudy's intent, demanding eyes, and then he said again: "But. Sometimes one rock holding firm attracts another, and another, and together they build something new. Or sometimes the person who has said, 'I will fight this battle but not that one, not today,' realizes one day that it is time at last to fight that battle. And sometimes one discovers that what at one time was, or seemed, unimportant, is actually central.

"You know the correct pronunciation of my name, Sayo Vawen. You come from my province; you know my family" (such an understatement!); "you are here, far away from home, wondering what of your culture you must abandon to fit in, to succeed. And you see me."

Cliopher paused, wondering how far he should go; but this was a small good, a small truth, upon which who knew what could hinge? He had never stopped before, regardless of whether something was uncomfortable, regardless of whether it was considered indecorous and uncouth to speak the truth one felt.

"You do not waver here, Sayo Vawen, on the small matter of what you know is correct, what is true, what is right. It may not matter, seemingly, to me; though you do not know how many bitter tears I might have shed for this small matter. But I can see very clearly in your face how much it matters to you.

"You are in a different situation—certainly than I am now, but also than I was when I first entered the Service, when I was a little older than you. I fought to be taken seriously, as a young man with a funny accent from very far away. I modified my accent, and let people misspeak my name, and learned to fit in. You do not need to."

He looked around the room again, at Zaoul and Kiri, at Aioru and Lord Eldo, at the pages and the secretaries and administrators who formed the heart of the government. They were all watching him with odd expressions, serious and troubled and, here and there, uplifted.

"The weight of general opinion is one of the strongest forces in the world. It is the current of human society. It is the motive force of change, the thrust of what gets done. It seems unstoppable, inevitable, immutable.

"It is not.

"It is shaped by the individual will saying 'yes' or 'no' and holding firm. The world changes one person and one decision at a time. None of us know what decision, precisely, is the telling one."

There was a long, long silence. Gaudy's eyes were glittering but his expression was unreadable as anything but 'puzzled'; the rest continued to stare, serious and troubled and uplifted still. Cliopher did not expect that any of them would know how to respond to such a declaration; he certainly would not have.

Eldo Vardes, taught social graces from infancy, was perhaps unsurprisingly the one to break the silence.

"When do you want the reports for, Lord Mdang?"

He did not quite manage the *a*, but he tried, and Gaudy looked very slightly taken aback to hear it. Cliopher smiled absently, as if his attention had already turned to his next task, and replied easily, "The day after next." He glanced at Kiri. "I'll need that report on the annual stipend tomorrow, Kiri."

"Of course, sir," she said, with a nearly straight face. He left the room, but though he was abstracted he was not so abstracted he did not notice the way Kiri smiled sympathetically at the young secretaries, nor the soft-voiced comment, "Oh yes, he's always like that. You'll learn."

CHAPTER THIRTY-THREE

TWO WEEKS INTO THIS PROCESS they had gone through half of the mundial ministries. Cliopher arrived a few minutes early one day, and found Kiri finishing her lunch in her office. She offered him a bowl of plantain chips, which he accepted happily. "You're right about the excellence of this year's crop," he said, enjoying the crunchiness with simple pleasure. "I am very pleased and impressed with their progress."

She ate a few bites of her salad. "You're riding them hard, sir."

He started. "Am I? Too hard? They're responding so well, I hadn't realized."

"Not too hard, perhaps, but I would be inclined to—perhaps you could express your admiration, sir. I think that would be beneficial."

"You're very good at managing people. I'll listen."

"What do you think of Gaudenius Vawen?"

He glanced sharply at her, but she was focused on fishing out a stray piece of slivered almond from her bowl. To be perfectly honest, Cliopher was so extremely proud of Gaudy that he felt he might burst every time his nephew answered one of his questions with wit, clarity, intelligence, and flashes of brilliance. He swallowed down praise-songs and said moderately, "He has much potential, I reckon."

"You're riding him noticeably harder than the rest, sir."

Cliopher paused, then said quietly, "And what do you make of that, Kiri?"

She smiled with sudden mischief at him. "Sir, if you were not particularly interested in a young man from your own very remote province you would be inhuman. If you did not expect more of him than anyone else because of that—or anyone else than Zaoul and Eldo Vardes—well, you would not be you. Why do you push Zaoul so hard? Eldo I can understand, but Zaoul ... He is responding marvellously, but I would have thought you would be gentler."

"He doesn't need gentleness, he needs a challenge. That is what he came out into the world for."

Kiri smiled slowly. "I had wondered if you ever saw yourself in the junior secretaries. I wouldn't have thought the Tkinele tribesman would be the one, but … it must be pleasing for you to have so many people who can keep up."

★★★

AFTER THREE MONTHS OUT OF the pages Gaudy had consolidated a place for himself with Eldo and Tully, Zaoul and the twins Iri and Iro. Cliopher tried to remember to compliment them on their excellence as they proved it, but he found it so pleasing to work with such undoubtedly brilliant young people that he kept pushing just to see what they would be able to achieve next.

They had gone through the entire review of ministries, the only hitch having been when Iri and Iro had asked to be excused from analyzing the Ministry of Fabrication, where their parents worked. Cliopher had set them to a side research project, and had been relieved that although Fabrication clearly could do with some changes, there was no hint of major corruption or wrongdoing.

Cliopher wanted to move onto the substantially more delicate task of assessing the provinces, and had decided to begin with the least contentious, Xiputl. The Princess of Xiputl was his Radiancy's great-aunt, and although her advanced age and high birth would have warranted a most comfortable retirement, she was a termagant—and her devotion to duty so admirable that Cliopher, if pressed, might have admitted he actively emulated her.

No one had ever thought to ask him this question, so he quietly watched her manage her province with dictatorial air and a pride so sublime it had the same effect as tender devotion. No one in Xiputl was ever in any doubt as to their place: but as it would have been far below Princess Anastasiya to fail in the least element of her duty, none of them could complain of any want except, perhaps, acknowledgement of their equal humanity.

She had been visiting a friend in Xiputl—then a marquisate under the Grand Dukes of Damara—when the Fall occurred. Her friend the marquis had died in the aftermath of the Fall, but Anastasiya Princess Yra, daughter and sister and aunt and great-aunt of emperors, had known her duty and had taken control over the region. There had been none of the violence in Xiputl that the other provinces had seen.

They were hashing out the best method for assessing the provinces—

after going through all the mundial ministries, his little group of under-secretaries had formed some decided, and quite disparate opinions—when the outer door opened and his Radiancy entered.

"It has been some time since I last observed the Service at work," his Radiancy said, gesturing them up from their surprised obeisances. "Let us not stand on ceremony. What are you up to today, my lord chancellor?"

"We are beginning the assessment of the provinces, my lord."

"With which do you begin? Amboloyo?" His Radiancy smiled at Eldo Vardes, who flushed slightly. Eldo would have been presented at court when he turned sixteen, Cliopher realized.

"Xiputl, my lord."

"Ah, reverse alphabetical order. That appears to be your method in populating your department as well—Oh, except for you two, sayora ... Olionnë, was it?"

After a panicked glance at Cliopher, Iro cleared her throat and said, "Olionnoë, Glorious One."

"How could I have forgotten the extra syllable? Most mellifluous were your names, I particularly noted them: Iri and Iro Olionnoë. I was no doubt distracted by your being identical twins. Do you have similar talents to each other as well as interests?"

Iro looked at Iri, who was generally quieter but also the leader. With a sort of fond look, Iri said softly, "Iro is better with analysis, and I with synthesis. We are both better with words than numbers."

"Whereas you, Ser Vardes, excel with numbers, as your mother before you, no?"

Eldo had been taught from birth how to move in the highest circles of society, and he showed no sign of the painful nerves of the twins. He did display two spots of red high on his cheekbones, something that Cliopher had noted generally happened whenever someone mentioned his family. "I am not a mathematician such as my mother, my lord, but I do enjoy numbers and quantitative analytics."

His Radiancy smiled at him and turned his attention to Tully, who sat behind the twins. "And you are the young woman from the Yenga—Tulliantha, was it not? You're Figar's daughter, if I do not mistake myself. You have his look."

"My father will be very honoured you know him, Glorious One," Tully said, looking flattered and slightly panicked at the same moment.

"You have come a long way from home."

She lifted her chin. "It was my desire to serve the wider world, my lord."

"Is that your motivation as well, ser Tkinele?"

For all his fearsome appearance, Zaoul was a gentle young man and somewhat shy. He nodded, then said, in the lazy voice that contrasted so starkly with his sharpened teeth and ritual scars, "I had many questions no one on the islands could answer."

His Radiancy looked sharply at him, his eyes kindling. The sense of his presence was noticeable, even to Cliopher who had spent so long in his company, and certainly to the young secretaries. Zaoul met the lion eyes without fear but with a certain widening astonishment and wonder.

After a long moment his Radiancy released him. "We are kin," he said simply.

Eldo Vardes breathed in so sharply he nearly gasped, but when Cliopher glanced at the young man his hot eyes were focused entirely on his Radiancy.

His Radiancy, of course, noted the response, but inevitably his own reply was oblique and addressed to the politely confused Zaoul. "*Devoga oha hav'eghan'oa, eloyiki?*"

Zaoul stared at him with blank bewilderment, then crashed out of his chair and flung himself down at the feet of the Lord of Rising Stars, somewhat to the alarm of Zerafin and Varro. He made no motion to touch, however. Shaking back his magnificent array of braids so that the beads and charms clattered, in a passionate voice he cried out: "*Indevoga e ngaloyiki, O rep'ekhan'oa!*"

"*Ega eghan'oa ne gaveghar o,*" his Radiancy replied, making a very deliberate but somewhat incomprehensible gesture over the young man. "You may return to your seat, Zaoul. I am afraid I do not know much more of the old tongue than that."

"It is far more than I ever thought to hear so far from home," Zaoul replied, sitting down but quivering as if he might be ordered to run at any moment. "Sweet my lord, how is it known at all to you?"

His Radiancy smiled, a slightly wry and sardonic expression that disturbed the serene mask with a glimpse of the inner man. The serenity returned a moment later, and his words were unemotional as usual. "When I was a boy I, too, was afflicted with the questions no one could answer. Or would, in my case; I'm sure my tutor knew many things he was forbidden to teach me. My usual punishment for misbehaviour was to learn minor languages of the Empire. He used to say that I was probably the only person still fluent in Renvoonran."

Cliopher could not help but wonder what sort of misbehaviours his Radiancy had perpetrated as a boy that ended up with him fluent in multiple dead languages. He himself had been sent off to Loaloa with Buru Tovo after falling headlong into petty larceny and pettier fistfights in the grief-stricken aftermath of his father's death by drowning.

It would have been nice to know Antique Shaian: but it was better to know the ways of the ancestors. And of course his family bore no comparison to his Radiancy's. Though, thinking about it, Cliopher mused, Antique Shaian *was* the way, or at least the language, of his Radiancy's ancestors.

Ignoring Cliopher's distraction, his Radiancy went on: "Antique Shaian began as one such punishment, but then I discovered the *Saga of the Sons of Morning*, and learned it for the sake of the poetry. When I was reviewing the treaties with Zuni peoples I discovered that modern Tkinê is very close to Antique Shaian—far closer than Modern Shaian—and I learned some of the words."

Zaoul gazed at him with an expression of adoration not very far from what Kiri occasionally permitted herself. Kiri's parents were priests of the Imperial Cult ... Cliopher wondered what beliefs, exactly, the Tkinele held. He had not asked such personal questions of any of them.

His Radiancy turned his brilliant eyes on Gaudy, and after a startled moment, laughed robustly. While they all stared at him he said: "Good heavens, but do you ever look like your uncle when he first came into my service! He has always looked younger than he is—no doubt to some disgruntlement when he wanted to be taken as a mature responsible individual. Of course, now he has the hat to display his respectability."

His Radiancy glanced at Cliopher to include him in the joke, still smiling broadly. "You seem to be progressing with your ambition, Gaudenius. Perhaps your uncle will create a position above Lord Chancellor for you to aim at—though you will have to wait until the new government for that. Well done, all of you. My lord chancellor has spoken very highly of your many excellencies, and I am well pleased with your work." His Radiancy nodded genially at the wider department, accepted the deep bow over her hands Kiri offered him as his due, and swept out again with Zerafin and Varro moving in unison behind him.

Everyone in the room stared at each other in stunned perplexity.

Kiri broke the silence first. "You've kept that very quiet, sir."

Cliopher met the furiously embarrassed Gaudy's eyes. "I have to admit it had not occurred to me that his Radiancy would be the one to mention it.

Well. Can we return to our work?"

Kiri stared at him in incredulity. "Are we just to ignore—"

"Yes, Gaudy is my nephew, and yes, obviously we had decided it would be better not to mention it until he had established his own reputation. Is there anything else?"

This was what it meant to be the *Lord* Chancellor: they all swallowed back their comments and returned valiantly to their interrupted tasks. Cliopher knew well enough that, since he did not want to lord himself over his department, he and Kiri would be having a fuller discussion once the younger secretaries left for the day.

He stifled a smile as he turned his attention back to the state of affairs in Xiputl. Gaudy might be annoyed, and certainly there would be an ample sufficiency of comments about nepotism to deal with, but Cliopher was glad indeed he could not take open pride in his relations, like everyone else.

CHAPTER THIRTY-FOUR

ABOUT A MONTH AFTER GAUDY's identity had been discovered Cliopher was deep in a meeting with his Radiancy about the developments in Nijan—of course—when someone knocked on the outer door.

Rhodin was on guard, and at his Radiancy's nod turned to open the door. He spoke briefly to the visitor. "My lord, Gaudenius Vawen is here with an urgent message for his uncle."

His Radiancy took one look at Cliopher and rang the bell. "He may enter. Kip, it is not necessarily—"

But Cliopher knew just how unlikely it was that anyone would interrupt a meeting with the Sun-on-Earth. Cold fears pinned him to his seat. Surely it wasn't Vinyë—his mother—his *mother*—

Gaudy hurried in, knelt to his Radiancy, and almost tripped over himself in trying to get to him before he had fully risen. He knelt beside Cliopher's chair, gripped his hands tightly. "Uncle Kip, it's all right, it's all right."

"My mother—your mother—"

"They're fine. Everyone is fine. It's all right. Everything is all right, Uncle Kip."

"Drink this," Conju said firmly, evidently having come in response to the bell. Cliopher took the cup of water he was handed and drank gratefully.

"I'm very sorry," Gaudy said, looking from him to his Radiancy. "I didn't mean to alarm you so much. I didn't realize that you would think—"

Cliopher sipped the cool water, and finally felt composed enough to straighten in his seat. "My apologies, my lord. Gaudy, if no one is—if nothing at home is amiss, what is so urgent?"

Gaudy flushed in embarrassment. He carefully went back to the proper spot for a report and knelt before his Radiancy. "My lord, your excellency, I am deeply sorry to have interrupted your meeting."

"Please explain yourself," his Radiancy said serenely. "We presume you have a purpose in doing so."

Gaudy winced. "My lord, there is an, er, embassy from the Vangavaye-ve here who—whom I thought your lordship and his excellency would like to know about immediately."

Now that he was no longer bracing for the worst possible news, Cliopher tried to think what else would be serious enough for the interruption. "It's not—please tell me it's not Cousin Louya?"

His nephew did his best to maintain an impassive expression, but he was not quite able to restrain a smirk. "No, although the Speaker does carry a letter from her signed by almost the entire family. It is Jiano Delanis of Ikialo village on Lesuia Island and his wife Aya inDovo Delanis. She claims kinship with you, Uncle—Lord Mdang—and I remembered that you spoke very highly of both of them."

"Jiano and Aya are *here?*" Cliopher asked in astonishment. "Whatever for—that fish farm?"

"Yes, your excellency. I gather they come as Speakers for the entire Outer Ring of the Vangavaye-ve and wish to petition for an audience with his Radiancy, as they do not feel that Princess Oriana is treating them fairly."

"We will certainly grant them an audience," his Radiancy said before Cliopher could respond. "They come as Speakers for the Outer Ring? Tell the Master of Ceremonies they are to be treated as equivalent to a high chief or a ruling count. We must finish our deliberations this morning, but Cliopher will see them after they have refreshed themselves. He shall determine what form the audience should take."

"Thank you, Glorious One," Gaudy said, prostrating himself, and at the gesture of dismissal took himself off.

"Are you composed?" his Radiancy asked quietly.

Cliopher ran his hands over his face. "I am, my lord, thank you. I'm sorry."

"Do not be sorry for loving your family, Kip. Bring Aya and Jiano here this afternoon for tea, if you see fit."

"Here, my lord?"

His Radiancy made a short gesture. "I like Jiano and Aya, and I do not wish to dress for a formal audience. Now, let us decide what to do about this bifurcation in the ranks of the Nijani population between the police officers and the duke's daughter's faction."

They did eventually come up with a temporary solution, temporary because Cliopher could not quite bring his thoughts to focus on the longer-term ramifications of the situation. He could tell that his Radiancy's thoughts were not focused, either, and sighed in fond aggravation at the whole concept of democratic government.

By the time he made it down to the Private Offices he was hungry as well as overset. Kiri drew him immediately into the back office. "Was that the wrong decision? Gaudy was quite insistent that you would want to know immediately, and his Radiancy too."

"No, that was the right thing to do," he said, looking longingly at her almost-finished lunch. "It was just ... Rhodin announced him as having an urgent message for me, and I was worried it was our family. Anyway, it's fine. His Radiancy has asked me to go see them, so I'm not sure what my afternoon will—"

She passed him the plate. "Eat the pork bun, sir. You seem unsettled. Take the afternoon to see to your countrymen and calm yourself. They might have good news of your family for you."

"Aya's my kinswoman," he murmured, swallowing the bun. "Are you sure—no, I don't doubt you! Very well, I'll leave you to your work. I was planning on—"

"It will keep until tomorrow, sir. Go."

***

HE FOUND JIANO AND AYA in one of the guest chambers of the Voonran wing. They were on the second floor, about half-way along, with a view across a set of gardens to the menagerie and the Grey Mountains to the west on the horizon. Aya answered his knock with a puzzled expression that turned to welcome.

"Oh, *hani*, I am so pleased to see you!" she cried, beckoning him in. "Jiano is bathing, he won't be long. What a splendid reception—we were sure you would assist us, but we did not imagine what a fuss there would be when we asked to be directed to you. We did not realize how important a person you are!"

Cliopher laughed ruefully. "It's a common refrain. Have you eaten?"

"Your nephew said he would send someone with food at the first hour."

"Very shortly, then. Splendid. I am glad to know Gaudy is treating you well."

"We feel very well welcomed," she replied gravely, but with a twinkle in her eyes. "Will you be seated? I will let Jiano tell you about our mission, but let me tell you how amazing this journey has been. I have this marvellous idea for a series set on the sea train—we met so many odd and wonderful people, the scenery is always changing, and if a murder happened in the middle of that long stretch between Little Paulo and the first of the Outposts, well, wouldn't that be just a delicious closed-room puzzle?"

"I'll take your word for it," he said, but he was inveterately curious about people's work, and added: "How do you work out your plots, Aya? I've been enjoying your books."

"You're very kind! Sometimes I start with my detective going somewhere and see what comes of it, sometimes I begin with the murderer—and sometimes I just have an idea for the murder."

He drew her easily into deeper conversation about her stories, her main detective series—fourteen books and counting, she reported—and her idea that the sea train perhaps needed a new one. They were interrupted only by the arrival of the food, brought by two pages. "She's getting on, my detective, you know," Aya said, pouring out coffee from the urn that had been included in the delivery. "About time for her to retire and tell stories to her young relations."

"Do you think that she would be content with that?" Cliopher asked. The question of what he would do when he retired had been occurring to him off and on as he embarked more deeply on the preparations for his Radiancy's quest.

Aya laughed. "That is a question, isn't it? Let me see. My detective—her name is Louya, not after your cousin—well, it is, sort of, because I used to hear stories about Loopy Louya Mdang when I worked at the provincial treasury and there was something about her name that just appealed to me— Anyway, my detective, Louya, has already had a couple of different jobs. Her day job was as a travelling accountant, that's how I manage to get her to all sorts of new places and meeting new people all the time. But I've made my way around the Ring and to the Isolates and basically everywhere within reach of Gorjo City, and I'm not sure Louya would be up to a long train ride, delightful as I found it."

She pondered a moment. "Although, the thing is, it was quite restful on the train. Jiano spent most of it worrying about what he's going to say to the Glorious One, but there was a lot of sitting on the roof looking at the stars or talking to other people, time to read, to draw, to write. They could do with a room for people to practice musical instruments in, because people *would* do it on the roof in the middle of the night. I could see Louya deciding it would be a nice vacation—for the Wide Seas are splendidly beautiful, you know, and the train is surely easier than the ships our ancestors used!—and then getting embroiled in a mystery halfway through, just about when she's decided a couple of months is quite enough of a vacation ... Ah, there's Jiano! And here's Cliopher, my love, he has just given me an idea for my next book."

"Wonderful!" Jiano replied, greeting Cliopher heartily. Aya pulled out a notebook from underneath her seat. "Is this food? Your nephew was wonderfully accommodating. Everyone else has been acting as if we are escapees from the menagerie."

"Until we said we were related to you," Aya put in, looking up from her notes. "I do hope that wasn't an imposition. We didn't realize things were arranged so differently here ..."

"I am delighted to acknowledge our relationship. Do you mind if I share your lunch?"

"Certainly! Fortunately, it looks as if your nephew intended you to, given how much food there is. Jiano, do you want some coffee?"

The business of serving food occupied a few minutes. After Cliopher took the edge off his hunger—for breakfast had been many hours before, and one pork bun wasn't really sufficient—he felt ready to focus on them. "Will you tell me what has brought you all the way here? Is it the fish farm?"

"Don't tell me the Princess has actually done something about it while we were on the train!"

"No! Don't worry—well, I'm not sure that's the right phrase. She has not gone forward with any developments, but she hasn't dropped them, either. My cousin Galen mentioned that Louya—my cousin Louya—had a bee in her bonnet about the fish farm, and that's the only major project I know about from the Vangavaye-ve."

That the princess was undertaking, he amended internally, for there were any number of major projects that he had set underway. Not so much against the princess' will as with her vague benediction and total lack of interest.

"Yes," Jiano said, and launched into a summary of the problems with it.

Cliopher listened patiently, interjecting a question here or there, until he felt he had a good sense of the matter. He was annoyed at himself for not having taken action after Galen's warning, but the change in his position after that holiday had thrown him considerably.

"I think it would be best if you presented your case before his Radiancy and the Council of Princes," he said finally, "but I will reflect on the matter. It may be that open court is the better option."

"Do you think the Glorious One will be favourable?"

"I do not make judgments on his behalf," Cliopher said dryly, "but he will certainly listen to you and judge you fairly."

Jiano sighed. "I have always wanted to see the Palace of Stars. I never thought to come as a supplicant."

"At least it's not as a prisoner," Aya pointed out cheerfully. "Cliopher, how are you? And your lord? And our other friends from your visit to Lesuia?"

"They are all well. I was meeting with my lord when Gaudy brought the news that you had arrived. He has invited you to come for tea this afternoon. We might go now, if you'd like. He will be free for another hour or so."

They responded with delightful alacrity, jumping up and arranging their clothing. They were wearing sarongs and efela necklaces, and looked from the Islands but not excessively so. As he ushered him out of the room, however, Cliopher caught a glimpse of their belongings through the door of the bedroom and saw that they had brought the elaborate grass skirts and feather headdresses of proper Outer Ring finery.

"Gaudy told us we were being treated as high chiefs," Jiano said as they walked towards the central part of the Palace.

"Yes, because you are acting as Speakers for the Outer Ring. It's a title used by various groups around the world, mostly up along the Xiputl arm or Southern Dair."

"Jiano will be doing the speaking; I'm just here for psychological support."

"And to keep track of the paperwork, love."

"That too." Aya kissed him on the ear, then looked beaming around. "What a truly glorious building this is. Can you tell us about it, Cliopher?"

He could tell them a bit, about the architect who had designed it and the successive Emperors who had built it. He explained its shape, its orientation relative to the Emperor, the location of the Throne Room, and the meanings of some of the symbols as they passed them.

They passed the apartments set aside for the Queen of Voonra, the equivalent of this wing for his own. Over three hallways, up two flights of stairs, past various upper nobility who bowed to Cliopher and looked wonderingly after his companions. He did not introduce them to anyone, but murmured identities—'There is the Prince of Southern Dair, that was the Princess of Jilkano-Lozoi, those are some of the court of the Princess of Mgunai'—and at length they arrived before the doors to the Imperial Apartments, where they were challenged.

"Jiano Delanis and Aya inDovo Delanis, by invitation," Cliopher said.

The guards saluted, the doors opened, and they said: "Lord Mdang and guests!"

They made their way through the seven anterooms, Jiano and Aya both looking around too curiously to become nervous, and finally launched into the study, where his Radiancy, who had evidently been pacing, stopped just in front of the portrait of himself.

Aya's gaze travelled from the man to the painting, and she blurted, "Then you're not Fitzroy Angursell after all!"

Jiano exclaimed, "Aya!"

His Radiancy's lips twitched. Cliopher ducked his head to hide his own smile. His Radiancy said, "I will take that as a compliment and not as treason, though I would suggest you refrain from discussing the topic in public."

"You're the ... the Sun-on-Earth," Aya said.

His Radiancy inclined his head. "Welcome to the Palace of Stars."

CHAPTER *THIRTY-FIVE*

JIANO PRESENTED HIS CASE to the Council of Princes lucidly, logically, and with no pretensions whatsoever. He made a perfect obeisance to his Radiancy, he bowed over his hands to Cliopher, and he addressed the assembled princes of Zunidh as equals.

Unsurprisingly, their responses focused almost entirely on his appearance, accent, and unaccountable nerve.

"Really, what can you expect?" the Princess of Jilkano-Lomoi said loudly to her neighbour, the Prince of Kavanduru.

The Prince of Kavanduru nodded wisely. "We all know, alas, what these ... Islanders ... are like."

Cliopher gritted his teeth and concentrated on keeping his writing even and light on the page. The only Islander the majority of the princes had met was him.

Jiano stood proud and tall in the centre well of the tables, his Outer Ring finery flamboyant and splendid as a cock bird-of-paradise. Aya stood at the side of the room near Cliopher, holding the case of documents they had brought with them.

After a few minutes of near-slanderous chatter, his Radiancy stirred. The room quieted instantly.

"Princess Oriana, you have our permission to respond to the case laid before you by your countryman."

Cliopher appreciated the ambiguity of 'countryman'. It was evident Princess Oriana did not.

She rose in her place. "Illustrious One, fellow princes ... Lord Chancellor ... this man's arguments are as absurd as his costume. Flashy, yes. Appropriate—hardly. Illustrious One, my province has few inhabitants and those there are show very little industry or interest in any form of development. This project is a splendid commercial opportunity and will put the Vangavaye-ve on the map."

His Radiancy glanced at the map of Zunidh that hung on the wall to his right, but said, "Speaker for the Outer Ring, how do you respond to your princess?"

Jiano looked as if he would have liked to contest that description, for a moment looking very much like how Cliopher remembered his father the Poz. He bowed over his hands to his Radiancy.

"Glorious One, the Vangavaye-ve is a wonder of the Nine Worlds for its natural beauty. We who are from there have no desire to spoil the land and the waters we have been given to steward and to love."

There was something of a stir from the Prince of Amboloyo, who was regarding Jiano very narrowly. Cliopher methodically wrote words and observed reactions, not his own thoughts. Any future historian, reading through the Council of Princes minutes, would see for herself the number of times Cliopher Mdang had argued that the purpose of government was to steward the resources of all for the benefit of all. All taken most widely.

"The fish farm project," Jiano went on, "is designed to benefit no one but its sponsor and the princess who will receive tithes on taxes on the proceeds."

Princess Oriana had been well coached by Earl Baljan. "The sponsor must invest a great deal of his own time and effort, as well as money, into developing the project. It is only fair he receive the benefits."

"To the detriment of the ecology, society, and health of the Ring? Glorious one, I have shown the princess a letter signed by a wide range of the population of the Vangavaye-ve—"

Princess Oriana erupted into genteel titters. "Yes, and the first name is a known crank and crackpot!" She poked the scroll in front of her. "Illustrious One, folly repeated a thousand times does not become wisdom."

"That is certainly one philosophy. Lord Mdang, please present this letter."

Cliopher rose from his seat and went to Princess Oriana. She stared past his head as he took the scroll. He made sure his expression was as unrevealing as possible as he crossed the open space and knelt before his Radiancy's throne to present the scroll to him on the golden tray used for the purpose.

The round tray had a further function besides the increase of ceremony and the protection of taboos. When his Radiancy invoked it, a spell replicated the tray's contents down along the silver chargers set before the princes.

This done, Cliopher returned to his seat and his own copy.

His Radiancy unrolled the original and scanned some of the names. At his gesture the rest of them followed suit. Numerous eyebrows were raised and glances exchanged as the princes saw the predominance of one particular name.

"My lord chancellor," his Radiancy said calmly after several moments. "It appears that a number of these signatories bear the surname Mdang. It occurs to us that you are of the Vangavaye-ve. Are they by chance related to you?"

"I believe I am related to all the Mdangs of Gorjo City, my lord," he replied, glancing very briefly at the scroll to see whose beloved names were there written in their own familiar or unfamiliar hands. Louya, Vinyë, Aunt Oura, Uncle Odo, Galen, Enya, Quintus, Zemius, Toucan, Bertie, cousin after cousin after cousin.

"You have not brought this matter to our attention previously, my lord chancellor."

"It had not come to mine in any official capacity, my lord." He was achingly aware of Galen's warning, the argument between Maya and the *velio* 'project manager', the repeated gossip about Earl Baljan and the fish farm. "As I am sure you have noticed, my lord, this petition is addressed to you."

It was not addressed to Cliopher because of how vehemently he'd rejected Cousin Louya on one of her mad starts, back when he had just started to come into a position of power and he had thought his family understood what he did, what they were asking him to do.

His Radiancy turned to the princess. "Princess Oriana, it appears that a substantial portion of your populace are sufficiently moved to sign a letter petitioning us on this subject. How do you propose responding to them?"

She gestured gracefully, looking every inch a jewel of the first water. Her garments were in Jilkano court style but made of ahalo cloth trimmed with foamwork and the golden pearls of the Western Ring. There were even a few flame pearls distributed about her headdress. Someone who didn't know the traditional patterns would probably take them to be Islander.

"Illustrious One, I am sure they are lovely people, but they are not, well, they are not exactly—that is to say, thanks to Lord Mdang's insistence on the annual stipend, they will hardly starve—and if they persist in disobeying their ruler, well, there are laws in place, are there not?"

She smiled brightly at Cliopher, who concentrated on making sure her words were written down with perfect accuracy.

The Prince of Amboloyo looked for permission to speak. "Are you suggesting, Princess Oriana, that the appropriate response is to, er, relieve them of their appointments?"

Princess Oriana tittered again. "Why, yes, Prince Rufus, and why not? It's not as if any of them do anything worthwhile, anyway. Lazy crackpots, the lot of them."

The sound of Cliopher's pen snapping in his fingers was, for a moment, the loudest sound in the room.

His Radiancy met his gaze blandly. Cliopher knew that he was permitting Princess Oriana to trip herself, permitting her allies to reveal themselves, permitting the convoluted personal and political dynamics of the Council to become clear. Usually Cliopher had no difficulties whatsoever in following his lead, interjecting a word or a movement or an argument wherever necessary to guide debates and decisions where he and his Radiancy wished them to go.

Usually.

Prince Rufus grimaced, his equivalent to a predatory smile. "I believe the Lord Chancellor might have something to say."

His Radiancy inclined his head gravely. A small part of Cliopher noticed the merriment gleaming in the lion eyes.

"Please speak your mind, Lord Mdang."

Cliopher took a deep breath to steady himself, rose, walked forward to stand next to Jiano, scroll in hand. Jiano smelled of fresh greenery from the leaves woven into his armbands.

"My lord, I thank you for the permission to speak." The formal phrases rolled off his tongue, steadied him. He turned to the princess. "Princess Oriana, I am amazed to hear you say these things."

"I thought your concern with the annual stipend was precisely to cover these sorts of situations, Lord Mdang. As for my response, well, you know the laws around disobedience, I am sure."

Cliopher inclined his head. "I do, ma'am, and am familiar also with the distinctions made in the law between lawful protest, civil disobedience, and treason. You mistake me: I am amazed that you would so blithely gut your provincial economy, and most admiring that you would so unhesitatingly sacrifice many of your own most appreciated comforts and luxuries to your principles."

Princess Oriana gaped at him before catching herself.

His Radiancy said, "Please expand, my lord chancellor. We are not all equally familiar with the economic and cultural activities of the Vangavaye-ve."

Cliopher bowed. Later perhaps he would be able to appreciate how neatly his Radiancy had played the room, how precisely he had set up the situation so that Cliopher's natural response was turned to advantage. For now he was simply furious, his stomach feeling as if he had swallowed a hard ball of righteous indignation.

He unfurled the scroll. "It was my impression, your highness, that you are fond of music—I note that the entire body of the Gorjo City Symphony Orchestra is listed by name, beginning with Vinyë el Vawen Mdang, my sister."

The princess' eyes widened slightly. She had large eyes, spaced widely, which she emphasized with makeup and by plucking her eyebrows to the point she looked perpetually surprised; but this was, he thought, genuine.

"I had thought you a patron of the ahalo cloth merchants, but I see here the names of all three of the cooperatives—beginning under Clia Mdang, my cousin." He unfurled the scroll a few more turns. "I believe those following Taro Nevan represent the toala guild, who are responsible for preparing the fibres used to create foamwork; after Nara Mdang—my aunt—are the dozen masters of the foamworkers' guild."

He unrolled more inches, letting the top end dangle over his hand, the variety of hands and inks visible.

"Ah, I see here the principal singers in the opera house—my aunt Malania and uncle Haido amongst them—and here, after Naua inDeana, are names I recognize from the pearl hunters of the Western Ring. And here, following Ghillian Poyë, who is in the provincial department of agriculture, are some fifteen or twenty names of her colleagues …"

He went on, picking out every name he recognized and giving their positions. He was astounded at how successful Cousin Louya had been.

Near the bottom were a cluster of elders—he recognized the honorifics in the Islander tongue—and then, as if a coda granting respectability, all the rest of his aunts and uncles, and last of all the matriarch of the Mdang family, his mother.

He said, "Even granting the idea that the Vangavaye-ve would function as a part of a Zuni society without trade goods or trades, I am simply astonished, Princess Oriana, to see you relegate Lazo Mdang."

She looked blank, as well she might, he thought viciously. He refurled the scroll.

"My uncle Lazo has no official position within the Vangavayen government, it is true. He is no chief. He is not even the Speaker for any group besides, possibly, the Mdang family. He is, as I imagine you might say, merely a barber."

Cliopher met the lion eyes again, this time by accident as he was sweeping his regard across the princes. His Radiancy showed nothing but lurking amusement, and that was, Cliopher knew, not directed at him at all.

"Lazo Mdang has no official position," he repeated, knowing they would never understand if he tried to explain the role of the *tanà*. "He is merely the lynch-pin of Gorjo City. He knows everyone, their strengths and their weaknesses, their skills and their pet peeves. He knows who works and who does not and why. He is where all questions come to be answered, all problems to be resolved, all crises to be calmed. The Vangavaye-ve could do without your support for interprovincial trade, for the university, for the departments of agriculture or finance or justice or the common weal. It cannot do without my uncle Lazo's barber shop. You certainly have the legal ability to close it down, your highness, but you would regret it."

He bowed over his hands, Vangavayen style, to his Radiancy, and at the nod returned to his desk. He spent a few silent moments preparing a new pen. Then he wrote, in precise lettering, *Cliopher Lord Mdang defended the people of the Vangavaye-ve against their princess.*

There, he thought defiantly, let history read that.

★★★

AFTER THE COUNCIL MEETING, HIS Radiancy bade Cliopher accompany him to his apartments. Cliopher presumed his Radiancy desired to go over the debate, which he did—but not the part that Cliopher expected.

It was late afternoon, and his Radiancy's terrace was in cool shadow. His Radiancy led him to the seats there, followed by Conju with a tray of coffee and cookies for them both. Then his Radiancy made the sliding gesture of the Wall of Silence. Cliopher's blood ran cold.

His Radiancy said, "While I am by no means disappointed in the results of today's council, I am somewhat concerned about you, Cliopher."

Cliopher dropped his gaze to his silver-chased glass. "My lord?"

"It has occurred to me that I can imagine no other circumstance in which you would permit a situation such as this to develop to the point where the people of a province sent an emissary to us against their prince. It was not so complicated a situation as to require it; it is not a matter of complete distrust and bad faith, though I can imagine it may yet lead there. You had at least two separate and independent mentions of severe dissatisfaction with Princess Oriana on account of this project that I know of, for I was present for them."

Cliopher's face was burning-hot and his stomach simultaneously congealed. He did not know what to do, where to look, what to say. "My lord ..."

"Two separate requests to consider a matter from established and trustworthy people? My lord chancellor, I know you do not ignore such requests—except, apparently, when they come from those you have most reason to listen to."

For a moment he thought he might actually vomit from shame. He swallowed repeatedly, staring with burning eyes out at the view before them, the city and beyond it the fens and on the horizon the distant sea.

"Kip," his Radiancy said more gently. "Kip, look at me."

"Please, my lord," he whispered, feeling the tears start to fall as he obeyed.

"Kip—I cannot claim to understand family dynamics, especially in a family such as yours. I have no experience. I don't ..."

His Radiancy trailed off. Cliopher's eyes were blurry, he could not see his Radiancy's expression, but his voice was ... not the voice of the Lord Emperor, but the voice of the man who came, every now and then, to his friend's apartments, with tea or wine or books.

"Kip, I do not understand why you are so vigilant against favouritism in yourself. I have never seen any indication it is a habit of yours—or even a propensity. Do you seriously spend your time wishing you could elevate your friends to high offices irrespective of their skills and talents?"

"Of course not, my lord."

His eyes were clearing now a little, could see that his Radiancy smiled. "I should not have added that rider, should I? Do you spend time wishing you could elevate your friends to high offices *because* of their skills and talents and the fact that you like them?"

This time Cliopher had to look down. "Sometimes."

"Some weeks ago Saya Kalikiri asked for a private audience with me. She wished my advice on what to do about the fact that although you very clearly liked and regarded highly and worked extremely well with a young man she had hired to the Private Offices, thinking that he would work well with you, a young man, moreover, who was the first besides you ever to come to the Service from the Vangavaye-ve, you were strongly resisting appointing him as a personal secretary precisely because he was from the Vangavaye-ve."

"My lord ..." He didn't know what he was protesting, trailed off.

"You described your uncle Lazo in terms that every person in that room knew for a description of yourself, your role in the world. It was abundantly clear you did not intend them to be a description of yourself. No one would cross my favour of you, because of who I am—and because of who you are. I assure you I would land heavily on anyone who even hinted of nepotism—but at the same time, I really do not understand why you actively work against those you love best."

Cliopher turned shocked eyes on him. "My lord!"

"You protest? You are consistent, Kip. You take no extra offices or moneys or honours for yourself; I must directly order you to accept gifts. You do, perhaps, ensure that the Vangavaye-ve is first when it comes to new developments and initiatives ... but then again, the princes are happy to let that one far-away and generally unconsidered province be the trial grounds for what they might well believe are amended developments and initiatives for their own provinces. That is it."

He swallowed again, his face feeling itchy as the tears dried. "My lord?"

"I mean: that is it. That is as far as your ... call it selfishness ... extends. You are so far from it, in fact, that you deliberately let your family believe your position to be significantly less important than it is." His Radiancy smiled wryly. "Inconceivably less important than it is."

His Radiancy waited. Cliopher cleared his throat. He could not find equanimity, felt himself to be entirely exposed, belly-up, defeated. He said, "They have never forgiven me for leaving."

"Have you ever forgiven yourself?"

Cliopher looked at him, met the lion eyes. Finally dropped his eyes in submission. "No."

★★★

JIANO WON, OF COURSE. THE only surprise was that only two of the Jilkano princes voted on Princess Oriana's side. The third was the Princess of Jilkano-Ngurai, in whose province was the island duchy of Nijan.

She understood, he realized from a few oblique comments, just how close Princess Oriana was coming to being deposed.

Four months later he received accounts of the Great Fish Farm Debacle from his mother, his sister, his aunt Oura, Ghilly, and four cousins. Only Quintus mentioned Jiano's journey to Solaara, and it was obvious that he had not himself spoken to Jiano or Aya, just heard that someone had gone.

None of them asked if Cliopher knew anything about it.

INTERLUDE TWO

A LETTER

MY DEAR CLIOPHER,

I read your latest proclamation today—I am behind-hand because I have been out at my little cottage painting the Pinnacles—and what can I say except, how wonderful! How astonishingly, magnificently, splendidly splendid! And knowing you, this is only the beginning. When you wrote to me last year to say that you were made the Lord Chancellor (as if I wouldn't have read the proclamations!—Eventually, at least!) and that you were hoping to achieve some of the ambitions you'd long since presumed would have to wait for some future generation, I thought you meant things like better health care. I was not expecting you to *begin* with an annual stipend for every single person in the world.

Can you imagine what is going to be the result of this?

—I am laughing at myself. This is your grand plan: obviously you can imagine its results! I'm sure you have all sorts of figures and analyses and charts and tables and endless support for why you think this is a good thing and what you expect to be the initial results. I wish I had been there in the Council of Princes chamber to see your face (and theirs!) when you argued it into existence.

I was there to paint you when you argued for what became the Indrogan Estates—the look on your face when you asked, no *demanded*, of the princes of Zunidh that they fulfil their vows to preserve the life and wellbeing of all their people ... Oh, how I wish I had been there to paint you when you asked the Prince of Amboloyo whether he was so weak he needed to rule by fear.

You see, I did read your letter.

Oh, my dear, I am so excited. I keep thinking of what a difference this annual stipend would have made in my life when I was younger—and so I think of all the young artists (and athletes and farmers and inventors) who will be able to look at their hearts and say, *yes*, instead of *no*. *Yes* they can take up that opportunity to study under so-and-so, or *yes* they can decide to spend a year seeing if they have what it takes to succeed—and what it takes no longer *begins* with *enough money to be able to say yes*. Now they can decide for themselves, not on the basis of whether their parents can (and will) assist them, but on the basis of whether they have the courage and the desire and the yearning to do it.

Cliopher, do you realize what you have done?

—I am laughing again. You had to figure out to the valiant the budget for this. You had to figure out a forecast for the effects on the world's economy and wellbeing of giving every single person, regardless of their origin, access to a standard amount of income. I've heard a few people mutter about why you would bother giving the rich and the aristos access to the annual income as well, and I have to confess I was wondering, too, until I started to think, first, that you probably know what's going on in those classes far better than I or the people I talk to do, and secondly, that one of the things I most admire about you is your commitment to fairness.

If it is fair that those from the bottom of society get to choose their futures regardless of their families' situations—well, is it not fair that those from the top should also get that choice? I have learned from my years under patronage that money, however benevolently bestowed, has its expectations. I have never wondered what kind of expectations there are on the shoulders of the children of the upper nobility, but now that I think of it, they must sometimes be heavy burdens.

But when it is a gift coming from the Lord of Rising Stars down to his people? The expectation is that one returns the tithe of the best of one's work—

Oh, Cliopher, when I painted you standing up against the world (in the form of the Council of Princes) arguing—successfully—for those who had nothing, I wondered where on earth you could go from there.

I should have known better. Oh, my dear, and this is only the beginning.

—With my love, and I enclose also a sketch from that day you stood up before the Princes (to hearten you when you stand, as you must, before them again), and one of my new paintings from the Pinnacles, to remind you of the wild areas of this world (for I know you care more for the people, but the ecology matters too)—

—Your Suzen

—One further thought: My hip is acting up again, I'm afraid, so I am not as mobile as I'd like and I don't think I can manage a trip to Solaara, but I should love to paint you in your full regalia as Lord Chancellor. Can you think of a reason to come to the City of Emeralds?

$\mathcal{A}$ $\mathcal{L}$ETTER

DEAR KIP,

I have to say, I was not expecting how surreal it would be getting letters from both you and Gaudy describing the same event. You write about whatever it is (I am thinking of your account of the open court when Gaudy and some of the other new secretaries came) the way you usually do, with a special focus on Gaudy and what you could see of his reactions.

Then he wrote with a description of the same event, but it's as if it's a totally different one. What is familiar to you is all new and strange to him; where you write about him (being the new element to you), he writes about you; where you glance off your own role in the proceedings he spends three paragraphs explaining why you were wearing what you were wearing. I had never suspected how important you are! It is all delightful and sheds such a different light on your life. I am starting to look forward to our visit in a way I never had before.

You sound (from both your and Gaudy's letters!) very busy, but you seem happy as well. Gaudy keeps writing about how hard you work, how much you get done. That's the Kip I remember, always so focused and almost scarily intent. I don't think Gaudy realizes how closely you're paying attention to him. It makes me wonder what else you noticed when you seemed focused on your present goal to the exclusion of everything else.

There's not much news to report from here. Cousin Louya is back into crazy territory with her theories that the entire mundial government is secretly run by a group who manipulate world events according to their mysterious plans. Why they should do this, and why you wouldn't catch them, she is unable to explain. It gives me great comfort, whenever she starts sounding the least bit plausible, to reflect that you are in Solaara making sure things run properly. She has never yet suggested that you are part of this shadow cabal!

Other than that: Toucan has finally retired, with a party thrown by Bertie and Ghilly. They invited me and Quintus, which was good of them, though I know they wanted you. It will be interesting to see what happens once they stop being happy about not working. Bertie seems thoroughly occupied by his yacht and fishing, but Toucan strikes me as someone who needs something purposeful to do. (No surprise in a friend of yours.) Perhaps one of your new plans will give him something to work on. It's a nice thought.

Mama is doing well, as are all the aunts and uncles and most of the cousins I can think of. Cousin Haro has been unwell, but seems to be doing better. Hillen is still obnoxious as ever, and seems to be settling in with intolerable smugness into his position in Common Weal. It's hard to believe he and Haro are related, even as half-brothers, they're so different. I have an idea for a music education program for those who might not come from musical families (there are some, even in the Vangavaye-ve!). I haven't tried to go to Hillen with it, though I think, from what you've told me, that Common Weal is where I should go to see about funding. You don't have any ideas, do you?

Give my love to Gaudy when you see him next, if that's not too humble a request for the Great and Very Busy Man my son informs me you are!

Love as always,

Vinyë

VOLUME THREE

THE HEART OF THE WORLD

CHAPTER THIRTY-SIX

CLIOPHER WAS STANDING IN THE middle of the outer Offices of State, finishing up a conversation with Kiri, when the lights went out.

"Damn," said Kiri. "Aioru, open the shutters the rest of the way. Lord Mdang, when will—what is it?"

Cliopher was not attending. He was standing shocked, reliving the worst day of his life, the worst day of *anyone's* life, the day Astandalas had fallen. He was waiting for the rest of it to happen.

But then the lights flickered, on, off, on, the magic in the globes faint and faltering, and he drew a shuddering breath, and knew what it must be, and, in tones as faint and faltering as the lights, he said: "My lord."

And then he dropped his papers and all pretence of decorum and ran, just ran, to the Imperial Apartments.

★★★

THE GUARDS LET HIM IN without question or challenge, though their eyes were wild and their bearing alert and dangerous. Cliopher skidded past shocked pages and servants and guards in the anterooms, bursting through the last door to the study where Ludvic Omo was kneeling over his Radiancy's prone figure.

The commander of the guards did not look up at Cliopher's entrance. He stayed where he was, hands cupped over his Radiancy's breast, pumping up and down rhythmically.

Cliopher stood with his own breast heaving, trying to catch his breath, trying not to whimper with grief and fear and alarm. Ludvic's hands slipped a little on the silk of his Radiancy's tunic, and he lifted them away before he quite touched his Radiancy's bare skin.

Above them the lights were flickering.

And then his Radiancy drew a shuddering breath, and even as Cliopher stepped forward, he saw his Radiancy's arms came up and before any of

them knew what he was doing his hands had clasped Ludvic Omo's forearms. There was a noise as of something snapping, and Cliopher, hands rising
involuntarily to cover his face, saw the expression of total horror cross his
Radiancy's.

Ludvic Omo said, in his stolid way, "I am here, my lord."

"Ludvic," his Radiancy said faintly, his hands gripping tightly.

"I am here, my lord," he said again.

"What—what was it?"

"Your heart, my lord. Do not strain yourself. Cliopher is here to take
care of things."

His Radiancy let his head sink back towards the floor, though he did not
let go of Ludvic. He stared up at the ceiling, tawny eyes swimming gold, and
he said: "They were calling my name ... Kip ..."

"I am here, my lord," said Cliopher, dropping to his knees beside his lord.

"Kip ... do not let them ... let them ..." His breath began to come more
rapidly, and he seemed greatly distressed, but could not get any more words
out.

Cliopher spoke as calmly and reassuringly as he could. "Do not worry,
my lord. I will not let them."

"Not again," his Radiancy managed.

"No, my lord."

"They could not hear."

"No, my lord. Be assured that I will not let them. For now you must rest
and recover yourself. I will see to everything."

"Mother Kip," he said, with a faint, ironic smile, and obediently closed
his eyes and seemed to concentrate on drawing the long even breaths that
Ludvic was encouraging him to take. His hands slid down until they were
gripping the guard's wrists. Cliopher looked for a long moment at Ludvic's
forearms, which looked as if they had been branded with gold, before he
stood up to take command of himself and the situation.

The only other person present was Pikabe, who had tears running down
his face even as he stood at full attention.

"What happened?" Cliopher asked him softly, going over to the bell-pull
and tugging it.

"His, his Radiancy was just walking to his desk when he, he said, 'They
are calling my name,' and then he clutched at his chest and fell before we, we
could think to—"

To break the taboo that might have seen Ludvic consumed by lightning or magical fire or some other horrible curse, thought Cliopher. "Did you send for anyone?"

Pikabe gulped. "No, sir. I'm sorry, sir."

"It's understandable," Cliopher said, only grateful that Ludvic had known what to do for someone having a heart attack or a stroke—even if that someone were his Radiancy—and strode through the seven anterooms past all the anxious guards to where the four pages sat awaiting orders and looking terrified. He chose the one who seemed least like she was about to faint. "Run down to the hospital wing for his Radiancy's physician, Domina Audry."

"His Radiancy?" quavered one of the guards.

"Run?" said the page, eyes wide.

Cliopher knew that a running page might cause panic—but—"As fast as you can. His Radiancy has had a heart attack. There seems no immediate danger," he added, with firm resolution, gesturing at the lights which were even now resuming their usual clear brightness. "But I think it is best his physician examines him as soon as possible. If anyone asks—on your return, mind!—I will be making an announcement of what is toward in the throne room within the hour."

The page swallowed hard and nodded, then ran off.

Cliopher looked at the other three pages. "Fetch Ser Rhodin," he said to one; and to the other two: "Fetch Saya Kalikiri and your replacements. There will, I am sure, be other messages coming shortly."

That first job done, he went back into the Imperial Apartments to find that Conju had appeared and was kneeling beside Ludvic at his Radiancy's side.

Cliopher joined them there. "I have sent for the physician, my lord," he said softly, noting that his Radiancy had still not relinquished his hold on Ludvic's wrists, and wondering how much that grasp was paining the guard. "She will be here very soon."

"Bed," his Radiancy said, with his eyes still closed.

Conju made an inarticulate cry of protest. "My lord, if you have hurt anything—"

"Bed," his Radiancy said, somewhat more firmly.

They exchanged glances, and then Ludvic said: "I hear and obey, my lord, but you must let go of my wrists that I may lift you."

"Not—no lightning?"

"No, my lord," said Commander Omo, his deep voice reassuring. His Radiancy's hands made a convulsive gripping motion, and then he let them fall. Ludvic gestured them back. He slid careful hands under his Radiancy's shoulders and knees, then stood with one smooth motion.

Conju hastily moved to open the doors leading into the private apartments. Cliopher and Pikabe followed them into the huge bedchamber, where Conju drew back the foamwork canopy and the opaque embroidered panels behind them, and Ludvic laid his lord into the great bed as gently as a leaf.

His Radiancy was silent for a few moments, his breath coming rough and hard, his eyes closed and brows drawn into a grimace of pain and distress. They all hovered awkwardly, Conju and Cliopher looking back frequently to the door to see if the physician had come. Pikabe stood with his spear up and his attention split between his Radiancy and the door.

There was a faint sound from the bed, and Cliopher turned his head sharply, to see that his Radiancy was reaching out, eyes staring.

"My lord," he said hastily, "what is it? What do you need?"

"Kip," his Radiancy whispered, "no, not—Ludvic—hand—"

And while they all stared at him, not at all understanding, he said, with the air of one making a tremendous final push, "Hand. *Please.*"

And Ludvic, who had gone to take up his position at the door, turned back to the bed and squatted beside it, and with the utmost gentleness took his Radiancy's extended right hand in both of his, and he said: "We are here, my lord. We will not let you go."

His Radiancy stared anxiously at him, as if waiting for the lightning to strike, and when nothing happened (or nothing, at least, that Commander Omo permitted to show on his face), he relaxed visibly and made a noticeable effort to smile.

Cliopher turned sharply away to control his own expression. He felt he had just done so when the door opened and Domina Audry came in, face set and workbag in hand.

"What has happened?" she said, taking in the tableau.

"His Radiancy appears to have had an heart attack," Cliopher said quietly. "Pikabe says that he clutched at his chest before collapsing."

"His Radiancy was in bed?" she asked, frowning. "Was he feeling unwell earlier?"

"No," Conju said, leaving his anxious hover to join their conversation. "He was in good spirits this morning. He bathed and ate as usual."

"He collapsed in the study," Cliopher offered. "Commander Omo was performing cardiac thrusts when I arrived, just in time to see his Radiancy regain consciousness. His Radiancy grasped Commander Omo's arms," he added, not quite irrelevantly. "He ordered us to bring him here."

Domina Audry gave him a sharp glance. She walked briskly up to the bed, where she used a variety of instruments to examine his Radiancy without coming anywhere near his skin. She asked a few questions of both him and Commander Omo, including asking the latter to count his Radiancy's heartbeats as she watched the time. Watching her face as she worked, Cliopher began to relax.

Just as she had put away her instruments and seemed about to make a pronouncement, his Radiancy suddenly arched in bed, his hand convulsing in Ludvic's grip, his face transfigured by agony into a rictus. His free hand came up to clutch at his chest, and he cried out in a voice that carried commandingly: "Stop! Stop! You are killing me!"

They all froze: Conju and Cliopher and Ludvic and Pikabe and Domina Audry. Commander Omo's phlegmatic countenance flickered briefly as his Radiancy squeezed his hand. Cliopher was watching his lord's face as the pain crested—and then his Radiancy collapsed utterly. The hand Ludvic had been holding slipped out of his grasp and thumped against the wooden frame of the bed.

Cliopher looked quickly up at the lights, but although they flickered they did not extinguish.

"His pulse, sir," Domina Audry said urgently to Ludvic, who picked up his Radiancy's limp hand gently and laid his fingers across his wrist. His own hands, usually a fine rich brown, were marked all over with smudges of gold.

Ludvic reported the pulse in a calm voice. Domina Audry frowned and began to search in her bag for various phials and a small crystalline dish in which she combined drops and dribbles of their contents. "His Radiancy must drink this," she said, pouring the mixture into a glass of water. "It will relax him and strengthen his heart until he has slept and—I don't understand quite what has gone here—it seems as if there is some magic afoot, or else—"

Or else there was something even worse going on, Cliopher thought, though what could be worse than magic that could affect his Radiancy he wasn't sure.

★★★

SOME THREE QUARTERS OF AN hour later, Cliopher made his way down to the throne room. It was packed with every courtier and civil servant and servant in the Palace who could cram into the space. He came in by the side door and climbed onto the lower daïs, very aware of the empty throne looming behind and above him.

When he lifted his hand for attention, the shocked and anxious whispers fell into an even more fraught shocked and anxious silence.

"My lords and ladies," he said, as clearly and loudly as he could. "You will have noticed the flickering of the lights. Some of you, no doubt, are recalling the Fall of Astandalas; others have heard some rumour. I am here to tell you that his Radiancy has had a heart attack—" he had to wait while a flare of outrage and outright fear swelled.

"Listen to me," he said intently. "His Radiancy has had a heart attack. He has survived: he is resting: there is every reason to believe he will recover entirely and soon. However, he will need rest and his usual activities will be severely curtailed until he has recuperated. Court is therefore adjourned until further notice. Any petitions or audiences intended for his Radiancy are to come to me as Lord Chancellor through the Offices of State. Once I have further instructions from his Radiancy, I will let them be known."

He nodded sharply and set off for his own chambers, never more grateful for the privilege of using the side door out of the throne room. He found he had a small constellation of pages, secretaries, courtiers, and even guards revolving around him, all of them clamouring for his attention. "Attend," he said even more sharply, and was extremely relieved to meet Kiri at his door.

"I thought you would come here," she said simply, as he gestured her in to the First Receiving Room. "I didn't even try the throne room. What was your announcement?"

"Court is adjourned until further notice, his Radiancy is resting and will need to recuperate, and ..."

"And you are in charge while he is doing so," she said sympathetically. "You know I will do all I can. What's first? Drafting letters to the princes?"

He felt one burden lift. "Yes, please do, and I'll read them over before signing them. Otherwise do what you do—I must return to my lord and see if he has any orders for me before I can make plans."

"You can do this," she said encouragingly. "This is why he chose you as his Lord Chancellor."

"It is practice for when his Radiancy leaves on his quest?" he said, with a faint flare of humour. He sobered almost immediately. "Oh, Kiri, I hope ..."

"Many people fully recover from heart attacks," she said. "They might need to change diet or stress, that is all."

It was a lot more than 'just that', Cliopher thought as he made his way back to the Imperial Apartments and was saluted in by the guards through all the anterooms. His Radiancy did not overeat or drink to excess; he swam daily, even if there was little other exercise beyond that endless pacing … and he spent fifteen hours a day, every day, working magic and managing people and governing a world and responding to the demands and requests and prayers of several more.

His Radiancy was lying back with his eyes closed when Cliopher was ushered into the bedchamber by one of the household attendants. His hand still gripped Ludvic's. Commander Omo had been brought a stool by someone—Conju, presumably—and his place on guard taken by Ato. He looked up when Cliopher came in, and said softly to his Radiancy, "Cliopher has come back, my lord."

Cliopher hurried over. "My lord, I am here."

His Radiancy moved Ludvic's hand in a way that suggested he would have liked to have taken Cliopher's in turn. He opened his eyes, which gleamed too brightly, and smiled very faintly. "Kip." He paused there to take a breath, but his breathing was more even than it had been, and Cliopher refused to let himself feel as worried as he would have liked to. "Kip. Orders."

"I am listening, my lord."

His Radiancy paused again, looking up at the delicately carved ebony of the bed canopy's frame above him. It was inlaid with mother-of-pearl and gold, and was easily the most beautiful item of furniture Cliopher had ever seen. His Radiancy bounced his hand, and Ludvic's, gently on the blanket beside him. "Not orders," he whispered, eyes closing. "Requests." He opened his eyes again. "Conju? Rhodin?"

Conju was hovering five feet away at a table on which was laid out his dressing wands and a flask of what was presumably medicine. He hurried over to stand on Ludvic's other side. Ser Rhodin was standing on the other side of the bed. Both men said, "We are here, my lord."

His Radiancy looked from one to the other of them with brilliant gold eyes. "Friends," he said softly.

Cliopher swallowed down the lump in his throat. "What do you ask of us, my lord?"

"If I die … no, listen … if I die, I have … please … last requests …"

"Whatever you want done, we will do," Cliopher said recklessly, meaning every word.

His Radiancy actually chuckled, though it turned into a cough and he wheezed for a long while before being able to accept the glass of water Conju held to his lips, and then his breathing evened out again and he gathered his strength and he said, weakly but clearly: "In my study there is a red book.

In it is my private will. I want you to promise me to see its clauses executed. Promise."

"Of course, my lord," said Cliopher, rather puzzled at the urgency with which this was spoken. "I cannot imagine any difficulties."

His Radiancy smiled and wheezed out another chuckle. "You have not seen it." He accepted some more water from Conju. "Promise me—the red book—see it published."

"Of course, my lord," said Cliopher again.

"It will be harder than you know," his Radiancy said. "Promise me you will see it published. There are instructions. Promise."

Cliopher exchanged a bewildered glance with Ser Rhodin; both Ludvic and Conju were frowning down at their lord. Ser Rhodin shrugged as if to say he had no idea what the book could be about, either, and why, if it were that important, his Radiancy had never before mentioned it, but that he was game for anything.

"My lord," Cliopher said unhesitatingly, "if it comes to that I will see the book published and all the clauses in your will fulfilled, though it cost me everything."

"Not everything," his Radiancy said, smiling at him.

"No," agreed Cliopher.

The other three men made their vows to fulfil his wishes, and his Radiancy listened intently, and then something seemed to let go within him, to the point that Conju leaned forward with a cry—but his Radiancy lifted Ludvic's hand to his cheek and then he said, very simply, "Thank you," and he slept.

CHAPTER *THIRTY-SEVEN*

BY THE END OF THAT first day Cliopher had learned just how great a difference there was between being the Lord Chancellor under his Radiancy and the viceroy in command.

By the end of the second day, with his Radiancy showing few signs of recuperation beyond a slightly stronger voice and a willingness to finally let go of Ludvic Omo's hand so that the commander could stagger off to bed, he was no longer wondering why his Radiancy had had a heart attack, only why it had never happened sooner.

At midnight on the second—or rather third—day he was signing his name to a seemingly endless series of letters, intended to explain his Radiancy's incapacity without completely panicking everyone, when a page interrupted him to say that a sky ship had been sighted.

Presuming that this was one of the nearer princes come in response to the letter, or possibly one who had already been travelling in advance of the next Council of Princes—and, hell, conceivably would not know the news— he finished his current stack and hastened up to the Spire.

The night was very black, heavy clouds covering the stars; only the Light shone brilliantly, like a giant star set not far above their heads. The air was warm and very humid, and he knew the rains were about to begin. Possibly right that night, he thought somewhat absently, not moving.

After exchanging greetings (and those of his letters that were sealed and ready to go) with the Light minders and making sure that sufficient footmen to bear the luggage were in the waiting room out of sight, he sat down on the bench outside the office, next to two quiet and sleepy pages, and stared at the moving points of light that were the only sign of the approaching sky ship.

It was coming from the west, so he assumed it was either the Princess of Mgunai or the Prince of Western Dair. He hoped it was not one of the Jilkano princes, who would not have heard.

It seemed to take forever to arrive. He closed his eyes at last, head aching, eyes aching, whole being aching, wishing he could sleep, wishing he did not know what crushing weight of responsibilities were waiting for him to finish that night, to begin again tomorrow. He nearly fell asleep: opened his eyes with a start: closed his eyes again so he could compose a list of what he needed to begin with in the morning.

A muffled laugh made him start upright again, cursing himself inwardly for being so unprofessional and discourteous, and then he stopped and stared as the lights from the ship and the Palace combined to show him the gathered members of his family.

"Why—Vinyë—Mama—Cousin Zemius—Leona—Cousin Quintus!"

Cousin Quintus winked. "I thought it time to see the capital, and given the breadth of the invitation ..." He shrugged.

His mother stepped forward to embrace him, with a fond kiss. "Dear Kip, you didn't need to wait up for us."

"Oh," he said, and stumbled over explanations and protestations.

"He's sleep-muddled," Vinyë said, laughing. "And no wonder. Captain Diogen, thank you so much for everything."

"It was my pleasure, ma'am," replied the captain, saluting Cliopher with élan.

Cliopher had just about managed to regain his composure, and thought ahead enough to wonder where he was going to put them all. He beckoned one of the pages over, who had brightened with this unexpected arrival. "Run ahead to my rooms and inform Franzel that my family has arrived. There are, let me see, six—"

"Eight," Vinyë said promptly. "Aunt Oura's sitting behind with Dora. She's asleep."

"Eight, then," he said. The page bowed hastily and quickly tumbled down the stairs. Cliopher turned to the captain. "I was expecting one of the princes, so there are people for the baggage ..." He made a gesture at the other page, who nodded and disappeared quickly through the door leading to the waiting room.

"Very good, m'lud," said Captain Diogen, saluting again.

Cliopher turned to his mother, who was watching this with a curious smile. "You must all be tired. Come along with me and we'll see about beds, and talk in the morning."

"That sounds remarkably sensible," his sister said.

His mother smiled at him and wound her arm within his. He smiled back, delight stealing through the weight of everything else, and he remembered that this visit had been arranged months before. In the commotion of his Radiancy's sudden incapacitation he had entirely forgotten: but it was clear when they arrived at his own chambers that Franzel had not, for his majordomo was waiting there to show them into the various rooms that had been prepared for them.

His short doze followed by the excitement of family (rather than the Princess of Mgunai, who was not in any way a person he would have wanted to be caught snoozing by) meant he felt capable of finishing his pile of letters. He signed the last at about the second hour, crawled into bed, and fell instantly into deep slumber.

★★★

SHOÄNIE, FRANZEL'S CHIEF ASSISTANT, WOKE him at dawn with a cup of strong coffee. Cliopher felt moderately refreshed despite the short sleep. He smiled at her as he sat up in bed and tried to gather his thoughts. "I'm sorry I had forgotten entirely about my family's arrival," he said. "You all performed wonders."

Shoänie smiled at him. "We had not forgotten they were coming, Sir," she said quietly. "Their rooms were prepared, and the notice you gave sent by the page was sufficient."

Whether that was quite true or not Cliopher was too grateful to enquire into. He thanked her again and sipped his coffee, and after a few moments felt ready to bathe and dress. Féonie had set out some of his more impressive robes; he put them on feeling rather as if he were girding himself for battle with the day.

He spent the first hour with another cup of coffee, sorting through the papers on his desk, finding as he did the letter sent down from the Light minders informing him that the *Eastern Wonder* had sailed and was expected back on such-and-such a date. He also found a note from Kiri reminding him that the second hour of that day was when the new appointments were being made, and he cursed and swallowed the rest of his coffee hastily and proceeded down to the Offices of State with barely five minutes to spare.

"I need an appointments secretary," he said to Kiri as soon as he had been bowed into the back office by various members of the Secretariat.

"You need a regular secretary, too," she said amiably, making a note.

"Can't they be the same person? I did both for his Radiancy."

She grinned at him. "You did everything for his Radiancy. You also have an enviable ability to organize yourself that is not shared by all your fellows. Will you take Zaoul and Tully or your nephew? Eldo's not back from Amboloyo yet."

"I am going to reassign Gaudy to my household for the next few weeks," he said with ruthless selfishness. "My family has just arrived, as was planned but as I had entirely forgotten, and I want someone to look after them."

"And who better than your nephew?" she said, making a note. "May I suggest Tully for appointments and Zaoul for dictations?"

"Not the other way around?"

Kiri grinned again. "Either way. Tully can wrangle thunder lizards; Zaoul is Tkinele. Either of them will do superbly. And I'm sure you will find some excellent use for your nephew afterwards."

"I had really not intended to show such favouritism," he said, sighing, as the pleasant prospect of working with Gaudy receded under this new concern.

"No one who has ever had anything to do with you, or with your nephew either, for that matter, would think such a thing. Those three and Eldo are the cream of their crop."

"Well ..."

"Tchah! Here are the daily reports for this morning. I'll assign your secretaries first, so you needn't stay for the rest of the appointments."

"Just as well," he murmured as he picked up the heavy pile of reports, and went back out with them to survey the dozen apprehensive junior secretaries sitting in the conference room. There was a soft murmur of surprise at seeing him there, and interest from the aspirants. His nephew looked briefly up at him, his face deliberately set into indifference, though his clenched hands showed his nerves. Cliopher would have smiled, but Kiri came in and he leaned back against the wall instead.

Kiri smiled like the sharp-toothed hunting cat she was named for. "We begin with the positions under the Lord Chancellor."

There was an eager buzz, and—Cliopher noticed—a number of speculative glances cast the way of Tully, Zaoul, and Gaudy.

"Given the unusual circumstances this week, Lord Mdang has increased the number of positions he requires from one to three. Tulliantha nai Vasiaan, Zaoul of the Tkinele, and Gaudenius Vawen, please join his excellency now."

There was a smattering of applause from the other secretaries as the three stood up and collected their writing cases and self-consciously came over to him. Cliopher nodded sharply, handed Zaoul his stack of reports, and set off for his office at a brisk pace, just catching the look the three friends exchanged behind him. He wondered briefly whether his Radiancy ever felt such mild chagrin at seeing his various attendants communicate half-behind his back, or if he felt pure avuncular amusement.

They turned a corner and nearly collided with a page, who skidded to a halt with gasping apologies and then said: "Lord Mdang, his Radiancy has summoned you."

"Very good," said Cliopher, and took the next hall accordingly. "Gaudy and Tully, go to my apartments and sort yourselves out. Zaoul, you will attend me upstairs."

Despite his fearsome appearance, Zaoul evidently was not without nerves, for he swallowed and then said, "Yes, sir."

"What would you like us to do, my lord?" Tully asked.

"Ah! You are to be my appointments secretary. There will, I am sure, be a multitude of people craving audiences. Organize them."

"And me, sir?"

Cliopher was thinking ahead to his day, but he was not so distracted he did not know that tone in his nephew's voice. He looked around briefly, to see that no one besides their party was in earshot, and he stopped and turned directly to him.

"First of all, Kiri informs me that you three are the best of the junior secretariat to come through in five years. I have need of the best. I expect you to work hard and demonstrate your abilities and ambition and worthiness of her regard and mine. Second, the full government of Zunidh landed on my head yesterday morning, and until his Radiancy has recovered, I require the most loyal, trustworthy, and competent assistants I can muster in order to fulfil my responsibilities, and it just so happens that my nephew and his friends are among that number."

"Yes, sir," said Gaudy, much abashed.

"And third," pursued Cliopher, "I am ruthlessly and very selfishly making use of the fact that you *are* my nephew, and that we have acknowledged it, because my mother and yours arrived on the sky ship at midnight last night, and I want you to see to them. We will come up with other duties for you once I have spoken to his Radiancy.

"Now, off with you, and make sure you tell Franzel you're my new secretaries. Tully, find a place in the outer rooms that seems useful for an appointments secretary, Gaudy, see to our family, and Zaoul, walk with me."

"Yes, your excellency," said he, following at a trot as Cliopher launched himself up the final set of stairs.

"When we get to the Imperial Apartments, I will have you wait in one of the anterooms. Go through that stack of reports and organize them in order of importance, please."

"How will I know what is most important?"

Cliopher smiled briefly as they arrived at the doors, where the guards saluted magnificently. "This is Zaoul, one of my new secretaries," he said to them, and repeated the point to the pages, and the second set of guards, within. Zaoul, who had been in their position only the year before, looked carefully sleepy as they passed through the second door and landed in the next anteroom, where he again introduced Zaoul to the guards; and again on the next, and the next, and the next.

Finally they entered the sixth anteroom, where there was a little-used desk and chair set in the corner for just this position. "Think of it as a kind of test," he finally remembered to say out loud, "so I can see how your mind works."

★★★

HIS RADIANCY LOOKED DRAWN, HIS golden eyes too brilliant and his breathing still overly noticeable. He was withdrawn in a more metaphysical way, as well; the bed looked far too great for its inhabitant, who could easily fill the throne room. Zerafin and Varro were on guard. Conju sat next to his Radiancy, looking as if he, too, had not slept, and as if he had been fruitlessly trying to get his Radiancy to eat more of the food set on a tray table next to him.

"My lord," said Cliopher, "you summoned me?"

The lion gaze was disconcertingly measuring. "Come here," his Radiancy said, his voice unwontedly thin, patting the bed with one long-fingered hand. The signet ring caught the light and flared.

"My lord," Cliopher said, going to one knee beside the bed.

"Nonsense," said his Radiancy, with a faint smile, but did not expand. "My lord chancellor, my physician informs me that I ought stay in bed and out of trouble for the next two weeks at least. It may be longer, she undertook to warn me, if I do not listen to her. She did not say obey," he added, the smile growing in irony, "but that was what she meant."

Cliopher did his best to imitate Commander Omo's phlegmatic nature. "Very good, my lord."

He had come to love his Radiancy's smiles. They had been so rare before that holiday.

"What news or gossip have you? Anything of great moment since yesterday? Conju has not left my side, he has nothing to report to me. He says there *can* be nothing to report while I am indisposed. It is most embarrassing."

Cliopher smiled involuntarily. "I announced that court would be adjourned until further notice and that all requests for audiences should come through me as Lord Chancellor. I almost immediately realized that this means I am in desperate need of some assistance, and have therefore appointed some secretaries."

"Whom did you choose? I hope you did not let your pride overwhelm your sense and spurn your nephew?"

"My lord ..."

His Radiancy chuckled slightly. "I take that to mean you very nearly did, but were persuaded against it by Saya Kalikiri."

"I cannot deny it, my lord."

"Is he waiting without?"

"No, my lord, for on Kiri's suggestion I assigned Tulliantha nai Vasiaan as my appointments secretary and Zaoul as my general secretary for dictations and so forth. He is the Tkinele tribesman you met. He is in the anteroom."

"Why not your nephew? Do you really fear gossip of nepotism so much, or is there another reason?"

Cliopher flushed, and then explained about his family's arrival. His Radiancy listened, eyes on his face, as if he could not quite get enough of looking. Cliopher found it very disconcerting, for his Radiancy had never been one to *stare*, and the power of his regard was searing. At last, his Radiancy said, "Bring them here to visit me."

"My lord, that may be too much excitement."

"For them or for me?" his Radiancy shot back. "Not all seventy-nine cousins came, I take it? They could hardly have fit on the sky ship."

"Fifty-nine," Cliopher corrected despite himself. "No, my lord, it is my mother and my sister, my niece, my aunt Oura, her granddaughter Dora, and my aunt's sons, my cousins Zemius—the scholar—and Quintus—who is a merchant."

"That is only eight. Why, this room has hosted as many as two dozen people, merely to watch me dress. Bring them here the second hour this afternoon."

And of course, that was a direct orde. Cliopher bowed, tried to avoid exchanging meaningful looks with Conju, and was dismissed forthwith. He collected Zaoul, who appeared about half-way done with the reports, told him he would get faster at discerning their import with practice, and went down to his own chambers. He realized partway along the lower hall that

Zaoul was hastening to catch up.

"You walk fast, your excellency," he said, his voice as ever languidly at odds with his sharp teeth.

"Much to do," Cliopher said, "though I didn't think I was."

"Practice will make me faster in this regard also."

"No doubt," he replied dryly, nodding at the footmen on duty and going through the door just as the bells struck the third hour of the morning. "Ah—Tully, you have made yourself at home. Good."

She had set a desk directly opposite the entry, with the First Receiving Room, the pink privy, the Second Receiving Room, and the Orange Lily Room, which Cliopher used as his semi-public office, behind it. She smiled brightly at him, and he reflected that it was going to be a delight working with such cheerful young people. "There have already been seven requests for audiences, your excellency."

"I think 'sir' is sufficient for both of you," he said, with a vivid memory of his Radiancy saying something similar to Leona, back home in Gorjo City, and was struck by a kind of swift nostalgia for the family who were in fact waiting for him and the lord whom he had just left. "We shall be working together a great deal."

"Very good, sir," she said, the smile lifting into a grin. "Do you want the list of requests? I have arranged them in order of importance, urgency, rank, and order of arrival."

"Might as well," he said, sighing. "You can make appointments starting at the fourth hour and going till the first of the afternoon, for a quarter-hour each unless they give you a very good reason why they need longer. Zaoul, you'll be attending me for those, so you can set yourself up with a desk through here in the Orange Lily Room—did someone explain how the door tiles work to you, Tully? Good. Explain them to Zaoul, please, and make sure you both get something to eat, while I see my family. I will be with them the rest of this hour."

"Very good, sir," she said again. "I believe they are having breakfast in the Tortoise Room." Cliopher made his escape with the list in his hand. The first name, he was appalled to see, was the Princess Mgunai. Whom, apparently, Tully had managed to put off. The Yenga clearly bred extraordinary fortitude. He opened the door of the Tortoise Room on a cheerful cacophony.

"There you are, Kip! Just in time for breakfast!" said Quintus, and he was enveloped.

He greeted them all affectionately, accepted coffee and a pastry from Gaudy, and sat down eventually between his mother and Vinyë. "Well," he said, as the conversation shifted back towards telling Gaudy all about the sky ship journey and attention landed back on the food. "I am glad to see you, Mama."

"I had not realized your chambers were quite so—big," Vinyë said, gesturing around them. "We were too tired last night, but when we woke up this morning and started to get lost in each other's rooms ..."

Quintus, seated across the table from them, heard this and laughed robustly. "It was like a game of Sardines, with Zemius being 'it'."

"I remembered about the tiles, but not which ones we were supposed to follow," Zemius said, grinning half-apologetically.

Everyone laughed again, and Dora started explaining what animals and flowers she'd seen so far on the doors. Vinyë turned to him. "What have you been doing already this morning, Kip? You were up as late last night as we."

Cliopher smiled ruefully. "Alas, the affairs of state do not wait on my pleasure. What have I been doing? I have finished a stack of letters and sent them off to the Light, I have cleaned off my desk for the fourth time this week, I have been down to the Offices of State to appoint secretaries—" He paused to smile at his nephew, who was still looking a bit miffed. "And I have been to attend on his Radiancy."

His mother's face went immediately sympathetic. "Gaudy has been explaining to us the situation. Your lord had a heart attack, he said?"

"Two—three days ago," he agreed. Gaudy was refusing to let him catch his eye. "His Radiancy has been advised by his physician to stay in bed for the next two weeks."

"He did not seem the sort of man to take kindly to his bed," Eidora said thoughtfully.

Cousin Zemius shook his head. "I have never seen anyone more dynamic in my life."

Cliopher thought of the drawn and withdrawn man on the bed, and he sighed. "We shall see. Or indeed, so shall you. I told his Radiancy of your coming, and he bade me bring you to him this afternoon."

There was what almost amounted to a shocked silence. Then Vinyë said cautiously, "All of us?"

He smiled at that. "Indeed! I trust you will not tire him exceedingly."

"But what are we to wear?" Aunt Oura said, nearly wailing, and the babble started up again. It was amazing how much noise nine people could make, he thought.

"Féonie will help you," Cliopher said. "She's my costumier. Zemius is acquainted with her—and I presume you already met Franzel this morning? And Shoänie too?"

"We've met quite a few members of your household," his mother murmured, with a lift to her eyebrow that Cliopher interpreted as a kind of mixture of pride and suppressed disdain. He was about to explain to her—or try to explain, at any rate—why he had such a great household, when a loud commotion broke through the breakfast-table noise. Before he could do anything, the door to the Tortoise Room was flung open and an irate woman in half court costume strode in.

The room fell dead silent, even Dora shrinking back against her uncle Quintus. The woman wore a northwestern sari in pink and green and gold, pink diamonds and emeralds and gold dripping from every possible location, from her elaborately dressed wig down to her toes. She glanced swiftly around the room before her gaze landed on Cliopher; she seemed, though it seemed impossible, to swell in yet greater fury.

"Who," she said, "do you think you are, sir, that you refuse *me* audience? Who are these people, that you give them precedence over *me*?"

Cliopher set down his coffee cup on the table and rose unhurriedly, and he said, in as mild a tone as he could manage: "I am the Lord Chancellor of Zunidh, your Highness, and these are my family. I believe my secretary will have told you I am not seeing anyone until the fourth hour."

"I am the Princess of Mgunai. They are common Islanders," she said, investing the simple statement with such disdain that it struck some answering chord of pure fury from deep within his heart.

"They are my family," he repeated, forcing his voice to remain mild. "And I am the Lord Chancellor of Zunidh, which is why you wish to see me."

"I *wish* to see the Lord Emperor, but his guards refused me admittance and informed me that I must speak to *you*."

"And so you shall, madam, at the fourth hour," he said, looking past her to see that Zaoul was standing indecisively in the next room out, surrounded by a gaggle of the princess' attendants ranging from a pair of guards through her ladies-in-waiting, most of whom were giving him half-fearful, half-eager sidelong glances.

Cliopher walked around the table and up to the princess, who was now staring at him in total consternation. But he had spent enough years in his

Radiancy's train to know how to dismiss someone. He smiled and bowed to her and turned towards the door, using his body language to half-turn her as well. "Zaoul! See that the princess has all that she needs while she waits. She might be most comfortable in the First Receiving Room."

"Of course, sir," he said, in his lazy voice, bowing and then smiling broadly at the princess. "This way, your Highness."

She stared at Zaoul, at the clear tribal markings: the filed teeth, the plaits hanging past his waist braided with various shells and carved charms, the ritual scarification, the skin as dark as her own. There was no tribe more famous, or infamous, than the Tkinele.

"You have a *cannibal*," she said, her voice faint with disgust and shock, taking an involuntary step forward as Cliopher set his hand to the door.

Cliopher did not have to feign his outrage, though he made sure she saw that he was not taking direct offence—yet. "Madam, I bid you remember you are speaking of a member of my household. I shall see you at the fourth hour."

And this time he managed to shut the door on her and turn back to his family, who were staring at him in about as much consternation as the princess had displayed.

He sat down with his coffee and tried not to shake with reaction.

"*That's* a bit of a change from when I was here before," said his cousin Zemius.

CHAPTER *T*HIRTY-*E*IGHT

THE PRINCESS OF MGUNAI, IT appeared, had been mollified by the assiduousness with which Zaoul plied her with tea and cookies. Zaoul had surmised (accurately, as far as Cliopher could make out) that she had just arrived that morning and that food would, perhaps, just perhaps, help mend her temper. It had: she was nearly smiling when Zaoul led her into the Tiger Room as the bells finished tolling the fourth hour.

Cliopher had had just enough time to see that along with the three neat piles of the reports, there was a small folder with notes for his upcoming audiences, written in a careful Chancery hand. The one for the Princess Mgunai stated that she wanted to be reassured of his Radiancy's health and also was quite concerned about the progress of her request ('application' crossed out) for a branch of the sea train to extend from New Dair, the current terminus of the line, to Port Nigarou, where a new tin mine was causing much interest.

"Your Highness," Cliopher said, bowing with great courtesy.

"Lord Mdang."

He gestured her to her seat and Zaoul to his corner desk. "I am sure you wish to be personally reassured of his Radiancy's wellbeing, your Highness," he said. "As I stated in my letter, his Radiancy had a heart attack three days ago. There is every reason to expect he will fully recover, but his Radiancy's physician has recommended most strongly that his Radiancy remain in his chambers for the next fortnight and limit the performance of his duties to the barest minimum possible."

He wondered if he had to spell it out for her, but the Princess grimaced very slightly and nodded. "I understand, Lord Mdang. There is one matter that is of the greatest urgency to my people—"

He managed not to look down at the sheet of paper. "I presume you speak of the sea train extension to Port Nigarou, your Highness?"

She looked surprised. "Why, yes, but I am not sure how you know that …"

He did not look at Zaoul, smiling blandly at the Princess instead. "It is my job to know, madam." Or at least appoint someone who would.

"Will his Radiancy grant leave to begin the works? The monsoons are nearly ended in Mgunai, and we could begin work within the next two months if his Radiancy permits. If we cannot, I shall be obliged to go into debt with Amboloyo to transport engineers and miners, or mortgage some of my jungles to Xiputl for their plantations, and these mines are already going to be five years before they are fully profitable."

The Prince of Amboloyo, as Cliopher's efforts at analyzing the state of affairs had shown him, very clearly (and fairly subtly, for Prince Rufus) was trying to increase his political power by seeking a foothold on the Dairen continent. He was already beginning to contest the ownership of the Dagger Islands, which lay between Amboloyo and the Xiputl Arm, and which Cliopher had not yet managed to turn into a self-governing political entity.

"I shall bring the matter before his Radiancy at the earliest convenience," he said. "Was there anything else you wished to bring before my attention this morning, Princess?"

She was already rising, and gave him a long flat stare. "We shall meet again soon, Lord Mdang."

"I shall be honoured," he replied, with a courteous and not at all subservient bow. Zaoul bowed her out, then came over to the desk and said: "The Lord Treasurer in Chief is next, sir."

"In five minutes, I suppose?" Cliopher looked down at the papers, and was not entirely surprised to see that next below the note about the Princess was one to the effect that the Lord Treasurer had a question about the taxes supposed to have been announced at court by his Radiancy that week. "How did you find out these details? I had presumed you had asked, but it did not seem as if the Princess expected me to know about the train."

Zaoul grinned. "I read through your reports, sir, and that with what I have gleaned in the past months at the Offices of State ..."

"Splendid," said Cliopher. "I can see you will shortly prove invaluable. Send in the Lord Treasurer."

★★★

THREE HOURS LATER HE HAD seen ten people, ranging in status from the Princess of Mgunai to the third undersecretary of the Imperial Minister of the Natural World, who was also concerned about the sea train to Port Nigarou but for a completely different reason, and took considerably longer to get rid of, as Cliopher wanted to be very sure he understood all of the details of the undersecretary's reservations.

He went back to his private quarters feeling that his head was about to explode, not least for the many details about salmon spawning the undersecretary had plied him with, and extremely grateful to the combined efforts of Tully and Zaoul.

His family were gathered, wearing a motley collection of courtly finery ranging from the outfit Lady Ylette had made for Zemius on his first visit to what Cliopher thought was probably what Vinyë wore for concerts. "You all look splendid," he said fondly, wondering why none of them had chosen any variant of Islander finery for the occasion, but deciding not to put them on the spot by asking outright.

"Liar," said Vinyë, laughing. "Your ordinary working outfit is far finer than anything we have."

Cliopher laughed in return, feeling his headache recede slightly. "This is one of the nicer ones, to be honest. Oh, it truly is wonderful to have you here. Would you believe I had in fact cleared my schedule so that I could spend time with you? Dora, you look very lovely. What a pretty frock that is."

"I even have my own purse," she said, proudly showing him a small woven-grass bilum lined with bright fabric.

He admired it dutifully, admired also the bag Quintus then proceeded to show him with even more elaborate pride, and was still laughing as he shepherded them out of his quarters.

"My old rooms," he said as they set up towards the Imperial Apartments, "were about a forty-minute walk off that way, at the end of the Alinorel Wing. It was Conju's idea to assign me these ones. It must be said they are much more convenient, though I miss the walk through the gardens. I shall have to take you through them, Mama."

"Captain Diogen said the rainy season was about to begin," Quintus said, as they passed through a delicately carved doorway and set off up an alabaster staircase whose carvings were, if anything, more beautiful.

"Ah," said Cliopher, smiling, "but this is Solaara, the City of Cities. It only rains at night, when it doesn't interfere with anything."

He didn't miss the look his mother exchanged with Vinyë, but they had arrived by then at the doors to the Imperial Apartments and were being challenged by the guards stationed there.

"Good afternoon," he replied. "These are members of my family. His Radiancy has bidden them attend him at the second hour."

"What are you holding?" Ghisan asked Dora, who was holding her uncle Quintus' hand tightly with in one hand and her bilum with the other.

She looked up at him and spoke with great dignity. "I have a present for Lord Artorin in my bilum to say thank-you for sending us the sky ship."

Cliopher blinked. Ghisan and his partner Cadro, both obviously trying not to smile, saluted magnificently and stamped their spears. The doors behind them opened, revealing four bored pages and the next set of guards.

"The Lord Chancellor and family to see his Radiancy," Ghisan announced, and without further ado the inner guards saluted and admitted them.

By the seventh anteroom only Dora seemed immune to a sense of intimidation. Cliopher said, "Why don't you wait here for a moment? I will see if his Radiancy is ready to receive you. The guards are Ingo and Auzevereän," he added, winning another salute and an appreciative twinkle in Auzevereän's eyes for being able to pronounce his name.

He hastened within, through the strangely empty study and past the somehow forlorn-looking doorway to his Radiancy's private study, knocked on the ivory door to the morning room. Lady Ylette answered and ushered him through to his Radiancy bedchamber, where Conju was still sitting attentively and his Radiancy seemed somewhat fractious.

"My lord," Conju said, "Cliopher is here."

"Kip," his Radiancy said, frowning past him. "Where is your family? Are they not coming?"

As if, Cliopher thought, anyone would refuse a summons from the Sun-on-Earth. He bowed deeply. "They are in the antechamber, my lord. I thought to ascertain you still wished to see them."

"Of course I do. I am bored out of my mind. Conju keeps telling me to rest, but he's the one that needs it. I hope they are prepared to talk to me."

"I am sure my cousin Dora will rise to the occasion, my lord."

His Radiancy actually laughed, and Cliopher, smiling, returned through the chambers to the antechamber. "Come," he said, and then as they entered the study, he saw how everyone faltered in astonishment and awe.

"This is—"

"Is that—"

"By the Emperor," Quintus said, looking at the vase Cliopher had spent so long admiring.

"This was my desk until I became Lord Chancellor," he said, pointing it out and sighing for those days, so happy and carefree in comparison to the present day.

(But, another part of him said, the Lord Chancellor of Zunidh was able to be his Radiancy's friend ... and that was worth all the work and headaches and stress ...)

"I have never seen such things," his mother said quietly

That reminded him of something. "We are going through to his Radiancy's bedchamber. His bed ... it is a foreign style, but so you know, the canopy is made of foamwork."

Aunt Oura's twin sister was the foamwork master. She raised her eyebrows. "A whole canopy?"

"It is astonishing," he said, and led them through to the ivory door, where Lady Ylette was waiting.

Pikabe and Ato were on the innermost guard. They smiled at his family on their entrance. Cliopher stopped several yards from the bed to make his bows. "My family, my lord," he announced, and at his Radiancy's nod, named them. They performed their obeisances somewhat raggedly, but less so than in Gorjo City, and Cliopher was sure they had been practising.

"Welcome to the Palace of Stars," his Radiancy said, making a vague gesture of benediction. "I hope your voyage was pleasant?"

"It was amazing!" said Dora, tugging her hand out of Quintus' grasp and advancing towards the bed. Cliopher hastily stepped forward to hold her by the shoulders. "I remember, Cousin Kip," she said indignantly. "I won't touch. I wanted to say my speech. I wrote it all out for you and everything, Lord Artorin."

After a brief pause, his Radiancy said, with the most magnificent air possible when lying recumbent on a bed, "Pray continue, Sayina Dora. We are most eager to hear you."

"It is in my purse," she said, with a defiant glance at first Cliopher and then the two guards. Cliopher, catching a flicker of an eyebrow from his Radiancy, let go of Dora's shoulders and stepped to one side. Dora pulled out two items from her bilum, the first a wax tablet of the sort used to practice writing or take notes and the second a flat stiff object wrapped in fancy paper.

She cleared her throat and stared fixedly at the tablet. "Dear Lord Artorin: Thank you very much for sending the sky ship to bring us to visit Cousin Kip. It was very kind of you and I will remember it always. Love Dora." She stopped and glared at him from under fierce eyebrows. "I also have a present for you."

"Ah! The proper thing is to give it to Cliopher—your cousin Kip—and he will pass it on to me."

"Why can't I give it to you directly?"

"Politics," he said, with a deliberately mysterious tone.

Dora giggled and gave the present to Cliopher with an elaborate made-up gesture. Cliopher, feeling very much on the spot, made the gestures and solemn bows as if it were tribute from some important prince, and presented it to his Radiancy in the same grand manner.

His Radiancy took it from him, face completely serene, eyes twinkling, and broke ritual sufficiently to open it right then. It was, Cliopher could see, a drawing framed simply in wood.

"Is this your work, child?" he said.

"Yes," Dora replied. "It's a picture of when you came to visit us. I wrote everyone's names in case you forgot any."

"I can see that," he said, and chuckled. "It's quite wonderful. Thank you. I can't think when I last received a present I liked half so well. Ah, here's your cousin Kip. I think I would have recognized him from his robes, even without the name."

Dora beamed and seemed prepared to list all the features of the picture, but Conju came in with a cup of tea on a tray and was immediately accosted by her. "Look, it's Conju! Hallo, sir! It's Dora."

"So it is," said Conju, after a brief glance at his Radiancy. "Your tea, my lord."

Cliopher took this as a hint that they had perhaps spent enough time entertaining his Radiancy, and was about to take his leave when his Radiancy said, "You have not brought refreshments for everyone, Conju."

Conju exchanged a meaningful glance with Cliopher, but said: "I shall remedy it immediately, my lord," and went out again.

His Radiancy resettled himself on his cushions and gazed thoughtfully on the grouping clustered somewhat fearfully on the carpet. "When I was Emperor," he said, "this room was filled with courtiers. Some of the rituals of Schooled magic required observers in order to be fully enacted. That is why it is so large."

There was a pause, as various members of Cliopher's family tried to look at the room again without taking their attention from his Radiancy. Cliopher tried to think of something to say, but he was not quite enough of a courtier to be able to spin nothings so easily. His Radiancy smiled gently and went on: "Domine Zemius, how go your studies? Will you be researching in the Imperial Archives while you are here?"

"With your permission, Glorious One."

"Of course. The Archives are now open to Scholars. Have you anything to add to your monograph or what we discussed on your previous visit?"

Zemius said, somewhat cautiously, "I have, I believe, managed to shed some light on the matter of the timing of the spell, Glorious One. There remain several books I should like to consult to be sure."

"Once you have done so, we shall be delighted to hear your elucidation. And you, Captain Quintus—Cliopher has told me you are a captain in a large merchant fleet?"

Cousin Quintus had not (or so he had whispered, with unexpected bashfulness, to Cliopher as they made their way up to the Imperial Apartments) anticipated being directly addressed by the Sun-on-Earth, and was briefly struck dumb before managing to say, "Yes, Glorious One."

"In what do you trade?"

"In everything, Glorious One."

His Radiancy raised his eyebrows. "It was my understanding that most of the shipping lines specialized at least regionally?"

Quintus swallowed. "The Vangavaye-ve is so remote, Glorious One, that we do not ... my company trades generally for everything the Vangavaye-ve needs and in everything that is produced." His glance travelled up to the foamwork canopy and down again to his Radiancy. "Generally speaking we trade out fine art, some spices, macadamia nuts, pearls, a few other shells, and fine woods, and we trade back everything else."

"Ah," said his Radiancy. "Who are your major trade partners?"

"We trade through the whole of the Wide Sea, Glorious One. Zangora-ville in Nijan is the central market for the Wide Seas, so we usually end our voyages there, and trade for what we need of the manufactured goods from Dair and Jilkano."

"How interesting. Have you ever had any problems with the Nijani police service?"

"No, Glorious One, only insofar as sometimes they go on strike and trade is delayed until they begin working again."

His Radiancy glanced at Cliopher, who said, slightly defensively, "That last round of legislative amendments has cut down their strikes by thirty percent in the last six months, my lord."

"I do not know how the Lord of Ysthar bears it," his Radiancy said reflectively. "The birthing process of a new form of government is exceptionally painful. Speaking of which, my lord chancellor, surely you have much to do this afternoon? You do not need to dance attendance on me. I shall not eat your family. Come back in an hour and a half."

"Very good, my lord," said Cliopher, bowing, and left without daring to meet any of his family's eyes.

★★★

AN HOUR AND A QUARTER was sufficient to work through one small stack of papers.

He discovered that Zaoul, left to his own devices, had sorted through his papers and rearranged them in order of significance. The Tkinele's idea of what was significant differed somewhat from the usual, showing a much greater emphasis on environmental and cultural concerns than politics or trade. After he'd finished the stack, Cliopher sat there for a few minutes, thinking about that.

When he passed Zaoul in the outer office, he smiled and said: "Carry on."

★★★

CONJU WAS WAITING AT THE ivory door for him. "Well?" Cliopher asked anxiously, pausing.

"He is laughing," Conju said, with a kind of confused air. "I have never seen him so ... merry. They are talking ... they are treating him like they treated me, when I first came with you."

Cliopher looked at him. "If it pleases his Radiancy, then we should be glad, Conju."

"I am worried he is over-stimulated."

"I shall see if I can draw them away," he promised, and with that Conju escorted him into the great bedchamber, where there was, indeed, a great deal of laughter and conversation going on. His Radiancy was at the centre of it, still physically drawn but seeming much more alive and engaged than he had been before.

"Lord Mdang," announced Pikabe into a lull.

"Ah!" His Radiancy looked at him through the gap that opened up between Aunt Oura and his mother. "Come here, Kip."

Cliopher rose from his obeisance and knelt next to the great bed. "My lord."

His Radiancy did look a little feverish, his eyes exceptionally brilliant and dark skin suffused with a faint blush. If he had been anyone else at all Cliopher would have put his hand on his forehead to feel his temperature, but as it was he contented himself with saying, "My lord," again.

"Enough, is it? Your mother and sister shall entertain me tomorrow morning. Bring them at the third hour."

"Very good, my lord," he said, knowing that his mother would not appreciate the phrasing his Radiancy had used, however conventional it was for the Lord Emperor. At the slight gesture of dismissal he rose, gathered his family with a comprehensive glance, and ushered them out the door past Pikabe and Ato and back through all the anterooms to the outer hall.

"Well!" began Quintus, but Cliopher had seen the distant approach of the Prince of Southern Dair, and shushed him.

"This way," Cliopher said, hastily leading them down the back stairs, past the rooms where the next-watch pages and guards waited, past a few curious servants who bowed to Cliopher, and thence to the hall leading to the back door of his own rooms.

"Here we are," he said. "Franzel, will you bring coffee, please? Did you have a good, er, audience?"

They looked at each other.

"That wasn't much of an audience," Dora said. "He wanted to talk about you the whole time."

★★★

AS THE ADULT MEMBERS OF the party were all somewhat overcome by the experience, Cliopher was able to leave them to their own quiet amusements for the rest of the afternoon while he did his best to work through the paperwork inexorably piling up. The first rush of panic was over, but now the responses to his initial letters were starting to come in, and he was obliged to read and answer most of them.

Franzel summoned him while he was deep in a letter of convoluted prose and torturous courtesy from the Prince of Amboloyo. There was something there, he was sure ... the Prince had addressed it to him, and there were subtle protestations of confidence and suggestions for how best to proceed buried in the grandiose phrases.

Franzel had to call him several times before he roused. He had long since sent Tully and Zaoul off-duty, and he blinked around his study at the dim light. The daylight had gone, and the clouds were massed thick and dark.

"The rains are to begin tonight," Franzel said, going to the windows to close the louvres.

"What time is it?" Cliopher asked, setting down his brush and rubbing his face wearily. The day felt a thousand hours long.

"Supper time," Franzel replied gently. "Two hours past sunset."

"Oh."

"There is time for you to bathe quickly, Sir. We have drawn the water."

Cliopher felt much better after the quick wash and change into his or-dinary clothes. He found his family gathered in the Tortoise Room, eating some sort of hors d'oeuvres and talking about what they had seen that day.

"Here's Kip," Vinyë said as he came in. She gave him a gentle kiss on the cheek. "You're looking worried, Kip."

He made an effort to smile brightly and to cast the Prince of Amboloyo's letter to the back of his mind. "Just thinking that I think I forgot to eat lunch."

His mother turned from where she'd been talking to Gaudy. "Franzel said the meal would be served as soon as you came."

"Then if you are all ready, by all means let us sit down."

He managed to keep his attention focused on the conversations flowing around him through the entire course of the meal. It was like having their let-ters come to life, he thought, smiling as Vinyë gave him an account of Cousin Louya's current start. The after-dinner coffee was served, along with little confections he had never been served before and quite liked, but he found he could not relax into deeper conversation.

"I've never had these before," he said, trying a white square that turned out to be some sort of gelatinous rice-and-coconut sweet. "They must be in your honour."

"Did you cook when you were in your other rooms?" Vinyë asked him curiously, as Franzel and Shoänie came in to clear away the dishes. "I don't remember you writing about it either way."

"I had a kitchen there, yes, and I prepared my own food some of the time. There are some cafeterias down in the working part of the Palace, and I used to eat there most of the time, or sometimes his Radiancy has done me the honour of inviting me to dine, or sometimes I am obliged to go to court and play at—oh!"

"Oh what?" Vinyë asked in amusement, as he stopped, struck by a sudden thought.

"That is what he's angling at. I must—will you excuse me, please? I must check something—"

"Of course," Vinyë said, though he could see a certain disappointment shading her features.

"I'm very sorry," he said, and made a distracted sort of bow to them be-fore recalling that this was (after all) his family, and hastening back into his office, where the thought of all those complex seating arrangements built out of custom, traditional rights, and the fluctuations of status, favour, and alliances had given him the key to the Prince of Amboloyo's letter.

He read the letter over twice more to be sure he had it correctly.

Stripped of its verbiage and delicate circumlocutions, its message was very simple: that the Prince of Amboloyo had realized (far more quickly than any of the other princes) that his Radiancy's indisposition and the consequent suspension of court meant that there would be a hiatus in the usually carefully controlled jockeying for power and prestige, and that this was an opportunity for a clever and ambitious man. The Prince had left it open to him to choose whether to interpret that last to include himself or merely the Prince in it.

It took him a considerable amount of time to draft a suitable reply, but at last he had a letter that stymied this particular bid without offence or—and he was quite proud of this—even definitely indicating that he, Cliopher, had actually received the message being sent him so subtly. He sealed the letter and gave it to the page on duty till midnight to deliver to the Light. Then he cleaned his pens and tidied his desk yet again, and went to the back sitting room, where Vinyë and Zemius were playing chess.

"Mama has gone to bed," Vinyë said neutrally when he came in.

Cliopher had listened to the chimes marking the hours without attending to them. Glancing at the clock, he realized that it was nearly midnight. "It's been a long day," he murmured, and stood watching them play out their game.

"You should go to bed. You're tired," Vinyë said, when he yawned for the fourth time.

"You're not?"

"I'm used to late nights," his sister replied. "I find it hard to sleep before midnight."

He watched them a while longer, feeling undercurrents and too weary to begin to address them. "Good night," he said at last, reluctantly acknowledging to himself that while he would always have said his family came first to him, when it came down to it, his duty to his lord was winning.

But he had not actually left the room when the door opened vigorously and rebounded off the wall.

Caught in the middle of another yawn, he turned in surprise, and didn't move his hand from his mouth when he saw that coming through the door were the two chief priest-wizards and Ludvic Omo.

Iprenna and Bavezh were in their formal costumes, including the accompanying masks. Commander Omo, for nearly the first time in Cliopher's memory, was wearing ordinary clothes, a sleeveless tunic and loose trousers both in unadorned plain linen. His bare arms still bore the vivid gold marks of his Radiancy's touch.

Cliopher's gaze was arrested there. Bavezh said formally, "Ludvic Omo wishes to make his farewells to you before his execution."

CHAPTER *THIRTY-NINE*

CLIOPHER'S GAZE JUMPED TO COMMANDER Omo's face, which was phlegmatic as always.

"I do beg your pardon, Magister?"

His voice came out in an eerie calm. He swallowed and forced himself to look away from Commander Omo's face and into the slit-masked eyes of the two priest-wizards.

Bavezh spoke self-righteously. "Ludvic Omo has broken one of the great taboos. The only remedy to restore the balance of things is for the blasphemer to die."

Iprenna added, "If this is done within three days of the offence, the curse will pass."

Cliopher had never particularly liked Bavezh and Iprenna, but in that moment, he hated them. He swallowed down his initial rage, trying desperately to maintain some calm reason, but when the three-quarter-chime struck and Iprenna turned back to take Commander Omo by the arm as if to lead him away, something snapped inside of him.

"You may not," he said, stepping forward.

Bavezh moved his head like a wading bird, perhaps a flamingo or a spoonbill. "You have no authority over us in the performance of our duties, Lord Chancellor."

"Does his Radiancy know about this?"

"The Lord Emperor does not need to be informed of every small detail of how we maintain ritual order."

Cliopher had just spent the past several hours contemplating the subtle manipulations of power being played out by the Prince of Amboloyo. It came to him in a flash all the changes that might come from the high priest-wizards overseeing the execution on grounds of ritual blasphemy of the Commander in Chief of the armed forces, and politically as well as personally he was appalled.

"You may not," he repeated.

Iprenna said warningly, "Be careful, sir! We have powers to ensure our duties are fulfilled."

"You have no authority over deciding the death of the Commander in Chief of the Imperial Guard, the head of the armed forces of Zunidh."

"He is stripped of his titles by his blasphemy," Bavezh said, his voice unctuous. "There is ample precedent, Lord Chancellor."

The threat was clear. And Cliopher did know a number of those precedents, for the executions of people ranging from a simple girl overcome with seeing her emperor all the way to one of the rival claimants for the place of consort to one of the great empresses.

It had been a long day. Cliopher took a deep breath, trying to maintain a polite tone, and had just begun to respond when Iprenna added, with an audible smirk, "You must see that it is no longer in our hands. The deed must be done by midnight."

Cliopher's temper broke.

"You have had any time these past three days to seek an audience with his Radiancy and inform him of the ritual requirements. You have—"

"I assure you, his Radiancy knows—"

"Do not interrupt me! You have had any time these past three days to seek an audience with *me* and inform me of this broken taboo and the potential loss of the Commander in Chief. You have—"

"You are over-rea—"

"*I have not finished!*" Cliopher roared. Bavezh rocked backwards; Iprenna, who was the one speaking, actually stepped away.

Cliopher went on: "You have had any time these past three days to make this announcement and permit Ludvic to say his farewells to his friends. You have deliberately left it till the last possible moment."

"There were—"

"*Do not interrupt me again.* You have over-reached your authority, your duty, and your responsibility, and you will take the consequences."

He strode between the two shocked priest-wizards and said to Ludvic, "This is far beyond my place to decide. Come with me." He took the guard's unresisting arm.

"My lord chancellor!" Iprenna cried, grabbing at his shoulders.

Cliopher shook him off with a strength born out of fury. "You have remembered my position! Good! Come."

"We cannot—"

"*Come.*"

Cliopher flung open the door and half-dragged Ludvic through the apartments, following the sun tiles to the outer hall, past the yawning pages and the surprised footmen. Iprenna and Bavezh followed behind him, twittering urgently and incoherently about the taboos and all the things that would be overset if they did not immediately begin the ritual execution. He ignored them in favour of the briskest march possible up the two flights of stairs and over the three hallways to the Imperial Apartments, where the outer guards watched the little procession arrive with expressions of total shock.

"We must see his Radiancy *immediately*," Cliopher growled.

Such perhaps was the expression on his face that they did not even challenge him: they stamped their spears to open the doors. The inner guards jumped into action, the pages scrambling away from the group.

Cliopher did not wait for any of the usual challenges and formalities: he cried, "Open the doors!" And for whatever reason it was, all the guards did so.

He strode through the dark study to the breakfast room, long familiarity with the room meaning he did not need more than the dim light coming in through the windows to see his way. He had never lit the lights in that room, did not know what spell or cantrip did so, whether it was the same handclap as lit the lights in public areas, or something known only to his Radiancy's staff, or to his Radiancy himself.

He knocked at the ivory door, but did not wait for it to be opened by Conju or Lady Ylette or anyone else: he turned the handle and opened it himself.

One of the lesser Tower servants was starting down the hall, shock and dismay in his face, as Cliopher drew Ludvic inside and the two priest-wizards, still hissing about the taboos, crowded behind him.

"You cannot enter!" the servant whispered. "His Radiancy has retired for the night."

"I would not disturb him if it were not a matter of the greatest urgency," Cliopher said. "Rest you assured that we will take all the consequences on our heads."

"But—"

"But *nothing*," Cliopher said, rather loudly, and pushed past the unfortunate man, who had, it appeared, been engaged in polishing one of the chandeliers, from the diamond drops spread across a low table in the anteroom. The brilliant sparkling jewels in the light of the single mage-lantern the man had on the table, all the rest swathed in layered shadows, burned suddenly brilliant in his mind's eye.

By the time he reached his Radiancy's bedchamber the guards had heard the noise. Ato opened the door, spear at the ready, to see who was arriving: when he saw them, his placid expression flattened into astonishment, dismay, and concern. He ducked back in and a moment later Pikabe came out, closing the door carefully behind him.

He spoke in an urgent undertone. "Commander Omo! Lord Mdang! High priests! What does this mean?"

Everyone, including Ludvic, looked at Cliopher. Cliopher said firmly, "We must see his Radiancy immediately, Pikabe. Wake him."

"Your excellency—" Pikabe looked beseechingly at his commander, who was looking down at the ground.

"Now," said Cliopher, not liking how Iprenna was reaching into the complicated knots of his sash for what appeared to be—

"You cannot draw a weapon *here!*" Pikabe cried in indignation, leaping forward to wrest the curved knife from the priest-wizard's hand.

Bavezh said in triumph, "It is nearly midnight! If the spell is not completed, the consequences will be terrible." He drew his own knife and advanced towards Cliopher and Ludvic Omo. "It will not hurt long, Commander, and then you will be with your family and the curse on your kin will at last be lifted and—"

Pikabe was still wrestling with Iprenna, whose clothes appeared to be enchanted. They were flying up around the guard and preventing him from returning to his post.

Ludvic was not trying to resist. Not seeing anything else to do, Cliopher pulled him forward, out of Bavezh's reach, and grabbed the door handle to open the door.

Several moments later he began to pick himself up from the corner of the wall and the floor.

"What," his Radiancy said in dangerously even tones, "is the meaning of all this? My lord chancellor, perhaps you can explain these remarkable circumstances."

Cliopher struggled to his feet with the help of a strong hand held out to him. He blinked around the room. Pikabe held Iprenna, now bound firmly in his own sash; Bavezh was lying huddled half in and half out of the doorway; Ato stood in front of the bed, spear held at the ready and expression suggesting that no one, but no one, was coming any closer. There was blood on the spear tip.

That left Ludvic Omo, who was the one who had offered his hand, and his Radiancy, who was sitting up in bed and regarding them with his most blankly serene expression.

First Ludvic and then Cliopher folded himself down into the obeisance. Cliopher lifted his head and caught his breath with some little difficulty—he felt winded and bruised from whatever or whoever had flung him across the room—and tried to make his voice come as calm as his Radiancy's. In the silence before he began to speak the midnight chime began to sound, and Ser Rhodin and Elish came in to take the next watch.

"It's too late," said Iprenna, and he let loose titter after titter of hysterical laughter.

"Be silent," his Radiancy said, and the priest-wizard was. "My lord chancellor."

"Fifteen minutes ago, Iprenna and Bavezh entered my apartments with Co—with Ludvic Omo, to inform me that Ludvic had come to make his farewells before his execution."

There was a stir from all four of the other guards. Cliopher did not look at them; he kept his eyes fixed on his Radiancy, who made no motion.

"When I enquired on what grounds he was to be executed, I was informed that it is the legal and ritual response to the breaking of the taboo against touching your Radiancy that the one so responsible be executed before the third midnight. While I do not discount the authority the priest-wizards have within their sphere, my lord, it is my belief that given the identity of the one affected, that order should come directly from you."

His Radiancy turned his head to look at Iprenna, whose eyes were rimmed with white like a frightened dog's. "Lord Wizard, what have you to say?"

"The law is clear," Iprenna said, and that the tremble in his voice was for the rituals, and not for his own situation, was clear in his next words: "My lord, that law has stood for thousands of years. On the three occasions it was broken and the ritual cleansing not fulfilled, the magic meant to flow outwards from the Sun-on-Earth was turned awry and caused grievous problems. My lord, due to the interference of the Lord Chancellor, we were not able to perform the ritual. He said we will take upon ourselves the consequences, but now we all will," he added, with a spiteful edge to his voice.

His Radiancy lifted his head and closed his eyes and was silent for some moments. Cliopher did not know what he was doing, if anything beyond thinking, but Iprenna began to tremble visibly in his bonds.

At length his Radiancy opened his eyes again and said: "Lord Wizard, your punctiliousness is noted. So too is your timing. We will consider what is the appropriate response."

"My lord, the ritual was not consummated!"

His Radiancy gave the priest-wizard a sharp glance, and Iprenna subsided, shaking more visibly now. "The magic of Zunidh is our concern, Lord Wizard. Go now. Do not leave your rooms until you are summoned to our presence. Pikabe, escort the lord wizard there and see that guards are set on his doors."

Iprenna gulped. "My lord ..."

"We nearly think you hesitate, Lord Wizard."

"Bavezh ..."

His Radiancy glanced at the huddle and his face softened. He spoke gently, "Lord Bavezh is beyond all mortal concerns, Lord Iprenna."

At his Radiancy's nod, Pikabe released the priest-wizard and undid the makeshift bindings. Hands free, Iprenna knelt next to his partner and friend.

The next minutes seemed very long. Cliopher tried to determine whether there had been any actual threat to his Radiancy—nothing deliberate, surely, though the rude awakening would probably cause the physician to have words with him. His Radiancy was inward-turned and very distant, but seemed physically unaffected.

After a decent interval, his Radiancy said, "Lord Iprenna, it is time." He added to Pikabe, "Summon two of the outer guards to bear the late High Priest's corpse to the appropriate place."

Pikabe saluted and led the blank-faced Ato and the weeping Iprenna out, leaving Ser Rhodin and Elish to take their places on either side of the door and Ludvic and Cliopher to stay kneeling where they were.

"Now," his Radiancy said once the outer guards had borne the corpse away. Cliopher looked up in alarm; Ludvic stayed staring at the floor.

"You may rise," his Radiancy said.

Cliopher did so, slowly, feeling every year of his age pressing down on him, but heartened by this sign of favour.

"You seem greatly concerned, Cliopher."

At the use of his name, Cliopher felt much of his immediate tension release, leaving the potential repercussions of this evening to starker relief. "My lord, though I must deprecate their manner, the priest-wizards do have a point regarding the law ..."

His Radiancy leaned back against his cushions, which Conju—when had Conju arrived?—solicitously arranged for him. He looked pointedly at Ludvic's arms. "It grieves me, Ludvic, to have hurt you so badly."

Ludvic looked up at his tone. "My lord, it is nothing for me to die in serving you."

"It is everything for me, Ludvic," said his Radiancy in a low voice.

"The law is the law, my lord."

"Yes: but the law is different for me than it is for you, in this as in so many things, and it was I who touched you. Go to your rooms, Ludvic, and breathe easy. You will have to go through the full ritual of purification, I expect, but though lengthy, tedious, and uncomfortable, it is not fatal. It does mean that you will have to be suspended of your duties until it is completed. Ser Rhodin."

"My lord?"

"You may wish to send for a replacement for the current shift. You will be Acting Commander until further notice."

Ser Rhodin looked down at his commanding officer, then at Cliopher, then back at his Radiancy. He saluted crisply. "As you wish, my lord."

"Cliopher."

"Yes, my lord?"

"Go to bed. We will discuss repercussions personal and political tomorrow at the second—" Conju made an abortive gesture of protest and his Radiancy smiled at him. "Very well! The third hour. I trust there will be no further crises tonight."

There were none, except that Zemius and Vinyë had put away the chess set and gone to their chambers, and Cliopher had to undress and lie down on his low bed and think about all the ways that could have gone differently.

At last he got up and lit a stick of incense at his little-used private shrine in memory of Bavezh, and with the aroma of Vangavayen sweetgum filling the corners of the room he did at last fall asleep.

CHAPTER FORTY

HE HAD ASKED FRANZEL TO wake him at dawn, for that evening saw the next meeting of the Helma Council. Cliopher had planned to work that day regardless of his family's presence, for the Helma Council was the most important of his many committees and waited on no one's pleasure but his Radiancy's—and since his Radiancy had deputized Cliopher to take his seat there, Cliopher had perforce to go.

Shoänie brought him strong coffee and chocolate pastries. He made himself get up and bathe, and after some thought put on his best official robes. The day would bring much chaos, and he hoped that the perfectly fitting resplendent outfit would loan him some countenance and dignity.

He kept seeing the glittering diamonds strewn across the polishing table, and the silver robes puddling around Bavezh's body. Poor Ato, he thought, thinking of the line of blood on the golden tip of his spear. Poor Bavezh. Poor Iprenna. Poor ...

He forced himself to put aside all consideration of the previous night's excitements. It would be necessary to address them soon enough, but he had to familiarize himself with the Helma Council's present agenda and remember his arguments and major concerns and his goal for this month's meeting, and there would surely be no other time in the day for it.

His inner footman, Havor, told him when his family started to emerge for breakfast. Cliopher had gone through the agenda and the notes he had begun during that period—so long ago it seemed now!—when he had been trying to work ahead in preparation for his family's visit.

He was pathetically grateful to see that Zaoul had worked his magic there as well. The Tkinele had added several pages of neat commentary drawn from gossip, the official reports, and miscellaneous of Cliopher's own files on the various matters up for discussion. It was such a *delight* to have a good secretary.

Dora and Aunt Oura were first, followed shortly by his mother and Quintus.

"What is the plan for today, Kip?" Aunt Oura asked after she had settled Dora into her chair with orange juice and a flatbread smeared with honeycomb.

"I imagine Zaoul will bring a stack of reports for me when he arrives," Cliopher replied, pouring himself coffee. "I must meet with his Radiancy this morning, which will no doubt guide the rest of the day, and there is the regular meeting of the Helma Council this evening. I cannot miss that one, I'm afraid. I was going to have to go to it even before my lord's indisposition."

"What is the Helma Council?" Aunt Oura asked curiously.

Cliopher had a rule for committees before he signed off on their formation: they had to be able to state their purpose in two sentences or less. This had affronted any number of bodies, but he had found it enormously helpful in assigning duties and secretaries and general governance practices. "The Helma Council oversees the financial activities of government. It meets monthly, and—oh, good morning, Vinyë—and Kiri!"

Kiri grinned cheerfully at him as he rose hastily to direct her to one of the free seats and made vague introductions. "Good morning, sir! Pleased to meet all of you at last. I thought that perhaps I had better corner you at breakfast, sir, given what the rumours are this morning. Dare I ask what happened last night? There is rumour of an attempted assassination on his Radiancy."

Cliopher said a curse that he had learned from Ser Rhodin, and immediately regretted it when everyone stared wide-eyed at him. "Forgive me. No. *No.* There was no attempt on his Radiancy's life last night."

"What, then?"

Before Cliopher could answer, the door opened again and Ser Rhodin himself walked in. He looked as if he had had even less sleep than Cliopher, but he was alert and presenting a cheerful front for all that. "Well, my lord chancellor," he said after a salute that took in the whole room, "what are your orders this morning?"

Cliopher sat down in his seat. "I beg your pardon?"

"Your orders, your excellency," Ser Rhodin repeated demurely.

"Since when do I give orders to you?"

"Since his Radiancy told me to take them from you. If you don't have— oh, thank you, Saya Eidora, yes, I will have some coffee. Cream, please, and honey, and cinnamon if there is any. What was I saying? Oh, yes. If you don't have any immediate orders, my first suggestion is that you have me assign a set of guards to you. Actually, that's more than a suggestion. Actually, I think

I might insist. In fact, I've already assigned them and told your household."

"I don't need guards," Cliopher said, discovering the headache that had dogged him for the past few days was back and fiercer than ever. Ser Rhodin raised his eyebrows at him. He sighed. "Why do I need guards, Rhodin?"

The guard sipped his coffee. "This is far better coffee than we get in the mess. Mm. Well, your excellency—"

"If you keep calling me 'your excellency' while we are at breakfast in my own rooms, Rhodin, I—"

"Yes?" Rhodin laughed. "I won't tease. To be brutally frank, you need guards because if something were to happen to you, the government would fall apart."

"I doubt that—"

"And last night you made some serious enemies. Oh, I can't imagine anyone would try anything directly, but if anyone has been considering, let us say, a change in the power dynamic of government, now is the time to act, with three of the four pillars of state out of commission."

"The four pillars of state?" Cousin Quintus asked.

"The bureaucracy, the priest-wizards, the guard, and his Radiancy himself," Rhodin replied, ticking them off on his fingers before reaching for a pastry he then ate in two large bites. "The princes are the fifth pillar, but most of them could be replaced without anyone noticing, and we let his Radiancy deal with them. Or Cliopher, as necessary, though they tend to get a bit miffed if he makes it obvious he's the one telling them what to do."

"What exactly happened last night?" Kiri asked, frowning intently.

Cliopher made a gesture at Rhodin, who shook his head at him. Cliopher sighed and said, "Bavezh and Iprenna, the two high priest-wizards, came to me with Commander Omo at a quarter to midnight. They informed me that Commander Omo wished to make his farewells before his execution."

"*What?*"

"That was pretty near my own response. They told me that it was the legal and ritual response to breaking the taboo against touching his Radiancy, and that it had to be done before the third midnight."

"And they came at the quarter-hour before the deadline?" Kiri bit back an obvious curse, glancing at Dora, who appeared to be playing obliviously with a little figurine of an elephant she'd brought to the table. "What did you do?"

"I, er, took exception, and we, er, sought an audience with his Radiancy."

"And?"

Rhodin shook his head again. "Stop being so missish, Cliopher. From what the guards said, Cliopher dragged Commander Omo and the two priest-wizards into the Imperial Apartments. They got to the inner door before midnight, and began to argue with the honour guards about waking his Radiancy. At this point Iprenna tried to fulfil the ritual.

"While Pikabe disarmed him, Bavezh took up his knife and made to attack both the Lord Chancellor and Commander Omo, but Ato says that Cliopher put his hand to the door—you should know better, Cliopher!—and triggered some of the magical safe-guards. As Bavezh was attempting to enter his Radiancy's bedchamber with a drawn knife and obvious intent to violence, he was killed by the guard on duty. That was just at midnight, when I came on duty."

He frowned suddenly at Cliopher. "Are you all right? Physically, I mean? You must have been thrown clear across the room when you touched the door."

Cliopher rubbed his shoulder, which was aching. "Some bruises," he admitted. "Now, Kiri—"

She said, "Let me see if I am correct. Of the two chief priest-wizards, Bavezh is dead and Iprenna—what happened to him?"

"Iprenna is under house arrest awaiting his Radiancy's pleasure," Rhodin supplied.

"I see what you mean about him making enemies last night. Right then. What happened to Commander Omo?"

"Commander Omo has been suspended of his duties while he undergoes the full rite of purification."

"Which I believe takes eighty-one days," Cliopher said, sighing. "No, that was for fruit. People are one hundred and twenty days—dear lord, that's four months. Ser Rhodin is Acting Commander in the meantime."

"And his Radiancy is still ... good heavens. Ser Rhodin, you are *entirely* correct that his excellency needs guards."

"I don't think anyone will try a coup."

Rhodin grinned. "All you need to do is take out the Prince of Amboloyo."

Cliopher stared at him. "To do what?"

"Good point," Rhodin said, not a bit abashed at suggesting Cliopher might want to try a coup d'état himself. "You're not a magus, so there's not really any further for you to go."

Cliopher took a deep breath, then decided it was better not to say anything about the balance of powers amongst the pillars of government, which he had spent quite a lot of time developing, and drank some more coffee instead.

"Well, I don't know about your family," Kiri said, "but I, for one, would be extremely chagrined to discover an ounce of prevention was all we needed. Take the guards, your excellency."

"I have no interest in rising above my place—"

Rhodin cackled. "There's nowhere for you to rise *to*."

"The princes—"

Rhodin snorted. "Let them stew. None of them look a span farther than their own interests."

Zemius came in the door, looking bleary-eyed and bumbling. He greeted them all vaguely, then focused on Cliopher. "Is your friend all right, Kip? That was such a scene last night."

"Yes, he will be fine, thank you."

"I didn't quite understand what it was all about."

Cliopher would not perhaps ordinarily have told them, but he was tired already and they were his family, and so he said, "Ludvic is the longest-serving member of his Radiancy's household and the chief of the Imperial Guard. When his Radiancy had his heart attack, it was Ludvic who saved his life. In the process, his Radiancy grasped him by the arms, and thus broke one of the great taboos. The priests were there to see things rectified."

"You were very angry."

Zemius stated it very simply. Cliopher snapped, "He is a friend of mine, and they were playing politics with his life. Not only that, he is a friend of his Radiancy's."

"*Hélouzithe, hélouzanth,*" Ser Rhodin murmured, the tag line of an old ballad about treason.

Cliopher turned to him. "Where has Ludvic been these past two days, that you didn't notice anything? He was fully prepared to die last night."

Ser Rhodin lifted his head back as if struck. "As it happens, Commander Omo had this week off, and since he was clearly feeling unwell from the, er, touch of the Sun-on-Earth, I decided it was best if he did in fact take those days. He has been in his rooms, naturally."

"Which are in the barracks," Cliopher said.

"Well, yes, the commander has never been one to seek out luxury."

Cliopher had only seen Ludvic's rooms once, during the course of overseeing renovations to the barracks. The commander was a very private man, and usually he came to see Cliopher rather than the other way around.

"Perhaps I should ask him to come stay with me here," Cliopher said, frowning at the dregs of his coffee. "Lord knows there's enough room in here, and I'm not sure ... if he's feeling that melancholic ... and if he has four months when he can't work, having to listen to all the shift changes and be there but not be able to—Do you think he would accept the invitation, Rhodin?"

"I think it's an excellent idea and you should insist," Rhodin said, with a slight lightening of countenance. "The commander's rooms are right at the back of the barracks, which is good for discipline and morale but less good for rest and recuperation."

"Will there be an issue with discipline and morale if no one is there?"

"My rooms as second-in-command are right on the main thoroughfare, so I can sit on anyone who makes a noise. They're good lads, and terribly enthusiastic about the fact that things are happening in the Palace."

"Meaning?"

"Meaning that no one has had to do anything for several hundred years, and then all of a sudden they get to use their careful training. There were numerous volunteers to join your rota."

Cliopher pinched the bridge of his nose. "Very well, when I speak with his Radiancy I will mention it. What else am I missing?"

"Breakfast?" his mother said.

"I had some pastries earlier ... but I will take some fruit, thank you." Cliopher accepted the orange segments his mother passed him, then turned abruptly to Kiri. "The princes are going to start arriving soon. The Princess of Mgunai has been to see me, and I saw the Prince of Southern Dair but didn't speak to him yesterday. Who else is here?"

She consulted a piece of paper from her pocket. "Western Dair arrived in the early hours this morning, and we are expecting the Princess of Xiputl and the Jilkano princes by noon, followed by Kavanduru, Amboloyo, and Old Damara. Lorosh is on the way. No one's heard anything from the Vangavaye-ve yet."

"Princess Oriana is useless," Cliopher muttered, then flushed as his sister and cousins laughed with half-scandalized agreement. "Er, well, I mean—"

"Oh, we all agree with you," Vinyë said, "but it's a treat to hear you say it. You're usually so politic, Kip."

Kiri consulted her paper again. "The new ambassador from Alinor is due in any day now, but at least you're usually the first one to greet ambassadors, so that's not going to cause insult. Um ... that leaves the Helma Council."

Cliopher swallowed half the orange, coughed, and then managed, "I've reviewed my notes. I'll need your department to check a few things before the meeting."

"Have you? That will make things much easier. I think that's everything for right now, sir."

More would come very soon, he knew. Oh, how he knew.

★★★

ALTHOUGH CLIOPHER OFFERED HER THE use of a footman, Vinyë preferred to carry her cello herself. He took her and his mother through the serving halls, which were slightly shorter than the main route. They passed only a handful of people, the hour being between the usual shift changes for guards and pages and servants.

Rhodin's two guards trailed along behind them. They were dressed in the lesser panoply, as they would usually wear for one of the princes or the lords magi of the other worlds. He had to force himself not to keep turning around to look at them.

As they went along his mother said, "You've mentioned Kiri in your letters. She's your assistant, is she?"

"She started off as that, yes," he replied, nodding absently at an upper servant coming by them. "My responsibilities changed well before my job title did, and Kiri's likewise. When my responsibilities as his Radiancy's personal secretary grew to the point I could not also oversee the day-to-day running of the Offices of State, she took over there."

"Mm," his mother said, and left it at that.

"What sort of music shall I play for his Radiancy?" Vinyë asked.

Cliopher glanced at her. "Whatever he asks you for."

"I've brought a good selection, but ... What if I don't know a piece?"

"Tell him so. Politely. His Radiancy is a very skilled musician himself, he will understand if you do not know everything."

"Is he? What does he play?"

"He plays an Alinorel harp, I know that, and he sings very well."

"Do you play together?"

Cliopher laughed. "His Radiancy has never asked me, but I fear he must know that I do not play the oboe anywhere near ... It has been some time since I regularly practiced, I'm afraid."

"You don't seem to take very much time for yourself, Kip."

Cliopher glanced sideways at her. "Don't take the current circumstances for my entire life, Vinyë. Usually I do have evenings and holidays."

"No!"

He chuckled, and was still smiling when they reached the door with the two guards. Perhaps unfortunately, the Prince of Western Dair was also there, arguing with them to let him in. As Cliopher approached, one of the outer guards—Midan, he thought—caught sight of him and fair broadcast his relief.

"Your excellency!" he said, saluting.

The Prince of Western Dair swung around to glare at him. He was dressed in half court costume, largely running in his case to hot pink and purple taffeta liberally festooned with pearls. He was a plump, not very tall man, and the overall effect of the various gussets and ribbons and carefully constructed folds of his court costume was to make him look like an over-bred fuchsia blossom.

Cliopher bowed courteously. "Your Highness. What is the problem?"

"I have an urgent need to see the Glorious One. The guards are refusing to let me in. Sir, I have heard such rumours this morning!"

"Ah. Your Highness, the rumours are overblown, but it is true that his Radiancy is not holding audiences, nor is he receiving visitors."

"He appears to be receiving you. And what are these ... people?"

Cliopher responded with a steady gaze and a calm voice. "His Radiancy has requested their presence."

"Oh, so *they* may go in, but *I* cannot."

"Until his Radiancy grants it otherwise ..."

"You have his ear, Lord Chancellor. They would not be coming if you had not suggested it!"

"I am sure you know well that his Radiancy is very fond of music, your Highness." Cliopher glanced at the guards. "We are expected at the third hour. If your concern is so very urgent, your Highness, my secretary will make an appointment for you and I will do my best to ensure that his Radiancy hears of it at the earliest opportunity. At present he is to concern himself with recovering his health, not affairs of state. Your Highness."

With poor grace the Prince shuffled over a foot and gave him a tight, grudging bow. The guards opened the door and announced, "The Lord Chancellor and musicians for his Radiancy."

Cliopher noted that the salutes given him were even crisper than usual this morning, and spent the time walking through the anterooms wondering about it. His guards stayed in the sixth anteroom, murmuring greetings to the guards on duty there. When he reached the ivory door to find Lady Ylette standing there, frowning, he remembered what Rhodin had said about their enthusiasm.

"Lady Ylette," he said, bowing with much more earnest respect than he had felt for the Prince of Western Dair.

"Lord Mdang." She glanced up and down his outfit and permitted herself a small smile before turning her attention enquiringly to his companions.

"My mother, Eidora saya Mdang, and my sister, Vinyë el Vawen saya Mdang, to play for his Radiancy. Lady Ylette is his Radiancy's costumier. Is his Radiancy ready to receive us?"

"I see the family resemblance," Lady Ylette murmured, regarding his mother sharply before turning to the tall and—so Cliopher had always thought—very elegant Vinyë. "Ah! What a treat it would be to clothe you both. How long are you staying in Solaara?"

"They have just arrived," Cliopher said, realizing he had no idea of the answer.

"Hmm. I shall consider. Come: his Radiancy is expecting you."

At some point the chandelier had been put back up, the blood on the floor scrubbed away, and all put back to rights. At the door to his Radiancy's bedchamber, however, there was a new set of guards on the outside of the inner door.

Cliopher knew there were several layers of ranking within the Imperial Guard, from the honour guard who stayed in the room with his Radiancy out in layers to those junior guards who were posted elsewhere in the Palace. As with anything else, the nearer to the Presence, the higher the rank.

He recognized Ingo and Auzevereän, who apparently had been promoted. Ingo said apologetically, "We must examine your instrument, Saya Mdang."

Vinyë said calmly, "Of course. Shall I open the case, or would you prefer to?"

"Please do so," he replied, and when she had done so examined the instrument carefully. Presumably this was for weapons or some sort of magical trap; Cliopher knew that the guards had ways to determine magical weapons. After a moment he nodded and said, "Thank you."

They saluted and knocked on the door, evidently a signal for Zerafin and Varro on the other side, for Zerafin opened it and announced, "The Lord Chancellor and the Sayora Mdang."

His Radiancy was looking very tired, was Cliopher's first thought after he rose from his obeisance and was beckoned closer to the bed. "My lord," he said softly, kneeling next to him.

His Radiancy smiled at him and set down his tea cup on the tray next to him. "Good morning, Kip. Sayora Mdang, you are most welcome. Conju is bringing you a seat, Saya Eidora. Perhaps you might set up your cello there, Saya Vinyë. I will speak with Kip first."

"Thank you, your Radiancy," they murmured, performing their obeisances and going to stand where he had indicated Vinyë should go.

His Radiancy had paused to take several deep breaths. Cliopher was alarmed to see how grey he was looking and how prominent the lines around his eyes and mouth were. "Now, Kip," he said at last. "Tell me what is of most importance."

Cliopher considered. "The princes have begun arriving. I have told them that you are not yet granting audiences."

"And is that working?"

"More or less, my lord. The Helma Council is tonight. We are discussing the annual stipend and the trade tax, as usual for this time of year."

"That cannot be all, my lord chancellor," his Radiancy said when he paused there.

Cliopher was watching his Radiancy's hands, which were twisting the linen sheet into spirals. "That is what is most important today, my lord."

The lion eyes met his and waited. Cliopher gritted his teeth and also waited.

Finally his Radiancy released him, sank back against his pillows, and murmured: "And to think I would usually have a full day of work out of all those not-so-important things."

"Your present work is to recuperate, my lord."

"And you will insist on it, will you? You are as bad as Conju."

"There is the matter of Lord Iprenna, the death of Lord Bavezh, and Commander Omo, my lord."

"Yes. We have been deliberating."

Cliopher arranged himself into all attentiveness. "What is your decision, my lord?"

"Write a letter of condolence to Lord Bavezh's family, explaining that he was over-zealous in the performance of what he saw as his duty and was killed in approaching our presence with a drawn weapon. He will not be attainted for treason, but his death was in all ways legal. That should prevent direct efforts at revenge. Bring the letter here and we will sign it."

"Very good, my lord."

His Radiancy gathered his strength. "By the strict interpretation of the law, Lord Iprenna should be executed for daring to draw his knife approaching our presence. Make certain he is aware of that. We shall grant him clemency for his zeal and punctiliousness. However, due to his deliberate delay and the effect, if not the intention, of destabilizing the command structure of the Imperial Guard , he is to be removed from his position. He will be granted a reasonable retirement in his family estates. Offer him the opportunity to suggest his and Lord Bavezh's successors."

"Very good, my lord."

"As for Commander Omo, he will have to stay in seclusion until the new high priests are chosen and the ritual of purification may begin. Ser Rhodin will assume all his duties and appoint a temporary second-in-command to take on his."

"Very good, my lord. With your permission, I had thought to invite Commander Omo to stay with me while he is undergoing the ritual."

"That is a good idea."

"Thank you, my lord." Cliopher looked carefully at his face, at the clear physical weakness, and the even clearer internal fury and frustration. He cleared his throat.

"Well?"

"There are rumours of an attempted assassination on you last night, my lord. I think perhaps I should make a formal announcement this afternoon. Is there anything else you would like me to say?"

His Radiancy chuckled softly, then wheezed for a few moments recapturing his breath. Cliopher regarded him some bemusement, not sure what was humorous in what he'd said. Finally his Radiancy said, "I shall consider. Set your announcement for the first hour of the afternoon, and come back here at noon."

"Very good, my lord."

"Ask your sister to play now. Any piece she likes greatly."

Cliopher smiled and did so. Vinyë thought for a moment, then grasped her bow and began a piece of slow intricacy and great beauty by the Voonran composer Ko Vai No, who had been at the Astandalan court in the early days of his Radiancy's reign. His Radiancy closed his eyes to listen, and Cliopher made his obeisances and quietly departed, with his mother's calm and somehow wondering glance resting on him.

CHAPTER FORTY-ONE

HE TOLD KIRI TO SEND word about the announcement, looked in on the rest of his family to ensure Gaudy had them all in hand, and went off to the barracks to speak to Commander Omo.

He found him sitting in his room in the dark, looking down at the golden smudges marking his hands and arms. When Cliopher (guided there by a visibly worried young guardsman) entered, he did not look up.

Cliopher waited for a few minutes, while his eyes adjusted to the dim room. He did not look at the commander's private belongings, kept his gaze very much on his friend. Commander Omo did not move.

At last Cliopher walked across the room and touched him lightly on the shoulder. Ludvic looked up at last, his eyes filled with a twisting pain Cliopher did not begin to understand but feared deeply.

Cliopher waited. In the distance he heard the bell chime away another quarter-hour of his morning, his day, his life. Ludvic stared at him, though what he saw Cliopher did not know. The real depth of concern and love of a friend and colleague? The bland expression of a career bureaucrat? He was never so serene or so apparently indifferent as his Radiancy. The best he could do was smile mildly and hide his true subject in other topics.

"I came to ask you to stay with me for a while," he said. "It is chaotic at present with my family here, but once they go it will be too quiet, and I would appreciate the company."

It was a transparent excuse, albeit a true one, but it seemed to be enough, for after another long wait the commander nodded.

★★★

CLIOPHER GAVE LUDVIC OVER TO Franzel for rooms and to his family for company, and went back to the Orange Lily room to where Zaoul was gamely endeavouring to get through the new stack of reports and urgent requests. Cliopher pushed his friend and his family out of his mind and sat down to draft the afternoon's announcement.

After a while Franzel brought in refreshments in the form of tea and gingersnaps. Cliopher set down the report he was reading summarizing the results of the last audit of the Treasury. Zaoul set down his brush and stretched out his hands carefully.

"How are you finding your new position?" Cliopher asked him, hoping desperately he wasn't asking too much, too soon.

Zaoul considered the question seriously. "I find it remarkable."

"Remarkable? How so?"

"At home, everyone does their own thing, and it is only when there is a dispute that the Paramount Chief gets involved. Here, you find out about everything and everyone wants you to decide what they should do."

Cliopher laughed weakly. "It is rather more complicated out here."

"It is like a very, um, complicated riddle. The world," he added, when Cliopher looked at him enquiringly.

"Yes, it is."

"Sir, may I ask you a personal question?"

Cliopher was immediately curious enough to put aside all thought of work for a moment. "Certainly, Zaoul."

"A few months ago it was Gaudy's birthday. You gave him an obsidian knife and a shell necklace. He told us that the note said they were things that you thought would be useful in the Service. At the time we did not know his uncle was you, we laughed thinking it was someone from outside. But I have been wondering ... why those things, sir? What did you mean?"

Cliopher regarded him for a moment. "What do you think I might have meant?"

"Knives are for strength, and the shell necklace, Gaudy said is not so dissimilar from our kina, it is money. Strength and wealth. But that does not seem quite right. Or not only that."

"I have spent my life far from home, from my own people," Cliopher said slowly. This was something he rarely articulated—but he did find in Zaoul something of a kindred spirit. Long habit prevented him from reaching up to touch the efela necklace hidden beneath his clothes.

"Like you, I was the first of my people to enter the Service. I found it very difficult at first, and was forced to assimilate to the dominant culture much more than I hope you will have to. Before Gaudy came I wrote to him with advice, practical things I thought he would appreciate knowing. Once he was here, I wanted him to know that he does not need to abandon all of who he is ..."

Cliopher found it impossible to say more. He fussed with his pen for a moment, embarrassed to have said so much. His own words about the difficulty of standing up for small truths erupted into his mind with brutal force. How much easier it had been to stand up against Princess Oriana on behalf of the whole Vangavaye-ve than it was to admit he had been terribly hurt by the necessity of assimilation.

At length he went on in a brisker tone, "Also they are practical, the knife and the shells. I have not been able to teach him as much of the old ways as I should have, as his uncle, but he knows enough that with those two things he could survive."

Zaoul looked at him with a sudden light in his eyes. "Do you know the old ways, sir?"

Cliopher thought in flashing succession of the unfamiliar feel of the tiller of Bertie's boat, the years (decades?) he had spent crossing the Wide Seas in a traditional boat of his own making, his Radiancy's question about the meeting-place of Iki and Ani, the lament his mother had sung when he left for Astandalas, and the fact that he had not spent enough time with Buru Tovo when he was last home.

After a moment he lifted his hand and untucked the efela necklace so that Zaoul could see it. He touched the black obsidian, the smooth facets familiar and comforting under his fingers, cooler than the golden pearls beside it. "They are not of very much use here, but yes, I know some of the old traditions."

And that was as much as he could say that was true, he thought, here where he chose his work over his family over and over again.

"Why did you decide to leave Tkinê, Zaoul?"

Zaoul met his eyes gravely. "I like complicated riddles. Also everyone was tired of my questions. My mother finally said that if I were so curious about the rest of the world, I should go there. I was the only one who stayed at the trade school after I could read. I wanted to know what else there was."

"And the Service?"

"We're very competitive, we Tkinele. When the teacher said it was a contest open to everyone in the whole world, and that no one from Tkinê had ever won it, that was something people understood. They did not understand why I wanted to leave, why I wanted to know things that other people didn't know, why I wanted to see all the crazy people out here. But they did understand why I wanted to win."

"I wanted to see Astandalas," Cliopher said, tucking away his necklace to its hiding spot. "I wanted to be where things happened. I wanted to be part of things."

I wanted to change the world.

"I understand."

"And now I am in charge of things, and you get to read all the endless reports of what other people are doing in the world. Hopefully you find it somewhat entertaining—you're certainly very good at it."

"Thank you, sir. I have much still to learn."

"Oh, we all do." Cliopher set down his teacup and pulled the next dispatch case over.

I will bring home a new fire to the hearth of the world.

Would he?

★★★

VINYË WAS PLAYING WHEN HE arrived back at his Radiancy's bedchamber.

Ingo and Auzevereän were still on duty, which meant that despite what it felt like it had been less than four hours since he left. They tapped quietly on the door when he approached, accompanied this time by Conju.

The music came through the door faintly, not the complex court music of before but one of the old familiar songs of the Vangavaye-ve. Both Vinyë and his mother were singing, Vinyë in her rich contralto, his mother soprano.

Eidora had been one of the famous sopranos of the Vangavaye-ve in her youth, skilled enough that there had been discussion of whether she should go to Astandalas to sing before the Emperor Eritanyr.

The opportunity had come, and was missed, when Cliopher's father died in a boating accident. A few years later, when her children were older and the opportunity came around again, Eidora had kept to a quiet retirement, and when her own mother had fallen into a lengthy and lingering illness, she had quietly taken on the nursing duties. She had sung at home and at family events, but never to Cliopher's knowledge again in public.

Cliopher slipped in between Pikabe and Ato and stood listening.

He thought that perhaps his heart might burst with joy and pride in his sister, his mother, his family.

As the song drew to its close, his Radiancy sighed deeply. "That was very beautiful."

His mother beamed at his Radiancy; Vinyë, turning her head in unexpected embarrassment, caught sight of Cliopher, and seemed surprised when he smiled at her. She fumbled with the bow of her cello, banging it softly against the strings. "W-would you like another song, Glorious One?"

"It is nearly noon. Kip will arrive shortly—ah! There you are, my lord chancellor. Is the world still running more or less as it ought?"

"More or less, my lord," Cliopher replied, still smiling, as he performed his obeisances.

"Tomorrow you shall give me a full report."

"As you desire, my lord."

"For today, however ..." His Radiancy trailed off, apparently in thought. He looked less grey and drawn than earlier, though still very tired and not at all well. Cliopher waited. The noon bells rang, and slight noises from behind him suggested that the guards were performing their small rituals of exchange as the new pair came on duty. After a moment his Radiancy, looking past Cliopher at them, said, "Yes, Varro, what is it?"

"The Princess of Xiputl wishes to see you, my lord."

His Radiancy considered this for a moment. "She is my great-aunt," he murmured so quietly Cliopher thought he was probably the only one to hear. More loudly his Radiancy said: "She may come in briefly, then. Stay until she is gone, Cliopher."

"Of course, my lord." At the vague gesture accompanying those words, Cliopher got up and went to stand next to where Vinyë and his mother sat. It was not appropriate to speak to them privately, so he contented himself with taking his sister's hand. His mother shook her head slightly, but she was smiling too, and Cliopher thought of his childhood, and his heart sang with that strange joy he had felt on hearing the old song.

Anastasiya Princess Yra of Xiputl swept through the doors which Zerafin and Varro opened for her as grandly as if she entered the Throne Room. She swept an elegant curtsey at the prescribed distance from the bed, rose up without really waiting for a gesture, got halfway through one of the formal greetings between vassal and emperor, and abruptly stopped.

"Was there something, madam?" his Radiancy prompted. To Cliopher's bemused relief his expression was one of suppressed amusement.

The Princess had been old when the Empire fell, but though her face and hands bore the signs of her great age, her carriage was as upright as ever. She was short, thin, and birdlike, and wore the iridescent green and purple of her jungle province in some ancient courtly style. Every time Cliopher had ever seen her she had seemed unhappy, her face marked with bitterness not all the artifices available to an imperial princess could erase. Yet he admired her sense of duty, her responsibility to her people, her shrewdness.

Now she looked as if she had unexpectedly stepped in something unpleasant.

"You have changed the bed."

There was a brief pause before his Radiancy lifted his eyebrows at her. "Whatever do you mean?"

"This is not the great bed of the Emperors!" She gestured at the superb ebony frame, the foamwork canopy, the intricately beautiful carved ivory finials, the inlaid gold. "This is ..."

Words appeared to fail her, and after a moment, his Radiancy said, "It is my bed."

"It is not right," she said, and Cliopher was astonished to see that her eyes were bright with starting tears. He caught himself from staring; remembered that the princess was his Radiancy's great-aunt, daughter of Emperor Lodyr, sister of Empress Anyoë, aunt of Emperor Eritanyr. The bed of the Emperors must have been where she had been born.

His moment of unaccustomed compassion was snarled when the princess did not retreat in polite confusion (or even polite disapproval) but instead gave vent to her feelings in language just barely the safe side of intolerable rudeness. Oh, the forms of her words were those of court courtesy, but her tone, her meaning, and her intensity were shocking.

His Radiancy lay back on his pillows and watched her with a serene and distant expression, tawny eyes hooded.

After a long and somewhat incoherent diatribe on the topic of bed curtains, she changed tack suddenly. "It comes of you being outside the true line. You were never supposed to become Emperor. You were never supposed to be seen."

Cliopher just barely stopped himself from hissing. He could see from his position how Zerafin and Varro were also trying hard not to respond. His Radiancy ignored them, attention focused on the princess. "And?" he said in a low and resonant voice. "You did not challenge the succession then."

"How could I? You were the Marwn: it was your duty to submit to your fate. And mine to submit to my own."

"Indeed."

She raised her chin and glared at him with glittering emotion. "Four Emperors have I seen buried. I will outlive you yet, Radiancy."

"It is not inconceivable."

"But mark my words, *Radiancy*: my dear Shallyr would have been a far different Emperor than you. He was born to the yellow, born to the throne, born to rule. You!" She gave a motion that suggested that if she had not been far too well-bred for the thought to even cross her mind, she would have spat in derision. "You have changed the laws, you have changed the customs, you have changed the bed. It is no wonder Astandalas fell under you."

Every word could have been counted treason, had his Radiancy wished. His Radiancy smiled somewhat sympathetically at her. This seemed to spur her to one further burst of venom, for she cried: "Oh, would that the Red Company had thought to take you!"

His Radiancy went very still, his face very blank, his whole body frozen.

The princess smiled, triumphant in having goaded this reaction, uncertain perhaps in its meaning, but exalted for having at last spoken.

His Radiancy said very softly, "If ever I may effect the release of Fitzroy Angursell, madam, it shall be on the condition he write a song about you. You have said your piece: go now, and find what peace you can."

The princess was not so angry she did not know her dismissal; and Cliopher had never known her to do anything but her duty. She went down into the full court obeisance, rose, and backed out of the bedchamber past the blank-faced guards.

When the door shut behind her his Radiancy looked over at Cliopher, who hastened over to his side. His Radiancy was back to his normal serene good humour, though physically he was once again drawn. "The princess was the younger twin," he said. "I don't believe she has ever forgiven her sister for becoming Empress. The old bed should be down in the Treasury somewhere—set someone to find it, and have it presented to the princess with our compliments."

"As you desire, my lord."

"As for the announcement ... what have you prepared?"

Cliopher preferred to keep his formal speeches as short as possible, so they were easy to memorize. He recited the one he had written that morning.

His Radiancy considered a few moments, then nodded. "Concise and sufficient to the day, as ever."

"Very good, my lord." Cliopher hesitated a moment. His Radiancy quirked his eyebrows at him. "What is it, my lord chancellor?"

Cliopher dropped his voice. "Fitzroy Angursell—"

"Yes?" His Radiancy's voice was suddenly sharp.

Cliopher backed down immediately. "My lord, forgive me. I do not mean to pry into matters that do not concern me."

His Radiancy met his eyes with a steady, considering expression.

Cliopher braced himself against the pressure, the magic, the glory. Finally his Radiancy said, "Something tells me that you think Fitzroy Angursell is a matter that concerns you."

"I have never heard anything but the wildest rumours of what happened to him, my lord. It seemed—it seemed as if you had more ... concrete ... knowledge."

His Radiancy settled back into his cushions, releasing Cliopher's eyes so that he could look at his canopy instead. "There was never any proof," he murmured. "But Kip ... there is an oubliette."

Cliopher ran frantically through all the possible locations. There were prisons under the Ystharian wing of the Palace, but he had never come across any mention of an oubliette in all his accounts or investigations or audits of the Justiciary. "In the Palace, my lord?"

"So I have heard." His Radiancy paused there, breathing evenly. Then he said, "Do *you* think Fitzroy Angursell should be freed?"

Cliopher hesitated. His mother and sister were speaking softly to each other on the other side of the room, a breach of etiquette his Radiancy was ignoring and which he was glad enough for. He said slowly, "My lord, the crimes of the Red Company occurred during the days of the Empire. The pronouncements regarding them stand, but ..."

"Yes?"

"They were always a special case. The people—"

"I do not ask for your political view. I wish to know what you, Kip Mdang, think."

Cliopher met the lion eyes steadily. "My lord, I have devoted my life to your service."

"And?"

"And I think that of all people, Fitzroy Angursell should be free."

The tawny eyes kindled slowly, and his Radiancy smiled, a disquietingly ironic expression. "The oubliette—it is magical in nature—it is hidden. Perhaps you may find it. No one else has, but then—no one else knows to look. And—"

"My lord?"

"And the Lord of Ysthar has won the game Aurieleteer. I am coming to the end of my reign. The Nine Worlds are at a point of change. Perhaps the Red Company will return, as so many call for."

Cliopher did not even ask how his Radiancy knew of the deep and abiding love of the citizens of the Empire for the folk heroes who were technically the last and greatest Terror of Astandalas.

"As for—yes, Varro?"

"The Grand Duchess of Damara desires admittance, my lord."

"We might as well get my family over with," his Radiancy said quietly to Cliopher with a quirk of humour. "Let her come in."

The Grand Duchess of Damara, Melissa Damara, Imperial Princess of Astandalas, was some decade or so younger than her brother, about Cliopher's own age. She wore half court costume in the Damaran colours of black and silver and white, the embroidery patterns of swans. She wore her still-dark hair dressed in court style, straightened, smooth, and cut into elegant wedges adorned with diamonds and pale blue zircons set in silver. Her eyes were dark brown, her skin ebony, her features recognizably similar to his Radiancy's even to the calmness of her expression.

She went gracefully into the obeisance and rose at his gesture, like Princess Anastasiya murmuring the formal greetings of vassal to Emperor.

His Radiancy responded equally formally. Then they both fell silent, not looking at each other. His Radiancy's hands were splayed calmly on the glimmering yellow silk of his coverlet; the Grand Duchess' hands were folded, equally calmly, before her. He was looking at her hands; she was looking not at his face but at the sun-in-gold on the richly embroidered curtains behind his head.

The etiquette was for his Radiancy to begin conversation, to set the tone, the topic, the formality, the intimacy. The Grand Duchess had undoubtedly been taught from infancy how to behave appropriately before the Emperor, be he uncle, husband, or brother. Cliopher looked at their faces: so similar in their calmness, their perfect lack of emotion, the almost imperceptible ways they were both betraying their awkward hope for some connection beyond the formal courtesies.

Possibly no one ever looked as closely at his Radiancy's face as he himself did.

Every year his Radiancy wrote to invite his sister to visit for the traditional family festival at Silverheart, carefully keeping the wording as neutral as possible so she did not feel constrained by etiquette to come, and every year the exquisitely polite negative came back.

"Thank you for coming," his Radiancy said at last.

She dropped her gaze not to his face but to his hands. They were perfectly manicured as ever, nails lacquered gold, the single signet ring his only ornament. His Radiancy had beautiful hands, Cliopher had thought more than once, long-fingered and strong.

"It was my duty," she replied, keeping her eyes lowered. Her voice was low, melodious, and soft. Cliopher knew from his reports that her people loved her fiercely, and although Damara had been very badly damaged by the Fall, its population decimated and its landscape scarred, she had guided it to a peaceful and fairly prosperous province much devoted to the arts of pottery and gardening.

"You have never failed in it."

Whatever else one might say about the old aristocracy of Astandalas—and there was a lot one might say about them—when it came to the remnants of the Imperial family left after the Fall, they knew their duty and unfailingly and uncomplainingly fulfilled it. The Princess of Xiputl was ancient, but she had been the only aristocrat to survive the Fall in Xiputl, and she had stood up without hesitation to organize the chaos.

Cliopher well remembered when the reports had started to come into Princess Indrogan's office. He had been a junior secretary; he had read them and condensed them for his superiors.

Most of the continent of Dair might have dissolved into anarchy, and the Vangavaye-ve could easily have dropped off the face of the world as half the continent of Kavanduru had in fact, but Damara under the Grand Duchess and Xiputl under the Princess Anastasiya had been stable, fed, and clothed long before anyone else had even picked themselves out of the rubble.

He dragged his attention back to the room when the Grand Duchess again spoke. "It came to me that I have never properly thanked you, my lord, for giving me the choice about my marriage when you first came to the throne. I was, and remain, very grateful. I know what you faced as a result of giving me that choice, and I wished you to know that I appreciate it."

The words were coolly spoken. The Grand Duchess might have been thanking him for a trinket given the day before rather than a major policy battle fought the first year of his reign as Emperor and every year thereafter until the Fall.

His Radiancy raised his eyes to her face, but by then the brief flash of honest emotion had faded behind the strict training of decorum.

"Thank you," he replied as coolly. She raised her eyes in turn, but did not meet his, and by then the even briefer flash of wistfulness had disappeared behind the opaque mask of serenity.

She evidently took that as her dismissal, or perhaps she really had nothing more to say—but Cliopher did not, could not, believe that—for she curtsied profoundly and backed out according to the protocol. His Radiancy watched her go with his face so blankly serene Cliopher's heart broke for him and unthinkingly he walked across the room without being summoned.

His Radiancy glanced at him sharply and away even more quickly. "So much for my blood relations," he said very quietly, with a ghost of a smile. "I am fatigued, Kip. I want no more visitors today."

"Very good, my lord," he said, wishing he dared say more, willing his lord to look him in the face and see everything he was not saying. His Radiancy, however, closed his eyes and lay back wearily, and when Cliopher still hesitated, said: "I will send word when I wish you to return or your sister or mother to play."

"Very good, my lord," he said again, and bowed and ushered his family out. His last glimpse of his Radiancy was an elegant hand coming out to close the curtains before Conju hastily stepped forward from where he had been hidden behind a corner screen to do it for him.

CHAPTER FORTY-TWO

"WHO WAS THE GRAND DUCHESS supposed to marry?" Vinyë asked at supper that evening.

Cliopher had been thinking about the week ahead and reluctantly dropping all the things he had planned to do with his family in favour of the work piling up relentlessly on his desk. They could go to the opera without him, he thought—and blinked when Vinyë repeated her question.

"Oh … his Radiancy."

"But she's his sister!"

Cliopher blinked again and forced his thoughts down to the here-and-now. "It wasn't against the law for the Emperor. They cared much more for the bloodline than for the question of incest. The Grand Duchess had been raised since birth to be the Consort, she was undoubtedly of the right bloodline, she was of child-bearing age, and she was healthy."

"It's still wrong."

Cliopher waited while Shoänie brought in the next course. "It's different for them. They were not raised like ordinary people—his Radiancy did not meet his sister until he had already become Emperor. I had not known he gave her the choice about the marriage, though I am not surprised. I don't think he would have held out as he did solely for his own sake."

"What do you mean, held out?"

"Don't you remember writing to me—every letter, almost—asking me when the Emperor was going to marry, when he was going to beget an heir? Imagine that from everyone—everyone. Every single person you meet is concerned about it. You are concerned about it. Your primary duty is to govern the Empire well: your secondary duty is to beget an heir to pass it on to.

"And then imagine that there are multitudes of laws around whom you may marry, but that it boils down to someone within certain degrees of relation to you, and that there is only one woman of child-bearing age in that category, and it is your sister. And you ask her if she, who has been trained since birth to be the Consort, to bear those heirs, to perform those duties, wishes to do so with you rather than the cousin she had been expecting to marry, and she says no.

"And imagine that you never tell anyone why it is you refuse to marry her, but give her the space to mourn her lost fiancé and retreat from the public eye and instead bear the entire brunt of the opposition and pressure on yourself."

Vinyë mouthed a silent, *Oh*.

"But you looked angry," his mother said.

"Did I? I must govern my expression better."

"Kip!"

He sighed. "Mama ... the Grand Duchess and the Princess are his Radiancy's only family. Their ways are not ours. But it hurts to see two people who could love each other—" He faltered. "These are not things I should be talking about."

"Kip—"

He turned to Vinyë. "I cannot imagine crossing the world to what might be your deathbed and saying nothing more than polite nothings and apologizing for something that happened before the Fall. Can you? They are two people who have never had the chance to learn how to be family. Undoubtedly it is proper etiquette, but ... he is still ... But then etiquette has never been my strength. Perhaps it is what they both prefer."

He shook his head and fell silent, addressing himself to his food. No one of his family spoke. Mindful of the unspoken currents, after a few moments he lifted his head, smiled brightly, and began to describe some of the things they could do while he was working.

★★★

THE NEXT MORNING, CLIOPHER WAS in his office reading over the law cases that were supposed to go before his Radiancy the next week and trying not to over-react to the horrible crimes in their dry prose. In the middle of a long description of complicated psychological assault and counter-assault, there came a tap on the door.

"Enter," he said.

Tully came in, cheerful face slightly worried. "Sir, the Grand Duchess of Damara is here to see you. She says it's a personal matter and quite urgent."

Cliopher stared at her. The Grand Duchess had never once spoken directly to him, let alone come to ask him for an audience.

"Sir? She's in the First Receiving Room."

"By all means," he replied, replacing the files in their dispatch case and standing up. "Will you send for refreshments?"

Tully nodded. "Zaoul's on it."

"Thank you."

The Grand Duchess was looking at one of the ancient pictures that Cliopher had left on the wall. She turned as he entered, and he bowed courteously.

She curtsied shallowly back. "Thank you for seeing me so promptly, Lord Mdang."

"To what do I owe this honour, your Grace?" he asked. "Would you like to sit down?"

She sat decorously, feet together and hands calmly on her lap. She was wearing informal costume in the Damaran style, loose trousers and long tunic in cool greens and blues embroidered with slightly darker shades. She looked beautiful, remote, and serene, but Cliopher, looking carefully at her face, saw that she was hiding tension.

Franzel came in with a tray of tea and lemon biscuits, poured for them both, and disappeared again on soft feet. Cliopher waited curiously and with mild trepidation.

The Grand Duchess picked up her cup, brought it to her lips, and set it down again without drinking. She then clasped her hands, bracelets clicking together gently. "Lord Mdang, I met your sister in the gardens last night."

He felt a thrill of cold fear run through his veins. He hoped he managed to keep it from showing on his face. "Indeed, your Grace?"

She gazed unsmilingly at him. "She introduced herself to me and begged for a few minutes of my time. I was curious, I suppose, and let her speak privately with me."

He had learned the hard way not to rush into speech. He sipped his tea and finally essayed a cautious, "Vinyë is very dear to me, your Grace."

She inclined her head. "That was evident."

She fell silent again. Cliopher waited, uncertain how he should respond. Usually he would take this for subtly expressed but nevertheless extremely serious criticism, but something in the way she held herself suggested that more was going on.

They both let the silence unspool for some time. The Grand Duchess gazed into her teacup as if reading the mysteries of the universe therein. Cliopher watched her, waiting, wondering, fear running up and down his back.

"You are a fortunate man," she said, still in her cool, unemotional manner. "You love and are loved deeply."

Had Vinyë *talked* to her about what Cliopher thought of—dear gods, he thought, that was so far from being done it was—

The Grand Duchess lifted her cup and this time drank from it. Her elegant throat was adorned with jewels both understated and flawless. Cliopher raised his eyes to her face. It came to him that behind the cool demeanour was an inner woman, perhaps as different from the outer as his Radiancy's inner self was from the Sun-on-Earth.

He leaned forward and spoke to that inner woman. "Your Grace, I have never known anyone to love as deeply as his Radiancy loves."

She sat back, showing just a hint of fluster. "The world knows your devotion, Lord Mdang."

"He is very ill," he said desperately. "He came to the brink of death. He has no family but you and your great-aunt. Can you not say something?"

He stopped. She stared at him, visibly shaken, meeting his eyes so he saw hope there, and desperation, and hurt, and bewilderment, and under and through all the fluttering emotions, like the bedrock underlying the Palace, pride.

"It is not my place to intrude where he has not invited."

"You are his only sister!" Cliopher caught his temper before it quite flew away. "Your Grace, every year his Radiancy has written to you in his own hand to invite you to the Silverheart festival. Do you need more invitation than that?"

She drew back, visibly affronted. "He has never indicated any true desire for me to come."

"And if he had expressed his desire?"

"I would have come. It would be my duty. When he desires me to attend other things, as the Council of Princes, he states so, and I come."

And there it was. "And what if he desired you to come not as his vassal but as his sister?"

She frowned at him. She was his Radiancy's sister: perhaps she was as brilliant and as trapped in courtly convention as he. (Perhaps?) "He is the head of my family and my house."

"Your Grace, Silverheart is the festival of the family. It is a time to celebrate bonds that are not only formal and political, but those of … love. His Radiancy is not a man to confuse obedience with love. He knows you are his loyal and devoted subject. The only way he can give you the space to show if you wish to be his sister is to withdraw as your lord. He has no way to show his love to you that is not also used by the forms of imperial benevolence."

She compressed her lips together very tightly, a gesture heartbreakingly familiar to Cliopher. After a moment, voice under control, she said: "You cannot understand."

She was not as opaque as his Radiancy: she had not spent her life in full public view. Cliopher could read her expressions, could see the layers of complex emotion and complicated history. He spoke gently and carefully to that inner woman. "I would be greatly honoured if you would explain, your Grace."

"The world knows your devotion—and your discretion," she murmured, more to herself than to him. Still softly, she went on: "Your sister said to me, *My brother loves your brother deeply, and he was angry for your brother's sake when you said nothing of love or care to him. I do not think you care nothing, so why do you not show it?*" She glanced at him. Her eyelids were lined in silver and pale blue powder, distracting the viewer from the emotion gleaming darkly in the eyes below. Cliopher swallowed hard.

"I believe I wish to tell you, Lord Mdang."

"I would be honoured."

Her posture was perfectly straight, her knees and feet together, her hands calm around her tea cup and saucer. The whole time she spoke she did not move except to glance once or twice up at him.

"I was twelve when I found out I had a brother. My father the Grand Duke had died, and my mother and I were in mourning. It was not long after the Grand Duke's death when my mother told me we had to go to our seat in Damara for some of the seigneurial ceremonies. We went to the Red House, where I had never been. I knew my mother had gone there with the Grand Duke every year for a few days for the ceremonies, and that she was always sad on her return, but she never explained.

"My mother gave me permission to explore the house while she organized things with the housekeeper. There were very few servants there. I found my way into a suite of rooms that had obviously been closed up for a long time. There were dust cloths over everything, and dust, too. I had never been anywhere so dirty before, and I fear I enjoyed flinging off all the cloths to see what was below them.

"There were wonderful things below those dust cloths, I thought: beautifully made globes of the nine worlds, musical instruments, a telescope, a microscope, old furniture. I had never seen things that were worn before, that were visibly *used*.

"I grew more and more curious: who had used these things? Why had they been left there, untouched? In other rooms in the suite it looked as if whoever it was had just walked out the door—there were pens and paper laid out on a desk, with half an exercise in Old Shaian written out. It was as if someone had gone, the servants had come in, thrown cloths over everything, and shut the door, and forgotten all about it.

"There were so many books—poetry and history and science and magic. Many languages. Then I found a closet full of clothes. A young man's clothes, out of fashion but of excellent make and materials. It was while I was looking at the clothes, trying to figure out when they might have been in fashion, that my mother found me. And she—"

Here the Grand Duchess looked at him and essayed a small, tight smile. Cliopher poured her more tea.

"You must understand, Lord Mdang, I was close to my mother, far closer than most Astandalan nobility were to their parents. Although there were other servants, nurses, governesses, tutors, my mother raised me as much as she could. She did not like to go to court, she left that to the Grand Duke, and she spent as much time as possible with me, teaching me the ways of court, the ways of our family. I know what familial love is, Lord Mdang, for my mother loved me fiercely and I her.

"She had taught me to submit to duty, for that was the most important lesson of all. And she had taught me, a woman of the Imperial House, what my primary duty would be—for Grand Duchess though I was destined to be, and now was, it was as Consort that I would be known."

Here she sipped some of her tea. "Lord Mdang, I still grieve for the grief I gave my mother that day, when I asked her in my innocence whose were those clothes, those books, those instruments. I had thought they were my father's, though the idea that he was young and slim once was almost incredible. It never once occurred to me that years before I was born my mother had had a son and been forced to give him up.

"My mother had told me, for she believed I needed to begin young to accept what my duty would ask of me, that she had conceived a child every year of her marriage until the Grand Duke grew too ill to beget one. Every year. I had thought I was the only one to survive. I had thought her sorrow was for all those lost children who had never come to term or past the first hundred days of life."

"She must have had the best physicians in the Empire," Cliopher said helplessly.

"So my mother did, and so too did Emperor Eritanyr's Consort," the Grand Duchess replied, her voice thin and cool. "Not all the medicine nor all the magic of the Empire could remedy the result of generations of close inbreeding, Lord Mdang. You cannot marry cousin to cousin forever. My mother had not yet told me the worst of Imperial policy. At that time I thought the—the malformed infants died naturally."

Cliopher took a long and unsteady breath.

"We were speaking of my unknown elder brother," said the Grand Duchess. "One who had, it appeared, been healthy in body and in mind— from what he left behind, intelligent and well-read and, let us say, interesting. I was very curious, and asked my mother many questions, until finally she told me—Stop.

"She sat me down, right there in what had been his rooms, and told me what she had been required to do: how when she had given birth to a healthy boy child, the third year of her marriage, she had been so delighted, so pleased, so gloriously relieved. She had been delighted to present her son to her own brother, the Emperor, not as Emperor but as brother.

"But it was as Emperor, not as brother, that Eritanyr looked at that healthy boy child, with the lion eyes of the ancient emperors, and it was as Emperor, not as brother, that he told my mother that the child would be his second heir, his Marwn; that she should not think to know him, for the boy belonged entirely and utterly to the Empire; that she should not let herself love him, for it would be crueller to withdraw that love later in life as she would be required to do.

"My mother was devastated, but she had been trained to submit to her duty, and submit she did. But she lost two brothers that day, for Eritanyr was her Emperor, not her brother, from that day forth, and their younger brother was so angry at Eritanyr that he renounced his name and his family and his rank and fled court before he committed treason. My mother gave up her son to the priest-wizards, and shortly after, she told me, his name fell out of her memory as if she had never known it.

"Thus I learned, when I was twelve, what might be required of me when I married the Imperial Heir. Thus I learned about my brother, the Marwn, the unnamed, the unknown, the unspeakable. I wondered about him very often, daydreamed of him, imagined myself escaping court life like my equally unknown uncle and riding off to find my brother. We would go have adventures, I imagined, we would be friends, we would be free."

She smiled wryly but with some gentleness for her younger self. "But of course, what I did was submit to my duty. I was Grand Duchess of Damara and I was training to be the Consort. I had to learn the ways of court, of sycophancy and of patronage. I had to learn what I could of medicine so that I would have the greatest chance of bringing children to term. I put aside my daydreams of adventure, as was my duty. When I was sixteen I was formally presented to the Emperor; when I was eighteen I was formally betrothed to his Heir.

"And then to that betrothal ball the Red Company came and gave me one brilliant glimpse of freedom."

Cliopher had forgotten that it was her betrothal party that the Red Company had crashed, when they stole the Diamond of Gaesion and six bottles of fairy wine (and, so said the song, one lady's maidenhead—though Cliopher had never heard any indication of truth to that story). He was too well-trained himself to ask all the questions he wanted to about That Party, about the Red Company, about the reactions of the court thereafter.

"I dreamed," said the Grand Duchess sadly. "I think everyone did. Perhaps only the Emperor and his Heir did not; they were angry. The Red Company had penetrated into the heart of the Empire, to the very throne room of the Palace of Stars, and they had not even tried to attack the Emperor or his Heir—they had simply shown they could."

She sighed lightly. "They had simply brought laughter and wonder and joy into what had been a cheerless—and I am come close to saying what I should not. No matter. Nothing else happened then. The Red Company went off after the White Stag. Life continued as it did."

She paused, sipped tea, smiled wryly. "Life continued as it did, until the day it did not. The Emperor died, and twelve hours later so did his Heir. Three days later my brother was recalled from his exile to take the throne of Astandalas."

Cliopher had wondered what it had been like for his Radiancy to ascend the throne after his exile. He had not, to his shame, thought of everyone else personally affected: never wondered what his Radiancy's family had thought.

The Grand Duchess shifted position finally, though only so she could set her tea cup down again. "I do not wish you to mistake me, Lord Mdang. I had no love for my cousin Shallyr. He was cruel, violent, stupid, self-centred, and arrogant beyond belief. I had been prepared since birth to be his bride, to become the Consort, to accept my duty to the continuance of the Empire by producing the heir. When my brother acceded to the throne, I already knew that I was the only available option for his Consort.

"I had dreamed, when I was younger, of what my brother might be like. I had imagined a brother from the stories—someone to have adventures with, to laugh with, to cry with, to cherish—someone to love. Not as a husband, but he would surely be better than my cousin—anyone would be."

She closed her eyes briefly against old memories. "I had spent my life studying the effects of inbreeding, Lord Mdang. I had spoken to Eritanyr's Consort, who was horrified by her sole living child. She gave me the advice of drugging myself before my husband's conjugal visits.

"I could not—I went to be presented before my brother, wanting a brother, knowing him for my Emperor and my husband-to-be, my imagination full of the cold reality awaiting me. It didn't matter if he were kind, gentle, loving: he was the Emperor. It didn't matter if he could love me: he was my brother. It didn't matter if he were intelligent, good-humoured, funny, handsome: we were so closely related it was almost impossible I could conceive a healthy child from the union.

"He was kind, loving, intelligent, handsome. He was not good-humoured when I first met him, flattened as he was by suddenly becoming Emperor. My mother—our mother—presented me before him in an informal setting. We were all dressed in full mourning. My mother brought me forward to make my obeisance, and she introduced me: 'I present to your Most Excellent Majesty the Grand Duchess of Damara, who stands ready to be your Consort if it should please your Glory.'

"And he, my brother, made some polite response I do not remember, for after he sent everyone away but his guards, and he invoked the Wall of Silence, and he asked me if I wished to be Consort."

She looked directly at Cliopher then, her eyes intent. "Lord Mdang, I think you will understand how completely astonished I was. I had never been given choice: it had never even been mentioned as a possibility. It had literally never occurred to me that I could say no. If he had ordered, I could not have said no. I was a loyal daughter of the Empire. I knew my duty and would fulfil it. And there was my brother—at that time we still did not know his name—less than a week in Astandalas, not yet crowned, asking me if I wanted to be his Consort.

"I could only stammer that it was his choice, that I was dutiful—I did not know him, none of us knew him! All we knew was that he had been raised to be Marwn, and now he was Emperor, and his word was law though he did not know it. I did not know if his temper and his self-love were as our cousin's had been. If I had said no, he could easily have taken it as treason.

"He knew, even then, that he was breaking etiquette. He told me, very seriously, that it had been borne on him that I was to be his Consort, for all the reasons I knew. He told me, even more seriously, that he could not in good conscience take me as his bride unwilling and ignorant. Ignorant of what, you might ask—I did not dare to, but he knew the question in my mind."

She laughed softly, the sound lacking true humour. "I never found out how he had learned the history of miscarriages, stillbirths, deformities, and infanticide lying between his birth and mine, in the long almost-barren years of the Consort's marriage. I do not think my mother told him. Perhaps he had studied breeding at some point in his long exile, when his life was so empty of people. But he sat there with me, my unknown brother who had become Emperor of Astandalas, and he said that as I would bear the children, it would be my choice.

"I knew my duty, and he knew his, completely changed as it suddenly was: but perhaps because he had spent the first thirty years of his life believing he would never have children, that his life was a solitary thing wholly consumed by his duty to the Empire, he did not see that he must destine me to twenty years of physical and mental and emotional torture in order to fulfil it.

"He gave me that choice, Lord Mdang. He was everything I had ever hoped for in a husband, everything I had ever dreamed of in a brother, everything one could desire in an Emperor.

"I knew what I was giving up in saying no. I was giving up court—which I did enjoy. I was giving up any hope of a husband and children of my own—for if I rejected the Emperor, who else could I wed? I was giving up any hope of family—for my only brother was that same Emperor."

Her voice dropped slightly. "But also … I was preventing the possibility, nay, the likelihood—almost the certainty—that the next emperor would be … broken. I knew how close the Empire had come to total disaster in Shallyr Silvertongue, Lord Mdang. No one better—I was his betrothed, his cousin, his subject, his own. I still bear the scars …"

She shuddered, hand falling from where it had involuntarily risen to her breasts. "I come to perilous waters. Lord Mdang, you have spent far more time with my brother than I have. You know the way in which the personal is public—for the Emperor, there is no privacy. What is very personal is for him a matter of public policy. I made the choice I did … I could not bear the thought of bearing another Shallyr, or worse, for were we not even more closely related than Eritanyr and his Consort had been?

"My brother never faltered, and he never said it was my choice. He maintained with utter steadfastness that he honoured my mourning for Shallyr, and that he would not require me to break my retirement. He was prepared to wait for our third cousin to grow old enough instead of forcing me ..."

She folded her hands more tightly together. "Of course I love my brother, Lord Mdang. But how can he look on me and not—he had to stand against the whole Empire—for me. He must have been so ..." She did not finish the sentence.

"Your Grace, his Radiancy did stand against the Empire for you."

"Our third cousin was twelve when the Empire fell. We all knew that when she was sixteen, she would be his Consort."

Cliopher tried hard not to show his revulsion (and tried even harder not to imagine his Radiancy stuck between his sister and some terrified little girl, and refusing to compromise despite all the weight of the Empire, focused entirely on political necessity, bearing down on him). "Your Grace, with all respect, that was a long time ago. The Empire is no longer. The question of marriage no longer applies."

"So we are left with the brother I still do not know," the Grand Duchess said, smiling sadly.

Cliopher was struck then with a moment of inspiration. "Your Grace, if I may draw an analogy from my own family?"

"Your family? I was under the impression that you are remarkably close to your family, Lord Mdang."

She made 'remarkably' sound as if it meant 'terrifyingly'. Cliopher smiled, concealing the pangs he felt about his family. "I do have a large and loving family, it's true. My mother was one of sixteen siblings, all of whom but one had children of their own. The uncle I am thinking of was somewhat idiosyncratic, and married a woman as ideologically driven as he. They went off to live on one of the uninhabited islands of the Outer Ring of the Vangavaye-ve, so they could live according to their principles and raise their children likewise."

"I believe I can see the parallel," the Grand Duchess murmured dryly.

Cliopher coughed. He reminded himself that the Grand Duchess was product of the same union that had produced his Radiancy. "They had three children. When they were about twelve, my aunt grew very ill, and my uncle decided to return to the city in hopes she might be healed by the physicians there. They came to live in my mother's house—my mother had cared for my grandmother when she grew elderly, and had the family house as a result—"

He realized the Grand Duchess was looking at him blankly, and he hastily returned to the main point.

"My three cousins were the same age as my sisters and me. We had grown up in the city, in the middle of dozens of relatives, in a great rambunctious extended family used to running in and out of each other's houses and offices and stores. These three cousins had never met anyone before. They were very intrigued, but they had no idea how to behave. They didn't know *how* to be part of a larger family. For the first few months, the three of them spent all their time together, usually hiding out in one of the rooms where the rest of us wouldn't bother them. It wasn't because they weren't interested, but they didn't know how to exist in company. They were overwhelmed."

"What happened to them?" the Grand Duchess asked with mild curiosity.

"After the first few months, we started to draw them out. I became good friends with the ones closest to my own age—Basil and Dimiter were twins. I was a bit more solitary than the majority of our cousins, so I took them with me on rambles or boat rides, where there weren't so many people. Over time, they learned how to behave in groups, in company, amongst strangers, and if you met them now, you'd never know they had such an odd childhood." He smiled as a thought struck him. "Well, you might have with Dimiter. The family called him Dimiter the Mad, because he decided to become an explorer. He died in the northern wastes of Voonra."

"And Basil?"

"Basil came to visit me in Astandalas once, travelled on to Alinor with Dimiter on an early trip, and fell in love with an innkeeper's daughter there. They eventually took over the inn and as far as I know, still live there."

"You miss them."

"I do," he admitted, then looked a bit sternly at her. "But we were not speaking of my family, your Grace."

"Do you think I need to learn how to be a sister?"

"Possibly, though to be honest I was thinking more of his Radiancy."

She stared at him.

"He has written to you every year in his own hand," he said softly. "Trust me, your Grace, it is an invitation."

"But what am I to do?"

"He has been pleased to have my mother read aloud to him. I think he finds it tiring to read at the moment."

"What should I read?"

It was in his mind to give her a few titles he knew his Radiancy enjoyed, but then he looked at her face and saw the resolution there.

"Your Grace, choose something you love to share with him. Remember the young man who left his instruments and his books behind when he was sent into exile. In his heart he is still that young man, as you are still that young woman who dreamed of having a brother."

She regarded him for an uncomfortably long moment, then smiled a secret, sad, smile. "My brother is fortunate to have you at his side, Lord Mdang. Few of our ancestors were so lucky."

★★★

"IF YOU HAPPEN ACROSS THE Princess of Xiputl," he said to his sister when he saw her, "do not on any account try to persuade her to tenderness."

CHAPTER FORTY-THREE

AT BREAKFAST THE NEXT MORNING, when Cliopher was trying not to think about all the things he should be thinking about, his mother said, "Cliopher."

She almost never called him by his full name, and it startled him out of his reverie. "I beg your pardon?"

The rest of his family fell silent and attentive, knowing as well as he did what the full name meant. His mother put down her spoon, folded her hands in her lap, and spoke carefully. "I have an apology to make to you, Kip."

He glanced around, but although the faces of cousins, sister, niece, aunt, displayed a mixture of emotions, none of them were of much help. Ludvic was looking very stolid and blank. Cliopher set down his own spoon. "For what, Mama?"

She met his gaze squarely. "I was annoyed that we'd come all this way to see you, and then you had no time for us. I wondered if you wanted only to show off the splendour of your rooms, your proximity to greatness, your fine clothes. I was very disappointed in you."

Cliopher blinked.

"No," she added, as he opened his mouth to respond (though how was he supposed to respond?). "Let me finish. I was annoyed, and I kept looking for confirmation—which I found, because you can always find evidence if you look hard enough. It meant I brushed aside all the other evidence, however. There comes a point when you are hurt and angry that you keep poking yourself with what makes you hurt and angry, and you don't see … Everything else. I'm sorry."

Cliopher blinked again. She didn't add anything else, and he thought, first and oddly, of how the refusal to accept an awkward half-apology had led to far too many wars in history.

His face was burning with shame and embarrassment.

He thought: this is my family. This, right here, is my mother, and I am about to leave her to go to a bloody awful Council of Princes meeting where I will be treated like something they found on their shoe.

He swallowed down his indignation and hurt. That would hardly help anything.

He said mildly, "I'm very sorry I led you to think that way, Mama. It was not at all my desire to make you feel unwelcome or to, uh, show off." Honesty compelled him to add: "Or not very much, anyway. I did want you to see the Palace."

Quintus made an abrupt, choked guffaw, and Cliopher, appetite gone, pushed his cutlery together. He forced himself to meet their eyes; Ludvic was frowning down at the table. "I can't promise things will be different, because I don't know what the days to come will hold, but ... I will do my best."

"That's all we can ask for," his mother said, forgivingly.

"Well," he said, and of course at that moment there came a knock on the door and Franzel entered.

"Sir, there's a Captain Diogen here to see you along with a person from the Grey Mountains. They say they have an appointment."

Cliopher had a disorienting moment of blankness, before he remembered what this was about. "Thank you, Franzel," he said. "Will you ask them to come in here, please?" He turned to his family as the visitors were ushered into the room. Captain Diogen saluted him and Ludvic, who nodded gravely, and the 'person'—a middle-aged woman dressed in the leggings and long white tunic of the Grey Mountains park wardens—bowed briefly.

"It's a beautiful morning for a flight," Captain Diogen said happily, genially refusing the cup of coffee Cliopher's mother offered him. "This is Sagora Adonde, your excellency, of the park wardens. She tells me the Liaau is at its peak."

"It is the most beautiful I have ever seen it, your excellency," she said earnestly. "The flame-of-the-forest and goldrain trees are in full blossom, and the waterfalls are perfect."

"I am delighted to hear it," Cliopher said, managing to smile. "Unfortunately I will not be able to join you today, but perhaps Commander Omo can take my place. Will you, Ludvic? It seems a pity to waste the spot."

Never had Cliopher wished more that he was the sort of man to throw over his obligations and head out on a pleasure junket for the day. He could see his mother once again withdrawing, his sister once again frowning, his family once again seeing him choose his work over them. He sighed.

"There will be other years for the Liaau, Lord Mdang," Sagora Adonde said encouragingly.

"Half an hour," Captain Diogen said, then turned to a suddenly excited

Dora. "What's that, young miss? Yes, you need your warm clothes. We'll not be going so high as on the journey here, but better to be prepared than sorry."

The bell chimed the quarter-hour. Cliopher started. "I will leave my family once more in your good hands, Captain. Sagora Adonde, thank you for organizing this for me."

"It was my pleasure, your excellency."

"Have a good day," Cliopher said generally, but with a searching look at his mother. After a moment she did smile: and with that he had to be content.

★★★

CLIOPHER USUALLY HAD ALL THE financial and bureaucratic operations of government under his direction, while his Radiancy dealt with magic and courtly politics. He still sat in on the Council of Princes as his Radiancy's secretary, but this was the first time he had ever gone in as Chair.

It was just about as bad as he had feared.

★★★

HE SAT IN HIS OFFICE late that evening, trying to concentrate on the reports that were once again piling up on his desk despite Zaoul and Tully's best efforts. Even knowing that the Council of Princes was usually a full-day affair when his Radiancy attended it, he had hoped it would be shorter under him, supposing that the princes at least would hate to listen to him any longer than necessary.

They did: but that didn't stop them doing their best to see just how much they could get past him while his Radiancy was indisposed. Hour after hour they had bludgeoned him with courteous words, one by one, in shifting alliances, in careful barrages of quiet voices and sudden loud bluster.

From a tactical point of view he was deeply admiring. He kept telling himself that there was so much he still had to learn; but he thought about how he had once seen sharks swarm a wounded dolphin.

He sat staring out at his reflection in the dark window. Finally he steepled his fingers over his face, hiding the dedicated bureaucrat from sight, and sat there with his knuckles pressed into his eyes.

"Are you still in there, Kip?" Vinyë said softly, tapping on the door.

He jumped, scattering a few of Zaoul's careful pages of notes. He picked them up in a fluster, finding his headache quadrupling as he bent over. He sank down against his desk and mustered a smile for his sister. "Did you have a good day?"

"It was wonderful," she said simply. "Thank you for organizing it."

"I'm sorry I couldn't go with you."

"So were we. The park wardens had arranged a special meal for you. And us, but it was obvious it was mostly for you."

"I must remember to write to thank them." Cliopher looked around somewhat helplessly. His usually neat and orderly desk was in disarray. Finally he found the notebook where he wrote memoranda, and extracted a pen. He made a note, then sat there staring down at the notebook, feeling guilty and regretful and somehow grief-stricken.

Vinyë slid her arm around him and sat down on the desk next to him. "Oh, Kip, don't look so sad."

He rubbed his face fiercely. "I was really looking forward to showing you the Liaau," he said, not able to look at her. "I'd spent all this time planning all the things I wanted to do with you, and then … I'm so sorry."

"Mama shouldn't have said that to you this morning."

"It was true. You keep seeing me choose my work over you. Over and over again. I know what it seems like—what it is like. I would always have said I would choose you first, but that's not true, is it?" His voice broke, and he squared the edges of the pile on his desk. "Oh Vinyë, I'm so sorry."

"Don't keep saying that, Kip. You don't have anything to be sorry about."

He felt her hand turning his head gently towards her. Her face was serious. "Listen to me, Kip. We're the ones who are in the wrong. We don't … we didn't know."

"I'm very tired," he said. "What didn't you know?"

She slid off the table, walked to look at the hanging on the wall opposite his desk, which she had given him. "We didn't understand … what did you do today?"

"I spent ten hours wrangling the Council of Princes."

"Did you have supper?"

He rubbed his face again. "I don't remember. I must have."

She looked at him, started to say something, then crossed the room again and put her hand on his shoulder. "Kip! Your shoulders are like iron. Come away from your desk and rest."

"I have to—"

"It will have to wait until the morning. You can't possibly do anything effective at the moment. Come, Kip."

He was so tired … He let her pull him upright and tug him gently out of his office and back into his private rooms. "Where's your room, Kip?" she asked. "I don't think I've seen it."

"The gold tree tiles. Right-hand door. Left. That one."

She opened the door to his bedchamber. The room was graciously proportioned but not so big as the one once given to the Lady of Zunidh; Cliopher had guessed it had once been intended for consorts or chief attendants. He found it comfortable, with windows giving on a fine prospect of the Dwahaii curving around to the sea, and he'd furnished it with simple but comfortable items. With his sister beside him his eye caught on the Western Ring carving on the wall, gift long ago from his uncle Lazo.

"Your bathing room?"

"The blue door. I can manage, Vinny."

"Can you?" she retorted, smiling suddenly, but relinquished her grasp when Franzel came out of the other door, which led to the dressing room. "Franzel, my brother has worked himself into a headache. Can you run him a bath and get him some food?"

"Of course, Saya Vinyë. The bath is ready, Sir."

"There you are, Kip. We'll talk in the morning." She pushed him gently after Franzel, who caught him with a shake of his head and guided him gently through the evening's ablutions.

★★★

HE WOKE TO THE SOUND of the bells falling away.

He lay there for a long moment, trying to gather the energy to get up and face the day. Surprisingly there was no Shoänie with his morning chocolate. And even more surprisingly, he felt rested.

He had not counted the bells. He looked to the windows, but someone had closed the louvres on the shutters tightly. He did not usually close them, as he was invariably up at if not before dawn, and he loved the view eastwards to the sunrise over the sea.

He got up and bathed and dressed in the clothes Franzel had laid out for him, a new official outfit that rivalled his previous best one in quality of materials and cut, though it was simple enough that he felt no need to go searching for his comfortable older ones.

It was obviously much later than dawn, though he could not tell how late exactly it was. He felt too well-rested to be as annoyed as he thought he should be.

He went through to the Tortoise room, where his family were finishing up what he was relieved to see was clearly breakfast.

"Good morning," Vinyë said, getting up and giving him a kiss on his cheek. "You look as if you actually slept long enough."

"Did you tell Franzel and Shoänie not to wake me?"

"No!" She laughed. "I doubt they'd take orders from me, would they? Even if it were for your own good. They must have decided on their own."

"Did you?" Cliopher asked Shoänie, who had come in with a fresh pitcher of chocolate.

She bobbed a curtsey. "No, Sir. The orders came from the Tower. There was a note for you. I'll bring it with your pastries, Sir."

"Thank you," he said, somewhat bemused, and sat down between Vinyë and Zemius. "What time is it, do you know?"

"Nearly eleven—uh, the fifth hour," Quintus said slyly. "We've been having a very lazy morning. Everyone was tired after the excitement yesterday."

"Tell me about the Liaau," Cliopher said. "It's one of my favourite places. There's a wonderful walk up through the gorge to the bottom of the waterfalls you can do in the dry season."

They described the outing, the magnificence of the flowering trees, the basins of clear water spilling over into waterfalls of astounding beauty, the birds and butterflies and the great thunder lizards with their bright plumage and deep calls.

The park wardens had arranged a quite remarkable day, Cliopher realized, showing his family some of their secret places where public visitors were not normally allowed to go. The guilt he felt about leaving them so often faded; but his own disappointment grew all the sharper.

Shoänie brought him his pastries and the note. He unfolded it curiously, and saw that it was in his Radiancy's hand:

> My Lord Chancellor—the Council of Princes is trying at the best of times, which this is not. I have ordered your staff to leave you alone for the morning to recuperate. Come at the first hour of the afternoon to discuss what happened; bring your sister to play for me after. A.

He shook his head, smiling, and folded the letter up again, then glanced up to see that his family were trying not to ask him what was in it. He smiled more broadly. "My lord gave the orders," he explained. "He felt that yesterday's council meeting would be trying. He has bidden you to play for him this afternoon, Vinyë."

"I should be delighted."

"Yes," he murmured abstractedly, taking a starfruit from the basket. "I am glad your outing was so good. In a few days I have planned a trip down the river to the port."

"Will you be able to join us?" his mother asked with careful neutrality.

Cliopher sighed. "Possibly. I shall have to see what's on my calendar now."

"Now?" Quintus asked. "You seem far too organized not to know your schedule."

Cliopher cut the starfruit into precise segments, enjoying the pattern of pointed lobes and interior seeds, the bright clean scent rising up. "I would be, usually, but things are topsy-turvy at the moment ... I was ahead on my work, you see, in anticipation of your visit. These are all things I would not normally be obligated to deal with."

"Because of the Glorious One being—"

"Yes."

"You care very deeply for your lord," his mother said in a softer voice.

"Of course," said Cliopher, his glance straying to the note. He was pathetically grateful for the order to take the morning off.

"You've never thought of getting married," Quintus said.

Cliopher looked at him blankly.

"It's not as if it was possible to ... with ..."

Cliopher flushed as he realized what his cousin was implying. "No. But also: no. That's not why ... That's not what ..."

"It would be understandable," his mother said.

"He is my lord and my friend," he said firmly. "That's all. Quite apart from the fact that it would be edging into blasphemy."

Quintus seemed disinclined to drop it. "But still, you never have—"

"She said no."

Into the short silence that followed his sharp retort, Dora looked up from where she was industriously drawing a picture of the Liaau to ask: "Who said no to what?"

Cliopher struggled with his temper—and with his long-buried private emotions. "A friend of mine from long ago. I thought we might get married, but she didn't want to."

"Why not?"

He thought of Ghilly and Toucan, married now these many years, planning their lives after work. Thought of how Ghilly sometimes looked at him, with a sort of speculation; and how she always turned back to Toucan with that brilliant smile.

"She thought I was too ambitious," he said quietly.

Dora smeared red all over her trees with a decided sort of gesture. "What does that mean?"

He kept his attention on Dora, but he was speaking to his family. "I would have stayed in Gorjo City for her, but she thought I would never be satisfied with what I could achieve there. She thought … and I suppose she was right … that I wanted more. That time when I came back after the Fall … that was when I asked her … and she said no."

"What do you want, Kip?" Vinyë asked.

"Now?" he laughed wearily. "Right now I want the time to spend with my family, but unfortunately past ambition is present work."

"You have these beautiful rooms, these splendid clothes, servants and guards and secretaries and all that. What more do you want?"

"Those are all trappings, Vinyë. Incidentals. Things I was given along with my position, not things I sought."

"What have you sought? What's taken you from us? What did we lose you to?"

Her voice held a note of sorrow that pierced Cliopher. "Vinyë—"

"*Explain* to us what is so important, Kip. Explain to us what you do. Explain to us what is so important that you have to drop all these things you arranged for us. Explain to us why you are never here. Explain to us what you are always doing."

"You've accused me of boasting and showing off just for having you here," he said, looking intently at her and his mother. "Do you want me—I have told you I am the Lord Chancellor of Zunidh."

"We don't understand what that means!"

He was so tired of them not understanding. "The government of Zunidh begins and ends with his Radiancy."

"That much we do understand."

Cliopher ignored her tone. "As the Lord of Zunidh his Radiancy is responsible for the world's magic. He has complex projects—he built the Lights, he integrates the sea trains into the world's magic, he cleansed the Fens, he has moderated the typhoons of the Wide Sea—"

"That has made a huge difference in the shipping," Quintus murmured.

"I am sure he would be delighted to know it."

"So your lord works great magic."

"The planning and actual work of magic usually take up perhaps a third of his Radiancy's time. Then there is the fact that he was, of course, the last Emperor of Astandalas, and he is very highly regarded by the other lords magi for his knowledge and wisdom and authority. He is very often solicited to assist in judgments, in making important decisions of state or justice or magic or—"

"We get the picture."

"Do you?"

Vinyë snorted. "His Radiancy spends a third of his time working magic as Lord of Zunidh, a third of his time helping other lords, and a third of his time running the government here."

"Well: a third of his day to eat, to hold court, to have any time to himself, to study, to be the supreme judge, to make decisions of policy, to ..."

"That doesn't seem very much time," Aunt Oura said diffidently. "He must be very organized."

"Under his Radiancy are the four pillars of government: the princes, the priests, the guards, and the civil servants. The princes run the provinces, the priests are responsible for spiritual and magical health, the guards keep justice and public order, and the civil service is responsible for basically everything else."

"We learned about that in school," Leona said suddenly. "The Council of Princes, the Ouranatha or College of Priest-Wizards, the Command Staff of the Imperial Guard, and the Lords of State are the governing bodies."

Cliopher nodded at his niece. "Yes, exactly. His Radiancy is the Chair of the Council of Princes, the Highest Priest of the College, the General Commander of the Imperial Guard, and the Great Lord of State."

"That doesn't seem to solve the problem of his time," Quintus said, dropping his air of disaffection and leaning forward. "Are those just figure-head positions?"

"It would be treasonous to suggest so," Cliopher replied dryly. "Certainly his Radiancy is the final arbiter of all decisions made by those bodies, but yes, he is willing to delegate to a certain degree. Ludvic Omo is the Commander of the Imperial Guard, for instance, leaving his Radiancy to focus on being the Supreme Justice and actually judge."

"And for the priests and the Lords of State?"

"He has specific ceremonies and rituals that must be done as Highest Priest."

"But surely the civil service runs most things?" Quintus said. "I mean, that's who we have to deal with the most often. We don't even deal with provincial authorities very often. It's always the mundial ministries of trade we deal with. What does his Radiancy do as Lord of State?"

"He listens to his Lord Chancellor, mostly," Gaudy said, when Cliopher balked at stating the truth.

A pause, then Vinyë said: "You're the delegate in charge of the civil service?"

"You could put it that way."

"But his Radiancy is abed. Wait—last night you said you'd been at the Council of Princes."

Cliopher rearranged his starfruit pieces on his plate as the door opened on Ludvic and Ser Rhodin. He smiled abstractedly at them. "Well, yes. At the moment, with his Radiancy indisposed, I am—"

"Kip! Are you saying you're *in charge of the government?*"

Ludvic blinked. Ser Rhodin, half-turned to close the door behind himself, started, turned around, and let out a huge peal of laughter.

"Sorry," he gasped at last, recovering himself to the point of wiping his eyes. "Were you only just now realizing that?"

Vinyë looked mortified; Cliopher's mother on her dignity; Aunt Oura very blank. "Rhodin," Cliopher said warningly.

"I will never understand the happily middle-class," Rhodin declared, evidently taking this as invitation enough and sitting himself down next to Quintus. "I presume you're all happily middle-class, you see, since Cliopher is so ... very ... determined ... about being ..."

"The scum that rises to the top of a boiling pot," Cliopher supplied, when Rhodin trailed off into vague ineffectual gestures.

"No! Who said that?" Rhodin asked, opening his eyes wide with shock and mild delight.

"The Prince of Amboloyo."

"The hell he said that to your face! When has *he* ever seen a boiling pot, anyway?"

"Who knows? He didn't say it directly to my face, to be fair. It was more of a loud aside."

"The Council of Princes is like a club for people with better blood than brains," Rhodin said. "If my brother had survived the Fall, he could probably have angled for one of the positions. He met the requirements."

"You don't?"

Rhodin chuckled and poured himself some coffee. "No, I have half a brain too many and half a parent too few." He paused. "That sounds better than it means. He was my half-brother: his mother was the first wife, and she was a fifth degree cousin to the Imperial House. My mother was a Voonran heiress, meant to repair the family fortunes, but alas she matched my father in her ability to spend, and they'd lost the house by the time I was fifteen."

"You did have a good sword-master," Ludvic murmured.

"True: and fortunately he was Alinorel and had a university education, because there wasn't anyone else for me to learn from." He glanced around at the bemused faces of Cliopher's family. "The glamorous life of a noble family of late Astandalan Ysthar. So the Prince of Amboloyo has progressed to name-calling, has he? He's about the only person who seriously wants your job."

"Some days I would be tempted to let him have it."

"Don't joke about that! World order would collapse with him as captain. He can't see further than his own ambition."

"What I need to find," Cliopher said thoughtfully, "is something exceedingly expensive and time-consuming that he can make his pet project."

"That *you* can make his pet project, you mean."

"The order would undoubtedly come from his Radiancy," Ludvic said.

Rhodin snorted. "Hah! Cliopher's come up with the majority of public works projects. No brilliant ideas surfacing yet, Kip? It's been a while since you last launched a major upheaval into society."

Cliopher flushed. Vinyë said cautiously, "What do you mean, Ser Rhodin?"

Rhodin set down his cup so he could tick items off his hands. "Let me see. There was the sea train—"

"That was Ngalo Bargouyen."

"Who everyone else thought was totally insane. You convinced his Radiancy and rammed the idea down the throats of every objector in the world. The sea train. The whole unified decimal currency—and don't pretend that came from his Radiancy! Finances are not his favourite part of government. I'm not sure if he's ever personally conducted a financial transaction in his life."

"When we were in the Vangavaye-ve …"

"He bartered, which as you pointed out at the time is a form of negotiation."

Ludvic smiled suddenly and unexpectedly. "Which possibly is his Radiancy's favourite part of governing."

Quintus looked floored. "The sea train *and* the decimal currency? They were really your ideas, Kip?"

Rhodin grinned at Quintus. "He doesn't look like he's a brilliant statesman does he?"

"Oh, are we discussing Lord Mdang's contributions to world govern-ment?" Kiri asked brightly, coming through the door in the wake of Shoänie with a fresh pot of coffee and grinning at him. "Don't look so morose, sir. There's the tax system—"

"The housing projects—"

"The postal service—"

"Enough," said Cliopher. "What did you actually come for, Rhodin? Kiri?"

Kiri's face sobered. "The auditors' report from the Ministry of Agricul-ture has come in. You'd better take a look at it."

Cliopher looked at her. "Hell. Agriculture, really?"

"It's pretty bad. They've been—" she glanced around the table. "You'll need to read it, sir."

Cliopher sighed. "Of course. Rhodin?"

"There are five cases due to come before his Radiancy at the Court of Final Resort next week. Are you going to be taking them?"

"Are you seriously suggesting I sit in the Throne of Judgment?"

"Well …" Rhodin made a superb shrug.

Cliopher told him, in brief and pungent language, exactly what he thought of this idea. Halfway through this he caught sight of his mother's confounded face, and he stopped abruptly.

He moved to lift up his coffee cup with slightly trembling hands, then sat there holding it, feeling shocked to the core of his being.

"Perhaps you might speak to his Radiancy about it," Ludvic murmured.

Cliopher gritted his teeth as outrage flared up within him again. "I think that is a very good idea. There is a line, Rhodin—"

"We know where it is as well as you do," Rhodin retorted. "We also know where you stand. What are you planning to do when his Radiancy goes on his quest? Will you refuse to sit in judgment then? Why would you not take this opportunity to practice when you have the finest legal mind in the Nine Worlds to give you advice?"

"I will speak to him." Cliopher sipped his coffee, hoping the motion masked his distress.

"I will leave the auditors' reports with you," Kiri said. "Do you have any special instructions for me?"

Cliopher closed his eyes, trying to ignore the insistent pounding at his temples. He had, he remembered vaguely, made a list the night before; but he had not brought his memorandum book with him. If he went to his office, he would be sucked into the whirlpool of things to do. He opened his eyes. "Gaudy, could you please go to my desk and find my memorandum book? It's got a blue and red marbled cover."

"I've seen it," his nephew said, sliding out of place.

Kiri followed his motion with a fond smile she then bestowed on Vinyë. "It's lovely to get a few moments more to speak with you. Lord Mdang's mentioned you often. I understand you play the cello? And direct the Vanga-vayen symphony orchestra?"

"Yes ..."

"She is a magnificent cellist," Cliopher said, then smiled brightly as Gau-dy re-entered with the book. "Thank you." He consulted his notes from the Council of Princes—the formal secretarial notes were no longer his to take, thank goodness, but Zaoul's—and then the scant to-do list he had begun be-fore weariness overtook him. "Yes, here we are, Kiri. The Princess of Mgunai wants to extend the sea train along the Dirigalo coast to that new tin mine."

"Seems like a good idea."

"It would be, except that evidently the route takes it through the pri-mary spawning grounds of five species of salmon, which it would entirely disrupt, to the ecological, environmental, economic, and cultural devastation of the entire western seaboard of Mgunai and half that of Western Dair."

She winced. "His Radiancy would never agree to that."

"Of course not, so we must come up with some suggestions. Will you set Aioru or someone onto researching alternatives? There is some haste."

"Of course there is. Anything else?"

"I need all the details about last year's budget—"

"Bedro and Jhurial have been working on a report for you. They should have it ready in the next day or two."

"Splendid. When is Kilina back from maternity leave?"

"Not for another six months."

"Pity," he murmured, winning a flashing smile. "Give her my regards, will you?"

"Oh, you hardly miss her now that you have Tully and Zaoul and Gaudy to fuss over."

Cliopher chuckled. "Tush now. The Ministers of Culture, Fisheries, Ae-rial Transport and Trade, and the Treasury are all up for renewal in the next session. Aerial Transport has already told me she doesn't want to renew for another term, but check with the others and ask the outgoing ministers for a list of suggestions. Remember that Treasury has a separate protocol for appointments. Try not to get the Treasurer's back up unnecessarily." He looked back down at his notes and saw the cryptic comment of 'Amboloyo', circled thrice. He stared meditatively at it.

"Sir?" said Kiri patiently.

He blinked, an idea suddenly surfacing. "I want you to draw up the formal declaration of a committee on public opinion of the state of affairs."

"I beg your pardon? Which—do you mean the one that's for your new government project? I thought you weren't planning on starting that till next year?"

"Amboloyo is encroaching, and I need something to distract him."

"Won't it be obvious that's what you're doing?"

Cliopher smiled at her with sudden pleasure. "Not the way I'm going to present it to him."

"Sir, it worries me when you smile like that."

"Will you take pity on a poor guard and explain?" Rhodin asked. "I know it's none of my business, but … If this has anything to do with public security …"

"The Prince of Amboloyo is ambitious."

"As we know."

"I am going to invite him to be the chair of my first Committee for the Reconstruction of the Government."

Rhodin blinked at him. "There's no way he could say no to that."

"And it will definitely be time-consuming and it could easily be quite expensive."

"Consider the draft drawn," Kiri said, grinning appreciatively. "Is there anyone else to invite for it?"

"That will be the Prince's responsibility," Cliopher said. "It will be interesting to see whom he chooses. I think that's enough for today, Kiri. I'm sure the dispatch cases are piling up towards the ceiling again."

She laughed. "That's where we all miss Kilina. It's funny, when she was a little girl and she would do those little magics, I never thought how very useful it would be to be move light objects a dozen feet across the room. She can't do much more than that, but between that and her gift at numbers—"

"I'm sure it's helpful for her as a mother, too. Especially with twins."

"I sure wish I'd had telekinetic magic when I was raising her and her sister," Kiri agreed. "Twins run in my family," she explained to Cliopher's. "Both my daughters entered the Service. One ended up in the Offices of

State, much to everyone's amusement—though we weren't nearly as good at pretending we weren't related to each other as you and your nephew, sir."

"What department is your other daughter in again?"

"Heritage. She's deep into doing a list of historically significant sites that ought to be specially conserved. Oh, that was your idea, too, wasn't it?"

"His Radiancy's."

Rhodin chuckled. "Cliopher, you sly dog, his Radiancy's ideas are things like 'There are too many poor people in the slums of Csiven and New Dair. What should we do about this dreadful situation?' Everyone else said: 'Raze the slums', you said, 'Give the people money so they're no longer poor'."

"And instituted the worldwide architectural competition to create housing so beautiful everyone else wants to live there," Kiri added.

"And then did all those social programs so that people who didn't know how to do anything could have meaningful work and artistic pursuits and get the appropriate health care and support."

"And then decided that a basic income would mean everyone could seek out meaningful work and artistic pursuits, and thus the annual stipend was born." Kiri smiled. "Which is a legacy well worth having, if you ask me. As you didn't, and I can see that you're starting to get fractious, I'd best get to work. Let me know when you want to meet after you've read the auditors' report, sir."

"Thank you, Kiri."

Rhodin got up to open the door for her, then sketched a salute. "I'll be off myself. There are recruits to boss around. I'll be on duty with his Radiancy this afternoon, Cliopher."

"To stand behind your rather sacrilegious suggestion? Very good. I'll be coming at the first hour."

They departed, leaving Cliopher to stare unhappily at the thick report that Kiri had left behind for him. "Are you going to go read that?" Vinyë asked.

"I should probably," he said slowly, and then firmly shoved it away from himself as a much better idea occurred to him. "But I will do so later. His Radiancy has given me the morning, and I intend to make proper use of my remaining hour. If I get my oboe to play with you, will you promise not to make too much fun of me for not practicing?"

CHAPTER FORTY-FOUR

A MONTH OR SO BEFORE his family were due to arrive, Cliopher had thought of what they could do, and had on Ser Rhodin's suggestion made reservations for them all at one of the restaurants down in the city. Ser Rhodin spent much of his free time exploring the food scene of Solaara, and could always be relied on to give good recommendations.

Cliopher had forgotten all about the reservation until Zaoul came by with a letter from the restaurant asking him to confirm the number of guests to be expected the next night.

The thought of just taking a whole evening off to be with his family was almost irresistible.

"You seem somewhat preoccupied," his Radiancy observed after the greetings were over and Cliopher was determinedly going through the list of things his Radiancy needed to know about.

Cliopher blanched and said, "I am sorry, my lord, if I am at all inattentive."

"I am sure your every thought revolves around me," his Radiancy replied with the blandest assurance and a mischievous quirk to his mouth. "What is on your mind, Cliopher?"

"I was wondering if it is entirely irresponsible of me to take tomorrow evening off to go to a restaurant down in the city with my family," he admitted. "I had booked the reservations before they came, but that was, of course, before …"

He trailed off, realizing he was getting into dangerous water. It was probably the fact that they were not in their usual places in the outer study, but in the breakfast room where his Radiancy, enveloped in rich robes, reclined at ease. "It is no matter, my lord. If we might turn to this next report from Amboloyo—"

"Kip."

"My lord?"

His Radiancy regarded him for a long and uncomfortable period. "Have you spent *any* time with your family since they arrived?"

Cliopher swallowed dryly and tried to look indifferent. "I have taken most of my meals with them, my lord. My nephew has been showing them around, and of course Vinyë and my mother have been most gratified to play and read to you, and—"

"I do not think the government will collapse if you take tomorrow off."

"My lord, there is a great deal to do."

His Radiancy resettled himself against his pillows and said amiably, "That is an order, Lord Mdang."

"My lord!"

His Radiancy chuckled. "I know: send Zaoul in to see me in the morning, and I will audit your work over the past ten days. Make sure you leave the Palace entirely, mind. Oh, and if your family will not object, take Conju with you, would you? He has been almost as assiduously overworked as you."

***

AND SO WHEN THEIR MEETING was concluded, Cliopher went to the Offices of State and told Kiri that he had been ordered to take the next day off so his Radiancy could audit his work. Once Kiri stopped laughing, she agreed to let Tully and Zaoul know, chivvied him away from the dispatch cases, and he went back to his apartments feeling guilty about just how pleased he was at the prospect of the next day.

"What is this?" Quintus said, laughing, when he arrived in the parlour his family had taken over for their socializing to find his cousin there by himself. "It's not even sunset, and yet here you are! Don't tell me you're actually done work for the day?"

A thousand and one tasks immediately jumped into his mind—but—"I am," Cliopher said firmly, and sat down. "Where is everyone else?"

Quintus settled himself in the chair next to him. "They went off to look at the menagerie again, on Dora's plaintive request. Having had my fill of lions and tigers and thunder lizards, I decided to spend the afternoon reading some of your very interesting books. You seem particularly interested in contemporary Ystharian culture from your collection?"

"I went on a diplomatic embassy to the Lord of Ysthar last year," Cliopher explained, "and was much amazed by the whole situation there. There aren't that many books written in Shaian. Apart from a handful of people, most of whom have returned from exile on the other worlds, they've lost

Shaian and developed a whole host of other languages. Some Alinorel Scholars have begun to work there, however, now that the Lord of Ysthar is starting to be rather more open to outworld visitors than he was before the end of the Great Game Aurieleteer."

"You went to Ysthar? I don't remember hearing about that! Probably I was out on one of my long voyages. Tell me more! Did you meet the Lord of Ysthar? What was the embassy for? Where did you go? What did you see?"

Cliopher complied, hesitantly at first, expecting as he was the questions to peter off, and then with more enthusiasm when they did not. He described the modest young man who was one of the greatest magi of the Nine Worlds, the strange city where he lived—as big as Csiven or New Dair, but very different in architecture and climate—and all the wonderful devices modern Ystharians used instead of magic, for after the Fall the magic of the world had broken so utterly the Lord of Ysthar had effectively banished its use while he worked to put it back together. Quintus asked eager questions, and he was thoroughly engrossed in the story when he realized the rest of his family had come in and were listening avidly.

They asked him so many questions he carried on over supper, making them laugh and exclaim with awe and amazement at the things he had seen. Finally Vinyë said, when Zemius asked him to repeat a detail, "Let him eat, will you?"

Cliopher laughed with exhilaration (and exhaustion; surely he was not usually so pathetic that interested questions from his family could shape his mood so entirely?) and said, "Now, tell me of your day," and listened with equal interest to Dora's enthusiastic description of all the animals they had seen, and how she had watched a rhinoceros give birth to a "little teeny-tiny rhinoceros baby," and how the hippopotamus had peed so vigorously he'd nearly splashed Uncle Zemius, and had Cousin Kip ever seen that?

"No, I haven't," he admitted, "though I did once see the pride of lions roaring in their sleep."

"You should go see the teeny-tiny rhinoceros baby," she said urgently. "We could go tomorrow!"

"Now, Dora," Aunt Oura said, "you know Cousin Kip is very busy."

"Ah!" said Cliopher, "but tomorrow, as it happens, I have off. I am supposed to make sure I leave the Palace grounds, however, otherwise it's all too likely I shall get drawn into something that is absolutely urgent and tremendously important. But if I'm not physically present, well, probably they will decide it will keep until the next day. It usually does. If you truly wish to go see the menagerie again, we can do so."

"You really and truly can come with us?" Quintus said.

"I really and truly can," Cliopher replied, smiling at their expressions of shock and pleasure and feeling a strong chagrin at how little time he'd spent with them. "His Radiancy has decided to audit my work, so I have the entire day to spend with you."

He addressed himself to the honeyed syllabub that Franzel had supplied for desert, but looked up again when he realized that his family were staring now with shock and concern. "What is it?"

"You're being audited?" Zemius said, in horrified tones. "You must be so worried!"

Cliopher began to laugh before he had quite finished swallowing, choked, coughed, and eventually managed to regain his breath. "Oh no, don't get the wrong idea," he said, grinning and trying not to start laughing again. "His Radiancy is auditing my work to ensure that I spend tomorrow with you. Possibly," he added conscientiously, "his Radiancy will find something he will wish me to change, but I don't imagine it will be anything very major."

"You don't?" asked Gaudy, tentatively, when everyone else besides Dora just continued to stare at him.

"Well, no," he said. "Why should he? I do my job thoroughly and well. If his Radiancy had any concerns or complaints he would have raised them with me already. He may have some suggestions for improvement, but I don't anticipate censure. This is something people never seem to understand about audits. They are there to ensure that standards are met and no one is doing anything underhanded or sloppy or otherwise undesirable, of course, but they are also there so that an outside observer can consider one's work in relation to the whole and provide suggestions based on that external perspective. Done properly they are a gift. In this case, doubly so, because I am exceedingly busy at the moment, as you know, and it would be impossible for me to take the day off without a direct order from his Radiancy. Which he has given me, and so ..."

"Why tomorrow?" his mother asked.

"Oh, I had reserved us tables at a restaurant down in the city a month ago, and, er, happened to mention to his Radiancy that I was not certain whether I could take the entire evening off, given the circumstances."

"To which his response was to give you the whole day?" His mother smiled approvingly. "I am coming to like your lord, Kip."

★★★

IN THE MORNING CLIOPHER DRESSED in the least fancy of his non-official outfits, which Féonie had made after a thorough and dismissive review of his entire wardrobe. Conju arrived as they were eating breakfast, also dressed in unofficial clothing and looking somewhat mutinous, but very pleased to see the various Mdangs.

"What is the day's plan?" he asked after accepting coffee and explaining that he had also been granted, or perhaps *forced to take* was the better phrase, the day off.

"We're heading out of the Palace and into the city, where no one is likely to waylay me for an audience or a committee meeting," Cliopher said. "We are going via the menagerie so that we can observe the baby rhinoceros and hopefully not be weed on by the hippopotamus."

"I haven't been to the menagerie in ages," said Conju, and was promptly collared by Dora so that she could describe all the wondrous animals he would shortly be seeing.

The menagerie was on the western side of the Palace, so Cliopher led them down to the ground floor and around the back of the Throne Room by some of the less-populated corridors, hoping thereby to avoid anyone stopping him.

Although a few people seemed inclined to hail him, he managed to avoid catching their eyes and instead had earnest if somewhat nonsensical conversations with Vinyë every time they passed someone. She was nearly breathless with suppressed laughter when they arrived at the side door to the Throne Room. Dora had to stop to refasten her sandals, and Cliopher, looking unwarily around, was promptly accosted by the guards on duty at the door.

"Lord Mdang," said one of the guards, saluting respectfully.

Cliopher searched his memory and managed to come up with the guard's name. By this point he had met almost the entire rota of the Imperial Guard on duty in the Palace. His Radiancy's outer guards rotated duties with those on the Throne Room, the various Palace doors, and a few other important places and persons—now including himself. "Mauron, isn't it?" he said, feeling a definite sinking sensation and hoping this was not the prelude to some knotted problem that would ruin his day off.

"Yes, m'lord. M'lord, Sayeva Ainura is within the Throne Room, and she asked us to notice whether you came by, and if so, if she could have a few minutes of your time."

"She hasn't asked for an audience ..."

"It was my understanding that it was something she only just now discovered."

Cliopher was about to state as firmly as he could that he was not having meetings today, when it occurred to him that it was not permitted to enter the Throne Room outside of court except under certain very strict protocols of admission and escort—and that between Sayeva Ainura, who was the Keeper of the Throne Room, and himself, those protocols would actually be met. And also, that Sayeva Ainura was a sensible woman and one of her word, and if she said she wanted a few minutes, she meant under ten.

"Very well," he said. "I believe that my presence and Sayeva Ainura's is sufficient for a private visit to the Throne Room, is it not?"

"If you vouchsafe for these people, then certainly, Lord Mdang."

"They are my family," he said simply, and Mauron and his partner (Jenar? Jonal? Jamol, that was it) both saluted magnificently—something all the Imperial Guards did exceptionally well—and then Jamol opened the door and Cliopher ushered them inside the little mirrored vestibule between hall and Throne Room.

"It's not generally permitted to enter the Throne Room outside of court," he said, as his mother shook her head in resigned amusement at him. "But it is worth the small delay it will take for me to deal with Sayeva Ainura for you to see it."

"Are we permitted to go in by this door?" Gaudy asked nervously. "I thought it was forbidden."

"You're with me," Cliopher said, pushing open the inner door and stepping to the side so his family could walk slowly into the most magnificent room in the Nine Worlds. It was even more spectacular without anybody in it, he thought: or without anybody besides the four people engaged in polishing the silver in the floor and the magisterial woman in Amboloyo garb talking with a short stout elderly white man in Alinorel Scholar's robes just behind them. Both of these latter looked over at their entrance and immediately crossed the splendid floor to meet them.

"Lord Mdang," Sayeva Ainura said, curtseying and eyeing his family curiously. "Thank you for coming so promptly. I don't believe you will have met Dominus Earthwright, now of Tara, my lord? He was the second-last Architect-Imperial before the Fall, and once he heard that his Radiancy had re-opened the Imperial Archives, came to complete some research. Dominus Earthwright, this is the Lord Chancellor."

"Yes, I remember your letter of intent," Cliopher replied, bowing slightly to acknowledge the man's more florid and foreign greeting. A few mostly-forgotten notes in Sayeva Ainura's accounts of her work maintaining the

Throne Room came to mind. "Welcome, domine. You were responsible for some of the structural maintenance done before the Fall on this room, were you not?"

"I was, my lord."

"That was what I was hoping to speak to you about, my lord," Sayeva Ainura broke in. "I know you are very busy, but if I could just speak to you for a few minutes—?"

"Do we need Dominus Earthwright?" Cliopher asked, smiling at the Scholar, who was observing the various Mdang family members' reactions to their first sight of the room with nearly proprietary pride.

Sayeva Ainura looked puzzled. "No, not unless you wish to ask him any questions afterwards."

"This is my family," Cliopher said. "His Radiancy has given me today off, but when Mauron mentioned your request, I thought that they might appreciate seeing the Throne Room. Perhaps Dominus Earthwright could take them around the room while we speak?"

"I would be deeply honoured and most pleased," replied the Scholar, bowing deeply again and then offering Cliopher's mother his arm. "Madam, may I escort you? You will observe that we stand now upon Eahh, which as the most remote of the outworlds is placed farthest from the throne …"

"Does your family live here, my lord?" Sayeva Ainura asked, as they followed the Scholar obediently.

"No, they are visiting from the Vangavaye-ve."

"So far! You must not see them often," she said, and then smiled at him. "And I know very well that you do not often have a day off! I am very grateful to you, and will be as brief as possible so you may continue on your way."

"You needn't be *too* brief," Cliopher said dryly, as the little tour party stopped some dozen yards away to marvel at something.

She laughed, and proceeded into a wonderfully concise description of a structural weakness in one of the pillars, Dominus Earthwright's convenient arrival shortly after its discovery, his suggestion for how to fix it, and the fact that it would cost most of the usual yearly budget to do so.

"Would that everyone with whom I had an audience was so concise and organized as you," said Cliopher, when he had absorbed this and been shown the pillar in question and the nearly-invisible fracture that was the problem. "What has caused the fracture?"

"The Palace has been very slowly settling since the Fall, and it seems that this part of the substructure has settled slightly faster than the rest."

"Are we likely to have more of this problem?"

"Hopefully not, though with your permission I will engage some structural engineers and wizards to examine the Palace foundations for any further erratic subsidence. We have caught this fracture early enough that nothing else is damaged, but, of course, if the pillar shattered ..."

"I will find you the necessary funds," Cliopher said, firmly telling himself that tomorrow would be soon enough to begin *that* joyful project. "I am merely grateful that you were able to discover the problem before it becomes more of one."

"It is thanks to you," she said, and when he looked confused (as he must), added: "When his Radiancy fell ill, and you announced that court would be adjourned until he was fully recuperated, you gave me permission to close the Throne Room and do a full clean. Thorough examinations are usually only done when his Radiancy goes on an extended state visit, and as there are none of those planned until he goes for his quest, it would have been a considerable time before we did discover the problem, if we did at all before the pillar started to flake."

Cliopher shuddered at the damage that could have caused to both the physical structure and mystical reputation of the room, and reiterated that Sayeva Ainura should begin her repairs as soon as possible.

Satisfied, she escorted him down the room to where Dominus Earthwright was explaining the window imagery, and, since it was not every day that Cliopher got to see the Throne Room in all its glory—and certainly not every day that he had the leisure to examine it as closely as it warranted, let alone with the guidance of an expert Scholar—well, he gave himself over as happily as his family to a consideration of its wonders.

***

THE RHINOCEROS BABY WAS, AS promised, very teeny-tiny indeed, and quite remarkably adorable. Everyone managed to avoid being pissed on by the hippopotamus, though it was a close call for Cliopher ("Ah," said Conju, laughing, "but you usually do contrive not to get splashed"), and by late morning they had left the Palace grounds behind, with only three more attempts at private audiences—all of which Cliopher was able to put off by sending the solicitors to Tully to make appointments.

When they passed the Imperial Guards at the main gates—who saluted him, to the visible surprise and curiosity of a few nearby bystanders—Cliopher began to feel the weight of his responsibilities slide away, and when they had wound their way out of the immediate open plaza and into the shade of the arcaded streets running down the hill to the main part of the city, he found himself very nearly relaxed, and when they stopped at a small café for coffee and gelato and the barista had obviously not the slightest idea who he was, he was delighted.

"You see," he murmured to Vinyë as they sat on the bench outside the café and watched Conju showing Dora how it was possible to eat gelato with eating sticks, "no one knows who I am down here. It is quite marvellous."

"Oh, Kip," said his sister, squeezing his arm. "Is it horribly selfish of me to want you just to myself for an hour?"

Gaudy was sitting on his mother's other side. He looked up.

"I could take them into the Museum of Natural History, Uncle Kip, and we could meet up again for lunch."

Since this idea was met with general approbation, after agreeing on a location where they would meet, Cliopher and Vinyë went for a walk through the upper city, admiring all the grand houses of the aristocrats who did not like to stay in the Palace when they came to court, and those of all the rich merchants who had made their fortune out of the rebuilding of Solaara after the Fall.

They talked of many things: Vinyë's symphony and her courtship with Hugon the trumpet-player, how Gaudy was doing in the Service, minor gossip about the inhabitants of those grand houses, and she teased him for not having told them what his job was before.

After lunch he walked through the Public Gardens with his mother, while the rest watched the inexhaustible Dora play with a group of local children in the fountains. As they admired the displays of flowers and foliage—especially the collection of water lilies, for which the gardens were justly renowned—they, too, talked, of all the little things they shared in letters but so rarely got to speak of in person.

"It's difficult," Cliopher said, after a companionable silence spent leaning on a railed bridge to admire a bevy of white and black swans. "I miss you terribly so often, but yet ..." He trailed off, shook his head. How could he say, *Here my life, my work, my skills are important; here I am known for myself, not for my relations; here I am able to make a difference?*

"I am not really irreplaceable, I know that." Or at least he had gone to some lengths to create lines of succession that suggested he was not. "But I am needed, and wanted, and I am good at my work and enjoy it. For the most part."

"You liked it better when you were your lord's secretary."

"I did. I did not ask to be elevated, let alone so high."

He wondered if he should talk about his dreams, which were so close now to coming into fruition. But that would be too much like boasting.

His mother smiled at him. "I am proud of you, my Kip. Not because of what you have achieved, though I am proud of that, of course. But I am proud to have as my son someone who is respected and loved by those who work under him and those above him. That tells me as much of your life here as your letters have done. I am very proud that you have never forgotten who you are."

I am Cliopher Mdang of Tahivoa. My island is Loaloa. My dance is Aōteketēta-na.

He had never said that aloud in the Palace, but it was, nevertheless, true.

Cliopher took his mother's hand, grateful in that moment for the simple pleasure of being able to do so (and, the thought came in a flash, not causing intolerable pain or permanent scarring as a result), and he kissed it, smelling her familiar scent, and he said, "When my lord retires I will come home to the Vangavaye-ve for good."

And that, he thought, as his mother gazed piercingly at him, was that.

CHAPTER FORTY-FIVE

THE RESTAURANT SER RHODIN HAD recommended was dark, poky, hot, and stuffed to the gills. The need for a reservation was obvious: Cliopher had to push his way past a quite considerable line-up of hopeful diners to reach the maitre d', who looked overworked, irascible, and blunt.

He murmured his name in the man's ear and was somewhat amused to observe how the bluntness was immediately tempered with a hint of court polish, though he was glad to note a dearth of court obsequiousness. They were ushered to a large table in a back patio, nearly private but for being off the route to the washrooms, and which (apart from said washrooms, which were on the other side of a low wall) had a superb view of the city and the Palace on its hill looking back at them.

After the small rituals of washing and benedictions, they settled into position to watch the sunset flight of birds back to their roosts in the Public Gardens and the fruit bats out on their nightly jaunts. The moon was nearly full and shone yellow on the distant prospect of the sea and the snaking meanders of the River Dwahaii, and there was music, too, from a chamber orchestra on the inner wall.

"Not bad at all," said Vinyë, listening to them.

They chose their meal and their drinks and sat there chatting happily—it was his family, Cliopher thought, awash in wonder and gratitude—and made occasional slightly rude comments about other patrons making their way to and from the washrooms, often on unsteady feet.

"The cocktails are excellently potent," Quintus observed, cocking his eyebrow at a young couple dressed in the height of city fashion—which this year included platform shoes and sequinned turbans—who were giggling over each other as they went stumbling back to the washrooms with obviously other intent in mind.

"Well, if you get too unsteady we can find a sedan chair," Conju said, and added to Cliopher: "Come now, don't be worried about the food. Ser

Rhodin never mistakes a restaurant."

"He never mistakes the trendiness of a restaurant, to be sure."

"The man isn't here to defend himself, but when has he led us astray?"

"There was that food stall in the Sun Plaza—though admittedly the food was very good. Just not their hygiene."

"Oh, yes," said Conju, somewhat taken aback, and on prompting told the story of how they had gone to check out the food stall (on Rhodin's urgent recommendation), and, despite the undoubted excellence of the spicy noodle dishes that were its specialty, had fallen afoul of food poisoning.

"That ended up with Cliopher instituting a license requirement for street food vendors," Conju added. "Which caused no end of trouble, and made for some very dull and expensive food options for a while."

"It cut down on food-borne illness by seventy percent," Cliopher pointed out.

"Ah, but no one has come close to those noodles."

"No doubt it was the decade-old grease they were frying them in."

Conju laughed and launched into another story of one of Rhodin's 'discoveries', and stopped looking quite so frequently back up at the brilliant lights of the Palace.

They were on the third course of the set menu when Quintus, coming back from the washrooms, bumped into a man going up. They exchanged apologies and then surprised greetings, for it turned out that the other man was another merchant captain and they had met in various ports around the Wide Seas over the years.

"But whatever are you doing here, Quintus?" the merchant said, casting a somewhat inebriated eye over their gathering. "You can't have started trading this far, or I'd've heard the news already. Visiting friends?"

"Family, Durig. I've got a cousin in the Lord's Service, and we decided it was about time we came to visit."

Durig brightened with interest, and made an exaggerated wink. "Anybody of influence? Because if your cousin is, you know, possibly there are opportunities ..."

Quintus looked at Cliopher, who tried to forestall him without saying anything, but his cousin merely grinned and said: "I believe he's a man of some influence, yes: he's Kip—er, Cliopher Mdang. Mdong, people say here."

"What, the Lord Chancellor? Strewth! You're not serious?"

"I am. Didn't you notice that our surnames are the same?"

"Captain Mdang ... Lord Mdang ... I suppose they are." Durig shook his head in drunken wonder. "Who'd've thought it."

"What sort of 'opportunities' are you thinking of?"

Durig looked immediately and quite remarkably alarmed, and hastily said: "No, no, ignore that. Don't mention it. Really, don't even joke about it."

Quintus, as Cliopher well knew, had a streak of mischief a mile wide running below his apparently respectable appearance, and now he said: "Come now, Durig, surely there's no reason to be so shy? My cousin—"

"You can't know your cousin very well if you think he'd do anything besides throw you out on your ear," said Durig, leaning on the table. "Strewth. Cliopher Mdang is your cousin. I would never have guessed. Never in a million years."

"What would he really do, do you think?" Quintus asked curiously. "If I said you'd been angling for preferment? I do know my cousin quite well, but of course his working life is here, and we don't see him that often, and not really in his official role."

Durig hesitated, then said: "You promise you won't say anything to him?"

"Not if you tell me why I shouldn't!"

Vinyë, Cliopher saw, was determinedly looking at her plate and biting her lip.

"Well," said Durig, with a great sigh, "I suppose I had better tell you. The Lord Chancellor is hell on kickbacks, bribes, backscratching, and any other sort of preferential treatment due to money or relation that an honest businessman might feel inclined to experimenting with.

"If you were to go to him and say I'd been angling for preferment on the basis of knowing you ... well, that wouldn't be anything direct and actionable, but I'd get nary a government contract going forward, and everyone would know why. No, that's not fair: and the Lord Chancellor is *very* fair. I'd get a government contract if it was absolutely positively clear that my company was the best for the job at hand. Anything where there's two or three bidders and they're much the same? I'd never get one. Aye, only if I could demonstrate that I was by far the best candidate."

"That does seem very fair," Quintus ventured.

"He is appallingly fair-minded," Durig said, sighing again. "I tell you, when he came to prominence there were people who thought he was going to be *such* an easy target. A nobody from the Islands? A coconut on the ground, as they say. The only question was whether it was money, power, or prestige he wanted most."

Now nobody was looking at Cliopher, not even Conju. Quintus cleared his throat. "And what was the answer?"

Durig snorted. "Neither. I don't think anyone knows what he wants, unless it really is just to make things run properly. Which is terrifying in its own way. The man is purer than a new fire and about as good an idea to mess with."

Cliopher wondered what the others thought of that particular analogy. The Mdangs were Those Who Hold the Fire; not that he ever spoke of such things with anybody. He glanced around, but they were all apparently riveted on Durig, who drank half of Quintus' water down before shaking his head at their imploring looks.

"I'll tell you a story I heard. I don't know if it's true, but everyone thinks it is. One day a good few years ago now, the Lord Emperor decided he wanted to reward Lord Mdang for something, and gave him a raise in his pay without telling him. Just went through the Treasury, I guess. Anyway, when pay-day came around, and he got so much more than he was expecting, do you know what Lord Mdang did? *He sent it back.* All of it, with a note saying the Treasury had made a mistake."

Conju made a choking noise and drank a hasty gulp of his cocktail. Quintus laughed robustly. "That does sound like something my cousin would do."

"Aye, and then you know what happened? He set up a system of audits through all the government ministries. That's what would happen, aye, if I started angling. First he'd put me on the List as a name to watch for contract biddings, then he'd go through all my paperwork, then he'd probably set his sights on the whole Ministry of Marine Transport and Trade and call for a full audit. And wouldn't they be happy when they heard why! Not that it mightn't be a good idea for some of *their* books to be looked into."

Despite himself, Cliopher made a mental note to suggest to Kiri that Marine Transport and Trade should perhaps move up in the list of ministries to be audited.

"Wouldn't the audit just, oh, show them some ways they could be better at their jobs?" Quintus asked, with a sly glance at Cliopher that Durig, fortunately, completely missed.

"Hah! If they were doing their jobs in the first place, aye, I'm sure it would. The State Auditors are hellishly thorough."

"Surely they'd appreciate that it was over and done with, if he audits all the ministries in turn?"

"That's the beauty of the system. Aye, he's fair as the sea and about as implacable, is the Lord Chancellor. It's done randomly, and sometimes the same ministry gets hit twice, even three times in a row. You see, in the beginning it was more regular, and everyone knew what ministry was getting done next, so they could prepare, aye, and make sure everything looked just right for the auditors. Then one day his excellency must have suspected something, for he sent the auditors back again a year later to—oh, I think it was Fisheries that time. And it turned out that Fisheries had agreed to all of the recommendations and hadn't put any of them into place."

"If it had only been a year …"

Durig chuckled. "Aye, they argued that, too. And the Lord Chancellor went through the reports—personally, I do believe it was—and pointed out every single recommendation that they should have done within the year, and he fined some of the upper bureaucrats and told them to get on with it. And of course all they did was a few of the easiest things, and then when they thought he'd gone on to something else they just went back to their old ways."

"And then?" Quintus said, in evident fascination. Cliopher contemplated kicking him, but wasn't sure he wouldn't hit Aunt Oura instead.

"And then Fisheries was audited a third time a year later, and that time measures were taken. I think the top sixteen people were charged with wilful negligence and desertion of duty, the Minister and three others were executed for *gross* negligence, and the rest of the ministry lost their jobs and had to reapply with everyone else to be reappointed. Something like only one in three was deemed sufficiently good to return to their posts. Ever since then people have been much more careful about implementing the suggestions."

"Oh," said Quintus, looking slightly stunned.

"After that the audits were assigned randomly, or maybe there's some other method, but it seems random outside those offices. Strewth, I can't believe I even started to joke with you about angling with the Hands of the Emperor. Might as well suggest asking the Emperor himself for a favour— though then again, probably he'd be more likely to grant one, since the Lord Chancellor is the one making sure everything runs tickety-boo under him. What a hell of a job that must be. Don't get me wrong, I think it's great he's cleaned up the Service. And it's great he's a nobody from the Islands, because it means he listens to people—really listens, I mean—and he's not at all snobby."

"That I am glad to hear," Quintus said gravely.

Durig snorted. "My wife's third cousin—see, Quintus, you're not the only one with cousins—works in the Ministry of the Natural World, and he was sent a couple of days ago to explain something to do with some extension to the sea train they're thinking of doing up in Mgunai.

"He's very small fish, is my wife's cousin, but he was granted an appointment the same day as the Princess of Mgunai, and the Lord Chancellor listened to everything he had to say and asked him for a full written report and analysis of the problem, and was very polite and everything, and you just know he'll weigh all that with whatever the Princess said, and make sure when the Lord Emperor hears about it he hears all sides of the topic. That's how fair he is. Why, it's said he's the one person the Lord Emperor trusts to make state decisions besides him. And that's how good he is at his job. And man, do I need the privy. Cheerio, Quintus, and don't say anything to your cousin. Lord Mdang, huh, really."

He pushed himself back heavily from the table, shook his head again, and made his way to the washrooms. Cliopher cleared his throat when he had gone, then couldn't think of anything to say.

Conju said, "I recall when that bit about your pay raise came out. I've rarely heard his Radiancy laugh as much as he did when he heard."

"I'm glad to know I provide some amusement to others," Cliopher replied, "as it appears no one thinks I have a sense of humour myself. Though I would like to point out that I had had six bribery attempts in the two months before that happened, and was feeling fed up with half the Service."

"Six?" said Vinyë, looking as if she didn't know whether to laugh or be appalled.

"It was when we were negotiating the Littleridge Treaty, and there were a lot of very worried people about. I received death threats, too." Cliopher shook his head.

Conju said slyly, "And when it all settled, everyone turned around and congratulated themselves on how brilliantly they'd solved all their problems, and your name was never mentioned at all."

He made a noise half of agreement, half of annoyance with Conju for bringing that up. Gaudy said shyly, "You introduced Sayo Oldis as working on that treaty with the Ministry of Culture. What was it for?"

Cliopher blinked and frowned. "Didn't you learn about it in school?"

"I think I remember it was mentioned in the *Ring o'News*," Zemius offered, when Gaudy looked mortified. "No one made much of it."

Cliopher took three deep breaths, released them, and said mildly: "The Littleridge Treaty was what established the current boundaries of the seventeen principalities, their hierarchy, their rights and responsibilities with respect to both his Radiancy as Lord of Zunidh and to their citizens, and concluded the Century of Wars with the peace that continues to this day. It is something that every Zuni child really should learn about as part of their basic education."

"Perhaps you need to revisit the Ministry of Education," Conju said with a grin, and added to the rest: "As you may have gathered, Cliopher was at the very centre of the negotiations as the Chair of the upper council, and, of course, as his Radiancy's secretary. It's a very worthy legacy. Even if your name isn't mentioned in the popular documents. Or by anyone."

Cliopher was grateful to be interrupted by the waiters bringing the dessert course and trays of coffee and liqueurs.

★★★

WALKING BACK UP THE LONG slope to the Palace, he found himself arm-in-arm with Quintus while Conju strolled with his mother. "This has been a lovely day," Cliopher said, refusing to think about what work awaited him for the next.

"You're easy to please," Quintus replied, chuckling. "What do you have planned for tomorrow?"

"It's the monthly market down in the lower city, which I thought everyone would enjoy. I'm going to have to see what's come up today, alas."

"And the results of his Radiancy's audit of your work. Perhaps he will give you another raise you can send back to the Treasury."

Cliopher laughed, knowing that Quintus was a far wealthier man than he would ever be, and not caring in the least. "We'll just have to wait and see."

But in the morning, as Cliopher was eating a relatively leisurely breakfast with his family and wondering where on earth Tully and Zaoul had gotten to with his diary of appointments, the door opened not on any of his secretaries but on his Radiancy himself.

"My lord!" Cliopher cried, shocked, as everyone scrambled to their feet, and blurted out his next thought: "The stairs!"

His Radiancy stopped with his hand on the back of the nearest empty chair to stare at him. "I beg your pardon?"

It was not Cliopher's place to offer any public criticism of his Radiancy, so he made the formal genuflection. "My apologies, my lord, I was surprised to see you here."

His Radiancy seated himself and made a gesture for everyone else to return to their seats. "To assuage your concerns, Lord Mdang, there are elevators running the height of the Tower. Certain of my forebears were incapable of managing the stairs up to the Imperial Apartments. While I am feeling much recovered, I assure you I am sensible to the suggestions of my physician and did, in point of fact, make use of them."

Cliopher felt himself blushing with embarrassment. "I rejoice to see you in such better health, my lord."

"I always worry when you begin with courtly phrasing, Kip." His Radiancy smiled and made vague gestures of benediction to Cliopher's family. "It is a pleasure to see you all this morning. I am here to discuss the results of my audit of your recent activities, Lord Mdang."

"Would you like us to leave, Glorious One?" Eidora asked promptly, making as if to stand.

"No, no," his Radiancy said. "I think you will perhaps find the results illuminating. Ser Tkinele, the books, please."

Zaoul was standing by the door next to Zerafin and Varro, Cliopher saw. He showed far more sign of nerves than usual, and brought forward Cliopher's familiar diary of appointments to set on the table beside his Radiancy.

His Radiancy moved several items out of the way with a carelessness that Cliopher found endearing, knowing as he did that Conju would have been fretting madly to see his Radiancy doing anything so manual himself. He then opened up the book, flipping through to a certain section, whereupon he placed them in the centre of the table. "Will you explain these pages, Lord Mdang?"

Cliopher looked down at the familiar pages. The spread covered the current ten-day period, with the hours down the side and each day separated out into columns across the pages.

He used a combination of coloured inks and scribal shorthand to block out the periods of time for each sort of activity; more specific appointments were now the province of Tully. These were all in the green he used for his personal time, with a few exceptions in the brown ink for the Helma Council and other budgetary matters, the black ink for attending on his Radiancy, the blue for his work in the Private Offices. It was not a full holiday, but it had been close.

"Those were my plans for this week and part of last, my lord," he said at last.

His Radiancy nodded and turned over the page to show the next spread. These pages were crowded, crammed full of a rainbow of inks that ran heavily to blue, brown, black, and the red and orange he used for the princes and other ceremonial tasks. From the first hour of the day through till midnight the appointments and sudden urgent meetings and the time blocked off for reports and responses and more reports proliferated.

Each day he had tried to put in at least four half-hour blocks of green for his meals and his family. Most of them were criss-crossed by a line in another colour when some emergency had taken him away again.

"And these?"

He was not sure whose eye he wished least to meet. "My lord, those record what I actually have done in that period."

His Radiancy flipped back to the original spread, which seemed remarkably light and open compared to the second. "Ser Tkinele, do you have a pen to hand?"

Cliopher, of course, did, and presented it to his Radiancy before Zaoul had managed to finish stuttering that he had one. "Thank you, Cliopher." His Radiancy regarded him for a moment and turned to the next two spreads. "I see that you had planned to go to the market in the lower city today, and tomorrow go down the river to the port, with supper at the River-Horse at the edge of the Fens."

"Yes, my lord."

He watched his Radiancy turn the page to the new schedule, which was only half-filled in from the last week's developments but managed to be so thoroughly full that Cliopher felt exhausted just looking at it.

His Radiancy lifted the pen and hovered it above the page for a moment as if looking for the best place to add in an item. Cliopher wondered what it would be, and hoped, with a savage, embarrassed hope, that it would be a line through the next Council of Princes meeting, which was set down in all its vicious red for the day he had hoped to be going down the river instead.

His Radiancy shook his head. "No. I have a better idea." He set the pen down and then ripped out the page with the new schedule. Cliopher made an involuntary sound of protest, which made his Radiancy smile before turning his head. "Ser Tkinele, you will act as my secretary for the next week. Cliopher, follow your original plan. We shall discuss the evident need to reform your job description once your family have returned to the Vangavaye-ve."

CHAPTER FORTY-SIX

THE LAST DAY BEFORE HIS family left, Cliopher entered the Imperial Apartments to find Varro and Zerafin standing at rigid attention, Zaoul looking as if he were trying to disappear into his desk, and his Radiancy pacing as he dictated, hands gesturing, robes flaring, mellifluous voice edged.

His Radiancy was having a bad day.

One of the things that had changed since his Radiancy's heart attack was that he now had bad days.

Oh, they were not bad days the way other people Cliopher had worked for and with had bad days—there were no flying objects, nor abrupt dismissals nor (perish even the thought) abrupt executions—but for someone who had hitherto displayed the most even and serene of tempers, the eruptions of visible impatience, frustration, even humour were disquieting.

Each day of his holiday Cliopher had checked punctiliously that he was not bidden to attend his lord, and each morning he had been firmly informed by Tully that he was not. The rumours around the Palace had him overstepping and annoying his Radiancy, and he knew that there were bets as to whether he had overstepped far enough to lose his position or his life.

Only he and his family knew the real reason for the sudden decrease in his responsibilities.

Cliopher cherished every moment of the holiday and did his best to keep from spending all his time thinking of how he and his Radiancy could use this furlough and those rumours to further their various political aims.

This morning was, alas, back to real work. Originally his family had been supposed to leave the day before, but the weather was inclement over the Wide Seas and Captain Diogen had preferred to wait for the storm to move north before he set sail.

Cliopher could not regret having an extra day with them, but he had not entirely minded that he had to return to work this morning, either. It was amazing what ten days of luxurious sleep and lazy occupation could do to make him once again eager to engage his mind with all the puzzles with which he was daily presented.

"And if my lord Chancellor were—ah!" said his Radiancy, swinging around suddenly from the further point of his pacing to see Cliopher standing there. "There you are. Go to, ser Tkinele. We shall not need you until after lunch."

Zaoul murmured something inaudible but no doubt polite, gathered his papers, made his obeisance, and fled. His Radiancy watched the door shut behind him as Cliopher knelt and was gestured briskly up.

"The best since you," his Radiancy said, "but for a Tkinele tribesman, he is remarkably soft-spoken."

"There are few who can, or choose to try, to stand up to you, my lord," Cliopher replied, setting his stack of dispatch cases down on the table. His Radiancy eyed them with noticeable revulsion, and Cliopher sighed inwardly at how difficult the next hour was going to be, since the first topic of the day was convoluted and dealt with a situation that his Radiancy had never been very keen on even before his illness.

"Hmm," said his Radiancy, swinging around so his skirts flared out. "I regret every day that you are no longer my secretary, but it must be said you make a superb Lord Chancellor. What is of first importance today, my lord?"

Cliopher opened the first of the dispatch cases. "It is the matter of the Nijani police service and the duke—"

His Radiancy opened his mouth to speak, looked dourly at him, and began to laugh. "Your face is a study in politics all by itself, Kip. I will not bite your head off because it is the Nijani police service, again. Come, lay out before me what has happened this time."

The Nijani police service was not even the worst of it, as Cliopher well knew, but he breathed an inward sigh of relief and laid out the matter as succinctly as he could. His Radiancy responded even more succinctly, Cliopher wrote the decision down in somewhat less pungent language, and turned to the next matter, a report from Mgunai on the progress of the sea train extension via a new aqueduct that promised to revolutionize the trains' possible usefulness on land if they could manage to make it work.

That was easily enough dealt with, and so too was the query from Southern Dair about a new provincial sumptuary tax they were considering, and a few other smaller matters. An hour and a half of solid work saw a month of Cliopher's work (and that of his department) finalized, formalized, and done, and he was feeling very pleased indeed with the day's results. There remained two hours yet of his Radiancy's time, and only one more issue to resolve.

Or, well, begin.

"My lord, the next topic is one you asked me to put on the agenda, regarding the next stage of preparations for your quest."

His Radiancy steepled his fingers. "Ah, yes. Have I mentioned how impressed I have been by your work when I was indisposed?"

Cliopher smiled. "You have."

"Would you like to be made the Duke of Ikiano?"

There was a pause. Cliopher stared at him. That was a title belonging to the Vangavaye-ve, empty since the Fall.

No. It was a title belonging to the Imperial power structure overlaying the traditional hierarchy of status in the Vangavaye-ve.

He could just imagine what his family would think if he announced he was taking on one of those Imperial titles. It was one thing to be the Lord Chancellor far away in Solaara, where all that was important about the position were the official proclamations coming down from the Offices of State and how it affected how often he wrote letters home. To have such a title at home ...

His Radiancy smiled mischievously. "I thought that would be your response." He sighed with mock regret. "Ah, well, I suppose I shall just have to make you Viceroy of Zunidh instead."

"My lord!"

"We will talk about the full ramifications next week," his Radiancy said. "To begin with, I would like you to speak with the Chief Archivist about the Imperial seigneurial ceremonies, those by which authority was delegated from the Emperor to the lords magi. Come now, Kip, don't look so thoroughly stunned! You must have been expecting something of the sort? Your family are leaving tomorrow: it is time to confound our court with the fact that you have been honoured, not disgraced, by the past fortnight's holiday."

Cliopher realized he was staring open-mouthed.

His Radiancy laughed, then glanced past him. "Yes, Zerafin, what is it?"

"The high priests, my lord."

His Radiancy sighed, good humour retreating behind the serenity. "You will get to experience this soon, Cliopher, little as you will relish it. I had forgotten the ceremony would fall today. It will not be more than a quarter-hour, Cliopher."

"I will attend, my lord," he assured him. He could assure him on *that* point, at least.

His Radiancy nodded at the guards to let the new high priests in. They were in their ceremonial regalia, one dressed as the Sun and the other as the Moon, in robes and masks of gold and silver. The Sun priest bore a brazier of smoking incense, the Moon priest a silver ewer of water. Cliopher did not yet know them well enough to identify as individuals. So far neither had shown any inclination towards playing the political games of their predecessors.

They arranged themselves around his Radiancy in the bare stone-floored corner of the room where his Radiancy performed certain spells. Cliopher went through his notes from the earlier resolutions and began to prepare the final drafts to be taken for copying down below.

He did not want to think about that blithe upturning of his world.

The ritual of purification outwardly involved chanting, complex motions of brazier and ewer, careful stylized washings of hands and feet, gestures and certain powders thrown onto the brazier to make poofs of coloured smokes that his Radiancy had to breathe, or run his hands through in certain gestures, or the like.

What was going on below the surface Cliopher did not have the magic to know, but he could tell, from the sparkles gathering about his Radiancy and from a certain crystalline quality to the chanting and the light, that there were very deep magics going on indeed.

The priests left after a quarter of an hour, and his Radiancy came back to his chair. He sat down this time, and looked, to Cliopher's concerned eye, as if he had spent the previous quarter-hour under torture. No longer smiling, even in his eyes where the laughter usually lurked unexpressed but just visible, he was drawn, bleak, tired, and his hands trembled.

"My lord," Cliopher began, but his Radiancy said, "It is what it is."

"My lord," he said again, and pulled over his notes of his first questions about the Viceroyship.

He spoke for a short while before it became clear his Radiancy was paying very little attention. He stopped speaking and waited patiently until his Radiancy noticed, frowned, and spoke. "You have stopped, Cliopher."

"My lord," Cliopher said quietly, "this can wait until another day."

His Radiancy looked at the dispatch case and then at the two stolid guards, and he sighed, and he said: "I should keep working, Kip. It doesn't help to be idle."

Idle was not a word Cliopher ever felt like ascribing to his Radiancy. He cast about for something useful to do that did not require focused attention, and after a moment was able to say: "My lord, there is a Scholar from Stoneybridge University on Alinor who has come to the Archives and has presented a request for an audience with you."

"From Stoneybridge?" his Radiancy said, with a very slight flare of interest. "What is his name?"

"She is Domina—Black," said Cliopher, consulting the notebook where he listed such incidental matters. "Professor of late Astandalan history."

"Black ... I have read one of her books," his Radiancy said, looking more intrigued. "She was very forthright and insightful in her judgments and opinions. I wonder if she will be anywhere near so forthright in person?"

Cliopher smiled. "Shall I send for her, my lord? She will be in the Archives below."

His Radiancy considered for a moment, looking down at the dispatch case, and at his hands, the signet ring and the gold-lacquered nails and the slight tremble, and his hands slowly closed into fists, and then he said, "Yes."

★★★

HIS RADIANCY DID NOT DISMISS him, so after sending the page Cliopher tidied away his papers and sat waiting for conversation, instruction, or dismissal. His Radiancy stood up to pace again, and after a few minutes said abruptly, "I told you how, as Emperor, I was magically disconnected from everything so that I might be joined again according to the rituals and orders of Schooled magic?"

"Yes, my lord," Cliopher replied, just managing not to add, 'more or less'.

His Radiancy stopped to look out the window at the city below him. "And although when the Empire fell that joining was broken in many ways, because the ceremonies and taboos were continued, many of the magical elements were retained ... I am being, for the first time, stripped of all the Schooled magic.

"It is ... hard, because the magic is not mine, it is alien to me, it is not part of my own magic, but yet ... for so long I have had to work within and around and through it, it is as if I—I don't know, as if my hands have been in gloves for so long they have become tender and almost joined to the glove. And now for the first time in so long the gloves are being drawn off, and although I know I will have much better ability to touch soon—"

He laughed, bitterly, at the phrase. "Not simply metaphorically. That will be later, when I will be able to touch with impunity. Now, I feel ... tender and vulnerable and sore and ... itchy."

"Itchy? My lord?" Cliopher said before he could stop himself.

"Itchy all over but inside myself," his Radiancy said, making a large gesture eloquent of frustration and skin-crawling revulsion. "I have been a hybrid mage for so long, with some of my inner powers quiescent, and now they are waking up but I am still within the bars of my cage, the ceremonies are barely begun, it will still be a year or more before I can... I am so *restless*, Kip."

"I am sorry, my lord."

"It is what it is," his Radiancy said again, "but I will be delighted when the process is over."

"I understand, my lord." Cliopher was remembering having chicken pox, and the unbearable desire to scratch oneself bloody to relieve the itchiness, and trying to imagine that being all one's inward sensation. He twitched in sympathetic reaction, and hastily turned back to his notes. A few moments later the guards announced Domina Black.

Domina Black was short and petite compared to most Zuni women. She was dressed in the simple black robes of an Alinorel Scholar, with bands of embroidery representing her university and discipline along its hems and lining the hood. Underneath she wore some sort of rich blue skirts that swished attractively as she walked and as she performed her obeisance. She had sleek black hair with some silver hairs mixed in, which she wore plaited and pinned into a kind of coronet. Her skin was a rich coppery brown, her features sharp and un-Shaian, not at all classically beautiful, and she looked, Cliopher thought, just about familiar—

He had a sudden image of her sitting on an elephant.

"Rise, domina," said his Radiancy, walking over from the window embrasure so he could see her better.

She rose up gracefully, and lifted her chin and regarded him.

Cliopher whipped his head around to look at his lord, who looked as if he were about to have another heart attack.

They stared at each other, Last Emperor and Scholar, his Radiancy's face shocked and nearly grim, his eyes wide with amazement and chagrin and regret and desire and a whole host of other emotions Cliopher could not even dare to begin to name.

She said nothing, but she did not drop her eyes, either.

After a very strained pause his Radiancy said abruptly, "We will continue this audience on the terrace. Bring refreshments." He swung around and strode to the terrace door, which opened as he neared. The guards fell into their places behind him and were gestured sharply to their positions by the door. Domina Black gazed after him with an arrested expression.

"I believe his Radiancy desires you to follow, domina," Cliopher prompted when she did not move even after he reached for the bell-pull.

She gave him a surprised glance, shook her head at herself, and smiled briefly at him. "Thank you," she said, and if Cliopher was feeling unsettled by his Radiancy's bad day, by the fear of another heart attack, by the threat of his own new position, by the sudden thought that this woman was quite possibly the love of his Radiancy's life—

Well, in that smile and in that brief phrase, he saw why.

He sat back, watching her walk across the familiar study to the terrace, with a smile for the guards and then a more guarded and serious smile for his Radiancy. He felt shaken to his core. He looked down at his hands braced flat on the table, then up at the superlative vase.

He could not help but wonder whether he had ever touched someone like that, in a lightning flash of spiritual illumination. After a moment he turned back to his papers, smiling ruefully to himself at the acknowledgement that his effects on the world were much less splendid. He was not an artist of anything but the hidden intricacies underlying government bureaucracy, and no one else actually cared whether those were beautiful or not.

But they were, he assured himself, attention stealing past the vase at the glorious man and woman who stood outside in their garments of black and gold and white and blue, light pouring down from a burnished sky upon them as if they were gods standing there. Cliopher's life might seem dull as a wave-worn stone, awaken no marvel or wonder or astonishment in an onlooker, but he had used it as best he could to build what he might, and he could be content with that.

★★★

THE CONVERSATION ON THE TERRACE was inaudible. Domina Black stood before his Radiancy, back straight, head high, eyes up, and said something that the wind whipped away. His Radiancy, looking down at her, visibly struggling for his usual serenity, shook his head and made the sliding gesture of the spell that ensured a certain degree of aural privacy for his conversation.

There was, of course, no visual privacy.

When Conju came in response to the bell-pull Cliopher directed him to bring refreshments for both lord and guest, the phrase his Radiancy had used being the code for that.

Conju brought out tea and ginger biscuits and at his Radiancy's gesture poured for them both before departing again. After a further moment of them staring straight at each other, his Radiancy directed the Scholar to her seat and took his own.

Domina Black sat down with perfect composure. From his desk Cliopher could see their two profiles, though not as clearly their expressions because of the angles of light and shadow under the terrace's awning. His Radiancy looked almost exactly as he did in the formal profile portrait used for coins; Domina Black, in deeper shadow but lighter-skinned, was starting to recover her poise.

Within two minutes she was passionate. Within five his Radiancy had lost his habitual serenity and was looking vibrantly alive and also thoroughly annoyed.

Cliopher did his best to work on his reports, but the gestures were as loud as the silenced words certainly were. The guards stood at formal attention, ready for the merest hint from his Radiancy that the Scholar was no longer welcome. But his Radiancy, fighting (as Cliopher could see) to retain decorum, never looked at them, and the Scholar, her colour heightening and her own gestures growing more energetic and wild, was utterly focused on him.

She reached out to touch his hand. His Radiancy recoiled.

His abrupt movement stopped the argument. They stared at each other without speaking for a while, the Scholar with her hand still outstretched, his Radiancy with his hands folded in his lap out of reach. And then she said something, half a dozen words perhaps, and waited.

His Radiancy looked at her with an expression of terrible yearning breaking through the blank serenity.

His Radiancy had not looked that way at the Moon, Cliopher thought, and wondered what the Scholar was offering him that the Moon Lady had not.

(*But that*, he had said, *is not my heart's desire.*)

But his Radiancy closed his eyes and shook his head and said, with a finality that could be felt in every gesture and must have resonated in the air, No.

Domina Black sat back in her chair and stared in disbelief and disappointment and something that Cliopher read as coming close to betrayal. After a long moment her features firmed, she recovered her own poise, and decorously asked something. To be dismissed, it appeared, for his Radiancy made the appropriate gesture and then, seeming to feel something, did her the unnecessary and once-unthinkable courtesy of getting up to escort her through from the terrace and into the study where Cliopher did his best to fade into the furnishing.

The silencing spell was local to the place in which it was cast, and so when his Radiancy said, "I am sorry, you know," Cliopher heard it.

Domina Black stopped and looked at him, and around the beautiful room with its superb furnishings, and with mockery and bitter disappointment she said, "Are you?"

And she performed the full formal obeisance with as much grace as she had on entering, and to his Radiancy's continuing silent glower she rose again and departed.

His Radiancy watched her go, his face stark with loss and devastation.

After a long, uncertain silence, his Radiancy staring at the closed door, Cliopher watching him, the guards watching with blank faces, his Radiancy turned to Cliopher and said with false heartiness, "What was that question about signing authority again?"

To Cliopher's considerable disbelief his Radiancy sat down in his chair and looked expectantly at him.

All his training and knowledge of etiquette and the rules of correct behaviour and his Radiancy's rank and preferences and everything he had done for all the long years of his service shouted at him to follow his Radiancy's cue, but all their considerable clamour was silenced by a sudden revolt in his soul.

"To hell with the Viceroyship!"

There was a short shocked pause, from the guards, from Cliopher's own mind, from his Radiancy. "I beg your pardon?" said his Radiancy, in a voice that Cliopher would usually have considered dangerous.

"My lord," Cliopher said with recklessness—but had his Radiancy not called him his *friend*? Almost his *family*? Who else was there to perform this office for him? "My lord, you cannot button it away."

"I nearly think you said I *cannot*."

"Oh, you *can*, no doubt: you can hide your feelings and suppress your heart and soul and all that makes you a man, and be merely the Last Emperor of Astandalas and the Lord of Zunidh. You can do so. But if you do, now, today, in this moment, you will lose your soul."

"How dare you speak so to me?" his Radiancy said, fury starting to spark gold in his eyes.

Cliopher set down his pen and stood up and stood with his shaking hands gripping the back of his chair and said: "Who else is going to? My lord, you have asked me to remember that you are a man. I am doing so. And I tell you, my lord, that if you let her go like that you will lose yourself for good."

There was a pause.

"You overreach yourself, sir. You are dismissed," his Radiancy said icily, and that, he supposed, was that.

CHAPTER FORTY-SEVEN

HE MADE THE FULL FORMAL obeisance and departed, feeling as if his heart were breaking in seven ways at once.

He made his way unsteadily down to his rooms, finding his mother and sister sitting in his back room. They took one look at him and came crowding round with concern and love, sat him down and plied him with coffee.

"I think," he said in response to a question, "that I have overstepped."

There was a pause, and then his sister said quietly, "What does that mean?"

Cliopher shuddered and hunched over his coffee cup and did not know what to tell them. He made a helpless gesture and then he said: "Possibly it will just mean I come back to the Vangavaye-ve with you."

There was another pause, and then Vinyë said, "Oh, no, Kip."

"Or," he continued grimly, trying to face up to the worst, "it may mean the executioner."

But that was not the worst. The worst was—was—

The door was flung open and Conju stormed in. "What are you doing down here?" he cried to Cliopher, who jumped and spilled coffee all over himself. "He needs you."

Cliopher swallowed. "He sent me away."

"His Radiancy sent you—what did you say to him?"

"Something Kip thinks is close to treason," Vinyë said when Cliopher just shook his head and tried not to think about how quickly one could destroy one's life.

"Close to *treason*?"

"Five steps past," Cliopher said, something sparking in him. "Did you think me utterly incapable of it?"

Conju stared at him and said, very simply: "Yes."

Cliopher looked down at the coffee staining his robes and willed them all to leave him to his misery.

What happened instead was that the door banged open again and again he instinctively looked up, to see Ludvic Omo storming in nearly as angrily as Conju. He halted in the middle of the room to stare and speak with dangerous intensity. "What did you *say* to him?"

"He says he has committed treason," Conju said.

"What the hell!" cried Ludvic Omo, with such force that Cliopher leaned back. "Treason? Treason, you call it! Treason? How could *you* possibly even *begin* to think—" He staggered off into oaths of breathtaking pungency, then stomped forward and grabbed Cliopher by the wrist.

Ludvic was many times physically stronger than Cliopher, and he had perforce to stand when the guard pulled him upright. "You are coming with me," he said through gritted teeth.

Cliopher dug in his heels. "Is that a formal request?"

Ludvic, tugging him unceremoniously towards the door, stopped abruptly. He looked with stricken face at Cliopher, who was trying to catch his breath. "You really think—"

"His Radiancy dismissed me," Cliopher said unevenly. "I have overstepped my place. Yes, Commander Omo, I really think this could be a formal summons."

Conju made a noise of dismay and disbelief. Vinyë and his mother were standing next to each other. Ludvic let go of his hand and more gently said, "What did you say?"

Cliopher swallowed hard. "You remember when we were on Lesuia and his Radiancy made that illusion of the woman on the elephant?"

They nodded, faces blank.

"She came for an audience today. I told—I told his Radiancy afterwards that—" He felt as if he had forgotten how to swallow, wiped his face harshly with his hands. "That—" It was far too personal, he thought, to say it—"He is a human being," he burst out, in a kind of wail. "Inside—despite everything—he has fought so hard to keep some part of himself free—and I could see when she walked out the door that he—he was losing—he was destroying, and I—how could I not say something?"

"Oh, Kip," Vinyë whispered.

His mother said, "But is that treason?"

Cliopher did not say anything. After a moment, Conju said carefully, "In a word, yes."

"There is no way," Ludvic burst out, "that his Radiancy would consider that treasonous from you. He loves you as a brother."

"He sent me away," Cliopher whispered, hearing that icy voice, seeing the inner man disappear behind the opaque Radiancy, guessing just a bit of what had made Domina Black sick with betrayal. If she had not had merely the admirable Radiancy—but had once known the inner man whose merest glimpses Cliopher loved so deeply—

Ludvic rocked back on his heels, looked down at the golden scars marking his hands. "You took me by the hand and dragged me to wake his Radiancy at ten minutes to midnight so that he would make the determination of whether the broken taboo meant death. You could have been chastened then—could very easily have been reprimanded."

"You did not see how he looked."

Conju said, "It sounds as if he is dismantling his private study with a private thunderstorm."

"Please come," Ludvic said. "You forget I am not on duty. I was asked."

"He *dismissed* me," Cliopher said, his voice cracking. "Are you suggesting I go counter to a direct order?"

They looked at each other intently, he and Ludvic and Conju, the air heavy with anxiety and fear. Conju backed down; but Ludvic said, in his usual phlegmatic way, "How deeply do you love him?"

The question hung in the air.

And Cliopher remembered then that his Radiancy had already been having a difficult day, that the purification ceremony had seemed to be something more literally torture; that his Radiancy had been trying to hold back his impatience for the period yet remaining before he could walk through the door of freedom; that his Radiancy could not touch or be touched; that he hated it. That the woman he still obviously loved after so long had reached out to him and in fear and horror he had recoiled, and lost her.

And that even if Cliopher was not Domina Black, did not walk through the world like a thunderstrike, nevertheless he could do his best, and that if that meant he was to be executed for his love, then he would do what he could beforehand.

And so it was that Cliopher walked up the two flights of stairs and over the three hallways to the familiar doors of the Imperial Apartments. No orders had been given; the three chief members of his Radiancy's household were saluted in without challenge.

Zerafin and Varro had been succeeded by Pikabe and Ato, both of whom were looking set and strained at the noises coming out of his Radiancy's private study. The main study itself looked exactly as it always did, formal and beautiful and calm. The noises consisted of thumps, sudden cracks, and a few sharp retorts and crashes. It was not in any way a happy sound.

Cliopher walked over to the long wall with the map on it and the one forbidden door, and he took a deep breath and in a gap in the noises knocked loudly.

There was no answer. He counted to fifty and knocked again. Again, nothing but the noises. He looked over his shoulder at Ludvic and Conju, who were standing uncertainly in the middle of the room. Had a sudden memory of his Radiancy coming down with champagne to ask whether his nephew had succeeded in the examinations.

If he was going to be executed for the treason of treating his Radiancy as a person, he might as well go all the way with it.

Knocked again, and this time into the ensuing silence he said: "Tor."

He felt, rather than heard, the shock of the four men behind him.

His heart was hammering in his throat. There was a dead silence, and then the door opened a few inches.

It opened inwards, and his Radiancy was standing behind it, his back to the light, his face in shadow. Cliopher guessed his own face was fully illuminated from the windows and lights in the main study.

"You were dismissed," his Radiancy said.

His voice was still icy, his eyes—pretty well all Cliopher could see of him—opaque, blank, and cold.

Cliopher said, "Yes."

His Radiancy said nothing for some time, stood frowning down at him, his power high and menacing. Cliopher did not try to match his stare, but thought of himself as a stone being swamped by the sea. If the sea truly wished to unseat him, he knew he would have no recourse.

But the wave ebbed. Ebbed from drowning Cliopher; and ebbed, he saw, from drowning that inner man whose name he did not know, save that it was almost certainly not *Tor*. But he had no other name to offer him.

"Tor," he said again, very softly, "please."

If he had heaved a stone through a window he could not seen a shattering as complete as what he saw breaking in his Radiancy's eyes.

Cliopher's stomach quivered with compassion at the tangled mess of emotions.

His Radiancy stepped back from the door and turned away, but he did not shut it, and after a moment Cliopher pushed it open the requisite span to let him enter. He shut it behind him, and looked tentatively around.

He had always assumed that his Radiancy's apartments were furnished to his taste, and that therefore the private study would be much the same, elegantly and sparely furnished with glorious works of art; restful, beautiful, serene.

This was not the case.

His first impression was of chaos. His second was that he had unthinkingly relaxed. His third was to notice that Dora's picture was pinned up on the wall over the desk.

The private study had probably once been a service room. It had a clerestory window high up on one wall; was perhaps fifteen feet square; and though even the service parts of the Palace were architecturally pleasing, that was about all one could say of it.

It was cluttered, crammed, full of—things. Books filled bookcases and overflowed onto every surface including the floor; cushions and fabrics jostled clashing colours; miscellaneous items, from stones to pens of every historical period to shells to mysterious objects decorative and possibly practical, were squished into the places between books and haphazardly all around the furnishings.

Apart from the several bookcases, there was a desk with a chair before it, a divan or eating couch of the old imperial style and, half-buried under the jumble of things, another table with a chair—seeming, in the circumstances, miraculously clear of clutter—placed puzzlingly on top of it. The harp from Navikiani was there; a lute was in the corner. There were probably other furnishings and who knew what else hidden under the mess.

"It appears that I am remarkably ordinary at heart," his Radiancy said. He was leaning against the desk, his face set into mockery as he watched Cliopher look at his private space, the only place in the whole of the world, the whole of the Empire, that was his, and his alone. "You are thinking that this is not so different from your inner rooms, and you are right."

The courtly answer would have been easy to say. Cliopher said nothing.

His Radiancy stared at him meditatively for an uncomfortable length of time. Cliopher bore the scrutiny, not trying to conceal his emotions, trying to figure out what was niggling him about that room, what was important. Not the clutter: his Radiancy rejected all efforts on the part of his staff to come in to clean or arrange it. No, there was something else it was showing him.

After a moment his Radiancy pushed upright. He walked over to a teetering stack of books leaning up against what Cliopher now saw was a wooden cupboard, undid a latch, and pulled out a wine bottle and two glasses.

Cliopher looked at those glasses, and deeply learned protest jumped involuntarily into his throat.

His Radiancy cocked one mocking eyebrow at him. "So far, and no further? Get yours from outside, then."

Cliopher swallowed, but surely his Radiancy had let him in once—*so far and no further.*

He was still holding on to the door handle. He edged around, not liking to take his eyes off his Radiancy, and blinked at the bright calm of the familiar room.

Conju and Ludvic were still standing in the middle of the room. Cliopher caught Conju's eye and, still not trusting his voice, made a gesture towards the table with the tray of water, wine, and glasses. Conju raised his eyebrows and walked over to it, hand on the bottles. Cliopher thought for a moment, but before he could answer Ludvic said, "Two."

And Conju nearly smiled as he put two wine bottles next to the ewer of water and brought over the tray for him.

His Radiancy had gone back to leaning against the desk and was staring into the brilliant red wine in his own glass. Cliopher looked around for a place to set down the tray.

"Here," his Radiancy said, moving a pile of books to the floor with quite magnificent unconcern for either the books or the fact that he was himself moving them. Cliopher nodded thanks and went down the room to set his burden down on the desk. He stopped awkwardly there, unable to voice any of the questions hammering at him.

With his own hands his Radiancy poured wine from his bottle into the glass Cliopher had brought down. Feeling stunned, Cliopher picked it up, held it loosely, until his Radiancy dropped his own glass and chimed it lightly against his.

"An old Alinorel custom," his Radiancy said. "To make a toast."

Cliopher stared at him. His Radiancy's mouth quirked, but his humour was still biting mockery, no joyful laughter. "Traditionally the first toast is to the Emperor, but in this case we will skip to the second, and make the toast to old friends who come with uncomfortable truths. Sit down, if you want. Move things wherever. There is no order in here."

"There is not much room to pace, either," he said, his voice feeling rusty with disuse, though it couldn't have been more than a few minutes since he had knocked on the door.

His Radiancy tossed back his glass and moved to pour himself another. "No, there isn't, is there?" He looked around the room with an indifference

Cliopher did not believe in for a second. "Not much what anyone expects of the Emperor of Astandalas."

"But he is not welcome here, is he?"

Cliopher managed to bite back *my lord*, but it was with enormous effort.

His Radiancy stared mockingly at him and said nothing.

Cliopher did not like that mocking expression. Did not like what it implied of his Radiancy's state of soul, did not like it aimed outward, particularly did not like seeing his Radiancy aiming it inward at himself. It was not the sort of self-aware humour that healed; it was a hard carapace to shield the wounds it was itself inflicting.

He said slowly: "What the Moon offered was not your heart's desire, and you rejected her. Yet when Domina Black offered you what is your heart's desire, you rejected her, too. Why?"

His Radiancy's expression did not shift. He did lift his hand and swallow down that whole glass of wine again, and poured himself a third, with a hand that was trembling. Cliopher watched the wine slopping into the glass and did not in any way think his Radiancy was drunk.

His Radiancy's voice came eerily commonplace. "Why? Why do you think?"

Cliopher thought of the shock of Domina Black's arrival, the recoil that had stopped the argument, the loss as the door shut behind her. Thought suddenly of Ghilly choosing Toucan—but he could see that Domina Black had not chosen another—or at least she had not until *after*—

So far and no further.

He spoke with the greatest compassion. "Will you not go down after her?"

He could see that his Radiancy was planning to say something light and mocking and unreal, but what came was a cry from the heart.

"Oh, Kip, don't you know that if I went now I would not come back?"

And he knew, as his Radiancy knew, that there was no way Cliopher was ready to take up the reins of government; that there were too many works of magic to be done before he left on his quest; that the purification rituals were only half-complete; that there were a thousand and one things that had to be done before he could leave.

Cliopher tried desperately to think how he could do it, how they could manage.

But what he knew, with every professional instinct in him, was that without his Radiancy there and without all the ceremonies of transferal and regency and so forth they had just begun discussing, without those formal

recognitions and safeguards, that the peace of Zunidh would fail in short order. That the Prince of Amboloyo would cease his tentative explorations and
launch into outright expansion; that the Princess of Xiputl would retaliate;
that Mgunai and Western Dair's delicate balance of competing trade and resources would collapse into acrimony; that Southern Dair would try to bully
everyone else into behaving, and fail; that—

"I'm so sorry," he said.

His Radiancy met his eyes, and to Cliopher's shock their respective efforts to smile broke his Radiancy's effort at poise. His Radiancy set his glass
uncertainly on the desk and slid down to the chair, and he lifted his hands to
his face and he wept.

He wept as one who never lost control: messily, loudly, shudderingly.
Cliopher stared, glanced wildly around the room, found his glance settling
on one of the many mysterious swaths of fabric draped over things. Why his
Radiancy had quite so much fabric in his study he had absolutely no idea;
but it was something.

He picked up a bolt of sumptuous violet angora, soft as a cloud to the
touch. He shook it out until he determined it was indeed a great swath,
enough for a cape or a court robe, and carrying it like a robe he stood up and
walked behind his Radiancy. He draped him with it and then he sat down on
the edge of the desk and with the cloth between them held the Last Emperor
of Astandalas as he cried.

CHAPTER FORTY-EIGHT

IT WAS, PERHAPS, A QUARTER of an hour before his Radiancy stirred. He had since ceased sobbing, but Cliopher continued to hold him until the shudders calmed, and even after that until his Radiancy finally shifted.

Cliopher edged back and nearly fell off the desk, his muscles cramped and unresponsive after the awkward position. He caught himself before he quite toppled over, wrenching his wrist slightly, and sagged down onto the divan.

His Radiancy wrapped the violet angora around his shoulders. He smoothed out the cloth with unnecessary care, face half-averted, and Cliopher realized with yet another shock that he was embarrassed.

It had been a matter of official state policy that the Emperor of Astandalas could not, by definition, be embarrassed. Embarrassment meant an acknowledgment of some equality between actor and audience. A true aristocrat was never embarrassed before his servants. The Emperor was embarrassed before no one.

Except, it appeared, before Cliopher Mdang.

Cliopher thought of how excruciating embarrassment was at the best of times, and that this was probably one of the worst of times, for a man entirely unaccustomed to feeling it would feel it all the worse for its rarity. He cleared his throat and said the first thing that came into his head that was not some asinine reassurance. "Why do you have so much cloth in here?"

His Radiancy looked up, startled, the embarrassment fading into curiosity. "I beg your pardon, Kip?"

Cliopher gestured at the violet mohair, the swaths of fabric elsewhere in the room. "It is idle curiosity, that's all, my—Tor."

His Radiancy reached out and picked up their respective glasses to refill them with the wine. Cliopher accepted his with a pretence of equanimity he assumed did not even come near to being convincing.

"Several reasons," his Radiancy said after a moment. "I get weary of yellow, white, black, gold. When I was Emperor there were so few things I could touch that … for some reason it is easy to purify fabric, and it was important to me to have things I could touch of—of different textures. And I suppose I have always liked how fabric looks draped around things."

"I had not realized there were so many taboos around what *you* could touch."

He bit back *my lord* again. It did not seem to be getting any easier, despite the room that was for once not designed to show off its central figure.

His Radiancy sipped at his wine, more slowly than before. "I felt like a ghost. No one could touch me, and I could touch no one. I cast no shadow, and shadows did not land on me. My slightest whim was obeyed, but any real desires I had were forbidden by the entire edifice of Schooled magic and Imperial policy. No one called me by name. No one looked directly at me. No one would ever ask me a personal question. If I asked anyone anything the response was grovelling sycophancy. Yet everyone was alive to the merest gesture I made. Everyone was terrified of me. Oh, I should clarify: not me. It was never me that anyone looked at, that anyone saw, that anyone thought about. It was always *the Emperor*."

Cliopher took a long and bewildered swallow of his wine.

"I used to lie awake at nights imagining what I would do, what I would say, when … she came. I thought … it never occurred to me that it was if, not when … it was the only way I could bear becoming Emperor. I thought she would rescue me—"

Cliopher tried to keep his expression compassionate rather than avidly interested and also slightly sickened.

His Radiancy swallowed back the rest of his glass of wine in one go. He looked at Cliopher's still half-full glass, made a twisted smile, and filled up both of theirs again. For a man who did not normally drink more than a glass or two at supper, Cliopher thought, his Radiancy was showing a superb disdain for both the time of day and the proprieties of drinking. And perhaps it was that he needed half a bottle before he could even begin to speak about his private life.

It appeared he could get no closer to the mystery of Domina Black yet, for he changed topics abruptly.

"There was this man—Lord Jedd, his name was—he was the Most Worshipful Lord of Titles and Master of Imperial Etiquette—oh, how I hated him. Everything he represented. He could not have liked me much, either, though naturally he never showed it. Naturally. He was responsible for teaching me all the taboos and rituals and rules about being Emperor.

"I had come from such a distant exile. I knew nothing of court life. I knew nothing about how the Emperor was supposed to behave. There were all sorts of rituals and ceremonies I had done as Marwn, of course, but I had been trained in them since birth and they were not ... they did not involve people."

He paused there, a muscle in his jaw working, his eyes luminously tawny-gold. The room was not brightly lit; only a few mage-lights glimmered here and there, and the oblong patch of sunlight high on the wall opposite the window.

"I hated everything about being Emperor. Everything. Everything. I hated how other people treated me, I hated how I was expected to treat other people, I hated all the taboos, I hated the total lack of privacy, I hated the magic that was turning me inside out. I hated being responsible for everyone and everything from money to spiritual salvation. Poor Lord Jedd bore the brunt of it. I don't know if he was afraid I would carry through with my anger ... he was a brave and courteous man ... and he was relentless.

"One day—I remember it so clearly—it must have been a month or so after I came to the throne, when the magic was settling down and I was beginning to be able to think and act rather than just react. One day Lord Jedd was going on about how I was treating people too politely, too courteously. Now, I had not exactly been raised that way, but I had spent enough time alone in my tower that it was something of a marvel to me to have people to talk to at all. And do you know what he said?"

Cliopher shook his head.

"He said, Lord Jedd, he said to me that he was surprised I was finding it so difficult. As the Marwn, he said, I must have been very used to being considered an institution rather than a person. And he said, when I looked at him much the way you are looking at me now, that if I learned nothing else from him, always to remember that from my bed curtains outwards I was only and ever the Emperor."

His Radiancy swallowed his wine down again.

This time Cliopher was the one to refill his glass.

"You don't seem concerned about how much I am drinking, Kip."

Cliopher met his glance for a brief moment before dropping his own eyes, unable to keep his equanimity and thinking that his Radiancy probably did not need to see how worried he was. "If you drank this much every day, my—"

"How do you know I don't?"

Cliopher blinked at him in genuine surprise, half-smiling at the incongruity. "Conju would have told me."

"And if I had ordered him to keep quiet?"

His Radiancy's voice was calm, enquiring, with a faint edge of challenge. Cliopher thought for a moment (for he did not drink much, either). "There would be indications, I think, even if ... Conju would not have asked me how many bottles, Ludvic would not told him two, Conju would not have smiled, when I asked for a glass just now. And—you could not do what you do if you were drunk or drugged."

"Drugged!"

Cliopher bit his lip. "Well ... it is possible, my lord."

"Conceivable?"

"I have conceived the thought, and immediately rejected it."

"Oh, Kip, I am become so boring."

"That you do not drink excessively is not boring."

"That was not what I meant," he murmured.

"What did you mean?"

The question hung there. His Radiancy stared at him, arrested, as if it were a question no one had ever asked him. "Once ... I was ..." He pushed away from the desk, stalked the four steps over to the desk with the chair on top of it. Didn't look back at Cliopher, looked down into his wine glass, the sparkling red wine. "I used to climb up here so I could look outside ... I used to dream ... I used to let myself imagine ... I used to hope ... I used to—"

"Yes, my ... Tor?"

"I used to be—oh, Kip, I used to be my own person—I used to *like* who I was—I used to be someone more than ... How can I go down to her? She asked me if I were only—if only I could—if only—"

His voice broke, and after a fierce glower, he dashed back his glass. "Next bottle. Are you certain you're not worried?"

Cliopher met his glance soberly, then smiled very deliberately and reached out his glass for a refill. "I could hardly countenance getting drunk on a regular basis, but once ..."

"I never get drunk anymore," his Radiancy said glumly. "Not that I remember it being particularly fun, but even so ... I don't do anything. She asked me if there was anything left besides the Emperor."

Was that the question whose answer had been that definitive no?

The wine was going to Cliopher's head even if it wasn't going to his

Radiancy's. "How dare she ask that? How dare you believe it?"

"How *dare* I?"

"Are you a man?" Cliopher demanded. "Prove it."

And his Radiancy, whipping around to glare at him, glared—and then he started to laugh, and magic shimmered into illumination around them, fell through the air, filled the room with sparkles and shimmers, and his Radiancy slumped down to a seat on the divan and raised his hands up to the magic raining down, and he laughed, and laughed, and laughed.

Finally he stopped and he looked at Cliopher through the shimmering magic and he said: "Will you speak so to me? Will you speak so *for* me? Will you speak so *about* me?"

Cliopher licked his lips. "If you desire me to."

"Will you go down to her? Will you tell her that I—will you tell her anything?"

"Anything?"

"Anything! Will you go down to her and answer any question she puts to you, will you tell her what you have said to me, will you—"

Cliopher clutched his wineglass. "Are you asking me to—to be your go-between?"

"Who better? Have you not done that on a thousand political fronts for me?"

"Um ... are you wishing to ... to ..."

"I want you to ask her to give me the chance to prove myself—to show myself—to be myself—"

The plaintive note was audible. Cliopher drank down his wine in one long swallow, then coughed until his Radiancy poured for him from the silver ewer of water, and he drank the slightly winey water and composed himself and then he said:

"I will go down to her."

★★★

IN THE END LUDVIC OMO went with him.

They had, Cliopher realized with shock, drunk three bottles of wine in under an hour. He had perhaps drunk half a bottle himself, and he felt it strongly. His Radiancy, two and a half bottles in, looked possibly slightly more leonine than usual, and the magic was still sifting down in sparkles like the end of fireworks, but otherwise his movements were certain, decided, and his voice and expression as clear and controlled as ever.

Cliopher emerged blinking into the public study. Conju and Ludvic were still hovering there; Ser Rhodin was now on duty with Elish.

Ensuring that the door was closed behind him, Cliopher rubbed his face and smiled ruefully at them. "His Radiancy will be out shortly."

Conju's prim reserve broke sufficiently for him to utter. "And …?"

"And he has drunk the better part of three bottles of wine."

"*Three?*"

Before Cliopher could reply the door opened again and his Radiancy strode out, looking not a wrinkle out of place. "I do apologize for worrying you all. Ludvic, you are off duty, no? Will you go down with Kip to speak to—Domina Black?—You are to answer her questions honestly, and if it occurs to you to offer any observations, do so. Cliopher will explain as you go."

"Very good, my lord," Ludvic said, saluting.

"Conju, attend me. It is time for a bath."

Conju nodded, then looked vaguely worried. "Ah … evening court?"

"They can entertain themselves without me watching them tonight. I'm sure they will appreciate the novelty. Come back after, Kip, it doesn't matter what time it is."

"Very good, my lord," he said, bowing, and then regretting it when his head swam. Ludvic Omo caught his arm before he quite fell over; his Radiancy had already turned to Conju and was explaining something with many gestures and quick words.

He turned to Ludvic and said apologetically, "I had to drink the rest, you know."

★★★

IT OCCURRED TO CLIOPHER AS he was changing into what Ludvic always called civilian clothes that he would prefer not to be recognized at the hotel, and so he wrote a letter of reference from himself in his role as Lord Chancellor. Since Ludvic was accompanying him, he was not obliged to take the trailing guards, and they walked down the Palace hill with him trying to feel sober, rather unsuccessfully.

According to her application at the Archives, Domina Black was staying at the Swan. The hotel was middling impressive, with high ceilings, lots of wicker furniture, and palm trees in pots. It was the sort of place Cliopher would have chosen for his family if he had not had the rooms to spare for them. He said as much to Ludvic as they entered.

"You wouldn't choose the Golden Lion?"

The Golden Lion was where lords stayed who did not keep houses in the city or have suites at the Palace. "A bit out of my league, don't you think?"

Ludvic smiled. "No."

Cliopher's retort was interrupted by the approach of the hotelier. She did not recognize them but did, presumably, recognize the quality of Féonie's tailoring, for she gave the two of them polite half-bows. "Gentlemen, is there any way I can be of service? Are you looking for accommodation?"

"Good afternoon," Cliopher replied. "We are looking for Domina Black of Stoneybridge, who is staying here according to the staff at the Imperial Archives. Could you direct us to her room, please?"

The hotelier hesitated, evidently torn between politeness and policy—a feeling Cliopher knew far too well. "I'm very sorry, gentlemen, but it is not the Swan's policy to divulge our guests' rooms to strangers."

Cliopher smiled in acknowledgement and withdrew his letter from the pocket in his sleeve. "I fully understand, ma'am. I have here a letter from the Lord Chancellor for Domina Black. Will you have it taken to her? We can await her reply here."

The hotelier's eyebrows went up as she took the scroll from him and examined the seal with some wonder. Cliopher wondered if she had ever had reason to see it before, but she gave no sign that she did not know what to look for. "This appears to be in order," she said, "though it is highly unusual for one of our guests to attract the notice of the Palace. You may wait in the chairs here, gentlemen. Would you like refreshments?"

"Please."

They sat down under one of the palms. "This is a nice hotel," Cliopher murmured, watching the hotelier find one of her underlings to take the letter and then return to her desk. "I think I would enjoy staying here."

"It would overset her completely to know the Lord Chancellor thought so," Ludvic replied.

They sat in silence for a few minutes. There were a number of small brightly coloured birds twittering in the palm trees and swooping down to peck at things on the floor, then darting in and out through the glass louvres on the windows. The hotel was built around a central courtyard in the South Dairen style, with a fountain in the middle of a richly flowering garden. The sun had set as they walked down through the city; magical lights were starting to glimmer amongst the plantings. Cliopher said, "Where would you choose, then? If you had to pick one of the hotels."

"This would have been on the very grand side of things for my family,"

Ludvic said after a contemplative silence. "I came from a very small village. My family were not chiefs or anything like that. Just carvers."

Cliopher noted the past tense, and decided not to ask anything further. A waiter brought coffee and a tray of mango tarts out to them. When he had gone Ludvic stirred sugar into his coffee and said, "My village was on Woodlark."

The entire population of Woodlark Island in the Azilint had died in what was the worst disaster in Zuni history apart from the Fall itself. How exactly it had started Cliopher had spent years trying to determine and still did not entirely know, but there were rumours of curses and forbidden magic, and certainties of drought, jungle fires, mudslides, and several sweeps of a pestilence that had maddened beyond all cure those who had not yet died. A quarantine had prevented the spread at first, but in the end his Radiancy had had to burn the island to bare ash to stop it.

Cliopher had been standing beside Ludvic when the commander gave the order to kill anyone trying to escape the quarantine on sight.

"I'm sorry."

Ludvic rubbed his left hand down the long golden scars on his arm. "It seemed right to me that I should die from his touch. For so long I have felt unworthy of living when they did not. At the end, when the priests came, I thought only that you were the Lord Chancellor, that you needed to know. Then I saw your face. I had not known you felt that way. Today when you went into his private study, I wondered if that would be it for you. I wanted you to know."

"That you are from Woodlark?"

Ludvic nodded slowly, watching as the hotel servant came back out of the doors on the other side of the front desk and approached the hotelier, who gestured towards them. "You have a loving family big enough to include Conju, and Rhodin, and himself. And me. I am grateful. That is all."

It certainly wasn't, Cliopher thought, but the hotelier had accompanied the servant back to them. "Our guest would be delighted to speak with you," the hotelier said. "She would prefer to meet in her room if you do not object."

"That would be best," Cliopher agreed, and they followed the servant up three flights of stairs and along one of the galleries to an elegantly carved wooden door. "Kiauru work," Ludvic murmured as the servant knocked.

The door opened on the woman who had managed to meet the exiled Marwn, and had not expected to see the same man in the Last Emperor of Astandalas.

"Come in, sirs," she said, with a splendid appearance of nonchalance.

CHAPTER FORTY-NINE

SHE ALSO HAD BEEN CRYING, Cliopher saw; her lustrous dark eyes were red-rimmed. She was composed now, however, as she stood back to let them through the doorway and gestured them to choose from the three chairs pulled up around a bamboo table.

Ludvic chose the seat facing the door, leaving Cliopher to sit with his back to either the bed or the small closet; he chose the bed, as the scroll he had sent to her was placed just closer to the other chair. She poured water from a glass pitcher into three glasses, taking hers last.

Finally she sat down in the remaining chair and looked gravely at them. Her steady, solemn gaze took in Cliopher's outfit and Ludvic's golden scars, which looked almost as if they could be deliberate mage-tattoos, if someone were so moved as to tattoo his palms and forearms in finger-wide smudges. She nodded at Ludvic and addressed Cliopher.

"You are the Lord Chancellor, I think."

Her accent was unfamiliar, but of course Cliopher had not heard many Alinorel speakers since the Fall. He nodded. "Yes. This is Ludvic Omo, the Commander of the Imperial Guard."

"It is an honour," she replied, inclining her head. "Your letter indicated you wished to speak to me, your excellency? Surely you might have summoned me to the Palace."

"We are not here in any official capacity, Domina. We are here on behalf of our lord."

"And is that not an official capacity, your excellency? It was my impression that all missives from your lord were official."

Cliopher winced inwardly. Ludvic, surprisingly, answered: "We are here as his friends, Domina."

"I suppose he wouldn't have deigned to come himself."

"Madam, that is unworthy of you."

"I'm not sure that's the best way to begin," Cliopher said, trying not to glare at him.

"It's true, though," Ludvic said.

Cliopher took a deep breath, then released it as a snort when Domina Black's lips started to twitch, a dimple appeared, and merriment lit her dark eyes.

"I think I must believe that you are here unofficially, for I have heard nothing to indicate you would ever be so gauche in your official business. So. Your lord has sent you down to me, why?"

"His Radiancy thought you might have some questions. We are here to answer them."

Domina Black stared at him, merriment fleeing again in surprise. Then her eyebrows went up, the dimple reappeared, and she seemed to savour the simple statement as if it betokened something far more complex. "He was always a humorist," she murmured. "What kind of questions? May I ask you about matters of the heart? Or am I limited to matters of state?"

Cliopher bowed to her with a certain ironic appreciation. "We are instructed to answer any question, domina."

She stared at them, frowning slightly. Then: "Do you think he enjoys being Lord of Zunidh?"

Even to hint doubt as to the answer was treasonous. Cliopher met her eyes and said, "No."

"Some parts," Ludvic said a moment later.

"That's fair enough," Domina Black said. "It would be unbearable to think he hated everything."

Her voice was musing, her thoughts clearly on the man she had once known. Cliopher thought of his Radiancy demanding that he *speak so for him*, and he said, for he wanted this stranger whom his lord loved to *know*: "I think he hated everything about being Emperor."

"You are very free with your words, sir."

"He cannot come down and speak for himself, domina, and so he has sent us."

Something about this struck her as exquisitely humorous, for the dimple reappeared. "*Can* he not? Is it not the case that the Last Emperor of Astandalas is worshipped as a god? It is hard to believe in such incapacity. Tell me truly: does he not mean he *will* not?"

Cliopher stared at her for a moment, the ground under his feet shifting. Who *dared* ask such things?

Who dared travel alone to the far ends of nowhere to dally with a man in such total exile he did not even know his own name?

—Unless, he thought in a moment of blinding insight, she had not travelled there *alone*.

Two weeks ago Princess Anastasia had lost her temper and told her great-nephew the Last Emperor that she wished the Red Company had thought to steal him.

His Radiancy had retorted that if ever he could effect the release of Fitzroy Angursell, it would be on condition the infamous poet wrote a song about her.

Two years ago, in Navikiani on Lesuia, his Radiancy had said that he had spent the night before his coronation praying for the Red Company to come.

He had formed an illusion of a beautiful woman—*this* beautiful woman—on the back of an elephant.

Cliopher looked at Domina Black, who was regarding him with high challenge.

Everyone knew the story of the Red Company and the Elephant. It had happened some time after the Customs House on Colhélhé and before they had gone hunting the White Stag, some time after the Bridge of Swords and before That Party in Astandalas where they had broken open the heart of Melissa the Grand Duchess of Damara. Some time after they had become famous, but before they had met the Imperial Heir on procession somewhere out in the middle of the Wide Seas on his way to Kavanduru.

Between the famous stories—between the sagas that Fitzroy Angursell wrote about those moments—

There were all the moments of travel and encounter, of anecdote and legend, of songs that did not belong to the great cycles and might have been about this moment, or that, this person, or that.

This morning Cliopher had been told he would become the Viceroy of Zunidh; this afternoon he had thought he might have overstepped all bounds of friendship and law and life; this evening he had been asked to go bear his Radiancy's heart to—

She was still glaring at him.

His heart leapt. He was not a soldier; it was not for him to wish to fence with swords, even with Pali Avramapul, the only person ever to have bested Damian Raskae in single combat. But to fence with *words* with her—

No wonder, he thought in marvel, that his Radiancy had not wanted to tell him his secret name. It was probably in a song that Cliopher had very deliberately never heard in any professional capacity but could sing word-per-fect in five variations.

He could think without any effort of four different songs that might have been the one. Could his Radiancy possibly have been Bellefontaine the Hermit? Ydar the Earnest Young Poet? Tamarill the—

"Your excellency?"

Her voice was even more challenging.

He started. "My apologies, Domina Black. I was reflecting."

She stared at him now in total astonishment. "I do beg your pardon, your excellency?"

"Please, call me Cliopher. It is my fault that his Radiancy could not come down—and I do use the word deliberately, I assure you. You are asking us, as he told me you asked him, whether there is anything left besides the Emperor."

"You are not giving me much reason to believe—"

"Madam, he is the Lord of Rising Stars, the Last Emperor of Astandalas, the Lord of Zunidh, the Lord of Five Thousand Lands and Ten Thousand Titles."

"I know his titles, sir," she said impatiently.

"Do you know what they mean? You know—I am sure you know—what power comes with them. Have you never thought of the responsibili-ties?"

She opened her mouth to retort and then stopped.

She was Pali Avramapul of the Red Company. Even if she were not truly Domina Black of Stoneybridge (though Cliopher did not discount the notion that she was), she had spent half her life fighting against the same corruption of the Empire that he had spent his life ameliorating. They had chosen opposite sides of the law to work on, but he knew that she knew at least as well as he what the Emperor of Astandalas was supposed to do, which very few of them had even attempted to begin doing.

The knee-wall of the daïs in the Throne Room listed the Red Com-pany as vanquished by the Empire. It was in the history books that they had been overcome by the restorations and reformations of Artorin Damara the Lion-Eyed, who had been earning the epithet of 'the Great' before the Fall made him forevermore 'the Last'.

Cliopher had spent his life learning to see and take advantage of the piv-otal moment in a conversation, an argument, a debate.

He leaned forward. "His Radiancy is planning on leaving on a quest to find an heir, according to the ancient traditions of the lords magi of Zunidh, a year and three months from now. Between then and now he must perform a full ritual of purification, so that he is able to touch or be touched by other living beings without causing the greatest hurt and magical impurities."

He gestured at Ludvic's arms. "Ludvic is the Commander of the Imperial Guard. He has served his Radiancy the longest of any in his household. When his Radiancy touched him he was given those scars."

Ludvic looked down, as if ashamed, though to Cliopher they were banners of love to be waved proudly. No one else had ever touched the Last Emperor after he became Emperor but for the Moon. No one else had ever *been* touched by him.

"Moreover, between then and now he must also prepare the world for the changeover in government that is to occur on his return. This involves many great works of magic—for he is, Domina, the Lord Magus of Zunidh—as well as a great amount of political manoeuvring and decision-making. There is much he must do before I stand in his place as Viceroy so that I will be able to uphold my promise to keep his world peaceful and prosperous and not thoroughly upended by his departure."

He looked searchingly at her. She met his gaze with that calm challenge, the core of strength in her magnificent.

She was the chosen champion of the Wind Lords of Kaphyrn. She had distracted the Sun when he had discovered there were mortals trying to steal the sheep of his pasture. She had travelled farther than anyone else Cliopher had ever met. She was, very likely, a Scholar of one of the greatest universities in the Nine Worlds.

She was Pali Avramapul of the Red Company, and so long as he did not name her neither he nor Ludvic had to do anything official about the fact that she had a price on her head that made the annual cost of maintaining the Throne Room of the Palace of Stars look stingy.

"I asked his Radiancy why he did not go down to you," Cliopher went on.

"And what did he say in reply?"

"He said that if he went down now he would not come back. Domina, I would give anything to have been able to tell him to go, but I am not ready—he is not ready—the world is not ready for him to leave. Please, please, give him the time to show you that in his heart he is still the man you once knew."

He stopped there, realizing his hands were out in gestures he had absorbed from his Radiancy's habit. She seemed to recognize them, for as he watched her grave expression lightened and the dimple reappeared.

"I had not realized he had one."

Her smile was dazzling. Cliopher matched her gaze steadfastly. She might be Pali Avramapul, a woman he could well imagine a man choosing over all the promises of the Moon, but he was persistent.

By all of his ancestors, he persisted.

After a long while she sat back without releasing his glance. "I can understand why he chose you."

For his emissary? For his Lord Chancellor? For his friend?

He waited. He was disoriented in time by the lack of the Palace bells, but certainly more than a quarter-hour went by before she spoke again. Ludvic, of course, sat there patiently; he was accustomed to it.

Cliopher waited, feeling the wine still coursing through his system, unable to refrain from inwardly rehearsing all the songs about Pali Avramapul that he knew.

At last she let out a deep breath, and he knew, as in other such conversations he knew, that he had achieved his aim.

She said, "Tell him that the next time I see him I will ask him for his name."

To someone else that might not have seemed a concession, but to Cliopher, to whom the question echoed through all his ancestral songs and stories, it was more than a concession: it was a victory.

★★★

WHEN, AN HOUR LATER, HE related this conversation—though not his inward speculations—to his lord, his Radiancy looked at him. "And what do you think of that?"

"My lord," he said, "she loves you."

INTERLUDE THREE

$\mathcal{A}$ $\mathcal{P}$ R O C L A M A T I O N

To be disseminated worldwide the third day of the seventh month:

FROM THE PRIVATE OFFICES OF THE LORDS OF STATE:

It is with the greatest satisfaction that his Excellency Cliopher Lord Mdang, Lord Chancellor of Zunidh by the appointment and grace of his Serene and Radiant Holiness Artorin Damara, announces the final adoption into law of a charter delineating the inalienable rights, freedoms, and responsibilities enjoyed by every citizen of Zunidh.

Copies of the full document are available in the provincial offices of the Ministry of the Common Weal.

By the sign and seal of Cliopher Lord Mdang, Lord Chancellor of Zunidh.

$\mathcal{A}$ $\mathcal{L}$ ETTER

The fifth day of the seventh month:

MY DEAR KIP:

You have no need to apologize for your preoccupation. We can understand, I hope, that you have built a life for yourself in Solaara that does not usually have us in it. It was very interesting to see the life you lead there, what it is you do with such engrossment. I hope it continues to give you joy and satisfaction as your duties change. We are proud of all that you have achieved.

Thank you for the good news of your lord's health. It was in all ways an honour and a pleasure to be invited to attend on him (a phrase you use so often! I understand it better now). I am glad to hear he is so much better in health and spirits. Zemius keeps coming up with new ideas from his research for the quest. Vinyë has told him to write to you with his results, which I hope you will think the correct thing to do.

I am not in the mood for relaying family gossip, and I imagine you are busy enough, with everything you are doing, not to mind. You will want to know this, however: my uncle Tovo has disappeared. It has been over two weeks now so we are assuming he has gone to join the ancestors according to the old custom. You know how much those traditions meant to him.

We will, of course, let you know when the sagali will be held, as I'm sure you will want to come home for that. We are sorry that you will be too busy to come otherwise.

Until then,
Mama

VOLUME FOUR

AŌTEKETĒTANA

CHAPTER *F*IFTY

"DO YOU HAPPEN TO HAVE a free evening?"

Cliopher looked up from the report he was reading. Rhodin was leaning in the doorway of his office. "I beg your pardon?"

"A free evening. I'm sure you're familiar with the concept. In most professions a minimum number are legislated."

Cliopher smiled and set down his notes. "I believe I might remember drafting that legislation, now that you mention it." He drew his diary of appointments towards him. "Was there a particular evening you were wondering about?"

"Tonight."

Cliopher had automatically flipped to the next week's spread. He looked up at Rhodin. "Tonight?"

Rhodin unfolded himself from the doorway and walked over to Cliopher's desk. "It's an hour after dawn, man. Do you ever *not* work?"

"Most people don't arrive unannounced at their friend's apartment at an hour after dawn."

"Most people don't have friends who—let me see that schedule—dear lord, Cliopher, I thought his Radiancy had spoken to you about making sure you take time for your health? No one wants you to have a heart attack!"

Cliopher looked down at the spread of the current week's schedule. He had been feeling quite proud of how much better he was doing about organizing his days. "No, look," he said, pointing at it. "All the things written in green are personal time."

"An hour in the mornings and the evenings and meals, except when those meals are at court or part of a meeting. Quite acceptable, all things considered. What does the green hatched with orange for tonight mean?"

"Er, that I'm working on something that is technically for work, but ..."

Rhodin made a face at him. "Yes, but?"

Knowing he sounded defensive, he said, "But that's really for me."

"And what do you mean by that?"

Cliopher looked at the two-hour block he had carved out of his schedule. "I was looking forward to reading those reports."

"You're sick, man," Rhodin said, shaking his head. "Sick. I think you should have supper down in the city—I notice that *is* in green today, well done—and come with me to the opening of the new exhibit at Hnala's Gallery."

Hnala's Gallery prided itself on having the most splendid collection of purchasable art in the world. Cliopher had not been in there for years; he knew his weakness, and his budget, too well. Rhodin knew this perfectly well, he thought mulishly. "Why? If it's the opening night, wouldn't we need an—ah."

Rhodin grinned at him.

"I'm sure they would let you in if you asked nicely."

"Yes, but they will *definitely* let the Lord Chancellor of Zunidh come without an invitation."

★★★

IT WAS A LOVELY EVENING, as it happened. The rains had finished but the heats of Solaara's long dry season had yet to set in, so the city was thronged with flowers but not yet too hot.

Cliopher walked down with Rhodin, who was dressed in a courtier's outfit for once, and looked quite different in his green and blue silks. Cliopher himself had dressed in what was nearly half court costume. He felt somewhat self-conscious about his splendour but also knew that it was the best way to ensure the evening went well for his friend.

They ate a very good, if somewhat strange, meal in what Rhodin assured him was the trendiest restaurant in the city (and whose host nearly fainted upon seeing the Lord Chancellor arrive unexpectedly at the door, for trendy the restaurant might be but haunt of the high aristocracy it was not), and then, as had been arranged, met his two guards in their lesser panoply. They followed him with greater-than-usual punctiliousness because of Rhodin's presence as they made their way along the great serpentine pergola all hung about with moonflowers and night-blooming jasmine that unspooled down the hill into the lower city.

"All right," said Cliopher before they quite reached the gallery, "thank you for the suggestion. What's this exhibit on, anyway?"

"It's the original paintings used in *The Atlas of Imperial Peoples.*

Apparently they've been sitting in some lord's storeroom since the first edition was published. The originator of the project was Lady Harktree—it's an Alinorel title, you know, but she was one of those caught up by the Fall in the Palace. Her heir's the one selling off the collection."

"Lord Zivuno," supplied Cliopher, who knew far more than he wanted to about the collapse of the man's finances. Lord Zivuno was very well connected to the Jilkano princes and particularly the Prince of Haion City. There had been a particularly long Council of Princes meeting the week before when the Jilkano princes had tried to persuade Cliopher that they would support him about making Nijan its own administrative district if he would help them keep Lord Zivuno from public disgrace.

Cliopher had stared at them in incredulity and demanded to know why Lord Zivuno could not learn to live on what they had always assured him was the excessively generous annual stipend.

"Mm," he said, and put his face into his court expression as they swept up to the door. One of his guards moved in front to announce him to the startled door-warden.

"His excellency the Lord Chancellor!"

The door-warden took one look at Cliopher and sank down into a genuflection.

And as easily as that they crashed the party.

★★★

RHODIN ACQUIRED FOR HIM A glass of what was undoubtedly very expensive wine imported from Ysthar. Cliopher, quickly bored with the press of fawning gallery-visitors and unable to get very close to the pictures, calculated the tariffs that ought to have gone into it.

He had just had a four-hour meeting with the Ministry of Intermundial Trade in which they did their best to persuade him he should increase their budget. Their argument had included numerous charts showing the benefits they provided, from specialty luxury items and scholarship to the taxes on said products.

Wine from Ysthar had not been on any of those lists.

He said as much to Rhodin, who had reappeared after going off to speak to the extraordinarily beautiful woman who was the assistant manager of the gallery and also, it appeared, the main impetus behind this evening's excursion.

Rhodin sighed. "You can take the man out of the work, but the work out of the man ..."

"I didn't say I was going to *mention* it to anyone in any official capacity."

"Let's go look at the pictures. Get your mind off work."

Cliopher smiled at him. "Rhodin, this is who I am. What about your young woman?"

Rhodin sighed again, but there was a wicked twinkle in his eyes. "The beautiful Sonya? I think we understand each other. She told me to make sure I could tell her something about the paintings when we see each other later. Come now, they're organized by region. Shall we start with Ysthar?"

"Certainly. You can show me the picture of your traditional cultural costume."

Rhodin cast him a surprised and very slightly affronted glance. Cliopher smiled to take away any offence. Rhodin was of an aristocratic (if impoverished) family: they were the ones commissioning *The Atlas of Imperial Peoples*, not appearing in it. Sometimes Cliopher forgot this. Rhodin did not.

They duly admired the (admittedly splendid) pictures of a wide range of peoples. Cliopher could not help noticing that the highest ranks displayed were Alinorel Scholars in their black robes and multicoloured hoods and a set of members of the Service in their various robes of office. Of course, the official state picture of the Emperor (Empress Anyoë, in this case) would have been on the frontispiece.

Between a Fifth-Degree Secretary (the highest rank he had achieved before the Fall) and the Emperor of Astandalas had been the whole range of the Upper Ten Thousand Families of the Empire, who had only to look up from their *Atlases* to see what their own traditional cultural costume was.

Cliopher appreciated seeing the garments and physiognomies of the peoples of the other worlds of the Empire, but he had spent many happy hours with the *Atlas* when he was young, and as he was, at heart, a local boy, he was most interested in the pictures of Zuni cultures.

To be honest, he was most interested in the picture of one particular Zuni culture.

They made it eventually to the picture of the Wide Sea Islander. The painting matched the rest of the set, the canvas about three feet by four, the portrait full-length to show off the costume.

Cliopher sipped at his (reasonably good) very expensive Ystharian wine and studied the picture carefully.

A young man stood proudly and looked at the viewer in great good humour and moderate challenge. He wore an elaborately plaited, woven, and dyed grass skirt, armbands decorated with feathers, greenery, and pearls, six layers of necklaces made of dark amber cowrie shells spaced with golden pearls, and a headdress that began with pearls and rose up to a crown of cassowary feathers surmounted with shimmering blue superb bird-of-paradise feathers. His face and torso were only lightly painted, in stipples and lines in red and yellow and white: colours for a trading festival.

"There are a lot more pearls than I would have expected," Rhodin said.

"He was a famous pearl hunter," Cliopher replied absently, his heart in his throat.

"I can see the relationship to what the people we met at that market on Lesuia were wearing. Vangavayen traditional costume is truly among the most splendid in the Empire."

Cliopher swallowed the desire to ask if Rhodin saw the relationship to him, but there were a dozen people close enough to hear him (and all agog to find some tidbit from the Lord Chancellor to share with everyone they saw the next day), and he did not like to wear his heart entirely on his sleeve. His family and his culture were private. He did not want them on display in the *Csiven Flyer*.

"Those were Eastern patterns, the ones we saw in Lesuia. This is Western Vangavayen."

"How can you tell?—Oh, there's Sonya coming, and that must be her boss with her."

The beautiful Sonya was making a purposeful line across the room towards them. For a brief, absurd moment Cliopher was afraid they were going to be evicted for having come without an invitation, but naturally what Sonya wanted was to effect an introduction of himself and show off to her boss that she had a connection, however tenuous, with the Lord Chancellor.

The boss was a woman of Cliopher's age, confident and assured in her bearing and her garments. She had no need to prove herself, he deduced from her appearance (from head to toe subdued, professional, and high-status), though that confidence was belied by a certain tension around her eyes.

Perhaps, he thought, she was concerned about the success of her exhibition. From what he had heard so far the audience was admiring but not particularly inclined towards purchasing. Figurative studies were not currently in vogue. People always paid for new portraits of their own families—his friend Suzen called such work her daily rice—but portraits of random people from around the five worlds of the Empire, be their outfits ever so decorative?

"Your excellency, may I present Saya Belardie? And Savela Hnala herself, if I am not much mistaken?"

"Your excellency, my gallery is honoured by your presence. Simply honoured. The world knows your belief—which takes such practical form, too—that the fine arts are a fundamental element in a good society, but to my regret I had not realized this extended to direct patronage."

Cliopher smiled blandly at her. "I have long admired the works in your collections, Savela Hnala. I have even bought a few in the past."

That threw her, he saw, for she could not place the Lord Chancellor as someone she had ever noticed buying anything. He could have told her of a dozen times he'd been fobbed off on the least of her underlings, but he kept that to himself.

She tried to regroup without exposing her ignorance. "I do hope they have given you delight?"

"Assuredly."

She did not look entirely reassured, and cast about for a way to regain control of the conversation. Cliopher sipped his wine, knowing he had probably spent too much time with his Radiancy, knowing also that he had never fully been able to suppress the pleasure he took in winning conversations. At least, he reflected, he had grown up sufficiently that he no longer looked at *every* conversation as an adversarial one; and he had learned from a lifetime playing at court how very subtle the games, and the satisfactions, could be.

"Are you enjoying your evening, your excellency?"

"Very much so, thank you."

She preened at the compliment, which cost him nothing to give. He smiled at her, giving her tacit permission to look around to see who was paying attention to her standing next to and conversing with the Lord Chancellor, and returned to his examination of the portrait.

"This is a splendid series," he said when he realized a few minutes later that she was still there. Rhodin and Sonya were too busy flirting to be paying attention. He gestured at the portrait. "This is an exceedingly fine painting."

Savela Hnala smiled at him in a way that he decided, generously, to take as approving rather than irritatingly condescending. "Yes, isn't it? The artist who painted it went on to great things. Splendid brushwork."

"I hadn't noticed," he admitted. "The representation caught my eye first."

She laughed indulgently. "Yes, people often find their first sight of a primitive striking."

Cliopher had raised his glass to take a sip so he did not say anything immoderate in response to the indulgent laughter, but at this he dropped it heedless of where the wine might slosh. "I *beg* your pardon?"

He was the Lord Chancellor of Zunidh. He held the power in this room. He could not respond personally to this. He *would* not.

Savela Hnala gave him a slightly surprised look, but it seemed he was governing his expression tightly, for she went on in the same vein: "Oh, do you take exception to my choice of word?" She laughed indulgently again. "It's not very politic, perhaps, but I prefer to use the *accurate* term. I suppose you would use something less charged, your excellency."

"I should use something less insulting, Savela Hnala," Cliopher said in a calm voice that everyone within a ten-foot radius around them heard very clearly.

She decided to try to laugh it off. "Your excellency, you may not be familiar with the terms used in art history. Islander culture *is* primitive, you know, in art historical terms. It is not meant as an *insult*."

He would not, he would *not* make this personal.

He shifted position until he stood in battle mode, feet firmly planted, head high, hands relaxed, stomach tucked, back straight, voice clear and firm and passionately reasonable, expression mild. "Savela Hnala, spare me the lectures on outmoded theories of art. You and I both know you what you mean."

Her face did not lose its tiny smirk, as if he and she were part of a club that *understood* these things, that knew that public adherence to such a theory meant, at best, an unthinking complicity with the whole superstructure of systematic prejudice that went with it.

"Your excellency, you see the best art of the Nine Worlds. Surely you understand the need to categorize what is excellent? I know your strong advocacy for a legal equality of all persons—the splendid document of the Rights and Responsibilities of the Citizen was, in a word, a triumph—but you understand, I am sure, that there is a rationale to rank and status."

She gestured at the painting. "It is a superb example of the Seventh Classical Mode. And more than that, as you yourself noted, the model is a splendid example of Wide Seas art. His cultural artefacts—" She pointed at the efela necklaces— "are truly magnificent. You could hardly find better in the Imperial Museum of Comparative Anthropology."

"I could hardly find better *art* in the Imperial Treasury."

It amazed him that anyone with a business successfully catering to the wealthy and status-conscious could be so totally blind to social cues, for to his increasing astonishment she seemed to take this as yet another secret indication that he was part of her cultural club.

She laughed again. "Oh, very good, your excellency, very good indeed.

You do have excellent taste—if I may make such a pun! Would you care to see some of the other paintings? It must be said that few other of our barbarian cultures have such a sophisticated visual language as the Wide Seas Islanders. They were not a literate people, you know, which I'm sure helps."

Rhodin said, "Lord Mdang—"

But Cliopher had gone beyond friendly remonstrances. He felt soiled by her implications, by her insinuations, by the very fact that she had spoken those words aloud in his hearing. He said, "Savela Hnala, I must admit you amaze me with your open bigotry."

Into the shocked silence he clearly heard someone whisper, "*Did he just say she was a bigot?*"

Savela Hnala finally seemed to realize he was not laughing along with her. "I—I beg your—your excellency's pardon?"

Too late, he thought grimly, and went on.

"Savela Hnala, upon what grounds do you base your assertion that this depicts the primitive art of a barbarian culture?"

"*Holy hell*," someone said in the crowd behind him. "*He's not—*"

Oh yes, he was, he thought, as Savela Hnala stared at him in deep shock.

"It is, I will grant you, a depiction of a person and the art of a quite *different* culture to that either of the original painter or of most of those who have been its audience over the years."

"That's what I meant," she said gratefully.

He raised his eyebrows at her. "Ah, but that is not what you *said*, Savela Hnala, and I must tell you, in my job I try to make sure I listen to what people actually say, and observe what they actually do. People do often find this somewhat disconcerting."

Her face slowly drained of expression. "I, er, your excellency, er—"

"What is your family's background, Savela Hnala?"

The repeated use of her name was starting to get to her, he could tell. It was one of the simplest and most effective techniques he knew for throwing someone off their stride.

The question stiffened her backbone. "I am from Haion City, your excellency. My family have been associated with the princely family, the Enobars, for many generations."

He nodded. "Haion City joined the Empire some eight hundred years before the Fall, after being conquered in the reign of the Empress Dangora XVII, if I am not mistaken. It was one of the last of the great cities of Zunidh to hold out against the conquest."

"The coming of civilization," she corrected him, the words jumping to her lips from childhood education.

"Indeed. The coming of civilization." He let her relax very slightly before he gestured at the painting again. "Perhaps you did not know that the Vanga-vaye-ve joined the Empire voluntarily in the days of Aurelius Magnus, some thousand years before Haion City. The Emperor voyaged across the Wide Seas specifically to request the Vangavayen Islanders' alliance and assistance. After an extended debate among the various councils and chiefs of the communities, they elected a Paramount Chief who agreed to the emperor's terms and thus passed into the fold of his magic and protection."

He did not let her respond. "Of course, the Vangavaye-ve has always been very far away from Astandalas, and subsequently from Solaara, and it is perhaps to be expected that a people would be best known by their exports. The golden pearls you can see are worn by the man in the portrait, who was himself a pearl hunter; one of the later developments of the treaties with Astandalas was that the majority of the ahalo cloth and foamwork created by Vangavayen artisans have been given as tithes."

His half court costume's upper layer (a kind of sweeping mantle in deep blue) was made of ahalo cloth. After two years of wearing it for court costumes he had almost managed to stop stroking the fabric when no one was looking. He stroked it now, the delicate, richly hued cloth catching the light in its famous soft iridescence.

He wanted to keep going, to rub her nose in her bigotry and folly, to scathe her to the core with his tongue—

But he was the only person in the room wearing ahalo cloth, he was the only person with two Imperial Guards in their lesser panoply standing at his back, he was the only person in the room who had the power to say these things to anyone he pleased.

And so, instead of all the other things he might have done, he smiled, and stepped back, and said: "The painting is superb. It reminds me of my own home. I will purchase it from you for my personal collection, Savela Hnala. Please make the arrangements to have it sent to me at the Palace when the exhibition is done."

She fell over herself trying to make apologies and express her gratitude and indicate that she knew he had just saved her from ruin. For he might not make much effort to set fashions: but everyone here would want to follow his example.

(And, he knew, with a tired, cynical part of him that he did not usually give much voice to, that the rumours of this evening's conversation would see all those people who disagreed with the Lord Chancellor's views of the hinterlands crowding round the gallery as the home of a kindred spirit.)

He let her express her emotions to see what she actually said, instead of what she wanted him to hear. The apologies, he noted, were all for the distress she might have caused him, and none of regret for what she had either said or intended.

And thus, when she finally wound down her phrases and had come down to a hesitant request for the best person she should contact (for the Lord Chancellor would not be relegated to her least-important minion!), he did not say for her to contact Tully, or even Gaudy, though he was tempted.

He said, "Thank you. When you have the paperwork together please get in contact with my secretary, Zaoul of the Tkinele, and he will ensure all is done to hand."

Everyone within hearing distance swivelled with one accord to look at a painting a few down from the one Cliopher had just bought, where a Tkinele warrior queen who bore a marked resemblance to Princess Anastasiya stood even more proudly and far more threateningly with someone else's head in her hands.

Savela Hnala looked faint.

Ser Rhodin examined the painting judiciously. "I must admit I had not imagined anyone could look fiercer than your secretary, but then, of course, he did not exactly go for the traditional profession."

★★★

AS THEY WALKED BACK UP the hill to the Palace, Rhodin said, "I'm sorry the evening turned sour for you, Cliopher."

Cliopher had been happily engaged in imagining the screeds he could write on the topic of the Wide Seas Islanders' contributions to Zunidh's history and culture—as if he did not already have enough to do—and it took him a moment to think what Rhodin was talking about.

"Please don't worry about it," he said, reluctantly deciding he would not, actually, have the time to write a long essay for the *Csiven Flyer* comparing the oral histories of the meeting of the last Paramount Chief of the Vangavaye-ve with the Emperor Aurelius Magnus (as recounted in song and dance in *The Lays of the Wide Seas*) with the written accounts from the Imperial Archives. He had, out of curiosity, once made the comparison; it was a minor regret of his life that he had not yet had the time to satisfy himself on the five or six points of difference as to which side had faltered in their accuracy.

He realized Rhodin was looking sidelong at him. He smiled reassuringly. "Truly, Rhodin, I enjoyed myself."

"How can you just let the insult go?"

"What insult?" He nearly laughed. "Rhodin, do you think I don't hear or read that every day? Yesterday the Prince of Amboloyo called me an octopus sucking the government dry. He's not very good with his natural history, it's to be admitted, but he is forthright with his views. So is nearly everybody else. I do not let myself take it personally."

Rhodin took a breath, then shook his head, obviously relegating this to the category of 'Cliopher is not a *true* aristocrat' (which was, Cliopher told himself, perfectly, and thankfully, true). "I'm sorry you felt like you had to buy that painting."

He did laugh at that. "Rhodin, I would have bought that painting regardless. Couldn't you see the family resemblance? That was a portrait of my great-uncle as a young man."

CHAPTER FIFTY-ONE

PRECISELY ONE YEAR BEFORE HIS Radiancy was due to leave on his quest, Cliopher woke up to a perfect hour.

He woke at dawn, the sky white with the coming sunrise. He sat up in bed to watch the light sweep across the sea and the fens and the city and finally reach his window, and when the orange sun had lifted itself above the horizon he got out of bed, wrapped a light robe around himself, and played his oboe for twenty minutes.

With music in his mind he then moved into the empty room beside his bedroom to dance.

The room had probably once been meant for attendants, but he had asked Franzel to clear it. He had had woven grass mats put down to make the surface more comfortable than its beautiful hard tiles and to muffle the sound of his steps.

One evening, after a long day spent biting his tongue so he did not say what he was thinking to Princess Oriana, whom he still had to shepherd through her budgeting process to make sure it came even close to facing up to reality (as if there were no competent accountants she might have drawn on in Gorjo City!), he had sat down on the floor with his silk robes puddling about him and used his scribal pens and charcoal to draw out the patterns of his family's dances.

After two and a half years as the Lord Chancellor he had finally reached the point where he could spend the first hour of his day not reading reports, not rushing out to see what emergencies had precipitated themselves through the night, not even catching up on his correspondence, but working on his own emotional and physical state of health.

Half an hour was enough for some of the common dances, the dances Cliopher had learned growing up, and which were in his bones. Many of them ought to have been danced with others, but he could not have everything, after all, and at least when he eventually did go home he would not disgrace himself.

Each week he danced one portion of the fire dance his Buru Tovo had taught him.

He kept waiting for the letter that would tell him the date of the sagali, the memorial feast, for his great-uncle. It would be held soon after the letter was sent, he knew, for the sagali was held as soon as possible after the shaman said the person's spirit had passed to the ancestors.

Cliopher had spoken of the matter to his Radiancy, who had obliquely apologized for him not being able to go home otherwise and told him that if he needed to drop everything to go, he ought to do so without hesitation. It had not, in fact, occurred to Cliopher that he might be expected to skip it.

Traditionally the sagali was held a year after the death, but in a case like this, where the person had quietly left the community to go to Pau'en'lo'ai, the Island of the Dead, to join the ancestors directly, the shaman could not tell except by doing divinations.

Cliopher had hung the painting (which had come with a note of fawning apologies from Savela Hnala, who, it appeared, had finally learned from someone that he was a Wide Seas Islander himself) in his sitting room, where every morning and evening he saw it and was reminded of who he was and how far he had come—and how far he had yet to go before he could go home. After three months he was still finding new details in it.

This morning he danced the middle passage, which once had shown him the way home.

His Buru Tovo had taught him the fire dance when he was eleven, that year when he had taken the young Kip to the Western Ring—to Loaloa, ancestral home of the Mdang family—to learn the ways of the ancestors. Cliopher had learned it all eagerly, loving the knowledge itself, and loving also the gift of respect suggested by the passing on of the knowledge, and loving also the old man—for Buru Tovo had already been elderly in his eyes, though in retrospect he was probably no older than Cliopher was now—who taught him.

Cliopher had never danced the fire dance at home. He had never claimed aloud, except that once to that seller of shells on Lesuia, to know *Aōteketēta-na*, the greater dances of the Mdang family. No one else had ever challenged him with the traditional words.

When he went home, he thought, as he stomped and whirled and angled his feet so carefully they never crossed the lines—as he moved his hands in the gestures that told the movements and strengths of the currents and winds of the Wide Seas—when he went home for the *sagali* he would make that claim.

His uncle Lazo was the *tanà*, in terms of having the role within the community that went with the dances, but though Cliopher was sure he had the deep knowledge of the songs, Uncle Lazo had a weak knee and could not perform the dances. Others knew the common dances of the Mdang family, the *Aōtētana*, but no one else that he knew of had claimed the greater ones, the ones danced over the coals.

It was possible that Buru Tovo had been disappointed that Cliopher had left the Wide Seas behind and had chosen someone else from his generation or that rising up below him to be the keeper of the dances. It was not something anyone wrote to him about, presuming, he had eventually realized, that his own silence about the old traditions meant that he was no longer interested in them. He had not known how to suddenly start writing with questions. And anyway, the traditions did not respond well to being written. They were *lived*.

In the sudden pause that fell between movements—if he had been singing the appropriate part of the *Lays* aloud he would switch at this moment between the historical narrative of the sons of Vonou'a and one of the lyrical passages—he heard the quarter-hour chime ring.

His thoughts had been far away. He stopped, breathing a little heavily from his exertions, and smiled with satisfaction to see that he had not smudged the charcoal overlaying the patterns across the mats.

★★★

THE REST OF THE MORNING was not so perfect, of course.

He met with the Council of Princes, whose habitual low-level disapproval turned into outright hostility when Cliopher informed them his plan for the reconstruction of the world government required soliciting the opinions of the world's people.

"I do not think I can have heard you correctly," Prince Rufus said.

Cliopher smiled at him almost pityingly. "Your highness, your committee has been doing excellent work in providing me with a basis for understanding the aristocratic perspective. As the proposed changes will affect everyone, from high to low, I wish to gather the perspectives from as many people as possible. You can see why, I am sure."

"I can see that you are letting your own partiality blind you."

"Your highness—"

"Lord Mdang." The prince emphasized the title. At the other end of the table Princess Oriana tittered. She had taken to tittering after nearly every interchange Prince Rufus had with the Lord Chancellor. Cliopher wondered if she had any idea how irritating everyone else found her.

"Prince Rufus. I would be grateful if you were to explain yourself."

"No matter what honours his Radiancy grants you, at heart you will always be a nobody."

He paused there while Princess Oriana tittered. Cliopher waited a moment, and, when nothing else seemed forthcoming, said, "Thank you."

This was evidently not the response the prince was expecting, for he beetled his brows in surprise, but quickly recovered his poise so he could square his shoulders and set his hands in a frank and forthright position on the table and in general provide every cue he was about to engage in a flight of oratory. Cliopher suppressed a sigh and made sure his expression was attentive even as he weighed within himself whether the prince was more likely to call him a barbarian or a lapdog before he was through.

He felt absurdly pleased when Prince Rufus climaxed his speech with both.

***

LUNCH HE TOOK IN HIS apartments with Commander Omo, who was finally back to his official position but had not yet moved back to his own rooms in the barracks. Cliopher had made no effort to encourage him to do so. Quite apart from the fact that he was still slightly worried about Ludvic's state of mind, he liked having him there.

He had been trying over the past month or so to get Ludvic to share with him his poetry. The commander had not yet relented, but seemed to be enjoying, in a perverse way, evading Cliopher's efforts to make him. While this occasionally took the form of outright refusals, most often Ludvic asked Cliopher a question that led him astray from his point in a flurry of enthusiastic response.

Cliopher had realized earlier that week that Ludvic might be a man of few words and those plain ones, but he was a master of tactics.

Today Ludvic did not wait for him to ask anything. As soon as Cliopher sat down, he said, "I have been wondering."

Cliopher was immediately reminded of the first time he had heard Commander Omo say that. He half-consciously repeated his Radiancy's words from that occasion. "Have you indeed, Ludvic? And what have you been wondering about?"

Ludvic nodded, taking the words at face value—or at least looking as if he did. "I have been wondering what you plan to do when you retire."

Cliopher smiled. "I will go home."

Ludvic nodded again. "Yes. But then what?"

"Well, I would like to …" He trailed off. He could not, in point of fact, think of anything he wanted to do besides be at home.

Ludvic waited.

"I would like a house."

That sounded reasonable. Cliopher ate some of his meal, then realized his friend was still waiting. He frowned. "Ludvic …" A thought struck him. "What do you want to do when you retire? Will you write poetry?"

Ludvic shrugged. "Perhaps."

Cliopher ate in a more thoughtful fashion. His Radiancy desired to— well, who knew, exactly? But even if Cliopher were not correct in his speculations concerning Domina Black (and he thought he was, although he had decided it was better all round if he did not ask outright), it seemed highly unlikely that his Radiancy would be content with a quiet retirement. Certainly not in anything like a monastery.

He looked at the commander, whose family had died with Woodlark, who had never married, who still carried in his heart the scars of having to make that dreadful command to uphold the quarantine. There was Conju— and Ser Rhodin—and Ludvic—and himself. None of them had married, none of them had families (well, Cliopher *did*, of course, but not of that sort), and all of them had devoted their entire lives to serving his Radiancy.

"Would you like to come to the Vangavaye-ve with me?" Cliopher asked.

He had thought this might be where Ludvic was going, but from the commander's expression, which had lost its usual phlegmatic calm in shock, the idea had been nowhere near the surface.

The bells chimed the hour. Cliopher pushed himself back from the table. "Think about it," he said. "I'll talk to Rhodin and Conju to see what they think. Not immediately: I have to see Kiri about the next phase of the Plan first. We have time to make our decisions. The fact that it would solve most of my concerns does not mean it will solve all of yours!"

He left Ludvic sitting there in stunned perplexity. Cliopher felt absurdly lightened by the conversation, by the thought that this was so simple a solution to his wish not to abandon his friends—any of his friends—by the idea of Rhodin and Conju and Ludvic all finding a home in Gorjo City, where they could be, first and foremost, themselves.

And his Radiancy? murmured a wayward thought that he did not let come into full expression, even in his own mind. Some desires were too dangerous to articulate, even to himself.

He opened the door to the main hall, greeted the footmen on duty, collected his honour guards from their positions, and set off for the Offices of State with his mind firmly turning towards the next task. He had disciplined thoughts. He was quite able to stop himself imagining a life where friendships could play out in hobbies and long leisurely conversations and the old traditional festivals and dances and—

He realized he had gone past the stair that led to the office. He shook his head, smiling at his guards, as he turned around, and therefore was the first one to see the upset page running up the stairs to him.

His mood sobered instantly. "What is it?"

The page skidded to a halt, tried to bow, gasped, tried to speak, gasped some more, and finally, as Cliopher was starting to get very alarmed, managed to get words out. "Oh, your excellency, there's a barbarian in the Palace who nobody can understand except he wants to talk to you, sir!"

Cliopher stared at her. "A *barbarian?*"

It was one of the worst insults a courtier might give. The girl's accent suggested she was of a high family, but then again, she might have been given the message by someone who meant the term quite literally. Cliopher strongly disapproved of using the word to describe anyone, even outworlders, even outworlders who had never been part of the civilized Empire; but not everyone did.

"He's coming up behind me," she wailed, in a panic he found disgusting.

"Don't be a fool," he snapped. "He's probably a member of a diplomatic embassy from one of the outworlds."

"He looks so savage," she said, looking about to cry.

He was strongly tempted to inform her that if she couldn't get control of herself and her prejudices she was not going to get very far in the Service, but before he could formulate the words into something approaching polite discourse he heard the noise of more remonstrations and confused people coming up the stair the page had approached by.

Those few who had not been talking when they reached the corridor started talking as soon as they saw him. He could not, at first, see the page's so-called 'barbarian'.

Leaving her to her crisis he walked between the guards (who smartly spun and fell in behind him) to see what, exactly, the gods had decided to land on him this afternoon.

"Well?" he said, in the voice he had learned from his Radiancy that could cut through any babble.

Everyone fell silent, so he could see who was there.

Guards, gossips, bureaucrats, minor courtiers, and in the middle, looking not a whit out of place despite being entirely out of his element, Cliopher's Buru Tovo.

CHAPTER FIFTY-TWO

CLIOPHER WAS HALFWAY THROUGH THE mourning process for his great-uncle.

He said, "But you're dead!"

This caused all the various courtiers etc. to stare at him in total horror. They melted away from Buru Tovo, who stood there, arms folded, short, scrawny, dressed in the outfit he could make himself by wandering into the jungle with a stone knife, frowning severely at Cliopher.

There was a pause.

"Buru Tovo! You're *alive?*" Cliopher might be the Lord Chancellor of Zunidh, head of the Imperial Bureaucratic Service, Hands of the Emperor, and so forth, but he was not so perfect a courtier or a bureaucrat that he could not be thrown entirely off his rhythm.

Buru Tovo unfolded his arms so he could cup one hand around his ear. "Eh what? Who's that? I'm looking for Kip Mdang!"

Two worlds collided in Cliopher's head and gave birth to the knowledge that his great-uncle was rather deaf and rather blind and probably had no idea Cliopher was the gorgeously-dressed person standing in front of him. From his hat down through to his jewelled sandals Cliopher looked like one of the upper aristocracy of the world. Féonie spent enough time and effort and public moneys ensuring it.

And, he thought, walking forward until he could grasp his Buru Tovo by the upper arms in the Astandalan style, he probably sounded like one, too, at least until he caught the familiar beloved accent of home.

"Buru Tovo," he said, then repeated it loudly and clearly and in as thick a Vangavayen accent as he could manage so quickly, "it's Kip. I'm here."

The old man peered at him. He smelled of coffee and caramel (not the usual stale fish), and his eyes were intent if slightly clouded. Finally he grunted and let Cliopher perform the ancient Islander greeting, forehead to forehead. "There you are. Why are you wearing that? I didn't recognize you. Tell these people to go away. I need to talk to you."

"Of course," said Cliopher, and turned to the still-horrified page. He had to think to lighten his accent to one intelligible to a courtly audience. "Inform Saya Kalikiri I shall be late and she should start without me."

He did not wait for any confirmation or response. He took his great-uncle by the elbow, smiled, serenely, at all the rest of the crowd of witnesses, and walked back to his own apartments with his head up and his heart high.

It had been a good long while since the last time he had started rumours half so delicious.

★★★

"I THOUGHT YOU WERE DEAD, Buru Tovo," Cliopher said.

He didn't usually repeat his thoughts quite this often. He was, he realized, a little flustered.

"Would you like something to eat? To drink?" He looked around the room helplessly. He was in working mode; he had gone to where he usually held audiences, the First Receiving Room. His appearance fit. His great-uncle's did not.

"Eh what? Why would you think something that stupid?"

Cliopher looked at him fondly. "You're over ninety, Buru. Mama wrote to me to say you'd disappeared. Everyone thought you'd gone to Pau'en'lo'ai to join the ancestors."

"You should have known better. Also, talk properly. I can barely understand you."

"Sorry, Buru."

"That's better." He sat back. "I came on that train."

Cliopher blinked. Franzel came in, eyebrows raised in silent enquiry, then departed again on quiet feet when Cliopher made a confused gesture at him. "You came on the sea train?"

"That's what I said." He scratched his side meditatively. "Lots of people on it."

"What about when you got to Csiven?"

"That's the big city? Lots of people, eh. Not too many Islanders, but I found a *wontok*. They knew the way over the mountains, to the capital. Lots of people talking about you, boy."

Cliopher contemplated the various proclamations he had had disseminated over the past year and did not find this surprising at all. He smiled in

wonder at how simply his great-uncle described the journey. He found a
wontok, someone who came of the same people, spoke the same language—
the same visual language, probably, for there were few outside the Outer
Ring of the Vangavaye-ve who spoke more than one or two words in the old
Islander tongue. And that *wontok*, meeting a stranger who claimed that relation, would do what it took to see him safely to his destination and successful
in his mission.

"But why did you come? Just to see me?"

"Lots of people talking about you, boy," he repeated.

"At home? Along the way?"

Franzel came in with coffee and pastries and a bowl of water and accompanying towel. He set these down on the table beside them and then retreated in astonishment at a glance from Cliopher. It was not often these days that
Cliopher himself performed the various tasks of the host to the guest.

Buru Tovo waved away his assistance. "What's this for?"

"Washing your hands."

"Washed them already, down in the yard."

"It's the custom here, Buru."

"Bah." He inspected Cliopher critically. "You keep any of the old ways,
boy? I didn't come all this way to see you all a fancy-man and foreign."

Cliopher stared at him for a moment, heart thudding painfully. "Why
did you come?"

He cackled. "Wanted to see the world before I go to the ancestors. Wanted to see you again before. Wanted—"

"Yes?"

Abruptly Cliopher remembered all the times his great-uncle had cuffed
him over the head and said *Listen, boy. Questions later.* He smiled, held up his
hand, though Buru Tovo hadn't done more than snort. "No! I remember:
Listen first. Questions later."

"Haven't forgotten everything, then. Go on."

"I beg your pardon?"

"You were going somewhere when I found you, no?"

Pearl-diver, fire-dancer, keeper of the old ways … which included knowing the ways of currents and tides, the movements of animals and fish and
birds. And men. Cliopher nodded. "I have meetings this afternoon."

"Go on, then. I'm tired. You're not old enough for that."

Cliopher had lived in a state of chronic exhaustion for long enough
he had mostly forgotten what it was to sleep more than six hours a night.

Though it was true he wasn't anywhere near a time in his life where he might nap through the afternoon! He pulled the cord that summoned Franzel from the mysterious back quarters of his apartments. When Franzel arrived, Cliopher said, "This is my great-uncle. He'll be staying with me for a while, so please show him to a room where he can rest and refresh himself."

"Very good, your excellency."

"Eh what?" said Buru Tovo, though Cliopher was fairly sure he was ribbing him this time.

★★★

HE STRODE INTO THE OFFICES of State only ten minutes late. He had with some difficulty put the thought of his great-uncle's arrival (and the gossip he had just caused; and what gossip there would be spread as a result of his arrival) out of his mind till later, and focused his thoughts on the topic at hand, which was a knotty question of intermundial trade as it related to his Plan. He found Kiri standing in the main office, evidently having just finished some sort of task with his group of secretaries.

"My apologies for my tardiness," he said, more aware than ever of the satisfying but foreign sweep of his garments as he strode up to her. "Is there something, Kiri?"

She was staring at him with a bemused expression he had not often seen from her. "Are you feeling homesick today, sir?"

His thoughts flashed to the startling vision of his great-uncle in the midst of all those court flunkies. But that was not homesickness, that was joy. "No," he said, deciding not to demand explanations, and turned to his secretaries. "Gaudy, look up the last Voonran treaty for me, please."

"Of course, Uncle Kip!"

He had turned back to Kiri when the words registered. He paused, then looked back at his nephew. "I beg your pardon?"

Gaudy was visibly mortified. "I'm sorry, sir."

"We've been working together for three years, and you've never once called me that."

Gaudy looked slightly panicked. "I'm very sorry!"

Cliopher was puzzled more than anything. Looking around vaguely to see that everyone else was staring at him did not help much. He sighed. "What am I doing differently than usual, Kiri?"

"Er—"

Into the silence that followed, Gaudy cleared his throat and said awkwardly, "You sound *very* Vangavayen, Unc—your excellency."

Cliopher closed his eyes and counted to ten and did all the little tricks that usually worked to lighten his accent and make it sound appropriately Solaaran-court. He turned back to Kiri. "My great-uncle just arrived. He is rather deaf."

"He's not dead?"

That was Gaudy, who seemed as thrown off his stride as Cliopher himself felt. Cliopher turned back to his nephew, feeling a bit like a dancer spinning circles. "No. It appears he did not go to Pau'en'lo'ai to join the ancestors as we'd thought, but instead got on the sea train without telling anybody. He has not yet vouchsafed me with a reason why."

"You don't seem worried," Kiri ventured.

Cliopher realized he was smiling foolishly, and tried to restrain himself to a more appropriate sobriety. "I'm not," he said. "I'm happy. He's a very important person in my life and I was waiting to hear he had died. I'm looking forward to hearing his reasons for coming so far. I'm sure they will be interesting."

Well, that was one word for them.

★★★

MINDFUL OF SER RHODIN'S MOCKERY (and his Radiancy's occasional request to see his schedule to make sure he did have those sections penned in green), when they finished their set of meetings and reports in the Offices of State, Cliopher did not pick up any of the multitude of other reports that were waiting for him, but instead announced to his startled secretaries that he was going to spend the evening with his great-uncle and they should do their best to cut his schedule for the next week to the minimum.

Leaving Tully to splutter and exchange glances with Gaudy and Zaoul, he strode back to his rooms, where he found his great-uncle looking through all of his personal belongings in his private sitting room.

"Good afternoon, Buru Tovo," he said, and then repeated it again in his thickest accent.

"There you are." His great-uncle looked him up and down. "Very fancy."

"It's the custom here." He realized he was apologizing, and grimaced at himself. He did not need to apologize for wearing the garments of his office and rank, surely.

"Bah. Sit."

Cliopher sat. His great-uncle squatted on the floor next to him, ignoring all of the four other seats available. Cliopher felt as if he were looming, and after a moment of Buru Tovo gazing up at him, expression masked in the maze of wrinkles around his eyes and mouth, he slid down to sit on the floor next to him. It had been a long time since he had squatted in the traditional way, so he made do with sitting cross-legged in the central Ystharian style he still had to do on occasion.

Buru Tovo grunted. Cliopher waited. He might have high office and rank, but his great-uncle was an elder, the oldest living member of his family, and the *tanà*. The *tana-tai*, even, eldest keeper of the knowledge. Cliopher did not get to speak first. He shifted position so his robes didn't bind about his thighs—not a problem he'd had when as an eleven-year-old he'd waited for lessons in his own grass skirt!—and then he waited. Any questions would only prolong matters.

Franzel came in with a tray, stared in horror at Cliopher sitting on the floor, tried to control his expression, set the tray down, and ghosted out again. Cliopher inhaled the scent of jasmine tea perfuming the air and slowly relaxed into patience.

The bells chimed the quarter-hour, and then the next. The scent of the tea dissipated as the liquid cooled. Buru Tovo squatted, arms loosely linked over his knees, eyes looking into a distance Cliopher couldn't see.

He regarded his great-uncle steadily, tracing out the features he had not had the leisure to look at the last time he had gone home, when he had passed him so briefly on the side of the Tahivoa lagoon. He had not made enough time for his Buru Tovo, who had taught him so much.

The old man's face still showed the pride and good humour displayed in the portrait. The challenge was masked now in twinkling eyes and wrinkles.

Buru Tovo had been out on a solitary sail to see what he could see when he'd encountered the cortege of barges and great ships assembled to take the Imperial Heir on progress around what would become his dominion. That had been Eritanyr, his Radiancy's uncle; it had been Eritanyr's son and heir Shallyr whom the Red Company had met on another progress a generation later.

Among those attendant on the Imperial Heir had been a painter charged with recording the Heir's progress and the more spectacular views of the Empire they came across. She had also been one of those painting the portraits for the *Atlas*. When she had encountered Tovo inDaina of Loaloa (as he would have described himself), she had decided he was the very image and type of the Wide Sea Islander.

It had never occurred to him before to wonder why Buru Tovo had had with him all his ceremonial regalia.

He opened his mouth to ask the question before remembering that he was here to learn. He subsided again, smiling to himself, at how easily the deep claims of family and culture overrode later-learned habits and expectations.

The bells chimed the third quarter-hour. Parts of Cliopher's legs were going numb. He did not want to think about physical discomfort. He thought instead about the text of his next proclamation, which was going to announce his ascension to the Viceroyship.

He always imagined Bertie and Toucan and Vinyë and Ghilly (and Quintus and his mother and all the rest) going to the town hall where such things were posted to read the text. He was constrained by the requirements of the form to compose them in a certain manner and style; but he did not compose them for any hypothetical demographic or audience, but for that specific image of Bertie before the board under the overhang of the hall. Bertie always scowled, in his mind's eye, reading the proclamations.

Cliopher cherished the hope that one day Bertie would write him with an unambiguous compliment about what he'd achieved, but that had not so far happened.

He had composed the draft and moved on to the next major item in his week, the Palace budget, when he realized he had missed the hour bell and the first quarter-chime. He opened his eyes to see that his great-uncle was watching him.

After the sweet notes fell into silence Buru Tovo said, "Lots of bells, eh."

Cliopher nodded.

Buru Tovo was quiet again. Cliopher sat quietly, no longer feeling as if he were *waiting*, exactly, though he was. He wasn't waiting *for* anything. He was sitting there with his great-uncle whom he had thought was dead, there in his private sitting room in the Palace of Stars, with all the shining and splendid glitter of his life as the Lord Chancellor of Zunidh puddled about him in the form of his robes, and all the deep history of his own life and culture there in the pain of his crossed legs and the faint, familiar scent of the dried leaves used to make a grass skirt.

Was this, he wondered, how Ludvic and Rhodin felt when they stood on guard? Meditative, patient, alert?

"Not so bad, boy. Thought you might have lost all the quiet here. Good enough."

He sprang up to a standing position, then cackled when Cliopher rather more slowly and creakily levered himself upright. "Need to move more, boy, or you'll be old before your time."

Cliopher smiled ruefully, brushing at his robes. "I'm afraid you're right, Buru."

He grunted complacently. "Got that right." A pause. "You want to know why I came, eh?"

The childhood response came unbidden to his lips. "Yes, please, Buru."

"Lots of people talking about you." Buru Tovo nodded, sucking at his teeth. "Lots of people. Thought it about time someone saw what it was all about."

"Mama and some of the others came to visit."

His great-uncle made a dismissive noise. "They came to see what they were looking for. Too close. Even that Quintus cousin of yours. He's a chief at heart, that one. Big ship, big man. He might dance *Aōtētana*, but he knows he'll never dance *Aōteketētana*. Not got the mind to hold the fire."

Cliopher felt a sudden, painful leap of emotion in his heart. "Buru, did you come to—" He stopped. One was asked to dance the great dances; or one danced them when the need came. One did not *ask* to be asked.

His Buru cackled. "Not so fancy to have forgotten everything, eh?"

"No, Buru."

"Speak up, boy."

But Cliopher knew he'd heard that quiet response.

"You've been a long time from home, boy."

"Yes, Buru."

"Missed a lot of the ceremonies. Barely know your island."

Cliopher looked down. "Yes, Buru."

The old man rocked on his bare feet, sucking at his teeth again. At length he said, "In the old days, the days of the voyages, they did the ceremonies at the right time. Didn't worry so much about the right place."

Cliopher looked up at him. He was not very clear on what particular ceremonies his great-uncle meant. There were plenty of common ones he'd missed, and undoubtedly there were secret ceremonies someone like Buru Tovo knew that he would not have been told of. He remembered vague rumours of initiations and secret knowledge passed down from generation to generation in secret places around the Ring.

He had been taught the fire dance, the dance of the Mdangs, and had imagined, for a while, that he would take his place as a keeper of the old traditions. Later he had left those traditions to go off instead to Astandalas, and although in his heart he had been trying to fulfil them (to go sit at the feet of the sun), to all external appearance he had snubbed his culture in favour of the court.

He had always thought the ceremonies were tied to their places, to sacred cave or secret cove. But it was true he was a descendant of the wide voyagers, the Wayfinders who had crossed the Wide Seas and discovered all those far-flung islands.

The sunset bell tolled, a deeper voice than the other bells. His great-uncle shook his head. "No sun, no stars. Need the bells to show the way, do you?"

Cliopher paused, then said, "I came to sit at the feet of the Sun, Buru."

Buru Tovo cackled. "Do you? You want the fire, do you?"

"Yes."

"Then bring me the sun and the stars, boy, to witness your life and see if it is worthy of the fire."

★★★

HE WALKED TO THE DOOR of his Radiancy's chamber turning over in his mind the utter impossibility of what he was doing. It was not a long journey—

—Or this portion of it wasn't. If he included everything that led to him even *attempting* to invite the Sun-on-Earth to drop everything else on short notice and come have dinner with his great-uncle Tovo, it was an extremely long and convoluted voyage indeed.

At the door to the Imperial Apartments the two guards saluted and reached to open the door before he had even taken a breath to speak.

"I don't have an appointment," he said, hesitating.

The guard on the right grinned. "His Radiancy's orders are that you are to be permitted entry any time of the day or night."

"Oh," said Cliopher, and then rallied himself. "Thank you."

The guards saluted again. The doors opened, and he went past the pages and the guards of the seven anterooms. The familiar study was empty, so he walked to knock on the ivory door.

Lady Ylette answered. He said, "Could you ask his Radiancy if I might beg the favour of an audience, please?"

She stood back and gestured for him to come in. When he balked she smiled, more primly than the guard. "His Radiancy has instructed that you may have access to his person whenever you request it."

He walked through the breakfast room, down the illuminated hallway, past the next pair of guards (who saluted without challenge), into the huge bedchamber. His Radiancy had not informed him of these privileges ...

Was it because he had wanted to see if Cliopher would ever reach again for a friendship deeper than the comfortable collegiality and occasional gift of intimacy they had come to?

He remembered telling his Radiancy's sister that his Radiancy had no way outside the forms of Imperial benevolence to show his love. All the verbal and gestural language of love was coopted by the strictures of how the Emperor behaved to his subjects. That did not go only for families, Cliopher thought. The language of friendship was used, too, in diplomacy and in the relationship between Emperor and his viceroys, the lords magi of the five worlds.

The dressing-room door stood ajar. As he walked up to it, Ato looked out at him, nodded once, and stepped aside.

Cliopher had not before seen the great illuminated mirrors that had been (he saw after a first blinded moment) hidden by what had appeared carved and painted panels. He stood dazzled by brilliance in the doorway of the dressing-room, his own reflection standing like a bronze-and-midnight shadow of his Radiancy's white and gold and black.

Ato and Pikabe were on either side of the door, watching. His Radiancy stood in the middle of the room on a low stool, watching Cliopher in the central mirror. Conju stood to one side, with a length of cloth-of-gold embroidered with tiny clear diamonds in elaborate floral patterns. The diamonds caught the lights and blazed fivefold in the mirrors.

"My lord chancellor," said his Radiancy, smiling at him through his reflection.

"My lord," said Cliopher, belatedly genuflecting. Conju continued with his careful arrangement of the cloth-of-gold, which he was winding about his Radiancy's upper body in the manner reminiscent of a Mgunai sari.

"What has provoked this unexpected pleasure? Nothing too terrible has happened in the world, I hope?"

"No, my lord." He took a breath. "Buru Tovo, my great-uncle that is, arrived in the Palace today. He came on the sea train."

"You must be greatly relieved to see him."

"Yes, my lord."

"Do you wish for some time off? I can imagine you have much to speak with him about."

"My lord is very kind."

His Radiancy smiled. "That isn't it, then?"

The cloth-of-gold was folded accordion-style, Cliopher saw when Conju paused in his winding to shake out another few feet of its length. The diamonds winked and glittered like sunlight on water. As the air moved in gentle eddies he caught the scents of flowers, sweet and rich and lingering, like the smell of fresh water after many days at sea.

"No, my lord."

"Well, then?"

Cliopher hesitated. His Radiancy was clearly getting ready for evening court. Then he said, "My lord, my great-uncle has not fully explained the reasons for his coming, except that it has something to do with old ceremonies he thinks I might be due for. He has asked me, in the way they do in the stories, to bring the sun and the stars of my life to bear witness to my life."

His Radiancy regarded him thoughtfully through the mirror. Conju shook out another three feet of cloth and began to drape it over his Radiancy's arm so it formed a perfect fan of pleats across his back.

"Something about your expression indicates that this is to happen soon. Even tonight?"

Cliopher nodded, and then said, "Yes, my lord," and then he thought about it again and added, "Please."

Conju paused in the cloth-of-gold draping. His Radiancy regarded Cliopher steadily through the mirror. Cliopher felt himself flushing hotly and didn't know whether to drop into the obeisance or back away or start spouting courtly platitudes or just keep standing there under scrutiny.

He kept standing.

His Radiancy smiled.

Conju started to unwind the cloth-of-gold.

"Go, then," said his Radiancy, "ask Rhodin and Ludvic. Conju and I will come down once we are dressed in our traditional costume."

CHAPTER ƑIFTY-ƬHREE

WHEN CLIOPHER RETURNED HE FOUND his great-uncle belabouring a mysti-fied Franzel with a list of foods the meal should include. Cliopher waded into the fray with his diplomat's instincts on high alert, but found that Franzel, far from being appalled by the demands to find breadfruit and taro, was delighted by the challenge.

"My lord is coming for supper as well," Cliopher said once he had trans-lated Buru Tovo's requirements into more palatable requests. "I presume they will have prepared his meal for evening court ..."

That did seem to astonish Franzel, but he quickly recovered himself. "You may rest confident in me, Sir!"

"I do," Cliopher returned wryly, and smiled at his great-uncle.

"Well, boy?"

"They will be here shortly."

"Good. You can clear the room. What kind of Islander needs all this fur-niture?"

★★★

IT TOOK HIS RADIANCY FORTY-FIVE minutes to dress in one of his infor-mal evening costumes. By that time Cliopher had just about persuaded his great-uncle that there was no way he could ask the Lord of Rising Stars to sit cross-legged on the floor, and also that his friends were not accustomed to the posture.

"Fancy men," Buru Tovo muttered, relenting. "Eh, who's this?"

Cliopher looked up to see Ludvic halting in the doorway. "This is my friend, the Commander of the Imperial Guard. He's joining us. Ludvic, this is my great-uncle, Buru Tovo."

Buru Tovo inspected Ludvic narrowly. "What is your name, what is your island, and what is your dance?"

Ludvic saluted. "My name is Ludvic Omo. My island is Woodlark in the Azilint. We do not have your dances, but the head of my carving is Odongai."

"Ey ana," said Buru Tovo, grinning. "What are your markings, there?"

"They are scars from my service."

"That's how you do it, boy," said Buru Tovo to Cliopher, and gestured at Ludvic to come sit next to him.

Cliopher smiled gratefully at the commander, who gave him a slow wink, and turned to ask Franzel whether everything was prepared.

"Yes, Sir, it will be ready at the usual hour."

"Thank you, Franzel."

"I hear the door, Sir. I believe your other guests have arrived."

Cliopher girded himself for the arrival of the Sun-on-Earth. It felt quite different to have him there as an invited guest than as an unexpected benison. Why, he was not at first certain, until his Radiancy walked in the door with Ser Rhodin and Conju, all three of them in lesser court finery, and he felt his jaw go slack with surprise when he saw there were no other guards.

His Radiancy smiled. "It seemed to me that this was a private dinner. They are on the outer door."

Cliopher stammered silently, then genuflected, then bowed over his hands, and finally said, "My lord, may I present my great-uncle, Buru Tovo inDaina of Loaloa? Buru Tovo, the Sun-on-Earth."

His Radiancy inclined his head. Buru Tovo bowed over his hands. "I met your uncle once, when he was a young man," he announced. "You don't look much like him. What should I call you, then?"

His Radiancy regarded him for a long moment. "Lord Artorin."

Buru Tovo nodded, and looked expectantly at Conju and Rhodin. Cliopher said, "Buru Tovo, these are my friends, the Cavalier Conju an Vilius and Ser Rhodin an Gaiange. Conju, Rhodin, my great-uncle."

Conju and Rhodin gave him identical surprised looks. It took him a moment to realize why; then he recalled that under the rules of courtly etiquette he had just indicated that Buru Tovo outranked them. Well, in Islander culture he did.

"So, boy, do we eat now, or talk first? It's your house."

"Er, the custom here is to eat two hours after sunset, Buru."

"Bah. Talk first, then. Sit down, Lord Artorin, I can't think where that boy's manners have gone. He used to know better."

His Radiancy said, "He is torn between two cultures, I think." But he sat down in the comfortable chair next to the stool Buru Tovo had dragged out from one of the other rooms.

Buru Tovo cackled. "Relax, boy, you look like you're waiting for a storm to hit. Lord Artorin, my boy there wants me to tell him he can claim the fire. He's trying not to look like he already has."

"Buru Tovo," Cliopher protested, flushing hard.

His Radiancy laughed. "What does he need to do to prove his worthiness to you? He said something about the sun and the stars?"

"Ey ana, that's the way of it. He'll tell us the way of his life by the signs he has used to direct it. Come, boy, get yourself ready already."

Cliopher was looking helplessly at the room, missing something—what? Not the guards—there was no hearth. He could not claim the fire without having at least a token flame in the space where they were speaking. He went over to the brazier placed out of the way in the corner, as he had almost never had the time to light it. Franzel had made sure it was laid ready to light, with wood in a beautifully decorated box beside it, a fire-starter to its side.

He carried the brazier over to the seating. Ludvic seemed to understand what he needed, for he moved the table to one side so that Cliopher could set the brazier in the centre of their grouping. He lit it with the fire-starter, knowing even as he did it that this showed a certain want in him. His great-uncle watched him narrowly, obviously noting the symbolic presence of the fire and the use of a Solaaran method of lighting it.

"So, boy, when was the last time you danced any part of the fire?"

Cliopher looked at him and said, "This morning."

★★★

HE EXPLAINED HIS DANCING AS simply as possible. His friends looked at him curiously as he described the mats and the patterns. No doubt the two guards had wondered what he did for exercise; something about Rhodin's expression suggested it. Buru Tovo nodded, revealing nothing of his thoughts.

"Good enough, boy," he decided eventually, when Cliopher faltered to a pause. (He could not call it a conclusion.) "So you haven't forgotten all the steps. What about the rest? What is your wealth?"

Wealth did not mean all the richness of fabric and art, of money in the bank or prestige in the world. It meant the knowledge Cliopher held in his mind, the songs he knew, and the symbols of that knowledge, the efela necklaces one earned, or bought, by exchange of that knowledge.

He got up from where he was sitting gingerly on the edge of his seat. Over on the wall of his sitting room, below the portrait of his great-uncle (who had yet to mention it), he had a large decorative chest. The chest itself was Voonran, bought cheaply in Astandalas when he had had the hours to spend looking around the second-hand shops. He opened the elaborate wrought-iron fasteners and reached in for the woven basket set inside.

The basket was from Western Dair, bought from a very young man from the then-slums of Csiven who had been doing whatever he could to eke out a living, but who had dreamed of a better life. Cliopher cherished the letter he had received from the man, no longer quite so young, a few years after the first of the Indrogan Estates had transformed the visual and economic landscape of the city. He had founded a little newspaper to describe the changes happening in his community; now the *Csiven Flyer* was read on three continents.

He set the basket on the low table between the seats. He fumbled a little with the stiff loop that held the toggle in place. He did not often open it.

It was traditional to lay them out in the order in which they came to hand. Cliopher would have been inclined to start with the least and build up to the most impressive, but that was not the way he had been taught.

The top necklace was the gold-ringed amber cowries from Lesuia. He lifted it out and held it up so the glossy shells caught the light. Forty-nine perfect cowries (he had counted them eventually), each about the length of his thumb, strung on a line made from the tough fibres teased out of Nijani flax.

Even there, in that room, before the Lord of Rising Stars, they were extraordinarily beautiful.

"Tell us the story of their coming to you," instructed Buru Tovo.

Cliopher took a breath. He gestured around to include his Radiancy, Conju, Ludvic, Rhodin. "We were staying on Lesuia, in Navikiani near Ikialo village. We were invited to a market at Ikiava. While we were there I stopped to look at a man with shells. I saw these in his collection."

"What did he ask you for?"

"He asked me my name, my island, my dances. Then he told me he'd heard of the three brothers who left, and asked me which I was. I said I went to sit at the feet of the Sun, and he asked me what I would bring home from the house of the Sun."

Buru Tovo cocked his head. "What did you say?"

Cliopher looked at the cool shells draped over his hand. Cowries had different significance in Jilkano, they were considered symbols of women's mysteries, gifts of the sea. Their shape lent itself to such interpretations, he thought, but the Wide Sea Islanders had always valued their beauty most.

"I said I would bring home the hearth-fire of a new life for the world."

He had meant it seriously. He still meant it seriously. Buru Tovo cackled. "What did he say?"

Cliopher smiled wryly. "He laughed at me like a kookaburra and said to be sure I did."

"You meet the Son of Laughter and tell him you're bringing a new fire to the Islands, you better believe he'll be watching. What else have you got in there, boy?"

"The Son of—" He stopped, for his great-uncle was grinning maliciously. "I know. Thinking first. Questions later if I can't figure out the answers on my own."

"Haven't forgotten everything, eh?"

He didn't dare meet his friends' eyes. He set the amber cowries down and pulled out the next string, which was made of tortoiseshell cowries set with gold pearls. It looked very like one of the necklaces Buru Tovo was wearing in the *Atlas* portrait, and he saw Rhodin look up at the painting and back down at the shells with a puzzled frown.

"This I bought on my visit home after I got the emergency stockpiles set up." He set it down, lifted out another, of tiny black cowries interspersed with purple-blue falao shells. "This was after the Indrogan Estates were established." Another, white cowries flushed with pale pink. "When Vinyë recovered from an illness she'd had."

He went through them all, twenty-five or thirty strands of a life, each of them marking some important moment, be it professional or personal. The ones from his younger days were shorter, the cowries smaller, more of them strung with other shells. Looking at them spread out before him he thought that they were all beautiful. He had not been able to afford the greater shells when he had first come home, but he had searched out to find lovely ones, meaningful ones, ones that he could place next to the gold-ringed amber cowries without shame.

Could that man who laughed like a kookaburra possibly have been Vou'a, the god of mystery? What did it mean, that his Buru even suggested it? Cliopher had never heard of anyone outside of stories meeting the gods.

Three nights after that encounter the Moon had come down to embrace the Sun-on-Earth.

Finally he came to the bottom of the basket and the last shell. It was not strung as a necklace. He had not bought it, nor traded for it, never been sure if it had truly been intended for him.

He lifted it out carefully. It was perhaps some sort of chambered nautilus, a spiral curve about the size of his hand. The shell was creamy white and iridescent green-blue, the colour of the feathers of a superb bird-of-paradise, of the heart of the Bay of the Waters, of the waters where the land fell away into the underwater caves where the toala guild members dove down and down until they could come up into the hidden caves where the star-spiders wove the silk that was made into foamwork.

He held it cupped in his hands to display to them.

"Ey ana," Buru Tovo said softly. "*Efani*. How did you come by that?"

Cliopher looked down at the shell. He could have been as concise in the account as he had been describing the origins of the other efela, but something moved in him and prompted him to say, slowly, the traditional words. "It's a long story of the sea to tell it."

After a moment Buru Tovo replied with the equally traditional words. "We sit by the fire ready to hear it."

Cliopher waited another few moments, breathing in and out, looking at the fire in the brazier, the shell in his hands catching its light. Ludvic got up and brought over another piece of wood, laying it carefully on the embers. Cliopher watched him, trying to find words, and then, as if he were making a report of his own experiences instead of the carefully objective (or at least, theoretically objective) observations he would use in a formal report, he began to speak.

CHAPTER *F*IFTY-*F*OUR

HE SET THE SHELL DOWN on the table, nestled in the coils of efela necklaces.

"After the Fall of Astandalas, I was for a time too busy to be lost. I had been in the Ministry of Health before, but the government had collapsed. I attached myself to Princess Indrogan and worked with her to rebuild. My job was to read the reports as they started to come in, write reports of verbal news, and summarize them."

He looked helplessly at his Radiancy, Rhodin, Conju, Ludvic, his great-uncle. "Report after report of disaster, death, famine, war. Anarchy in the south—flooding in the west—lava flows in the north—monsters in the sea. Magic gone awry, the weather mad, even time no longer working properly. I read them all and collated them into coherence, into reports that Princess Indrogan and others above me could use.

"And from east of Amboloyo and west of Jilkano, silence."

He smiled twistedly. "I was so excited the first time a letter came from the City of Emeralds. It had been sent by carrier pigeon across to Southern Dair, and then people had passed it hand over hand until it reached me in the Palace. At last, I thought, there was a sign of life in the Wide Seas.

"They reported a tsunami had destroyed the city and they had seen no lights from Zangoraville since. They had lost all their ocean-going ships. They had no food, no medicine, no magic, very little fresh water. There was dysentry, cholera, epidemics of diseases that had been unknown to physicians except as something people in the outworlds faced. Plagues. Pestilences. Roving bands of desperate people.

"And across the Wide Seas, they said, a wall of storms."

He swallowed, looking at the shells symbolizing the important parts of his life. The gold-ringed amber cowries, gift perhaps of Vou'a, the Son of Laughter, the god of mystery, to whom Cliopher had in his pride and his folly claimed that he would bring a new fire home to his people.

"I wrote letters. I sent them out with every person who was going anywhere, following the example of those seeking to find out what had happened, find someone to help them rebuild. I wrote letter after letter to my family. One kept coming back, and I kept writing addenda, explaining what I had done since its last return. It never got past the edge of the continent."

Ludvic got up and put another branch on the fire. Cliopher watched it catch. He did not know what he was trying to say, except the story. He had given those theoretically objective reports to his Radiancy, about what he had seen, when he came back.

He gestured at his Radiancy. "One day the Last Emperor awoke. Hope began to move, in a way that it had not before. People began to say to one another that things could be rebuilt, that the world could once again know peace and prosperity and good government.

"An admiral came. She had been caught on the seas when the Fall occurred, up in the corner of the Xiputl Arm. She had seen the lava flows overrun Northern Dair and run into the sea. She had seen strange creatures in the jungles of Xiputl. She was enough of a wizard that she felt the call that you sent out, my lord, to all who could hear, to summon them here to Solaara to find the news. She brought with her messengers she had found along the way, sent out of Damara with tales of their continent.

"From Kavanduru, stories of mad magic, of trees that flew and stones that walked, of rivers that burned and animals that spoke. Damara alone held anything resembling government, they reported, because the Grand Duchess held her people safe by her will. She sent messengers out in every direction to spread the news. Eventually their reports reached here, told us what they could, of the deaths, the destruction, how they had watched Kavanor fall into the sea.

"And across the Wide Seas, they said, a wall of storms."

He stopped, trying to catch his breath, trying not to say all the weight of his memories. They had their own memories of those days, his friends. Conju and Rhodin had lost all their families. His Radiancy had been comatose for a hundred years. Ludvic ...

He looked around, met their gazes carefully, including the tawny gold of his Radiancy's, his great-uncle's clouded brown. Took another careful breath to steady himself.

"The admiral was from Jilkano, but her family had travelled to the Vangavaye-ve just before the Fall. It was known as a wonder of the Nine Worlds, of course. She decided to go find them. I ..."

He took a deep breath. This was one of the sharpest regrets of his life. He did not know how to say how much it pierced him to know he had made this decision.

"I gave her the letter—the one that kept coming back—to take. I did not go myself."

He could not meet anyone's gaze. He looked at the brazier, at the coals, at the newer wood burning cleanly, the scent of acacia from the Solamen Plains, not the scent he knew from home. The shell Buru Tovo had called *efani*, Ani's tear.

"I didn't go. I went to Princess Indrogan to ask her leave, and she would not give it to me. I should have gone. As soon as I saw the ship go I knew I should have gone ... I ..." He stopped, breath catching again. "I didn't go. I let her go without me. I did not stand up for what I knew was the right decision."

He was silent for a long while, trying to collect himself. Buru Tovo watched him, eyes narrowed, all the wrinkles of a life of laughter and wisdom hiding anything but the good humour and deep knowledge he possessed. His Radiancy said softly, "Princess Indrogan was one of the strongest personalities I have ever encountered. And she could not have wanted to lose you."

Cliopher closed his eyes, feeling tears starting. Was it as simple as that?

"I was weak," he said. He realized he was bunching the fabric of his robes in his hands. He smoothed the fabric out slowly, trying not to shake. "I should have gone."

"You didn't," said Buru Tovo. "What did you do?"

"I worked. I wrote letters that disappeared. I counted out the months it might take for the admiral to get to the Vangavaye-ve: back across to Kavanduru, across the Wide Seas ... into that wall of storms. I counted out the months, and the years, and finally one day I could not bear the silence any longer and I went to Princess Indrogan and I resigned."

He stopped there for a moment. He had told his Radiancy this, on the sky ship (or was it on the sand bar? Or the bench outside the lighthouse on the Palaoa lagoon?). He had not told anyone else this story. No one had asked, and he had not made them listen.

"She told me all the reasons why I was an idiot to leave my position, that she was a rising star in the Emperor's new court and that she would take me with her. But by then ... I can be stubborn. I persevered.

"So I went. I went south, overland, with a detachment of the Guard who were setting up an outpost in Southern Dair. I spent months prisoner of one of the mountain tribes, who thought I was sent as a spy. Finally they agreed that if I were a spy for the Plainsmen the most obnoxious thing they could do to me—besides killing me, obviously, but I managed to persuade them not to do that—was to set me down on the other side of the mountains, so they took me through the rope bridges across the Southern Grey Mountains and abandoned me on the western side.

"I made it down to the port of Csiven, by which point I had no money and nothing to trade except for an ability to write chancery hand and knowledge of conditions in the world. I made enough as a news-crier to eke out a few weeks while I waited for the trade winds to start. I found someone who was taking a party of hunters to the Yenga—there was famine in Western Dair and they were even willing to take on the thunder lizards for food—and the captain agreed to drop me off at the guano mines on Do Alouak."

"What did you expect to find there?" Rhodin asked him, frowning.

Cliopher smiled slightly. "Guano. I was just trying to get as far west as I could, and I reckoned that Do Alouak was the last port between Western Dair and Jilkano where people could take on water before embarking across the Nearer Western Sea. As it happened, I saw nothing of Do Alouak because there was a ship just readying to sail when we came into sight. They waited for our news, but the winds were unsettled and the captain was afraid he'd be driven onto the rocks if they turned, so I got on with about two minutes of explanation that I was coming from Solaara and going west."

"Who were they?"

"A pirate ship—well, they'd been part of the Zuni division of the Imperial Navy, and had struck out as 'free merchantmen' after the Fall. I spent an educational few months with them going around the Southern Hook of the Yenga and then through the Pinnacles of eastern Jilkano. The captain was eventually taken up for piracy," Cliopher added reflectively, "many years afterwards."

"You testified on his behalf," his Radiancy observed.

"He did treat me with courtesy. The pirates dropped me off on a deserted beach on the Jilkano mainland, and I walked from there to the City of Emeralds. There was so much fear, so much anxiety. I went from village to village along the old walking routes, earning my supper by telling the news. Over the Massif to the City of Emeralds, and there in the ruins I saw the shadow that lay on the Wide Sea. No one wanted to sail west. But I persisted. Finally I met a merchant who was from Nijan, and he said he would take me there. We set off one morning ... in good weather it's what, six hours' sail from the

City of Emeralds to Zangoraville? You can see Mount Glory on a clear day.

"It took us—well, it felt like two weeks. Possibly it was years. We entered the darkness on the second day, and, well ... the gods smiled on us, and sent us a frigate bird. We followed him, in this little trading boat that was meant for the Leeward Sea, rowing, sailing when we could, getting hungrier and thirstier, wondering if we would ever see daylight again ... then we broke through and landed at last in Zangoraville."

"There had still been no news at that point?" his Radiancy asked.

"None. Their harbour was all right, and at first I was heartened, for it was full of all sorts of vessels. When we came ashore, however, and were greeted, we discovered that although a few people had made it to shore, there were not many, and they were ... marked, I suppose, by the passage through the darkness."

"Everyone was marked by the Fall," his Radiancy said softly. "Some more obviously, or more deeply, than others."

Cliopher shrugged uncomfortably. He had never considered himself marked in that way. Had he not come through unscathed, when so many had not? He had not lost his family, his homeland, his life.

He took a breath. This was the point of this story. "In Nijan there were stragglers, most of them from right after the Fall. They were desperate for news—they knew that there had been some sort of major cataclysm, but not what it was, what it meant. I lost my voice from telling the news over and over again.

"For a while I thought I was going to be stuck there with them. No one wanted to go west—no one had come back from the other side of the barrier reefs, and they had lost all their ocean-going ships. There was a wall of storms across the Wide Seas, I was told by the people who had been caught on the water when Astandalas fell, by the fishermen who went to the edge of the reefs. I asked everyone—I persisted—I am good at persisting—I had not come so far to stop there—and finally I was told of a mad artist who was a Wide Sea Islander."

"She was *wontok*?" asked Buru Tovo.

Cliopher nodded. "Yes. She spoke the same language—is of my people," he added for the benefit of the others. "She was actually a Scholar originally from Lobau, which is one of the Isolates. She was long since retired, and spent her time trying to reconstruct the old knowledge from what she had learned as a child and what she could find in the libraries. She was a bit cracked, I suppose. So was I, by that point. At any rate, when she told me she could show me how to make an old Voyager boat, I said ... yes."

"You made a boat? The old way?" Buru Tovo asked sharply.

"Yes. At the time I did think how much you would approve—and how much I already knew how to do, once I was reminded, thanks to your teaching. I knew how to plait grass, make lines, what plants to use for weaving and which for sewing ... I knew how to make a drill out of a bow and a piece of obsidian, a knife, a fire pot. Saya Ng—that was the old Scholar's name—she showed me the shapes to cut the wood, how to build an outrigger, how to shape the sail. She wasn't strong enough to do it herself. She sat there under an umbrella at the edge of the clearing where we worked and shouted vague instructions at me."

"You always respond so well to that," his Radiancy murmured.

Cliopher smiled. "Yes, my lord. Eventually there came the day when we thought the boat was ready. She was still worried that I didn't know how to navigate properly. She was Nga, Buru Tovo," he added.

His great-uncle snorted. "Ey ana, they never think anyone else can read the stars. She went with you?"

"Yes. She said to me that I was mad but she was old, and though it would be the last thing she did she would sail the Wide Seas as her ancestors had before her. She said I could carry the fire, but she would read the wind."

"Nga," Buru Tovo said, shaking his head. "That's why most of them ended up in the Isolates. Mad as albatrosses."

"So you set out in a boat you had built—out of what?" Rhodin asked.

"Bush materials. Pandanus leaves, coconut fibres, balsa wood, Nijani flax, kauna wood, that sort of thing."

"And for food you had ... ?"

"We had a great many coconuts. Taro, manioc, breadfruit, dried fish ... and our lines and our hooks and our knowledge. We didn't know how long it would take to reach Odou'a, the first of the island archipelagos west of Nijan. Our boat wasn't really big enough for an oceangoing voyage. We should have had a fifty-foot double-hulled canoe with two sails and twenty or more crew. Instead it was about twenty feet long and just the two of us."

"And the Nijani just let you go?" Rhodin asked, leaning forward. "They must have thought you were insane!"

"They wanted to give us our funerals before we left. They promised to pray for our souls. We went on an outgoing tide through the barrier reefs just at sunset, and then Saya Ng pointed us towards the Fisherman and the Wide Seas, and for several hours we thought we were doing fine. The second day out we hit the first of the typhoons."

Cliopher wanted to skim lightly over the subject, but this was the heart of the tale, and he could not. "We made it through the first typhoon in one piece, but it took us a long way out of our way, and although she had the knowledge, she did not have all the long practice of it. She'd stopped when she was a young woman, her teacher had died and her family wanted her to leave the old ways. They had moved to Zangoraville, left their island."

"Different in Nijan," said Buru Tovo. "Go on, boy."

"We held our course as best we could towards Odou'a. We thought we should reach it on the seventeenth day, but the typhoon meant that we did not know if we had lost our latitude. We started seeing land birds on the twentieth day—noua, white terns."

"Ey ana, you were close, then."

"We were close to somewhere. Saya Ng knew that they fly out quite far, so we could not expect to reach their island that night. They sleep on islands," he explained to Rhodin and the others. "Then they fly out to sea in the morning to feed. They fly close to the surface when feeding, then as the sun begins to set they rise and set off back to land. Watching them, you can chart a course based on their direction, find even a low atoll that way. That was what we did. The only thing was that each type of bird goes out a differ-ent range—the noua go further than the naua, the brown terns, for instance.

"We were so relieved that we were coming close to land, that we might have a chance to rest, to sleep, to get more food, to catch fish ... we did not pay enough attention to the signs."

"A storm?"

Cliopher sighed. "Yes. Another typhoon, or close to it. It seemed to come out of nowhere. I had begun to learn the feel of the waves of the open ocean, like you showed me, Buru, for the Bay of the Waters, but I did not understand all the changes, that the voices of the winds were different. We did out best, but so soon after the last one ... we were exhausted, both of us." He looked at the shell. "Saya Ng was old and not as strong as I was. She went over ... I could not find her again ..."

Buru Tovo spoke sternly. "Her body went to the waves and her spirit to the call of her ancestors, guiding a fire-tender across the Wide Seas. She was Nga. She died valiantly. You may let her go from your hands."

Cliopher looked up at his great-uncle, his mouth dry. "Have I been hold-ing her all this time, Buru?"

"Ey ana," he said more gently, reaching over and patting him on the shoulder. "You kept her flame burning long and long. You offered to hold the fire so that she could follow the call of the sea to the sunset, as her ancestors before her. You can do no more. You could do no more. We all must answer when the gods call us."

Cliopher bowed his head, looking at his hands cradled in the bronze and blue silk of his robes. His friends were silent, letting him speak.

"After many days alone in the storm I had no idea where I was. I missed the island the noua had shown me. I ended up at last finding land almost by accident ... I saw one frigate-bird flying high, and followed him through the reefs to an island. It was big enough to have trees, coconuts and breadfruit and pandanus. No water, but I had collected enough in the storm that I was not totally lost, not with coconuts there.

"It was very beautiful. I dragged my boat up onto the sand and I built a fire and I sat there as the sun went down and the stars came out and thought that it was one of the most beautiful places I had ever been, and I was from the Vangavaye-ve, the home of music."

"Where was it?"

Cliopher smiled at Rhodin's question. "I have absolutely no idea. Somewhere in the southern part of the Wide Seas."

They all looked at him. After a bit, his Radiancy said, "You're not a wizard. You can't tell by magic ... how did you find out where you were? For I perceive that you are now here, rather than a wild hermit on a remote isolated island."

"I danced."

Buru Tovo said sharply, "Explain, boy."

Cliopher felt as he had as a young boy, using what Buru Tovo thought too impertinent a tone. He made a gesture of apology, palm over fist in the Vangavayen style. "I repaired the boat. I rested and regathered my energy and my resources. I watched the sky, the sea, the birds, the fish, the sun, the stars. And all the time I worried that I would die there, on that island, alone and of no use to anybody.

"Eventually I finished the work, and as we have always done when the work is done, I danced. I danced all the old dances you had taught me, Buru, and the ones we do when we sing the *Lays*, over and over again. One day I built a great bonfire and when it was burned down to coals I raked them into the patterns of the fire dance.

"And when I danced that fire dance I remembered that you told me that this was our store of knowledge ... is it permitted, Buru, to speak of these things, before *velioi*?"

"They are the sun and the stars of your witnessing, boy."

Cliopher nodded, found his voice again. "You had told me that the dances showed the way, that the fire dance was the record of our family's journeys, all that had been done in old days when we crossed the Wide Seas. And as I danced it, I came to wonder if it was not perhaps a map of those journeys. If only I could figure out where in the dance I was, perhaps I could figure out where to go."

"And you did?" said Rhodin intently.

"Yes. It took me ... I don't know how long. Months. Years. I don't know. I danced it over and over again, drawing the patterns on the sand, in coals. Dancing it at night, in the morning, at noon, in the evening. Dancing it as the stars turned ... Dancing it, trying to figure out what the key was, what it said beyond the words of the songs, the movements of the dance. That was what I did. I danced. I went fishing, swimming, hunting octopus and crabs and sea turtles. I took my boat out to see what the currents told me, the winds, the waves, the sky. I studied the ways of the birds, the fish, the dolphins, the whales. Then one day I finally remembered you telling me, Buru, that all of what you had taught me was only practice, because the proper time for the dance was at sunset when the moon is is a new crescent when the Fisherman—that's one of the southern constellations—stands upright."

Buru Tovo nodded. "Four days from today."

The longest Cliopher had spent out-of-doors in the past year had been his evening with Rhodin. He had had no idea what the current phase of the moon was. Once he had known it as intimately as he now knew the bells.

"I waited until the moon was new, the Fisherman stood upright. I set up the coals, and this time when I danced, as I moved my hands, set my feet in the patterns, I realized that at one point in the dance, the turn I was making, the shape my hands made, the way my feet moved, the rhythm of the words, the line of the coals ... all of those things together were the shape of the place that I was. They told me the shape of the currents, the winds, the stars, the waves."

He found he was half-making the gestures, holding his hands in the arc that pointed (he had finally realized) exactly to the point where the sun had set—but only when he stood at the right point of the dance for where he was in the sea, with the pattern oriented properly to the cardinal directions, at the right time of day at the right time of the month in the right time of the year.

He set his hands self-consciously in his lap again. "Once I knew where in the dance the island was I had to figure out where the Vangavaye-ve was ... but we always call the end of the dance *coming home*, and this was the dance of my family, my ancestors who had come to the Vangavaye-ve, to Loaloa in the Western Ring. The dance was a kind of map, of the currents and the winds and the relations between the islands of the Wide Seas. Once I knew where I was, and where I was going, I could plot my course."

Buru Tovo was nodding, quite as if this was exactly what he had expected. Perhaps he had. It was possible that the key of the map was common knowledge, or at least was known to the *tanà* who kept the deeper knowledge of its meaning. If Cliopher had not left the Vangavaye-ve in the first place ... if he had stayed, if he had rested content within the Ring as almost the whole of his family did, if he had satisfied himself with the life he could have led there ...

Well, perhaps he would be sitting on the verandah of his own house, watching his own children (even grandchildren!) play, growing deeper and deeper in the wisdom learned from the sea and the stars and the sky.

But he would not be sitting in a room with the Sun-on-Earth; and he would not have sailed the Wide Seas in a boat of his own building; and he would never have done more than dream the vaguest idea of a new fire for the world.

"I sailed home," he said simply.

Years it had taken him, or perhaps decades, or perhaps even centuries, in those days when time had not followed hour after hour as it did now. Zigzagging from island to island, learning the ways of birds whose names he never learned, of the winds named in the old *Lays*, of fish and sea-going creatures who never came close to shore.

He had seen wonders, phosphorescent waves, a sea full of jellyfish like the magic-illuminated globes that lit the Palace, flying fish catching the sun like jewelled bronze.

He had learned to sleep with his body listening to the waves, how they changed in the night, how they shifted the course his small boat took.

He had gone through more storms, each time despairing, each time spun out of his course, limping with torn sails or broken rudders or spoiled food to the next uninhabited atoll or sudden volcanic mount. Waited for the stars to be in the right position, so he could build a new fire, out of seaweed and driftwood and coconut husks, rake out the coals into the old patterns, find again the island, the way.

And finally, after so long at sea he had forgotten the sound of his own voice raised in anything but the songs of his ancestors, telling him their deeds, raising his spirits, showing him the way, he had heard the birds crying and the surf booming and smelled suddenly on an evening breeze the flowers of the Outer Ring.

"I sailed home," he said again. "I came to the Gate of the Ring at night, and I cast the sea anchor to wait for the morning. I could hear the birds crying on Pau'en'lo'ai. I thought they sounded like the voices of the dead. By then I did not mind. The ancestors had shown me the way home."

He reached forward, picked up the shell, which Buru Tovo had called *efani*. He knew the word, mentioned in one of the *Lays* as it was, the shell sacred to Ani, the Mother of the Mountains, the one who had sung the great lament, the first song, when her son sailed away from her to see what lay on the other side of the horizon. *Efani* was the tear of Ani, which she had shed not on his going but on his coming home.

"That night I could not sleep. At first I thought it was because I was worried about my anchorage, so close to the reefs as I was. But by then I knew the sound of danger on the water. Then I thought I was afraid of the toll-keepers, that I would not know the right things to say. I had never tried to pass them, was not sure if the stories were true. Then I thought I was afraid of what I would find on the other side of the Ring. What would I see, when the sun rose in the morning? Would I see what I had come so far to find—or would I see something like the destruction I had found in Southern Dair, in Western Dair, in Csiven, in Jilkano, in Nijan?

"It was a dark night. I sat there, awake, watching the stars move overhead, in and out of clouds, listening to the birds crying in the night. Slowly the night turned to dawn. The Gate faces towards the sunrise. As the sky lit before the sun rose above the horizon I readied the boat to sail the rest of the way. Just as it became light enough to see, I saw floating on the water beside me this shell."

He looked at his great-uncle. "That is it. I saw the shell, and it seemed … I wasn't sure. I didn't know what it was, that it was *efani* of the stories. I wasn't sure if I should take it, if it was meant for me, or if it had been intended to sail out of the Gate and into the Wide Seas. If I took it, was I preventing someone's prayer from going home? Later I wondered very much. But I could not help but think it was a gift for me. The birds had finally stopped crying. I reached and lifted it out of the water. The sun came over the horizon and struck a blaze on the shell as I touched it, so I was nearly blinded for a moment. I almost put it back, then, but I decided that it seemed as if I had been marked by it, by the sun and the sea, and so … and so here it is."

He sat back to indicate that he was done. Buru Tovo had closed his eyes, not showing either approval or disapproval.

After a moment Cliopher remembered the traditional closing words. "So far did I go over the seas, gathering together the words of my tale that I have told you today."

Buru Tovo spoke without opening his eyes. "May the story be remembered as long as fire burns."

There was silence. Cliopher felt his heart thundering in his ears. He looked at his friends, at Rhodin and Ludvic and Conju and his Radiancy. They all sat there in silence, faces solemn, the brazier crackling softly and the shells winking in its light.

Finally Buru Tovo opened his eyes. He transfixed Cliopher with them. "Never have I heard that you sailed the Wide Seas in a boat of your own hand's shaping, boy."

Cliopher's insides congealed with something like guilt or shame. He was unable to keep his own eyes up. He looked down at the shells. He had never consciously noted how much the vase in his lord's study he loved so much was the same colour as this shell. "No, Buru," he replied quietly.

"And why not?"

The story of that homecoming was not one he could bear to tell. His heart felt raw from the tale of his voyage. He said, "At the time, no one asked me how I had come home, and I did not choose to speak of it later."

Rhodin said incredulously, "Didn't your family want to know how you'd crossed the Wide Seas? How could they not *ask* you?"

Cliopher compressed his lips to hold back—not words, precisely, but emotions that were old and dead and irrelevant, surely.

"My grandmother, the matriarch of our family, was dying. She had been telling everyone for months that she was waiting for me to come before she went to join the ancestors. They had had that one letter from me ... the admiral had made it to the Vangavaye-ve, though her ship had foundered on the reefs coming in. They knew I had survived the Fall ... and they thought I had chosen to stay in Solaara. When I walked in the door they were all focused on her ... I don't think anyone even noticed I was wearing a grass skirt. It was not the time to speak of myself, not when my grandmother was in that state, and after she had passed on ..." He shrugged, managed a smile. "Afterwards the questions were all about the future, not the past."

"And you never ..." Rhodin stopped, shook his head. "You've never said."

And until there came a necessary moment of intimacy, Ludvic had never said that he was from Woodlark, that when he had given that order to shoot anyone trying to escape the conflagration visited upon the island by his Radiancy's magic to stop the spread of the pestilence there, it was his own family and people and island he was condemning.

And Conju had only ever hinted at the grief he had felt, that he still held within him, for that long-ago friend of his who was a wild mage and had fled the Empire, and who had not wanted to ask Conju to choose between the Empire and him.

And his Radiancy had only ever wept once for all the years he had been a god and not a man, in that private study of his, when Cliopher had done his best to give him the comfort of someone else's touch.

And Rhodin himself had never spoken of what he had lost when Astandalas Fell.

"No," said Cliopher, quietly, meaning many things he could not say in better words. He found his hand had strayed to the one efela he wore. He had made that necklace under the auspices (and vague instructions) of his Buru Tovo. Each hard-won pearl, each even more hard-won hole drilled through for the line, the smoothly faceted obsidian centre pendant, the knotted string that had never once come undone no matter how he abused it.

"Efela ko," his great-uncle said, nodding at it. "And to you?"

"All that I am is held in my beginning," he recited duly. "Pearls of the sea, cord of the land, stone of the fire, circled around my throat that breathes and the voice that sings."

Buru Tovo reached over and picked up the *efani*. He turned it over in his hands, as if reading something written in the pattern of iridescence and cream, of chamber and spiral, of story and silence and the sound of the sea when it was held to the ear.

"It is the crescent moon four days from now," he said. "The Fisherman stands in the sky. You will dance *Aōteketētana* then before your community here."

"You will dance it in the throne room," said his Radiancy, equally firmly, and then he smiled. "At the feet of the Sun."

CHAPTER ᏻIFTY-ᏻIVE

"BUT, LORD MDANG, YOU MUST——"

Cliopher swung around in the middle of the outer office to see that the Master of Ceremonies had followed him in. He bit back his first expostulation as intemperate and said, "I'm afraid I don't see what your problem is, Lord Lior."

Lord Lior, the Master of Ceremonies, stared. Kiri and Aioru and Gaudy and everyone else in the room stared. Cliopher was at the very edge of losing his temper, and so he, too, stared—in his case at Lord Lior, whom he had just asked to organize the court to accommodate the unusual orientation required by the fire dance.

"Lord Mdang," said Lord Lior, all sweet reason and immutable custom, "you are asking me to flout the courtly manners of thousands of years of civilization in order to perform some——"

He stopped.

Cliopher found control over his tongue slipping. "Do say the word you mean."

Lord Lior retreated. "Lord Mdang, I ask you, as a reasonable man—you *are* a reasonable man—you understand the impossibility of what you are asking. It will not do, your excellency—it is a longstanding pride of mine, of my office, that the throne room of the Palace of Stars has never been sullied by——"

He stopped again.

"By what, Lord Lior?"

"Lord Mdang, you know of what I speak."

Cliopher counted to ten. He had never particularly liked Lord Lior, but he'd never disliked him either. This current tone of jocular fellowship, of we-belong-to-the-same-club-ness, of intimations that they stood together as bulwarks of civilization against the barbaric hordes thronging outside the walls—

Oh, it got his back up.

He had for too many years smiled and not said what he was thinking. He was always only tolerated on the edge of the inner circles, and did not care except insofar as he needed access to those sanctums if he were to fulfil his aims.

"Say it," he said.

His voice was still controlled. He probably looked much the same as always. If he did not lose control of his tongue no one would know how angry he was. No one did; he had heard rumours occasionally of how even-tempered he was. He smiled and said nothing then, either, his Radiancy's words coming to mind. *That I do not display my emotions does not mean I do not have them.*

"Lord Mdang, surely we understand each other well enough. The entertainment you propose ..."

"It is not an entertainment."

"Exhibition, then? Lord Mdang, the appropriate place for such an event is the Museum of Comparative Anthropology. The Gallery of Primitive Cultures——"

Cliopher gritted his teeth. He had to work with Lord Lior for the Viceroyship ceremonies. "*Primitive* in the art historical sense?"

"Oh, very good, your excellency. Yes, precisely. Lord Mdang, we all have embarrassing relatives who make intemperate demands on us. We may try to fulfil them, privately, if they are not too onerous. We do not upend the entire court."

"I am not embarrassed by my relations, Lord Lior."

Lord Lior said, "Of course not!" in a tone of voice that meant *you should be,* and Cliopher's tenuous hold on his temper broke.

He took a step forward. "Lord Lior," he said, "you should be grateful on your life that I am not truly one of the upper aristocracy, because you are grievously insulting me and mine. How *dare* you respond to my request for you to arrange the courtiers appropriately in the Throne Room by suggesting I should hold the ceremony in the Gallery of Primitive Cultures in the Museum of Comparative Anthropology?"

"Lord Mdang, I meant only that——"

"Ah, Lord Lior, you seem unaware of my propensity for taking what people say at face value."

He took a breath. Lord Lior jumped in with, "Lord Mdang, you overreact! I mean no insult to you and yours——"

"Really? And here I had always been under the impression that it was precisely your job to know how to avoid or give insult at will."

He watched the Master of Ceremonies cast about for some way to mend this situation. Cliopher made no attempt to help him, to de-escalate, to behave in any way like the diplomat, the politician, the smoother-over of rough waters and ruffled spirits.

"Lord Mdang, I am sorry if in any way I spoke, ah, intemperately. You are a reasonable man; you understand the need to obey the rules; you are very skilled in the courtly dances."

"Yes," Cliopher said acidly, "I have always enjoyed playing dress-up."

Lord Lior stepped back as if that had been a physical blow. "Your excellency—we have worked together for many years—you have never been so bold as to suggest—you are a reasonable man—"

"Whereas you are a soft-spoken hypocrite."

"Lord Mdang!"

"You have done your best to keep from committing yourself to anything, but I must admit I find that reprehensible. I cannot respect your preference of the forms of courtesy over every substance of virtue."

"You have always been held as the very model of successful assimilation—"

Lord Lior took another step back, at the expression on his face, Cliopher assumed, for he had not himself moved. He took a deep breath before he spoke, though not to calm his temper; simply to make sure he could speak clearly and not shout. He looked around, not at anyone, just to gather his thoughts, but he saw the faces watching him in various attitudes of shock.

Kiri, Eldo, Tully, the half-dozen others who came from courtly or long-standing bureaucratic families, all of them astounded and confounded by the even-tempered diligent Cliopher Mdang losing his temper at the Master of Ceremonies, symbol of all the hierarchy of which they were a part.

Gaudy, Zaoul, Aioru, Iri and Iro, the half-dozen others in the office who came from the far-flung hinterlands of the world, from the lower classes and the distant provinces, from those cultures depicted in *The Atlas of Imperial Peoples*, and from all those ancient civilizations whose arts and artefacts were displayed in the Gallery of Primitive Peoples in the Imperial Museum of Cultural Anthropology.

What he said now *mattered*. It mattered to them—to Gaudy, who was family! To Zaoul, who was Tkinele!

It mattered to everyone who had looked at him and wondered if making a difference in the world meant abandoning all they loved of their homes.

It mattered to those others, to Kiri and Eldo and all those like them, to

Lord Lior himself, all those whose cultures were not shown in the *Atlas*, who would never be asked to be ashamed of what they were, who would never be praised for *assimilating*.

And, by all his own ancestors, it mattered to him. How could he claim the fire if he ran from its burn?

He said, "Lord Lior, I would respect you more if you came right out and called me a savage."

That caused the first audible response from the audience, a shocked gasp. Lord Lior tried to say something, but Cliopher talked right over him.

"I do not flaunt my culture in the faces of the ignorant and the abusive. It is *mine*. I do not come to court in Islander finery, because I respect your cultural traditions and prejudices. I have my own."

He stopped, swallowing. He had thought losing his temper would be like opening the door of a pen, as if all his emotions would rush out, but he had kept them silent for so long he had to dredge deep-down to find the words to express them.

"Lord Lior. You were in the Palace through the Fall of Astandalas. Do you remember what happened in the immediate aftermath? What did you do?"

"A-after the *Fall*? Lord Mdang—"

"Answer me, Lord Lior."

Lord Lior's eyes were wide. "I—I went with the others to the Throne Room to find out what had happened."

"And?"

"And ...?"

"And what happened then, Lord Lior?"

"I, I, I don't remember. It was so awful—and so long ago!—we were all talking, Lord Mdang, you cannot know what it was like, all the fear and the uncertainty."

"I was there, Lord Lior. I know what it was like. What did you do?"

"*You* were here in the Fall?—No! No, I will answer!"

He frowned, closing his eyes, obviously far happier to humour this strange tangent than face Cliopher Mdang in a temper. Well, he was not stupid, not usually.

"We all stood there, trying to figure out what was going on, afraid and uncertain and hoping someone would take control—and then, yes, I remember, the servants started bringing out hot soup." He laughed nervously. "Lord Mdang, I had forgotten that until now, though at the time I swore I would never forget how comforting that bowl of soup was ... It was like being a child and given comfort when you most need it. I think I can see your point. Lord Mdang, we owe respect to our families who took care of us—"

"That is not my point, Lord Lior, though I am glad to find you not entirely without emotional attachments. Do you know *why* there was hot soup in the immediate aftermath of the Fall?"

Lord Lior blinked. "Obviously the cooks prepared it."

"Let me tell you. Before I myself went to the Throne Room to see what was toward, I went down to the cafeterias in the lower parts of the Palace. There were very few survivors down there. There had been a skeleton staff in the kitchens, the rest of the staff having been given the night off for the Silverheart celebrations. One of the cooks was there, weeping, because all the magic had failed. The cold rooms—the hot water—the stoves."

"The soup was *hot*, I tell you."

Cliopher smiled thinly at him. "It was hot because I know how to light a fire without magic, without matches, without anything but two sticks and a string. I lit the first fire in the Palace after the Fall of Astandalas—and I tell you, sir, *I have not let it go out since.*"

"Lord Mdang—"

"I lit that first fire, Lord Lior, deep in the cold heart of a Palace that had lost its way. I went to the Throne Room and found there Princess Indrogan starting to organize people, and I attached myself to her to assist any way I could with the rebuilding of the world. I built that fire and I have tended it all the long years of my life since, because I am a Mdang of the Vangavaye-ve and our dances are the Dances of Those Who Tend the Fire.

"My ancestors carried fire across the Wide Seas, from island to island, bringing with them light and music and art and all the other necessities of civilization. You do not get to tell me that my culture is primitive, Lord Lior. My culture is ten thousand years older than yours. Our songs go back before the coming of the Empire. When Aurelius Magnus was fighting a losing war and needed allies, he had heard of my people, and he asked for our assistance and our knowledge, to show him the way across the sea. We are not a warlike people. We are sailors and musicians: but we know the way, by the Sun and the stars and the winds we can find our way."

"Lord Mdang—"

"You say I am the model of assimilation? I was the first person from all the Wide Seas to enter the Imperial Service. I learned early the importance of not being seen to rock the boat."

He paused a moment, to let that phrase sink in, but Lord Lior stared at him with wide, uncomprehending eyes.

The hell with that, he thought. He wanted the man to *understand* what he was saying.

He gestured at his outfit. "Lord Lior, I am willing to dress the part. I am willing to speak the part. I am willing to let people mispronounce my name. I am willing to overlook being called everything from a *savage* to an *aristocrat*.

"I am not, and have never been, willing to compromise my principles. When I look back on what I have done with my life I rest content knowing that when I have made mistakes, I made them from my principles and to the best of my knowledge, and that I was able to learn from those mistakes and do my best to fix them. I learned in a hard school, Lord Lior, that mistakes can kill. My father died from such a mistake made in the face of the sea. Mistakes of philosophy or policy do not seem like they can be so deadly, but they are."

He paused for another breath. He had not even launched headlong into the core of the problem. He had never laid claim to these feelings, never articulated them, and he—who spent his life articulating the impossible!—found the words coming hard.

Lord Lior, unwisely, thought it a good moment to interject a soothing platitude. "Lord Mdang, you are well respected for your accomplishments. We all know you work very hard for the good of the world."

"I do thank you for noticing."

The Master of Ceremonies winced. "Lord Mdang, you are a great diplomat. You understand the importance of compromise. Perhaps there is a way to—"

"The only reason anyone has ever thought I compromised on anything, Lord Lior, is because they don't have a clue what my aims are."

"You are currently riding high on public opinion. But your excellency, please think! The customs are there to guide us in uncertain times, when we do not know what to do. At some stage the wind of opinion will shift, and then where will you be in all your vaunted reforms and work?"

Cliopher pounced. "You appear to have forgotten at some stage in our conversation, astonishing though it is, that I am from the Vangavaye-ve. I am a descendant of those who settled the Wide Seas. I don't care two shakes of a stick for the direction the wind blows."

Lord Lior stared at him some more.

Cliopher realized this was the way. Something lit in him, a fire perhaps, a wind, a star—the realization that this was his direction, that this was his way home, to being who he was, to stating clearly and firmly for once exactly what he believed.

He almost smiled with exultation, as if his soul was a sail and he had set the angle just right for it to be filled, for it to take him the direction he wished to go, home—home—*home*!

"You look at me and see the model of successful assimilation, the primitive, the barbarian, the *savage* from the proverbial end of nowhere who made his way up the ranks of society to land before you the Lord Chancellor of Zunidh. I am dressed that way. I speak that way. I permit you to instruct me in the behaviour appropriate to that position, and I follow it.

"And because I do those things, you believe that I have sloughed off my past, my family, my culture, my origin, my home, and embraced without remorse or regret or recidivism the height of civilization as embodied in the hierarchical structure of the Solaaran court."

He paused for a moment, swallowing, gathering his thoughts. "You are wrong."

Someone moved in the corner of his eye, but he could not see who it was, and he did not care. "I have heard it all, Lord Lior. I have heard myself called a savage, a barbarian, a primitive—"

"Lord Mdang—"

"—Backward, uncivilized, uncouth, untamed—"

"Lord Mdang, please—"

"Radical, revolutionary, rebellious, revolting."

"Lord Mdang, I—"

"I have heard myself called a loony, a lowbrow, a lowlife—and also a lackey, a lickspittle, a lapdog, a tool. I am considered by the conservative outlandishly radical, and by the liberal the toady of an outmoded system."

"Lord Mdang, I assure—"

"When the wind blows from the middle classes, I am a pawn of the aristocracy. When the wind blows from the upper ranks, I am a barbarian set to destroy civilization. When the wind blows from the hinterlands, all my work is for the city; when it blows from the cities, I am only concerned with the provinces. The poor complain that I work only for the wealthy, the rich that I care only about the poor. To all the people of Zunidh I am a scandal."

He smiled at Lord Lior, who would never have dared to say any of those things to his face, though he had certainly thought half of them.

"I am the Lord Chancellor of Zunidh. I am the Secretary in Chief of the Offices of the Lords of State. I am the Chair of the Helma Council. I am the Hands of the Emperor. I am equal in rank to the Council of Princes as a body.

I asked you to assist me because we have worked together for many years and I respect your skill at your job."

He paused for emphasis, then continued: "Having clarified your personal opinion of me, our interactions are now placed firmly in professional relation, and under that category, Lord Lior, you know far better than I exactly how much I do not need to *ask*."

Lord Lior opened his mouth and then shut it again.

"I am Cliopher Mdang of Tahivoa in Gorjo City of the Vangavaye-ve. My island is Loaloa. My dances are *Aōteketētana*. I am a Wide Sea Islander.

"My ancestors sailed across the Wide Seas in boats of their own hands' building—as have I. They carried the fire of civilization from the House of the Sun to the islands they claimed as their own—as have I. They learned the ways of the winds and the seas and the stars, of the birds and the fish and the animals, and very certainly also the ways of men—as have I. They did not store their knowledge in writing, so easily lost or damaged in the seas, but in their minds, in their dances and their songs and their designs, and in the knowledge they passed on from generation to generation.

"I left the Vangavaye-ve so that I might go sit at the feet of the Sun. I wished to see the heart of the fire. I wished to know this Empire of which we were a part. I wanted to know what was said of the meeting of the Emperor Aurelius Magnus with the Paramount Chief Elonoa'a of the Vangavaye-ve in the halls that had been built by the descendants of the Emperor. I wanted to see what I could do to make the world a better place. I wanted to bring what I had learned from my family, from my elders, from my culture, and see what I could bring to the Emperor as my tithe of service and loyalty."

He made a gesture. "You think I have assimilated to the culture of the court? Lord Lior, only children think that external appearance is a perfect representation of interior reality. You should know better. Have you never paid any attention to what I have *done*? How can I be both outlandishly radical and the toady of an outmoded system, both provincial oaf and urban elite, both primitive fool and high-ranked politician, unless I have drawn a line through the middle and followed it?

"When I was a Fifth-Degree Secretary in the Ministry of Health I worked in an office in the bowels of the Palace. The Department of Censorship was to my right and the Department of Internal Security was on my left. The torture chambers were on the other side of the wall. Sometimes we could hear the screaming."

"Lord Mdang—"

"I do not believe I need to spy on or censor or *torture* the people of the world in order to have a good government. *You* are not afraid of me, Lord Lior! You do not stand before me fearing that I will have you strung up by your toes and disembowelled while you watch for the things you are saying to me!"

Lord Lior went a satisfying grey as he recalled all those previous Ministers in Chief who would have done just that.

Cliopher went on intently: "I am not afraid of my people, Lord Lior. And you know what?"

The Master of Ceremonies shook his head, his eyes wide and shocked.

Cliopher made a wide gesture. "The Department of Censorship is no more. The Department of Internal Security is no more. The torture chambers, you may be very sure, are no more. That entire floor is no longer used for offices. But I am here, Lord Lior."

He let the silence go for a moment as he tried to hammer his feelings into coherent words.

"When I sat down in that horrible office, hearing screams on the other side of the wall, I conceived a plan for what I thought would be a good government. One that did not rely on fear or force to govern. One that would mend structural biases and systematic problems. One that would enrich the poor and not impoverish the well-off, which would permit anyone, whoever they might be and wherever they might come from and whatever their status or wealth might seem, to follow their vocation to the betterment of their community and the world."

He made one sweep of his glance around the room. "I was twenty-five when I made that plan, and put it aside as absurdly idealistic and impossible to realize. I am two years off from its completion. Look around you, Lord Lior!"

He pointed at Zaoul, sitting next to Eldo, both of them with their faces stunned. "When I was that Fifth-Degree Secretary in the Ministry of Health, do you think a Tkinele tribesman and the son of a provincial governor would ever have found themselves next to each other?

"What did you think, when you were sipping hot soup in the Throne Room of the Palace of Stars and wondering what had happened to destroy the greatest civilization the Nine Worlds had ever seen? Did you ever think the world could be *better*? I did."

He paused again, spoke a little more softly. "I did. I took everything I had ever learned from my family, and especially from my great-uncle, who is the *tanà*, the tender of the flame, the one who keeps the old traditions of our family alive and passes them on to the next generation. I took what I had learned, which was to set my course by the Sun and the stars, and by my own skill and by the works of my hands, and by those of those I trust to work with me, to sail the line of my voyaging to my destination.

"When I go to my ancestors I will be able to hold my head high when they ask me for the tally of my days. Can you say the same?

"I am a Wide Sea Islander, Lord Lior. I do not care which way the winds blow. I can sail through a typhoon as through a calm. I can sail with the wind full behind me, and with the wind across me, and with the wind athwart me. I can weather the storms and when the skies clear I can rebuild my boat with the skill of my hands. I can determine the direction of my destination through the songs of the ancestors that have taught me the ways, and with the Sun in the heavens and the bright stars my guides I can keep going."

He lifted his head and spoke forth the old words with new resolution. "I am Cliopher Mdang of Tahivoa. My island is Loaloa. My dances are *Aōte-ketētana*. I left the Vangavaye-ve that I might sit at the feet of the Sun. From the Sun-on-Earth have I learned my destination, and with the stars of my principles to guide me, I know the way.

"Let the winds of public opinion blow how they may. Let people call me what they will. Let them think I have assimilated, or not, as they wish. I do not care what anyone thinks of my work except for the Sun-on-Earth and my own heart's conscience.

"But when the eldest living member of my family, the *tanà* of my people, the man who taught me so much of the ways of my ancestors and of myself, comes and asks me to perform one of the most sacred and solemn ceremonies of my people—Lord Lior, when I am asked such a thing by a man I hold to be worthy of respect above all others in this world save for the Lord of Rising Stars himself—when I am asked such a thing, I do not think that it is an embarrassment, nor an onerous burden, nor a thing to shunt aside as a possibly picturesque but certainly uncouth custom from a primitive culture. Instead I am honoured.

"I invite the court and clerks of Solaara to come to the ceremony because it is intended to be done with the witnessing of one's community, and my great-uncle the *tanà* has decreed that since I have spent so much of my life working here, far from home, in a foreign community that does not know the names of the currents or the winds or the stars of the Wide Seas, that it should be those with whom I have worked and lived as witness, that they might learn something of the world of which they are only a small part.

"I am Cliopher Lord Mdang of Tahivoa. My island is Loaloa. My dances are *Aōteketētana*. I am the Lord Chancellor of Zunidh. I am Secretary in Chief of the Offices of the Lords of State. I am the Hands of the Emperor. The Emperor my lord has given his permission for a high and solemn ceremony of my culture to take place in the Throne Room of the Palace of Stars before the assembled court and any others I might choose to invite out of my wider community."

He waited for three heartbeats, then inclined his head in dismissal. "You have your instructions, Lord Lior, as to the special requirements for the event. I presume you have no further quibbles."

He did not wait to see the Master of Ceremonie' response. He turned to Kiri. "Give me something to work on that has nothing to do with the bloody aristocracy."

CHAPTER ℱIFTY-𝒮IX

CLIOPHER SAT DOWN AT AN empty desk in the outer office with a pile of dispatch cases. The familiar work and the focus necessary to do it slowly began to work their magic, softening his emotions and taking the edge off his anger.

He could hear faint sounds from the other secretaries, who were undoubtedly trying to tiptoe around him and not make any of their usual noises. He might have told them not to bother, that their sounds were soothing—even the thump as someone knocked something to the ground, the muffled exclamations, the guilty laughter—but that would have required bringing his attention back to the surface, and if he did that he was not sure what else he might say.

He worked steadily through the files. They were not problems that he usually would have dealt with personally, not any longer, though once they had been the 'daily rice' of his days.

(He should write to Suzen the painter, he thought distantly at one point, turning over a page. She would be glad to know he had bought the painting from the *Atlas*. It had been too long since he had seen her in person, longer still since the days they had been lovers, when she lived in rooms just down the hall from his old apartment, come as a painter to record events at the court and produce one of the new state portraits of his Radiancy.)

He read accounts of agricultural developments in Southern Dair and studies indicating they might, or might not, be of use elsewhere in the world, and requests to solve problems of funding, patronage, weather, magic, storage, trade.

(Would there be time to invite Suzen to come to see the fire dance? She was one of the few he had ever spoken of his culture to, driven in her case by an interest in its visual arts. She was from Jilkano, the City of Emeralds, and when they had first become friends she had told him she had grown up with Mount Glory of Nijan on the horizon and never wondered about the people who lived in Glory's shadow, let alone those who lived on the other side of the horizon. He had told her that Zangoraville was the trade centre of the Wide Seas, but even though it was within sight of Jilkano, few were the Islanders who crossed the strait to the mainland.)

He read accounts of the ongoing progress of the sea train extension up the coast of Mgunai. They had eventually sent engineers to Ysthar to learn about raised aqueducts and viaducts, something he had suggested, from a vague memory of something the present Lord of Ysthar had said to him about Ysthar's own land-based train system when he had been there on that embassy after the end of the Game Aurieleteer.

They were now in the process of creating a system of locks whereby the train could be lifted from sea-level up to the new above-sea-level viaduct. The canal was raised on piers rather than a full reef, and therefore did not prevent the salmon and all the other migratory sea-species of the region from accessing their spawning grounds. It also promised to completely revolutionize trade on land, for once the sea trains were built, they were much the cheapest way of shipping large quantities of goods—and people.

(No. Probably not time enough, alas, for even a sky ship to get to the City of Emeralds and back. But he could try. Also he should invite the curator of the Gallery of Primitive Cultures from the Museum of Comparative Anthropology. That would be the best way to show why the name should be changed; and in the days, back when he had the time, when he had spent many hours in the gallery, homesick for a place where all those familiar things were used, not behind glass to be gawked at, the curator had been kind.)

He read about the mines of Amboloyo and how their productivity had improved over the past year. He thought to himself that he much preferred the Prince of Amboloyo's bluntness to the Master of Ceremonies' insinuations; and then, as he finished the last page of the report and the last note of his own thoughts, which fell out of his mind as soon as his brush lifted from the paper, he thought that perhaps he had some apologies of his own to make.

He cleaned his brush and tidied away the documents into their respective cases. When he stood up everyone in the room immediately stopped what they were doing to watch him. Aioru was at the door to the inner office; he ducked back in, and after a moment Kiri also came out.

Cliopher found he was more amused than anything by this. He strode forward and handed his dispatch cases to Aioru. "Please go over these before you send out the replies. I would not like to have let my temper cause me to miss something important—or lead me to say something I ought not."

Aioru murmured something that sounded polite. Cliopher smiled briefly at him, then searched around until he could meet Eldo's eyes. "Lord Eldo." He looked again, waiting until people met his gaze. "Saya Kalikiri. Saya Urda."

There were a few others he knew were of the aristocracy but who went to some lengths to avoid being seen as such, and so he did not name them.

"I wish to apologize to you, and the others in this room, most especially to you, Lord Eldo. We all have our biases and prejudices. I am sorry if I in any way suggested that I condemn the entire upper aristocracy to folly or bigotry because of the actions of one or a few. I hope I do not do so; but we all know that when we lose our temper we can speak things that do not belong to our better selves."

The fraught silence turned to one, he was slightly bemused to note, of almost-amused astonishment. Eldo was flushing red, though Cliopher could not read whether the emotion was embarrassment or anger or shame or something else.

"Sir," he said, after looking around at the room to see if anyone else was going to say anything, "when I told my father I had passed the exams and intended to join the Service, he disowned me."

Cliopher stared at him.

Eldo took a deep breath. "I went to the Department of Common Weal in Boloyo City and applied for the annual stipend, that I might pay my own way to Solaara. The person ahead of me was a wild man from the mountains, who had come back to the city for his granddaughter's wedding. He wanted to surprise her with a gift, with looking respectable. The person behind me was a middle-aged woman who had just left an abusive husband. We all received the stipend. It is not only the poor to whom you have given freedom and—and hope."

Cliopher stared some more. And then he said, "Your father is proud of you. I saw his face when you took the oaths before the Emperor."

Eldo smiled. "My father likes people who stand up to him."

"He thinks I'm an octopus sucking the world dry. That's not what octopi do, but I haven't belaboured the point."

"Sir, I wanted to join the Service ever since the time my father came home and ranted about you for three days straight. I wanted to know who this person was, who stood up to him—not many people do!—this commoner who wanted to change the world's government. I had no idea you had started planning it so early."

"I don't think anyone did," Kiri said. "Sir, you've truly been working on this plan all along?"

Cliopher stared at her, for a change of direction. "You didn't think I pulled it out of my sleeve on short notice? That I simply said to his Radiancy, 'Oh, of course I can completely restructure the entire system of the mundial government in five years, no problem'?"

"You didn't say otherwise," she said, laughing. "And we who work with you have come to expect such miracles of organization."

Cliopher shook his head. "Here I am giving away all my secrets. But how could you not see it? You read the same reports I do, Kiri." He gestured at the office. "You all read the raw material for those reports and write them. Have you not seen the changes? They were incremental for many years, but they add up to a sea change. Kiri, you've noticed the shift in the composition of this department, of the whole Service."

She nodded, though her expression didn't fully clear. "Yes. When I started it was eight-five percent drawn from the middle and upper classes of the central provinces. Now it's a third from the hinterlands, and well over half if you look at the lower classes." She smiled at the room, who were all looking at each other as if they had never fully realized this.

Cliopher said, "The point is not those surface numbers, but what has led to them. They are symptoms of the change—and to a certain degree, agents of it as well. But the real changes are in the education system, in travel and trade and health, and in the dropping of certain elements of the examinations to avoid the biases that used to deflect anyone who wasn't of a certain class and origin."

"You got in, sir, under the old system," she protested.

Cliopher caught his nephew's eye and found himself laughing. "Yes—but as Gaudy can tell you, only after five tries! And I spent a long time aggravating people in the Lower Secretariat before I ever got to a position of any influence whatsoever."

"Surely not," someone murmured, without sarcasm as far as Cliopher could tell.

He laughed again. "I used to labour under the misapprehension that if I just told people what they were doing wrong, they would gladly fix it. This did not go over particularly well. I also was known—something else Gaudy can tell you, eh?—for having a wicked tongue."

"I would not have believed it, but can now," said Kiri, totally seriously.

He smiled ruefully. "We'll see what the haul of that casting is. I am comforted by the recollection that the upper aristocracy no longer control ninety-eight percent of the wealth and power of the world, but only forty percent of it."

They stared.

He sighed. "Come now, my friends, this passes through your hands every day!"

Kiri said, "I think this might be why you have the position you do, sir."

Cliopher said, "It's obvious, surely?"

"To you, sir."

He couldn't remember what he'd actually come in to the Offices of State to do, and Tully had not yet made any indication he should be doing something else. "Very well, then," he said, taking the case that held the agricultural reports from Southern Dair back from Aioru. "Gather round, and I'll show you what to look for behind the things that you see."

He handed around the summary of the report and waited while they read it. After it had come back to him, he said, "Very well, what can we learn from this?"

Ashendra put up her hand. "The state of agriculture in Southern Dair."

Cliopher nodded patiently. "Yes, certainly that is the primary information. What else?"

She subsided in puzzlement. Everyone else looked at each other. Finally Gaudy put up his hand. "We could compare it to reports from elsewhere and see how the overall state of agriculture in the world is changing?"

"Indeed, that would certainly be a good thing to do. What else?"

He waited, until finally Eldo said, "Why did this come to us, sir? This isn't just a report, it's full of questions and requests. Why didn't it go to their Prince?"

"Exactly. But you can answer that, I think."

Eldo said slowly, "Because we are the ones who can answer the questions and grant the requests."

Aioru said, even more slowly, "That didn't use to be the case. This never came to us before you created the Ministry of the Common Weal. I remember now, the Council of Princes said that if you wanted to listen to every niggling little complaint that came in from the people, they'd let you."

"Yes," said Cliopher, and looked seriously at them. "Let this be a lesson to you all: whoever takes the responsibility gains the power. By giving up that task to us, the princes gave up also the power involved in performing it. They were able to become more efficient and focused in areas they thought important; I have been able to guide the Secretariat into taking responsibility for the things I think are important. And over time, we have gathered a considerable amount of power."

"And nobody sees it," Aioru said wonderingly, glancing down at the paper. Cliopher could see his thoughts racing, as he started to make connections he'd never thought of before. "It's all there, in plain sight but—but nobody sees."

"But we don't seem to have any of the privileges of power," someone said from behind Eldo. "We don't get to stand in court looking magnificent—well, you do, sir, but not the rest of us."

Cliopher smiled. "The question of whether the form of power, or the reality of it, is more important to you is one that only you can answer. I stand in court as I do because it is part of the game to show that I have the prestige, and because I do not intend to destroy the princes—far from it! I do not wish them to lose their culture any more than I do my own. You do not, the Upper Secretariat does not, because the transferal of power is not complete, and I have no intention of it remaining with us—with me, with you, with this department, even with this part of the government—for much longer."

He gazed solemnly at them, meeting each one's eyes. "We are responsible for tending the fire on the journey so that we might hand it over to the next community who needs it. We have gathered the responsibilities and done our best to find ways to fulfil them. The next stage of the process is to start returning the powers—and the responsibilities—back to the provinces."

"Why take them from the princes if you're just going to do that?"

For some reason that made Cliopher recall what his original purpose in coming to the Offices of State had been. He nodded at Aioru, who'd once more spoken, and said, "Aioru, all the rest of you, you are in the thick of the new developments. I think that now you have an idea of what to look for, you will be able to see where we are going."

He turned to Kiri, who was smiling oddly at him. "Kiri, I have recalled that I came not to lose my temper nor even to show my purpose, but to appoint a new secretary for his Radiancy."

She said, "Oh, no, Huara didn't work out?"

Huara hadn't, but had not yet been told that when she'd sprained her wrist. His Radiancy had made it clear that he wanted someone else, however, and had hinted that maybe Zaoul would be a good option, though not if Cliopher could not spare him.

Cliopher had in fact been intending to make that sacrifice (much as he did not want to lose Zaoul) before he'd encountered Lord Lior, but that argument had shown him two things. One was that if he appointed Zaoul (who would almost certainly work out), it would be considered a severe insult to all those who would already be insulted by his argument with Lord Lior and that little interaction down at Hnala's Gallery a couple of months ago. And the second was that Eldo had been the first one to see the wider implications of the agricultural report.

He nodded at Kiri. "She's injured her hand, but I think there might have been a request even so."

"Very good, sir," Kiri replied. "Is there anyone particular you think should go next?"

"Yes: Lord Eldo. Please attend his Radiancy at the third hour tomorrow morning."

★★★

WHEN HE GOT BACK TO his apartment he found his great-uncle talking with Féonie about his grass skirt and headdress.

"It will still fit him," she was saying as he entered the sitting room and found her examining the garments, which were laid out on the table.

"It's not suitable for the dance," Buru Tovo replied firmly. "Eh, there you are, Kip."

"Good afternoon," he replied, amused to see that his great-uncle did not appear to have any trouble with Féonie's Mgunaivë accent.

Féonie said, "Why have you not told me about your family patterns? We should have been using them in your clothing!"

Cliopher had never thought of them in that way. "I suppose I didn't ..."

"If you were of an old family of Solaara or Astandalas we would use your family's crest," she informed him. "You come of an old family with its own designs. You should be using them."

"Oh," he said lamely, the Master of Ceremonies' criticisms filling his mind. But this—Féonie's simple acceptance of his own cultural traditions as worthy, as *equal*—was exactly what he had been trying to accomplish. He felt, for a brief moment, as if he might cry.

Then Buru Tovo stabbed his finger at the grass skirt. "What's this?"

"You know what that is, Buru. What would you like me to do about it?"

He wished a moment later he hadn't phrased it like that, for his great-uncle told him.

★★★

"HOW ARE YOU GETTING ON with your preparations, Kip?" his Radiancy asked on their next meeting, which was an hour before Eldo was to start.

Cliopher weighed the various ways he could answer that. "I have discussed the arrangements with Lord Lior and I have begun collecting together the elements of the traditional costume. I did wish to ask you about that, my lord—my lord?"

His Radiancy was laughing. "Cliopher, from what I have heard you gave Lior a tongue-lashing such as no one can believe came out of your mouth—or that he prompted! Did he really call your great-uncle a savage?"

"I should not like to put words in his mouth, my lord."

"Really? You amaze me. Come now, I hear you called him a soft-spoken hypocrite. What did he call you to prompt that?"

Cliopher bit his lip. "A reasonable man."

"A strike to the heart! My dear Kip, do not look so mulish. I would never stoop so low as to call you reasonable. You are quite the most radical idealist I have ever known—or at least, the only sane one. Please, continue with your query."

"Thank you, my lord. First, I need to acquire certain materials, and I was wondering if you would object if I took them from the menagerie and gardens."

"Feathers and grasses and so on?"

"Yes, my lord. Also, er, a pig."

***

ALONG WITH THE PIG HE had to supply a feast. He was not, he was grateful to learn, required to kill the pig.

"Nah," his great-uncle said, "we're not Vargas. Let them be the hunters."

"My father was a Varga."

"You learned the dances from me, boy."

And that, therefore, was that. Cliopher went down to the kitchens to speak with the chief cook, who told him, first, that he ought to have summoned her to his office, and then, when he explained what he needed her to prepare, got very excited and informed him that she was from Csiven and her grandmother had been an Islander and she had always wanted to do one of the traditional feasts. He left, smiling, light-hearted, and went upstairs to tell Gaudy to go down to the Museum of Comparative Anthropology to invite the curator and ask to borrow the kona'a drum.

CHAPTER *F*IFTY-*S*EVEN

CLIOPHER SPENT THE MORNING MEETING with the various ministers of trade, the first part of the afternoon meeting with the new high priests to learn about the extremely elaborate and lengthy purification ceremonies that would begin the next month (so, they told him, he could properly adjust his schedule that they might be fit in at the correct times and places), and the last part of the afternoon in an emergency meeting with the Lord Treasurer, who had found some discrepancy in the tithes coming from Xiputl and wanted to know what to do.

When he finally got back to his apartment in order to prepare, he felt entirely unready. At home he would have spent all day leisurely joking with family and friends while they dressed in their finery.

Féonie bustled round to help him attach the headdress into place. Cliopher dismissed her at the end to stand alone before the tall mirror in his dressing room, looking at the picture he presented.

He was not so slim or muscular as he had been as a young man, of course. He was thicker around the middle, flabbier around the arms and shoulders. His legs were strong, from all the walking, dancing, stair-climbing, kneeling. Barefoot, the scars from learning the fire dance were visible on the sides of his feet, the skin there still shinier and pinker than elsewhere.

He settled his efela ko (he'd forgotten that name for it), finding it odd to have it so displayed.

The grass skirt—actually made of pandanus leaves from the botanical gardens—was not as elaborate as it might have been, since he had not had the time, nor Féonie the knowledge, to dye the leaves and weave them in all the traditional patterns that should have gone into it for such a dance. As a result it looked much like the old-fashioned grass skirt worn by the seller of shells in Ikiava market, who might or might not have been Vou'a, the god of mystery.

The headdress, too, was simple. Pearls from the Treasury, cassowary feathers from the menagerie, woven together with Féonie's silk threads. It was surmounted by the reddish-orange tail-feathers of the royal bird-of-paradise, since there were no specimens of the superb in the menagerie.

He was not wearing the body paint that he would have for other ceremonies. The fire dance did not require it.

He was twice the age, at least, of his great-uncle when Buru Tovo had gone sailing out into the ocean and met the Imperial Heir on progress. Cliopher did not look exactly like the portrait of the Wide Sea Islander from the *Atlas*, but the family resemblance was very strong.

The quarter-chime rang the quarter before sunset.

He took a deep breath, adjusted the efela ko once more so that the obsidian pendant sat properly, touched the headdress to make sure Féonie's efforts had indeed secured it. Then he strode out, past the footmen on the front door, where he collected the two guards in their lesser panoply, and walked with his head high and his bare feet padding softly on the stone floor down to the Throne Room of the Palace of Stars.

★★★

IN THE HALL WERE GATHERED the courtiers, half the Secretariat, and the majority of the Imperial Guard.

For an ordinary court the courtiers would be arranged according to the ceremonies expected and the ranks involved. Closest to the throne was, always, highest in rank. For meals the seating arrangements were complex and changed nightly as the courtiers played games of status and alliance and enmity. Though he was insulated by the demands of his offices from such movements, Cliopher watched the games more closely than he let on, having learned early from his Radiancy how valuable that knowledge was.

Lord Lior had taken the customary requirements Cliopher had given him and applied them to the ranks of courtiers, bureaucrats, and guards (as well as the handful of others Cliopher had invited personally), orienting them along the axis formed by his Radiancy's throne on its daïs and the great rectangular bed of burning coals that made up the dancing ground.

Buru Tovo and Gaudy had spent the day raking the coals into their position. As Cliopher entered, quietly, as befit the one who had not yet successfully performed the dance, he saw the ranks of brightly-garbed aristocrats in full court costume, the Secretariat in their official robes, the guards in their panoplies. The Throne Room was illuminated by the deep-orange sunset light coming through the western windows and the deeper reds of the fire bed.

Gaudy, dressed in Cliopher's old finery, knelt beside the kona'a drum, looking fixedly at the coals. He would be playing the beat of the dance, which Cliopher had always before held within himself or sung aloud.

He stood in his usual position, on the daïs, below and to the side of the throne, where he could easily see his Radiancy's face and also look out across the room.

He looked up and met the lion eyes. His Radiancy nodded once, gravely, and then made a gesture for silence. The room quieted instantly.

"The Lord Chancellor has arrived," his Radiancy said. "His excellency will commence the ceremony to which he has invited you to be witness shortly. Before he begins, we wish to declare that, knowing our most beloved servant's diligence and care for all the duties, large and small, with which we have entrusted him, we have enchanted the floor of the room that it might not be damaged by the coals laid across it. We wish also to declare that that is the sole enchantment at work on the fire. If Lord Mdang touches the coals, he will be burned."

Cliopher felt a tiny, niggling concern in the back of his mind relax. He had been worried about the floor, at the effect of all that heat on the silver and the gems. He had not relished the thought of trying to find enough perfect lapis to delineate the Wide Seas to replace it.

His Radiancy said, "We are greatly honoured and privileged to be invited to witness this, the legendary fire dance of the Seafarers. It was last performed for an outside audience before the Emperor Aurelius Magnus, who wrote that it was the most magnificent dance he had ever observed."

Cliopher, breath falling into the slow, steady rhythm he had learned so long ago, eyes on the coals, heard the susurration of the assembled crowd as they murmured over to themselves whatever stories they had heard of the fire dance of the Wide Sea Islanders. Cliopher did not know exactly what those stories were, and wondered distantly, vaguely, where Aurelius Magnus had written his description of the dance. He had not found any such account when he had researched the coming of the Emperor over the sea to the Vangavaye-ve.

His Radiancy said, "This ceremony is one that at once challenges, enacts, and acknowledges Lord Mdang's claim to be the holder of certain traditional knowledge and skills. We all know his excellency's great ability at negotiating metaphorical fires. Let us now see the literal manifestation of the knowledge that has guided him his whole life long."

Cliopher knelt to his Radiancy in the court style, then walked to the head of the stairs. He paused there, waiting his great-uncle's signal, and regarded the room.

The audience stood on either side, with an aisle open between him—or rather his Radiancy—and the fire bed, and between the fire bed and the great double doors. Guards stood at each corner of the pattern, for display more than anything else, as heat distorted the air in heavy waves above the coals and no one would be fool enough to approach it.

Buru Tovo had laid out the pattern across the map of the hemisphere of Zunidh that contained the Wide Seas. Cliopher had wondered, at times when the movements of the courtly dance revealed the jewelled floor, what he would learn if he were to overlay the map with the pattern of his dance.

From here he could see no blue, only flashes of gold and green and crystal as the coals burned and the gems representing islands picked up their colours.

The map was oriented correctly for the theological and ceremonial east, which was the Sun-on-Earth on his throne. Back in the days of Astandalas the throne had been precisely east. Whoever had inscribed the map had done so with the proportions Cliopher had learned by the scars on his feet.

At a signal from Buru Tovo Gaudy began to beat the drum. Cliopher took a deep breath and descended the stairs. As he walked down the aisle left between the courtiers he let the drumbeat fill him, the deep-voiced kona'a speaking forth his heartbeat. He walked at its pace, warming his muscles for the dance, focusing on the pattern, on the song of the *Lays* that called to him. He could not focus on the fire: that was the sure way to be burned.

For the *Aōtētana*, the ordinary dance, the dancer was also the singer. It was difficult to do both without fumbling, and there were not many, even among the multitude of Mdang cousins, who had successfully danced it at one of the festivals. Cliopher had always thought the *Aōteketētana* simply added the fire, if such an addition could be simple, but his great-uncle had informed him that he had a lot to learn, boy, before he could sing the correct song.

"*Tanà* first," he had said. "*Tana-tai* comes later."

And so Cliopher did not have to draw enough breath through the heat waves to sing. He had worried that not having the song in his throat would throw off his dancing, for even in his own morning dances he sang the words softly, under his breath, to keep himself in time.

The drumbeat was louder at every step. The coals glowed more brightly as the sunlight left the windows. By the time he reached the edge of the fire bed he was nearly in a state of trance.

He waited at the edge of the fire. He could no longer see his audience, no longer see anything but the coals and the wavering air above them and the brilliant gems of the Islands in the spaces between. He could not hear anything but the combined drumbeat and heartbeat in his breast. He could not think of the heat: only the shape of the fire.

The first test was to know when to begin the dance. On the beach of those islands where he had learned his way home he had been able to see the moment the sun touched the horizon. In here, inside the Palace of Stars, he had none of the cues of the natural world.

But he had followed the bells, day in and day out, and knew as well as anyone could the moment they would strike.

At precisely the moment the sunset bell began its sonorous toll Buru Tovo's voice began the song and Cliopher's foot touched the first space within the coals.

He gave himself over to the dance. The song was familiar from the words he knew and familiar, too, from the songs his great-uncle had sung him on Loaloa. Over and over Buru Tovo had sung the *Lays*, until Cliopher half-forgot how to think in anything but its words. His conscious mind knew that half his ideas of government were drawn from its stories; his body still remembered things his mind had long since forgotten.

His feet landed precisely. His hands moved in the gestures, pointing to the west or the east or the north, to the Sun-in-Glory on his throne or a certain constellation set into the ceiling. Here, in a room decorated to show the vastness and wealth and power of an empire that had spanned worlds, Cliopher had never felt so much an Islander, nor so much at home in it.

The familiar voice, rough-edged but true-pitched, rose and fell in the old words, the familiar rhythms, the ancient story of the journeys of the Wayfinders as they found their way across the Wide Seas to the home of the Mother of Islands, to the Vangavaye-ve, the home of music.

Cliopher danced their journey, his hands shaping the winds, his feet pointing the currents, his twists and his turns and the angles of his arms pointing now to the Fisherman, now to the Sun, now to the Moon, now to the Sixteen Bright Guides who marked the houses of the sky and who had been the reason his grandmother had had so many children.

She had promised the Mother of Islands that she would bear children in honour of the Bright Guides—the brightest stars of the southern sky—if her new husband came home safely out of the greatest typhoon to hit the Vangavaye-ve in the people's memory.

He had come home, and laughed at her vow, and told her, later, that he had promised Vou'a that if he returned home safely to his wife he would cultivate a garden whose bounty would spill out across all the Ring to the honour of the Son of Laughter.

Sixteen children had she borne, and fifty-nine grandchildren in their turn, and the seed of the gardens both real and metaphorical of his grandfather were spread far and wide around the Ring and even so far as here in Solaara. There was a *tui* tree in the botanical gardens, the only one to be found east of Nijan or west of the Isolates, because Cliopher had once, very carefully, in the days when he took the sea train, brought a seedling from the garden his mother grew.

The sweat ran down his face, his shoulders, down the furrow of his spine. He could feel the heat in his feet, his calves, his knees. The edges of the grass skirt were singeing; mixed with the sweet smell of the coals was a fainter scent of charcoal and the less-pleasant odour of singed hair. If he had touched the coals directly he could not tell from the feel.

The song rose and fell, sometimes in the old language, mostly in the words he had learned from the *Lays*. His hands pointed to gemstone stars and moon window and Sun-on-Earth. His feet landed in the narrow channels of safety between the wide swirls of fire. The drum beat his heartbeat. His breath came as evenly as he could manage, though the fire stole away the oxygen and the room was more enclosed than the clear wide beaches he had never fully appreciated.

He danced himself out of himself. He was, at the end, the beat and the song and the fire and beyond the fire the darkness filled with a faceless audience who might have been the hosts of his ancestors but were instead the unknowing members of court and guard and priesthood and secretariat.

The five pillars of the government witnessed *Aōteketētana*, there in the house of the sun, where Cliopher had quietly striven to light a new fire and tend and build it until it would become a light to the world and the hearth fire of a new civilization.

And finally, he danced himself home.

Coming home was what they called the final steps, the triumphant circle around the Vangavaye-ve, the twirling dash to the Isolates and back before, at last, the pattern ended exactly opposite where it had begun.

Both feet landed outside the coals as drum beat and song finished and the great bronze bells of Zunidh tolled the hour.

Cliopher was facing his Radiancy: facing the sunrise, as the dance finished, facing where he had come from in the dance. His ancestors had come from the west and sought first what lay behind the sunrise. They had reached Nijan and turned again and sought the sunset and the islands they would settle as their own.

The only sound he could hear was the faint sizzle of sweat as it dripped off his hands and landed on the nearest coals.

He looked at the fire and was glad to see its pattern was undisturbed. In the dances he had done on those desert islands he had sat afterwards in the sea to cool his legs; he would have to wait a little longer to return to his rooms and the cold bath he had asked Franzel to draw for him. He would not have direct scars from this dance, but despite the protective unguent he had slathered on earlier he had more or less roasted himself for an hour, and his legs would be a long while healing.

It was traditional to meet the eyes of the audience before departing. Cliopher looked around, left to right as he had been taught. Immediately to his left was Lord Lior, who had given himself a position at the front.

Cliopher looked at him for a long moment. He could not have said anything even if it had been customary for him to do so. His voice felt tucked deep inside himself. Nor did he know what expression was on his face. He knew he was still breathing hard, his pulse pounding his throat and ears, the sweat running down his skin. He had never had an audience before. He could barely hold on to what he was supposed to do to formally finish the dance.

Lord Lior looked at him with an intense expression Cliopher could not, in that state, decipher.

Then the Master of Ceremonies bowed his head and sank down into the obeisance that was intended to show the greatest honour and respect to someone not the Emperor. It had been done for generals coming in triumph, for heroes being recognized by the Emperor, for artists presenting the most sublime works of art.

In a deep rustle every other person but the guards and the Sun-on-Earth and Buru Tovo followed suit.

Cliopher looked around at all the court of Solaara doing the highest honours to him. The guards were saluting. Buru Tovo was watching him from down the length of the fire bed.

Finally Cliopher looked up at his Radiancy on his throne. He was too far away to see his face clearly, could not truly meet his gaze.

He bowed over his hands, palm over fist, in the Vangavayen style. His Radiancy inclined his head.

The assembled court rose in another deep rustle.

I am Cliopher Mdang of Tahivoa. My island is Loaloa. My dances are Aōte-ketētana.

The Lord Chancellor of Zunidh turned and walked out of the room, his head high and his back straight and his feet ringing as they struck the jewelled floor.

INTERLUDE *Four*

An Announcement

To be disseminated worldwide on the seventeenth day of the eighth month:

A PROCLAMATION FROM THE THRONE OF GLORY:

Pursuant to Our coming temporary absence from the seat of government, and ever-mindful of the great diligence and skill with which Our most beloved and loyal Lord Chancellor has undertaken every task of governance and legislation with which We have entrusted him, We are most pleased to announce the evolution of his Excellency Cliopher Lord Mdang, presently Our Lord Chancellor and head of the Imperial Bureaucratic Service, to the position of Our Viceroy of Zunidh.

The world has long reaped the fruits of Lord Mdang's many efforts on Our behalf and in Our name. In order that Our people may celebrate and honour him as We do Ourselves, the Viceroyship ceremonies will be performed in a progress through each province of Zunidh. The final ceremonies will be conducted in the homeland dear to Our minister's heart, the Vangavaye-ve, that his family may share in Our delight and confidence as We entrust Our world of Zunidh to him.

By the sign and seal of His Serene and Radiant Holiness, Artorin Damara, Last Emperor of Astandalas and Lord of Zunidh

An Invitation

The eighteenth day of the eighth month:

My dear Bertie—

 I write to invite you and Irela to the coming viceroyship ceremonies. I think you will find them interesting from an anthropological perspective. You will get to see me in a particularly splendid outfit, at the least.

 —Kip

$\mathcal{A}$ $\mathcal{R}$ESPONSE

The twenty-first day of the eighth month:

Dear Kip,

Thank you for the invitation. We will certainly do our best to come. Your outfits always sound intriguing, and it will be fun to see you in one at home.

Can you tell me what the situation of Zangoraville in Nijan is? I know you've been there quite often.

Bertie

A REPLY

The twenty-third day of the eighth month:

Falbert—
I cannot respond to questions about the government. Please don't ask me.
Cliopher

Volume Five

The Song of the Home Fire

CHAPTER FIFTY-EIGHT

THEY CAME AT LENGTH TO the Vangavaye-ve for the final stage of the regency ceremonies. Cliopher had been feeling mostly at peace with the whole thing, until the familiar first glimpse of the Outer Ring came into sight, whereupon he dissolved immediately and unexpectedly into tears.

He had been sitting with his Radiancy in the Sun Cabin's balcony, discussing the order of affairs, when his Radiancy had pointed out the Outer Ring mountains. Cliopher looked up eagerly, disentangled the green jungle from the blue ocean, was half-blinded by a gleam of sunlight reflecting brilliantly off a waterfall—and then, the tears.

His Radiancy waited patiently until they stopped, as abruptly as they had started. Then he said: "You are feeling it, then. When we come to Gorjo City, take the first two days to visit your family and friends."

"My lord, I thought—"

"Kip."

★★★

SER RHODIN CAME ALONG WITH him, and a footman to carry their luggage. Rhodin was carrying his spear and had his sword belted at his hip, but he promised Cliopher that he would content himself with hidden weapons once they were out of official duty—which was inside the door of his mother's house.

Before they arrived there, however, they passed close by a house Cliopher knew as well. The Kindraa residence was another rambling multigenerational building, with jumbled outbuildings connected together with breezeways and little courtyards. As they neared it, a pair of young men, stripped to their cotton trousers for the work, were striving to move a very large pianoforte out the front door. A small crowd had gathered about to watch and shout good-natured advice that the two men were steadfastly ignoring.

"Why do you think they need to go out the front door?" Rhodin murmured, as they drew to a halt a discreet distance away to wait for the narrow passageway between canal and house to clear.

"That piano was always in the lower house," Cliopher replied, trying to see if Falbert was in the throng. "If they're moving it to the Birdhouse, they couldn't go through the middle—there's a pool in the way."

"A pool?"

"For the boats. And fishing, of course."

"What a strange set-up. Do you know them? Are they cousins?"

"Yes—they're not cousins—Bertie was my closest friend when I was young."

"We met him in the restaurant when we were here before."

Cliopher was surprised that Rhodin should have remembered this. "Yes, he was. Why do you—" But he broke off as Falbert, as large and loud as ever, came out behind the second of the men to shout genially at everyone to move out of the way.

"That includes you two *velioi* over there," he called.

"*Velioi?*" repeated Ser Rhodin suspiciously.

"'Foreigners'." Cliopher walked a few steps closer, though not so close as to get in the way of the piano-movers. He raised his voice. "While I have to admit Rhodin's from away, I was born and raised not three canals over from here, Bertie, and I take insult."

Falbert looked over at them more sharply, then made an extraordinary noise and fair leaped over the piano. He enfolded Cliopher into a huge hug, pounding him on the back and roaring a bit incoherently. After a moment he stood back, hands on Cliopher's upper arms, and stared searchingly into his face. "Kip."

Cliopher caught his breath from this remarkable greeting. "Or then again perhaps I won't." Out of the corner of his eye, he saw Rhodin's right hand relax away from the hilt of his sword. "Retirement must be suiting you, Bertie. That was an impressive leap over the piano."

Falbert turned back to see that the piano-movers had set down the instrument to stare at them. "Oh yes," he said. "We're moving it to the Birdhouse. My grandmama died, you know, and I'm getting the piano."

"I'm sorry about your grandmother."

"It was a mercy. You know how ill she'd been. She was seeing my grandfather everywhere at the end. I think she was glad to go to him. Now. What are you doing? Are you going home?"

The simple question rattled Cliopher badly. Home—he'd never felt so in need of it being *home* as after the gruelling past six months taking up the viceroyship—and never so far from it being so. "Yes."

For all his bluster, Falbert could be insightful. He obviously saw something in Cliopher's face, for he said: "Are they expecting you at any time? Can you come in for coffee?"

Cliopher glanced at Rhodin, who shook his head with a pleasant but stubborn smile. He sighed. "I'd love to, Bertie, if you don't mind Rhodin joining us? Havor can take our things to the house."

He nodded at the footman, who'd been gawking at the to-him exotic surroundings of Gorjo City, and preening himself a little on the reactions of the locals to his to-them exotic livery. "Go two more streets up, then over three canals, Havor, and it's the big red house with a jacaranda tree in a pot out the front. If you don't see it anyone can tell you where the Mdang house is. Tell whoever answers the door that Rhodin and I are visiting with Bertie Kindraa and will be along later."

"Yes, your excellency," Havor said, half-bowing.

"That's the Lord of Zunidh's livery," Falbert said, frowning suddenly at it. "Orange and dark blue with gold trim. Why are you using that? And—'your excellency'?"

"Let's go in," said Cliopher, pushing him towards the next door.

"What are you just standing there for?" Falbert said, disentangling himself to frown at the piano-movers. "The sooner you get that moved the sooner you can go fishing."

"Sorry, Papa," the older of the two said, grinning. "It's not every day we see you jump over a piano."

"Or every day that you see one of the Imperial Guard," the younger added, looking admiringly at Rhodin.

"Bertie's sons, Faldo and Parno," Cliopher supplied for Rhodin's benefit. "This is Ser Rhodin."

"Not Ser Rhodin an Gaiange, the Deputy Commander of the Guard?" Parno asked, eyes going wide with amazement.

"I have that honour," Rhodin replied. He did not need to stand any straighter, but he managed somehow to give the impression of being even more on his dignity.

"How did you know that?" Cliopher asked curiously.

"It was in a book I read. I've always been very interested in the Guard, sir, I've read everything I could about it."

"Spends all his money on fighting lessons," Faldo said, with an indulgent air that made Parno flush angrily.

"Why haven't you applied?" Ser Rhodin asked. "I would have noticed someone from the Vangavaye-ve."

Parno stared at him in consternation. "I—I didn't know I could—sir. Don't you only take the best?"

Rhodin gave him an appraising glance, taking in the rippling muscles of his torso and arms. "How do you know you're not good enough unless you apply?"

"But how—how could I—how would I even get to Solaara? And what would I do if I got there? No one would look twice at me."

Ser Rhodin gave him a totally blank look. "Your father is Cliopher Mdang's oldest friend."

"But how would that help me with the guard? He couldn't get Gaudy a position in the Service, and that's his own nephew."

"Couldn't? Hardly. But even he would hardly consider telling me there was an applicant to be nepotism."

"I'm right here," Cliopher said. "Can we go in, Falbert?"

Falbert started. "Of course. I'd be honoured to have you in my house, Ser Rhodin. This way, please."

Rhodin smiled and waggled his spear. "Oh, I'm still on duty. I'll come behind."

"Rhodin."

"It would be my head if something happened to you."

"Oh, but Papa—"

"Move the piano first, and then we'll see." Falbert frowned at his sons, but fierce eyebrows and fiercer glower could not hide his obvious love and pride in them. After the two had shouldered the piano again, he led Cliopher and Rhodin inside, then through the warren of rooms and stairs to the Bird-house, the airy tower where Falbert and his family spent most of their time.

Once there, he showed them to comfortable seats on the balcony, which had a lovely view of the central pool, and, through the narrow channel leading to the public canals, a glimpse up to the royal palace on the slopes of Mama Ituri's Son.

"What can I get you?" Falbert said. "Water? Coffee? Something stronger? I have a very nice white here from Looenna."

"White what? They're never making wine in Looenna."

"But they are! Up on the ridge, where it's cool enough to set the grapes.

Ghilly can explain it to you. You've been away too long this time, Kip. We've missed you. I'll get a bottle and you can decide for yourself if it's any good. It probably doesn't compete with what you get in Solaara, mind."

He disappeared inside while Cliopher was trying to come up with a response that even began to explain the past six months. He sat down slowly into one of the chairs, smoothing out the fine silk of his garments. Rhodin stood beside the door at attention. "Do you have to stand there?" he asked at last.

"I'm still on duty, Cliopher—Kip."

"Falbert is my oldest friend."

Rhodin looked at him for a long moment. Then he inclined his head. "It is easy to forget you have your pride, Kip. I'm sorry. When your friend's sons come in I will speak to the young man about the guard."

Falbert came back in with a wine bottle and three glasses. He said, "Please do sit down, Rhodin. Kip's mentioned you in his letters. You're quite the gourmet, aren't you? I think you'll appreciate this wine. Even if it is from the Vangavaye-ve."

"Many good things come from the Vangavaye-ve," Rhodin replied, unbelting his sword, and sitting down in a chair that faced the door and stood between balcony and Cliopher. He set his sword down on the floor beside him and tucked the spear half-under his feet. "Kip Mdang, for instance."

"That's a bad example," Falbert said, chuckling.

Rhodin raised his eyebrows at him even as he swirled the wine around in the glass. "How so?"

"Kip had one great ambition in his life, and that was to join the Imperial Service, though none of us ever really understood why, especially when he used to love the old ways so much. And it doesn't seem to have earned him anything worth having except for fancy clothes and tired eyes. What good's being the Lord Emperor's secretary if you never get to live? It took him a ridiculously long time to pass the exams, and well … I don't think he's ever quite lived that down."

Cliopher said nothing. After a moment, Rhodin said, "He's not the Lord Emperor's secretary now."

"Oh, aren't you? I'm sorry, Kip. I've put my foot in it again, haven't I? I'm forever doing that. But you see, Rhodin, Kip's atypical. He wanted to leave—and he left. Oh, I'm sure he's done good work there, but just think what he could have achieved here, where everyone knew him. He could have done so much here. He was so brilliant … We were all just waiting for him to shine—and then, nothing. He went off and got swallowed up in Astandalas. It was such a waste."

Cliopher felt as if he were going to dissolve into tears again. "Falbert," he said, but his voice cracked away into silence and they did not look at him.

"And after the Fall—we thought he'd died—and then he came back, and we thought he was home to stay, we thought he'd given up that foolishness and was going to stay where he belonged, with people who loved him, with people he loved, with *us*."

As if there was no possible way he might have met people worth loving elsewhere; as if he had not come home, when Basil and Dimiter had not. But somehow it was acceptable, or at least accepted, that Basil and Dimiter would not, and Cliopher, who made every effort to come back as often as he could, was given ... this. Love and welcome and reproaches and a stubborn refusal—an unbelievable insular *denial*—of all that he'd ever achieved.

"But then he went away again to Solaara, and it was clear he was never going to come back. Not to stay. Hardly to visit. You say he's a good thing to come from the Vangavaye-ve? He was the one with the dreams and the ambition and the mind and the heart to change to the world—but—why do you think I didn't want my son to—" His voice broke. "His heart would break if he tried and failed. Don't you think some dreams are better kept dreams? It's better not to care so much! How could I want my son to end up like—"

"Like me?" Cliopher said in total disbelief.

"You followed your dreams and it destroyed—Kip, you're the perfect bureaucrat. The perfect example of the New Shaian gentleman." Falbert looked him up and down. "Everything tucked away into its place. You. Of all people, how could *you*—you used to be—we all thought there was so much possibility in you. We were all waiting to see what you would do. We thought you might be the one to take the Islands to—" He stopped harshly, then went on, spitting out the words: "Instead, we got this ... this *secretary*."

Cliopher thought of Ghilly telling him he was too ambitious, that she refused to come always second. His family, coming at last to see him, and seeing him choose his work over and over again instead of them. His friends, never coming at all. He looked down.

Rhodin sipped from his wine glass. "You're right," he said meditatively, "this is a very fine white. Tell me, Sayo Kindraa: what do you think of the changes since the Fall? You've obviously heard the term 'new Shaian' for the court culture. What of the rest?"

"The rest?" Falbert sounded bewildered. "Kip writes about the court. What has that to do with anything?"

"The Vangavaye-ve hasn't changed very much," Cliopher murmured.

"That's true—well, except with things like—the annual stipend, the sea train, oh, the Lights. The postal service is better than it ever was, eh Kip?—the government is starting to make more sense—I like the way they do tithes now—what has this to do with anything?"

Rhodin smiled enigmatically. "What do you know about the ceremonies at the end of the week?"

"Up at the palace? Something about the government when the Lord Emperor is away on a state affair. It didn't sound very important to me, but then I don't have anything to do with the princess' court. I guess people who trade outside the Ring might care. Kip invited me along, but—"

"Ah. I see," said Rhodin, and shook his head.

"What?"

But the door opened, and Falbert's two sons, washed and dressed properly now, came in with sheepish grins. Parno was suddenly shy in Rhodin's presence, and even Faldo grimaced some sort of awed greeting that suggested Parno had spent the interval explaining to his brother how important Ser Rhodin was.

After the greetings, Parno said tentatively, "Why are you in your uniform, sir?"

"I'm on duty until I get Kip safely home. But he is, as he says, in his oldest friend's house, so let us go into the next room and let them talk, and you can show me if you live up to your ambition, Parno. Call if you need anything, Cliopher."

Falbert poured them more wine and they sat back to regard each other. Cliopher realized he was twisting his hands into the delicate fabric of his over-robe and made them relax. Féonie would be most distressed at the wrinkles. Against his throat his *efela ko* felt tight and awkward.

Falbert looked at his hands, then up into his face again, and frowned as fiercely as he had previously glowered at his sons. "Why are you being guarded?"

Cliopher clasped his hands around the stem of the wine glass to keep them from twisting the fabric again or trembling too obviously. "My lord desired it."

"That's not an answer. Is he expecting some mischief?"

"Ex-expecting? No, I don't believe so."

Falbert continued to glower. "Have you let the fire go out entirely? You would have been spitting angry, once."

Cliopher did not feel angry. He felt as if it were only his habitual self-control that was holding him back from some great emotional precipice. He was so tired. All he wanted was someone to comfort him, he thought plaintively, and tell him that this was all for the good, that all the magic, all the regency ceremonies, all the power, all the responsibility, all of that was worth this.

He should have been infuriated at the insinuation that he had *let the fire go out.*

Falbert said nothing, continuing to glower instead. Finally Cliopher said, "If Rhodin accepts Parno for the Guard, will you let him come to Solaara?"

"If Rhodin—you cannot be serious!"

"He seemed to be."

"It's all very well for Parno to dream, but he's coming to the time when he should put away youthful ambitions and find real work."

"Lest he become like me," Cliopher said dully, tipping his glass from side to side to look at the light caught in the wine.

Falbert let his breath out noisily. "I did put my foot in it. Kip, I didn't mean to insult you."

"Insult me? I wasn't insulted. I probably should have been. Rhodin thought I should be. But he's nobility. They have a different idea of honour."

"If Parno—Kip—you're a husk. You look so grand I didn't recognize you at first when you came along the canal. I thought some great lord had gone astray. You look different—you walk different—your voice is different. You have servants and guards and I don't know what else. Kip, I was a museum curator. I know the first quality of silk when I see it. Your robes are magnificent. Is it worth it?"

He closed his hands around the glass, which was threatening to tip. He wanted so badly to bare his heart—but Falbert went on without leaving him space to bring the words out.

"I don't—I'm scared of people who go after their dreams. What might Parno become, following his? What might he lose? He's a good boy, kind and careful and smart."

Cliopher found he had some words, after all. "What happened to your dreams? You had them. We used to sit around at night talking about all the things we would do. You had that dream to sail all the way around the world."

"And you used to say you would go to Astandalas and win the Emperor's favour by showing him what an Islander could do, and come home covered in glory to marry Ghilly. Why didn't you?"

"She wouldn't have me. Why didn't you?"

"Because I grew up! Because I got the job with the museum, and I was good at it and wanted to be promoted, and it was good to have money. And then I met Cora and we got married and then the boys, and ... But this isn't about me. It's about you. Why didn't you come home? We all expected you to. We never thought you would actually *leave*—Kip!"

The stem of the wine glass had snapped in his fingers. Cliopher looked down at his hands in amazement, at the dampness spilling across the deep blue of his over-robes, at the beading line of blood. He took several deep breaths to steady himself. The blood glistened red, a superb complement to the robes. The glass lay in pieces on his lap, the broken edges catching white in the light.

"Kip," Falbert said, and his voice was so uncertain and unlike him that Cliopher looked up. "Kip, talk to me. Don't—don't look like that. Just—don't. Have you cut yourself badly? Let me look at your hand."

Cliopher shook his head. He felt light-headed. All he was sure of was that if he spoke, his control would probably snap. He sat there, not resisting as Falbert took away the broken glass and examined his hand. He wrapped a cloth around his palm, muttering something about it not being serious. Cliopher set his hands in his lap, the white cloth even more brilliant against the blue, and wished with a sudden aching ferocity that his sister Navalia were there.

But Navalia had died before he joined the Service.

He firmed his lips against the memory of her telling him not to give up, that if he had something to offer the Empire, then he should give himself wholly to the offering of it.

Would she, too, have said he had wasted his life for having done so?

"Parno's not chasing a *viau*, Bertie," he said. "Rhodin wouldn't even have hinted he might take him if that were so."

Falbert showed no sign of relief, or even that he'd heard this. He said, "Tell me, Kip, why you didn't come home to us."

He had, and they had not wanted him, not the Kip who came back. He could not say that. There had never been the room to say that. For he had chosen to go ... and go, and go. And if he made proud claims to bring home a new fire ... oh, even his Buru Tovo had laughed at him for saying so, let alone the Son of Laughter himself.

He said, "It's been so long—does it still matter so much to you?"

"You know it does!"

And for whatever incomprehensible reason, that—that!—was the last straw.

CHAPTER FIFTY-NINE

CLIOPHER CLENCHED HIS FISTS, FEELING the cloth tighten around his hand. This time when he spoke his voice was thin, brittle, sharp as the broken glass.

"Do I? How? You tell me each time I come that you miss me, that you wish you saw me more often, that—yet you have never come to see me. You have never even suggested you would come. You used to say that you would make seeing me the goal of your trip around the world—but then you stopped talking about that. Instead you'd say you wished there were some other way of getting to Solaara, some safer way.

"I gave you the sea trains—I made them build them all the way out to Gorjo City—the *second* line was all the way out here!—did you think Princess Oriana did that?—and you said they took too long. You couldn't take so much time away from your work, you said. You didn't have the holidays I did, you said. I had so many more people to visit, you said. It only made sense for me to come here, you said.

"You never asked me what it took for me to get that leave—never thought to ask what I had to give up to get six months at a time to take the train for six weeks here. You know that after the Fall time worked strangely—it was longer in Solaara than here—I had three weeks free holiday a year, back then. I saved them up—so that every eight or nine or ten years I could come to see my family and my friends.

"Friends who never *once* tried to come the other way. Who told me all the places they went, the holidays they took, the visits they made, by train, by ship. You sailed all the way to the Isolates once, back when you had a whole year's sabbatical from the museum to do your own research.

"I remember when I got the letter saying you had been granted the sabbatical. A whole year, you said. You were so excited about all the things you could do with that time. You wrote to me about them at length. And I kept turning the pages, waiting to see when you would say you would come to Solaara, when you would come to me—when you would come to look at the Imperial museums, at least—and I got to the end of the letter and you never even mentioned it.

"All these wonderful things you were planning to do, people you were excited to see—and it was like I was—not invisible—but—meaningless. I was just someone you wrote to sometimes, out of habit. I realized I wasn't a real person to you any more—that if I wrote once more to say, *Please come visit me*, you would just look at the letter and laugh and say what a joke, how Kip always did love a joke, and keep on saying how one day you would sail around the world to see me, and never come."

"Kip—"

"I know that you've made lives without me. I know that you have families, friends, hobbies. I know that your life is full. I know that you like it when I come to visit—that you enjoy reminiscing with me about old times, that you like gossiping about people I know, or used to know, or you think I should know, here. Always here. I know that you're always very glad to see me when I come—and I know that you hardly notice when I'm not here."

"That's not true!"

"Isn't it? After that letter about your sabbatical I didn't write to you for *eight years*, and you never noticed. You just wrote to me every once in a while, gossip and plans and you working through what you were going to do next, or what article you were writing, or what exhibit you were organizing. You never asked me anything about what I was doing. You didn't even seem to think I *was* doing anything. Finally you asked me about some artifact in the Imperial Museum, whether I could go have a look at it for you.

"I sat there with that letter and thought and thought, and finally I decided that in memory of what a friend you'd once been to me I would go and look at the thing for you. It took me months to get to it—they were refurbishing the museum and half the curators were gone, and no one knew where it had been put, and I had very little free time because I was working on the Littleridge Treaty—and then I was sick—well, never mind—until finally I—well, anyway, finally I found it, and I got the details you wanted, and I wrote back to you. And then in your next letter you said it didn't matter, you'd found something else that disproved the theory, and—you never even thanked me. I'd gone to all this trouble for you, and ... Never mind. It doesn't matter now."

Falbert had taken off his glasses so he could rub his eyes. "Kip ..."

"What? You think I have wasted my life—or worse than wasted—that I have *ruined* my life, that I am something you need to warn your children about. Look out for the dangers of ambition, for you might be like Kip Mdang, and achieve yours! And then where will you be? Your family and friends will hate and despise you for daring to want something different— and for showing them that it is possible. Is that the problem, Bertie? That in achieving my ambition, I remind you that you—what? That I was willing to work that hard, make those sacrifices, dedicate that time, that energy, that— that devotion—and you weren't?

"Why did you even invite me in? Was it to tell me how I've wasted my life? Was it because you were afraid I would put ideas into your son's head? Or was it just out of habit—here is an old acquaintance who used to be my best friend, inside he must come?"

Cliopher stopped there, a little short of breath, a little ashamed and a little frightened of himself. He felt exhilarated, tightly wound, vibrating with tension like a stringed instrument. If Falbert plucked him, surely he would sound out like his Radiancy's harp.

Falbert said, "Come with me." He stood up and led Cliopher off the balcony, through the room next door, where Rhodin was talking to Parno and Faldo, up the winding openwork staircase to a bright, airy room full of boxes and books.

While Cliopher watched, waiting for a word he could lash back at, Falbert went to a bookcase that held nothing but stacks of identical wooden boxes, each neatly labelled. He peered at them for a moment, then pulled out one of the boxes on the second shelf from the top. He set the box down on the large wooden desk facing the window, took off the lid, and then lifted out bundle after bundle of neatly stacked papers.

Each bundle was tied with a ribbon, and each had a tag tied to the ribbon with twine. He glanced through the tags, came up finally with the one he sought. He undid the ribbon, spread out the papers, cleared his throat, and read:

> *Falbert—*
> *I went to the Imperial Museum of Culture to look at the Beaker Pottery. The curator (one Dominus Murdry, originally from Alinor as I gather) assisted me with taking the measurements etc. you requested. The details are all on the enclosed sheets.*
> *I haven't much time for writing today. Give my regards to your family, and to Toucan and Ghilly of course.*
> *Kip.*

There were a number of other papers in the same bundle. Cliopher could identify his own letters at a glance from the colour of the paper. The others were of a type much more common in the Vangavaye-ve. Falbert picked up one of these, and read:

> Bertie—Good heavens, can that really be a letter from Kip? I've never seen one under two pages from him! But at least he's writing to you again. I wonder if we missed a letter where he explained—it seems so unlike him not to reply to your letters—but of course, he's gotten less and less forthcoming over the years about himself, and it's so hard to tell now what he's actually feeling.
>
> Do you think he's sick? I've just asked Ghilly, and she says he must be, as his letters to us have been shorter than normal, too. Now our question is whether we mention it or not—if he's sick making him feel guilty for shorting you would be the worst office of friendship—we'll have to see what his next letter says. T.

Cliopher looked at him, and at the shelves of boxes, and he felt some of the tension start to slide away, leaving a cold, shaky sort of feeling in its place.

Falbert raised his bushy eyebrows in challenge, then carefully folded the letter, set it down, and pulled out the next in its pile.

> Falbert—
>
> I am sorry to hear about your troubles with the Chief Curator. Perhaps one day you will have that position, and you can browbeat poor under-curators into excellence yourself. Of course I will not say anything about the Beaker Pottery theory you have had to drop. I don't think it's anything to be ashamed of, to change your theory when new evidence is found—isn't that the heart of good scholarship? Change the theory to suit the facts, rather than the facts to suit the theory—which is fraud.
>
> Kip.

★★★

> Bertie—I've just realized, in both these last letters Kip's called you Falbert. Does that signify anything? Does he often call you that? Ghilly says he's been getting more formal lately, but she reckons that might just be court fashions.

(Fancy our Kip following court fashions! I always look at the coloured plates in the fashion books from Solaara and imagine our Kip wearing the court costumes, and then I have to stop and lie down and my mother steals the fashion books back. She says that Kip has better taste in his smallest finger than I have in my whole body, and mourns that he went into a profession with a uniform. She wishes he'd wear it when he comes home. I tell her this is contradictory, but she doesn't care. I do wish we could go see him—but Ghilly's barely gotten over bonebreak fever, and Cora is—well—what a waste of our grand plans for your sabbatical, eh?)

Anyway, back to Kip's letter—Ghilly and I reckon he wouldn't tell us if he were sick. In his last letter to us (which arrived last week, I'll send it to you along with this so you can read it) he mentioned something about the Palace being crammed for some conference or other, so there could well be something going around. You know how conferences are.

We reckon we should all write him long light letters and make him forget his troubles. After Navalia died he never wanted to talk about heavy matters—but I don't need to go into that with you. T.

★★★

Falbert—

I hadn't realized I was missing the event of a lifetime when the Flying Fish Festival met up with the boat race across the Bay of the Waters. It may be hard to believe it, but I was working, and quite forgot they were on. Shocking, I know. My regards to everyone.

Kip.

★★★

Bertie—What is up with Kip and his ridiculously short letters? It hardly seems worth writing at all, if all he's going to do is write two sentences and send it off. Unless he's so worried about the post losing his letters he dribbles all his news out in pieces, one bit to you, one to Ghilly, one to his mother, one to me …

Not that we have much more news from (or of) him, but Ghilly saw his sister yesterday and she (Vinyë) said they've been getting short letters, too, but they reckon he's just busy.

It's funny how hard it is for them to say they're proud of him—you can see it when they talk about him, but all they ever say is how they hope he is working hard and being good. It's Kip, I said to Ghilly when she told me this, what else do they think he would be doing? And she said, he has been writing a lot about compromise lately … Which he would hate particularly, of course.

We reckon we should take turns to write him, so that he gets letters at decent intervals. Assuming the post works, that is. It would be nice if it were as reliable to get a letter to Solaara as it is to get across the Bay …

Pity Kip isn't in charge of the government so he could fix the post … T.

That was the end of the first bundle. Falbert spent a few moments re-folding the letters and tying them up in their ribbon. When he had replaced everything to his satisfaction, he closed the box and put it back on its shelf. Cliopher started to say something, but Falbert held up his hand in a gesture for silence.

Then he took the second box from the top shelf, slid it down with some effort onto the desk, and from it extracted another bundle. The same ritual of untying ribbons and carefully unfolding old paper. Then:

My dear Bertie—

I keep beginning this letter, stopping, starting, stopping again. I don't know how to write about what happened today. It was important—the most important day since the Fall—and—I—

Let me begin at the beginning, and carry on.

I think I told you in my last letter how I am now an undersecretary for the Princess Indrogan.

I wish I knew whether any of my letters were reaching you. Do you even know that I survived the Fall of Astandalas? Fortu-

nately I had not gone to any parties down in the city this year, and was instead in my room at the Palace trying to figure out when and how I could get back to Gorjo City when suddenly the lights went out and the earthquake &c hit.

&c. Shorthand for an apocalypse.

When I woke up the Palace was plunked down in the middle of a village that turned out to be Solaara, just by the Imperial Necropolis in eastern Dair. We are all deeply puzzled and worried about this, but the Emperor is not dead—just—asleep—and no one wants to build a tomb in case he does die, and we go with him the rest of the way.

I have no idea what happened or why we ended up on Zunidh when we were on Ysthar, and neither does anyone else. I seem to be the only person pleased to be on Zunidh, even if it is still too far away from home.

So: I am an undersecretary for Princess Indrogan. That means there are some five or six secretaries above me (and one even more junior one below), and mostly I get to make reports of the things everyone else gets to make decisions on. Not that secretaries ever get to make decisions, of course. I don't mind the work—someone must put all these reports together to make sense of them—though sometimes I get drawn into what I am synthesizing and think about it, which I am not supposed to do, of course. Curiosity has always been a weakness of mine—that and my sense of humour are forever getting me into trouble.

(Princess Indrogan has no sense of humour whatsoever. This is why it is good I am merely an undersecretary.)

Anyway, there was a meeting today to discuss what should be done about southern Dair, which apparently has dissolved into anarchy. I took my notes and tried not to look too curious.

(Shall I ever be able to manage a properly bland public-servant kind of expression? I fear I shall never be a properly bland public servant ... it does seem a strange thing to desire to be, doesn't it? Perhaps I should say, a proper public servant. The blandness is surely not obligatory.)

The meeting dragged on and on, I think because the Princess was trying to get some of the other nobility to support her. (I have to write vaguely; I'm sorry.)

We started at nine—the third hour (have I told you [did you even get the letter in which I may have told you?] that we've gone to this strange revolving six-hour clock here? Solaara is right on the Equator, so the days are exactly twelve hours long and the nights too. People have started saying 'the first hour' to mean the first hour after the dawn bells [that is, the seventh after midnight], 8:00 is 'the second hour', and so on till noon, then we start again with the 'first hour after noon'. The same after sunset and again after midnight. I'm not sure why anyone thought having four of each hour is an improvement over having two, but there you have it, I am not in charge of the government.)

When I am in charge of the government, the first thing I shall work on is the post. How I miss the Astandalan service—

Isn't it strange that the things I miss most are the postal service and the food.

Being sure that the Vangavaye-ve is still there, not fallen off the face of the earth like eastern Kavanduru.

Anyway, the meeting started at the third hour and was still going strong at noon. We were all waiting for the noon bells, I think, because the Princess invariably takes a break then to do one of her old rituals, and that means the rest of us can get food &c. Usually the bells—invariably the bells—sound the same. There's a certain bell that rings each of the four quarters (dawn, noon, sunset, midnight) and then a different hour-bell and a third one for the quarter-hours. The room we were in you can't hear the quarter-hour chimes. This time, however, after the noon bell ALL the bells pealed at the same time—and then didn't stop.

We sat there staring in amazement at each other as the bells just kept ringing and ringing. Finally the Princess sent the most junior secretary out to find out why all the bells were ringing like that. Then she did her noon ritual (those Astandalan aristos never, never, never miss one of their rituals) and the rest of us had some food that had been laid out in the next room, as usual, and we waited.

That vigil felt as if it occupied centuries. I suppose it might have. There are very odd reports coming in from some of the hinterlands.

Eventually the bells stopped ringing—I think it was a full half-hour later if not more—and we could hear this weird sort of echoey noise, as if the Palace was whispering to itself. Princess Indrogan wanted us to get back to work but everyone was too distracted and jumpy. It didn't feel like when Astandalas Fell, but it was somehow akin to that—but not bad. I never felt it was bad.

Eventually Pito (the most junior secretary) came back, shaking with excitement, and told us that the Emperor had awoken!

And then, of course, no one even tried to get back to work. Princess Indrogan went off to the Lady of Zunidh's apartments (where Lady Jivane has been holding audiences) to see what was toward, and the rest of us went back to our rooms. There are loads of spontaneous parties going on; I can hear people singing the anthem of Astandalas through the window of my room.

I have nearly run out of paper, and the Palace is in such uproar I don't think I'll be able to get any until tomorrow. Not that I have any idea when I'll be able to send this ... or if you'll get it ... I keep writing letters to you and Ghilly and Toucan and my family, and I hope you're getting them, but apart from one I keep being given back and sending out again, they keep disappearing. And no one has had any news of the Vangavaye-ve at all. I don't think anyone else in the whole Palace is from there—and I suppose it's fair enough, when one has lost whole worlds one does not care so much about a small archipelago way out in the Wide Sea, even if it is the most beautiful place in all Creation...

If you get this, tell my family I am well and I love them and I will figure out a way to get home one day. And tell Ghilly—you know.

Kip.

That bundle had only one other letter tied up with it. Falbert unfolded it solemnly.

> *Bertie—oh, Bertie—I have just heard the news from Elisa Varga, who had it from Aerope Vawen, who heard from Quintus Mdang that a letter has come from Kip for his mother, and now you have one, too? Oh, Bertie—please say it's true! Does he sound well? Where is he? How did he get there? What happened? Tell me everything! I must stay with my great-aunt through the next two full moons, please write to me and tell me what you know. Oh Bertie, Kip is alive! Ghilly.*

Cliopher looked at the rows and rows of boxes. He cleared his throat several times. "You kept all my letters?"

"I do hope you've kept mine. It would be nice to have the whole collection together at some point."

"Of course I did. I am the perfect bureaucrat, after all. We always keep papers."

Falbert smiled ironically at him. "And I am a museum curator. We always keep artifacts of interest."

"Neatly labelled and tidily stored, I see."

"Wouldn't want them to get mildew or moths, would we. I think perhaps you should listen to one or two others."

"Bertie ..."

But Falbert went back to the bookcase and pulled out a box from a lower shelf. This bundle was fat and full, alternating the familiar palace stationery with the other stuff. He pulled out a letter from the middle of the pile.

> *Dear Falbert—*
>
> *I stand justly chastened. You must realize I can't write any details about my work, however. My lord is not someone I care to gossip about. He was, I believe, quite pleased to meet you. He does not often encounter such enthusiasm—and I think it amused him to see me in my own milieu, as it were.*
>
> *Gaudy has indeed passed the exams and is coming to the Palace soon to take his oath of service. I am exceedingly proud of his accomplishment (and reminded, of course, of how long it took me to do the same ...). I can't claim much of an influence on him*

besides the fact that I did manage to pass the exams in the end and achieve a position of some status.

I do not have much time to write today, I'm afraid. After the holiday, the work recommences ...

My regards to everyone, especially Irela, whom I am delighted to have finally met.

Kip.

PS—Now that you are retired, will you not take your boat and sail across the Wide Seas to visit me? Just think of the museums there are in Solaara. And the typhoons are not such a problem any longer.

"Bertie ..."
"A couple more."

Bertie—Are my eyes deceiving me, or did he finally actually invite you for a visit? Do you think we pushed him too much by joking about it? Also— 'a position of some status'? The personal secretary to—well!—And can he really think he has no influence over his nephew? How many times Gaudy's come round to ask us everything we know about Kip and his job and the Service and how he got in and can he read his letters and and and ...

I saw Zemius Mdang yesterday, back from his trip to the Palace. He is still dazed at having an interview with the Glorious One. (I quite understand: I am still dazed from realizing we met the Glorious One. How can Kip be so calm?) He's never a very easy person to get a straight answer from, but after many questions I managed to pin him down to admitting that Kip seemed out-of-sorts with his promotion.

Anyhow, Ghilly will be back from her tour of inspection next week, and if you'd like to come for supper we can have a confab about Kip. T.

★★★

Falbert—

I cannot respond to questions about the government. Please don't ask me. —Cliopher

"Don't say anything. One more."

Bertie—He signed it 'Cliopher'? Hell. And that was after you asked him whether he thought it likely there would be any problems in Nijan, wasn't it? Hardly a question about state secrets, I would have thought, especially as it should have been obvious to Kip that you were planning a voyage.

Ghilly is right, something is wrong. We'd best bring our letters over and have a proper read-through, like we talked about doing last year. We'll do it at the Birdhouse, you've got more space in your office. Will the day after tomorrow work? We can come by in the early afternoon. T.

Falbert refolded the letters and tied up the ribbons and replaced the boxes. Cliopher watched him numbly. His mind felt blank.

"You're twisting your robes," Falbert said, nodding at his hands.

He had mangled the silk so badly the creases stood out in little bunches. He tried to smooth them out ineffectually. His hands were trembling, but that was not new, that had started with the first of the regency ceremonies. His Radiancy had told him it was a normal physical reaction to the magic involved, and that it would improve after the final ceremony completed the ritual transfer of power.

He swallowed dryly. "That letter must have come recently."

"If you call it a letter. Yes, just the other day. I was surprised at how quickly you responded. I wasn't expecting you to show up here immediately after."

"I was in Nijan. Not far to go."

"What were you doing there? Or is that a state secret, too?"

Cliopher stared dumbly at him, and then the doorbell rang suddenly, sharply, once, and as if that were a signal he sat down in a heap on the floor and started to cry.

CHAPTER SIXTY

THERE WAS A CONFUSED MUDDLE of footsteps and voices. He distinguished Rhodin's clear, aristocratic tenor through the deeper rumbles of Bertie and Toucan, saying something about exhaustion and ceremonies. Then somebody—but he knew it was Ghilly, from her scent and her touch and just because of course it was Ghilly—knelt beside him and hugged him. He thought of hugging his Radiancy while he cried, through the soft robe, and he was never so grateful that he was not his Radiancy, that he was not bound by those taboos and restrictions.

After a while he stirred in Ghilly's arms, feeling guilty for enjoying her embrace. He wiped his face with his hand, forgetting about the bandage on it. Blood had seeped through one section, and was probably now smudged across his face. He sighed. He was not behaving very much like that perfect civil servant, that New Shaian gentleman, the Lord Chancellor of Zunidh.

The Viceroy of Zunidh. To people unversed in the language of diplomacy and court politics, that probably did not sound like it made much of a difference.

He took a deep breath. He had to hold on to who he was. And who he was was Cliopher Mdang, the Lord Chancellor of Zunidh, who had danced the legendary fire dance of the Wayfinders in the throne room of the Palace of Stars.

It seemed more than a world and a lifetime away, for all that it was a mere year and half a world distant in fact.

Why was it easier to claim the fire far away from home?

Oh, how glad he was he had asked Féonie to use his family designs, that surprisingly sophisticated visual language of the Wide Sea Islanders, in the court costume he would be wearing for the investiture.

"Come down to the comfortable chairs," Falbert said, and pulled him upright by his uninjured hand. Cliopher followed his friends downstairs. Parno and Faldo had disappeared, to go fishing, Rhodin said.

They gave him water and a short while later coffee, and after he had sipped some of the hot brew—no one made coffee like Bertie, he thought—he felt somewhat recovered, if mortified. He forced a smile. "Sorry for that. I'm over-tired."

"Is that what you call it?" Ghilly asked sceptically. "You look dreadful. And your hands are shaking."

He clutched at his robe again to stop the trembling. "It's—it's nothing, really. How are you? Toucan? Ghilly?"

"Kip, this is ridiculous."

He stared pleadingly at her. "Ghilly …"

She picked up two letters from the table next to her and waved them at him. "We were already coming to see Bertie about you today, then this morning we got these—letters. One from you, asking if we'd be able to meet you tomorrow, very formal and official-sounding, and then—this one—which I'd take for a prank except the paper is far too lovely."

Cliopher focused bleary eyes on the second letter. The heavy creamy paper was very familiar to him, as was the slanting untrained hand of the writer. "That's his Radiancy's hand," he said, curiosity piercing through the dull fog. "What—what did he write you for?"

Ghilly looked disbelievingly at the letter. "What do you mean—his hand?"

"That's his handwriting. Not Eldo—his secretary's. His own."

"I thought you were his secretary?"

Falbert made a warning sort of gesture. "Not any more, he told me earlier. Well—what is the letter about?"

"It's an invitation to that shindig up at the palace. It—it makes it sound important to you." Ghilly looked searchingly into his face. "Is it, Kip? Is it important?"

Cliopher actually opened his mouth, but had no idea what to say to this. Was it *important*?

"Will you read the letter?" Falbert asked.

Ghilly handed it to Toucan without taking her eyes from Cliopher's. Toucan cleared his throat. "It was just addressed to 'Toucan and Ghilly, Gorjo City'.

To Toucan and Ghilly:

By right of your long friendship with Kip Mdang, you are invited to witness the viceroyship ceremonies taking place at the Palace of the Vangavaye-ve on the fifth day of this month. The formalities begin the hour before sunset. A.

"It's signed with a sun—you know, with rays—that's what made it seem like a prank—a Sun-in-Glory, I guess. Huh. We shall frame the letter as an artifact of greatness. But—what is it for, Kip? Why is it so important that your lord would write to invite us? He obviously didn't ask you for our surnames."

"We couldn't remember them," Rhodin said diffidently. "His Radiancy asked Ludvic and Conju and me if we could, but all we could remember was your nicknames—Cliopher doesn't talk about you formally very often, it's always 'Bertie' or 'Ghilly' or 'Toucan'."

"I don't think I know your real first name, Toucan," Cliopher said with an attempt at a smile.

"It *is* Toucan—I was born with the big nose, and my parents had said my older sister could name me, and, well, the story is that when she first saw me she starting laughing and laughing about my nose, and said I looked just like a toucan, and ... Toucan I have always been. But that doesn't answer Ghilly's question, Kip. Obviously if we're invited by your lord, we'll go, but—what is it? Why should it matter that we're your friends?"

Cliopher looked beseechingly at Rhodin, who was back to holding his spear over by the door. Rhodin shook his head. "No, Kip, this is on you. I don't understand why you've never explained before, but that's your lookout."

"Explained what?"

Cliopher bit his lip. How had they not *understood*? He had tried so hard to make the proclamations clear. No one else but those whose opinions he cared most about had found them difficult to understand.

He thought of certain other moments in his life when he had failed to take something seriously in the context of his work (that fish farm, for instance) because of the emotional colouring of its origin. It did not take much to see how that could work the other way.

His Radiancy had put things into place so that if Cliopher ever reached out, he would find himself welcomed. He had not initiated friendship, because the custom was that he *always* initiated, and he had wanted someone to reach out to him for himself. And one day Cliopher had, and found ...

Cliopher had never fully explained, because he had wanted—so desperately had he wanted—his friends, his family, to ask him first. But perhaps they had never asked, wanting him to reach out first to them.

He had no idea how to bridge that.

He said awkwardly, "His Radiancy is going on a quest to find an heir. I'll be the person left in charge when he goes."

Ghilly quirked her eyebrows at him. "Aren't you always the person he leaves in charge?"

"This time is more ... official."

And even then, at that moment, they could not bring themselves to say *Congratulations, Kip*; and he could not bring himself to say *Why don't you care?* for fear they would answer.

Ghilly said, "Why didn't you tell us before?"

Cliopher looked involuntarily towards the staircase and the boxes and boxes of letters. He swallowed. But there were all the proclamations ... Unless he was wrong there?

He felt dizzy with the thought, pinching his fingers together until the twisted fabric made them throb. It made so much more sense, that they simply *did not know*—

But—

How could he be wrong there? Ever since he had become Lord Chancellor, every quarter-day he had conscientiously sent out proclamations with news of the mundial government's developments.

And each time he got a letter or two from home with a dribble of lukewarm praise for what had taken a whole lifetime of dedicated work to *begin*.

And when he wrote to Toucan with jokingly hypothetical problems, asking for advice for how to reconcile the *Lays* with some current or prospective crisis, Toucan would write back, serious about teasing out a formal political philosophy from the songs and dances, jocular about the hypothetical practical applications that were every quarter coming to reality in suitably pretentious court proclamations.

He remembered suddenly Toucan's cousin Maya, quarrelling merrily with that Jilkanese man about the fish farm, winking at him when she declared that there only needed to be *one* Islander in the government to make a difference.

He swallowed against the bitter knowledge that his best friends and his family had a picture of him in their minds that was so strong and so positive that they were able to dismiss everything that contradicted it, good or bad.

And what was that picture? That Kip Mdang had left the Vangavaye-ve—*left the Islands*—and assimilated into the Solaaran court, where he had achieved a position of some status—they did grant him that, in their letters amongst themselves, at least—at the cost of almost everything they believed he had once considered of the utmost importance.

But yet ... Cliopher glanced at the boxes and boxes of letters, the evidence of how much they meant to him—didn't Bertie realize how much *time* it took to write all that?—and Bertie's collection was only the beginning of Cliopher's correspondence.

But yet, how could he be so bitter and small-minded after seeing such evidence of their care, their thoughtfulness, their ... love? For love it was that kept them writing, kept them wanting their Kip to come home to them.

He tried to think of ways to phrase his desires in such a way that he did not destroy their friendship, and failed. He had accused Bertie of it being only habit and the recollection of friendship that made him continue to write, and Bertie had harrowed him with his own assumptions.

For now that Cliopher thought about it, he could not deny that there was a difference between the older letters and the recent ones. Nor that that difference was solely to do with his more limited time for correspondence.

And he was so very tired. He did not have the emotional energy to start another quarrel. He felt a quirk of humour, not quite enough for a smile, at that thought. *Their* Kip had never backed down from a quarrel over principles.

Well, it was a matter of pride to *Cliopher* that he had never backed down from a quarrel over principles. At one level he was appalled that he was even considering starting now.

What could he *say*?

He bent his head over his coffee, trying not to start crying again. At court this admission of weakness would have been devastating.

Falbert spoke over him. "We should have gone to Solaara."

"Oh," said Ghilly, as if her heart were breaking.

Cliopher struggled uselessly to regain his composure, not at all sure why her heart would be, even less sure why his own seemed to be cracking under the strain of not ruining his oldest friendships in a foolish and unproductive display of temper.

★★★

HE WENT HOME A WHILE later, feeling muddled. He rang the bell to warn of his and Rhodin's arrival. It was answered by his sister, who said that their mother was just going out to call on all their relatives.

His mother and Aunt Oura arrived in the hall while he was still trying not to be too disappointed that Vinyë, too, said nothing about his becoming the Viceroy of Zunidh.

Not even a 'congratulations'? Cliopher thought in a small, pathetic voice, feeling as he had as a boy, as a young man, as an adult, every time he had reached some hitherto-impossible milestone and his family had responded with pointing out the next. Learn how to dive for a golden pearl, and they were dissatisfied he did not find one marked with fire.

Of course, they thought he had turned onto the wrong road long ago. No wonder they were so insistent on showing him what they saw as the right road, the way to cut back across, the way home.

But—

It was not that he wanted the parades that had been held (not organized by him!) in Nijan or in Haion City or, might the gods laugh, in Amboloyo. The combination of the most incredibly lofty imperial ceremony with the elevation of a commoner—and not just any commoner, but a Wide Sea Islander, a *tribesman*—to the highest achievable position had been felt, at least by most people, justly worth celebrating.

Cliopher had gained a sense of what his Radiancy had meant about being the centre of all attention and yet, as a human being, invisible; but he had looked out at those cheering throngs and been satisfied that some of what they were cheering was the new possibility that any of them, or their sons or daughters, could break through the ossified hierarchy and change the world.

He had not wanted a parade in the Vangavaye-ve. He had not wanted cheering throngs to follow him down the street. He had not even wanted things to change.

But he would have liked someone to say 'congratulations'.

His mother embraced him, followed by Aunt Oura, who then held him out at arm's length to inspect. "You're looking very tired, Kip," his aunt said. "But so beautifully dressed you'd hardly notice. You'll feel better once you've had a chance to visit with everyone—we've been missing you."

"Where are you going?" he asked, trying to make his tone at least acceptably enthusiastic. He still felt shaky after the emotional visit with Bertie, aware that if he went out again Rhodin would accompany him in his panoply, and totally disinclined to face his family's critical assessment of his appearance—in all senses of the world—with the savage certainty that if Bertie and Ghilly and Toucan and Vinyë and *his mother* all refused to offer him any form of congratulations, then no one else would, either.

"Off to see Lazo first, then Malania's having a drop-in this afternoon. She'll be ecstatic you're here."

Cliopher looked from his aunt to his mother, who was looking gravely at him. He remembered with still-vivid embarrassment the backhanded apology she had given him on that one visit to Solaara, when she had seen his desperate attempts to keep from drowning as cock-of-the-rock gestures to show off his importance.

He realized he was dressed in what had become ordinary clothing to him, but which was of an entirely different order of expensive to anything his family would ever own. *Boats* cost less than his outfits.

Buru Tovo would have snorted at the idea that either boats or outfits needed to cost anything at all but your skill and some time.

He felt as heavily as ever the unspoken mountain of expectations that weighted down that apparently casual invitation. Reached deep inside himself to find that store of amenability, geniality, common courtesy, that usually saw him through all the multitude of encounters he faced every day when all he wanted to do was never see another human being again.

There was nothing there.

He tried again, tried to vocalize the polite assent he always said, tried to force himself to smile, tried desperately not to start crying again.

"We should get going," his mother said, still watching him. "Come along, Kip."

For the first time in almost his entire adult life Cliopher said, "No."

CHAPTER SIXTY-ONE

VINYË WAS THE ONE TO speak first. "Kip? You're not going?"

Cliopher stepped away from the doorway. Rhodin moved silently to stand behind him, the motion kept unassuming. Sometimes his guard's movements were intended to show off; on those occasions Cliopher had to brace himself not to be as visibly impressed as everyone else. But when they wanted to be unassuming the guards were nearly invisible despite their panoply.

He took a deep breath, seeing the frown in his mother's face, the surprise in Aunt Oura's, the concern in Vinyë's. He looked at his sister, back at his mother, tried to find an acceptable excuse.

His mouth spoke forth the truth without him quite intending it. "I'm going to climb up to the Reserve. I haven't been up there in years."

"You haven't been *here* in years," his mother said.

The pathetic little voice whispered something about irreconcilable difference of priorities. Cliopher was stung, and—like any one of a thousand diplomatic fracas involving *irreconcilable differences of priorities*—he lifted his chin, smiled his best diplomatic smile, and said mildly but implacably, "Please give my apologies to everyone and say I will be delighted to see them tomorrow or, failing that, at the ceremonies the day after. I am sure that if you explain it to them they will understand that I need a few hours of peace and quiet after all the work this year."

His mother kept frowning. Aunt Oura's glance shifted quickly from him to Eidora to Vinyë. Then his aunt smiled, patted him on the arm, and said, "Of course, Kip, you must be tired. We'll see you later."

And just like that, so much easier than he had ever imagined, they left. They also left the mountain of unfulfilled duties sitting there; but Cliopher was used to mountains of unfulfilled duties, and routinely conquered them.

Vinyë said, "Well done!"

Cliopher started weakly to laugh.

★★★

HE CHANGED INTO ONE OF the outfits he'd left in his bedroom, Vangavayen in style and make: tunic and trousers both of loose cotton. They were both rather looser on him than the style warranted, as it appeared he'd lost weight, though when he straightened his shoulders the fabric bound.

For a moment he was startled, wondering if he'd somehow managed to put muscle on, then snorted softly at the realization that *these* garments had never been fitted to him. He looked at himself thoughtfully in the mirror.

There had been a few times over the past couple of years when he'd wondered whether the subtle changes in his appearance were due to physical change or simply the ever-evolving wardrobe Féonie made for him. He was quite certain she would have made him look magnificent if he'd put on rolls of fat like a Cinthri wrestler or a Mgunaivë chieftain (for whom authority was measured in gravity, and who held that the wealth of the village should be shown in its populace; the naturally slender were always at a disadvantage).

He had noticed the grey hairs; the recent trembling; the occasional complaint from joints and muscles. He had tried to exercise more, to eat better, to sleep enough. He had thought he was holding total unfitness at bay, at least. He had not noticed that at some point he had crossed some invisible line and was now … old.

He went back to his wardrobe and through the neatly hung ranks of a lifetime of clothing, pulling out tunics and trousers to try on. He had to go back quite a long way, judging by the fabric, before he found ones that fit.

He straightened his shoulders, lifted his chin, and the ill-fitting old clothes suddenly shifted on his frame and made him look like the Kip who had (he remembered now) proudly bought them with the first real surplus of money he had ever had. He and Toucan had gone to what they thought of as the *expensive* shops, and Cliopher had found the fabric (oddly enough, the same colours he habitually wore now—blue and orange and white—but all much brighter than the rich hues of the regalia of Zunidh), and had the clothes made, and they had gone out to—where was it? The Parrot, that was it, the café-bar at the university, and celebrated.

He tucked his *efela* below the collar, thumbed his nose at his own image, went out to ask Vinyë if she wished to join him, and crashed back into his current life at the expression on Rhodin's face.

Cliopher discovered he was fed up with court conventions as well. He lifted his chin and said, "We're going rambling. Vinyë, would you like to come?"

She was dressed in suitable clothing, but she hesitated. "Are you sure you don't want solitude?"

"I don't want to sit making small talk and being raked over the coals for not coming home for three years," he retorted. "If you can refrain from either of those things, I'd love your company. We'll stop by and see if Ghilly and Toucan are still at Bertie's and want to come."

They were; and when they saw Cliopher something in their eyes shifted, as if he had settled into place.

★★★

THE RESERVE COMPRISED THE TOP half of Mama Ituri's Son. To get there one walked up through the university grounds, across the lowest of the Palace gardens (kept open to thoroughfares only by dint of much protest), and through the wrought-iron gate in the wall bounding the garden. On the other side was jungle laced with paths. It was a friendly place, with seats at good viewpoints and occasional signposts, and was a popular destination for anyone who fancied a walk with a view.

Cliopher set a strong pace. He was grateful for his friends' company, but he did not, at first, want to talk. He wanted to push through the muddled emotions, get himself to the point where he could laugh at the fact that they all responded so much more easily, more positively, to him wearing decades-old clothing than to the elevation in rank.

He kept taking the paths leading upwards. He truly had not climbed the Reserve in years, not all the way. There had been a few gentler and shorter ambles in the lower reaches with friends and family. He ignored those turnings without even thinking about it, feet following the path he used always to take.

Up, and up, and up, and around the shoulder of the mountain, and up some more to the peak, where he finally stopped to rest.

Ser Rhodin was not winded, but he looked at Cliopher with respect. "I had no idea you were fit enough for that."

Cliopher smiled ruefully, breathing long and slowly, lungs burning. "Neither did I. Maybe we'll take it a bit easier on the way down."

"Here come your friends."

Ghilly was first, then Vinyë and Toucan, and at last Bertie, who was snorting and puffing but hauled himself to the summit cairn. He scowled ferociously at Cliopher. "Let your spleen out, have you?"

Cliopher ignored him so he could soak in the view.

Gorjo City lay spread about the lap of the mountain below them, a jumble of canals and bright houses and pools and boats and people. To their right and a little below their level was the top of the Spire, the sky ships jostling each other at the too-small dock. They blocked the view towards the Gate of the Sea. Out the other direction was the Bay of the Waters and the Outer Ring rising up around them.

"I love this view," he said quietly to no one in particular.

"You always used to look out," Bertie said, scowl directed at the sky ships and the opening in the Outer Ring behind them.

"Well, priorities shift over time." Cliopher did a full circuit of the summit, hand resting on the topmost stone of the cairn. It was smooth and shiny from generations of people doing the same. He smiled at Rhodin, who shook his head. "Shall we start down?"

This time he walked more moderately, next to Ghilly. He asked her about the wine-makers of Looenna, and was deep into a discussion about the various grants the farmers could apply for when they abruptly came out of a thick belt of jungle and he recalled the main reason why he had not taken this route since he was a young man.

They had emerged just below the outlet of a hanging valley. The stream that had made it launched itself off the cliff in a triumphant spray like an outflung piece of foamwork. The path itself came to the edge of the cliff and started up again on the far side of the dropped valley, with an ancient rope and wooden bridge between them.

Once upon a time Cliopher had been the one who had shaken the ropes to annoy and frighten his sisters and friends. He had loved this hike, the view up and out, the waterfall's ever-changing beauty, the slight frisson of fear crossing the bridge, seeing the water dropping down to an inlet of the sea far below.

Once.

He had not consciously realized, not until he set foot on the threshold and his hand on the rope railing and froze, just how much that had changed.

With enormous effort he pulled his foot back from the start and removed his hand from the rope. He smiled at his friends, who had not yet noticed anything odd—and would not, if he could possibly prevent it. He carefully did not look at the bridge, the drop, anything but the familiar beloved faces. They were not the whooping and hollering war-party that had chased him across the rope bridges of the Southern Grey Mountains. They were his family.

His logical mind said that perhaps it was because they were behind him that the fear had gripped him that way. If they went *first*, he reasoned, it would not seem that he was being chased.

"After you," he said lightly, with a sketch of a court bow to Vinyë.

She laughed and set across, Ghilly close behind her. Toucan stopped for a moment to let Bertie get ahead of him. "You won't shake it, will you, Kip?"

Cliopher resolved that as soon as he was across the damn thing he would apologize to Toucan for those ill-chosen pranks. "I promise I won't," he said. "I'll even wait until you're all the way across."

Surely that would do it.

"Just don't rock it the way you used to," Toucan said, and cautiously set out.

Cliopher turned to Rhodin, who said, "Your sister's across. It looks sturdy enough."

And he waited expectantly. Cliopher knew just how inflexible Rhodin could be when on duty, and told himself that one person behind him was entirely different, was actually rather nice, not frightening at all.

He gritted his teeth, gripped the rope with both hands, and stopped.

Remember your hands, he told himself. You are free to grip, to hold. Don't look at the boards—

But of course he looked at the boards. In the chinks between he could see the blue and white water swirling against the rocks down below, the exact view shifting wildly as Toucan's motions rocked the bridge from side to side. When the motion stilled—he was being kind, Cliopher told himself, waiting until Toucan had reached the other side—he inched his foot forward again.

After what seemed ages his foot slid onto the first board. He sighed with relief and focused on getting his left foot onto the board with it. Was there, and feeling triumphant, when Rhodin said, "Are you all right, Cliopher?" from right behind him.

The voice was fine, but the sun was behind them and cast Rhodin's spear in sharp shadow over his own. Cliopher bit back a whimper and found that without conscious intent he was now back on the firm land facing his friend.

He forced another smile. "Will you go across first, Rhodin? I have ... I was once ... Do you know that old rope bridge across the Haren Gap? The one they replaced with the stone one a few years ago?"

Rhodin looked mystified. "Yes, why?"

"I was once chased across it by some people armed with spears. Will you please go across first?"

"When on earth—on the other side, yes, of course. I will ask you for the story, you know!"

"It's a long one. Please—"

Rhodin nodded, mystification replaced with intense curiosity, and stepped lightly across the bridge to join the others. Cliopher looked around to make sure no one else had sneaked up behind him unawares, chided himself for such a foolish fancy, and once again inched himself forward to the entrance.

And there he stood. Sweating, heart pounding, waves of shivering cold and burning heat washing over him in succession, mouth dry, quiet whimpers getting past all those years of training to keep his feelings to himself.

And he kept thinking that there he stood on one side of an impassible gap, his family on the other, and he could not cross the bridge between.

Again and again he tried to make himself step onto the first plank. Again and again his body refused. His mind threw up images to torment him with, nightmares and memories of broken bridges, broken cross-lines, broken people.

He shoved the images ruthlessly to one side, refusing to believe in them. Told himself through gritted teeth that he had persevered against all opposition all the way to being the Viceroy of Zunidh, and he was not going to let an old memory defeat him. He had not been defeated then! He had made it across the bridge. Made it all the way home. And the bridge had not even been the hardest part of that journey.

He closed his eyes and stepped blindly into space. He was heartened by the rough rope in his hands, the width of the planks under his feet, the merest sway to the bridge.

He got quite a ways out when his sandal caught on something. He opened his eyes automatically to see what it was; found that the lacing had caught on a large splinter. He had a moment to think through how to release it before his eyes lost their focus on the bridge and went instead for the water and rocks a hundred feet down.

Their roaring filled his ears. He stood there as the wind picked up, the bridge swayed around him, trying to break the hold of fear on himself, unable to succeed. Sure that any moment he would lose his grip on the ropes—he could see the sequence of events so clearly!—would try to release his foot—would overbalance at just the same moment as a strong gust of wind—and—more roaring.

He had not *listened* before. This time he thought there might be words, and since he was otherwise caught in the trap, he tried harder. It was Bertie.

"Kip," he was saying, over and over. "Kip. Kip. Kip."

Cliopher thought how strange it was that the roaring had Bertie's voice. Then big warm hands enfolded his cold, tense ones, and the surprise of the touch was so great it broke through the roaring and Cliopher looked up and away from the bridge.

Bertie was right in front of him, scowling.

"I love your scowls," Cliopher said, the first thing that came into his mind. He could feel the fear creeping back, a great roaring nothingness all around him, behind him, behind Bertie. He focused hard on Bertie, who was trying to make him release his grip. "Don't do that, Bertie."

"You need to come with me, Kip."

"This is fine," Cliopher said shakily. "Atmospheric, even."

"Kip, if I take one of your hands—"

But the moment that Bertie turned and ceased to block the view, the roaring surged, and Cliopher swallowed back whimpers but not soon enough.

Bertie turned, stepped towards him until his bushy eyebrows and wild hair filled Cliopher's vision. He placed his hands back on Cliopher's, leaned forward gently and touched his forehead to Cliopher's, the ancient Islander greeting. "Come, Kip, it's time to go home."

Cliopher closed his eyes, trying to ignore the swaying, the wind, the roaring. Said softly, "I don't know that I can, Bertie."

They stood there for a moment, foreheads touching, hands touching. Cliopher thought again of his Radiancy, who never had anyone to hold him against his fears. Missed him suddenly, fearfully, frighteningly.

Bertie said, "Can't, or won't? *Can't* can be fixed."

Bertie did not mean the bridge. Bertie meant … everything else. Cliopher said, voice trembling, hands trembling, heart trembling, "Can't."

"Then we will fix that. First of all, we must get across. *Give me your hands.*"

The order was snapped out, Bertie all authority, and Cliopher found his hands loosening on the rope until his fingers ached with how hard he had been gripping.

"Good. Good," Bertie said, sliding his big warm hands into Cliopher's so he could no longer feel the rope. "Now, Kip, I want you to step with me."

"Don't let go," he said urgently as Bertie stepped back, feeling all the space between them yawn open into vertigo. "Bertie!"

"Right foot!"

"Bertie, I can't!"

"You must!"

"Bertie!"

"Close your eyes, Kip, and *trust me.*"

Cliopher had always responded well to direct orders from those he greatly respected. He closed his eyes.

CHAPTER SIXTY-TWO

"YOU CAN OPEN YOUR EYES now," Bertie said gruffly.

Cliopher opened them warily. The ground was solid beneath his feet; his heart was still hammering wildly. But he was across the bridge.

He was overwhelmed in a rush of embarrassment. "Thank you." He looked around, still warily, at the concerned grouping of his friends, and the still-swaying bridge. He shuddered. He forced himself to smile amenably. "Could we sit, do you think, for a moment?"

He did not wait for an answer, but plunked down on the bench placed to look out over the chasm and the sea. Rhodin planted himself to one side, conveniently blocking the bridge. Vinyë hesitated a moment and then sat beside him. She took his hand; it felt very cold in hers. "That's new," she said, rubbing it gently.

"Not really," he replied, breathing slowly and deeply to regain control. "I'd forgotten why I avoided this path."

"What happened? Did one break under you?" Vinyë asked.

He felt entirely disinclined to explaining. Rhodin said, "You said you were chased across that long bridge over the Haren Gap in the Grey Mountains. I've been trying to think when that might be. It must have been when you went—came—home after the Fall? I seem to remember you saying you were captured by one of the mountain tribes."

Cliopher watched some white gulls float past them. One, two, a dozen, soaring on some updraft, shining white against the black rock and the blue sea.

"Yes," he replied at last. "They thought I was a spy for the Plainsmen. Eventually they decided the best thing to do was force me to run barefoot and bound across the rope bridges. They could have caught me at any time, of course, but they enjoyed making me run. The last bridge, the long bridge, was the worst. They hadn't kept it in good repair, there were many missing planks."

"You can't go across rope bridges very often,"Toucan said encouragingly.

Cliopher laughed, though it sounded more like a whuffle. "Every time getting on or off one of the sky ships … the only saving grace of those is they're not very long."

"I don't remember you talking about this," Bertie said, scowling.

Cliopher sobered. "No.You were never very interested in hearing the account of that journey. Anyway. I'm feeling better. Shall we continue down?"

"Kip—"

But Vinyë said nothing else. Cliopher stood up and started walking, so that perforce they had to come with him.

And of course, they said nothing else; and he said nothing else; and all the things they were not asking, and he was not demanding, accompanied them down the mountain like the gulls.

★★★

THE PARTY THAT EVENING GOT perhaps slightly out of hand.

It was an impromptu affair, mostly in honour of Parno, partly in honour of Cliopher, though he was muddled as to what, exactly, anyone thought they were honouring. He kept almost asking, and then falling silent; and Ghilly and Toucan and Bertie and Vinyë all almost said something, and then instead turned the conversation towards family gossip and local news, and he sighed and accepted another drink and wished Basil were there.

Probably Basil also would prefer the old Kip.

They had come down off the mountain to find the older generation still at Aunt Malania's and Irela demanding of Bertie what he was thinking to disappear when Parno had such a thing to celebrate. Bertie scowled good-naturedly, Irela said a large handful of Parno and Faldo's friends had gathered in the Birdhouse, Bertie promised to shift them so that Irela could have some peace and quiet, and off they went.

Cliopher could not help reflecting that he would have enjoyed the evening very much had it ever been acknowledged outright that he, too, had cause to celebrate. Somewhere around the second bar and the third drink he decided that even if not a single one of his friends or relations felt moved to congratulate him for being made the Viceroy of Zunidh, nevertheless they all seemed assiduous in welcoming him home and that, at least, was something he could be glad of.

Eventually word came trickling down that Cousin Zemius had finished teaching and had found them places at the Parrot, a café-bar tucked between palace gardens and university grounds where Cliopher and his friends, like many generations of students before and after them, had spent many happy hours.

By that point they were all at least tipsy. They reached the Parrot and more or less took over the whole place. The bartender knew Zemius and Bertie well, and accepted this invasion with equanimity. Freed of the restraints of being in a residential neighbourhood, the party increased in volume and enthusiasm. It was all very cheerful and very fun and something Cliopher had not experienced since he was a young student himself. Probably the fact that he still wore his old clothes helped everyone.

Some time well after dark he went out to the privy and on his return stopped at the bar to ask for a coffee. He was recognized by Haldo, the owner, and stopped to talk.

They exchanged greetings and proceeded to reminisce, Cliopher complimenting him on the coffee (which was, of course, made of Vangavayen beans roasted in-house) and how he never quite managed to find the right kind of bean in Solaara.

"What, you can't buy good beans there?"

"Not Vangavayen beans," Cliopher replied, inhaling appreciatively. "I've missed your coffee, Haldo."

"Get away with you," Haldo retorted, laughing.

"Are you talking about coffee?" Rhodin asked from behind him. Much to Cliopher's embarrassment, Rhodin had insisted in accompanying him to the privy (though not, thankfully, inside), but he was being exceptionally discreet about it.

"We'd better have a second one," Cliopher said to Haldo. "Rhodin's a great connoisseur of such things."

"I'd better not disappoint him, then, eh?"

Haldo turned back to the coffee machine, which made a loud hissing noise as the internal steam works raised pressure again. Cliopher, watching him idly, was made aware of the altercation beginning behind them by Rhodin's hand on his arm.

He turned to see a pair of gorgeously dressed young louts making loud mock of Parno and his girlfriend. As they became aware that the attention of the room was turning to them with shock and disapproval, they extended the range of their taunts to encompass them—and all their class, occupation, and relations. Parno stared open-mouthed at them, at their extremely fine clothing, their dark skin, their shaven heads, their jewels, all the marks of the privileged nobility.

Cliopher exchanged a glance with the appalled and irate Rhodin, and set off not directly for the front of the room, but to the table just behind Parno's where he could see Falbert starting to rise into high temper.

Before he quite made it a smooth aristocratic voice said, "Insolent puppies! Down."

The two louts' grins faltered. Pushing between them came a woman of about Cliopher's own age, dressed in an Amboloyan mantle of the finest embroidered silk. She wore fewer jewels than either young man, but her carriage was proud and her bearing superb. She appeared half-Voonran, like Rhodin, her skin was a creamy bronze colour, her almond-shaped eyes an unusual blue, and her sleek hair silver-touched black and dressed into curls. Next to the two overdressed louts she looked like a calla lily in her green and white.

"Lady Rusticiana," one of the louts said in protest. "How can you embarrass us like that?"

She quelled him with a glance of such perfectly demonstrated disdain Cliopher immediately began to wonder how often she practiced it and what exactly she did. He did not recognize her, though she seemed strangely half-familiar. "I'm sure if you think about it for a moment, Lord Balo," she said coolly, "you will see that it is not I who am embarrassing you."

Balo was cousin and heir to the Vangavayen princess, son of an important nobleman from Jilkano, and from all repute not at all accustomed either to thinking or being reprimanded. He opened his mouth on another poorly-articulated protest, which Lady Rusticiana quelled with a single glance.

"Insolent puppy," she said again, her voice dangerously smooth and quiet, her accent pure Astandalan court. "You dishonour yourself and your family. You demonstrate nothing but the most egregious idleness of mind and pusillanimity of spirit. Were you a child of mine I should not let you out in public; were you a student of mine I should have you scrubbing the university toilets for a year."

"Lady Rusticiana, you cannot possibly—" the second lout tried.

"Silence, boy!"

She turned to the room of dumbfounded Vangavayens and swept them a curtsey of second-degree apology, which surprised Cliopher considerably more than her words. For words were, if not cheap, then at least easier for most aristocrats to bear than the embodied ritual of apology and humility.

Her voice rang out in the room, "Good citizens, it is with sorrow I must apologize for these young idiots. Be you assured I will be speaking with their guardians about their atrocious behaviour."

Cliopher looked at Rhodin, who mouthed, 'Radical' at him—which made only marginally more sense. *She* might be a radical, but little of what Lord Balo and his friend were saying would be considered an embarrassment by the aristocrats of the world. They did not grant enough equality to commoners to feel it. And Balo was heir to the Vangavaye-ve.

And who *was* she? Cliopher thought he knew all the great aristocrats of the world, by name and by sight at the very least, and Lady Rusticiana surely was one such.

Before he could respond, the door opened behind Lady Rusticiana and four women in evening court dress came in, followed by Princess Oriana. The princess did not even look at the room: she focused on Lady Rusticiana with well-bred alarm.

"Lady Rusticiana, this is not the company or the place for you."

"Whatever do you mean, Princess?" Lady Rusticiana replied.

Princess Oriana made a gesture of polite disgust. "I do not feel I should have to tell you, my lady, that while hot-headed young gentlemen might choose to demean themselves by consorting with the lower classes, it hardly behoves a lady of your rank or mine to do so, let alone to engage with such creatures."

"Hot-headed young gentlemen?"

Princess Oriana tittered. "Labour monkeys, to be dreadfully vulgar. They are incapable of anything resembling polite behaviour or correct judgment."

Cliopher walked forward the necessary few steps to be able to put his hand firmly on Falbert's shoulder and press him down into his seat. No one else paid any attention to him or his movement. Lady Rusticiana appeared to be swallowing down fury and trying to decide how best to respond to the princess—who was her host and the reigning monarch, of course—without abandoning her (definitely radical) principles.

Although Cliopher was rather curious about how far she would go to defend them, he was more certain that he wanted to head off more vile insults slung at his friends and family.

"Princess Oriana," he said therefore, quietly and clearly, making sure his accent was his court one. He wanted Princess Oriana to have no excuse for misunderstanding him tonight. He kept his hand heavy on Falbert, who showed definite signs of wanting to rise.

The princess and her party swung around in outrage at this address out of the undifferentiated mass of nonentities facing them, and for a moment hung fire in shock and indecision.

Cliopher met the princess' eyes calmly. Princess Oriana was vain and vapid; when she had been informed that she had inherited the throne of the Vangavaye-ve—by Cliopher, acting on his Radiancy's behalf—her response to hearing that her cousin and court had perished in a volcanic eruption had been, 'Oh, wonderful, now I shall be permitted to wear *ahalo* cloth!'

She was, however, not wholly stupid. Cliopher could watch her mind at work; could nearly identify her thoughts as they occurred to her; could see the moment when she realized she had just offered the new Viceroy of Zu-nidh mortal insult.

She said, "Lord Mdang," and promptly sank down into the curtsey of a first-degree apology.

He stared down at her. He knew he was a little drunk, knew that he had intensely disliked her for all the years he had known her, knew also that he had spent the day having it thrust in his face that he could not trust his emo-tions or his judgment when it came to the Vangavaye-ve.

She held the curtsey. He stared.

If she had emulated the Prince of Amboloyo and ever said such a thing to his face—

If she had merely stopped with *labour monkeys*—

If she had been someone he had ever had the least morsel of respect for—

If she had ever done a moment of work that was not immediately for her own gain—

She was starting to tremble slightly. Her face was frozen in a court smile. And he?

He made the gesture permitting her to rise. She rose, fear and frantic apology in her bearing, in the angle she held her fan and the way she kept her eyes lowered. She waited for him to speak.

If this had been the ruler of any of the other sixteen provinces of Zunidh, would he have accepted the offer of fealty?

How could he for one moment think that he was being fair when he bent over backward to save her from her own mistakes?

How could he *do* that to his own home?

How could he *have done* that?

"Princess Oriana," he said finally. "I think you had better inform his Radiancy of your opinion of me."

CHAPTER SIXTY-THREE

ONCE THE DOOR HAD SHUT, Cliopher relaxed his pressure on Falbert's shoulder and sat down.

Rhodin passed him his coffee cup. "Well done."

Cliopher smiled ruefully, knowing this was for him not *completely* losing control of his temper. "Thank you."

Falbert, Vinyë, Ghilly, Toucan, and Zemius all stared at him. Toucan cleared his throat and spoke first. "Why are you smiling like that? That was the Princess! She could make our lives hell for annoying her!"

Rhodin chuckled. "Yes, but Cliopher just—ah, put her in her place," he amended hastily at Cliopher's sharp glance. Not that Cliopher *minded* his family knowing—or rather, guessing—but it would be highly improper of him to *announce* anything of the sort before his Radiancy officially told him to. "That was very nicely done indeed, Kip."

"Thank you," he said again. "Do you know who Lady Rusticiana is?"

"Never mind Lady Rusticiana for a moment," Ghilly said. "Let's go back to the point of what we can expect to come out of that interchange."

Cliopher was just drunk enough to say what he was thinking. "Ghilly, you are a very smart woman. I'm sure you can figure it out. I can't say more than I already have."

"Kip—"

"I can't say anything until I have some official communication from his Radiancy," he expanded, and at her look of startled comprehension smiled. "Lady Rusticiana, Rhodin?"

"She's a sister of the last Prince of Katharmoon on old Ysthar. Weren't you at court when she was presented? It was the great scandal of the year. She threw over the Grand Duke of East Voonra because he was a 'great bully of a buffoon who thought his money and rank meant he had no need to think'—ah, the caricatures!—and ran off to live penniless with wandering players on Alinor."

"I think I do remember hearing about that," Cliopher said, "though I wasn't exactly at court in those days, Rhodin—I was down in the bowels of the lower secretariat with the other labour monkeys."

"You're so deliciously disapproving," Rhodin said, chuckling.

"Well, she's a fool."

"You must be a little drunk, Kip, you're being blunt."

Ghilly seemed to take this as a suggestion, for she topped up Cliopher's coffee with the rum. "Come now, explain. You seem to have had a completely different conversation than we heard. Princess Oriana came in, and you came forward and put your hand on Bertie's shoulder to keep him from getting up and making a ruckus, and said, 'Princess Oriana', very deferentially, and—?"

"Oh, I wasn't being deferential. I was being mild."

"The difference being ..."

"The difference being that one defers to someone one respects."

"Ouch. Right, she curtsied?"

Cliopher knew he should probably stop drinking, but he was thirsty and the coffee was there—and it was delicious—and he was at the point where he didn't much care. "As soon as the Princess recognized me, she knew that she had to act quickly to remedy the situation, because first her cousin and his friend and then she had offered me mortal insult."

Vinyë frowned. "But she didn't know you were here."

"She knows I am a commoner of Gorjo City—"

"By birth," said Rhodin.

"His Radiancy's favour notwithstanding, I *am* a commoner, and obviously if I am attending a party in the city, it's because the people at the party are friends and family of mine. It's one of the better aristocratic traits that an insult to one's family is an insult to oneself, so even if I weren't here, and I just heard about it, I'd still be expected to respond. Which is one reason there won't be any retaliation. Not that there will be, because she submitted to me."

"This is the bit I don't understand. You just stared at each other."

"There are rules to court etiquette." Cliopher looked around at their blank faces. "You really didn't see? All right: when she greeted me, she curtseyed. You saw that."

Falbert snorted like a breaching whale. "Yes, but it was weird. Didn't look like a normal curtsey."

"That's because it was an apology in the first degree, and people don't do that very often. When Lady Rusticiana apologized to you, her curtsey was in the second degree, which is still very remarkable but not quite as unusual. An apology of the first degree is to head off the sort of insult that ends up in war. She knew, you see, that she had just called me and mine what any nobleman would take as an intolerable insult."

"But you're not really a nobleman," Vinyë said.

Cliopher moved his head in a noncommittal gesture. "Not by birth, certainly, nor by intent, but … by his Radiancy's favour I do outrank her."

Rhodin chuckled. "You outrank everyone except the lords magi and his Radiancy. And you can well believe if she'd offered that sort of insult to any of them, she would be up in her palace right now committing ritual suicide before she was publicly executed for her impertinence and disrespect. Maybe she is, come to think of it."

"It would muss her clothing too much."

"And you told her to go tell his Radiancy what she thought of you." Vinyë frowned at him. "Are you *sure* that's not going to hurt you?"

Cliopher said, "I am more than happy to wait to hear what his Radiancy thinks."

Haldo frowned at him. "I think you've had too much to drink. I really don't—cripes, that white lady's coming back."

Cliopher looked up to see that the door had opened on Lady Rusticiana, who strode across the room towards him. Being a polite man (most of the time), and having been favourably impressed by her response to Lord Balo, he rose. "Lady Rusticiana, I believe?" he said. "What can I do for you?"

"Lord Mdang," she replied, sweeping him a court curtsey of sumptuous elegance. "I am reluctant to interrupt your time with your family and friends, but if I may say three things to you?"

"Certainly."

"First—I am utterly despondent for being in the least associated with those insolent fools who call themselves lords of men, and I must apologize once more for them and for their behaviour to you and these good people." She gave the second-degree curtsey again. "Second, I have been wanting to meet you this age, Lord Mdang, to ask you some questions about your political reforms, and although now is clearly not the time, I wished to let you know in the hopes that you might be able to make some time for it."

"And third?" said Cliopher, who wasn't sure what to make of this.

"And third," said the lady, her blue eyes sparkling with amusement, "that was one of the most elegant and subtle displays of power it has ever been my privilege to witness, and I must thank you for the pleasure of the experience."

"Oh," he said, and then, because there wasn't anything else he could think of to say, he added, "Thank you."

"You are most welcome," she said. "I will not keep you—I know you do not have much time at home. I am very much eager to witness the ceremonies this week. The Vangavaye-ve is noted for its remoteness—and its beauty. The histories will be rewritten to include you."

And with that, while Cliopher was feeling stunned, she curtsied again and departed.

Haldo said, "Another drink?"

"I'll have one too, please, Haldo," Quintus said, pulling up a chair and causing the rest of them to shuffle around. "I just docked and heard the party was up here tonight. We celebrating anything particular?"

"Bertie's son Parno has been accepted into the Imperial Guard," Cliopher said, accepting the glass Haldo offered him with resignation.

"No, has he really? That's extraor—*Kip*? You're here!"

"I am," said Cliopher, grinning at him. "How are you, Quintus?"

Quintus was staring at him in consternation, though when Cliopher raised his eyebrows in silent enquiry he shrugged and made a gesture with his hand as if to say 'later, later'. "I'm fine, thanks, Kip—and hello to everyone. Who was the lady? Friend of yours, Kip?"

"She sure hopes to be," Toucan said, grinning.

Quintus cracked a guffaw. "Just as well she's gone. Cousin Louya's coming up behind me. You probably haven't heard her last mad start, have you, Kip?"

Cliopher stifled a groan. "When did she come up with it? I didn't write back to her last letter, which was about six weeks ago." He contemplated Cousin Louya's letter-writing habits gloomily. "There's probably another one following me around the Wide Seas with whatever—and here she is."

On another person Cliopher might have admired the dedication to personal style over convention or custom. He looked at Louya's peculiar mix of Outer Ring headdress (not in the Mdang family patterns, but in a version of Louya's paternal Faopao), Nijani-inflected batik-dyed skirt in indigo and green, and a strange multicoloured shawl-like mantle that teased at his memory of old Voonran costumes, and he merely felt weary. Féonie would have clicked her tongue at the colour combination. He felt cheered at that thought, and managed a welcoming smile. "Cousin Louya."

"Cousin Kip. I didn't realize you were down here."

This came out fairly normally, and for a moment he thought they might be able to have a normal conversation. "Oh, I have a couple of days before I have to get ready for—"

"That's not long enough," she announced.

"I beg your pardon?"

His fleeting thought that she could hardly care very much for his holidays or lack thereof was immediately borne out when she held out her hands to cup the air on either side of his head. He shifted back instinctively, though he held his hand to Rhodin to prevent him from doing anything just yet.

"Hold still," she said insistently.

"Louya, I have no idea what you think you're doing, but it's rather strange and not very polite."

She withdrew her hands so she could put them on her hips and glare at him. "Polite? Does *polite* matter when it's a matter of the world's security?"

It had taken some hard lessons, but he had learned just how effective courtesy was as a weapon. "Absolutely," he said, smiling.

"Cousin Kip!" She actually stamped her foot. "You are not being reasonable. Do you not realize how fragile the world's peace is?"

"Yes," he said, though it would be a lot less fragile come the day after the viceroyship ceremonies were completed … and as stable as he could make it before the new Lord of Zunidh came to the Palace.

He took another sip of his drink. Cousin Louya gave no indication she had heard him say anything.

"Do you not know how close we all are to complete erasure of our culture? Even our lives? There are people, Cousin Kip, who seek nothing less than the destruction of all who are unlike them! They are *everywhere*. They spend their lives plotting the complete destruction of the world's government. They have spent the past decades infiltrating it, hiding their true nature with cunning masks, waiting and biding their time to strike at the heart of civilization. The government doesn't know what to do about them—they don't hear what I hear—"

"I assure you, Cousin Louya, that not only do I read your letters, but I share them with other people in my offices."

"They don't know. You do not know. You don't understand the ruthlessness of these people. The government is useless—useless, I tell you! These people, this secret organization, they have taken over all the important ministries. They run trade, the treasury, the common weal—all of it is part of their plot! They have spent years working secretly to do this. And all the time those in charge of the government sleep, thinking that these changes are their own idea, when it is all secretly to the maintenance of the secret society who is truly running the world! Cousin Kip, you must use your influence to stop them! It's not too late—I can tell you what you need to know! If you haven't been thoroughly corrupted yourself, you can still stop them destroying everything important. You need only to listen to me."

She stopped for a moment to catch her breath. Cliopher drank back the rest of his drink in one swallow, which he shortly remembered was not the best way to keep control of his tongue.

He said, "Cousin Louya, do you have any idea how stupid you sound?"

She stopped her impassioned gesturing in shock and affront. "I—what?"

"Make up your mind, cousin." He gestured at himself. "Am I the idiotic tool of this secret society you think are running the world, or am I a man of influence and reason? It's hard to see how I can be both—and that's not without going into the details of this plot, which—please—I beg you not to recount to me again. I did read it in your last letter.

"As it happens, I was unable to reply because I have spent the last six months travelling the world in order to more effectively govern it, but I assure you, I did ask Aioru, the Deputy Minister of the Common Weal, to look into it. He has investigated many of your previous insights in order to determine any minor grain of truth there might be. He sometimes finds something—much more often, as in this case, he finds not the slightest shred of likelihood in any of it.

"Do you not realize how totally irrational it is? If you don't, you need medical and spiritual help. If you do, and this is all an elaborate prank, you, personally, waste more of the government's time and resources than any other single individual outside of the upper aristocracy. This may please you, but it is not a distinction I relish in a member of my family."

He regarded her outfit more obviously, and recognized this time the point of the tiny red coral toya beads in her headdress. "I can be thankful for small mercies that you do not claim Mdang patterns in your garments. The bastard offspring of south Nijani batik and pre-Fall Voonran mysticism along with a peculiarly hybrid Faopao and Nga headdress suits you."

She opened her mouth and shut it several times before finally coming up with a retort. "At least I'm wearing *proper* clothing."

"Yes," he said, smiling, "I'm afraid I didn't bring all my *efela* home with me."

She tried for a moment to rally, glaring at him, then looked for support from the others. This did not appear forthcoming, for she spun on her heels and flounced out.

It took until the door closed for Cliopher to realize he had said all of that out loud and not in the safe privacy of his own mind. He sat back in his seat, rearranged his robes with his once-more trembling hands, and smiled apologetically at the table. "Sorry."

Toucan reached into his sleeve and pulled out a handkerchief—which he handed to Falbert.

"Bertie!" Cliopher said in astonishment, overwashed with the embarrassment taught him by a lifetime spent at a court where emotions shown were vulnerabilities to be exploited, not strengths to be admired.

"Oh, Kip," Ghilly cried, "we thought we'd lost you—we thought *you'd* lost you—it's been so long since we've seen you launch into a rant."

"I lost my temper," he said. "It's nothing to be proud of."

"Cousin Louya doesn't need medical help," Vinyë said. "She needs something less mischievous to do. She also needed you to stop humouring her. And what do you mean, it's not something to be proud of? Kip, you never stand up for yourself."

It was Cliopher's turn to open his mouth and shut it again.

Rhodin peered into the coffee pot and made a face when he saw it was empty. "You haven't come to visit him for dinner and found him pacing angrily about the injustice of something-or-other. I'll never forget the postal service one. That was truly epic—he didn't stop talking about it for four hours."

As Cliopher tried to disclaim this, his friends all started laughing. Zemius said, "I feel as if I'm missing a joke here."

"After the Fall," Toucan explained, "in nearly every letter Kip would say something about how when he was in charge of the government the very first thing he was going to do was fix the post."

Vinyë laughed. "That's true, Kip, you did write that a lot. Of course, then the post was improved, and—" She stopped abruptly, and gazed searchingly in his face. "Did you really do that?"

"Did he ever," said Rhodin. "Some letter had taken eight months or something to get to Solaara from here. After ranting to us—Conju and me— all evening about the sorry state of the post, he must have stayed up all night devising a new system, because I was on duty the next morning when he came in and presented his Radiancy with his proposal. And then you ranted at *him* for forty minutes."

"Oh, I don't think I'd say that."

"I don't doubt you wouldn't, but nevertheless, that is what you did. Same thing when you were arguing for open access to the Lights. Or indeed for the rights of those fishermen on Copper Eyot. Or—"

"Thank you, Rhodin."

Rhodin grinned at him.

"We should talk about something less embarrassing,"Toucan said."Hmm, I know, the interest being shown you by radical royal scholars of a certain age and very definite beauty who come soliciting introductions and want the opportunity to speak to you in private, later ..."

"No one is that obvious," Cliopher said, flushing hard.

Rhodin grinned again. "You may prefer absurdly discreet liaisons, but it isn't unknown for people to signal their interest in others by, oh, being visibly interested."

Haldo had brought him fresh coffee and he sipped at it to cover his embarrassment. Ghilly raised her eyebrows at him again."What sort of absurdly discreet liaisons do you have, Kip?"

Cliopher set his cup down in incredulity. "We are in a public place."

"We're all friends and family here."

"Haven't you ever *read* any history? Ask Rhodin, since he knows so much."

Rhodin shook his head. "All I know is that you're absurdly discreet about your affairs."

"How do you know I have any, then?"

"Well, when his Radiancy sends for you unexpectedly in the middle of the night, and you are not in your rooms, and neither Conju nor I know where you might be ..."

"I might have been walking in the night gardens."

"True—or you might have been climbing trees in the gardens of the Sun."

Cliopher flushed again as everyone laughed. Rhodin waited until the laughter died down slightly, then said thoughtfully, "The only name I ever heard definitely connected to yours was Adelia Ealoapeha."

"Oh, tell us about her!" Ghilly said, leaning forward in eager interest. "Was she smart? Beautiful? Elegant? Where was she from? What did she do? What happened?"

Rhodin said, "She was very lovely and definitely elegant—half the court fell in love with her when she arrived from Jilkano as one of the new princess' ladies-in-waiting. She could have had practically anyone, and she chose Cliopher."

"You sly dog," Falbert said. "You never mentioned her in your letters."

"It wasn't a very long relationship," Cliopher muttered, willing Rhodin to stop talking about it, but since he didn't actually say that aloud, of course Rhodin kept on.

"The fire burned hot and fast—and went out very quickly. I wasn't there when the end happened, I'm afraid, because I had to go to a training camp in Kavanduru and when I got back, no one was talking about it." Rhodin smiled fondly at Cliopher. "Least of all Kip. Not that he'd actually been talking about it before, but you could see it when he looked at her. When I got back the princess had gone back to Jilkano and the lady with her."

"What happened?" Ghilly asked sympathetically.

"It must be difficult to have your love affairs talked about through a whole palace," Vinyë said, even more sympathetically.

"Fortunately, I'd had the practice of being related to most of the major gossips of Gorjo City."

"You were pretty cut up about it," Rhodin said.

Cliopher sighed. "Because she was using me. She was a spy for the Emerald Conspirators. She didn't go back to Jilkano—she was executed at the block for committing high treason. I was fortunate I didn't go with her."

Rhodin made a gesture almost as apologetic as Lady Rusticiana's. "I'm sorry. Conju warned me not to talk to you about it, but he didn't say what had happened."

"It was classified information, for the princess—anyway, there were a lot of things that had to be kept quiet."

"Being seduced by someone who turns out to be a spy isn't a crime," Ghilly said.

"It is when you're the Sun-on-Earth's personal secretary," Cliopher replied dryly. He raised his cup and drank the coffee appreciatively, surprised anew to notice his hands were trembling. He folded them around the cup to hide it, but not before Ghilly, who'd been looking at him through narrowed eyes, followed his dropped gaze. She reached out and took one of his hands in her own.

"It's nothing," he said, aware that everyone was watching this, but it was far too late.

Vinyë said, "Have—have you developed the palsy, Kip? Or ..." But she could not say aloud the worse diseases that caused involuntary shaking.

"No. It's not—it's not a disease."

"Stress and overwork, then?" Ghilly said, letting him withdraw his hand again. "For someone who appears to spend a great deal of time ensuring other people have the opportunity to follow their dreams, you don't seem to take much time for yourself."

"But my dream was to change the world."

He intended to speak lightly, but his voice came out jarringly serious. Vinyë, reaching out to take his hand, sat back, a troubled look on her face. "Kip ..."

But Falbert said: "So it was. And we sit here and complain that you were too ambitious and left us behind."

Ghilly winced and looked away. Cliopher caught Toucan's eye, then dropped it, unable to maintain eye contact. "The trembling is a side effect of the magic in the regency ceremonies," he added hastily. "My lord tells me it will improve once the final ceremony is completed."

Showing a surprising grasp of the conversation's subtleties, Zemius said, "That's what's happening this week?"

"I sent you invitations months ago."

Vinyë looked guilty. When Cliopher raised his eyebrows at her, she said wretchedly, "We didn't realize ... I don't think anyone took them very seriously. I mean, we're to play, but ..."

He took a deep breath, and then another, and finally he said in a tolerable imitation of a calm voice, "I came to your wedding, Vinyë, and yours, Ghilly and Toucan. I came when you were appointed to your professorship, Zemius. I came when your children were born, Bertie. I came when you were given your ship, Quintus. I—I have never married. I have no children. I have never asked you to come to *anything* of mine except this—and you are telling me you don't think it's serious?"

"Kip, we—we didn't realize it was so important."

"Do you know, we planned the order of the ceremonies so they would finish up here, precisely so you could come. They should have concluded in Solaara. I sent you invitations as soon as I knew when they would be. I thought—"

His voice shook, and he had to pause a moment to regain his composure. "I thought you would realize that it was important *to me*. I thought you might like to share—to celebrate with me—that you would realize I wanted to celebrate with *you*. I thought that you would be willing to spend a *day* doing something for me. But of course I chose to go away, and therefore nothing I have ever done truly matters." His voice twisted into bitterness, and he stopped speaking.

"Kip ..."

"We know you've achieved a high position," Toucan said over top of Vinyë.

"I am so tired," he said, the tears threatening to come again in a mixture of fury and frustration. "It's hard, you know, being neither fish nor fowl. To you, I left—I have a title, I have all the trappings of wealth and rank, I have left you all behind—and you're so determined to punish me for it that you treat me as if every time I come home I spend all my time lording over you and thinking myself so much better than you and boasting of all my important friends and all the things I've done."

"Oh, no, Kip," said Ghilly.

"To the rest of the world I am this jumped-up tribesman from the back end of nowhere with no rights to do any of what I am doing. Do you think what Lord Balo and Princess Oriana said was unusual? Do you think I haven't heard that, and worse, nearly every day of my life? If you think the aristocracy of the world are happy about my being elevated and welcome me into their midst, you are much mistaken."

"But if you have done things like the post," Ghilly said.

"Do you want me to boast? Fine! I instituted the annual stipend, the postal service, the sea train, the graduated taxation for small merchants and manufacturers, the hospital system, the new teaching colleges, the protection of the kula ring, the audits of government departments, the decimalization of the currency—oh, I have done many things in my time in government. And let us think who these things benefit. It's not the princes and the upper classes."

"Or the wizards or the guards or even the bureaucracy," Rhodin said quietly.

"I have done my best to root out corruption—bribery, profiteering, insider trading, price fixing, protectionism, false weights, fake measures—I established interprovincial treaties for movement of goods and people—I opened access to the Lights, to the sea train, to the universities—I chaired and drafted the Littleridge Treaty—I set the annual budget—I negotiate intermundial treaties—I audit each and every department and ministry in the world—

"I have spent the last three years running the executive and legislative arms of the government while simultaneously performing a thorough review of the state of the world and the results of all these efforts of mine. They've not all been positive. His Radiancy has tasked me with restructuring the government so that he can hand it over to his successor with a glad heart."

He glared at Toucan. "How many letters have we written back and forth planning a new system of government? How could you possibly think I would not seize the opportunity to put it all into effect? Forgive me for wanting to share that with you—for thinking that you might, I don't know, just possibly you might be slightly *proud*."

He managed to draw breath then, painfully aware of his vaunting, of the blankly dismayed faces facing him.

Quintus cleared his throat. "Clearly we need to get you drunk more often, Kip. Of course we'll—oh, here's Enya."

"Hi everyone," Cousin Enya said, bounding in the door. She was still in her chef's outfit and carried a bulky paper-wrapped parcel in her hand. "I heard the party was up here tonight. I brought crab cakes. Say, Vinyë, do you know what's going on with that thing at the palace? Galen was cleaning out the desk and found Kip's invitations, but—"

"Kip's here," Vinyë said urgently.

"Oh, so he is! I didn't recognize you in that outfit from the back. You've lost weight—and your hair is so grey—" She stopped abruptly. "You look very distinguished. Anyway, since you're here, I can ask you: is this thing at the palace very important?"

Cliopher put his head down on the table with an audible thunk.

CHAPTER SIXTY-FOUR

THE CRAB CAKES, UNSURPRISINGLY, HELPED materially to improve his mood. By the time he had eaten his fourth, he had regained his equilibrium and was able to enter into the deliberately light family gossip that was frothing about him. Possibly this was assisted by Haldo bringing him some sort of devilishly smooth sweet cocktail with a muttered comment Cliopher could not entirely hear but seemed to have something to do with his mother and the sea train.

He had relaxed enough to laugh at the story about Cousin Arnie's son falling into the vat of ink at the *Ring o' News* and Toucan's efforts to give Rhodin a primer on the various factions of the Mdang family.

"We don't have factions, surely, Toucan," Cliopher protested.

"Would you prefer tribes?"

Quintus said, "I like to think of it more as houses, like in an Astandalan novel."

"Have you given these houses names?" Rhodin asked.

"We should get Polly to," Enya said.

"Polly's Aunt Leonora's daughter, Rhodin. She's a writer."

"Do you know, I very much doubt I am going to remember anyone besides the people I've actually met. I'm sorry, but it's true. Sixteen aunts and uncles and sixty cousins and all their spouses and children is, well, somewhat excessive, if I may speak frankly."

"We made flashcards when we were little," Cliopher said, grinning suddenly at the memory. "Do you remember, Vinyë? Every time someone else was born we'd pull them out and add another one. I wonder whatever happened to them?"

"They're still in your bedroom at home," his sister replied. "I found them a few weeks ago when I was looking for something. I noticed you'd kept them updated as far as Dora's birth."

"Well," he said, flushing uncomfortably, "it would be embarrassing to come home after being away for so long and forget the name of someone

I'm related to."

"Even unto the third degree?"

"I like seeing the patterns in things. Naming traditions, numbers of children, intermarriages ..."

Quintus laughed. "Are you serious?"

"Why did you never go into scholarship?" Zemius asked. "You've got the mind for it. You could have been a great scientist."

The crab cakes and the sweet cocktail had mellowed his mood very considerably, Cliopher thought, smiling at his cousin without any of the edge he had felt earlier. "One of many things I could have been, I suppose, though I don't think science ever occurred to me—I was going to go for accountancy if I didn't pass the exams."

"Were you really?" Rhodin asked.

"He had all sorts of offers," Toucan said, "but he would insist that he wanted to go to Astandalas."

"Of course." For Rhodin, there was nothing mysterious at all about such a desire—he came of a society where everyone wanted to go to Astandalas, and most people did.

"These are very nice crab cakes," Cliopher said to Enya. "Are you still at Potlatch?"

She smiled at him. "More or less. I've been taking some extra catering jobs to raise up cash for renovations. Rising damp is such a pain. Galen and I are working on opening our own restaurant—hopefully within the next year or two. Do you think you might be able to come to the grand opening?"

"I shall do my best," he said, pleased at the invitation and aware of the irony of its timing. "Send me the date as far in advance as possible, please, and I'll try to make it work."

Vinyë and Toucan both gave him strange looks. Toucan said, "When are you going home?"

Cliopher said, "I don't know, it'll depend on how well I can organize things. I hope about six months from now I'll have time."

Toucan gave him another strange look. Cliopher, thinking over his sentence, was confused at why Toucan was confused, and decided to eat another crab cake. Enya, missing all this, drank some of Quintus' rum, sighed happily, and spoke dreamily. "What's your favourite food, Kip? Anything you particularly miss from here? I keep meaning to ask you."

He considered for a moment, but he knew the answer. "Lotus buns. I'm never here for the Singing of the Waters, because it falls so close to the Lord's

New Year, and I always have to be at court for that. There's a Jilkanese restaurant in Solaara where they make lotus buns, but they're not the same—I don't know if it's a different sort of lotus, or what, but they're never ... I always buy them for the day of the festival, but it's not the same. And then no one here makes them any other time of the year."

"I would have made them for you if I'd known you missed them," Enya said reprovingly. "What's the point of being a chef if you can't make the foods your family wants? How long are you here for this time?"

"I've got tomorrow down here, then there's a day of purification ceremonies at the palace, and the regency ceremonies, and then I think his Radiancy said we would stay another day after that, didn't he, Rhodin?"

Rhodin looked at him. "You *are* drunk, aren't you? We're to leave a week from tomorrow."

"This is what comes of delegating to secretaries," Cliopher responded wisely. Rhodin made a choking noise, echoed by a gasp from Ghilly as she looked past him towards the door. Cliopher twisted around to see who was coming in now, and was for a moment entirely befuddled to see a rain-haloed Zaoul standing there, as if the mere mention of his secretaries had summoned one.

"Who is *that*?" Ghilly asked in a breathless whisper.

"That's my secretary," Cliopher said, recovering himself and smiling at the young man. Zaoul visibly relaxed and approached their table. Accustomed as he was to the Tkinele's appearance, it took Cliopher a moment to realize why everyone else looked so wary and intrigued. Dressed in the dark blue and orange of Cliopher's household, with ritual scars along his arms and long braids with their clacking ornaments, he looked fierce and dangerous. "Please tell me there's not been an emergency up at the palace, Zaoul."

"Not to my knowledge, sir," he replied easily, his deep voice calm and leisurely as ever. "Only I was expecting Gaudy and Tully to arrive first, and wasn't sure if I had the place right. We weren't expecting you to be here, sir. I was sent into the city by his Radiancy on an errand. I'm off duty now," he added a moment after.

"Of course," Cliopher replied, nonplussed. "So am I."

"Yes, sir."

"Gaudy's coming here?" Vinyë asked eagerly. "Wonderful!"

"Yes, ma'am."

"This is my secretary, Zaoul of the Tkinele," Cliopher said, and made the introductions all round for those who had not yet met him. Zemius wordlessly pulled up yet another chair, and they all shuffled around to make room.

Once he had settled, Enya said, "I don't know anything about the Tkinele, Zaoul. We were just talking about festival foods that Kip misses. Since you're here, may I ask you what you would eat at home?"

Zaoul looked a bit panicked by this question. "Fish, yams, taro, that sort of thing."

Enya nodded. "Of course. But what about festivals or special occasions? What sort of dishes would you eat then?"

Zaoul cast a glance at Cliopher, who did not know what to suggest to him, and then said, reluctantly, "*Doletho*. Er, long pig."

"Long pig? What sort of occasions do you eat it? How do you cook it?" Enya asked eagerly, fishing in the pockets of her wide trousers for a pencil and notebook. Then she noticed that Zaoul was staring at her wide-eyed. "Unless it's secret? I don't mean to pry. I'm a chef, you see, I'm always looking for new ideas, and I've never heard anything about Tkinele cuisine."

"Really?" Quintus said faintly.

"Really, Quintus, you know how I like to hear about these things! Sorry, Zaoul, please do go on, if you don't mind."

Zaoul cast another beseeching glance at him. Cliopher cleared his throat. "I think Zaoul may be referring to the Tkinele practice of, er, ritual cannibalism. Is that right, Zaoul?"

"Yes, sir," Zaoul said, obviously relieved at his cool and matter-of-fact manner.

Enya stared at Zaoul for a long moment like she was modelling for the illustration of 'cultural shock'. Then she closed her mouth, blinked twice, and said: "You've really and truly cooked and eaten *human beings*?"

Cliopher had never dared to ask the question outright, and was ashamed at how eager he was to hear the answer. Zaoul cast him another plaintive look, squared his shoulders—which made him look massively muscular and dangerous—and said, as one going to his execution and determined not to make a mess of it: "I have."

There was a silence pregnant with unspoken emotions. Finally Enya said, "What does it taste like?"

"Pig, presumably," Cliopher said, giving her a quelling glance. "Zaoul, you—you do know that it's—that is to say, I don't expect you to be ashamed of who you are and where you come from."

Everyone looked at him, but he kept his gaze on the young Tkinele, who met his eyes slowly.

Zaoul's skin was as dark as his Radiancy's—far too dark to show blush-es—but Cliopher was accustomed to reading the minutest expressions of his lord's face, and he knew without shadow of a doubt that Zaoul's face was on fire with embarrassment.

Zaoul's eyes belied the scars and the muscles and the hair and the filed teeth and the reputation: they were the eyes of a gentle soul, a poet, a dream-er, an artist, a scholar, of the sort of person who asked the questions no one else was curious about, who dared to leave the familiar islands for the unfa-miliar and often hostile world beyond.

"You've never asked me if I were a cannibal," he said very quietly, but the table was so silent his voice fell clearly into the air.

Cliopher did not look away. "It didn't seem particularly relevant to whether or not you could be a good secretary. Is it?"

Zaoul hesitated. "Other people seem to think so."

"As you may have gathered, Zaoul, I do not pay very much heed to what people other than his Radiancy think of how I ought to do my job. I am very happy with your work. I would have found you another position if I were not."

"People say I'm a monster. A murderer. Evil."

Cliopher paused a moment, wondering how best to reply to that, and then he said, simply: "They've said that about me, too. I once had a very dedicated correspondent who wrote me every day for six years to lay out in excruciating detail how I personally was the incarnation of Bak Ailonguwak, the soul-stealing, child-killing demon of west Kavanduru.

"Other people have spent their time somewhat more profitably collect-ing together lists of every ill effect of my actions. All the people who died building the sea train, venturing into the jungles of Xiputl after precious jew-els or possible medicines, who were slaughtered by the armies putting down revolts. All the people who lost everything because of my decisions.

"I do not think I am evil because I have been willing to make those decisions, day after day, year after year. I do not think you are a monster be-cause you are from a tribe whose name has been one to conjure fear with for centuries. I admire you for daring to go into the wide world—and not as a curiosity and a freak, nor trying to capitalize on the reputation for ferocity your people have, and which you could easily pander to." He smiled crook-edly. "People would have understood better if you had entered the Guard."

"I don't like violence. It's bad enough to kill someone for food, but how much worse to kill them simply because you are angry! It's murder." He

VICTORIA GODDARD

glanced suddenly at Ser Rhodin, whose face was blank. "I'm sorry, sir. I know it's your duty, but I don't understand that sort of violence."

Rhodin made a sort of forgiving gesture. Cliopher, curiosity raised, asked, "Does no one in the Tkinê islands ever kill out of anger or wickedness?"

Zaoul furrowed his brow, which made him look even fiercer. "Very rarely, sir. To take someone's life, that is a matter of much *yola*, much importance, and if you do it lightly, the spirits get very angry. To be haunted by the dead— no, that is no good thing. There was one such on Tkitidola—she had killed her husband for turning to another's bed." He shivered.

"That sort of crime of passion is understandable," Toucan said. "There are special laws governing them."

"She should not have killed him as she did," Zaoul replied firmly. "Without ritual, without ceremony, without the right knives—she gave him no chance to set his soul right, no chance to be make his peace with the spirits, no chance to be reborn, no chance for his family to mourn him according to the rites. When someone is killed outside of the rite, it is *ne yolanga*, bad magic. His soul leaves the human realm."

"What was her punishment?" Toucan asked, adding, "I spent my career in the Provincial Court of Justice. I am always interested in other legal processes."

Cliopher thanked him silently for calling the Tkinele practices 'legal processes'—which they were, of course, but few were those able to get past the basic fact of cannibalism to see the intricate social structure that had produced it.

Zaoul glanced at Cliopher again. "She was shunned. She had brought *ne yolanga* to her island. She was—there has to be balance, you see? Male and female, living and dead, night and day. She had cast her husband out of the human realm in death, so she was cast out of the human realm in life. He is a ghost in his spirit, she is a ghost in her body. No one looks on her, no one touches her, no one speaks to her. Her name is not spoken. She is no longer human."

For a brief, shocked moment, Cliopher heard his Radiancy's voice echo in his mind: *I felt like a ghost. No one looked at me, no one could touch me, no one would speak directly to me.*

So felt the Sun-on-Earth on his ascendancy, above the human realm instead of below it, but as cut off and removed from human intercourse as a murderer.

"It is very interesting," Falbert was saying, "how many taboos each culture places around death and food—sometimes anthropologists argue that the rituals of eating are to deny cannibalism, but would I be right in understanding that in your culture, the rituals of cannibalism exist to prevent murder?"

"The gates of life are always marked by death," Zaoul said, "and to keep the balance, so the gates of death are marked by life. You asked me what we eat on festival occasions," he went on, turning solemnly to Enya. "We eat *doletho*, because that is how we were taught by the gods to honour both the spirit world and the human world. When a child is born, the blood that comes after is eaten by the mother. When a person dies, their body is prepared according to the rites and their family partakes. The person's soul then has the chance to be reborn in their family, to stay within the human realm, or if they have broken free of the cycle, then, too, they may give their gifts to their family and move on knowing they have nourished their family in death as they did in life."

"So you don't actually go out and kill someone for the purpose of eating him?" Falbert asked.

Zaoul hesitated again. "For the other great feasts ... that is how you pass into adulthood or ... there are some other times. To become an adult, there comes a time when the children of the year must go to a certain place. You are stripped of your children's clothes, your children's tools. You are left naked as the day of your birth. You must make your way to one of the other islands—one of the other clans' territories—and with weapons of your own fashioning hunt and take ... someone.

"You must bring your captive back to the sacrifice rock, and perform the sacrifice. At the feast the *doletho* is shared out, and you are welcomed into the circles of the men or the women, and the shamans give you the marks of your lineage, your tribe, your family."

He ran his hands down the scars on his shoulders. He looked very remote; looking into his eyes, Cliopher was startled by their brilliance, as if the young man was holding back tears.

"How old were you?" Vinyë asked in a hushed voice.

"Fourteen. His name was Mydon. He came from Elgyaki, the farthest island. He had taken my brother two years before for his wedding feast. My family wished my brother's spirit to be returned to us."

There were all sorts of unspoken expectations and familial dynamics packed into that sentence, Cliopher thought, in the quiet voice, the unemotional tone, the faraway look, the way he visibly embodied the ideal of a Tkinele cannibal warrior, the lazy good humour and hidden intelligence with which he did the work of a secretary in the Service. Cliopher wondered if his family had wanted him to be a warrior, or—given that deep well of intelligence—a shaman; and if by leaving the islands he had left for good.

And he wondered if, having once gone out naked and alone to hunt another man and bring him back to be eaten, you could ever quite look at people the same way again.

And then he realized that it was going out into the wider world that had caused Zaoul to look at people differently, to see himself differently, to be called 'monster' and 'evil' and 'murderer'.

"Thank you for telling us about your people," Cliopher said formally. "It is never easy to be so different. It is especially difficult to be the only experience others have with your culture, with your people. You bear the weight of teaching everyone what it is to be Tkinele."

Zaoul grimaced, the sharpened eye teeth noticeable. "I am not a very typical Tkinele. I left. And not to join the guard."

Cliopher smiled at him. "Ah, but by making the choice to join the Service, you have shown the world that the Tkinele are not only fearsome warriors who never leave their islands. You are a truly excellent secretary, Zaoul. I consider myself fortunate not to have lost you to his Radiancy's household—at least not yet."

"Gaudy and Tully—" Zaoul began.

"Your talents, skills, and personalities complement each other so admirably, I am at a loss for how I managed before." Cliopher smiled a bit crookedly. "I suppose I didn't, as I was going through secretaries nearly as frequently as his Radiancy before I selected you three. It is a very demanding job I ask of you."

"We are honoured by the challenge," said Zaoul earnestly, then glanced past him. "Aren't we?"

Cliopher turned around in his seat to see that Gaudy and Tully had arrived. He wondered how long they had been standing there. Tully was looking thoughtfully at Zaoul, Gaudy at himself.

"We are, sir," said Tully. "Sorry we're so late, Zaoul, but there's a bit of an uproar in the palace and we wanted to make sure we weren't needed."

"What happened?" Cliopher asked, bracing himself.

Gaudy glanced at Vinyë and then back at him. "Don't worry, sir—Uncle Kip—you're not to be concerned."

"Though you *are* concerned," Tully added. "Don't glare at me, Gaudy,

Lord Mdang would find out about it soon at any rate. We weren't told *not* to tell him—and nor was anyone else. His Radiancy clearly intended it for an example."

Cliopher found his curiosity deeply roused. "Why, what has happened?"

"You tell it, then."

Tully composed herself as she often did when asked for a report. "We had finished up our tasks for the day, sir, and were returning to your rooms to change before we came here to meet Zaoul. As we were nearing the corner at the top hallway, we came across one of the princess' court—"

"Earl Baljan," Gaudy put in, scowling.

"He was talking to one of his friends, and they were both obviously a bit drunk, but still, they shouldn't have been ... anyway, he was talking about you, sir, saying some very unpleasant things. He clearly meant for us to hear them, for he kept smirking at us as if daring us to do something about it. I don't think he knew that Gaudy was your nephew, he could just see that we were in your colours, sir."

"What did you do?" Cliopher asked in some trepidation.

"Tully held me back," Gaudy said, still scowling. "I didn't know what we should do. He outranks us—but he really shouldn't have been saying those things. He wasn't saying *treasonous* things about you, or at least not quite, but they were very poisonous and wrong. I felt we should go and tell him he was edging close to betraying his superiors."

"Earl Baljan?" Quintus said in amazement. "He would have broken you. He's a brute and a blockhead, and vicious to boot."

"To table, rather," muttered Tully, who was now trying not to grin.

"Tully!"

"Come now, Gaudy, you must see the humour in it? What happened next, sir, was that it turned out his Radiancy was coming down the corridor on the other side of the corner, and had heard what the earl said."

Cliopher looked automatically at Rhodin. Rhodin said, "His Radiancy would not like to hear that."

"No more he didn't," Gaudy said fervently, and Cliopher could see now that his scowl was hiding a kind of unholy amusement. "His Radiancy swept around the corner and when the earl and his friend had gone down into their obeisances, he told him off—and then turned him into a table."

"I beg your pardon?"

Tully shook her head in amazement. "It was like something out of a book of fables, sir. He said that the earl was unworthy to sit at the same table as you, that if he had ever done one-tenth of what you have done for Zunidh he would be a great man, that he was a snivelling coward and bootlicker when he wasn't being a bully—"

"But the table?" Quintus interrupted urgently.

Gaudy took a deep and unsteady breath. "We were all—there were other people who had been following along behind his Radiancy, plus us, plus some of the palace staff, including Aunt Jouna—we were all staring and amazed, because his Radiancy is not usually so vehement—when suddenly his Radiancy stopped speaking, frowned at the earl, and said, 'If you are stupid enough to publicly denigrate our Lord Chancellor and suggest that our choice of him for our Viceroy was a result of blind partiality, you are unworthy of your title, your lands, your honour, and, by your choice of targets, your life'."

One of Gaudy's more remarkable skills was his facility for remembering conversations verbatim, so Cliopher had no reason to doubt the language.

"And then," Tully went on, "one of the other courtiers made a sort of sobbing sound, and his Radiancy turned to her and—"

"He said, 'Madam, the earl has suggested we are a fool and ill-served in our judgment. What say you?'"

"And she said—'Glorious One, Sun of Righteousness, Lord of Justice, have mercy.'"

"His Radiancy said: 'Madam, he has called our Lord Chancellor a carbuncle on the face of society.'"

"That's not very original," Rhodin murmured.

"Well, that wasn't all he called him," Gaudy admitted.

"Anyway," Tully said, "his Radiancy stared at her for a while, then he turned back to Earl Baljan and stared at him for a while. The earl was sort of halfway crouched down, with his rear in the air, and well, I guess his Radiancy thought he looked like a table, because he waved his hand in the air and suddenly the earl was a table. And his Radiancy said, 'We are sure the former earl will be much more useful in this capacity.'"

"His Radiancy turned Earl Baljan into a table?" Cliopher repeated.

"Yes. I didn't know anyone could do that, outside of stories."

Cliopher hadn't, either, but he was absurdly pleased by the notion that a wizard from a book of fables would turn someone into a table on *his* behalf. "And then what did he do?"

"His Radiancy? He walked around the table and continued on to his rooms. Everyone else followed him, giving the table a wide berth. It's still sitting in the middle of the hallway, as far as I know. No one wants to touch it."

After a moment Cliopher thought to ask, "Had Princess Oriana come in at that point?"

"No," said Tully, "we saw her going to talk to his Radiancy just as we were leaving."

Cliopher could not keep himself from smirking as he imagined the reception she would find.

CHAPTER SIXTY-FIVE

THE NEXT MORNING CLIOPHER WAS, naturally, ashamed of the outbursts of the day before. He had been tired, even exhausted, but that was no excuse for losing his temper with all those he loved. At least he had not shouted at Rhodin at any point, and Ludvic and Conju were with his Radiancy at the palace. He had managed to aggravate nearly everyone else who was close to him.

He dressed in his least fancy civilian clothes, aware as he did so that they were of a style, cut, fabric, quality, colours entirely foreign to those of his family and friends. But they were what he had; and he might at any moment encounter someone who did care what his position was, and expect him to be dressed appropriately.

And besides, he liked them.

He had slept for well over fourteen hours, and it was late in the morning when he made his way through the warren of rooms to the kitchen. He found his Aunt Oura there, baking rolls.

"Good afternoon, Kip," she said slyly.

"Good morning, Aunt Oura," he replied, with a florid bow. He eyed the tray of steaming rolls she had just drawn from the oven. His stomach reminded him that four crab cakes was not really an adequate supper, even if combined with excessive amounts of coffee and dark rum. "I don't suppose any of those rolls are ready to be eaten?"

She pretended to consider—or possibly did consider. Aunt Oura baked to distract herself from the woes of her monograph, but she could be equally chary about sharing the results of either. "I suppose I could let you have one or even two. Just to tide you over. The ones on the left are chocolate, the right curd cheese."

"Curd cheese? Where did you get fresh cheese here?" Cliopher turned to the sink to fill the kettle. His aunt took it from him to put on the hob.

"Looenna. Some women moved here from Amboloyo, of all places, to start a vineyard halfway up the mountain. They have cattle wandering around grazing between the vines, and started making cheese last year."

Cliopher nibbled at the pastry. Solaara was too tropical for most cheeses; some of the local goat herders made a fresh herbed cheese, but no one made the hard melting cheeses of the north.

"It's very good," he said, swallowing. "I always like visiting Amboloyo for the cheese. I miss it from Astandalas."

Aunt Oura wiped her hands on the apron. "Do you know, Kip, that must be one of the few times I've ever heard you mention Astandalas. Did they have much cheese there?"

Had he truly never spoken of Astandalas? But no one had ever asked him about the fabled city, not after the Fall, and he had not come home before.

"Hundreds of varieties. There was this cheese shop in a place called Zangora Square, not too far from the Palace, which prided itself on having the most kinds. It was all set out like a jewellery store. Dramatic lighting, a quiet hush, very attentive and polite staff, that sort of thing. They used to import cheese from Alinor, plus all the kinds made around Astandalas the Golden itself."

He chuckled, looking down at his fine clothes. "Not that I could afford to go there very often. A little farther along was a much more ordinary cheese store, which had almost as good a selection, but they didn't have anything like the ambience."

"You used to write about the city, how you were exploring it, how interesting it was. Sometimes we wondered if you weren't exaggerating in defiance—but of course we wanted you to come home."

"Of course," he murmured, taking one of the chocolate rolls. He broke it open with his fingers. "I had a very difficult time of it in Astandalas, especially at first. There was a proverb—they might still say it places, Alinor perhaps—they used to say 'as far away as the Vangavaye-ve'. Meaning, the farthest conceivable place. 'People must do that in the Vangavaye-ve'. 'They probably think that in the Vangavaye-ve.'"

Except that in those days they had said 'Vonyabe'. Or they had until they encountered Cliopher.

"The first time I heard it I nearly got into a fight with someone. I just heard 'Vangavaye-ve' and I was so homesick—I turned and asked them what he had said, if he were from there, going there. He was talking about something stupid—I don't even remember what—and he'd just used the phrase as part of it."

"And the fight?"

"I was annoyed about his language, and called him out on it. I don't think he realized that the Vangavaye-ve was a real place—in his mind it was something out of a book of fables. When I said I was from here, he looked at me like I was a freak. But instead of fighting he asked me to join his friends for a drink and we went and talked about where we were from for hours."

"So you made a friend."

Cliopher smiled ruefully, remembering Dwian fondly, and remembering also how that acquaintance, though remaining friendly, had never blossomed into true friendship. Dwian had been from the city, and had gone to a friend's party the night of the Fall. He had not invited Cliopher along, which had hurt tremendously for the first half of the evening.

"I'm talking too much," he said, splitting the chocolate roll neatly in half. "How are you, Aunt Oura? How's your monograph coming along?"

She crooked her head quizzically to one side, examining him much as she did her specimens. "Why don't you like talking about yourself, Kip?"

"Habit, I suppose," he replied lightly.

"But why start that habit?"

He laughed. "Have I ever like being the centre of attention, Aunt Oura? Not to mention I'd be asking for trouble if I talked too much about my work."

"We like to hear your stories, you know."

He felt his smile fading as that simple statement crashed against a lifetime of experiences. All those letters that never asked him about his work. All those visits home when he was never asked about his life in Solaara. All those times he had started to say something, and his family had looked at him with indifference or disapproval or reproach, and he had changed the subject and seen their expressions relax and turn glad.

Aunt Oura said, "What is it?"

He looked down at the shreds of the roll in his hand, the smell of chocolate rising up. He smiled painfully. "I will have to think of ones you will enjoy, then."

She said, "That would be good." And then: "Did you hear about how Arnie's son fell into the vat at the *Ring o'News*?"

★★★

HIS FRIENDS ARRIVED SHORTLY AFTER. He was still in the kitchen, and therefore made it to the front door at the same moment as Leona. His niece grinned at him as she opened the door. "Are you expecting anyone, Uncle Kip?"

"I am, as it happens" he said with mock indignation. "Are you?"

"Not really, but I was bored with my homework."

"May we come in, or must we stand here while you're deciding who gets to greet us?" Falbert asked in robust tones. Cliopher and Leona hastily stepped aside, both laughing.

"Gaudy should be coming down later today," Cliopher said to Leona.

"I'll finish my project," she promised, and hastened off.

Cliopher greeted his friends properly in the Astandalan style. "Thank you for coming."

"You sound very official," Toucan murmured. "Is this?"

"No, you need not be worried." Cliopher had been intending to ask them to help him with a few parts of his Plan, but he felt so battered by the day before he decided to wait until after the investiture. "Do you want anything to drink? My aunt Oura's been making rolls, and said I could share them with you. Chocolate and cheese. Rather, chocolate or cheese. I want to hear more about these Amboloyan farmers on Looenna, Ghilly. You didn't mention the cheese yesterday. I am most intrigued by what they're doing."

"You and half the city," she said. "The other half feels that they're a little *too* foreign."

"I'll help you," Falbert volunteered.

"Thanks," Cliopher said as they loaded two trays with the rolls, fresh fruit, and pitchers of water, chocolate, and coffee.

"I imagine it's been a while since you were last loading your own trays."

"I'm sorry about yesterday," Cliopher said. "I was very tired, but that's no excuse."

"You know I think it's important to vent. I can't believe you were stewing over all that for so long. That hurt more than anything, I think."

"I don't actually stew over it all the time. It's been a stressful couple of years."

Falbert looked at him, bushy eyebrows beetling. "Pax?"

Cliopher grinned at him. "Pax."

They carried the trays upstairs together. Halfway along one of the halls, Falbert said, "Do you remember what that first argument was about?"

"The one that led to your grandmother declaring the Pax Astandalatis on us? It was—" Cliopher stopped and burst out laughing. "I have no idea, Bertie, do you?"

"I thought you might remember."

"I'll put my mind to it." Cliopher kicked open the door with the knack that had never left him, despite all the years he had spent away.

"Given how much else you have to put your mind to, please don't."

"I can think about more than one thing at once."

"You can probably think about fifteen things at once," Ghilly said as she and Toucan relieved them of their trays. "The best secretaries always seem to be able to."

"Oh, Kip always could do that," Toucan said, and as easily as that the conversation spiralled into reminiscing about the days before Cliopher had even begun to think about leaving.

Cliopher felt mildly ashamed at how disinclined he was to push the conversation anywhere else.

But he enjoyed the reminiscences—

And it was true that his friends laughed and encouraged him in *these* stories.

★★★

IN THE MID-AFTERNOON THEY WERE brought more rolls by Vinyë, who was looking so disconsolate Cliopher was alarmed, and said so.

His sister smiled wanly and waved a letter at him. "Just disappointed, Kip. I'd applied for a grant for this project on increasing musical education—"

"Yes, I remember you writing about it," said Cliopher, who had in fact composed the grant based around her project.

"We were supposed to hear back today, so I stopped in on my way home from practice, and, well, I didn't get it." She frowned at the letter. "I really felt as if I met all of the requirements, too."

Cliopher blinked. "What does it give as a reason?"

"Oh, that by some law I am ineligible, and—"

"May I see the letter?"

With an air of surprise, for he rarely interrupted anyone, she passed it to him. He read it over several times with an increasing sense of outrage. "This is entirely wrong."

"Oh, Kip, don't worry—I'll get over the disappointment. If that's the law, that's the law."

"That is not the law. I wrote that law. This is not what it says. And you are definitely eligible for this grant—I wrote it for you. How late is this department open?"

"Till three, but really, Kip—"

"Rhodin?"

"I'll change," the guard replied, smiling slightly.

Gaudy jumped up with alacrity. "Shall I change as well, Uncle Kip? Are you going to go see them?"

"I certainly am." Cliopher glanced at his friends, who were looking intrigued. "Will you come as witnesses? This has the potential of being exceedingly messy. Vinyë, what relatives do we have in the Department of the Common Weal? Isn't Cousin Hillen there somewhere?"

"He's the Director," his sister said after a moment.

Cliopher paused, for he could see no way the letter's indication of wrongdoing would not implicate the Director.

"We've never liked him anyway," she said encouragingly.

"Just as well," he muttered, frowning at the letter, which was signed by someone named Lina Erzan on behalf of the Director of the Common Weal of the Vangavaye-ve. "Someone is going to pay dearly for this."

"Not for refusing me the grant, surely!"

He had already started to think about the ramifications, and had to restrain his mind to answer his sister. "Someone has deliberately misrepresented the law. That cannot go disregarded."

Gaudy returned in the dark blue and orange of his service, carrying Cliopher's writing kit. Rhodin was only a few steps behind him, in the lesser panoply with spear and sword. He saluted crisply on entering. "Koloi and Mbangele are at the hostel down the lane."

"What, they've been staying there?" Cliopher said.

Rhodin grinned. "His Radiancy insisted."

Cliopher forbore commenting further. "Very well, let us go down to the offices. Are they still on the Lotus Canal, Vinyë?"

"No, they're over by the Cockatiel now. Can I come?"

"Certainly."

They were, therefore, a fairly large party: Cliopher, Rhodin, Vinyë, Gaudy, Toucan, Ghilly, Bertie, and the two younger guards, who had been playing dice in the courtyard of the hostel and appeared delighted to have something to do. Parno joined them by the Kindraa house, and a few streets on they collected Quintus as well.

Cliopher did not really want so many, but could see no polite way to send them away. He dismissed the thought, focusing instead on what would be the best course of action to determine what exactly was amiss with the department. He was annoyed at himself for not having caught the wrongdoing earlier. That he had been very busy over the past few years was no good excuse.

By the time they arrived at the department offices he had governed his temper to a low simmer and was able to smile politely, if thinly, at the receptionist, whom he vaguely recognized from his university days. She looked askance at him, slowly out at the rest of the group, lingered on the three guards, and then back at him.

"You're Kip Mdang, aren't you? Dressed up for your visit home, are you?"

He inclined his head. "I would like to speak to Lina Erzan, please."

A woman from the back of the room got up and sauntered over. Slowly. Smirking. "What can I do for you, er, Kip?"

As had happened facing Princess Oriana, facing Cousin Louya, the night before, Cliopher felt something snap inside him. Not control, or not exactly, but that part of him that was usually very happy to stay modestly in the background doing his job.

Perhaps he had been spending too much time with his Radiancy.

"The proper address is *your excellency*," he said crisply, and moved behind the receptionist's counter into the office space behind before anyone reacted to his words. "I see that your name is on this letter, Saya Erzan, in place of the Director of these offices. Will you please explain to me your position?"

She put up her hands in protest. "Hey, you're not allowed to come back here!"

He raised his eyebrows at her. "Is it possible you are unfamiliar with my position?" He let his glance rove around the room, taking in the dozen other officials, who had all ceased pretending to work and were watching him avidly, and the two dozen or so people in the waiting area.

"I don't know who you think you are—"

He *had* been spending too much time with his Radiancy.

"And yet," he interrupted, voice even and calm and perhaps even serene, "it is *my* name and title on those signs, it is *my* name and title on this letterhead, and indeed, it is *my* name and title on the letters of appointment for every person within this office. I am astonished, Saya Erzan, that you are so ignorant of the hierarchy of the Service of which you are a part. I am Cliopher Lord Mdang, Saya Erzan, Secretary in Chief of the Offices of the Lords of State, head of the Imperial Bureaucratic Service. I have *every* authority to be on this side of the counter. I shall repeat my question once more, Saya Erzan. Will you please explain your position to me?"

She gawped at him. He waited, but she did not answer. He made a show of looking at the letter, which he still held in his hand. "It says in this letter that you are writing on behalf of the Director of the Common Weal, and in that position—whatever exactly it entails—that you have rejected this application for the new artistic education grant."

There was a slight stir in the waiting room. Many of them must be waiting for their own results.

Lina Erzan swallowed, her smirk fixed, eyes rolling towards the closed door at the back of the room. "Hillen asked me to write them because he was too busy. He told me which ones to pass—he'd already decided—I didn't do anything wrong!"

"I shall be the determiner of that," he said. "What *is* your position, Saya Erzan?"

"It's—that is—I'm not really a member of this department—"

"She's his lover," someone said from behind him.

Her smirk malformed into vicious hatred, but she did not deny the statement.

"Do I understand correctly?" Cliopher said in tones of reproof as mild as he could manage. "You are not officially a member of this department—that is, you were not hired within it?"

"I'm *paid* for my work," she said, with a re-emergence of bluster.

The helpful informer behind him said, helpfully, "That doesn't make it better, Lina."

"Why, you gossiping son of a—"

"That is enough," Cliopher said, and pointed to a bench against the side wall. "Sit there while I continue my investigation of this department, Saya Erzan."

"Here, you can't do that!" she cried.

"Your excellency," he reminded her. "Ser Rhodin."

Ser Rhodin walked forward, broadly muscular and visibly armed. Saya Erzan made a shrill squeaking noise long before he came within arm's reach, and retreated in what amounted to a hop to the bench, where she sat glaring balefully.

"Thank you," Cliopher said to Ser Rhodin, who inclined his head, face perfectly straight, and made his way to stand next to the bench.

Cliopher turned his attention to the rest of the office, but as he began to decide which person to go after next, the back door opened and his cousin Hillen came out.

Hillen was a burly man. He'd played sports seriously for many years until a knee injury had seen him turn his attention first to local politics and then, it appeared, to the Department of the Common Weal. He had gone slightly to fat, but his self-satisfaction was as plain to see as it ever had been. His father had been rather better-to-do than most of the Mdang family's inlaws, being a distant connection of Earl Baljan's, and Hillen was his only child.

He smiled jovially, genially, and expansively.

Everyone in the vicinity looked at him, most of those in the waiting room with apprehensive or resigned expressions, most of those in the office with expectant smirks.

Cliopher was a strong believer in the notion that a leader was responsible for the attitudes of those below him. He was also a long veteran of the court and the Service, and he could read as plainly as a book that everyone expected him to be cowed before the charismatic and powerful Director, a man who had bullied him (and everyone else, for that matter) as a child.

Hillen ignored the presence of Ser Rhodin, which was impressive, winking instead at Lina Erzan. He beamed around the room until his even slower saunter brought him before Cliopher, at which point he made a great show of recognizing him.

"Why, it's Cousin Kip!" he said, beaming. "We haven't seen you in an age. Whatever have you been doing with yourself? You're looking very grand. Very grand indeed. What brings you down here to make a fuss in my department? Nothing too serious, I expect! Shall we go into my office and settle things amicably? I've got a very nice tipple you might enjoy."

"No, I think I'd prefer to stay out here with the audience," he replied. "You're the Director, Sayo Mdang, are you not?"

There was a definite stir.

Hillen laughed. "*Sayo*, is it? Eh Kip, that's a bit ripe."

"I am the Lord Chancellor of Zunidh, Sayo Mdang, as you will know from your official correspondence with the upper ministries. You will address me as *your excellency* or as *Lord Mdang*, as you prefer. I have several questions to ask of you."

"We definitely must go into my office, er, your excellency. I'm not really sure why you're so upset, but really, I'm sure it's nothing that can't be resolved with a friendly discussion."

"I shall begin with asking you, Sayo Mdang, how many people are currently on the roll for this department?"

Hillen had been making come-hither motions, and stopped to frown at him in total puzzlement. "I beg your pardon?" Ser Rhodin stepped forward meaningfully. Hillen, who evidently *had* noticed him, rolled his eyes. "I beg your pardon, *your excellency*."

"How many people, Sayo Mdang, currently work in this department?"

"Oh, fifteen, sixteen, something like that. How do you expect me to know that? I'm a busy man. Perhaps you do things differently in Solaara."

"I imagine we do. How differently I intend to determine. You have fifteen or sixteen people in this department. Do you include in that number Saya Erzan?"

"Lina? *Lina?*" Hillen laughed exuberantly. "Dear me, Lina doesn't work *here*. She works for me, you know."

"Yet her name is signatory to this document, which is an official production of this department."

Hillen's smug smile faltered very briefly. "She was following my instructions—I was the one who'd decided on the grants—I gave her the list—"

"And yet this application was rejected?" Cliopher's voice was all polite reproof. Hillen's hackles slowly settled, the smile plastered back on.

"My dear cousin—*your excellency*, if you're going to insist—"

"Oh, I do believe I am, Sayo Mdang."

"If you are to look closely at the document, which I drafted personally, I assure you, *your excellency*, you will see that the reasons are given clearly and in agreement with the policies set forth in the department manual."

Cliopher looked down at the letter. "This paragraph, do you mean? *Whereas it is seen in paragraph 8 of the third section of the Seventh Law of the Charter of Public Ministries that any person in a government ministry is not eligible for any monies to be granted according to public reward*—that is what you are referring to, Sayo Mdang?"

"It certainly is," Hillen said, all bluster and injured innocence, but he was no match for the great courtiers of the Palace, and Cliopher could read the cunning and the malice behind the bonhomie. "Really, Cousin Kip—really, *your excellency*, how can you argue with the law? I'm sorry your sister did not get her grant, but she is the Director of the Symphony, and that is a government ministry, last I checked." He chuckled. "You live far away, Cousin—oh, really? Fine! Your excellency!—perhaps you don't read the laws often enough."

"I have been known to argue with the law when it needed to be changed," Cliopher said, in a quiet tone he had learned from his Radiancy and which could cut through any ambient noise whatsoever.

"In fact, if you consult your copy of the *Charter of Public Ministries*—you were sent the new edition six months ago, but any of the past nine editions will do—oh! I see that you have the last four on the shelf behind you, if you care to consult any of them at this moment—no?—you will see that the Seventh Law was changed three iterations of the *Charter* ago. The third section does indeed treat the subject of government grants and bursaries as it relates to those in the public service in one form or another, but this is not, and has never been, either the wording or the purpose of the paragraphs in question. I am very familiar with the specific wording of the law, for I wrote it."

Hillen blinked. "You can't just *rewrite* the law!"

"I am glad to know your sense of justice is not entirely atrophied, Sayo Mdang. There are procedures in place for addressing laws that need to change, whether because the Empire Fell or because injustice is discovered to be calcified in our instruments of justice. However, since your reading of the law is, shall we say, unjustified, I will ask you to revise your decision on this application."

Hillen snorted. "What, after I've gone to all the trouble to make it? I don't think so. Why, everyone would be knocking at my door for me to change my mind—and it's not as if that was the only reason not to give her the grant."

"Indeed? It is the only one listed. Do enlighten me, Sayo Mdang."

"We really should be doing this in the back office—we don't want everyone to know how—"

"Are you suggesting that there is some desirable lack of transparency about your procedure, Sayo Mdang?"

"What? No! No, of course not—don't be ridiculous. It's just that surely you'd be much more comfortable—there are good chairs, some nice wine, even a little tea if you're so inclined, and there are certainly other considerations a man of sense might want to—"

"Sayo Mdang, this is our first official encounter and as such I will give you one warning, which is that it is a capital offence to attempt to bribe me."

There was a very definite silence of shock in the room. Hillen, who was beaming jovially again, faltered.

He *had* been spending too much time with his Radiancy. He was starting to enjoy this.

Cliopher took three steps forward. Hillen took an instinctive step back, trying to regain his control, but his jaw was working—not with true injured innocence, but indignation underlain with fear.

"Look, your excellency, if that's what you're going to insist on, I don't see what right you have to come down here, all la-di-dah and stuck up, and interrogate me about the doings of my department. This is *my* department, do you hear? Mine! It's my place to run as I see fit. I make all the decisions—"

"And do you stand by them?"

"What? What? Of course I do! No one else has a backbone in here. No one does any work! I'm the one who has to deal with the finances, I'm the one who has to hire people, I'm the one who has to decide whether people get their grants, I'm in charge, and I do not take kindly to my upstart little cousin coming in and telling me I'm to call him *your excellency* and telling me how to do my job!"

"Magnificent," he said, after a long and measuring stare that made Hillen lose all the posture he had built up in his little speech. "Perhaps you will in time be able to find a new career on the stage. The timing, and indeed the possibility, of any further career will, of course, be determined by what I discover after the auditors give me their final report and what judgment I make."

"What do you mean, a new career? I have friends of high rank, I have money, this is *my* department—how *dare* you! What am I supposed to have done that's so bad, invited you to have a drink and sort out your issues in a civilized fashion?"

Cliopher folded his hands before him the posture of official decrees, which probably no one but Ser Rhodin and Gaudy recognized, but was the way these things were done.

"Hillen Sayo Mdang, until the auditors have finished their report I cannot say with any exactitude what your crimes have been, but on the scale from negligence to treason I expect they will fall somewhere in the higher end, with the more serious charges including incompetence in a position of power, deliberate misrepresentation of the law, falsification for personal gain, bribery both given and received, and, of course, embezzlement in excess of one hundred and fifty thousand valiants. It may be considerably in excess of that sum, but at the moment I do not know precisely how long you have been falsifying the number of employees in this department so you can pocket their salaries yourself."

There was another incredulous ringing silence. Hillen opened his mouth and then shut it again. Every line of his face proclaimed a guilty conscience. Finally he blurted, "How did you know about—" He stopped, but it was by far too late.

"You ask my authority, Sayo Mdang? Is it possible you have never noticed whose seal, whose title, and whose name it is on the ministry documents? The Common Weal is *my* ministry, Hillen: I founded it, I structured it.

I wrote its policy documents, and I continue to take a considerable interest in its workings in the various provinces of the world."

Cliopher turned to his party, who were all staring at him as if he'd grown a second head. He met Toucan's eyes gravely. "Sayo Nevan, if I recall correctly there is a police station not far from here. Would you accompany Ser Rhodin as he escorts Sayo Mdang there?"

"Of course, your excellency," Toucan said after a small pause.

"You can't just *arrest* me!"

Cliopher spun around and fixed Hillen with a stare so fierce he took another step back.

"I am the Secretary in Chief of the Offices of the Lords of State. I am the head of the Imperial Bureaucratic Service. I am the Hands of the Emperor. I am the Lord Chancellor. As of the day after tomorrow I will be Viceroy of Zunidh. In all the world I am second in authority to the Sun-on-Earth, and to the Sun-on-Earth alone. I assure you, sir, I am perfectly within my rights—and my duties."

Hillen was shocked with disbelief and dawning awareness. Cliopher held his gaze for a long moment, the room dead silent, and then he very deliberately smiled.

"It is, however, true that you are my cousin. For that reason I shall do everything in my power to see that your case comes up before the Lord Emperor before he leaves Zunidh rather than before me afterwards—and for that reason I shall also ask Ser Rhodin, who is Deputy Commander of the Imperial Guard, to make the actual arrest."

"With pleasure, Lord Mdang," said Ser Rhodin, and did so.

Toucan and Parno accompanied Ser Rhodin and the faintly protesting Hillen out the door. Cliopher took a deep breath and looked around the room. "Who is in charge of the financial records?"

Someone in the back raised a trembling hand. When Cliopher nodded at him, he said, "Er, your excellency, the Director."

"Who is in charge of the policy documents? Also the Director? And the records of decisions—of course. Well then, sayena, what do *you* do?"

None of them could give him any better answer than Lina Erzan, who was still sitting on her bench in shock. After a few minutes of interrogating them, with the end result only increasingly incoherent babbling, Cliopher turned to the least incoherent of the lot and bade her bring him all the grant applications and their decisions.

"They're in the Director's office," she said.

"It is not, I trust, the Imperial Apartments?" Cliopher said. At her pan-
icky look, he sighed with carefully evident disappointment. "Saya Erzan, you
appear to be more familiar with that office than the officials of this department. Bring me the papers I requested. Gaudy, accompany her."

"Yes, your excellency."

When the untidy and somewhat food-stained stack was brought to him,
Cliopher made the receptionist move out of the way. He took his writing kit
from Gaudy, set up his pens, and then said: "In the somewhat unlikely event
that any of you manage to regain a job in this or any government department, this is how it is done."

He read through each application quickly but carefully, making a few
comments as necessary to clarify the projects or amend them for sense or
effectiveness, and finally signed his name to those he felt passed. Everyone
watched him breathlessly, which usually would have confounded him but he
was still so angry and yet half-amused at the whole situation that he could
not find it anything but humorous. How much his Radiancy would laugh
when he described it to him.

"Very well," he said, setting down his pen and looking at those in the
waiting area. They seemed to have increased in number since his arrival.
That was probably to be expected: gossip moved as fast in Gorjo City as it
did in the Palace. Even as he looked, a swaggering young scion of the lesser
nobility came through the door, followed discreetly by Ser Rhodin, Toucan,
and Parno.

"Carletta Vardes," he said, and a plump, apprehensive woman got up and
approached him. He smiled reassuringly at her. "This sounds like an excellent
project. Good luck with it.—Strigo Mden."

There were two dozen or so applications. Two in the middle had to have
amendments agreed to before he would sign his name. A couple that had
been passed by Hillen were rejected; the majority that had been rejected by
Hillen were passed.

Finally he was left with one application. "Kio Baljan."

Kio Baljan was some connection of the Earl, Cliopher gathered from
both resemblance and name. He was the late swaggerer, and he sauntered
over with a confident sneer and a poor attempt at aristocratic hauteur. "Well,
hand it over, then.—What the hell? This is *rejected*?"

"Your project fulfils half of one of the nineteen criteria. Surely you did
not expect it to pass?"

"Hillen promised me I'd get the money—that was five cases of Amboloyan wine that cost me, you know!"

"I didn't, as it happens, but if you would like to testify to bribing Sayo Mdang in court, it is possible that your own sentence will be commuted. I promise nothing, because of course the full charges have not yet been laid, but it is a possibility."

"What the hell."

"Ser Rhodin, if you would be so kind—"

"Of course, your excellency," Ser Rhodin murmured, face blank and eyes gleaming, and promptly charged the man with bribery of a public official.

Cliopher surveyed the waiting area. "Who would like to go next?"

There was a long and awkward pause before someone tentatively raised her hand in the back. "I had a question about the annual stipend—?"

Her problem was not complicated, and Cliopher was able to send her happily on her way in a very short time. He cleared out the waiting area as decisively and efficiently, forcing the department officials to find papers, policy documents (for he did not have them all memorized), forms, and sundry other items. Finally all that was left were the officials themselves and his own party.

He opened his writing kit again and removed a sheet of the heavy magically-enhanced paper and the bottle of ink he used for official declarations. Without comment he wrote out that by order of the Lord Chancellor the Vangavayen Department of the Common Weal was closed until further notice for auditing and restaffing, and that any applications for positions in the new department would go through the Ministry of Public Goods of the Wide Seas—which had just been audited and which he knew was in good, if somewhat ruffled, order.

He affixed his seal to the declaration, handed it to Gaudy, and surveyed the nervous officials. "This department is now closed for a full audit and review. You may reapply for your positions in the general applications that will begin two weeks from today. You may take your personal belongings out of your desks but all other materials and papers are to be left here for the auditors to assess." He pointed at the person nearest the door. "We will begin with you, sir."

"What—what do you mean?"

Cliopher raised his eyebrows again. "Come now, you cannot expect me not to observe what you take out of the building with you?"

CHAPTER SIXTY-SIX

HE WAS SOMEHOW SURPRISED TO see that it was still brilliant afternoon outside. The sixteen bewildered and upset officials—he had counted them as they filed out—had filtered away down the street, he had confiscated all the keys and locked the door, then asked Rhodin to seal the offices magically until the auditors arrived. He affixed the declaration to the door, wrote a note to Kiri to send a team of auditors—on second thought, *all* the available teams—post-haste to Gorjo City, and then considered his party.

"Parno," he decided. "You've always been a strong runner. Will you run this up to the Light for me, please? I want the auditors to get here as soon as possible."

"Of course, uh—"

Cliopher felt himself abruptly relax. He laughed. "Gaudy manages to figure out what he calls me when. I'm sure you will as well. In the meantime, if no one has any objections, shall we begin our way home?"

They were all still staring at him. Parno glanced at his father, then took the letter and began self-consciously to trot down the canal towards Mama Ituri's Son. Cliopher took in the shocked faces and said lightly, "Unless there are any other ministry departments you think I ought to take a look at this afternoon?"

"Most of them will be closed by now," Falbert said.

"Then they shall have to wait until the auditors have finished with this one. Gaudy, when you have the chance, please write up a report for me on what just happened. I'll need it for, hmm, three days from now."

"Of course, sir. Uncle Kip," he added, grinning, when Cliopher smiled at him. "Do you want me to carry your writing kit?"

"No, I think I can manage," Cliopher said, who had tucked it into the familiar position in the crook of his arm and thereby realized how much he had been missing it. The Lord Chancellor was not really supposed to carry his own burdens. As for the Viceroy of Zunidh ... he would be lucky if no one tried to prevent him from *walking* on his own. He'd seen Franzel and Féonie with their heads together over a catalogue of sedan chairs.

"Are you always like this at work?" Toucan asked curiously.

Cliopher started to stroll back towards their part of town, smiling at the familiar landmarks with the satisfaction that being incisive always gave him. "What do you mean?"

"You're so—efficient."

"*This is how it's done*, indeed," Ghilly said, smiling at him before tucking her arm into her husband's. "I've never seen anyone in that department do as much work as you forced them to do in an hour."

"I can't believe you arrested Cousin Hillen," Quintus said, chuckling. "Is that a secret, or may we tell people?"

Cliopher looked at him in amused disbelief. "There were over forty people in that office, Quintus, and that's without counting all those along the route to the police station. Did you have any problems, Rhodin? Toucan?"

"Hillen tried to bribe us," Rhodin said. "Poorly."

"Five cases of Amboloyan wine were not sufficient?"

"As it happens, I prefer my head."

"What a pity that Hillen doesn't appear to. I do hope I can get this before his Radiancy before he leaves."

"What happens if you don't?" Ghilly asked. "Does the case wait for his return?"

"No, it'll come before me. There's no one I can recuse a case to except his Radiancy. And this is my department. Serious crimes in government ministries come before the Crown."

"Do you think it's fair to condemn someone to death for embezzlement?" Toucan asked, more curiously than aggressively.

Cliopher regarded him seriously. "Embezzlement is only part of it; falsifying the law is the bigger crime. That is the law as it stands, and I neither can nor should be able to change those laws without going through the entire machinery of government and having his Radiancy's approval. However, it may be that it is a calcified injustice, in which case it ought to be changed."

"And just like that—" Ghilly shook her head. "You're so blasé about all this, Kip. As if turning people's lives upside-down is something you do every day, and then on to the next task."

"It's not quite every day, but it is fairly often. Ghilly, this *is* what I do. I am the solver of problems, big and small. It's my job to make sure the government is working properly. It's not usual for me personally to upend a department in the provincial secretariat, but that's because I spend my time in the upper levels. It's not usual for me personally to fill in the forms and accept the applications, but I can do that, too."

"Efficiently, calmly, effectively, and ruthlessly."

"Ruthlessly?" Cliopher laughed, aware of ironies and ramifications far beyond what they saw. "Do you think so? None of those people will starve or lack housing, clothing, or the opportunity to find work. Most of them will get jobs fairly quickly. I did not charge Lina Erzan with anything, though she is undoubtedly culpable in what Hillen was doing. I did not charge any of the other officials with gross incompetence or negligence, although they displayed every evidence of it. I did my best not to humiliate anyone who was not trying to bully me into getting his way."

"But you fired all of them because they were intimidated by the questions you were asking—"

"Vinyë," he said, turning his head abruptly to her. "What is your position?"

She blinked at him. "I'm the Director of the Vangavayen Symphony Orchestra."

"And what does your position entail?"

She smiled slightly. "I am first cellist; I organize rehearsals, I oversee the performance and practice spaces, I advertise and audition and hire new players, I find new music ... There are other elements, too, of course."

"Quintus, what about you?"

Quintus was grinning. "I am the captain of the merchant ship *Gold Pearl* and a member of the Board of the Merchant Navy of the Wide Seas."

"But it's easier for them," Ghilly objected. "They have clearly defined positions."

Cliopher sighed in exasperation. "That department has clearly defined positions! For a region the size of the Vangavaye-ve there should be between twenty-three and twenty-five officials—all of whom have clearly defined titles, duties, and requirements, all of which are laid out in the fourth appendix to the *Charter of Public Ministries.*"

"Maybe they didn't know about it," Bertie said tentatively.

Cliopher snorted. "I assure you, I pay attention to the reports that come up from the Vangavaye-ve. As Director, Hillen has put in for twenty-four employees for *at least* the past year—so when I arrive and find a shoddy, shabby, ill-run, and disorganized department only two-thirds full of people unable to give the least indication of what they do, let alone what they are supposed to do, and who cannot find without assistance the most basic items of any department—heavens above, Bertie, one of them couldn't find the *paper*!"

"You can't expect them to work the same way they do in Solaara."

"I don't care *how* they do their work, so long as they *do* do their work and it doesn't involve bribery, cronyism, and major corruption. They could finish their work by noon and spend every afternoon fishing for all I care— so long as they do their work first!"

Vinyë said suddenly, "What do you mean, you pay attentions to the reports from the Vangavaye-ve?"

"What do I mean? I mean I read them. Of course, I read the general reports for all the provinces, and selected ministerial reports, but I read all the ministerial reports for the Vangavaye-ve."

"That must take a fair amount of time."

He shrugged, but Gaudy made an involuntary noise. Cliopher raised his eyebrows at his nephew. "It's what, an evening every few weeks? It's not as if I make you stay overtime for it so I can dictate at you, Gaudy. Every once in a while I catch something, or there'll be a nice mention of someone—" He stopped, realizing that made him sound dangerously sentimental, and made a show of looking at their surroundings. "I think I've gotten turned around. Are we anywhere close to Erno's café on Saloa?"

Vinyë and Bertie both looked at him hard, but let the matter drop. Toucan cleared his throat. "It's down Salter."

"Shall we? Will we lose Parno, Bertie?"

"I'm sure he'll be able to find his own way home."

They walked down the familiar streets, the others greeting acquaintances as they passed them. Many knew Cliopher, and he returned their greetings and turned aside their comments about his clothing, his hat, his accent, his bearing. He did his best to maintain an even temper and respond with smiles and polite words. It was not as if the fourth or sixth or eighth cousin or neighbour or old schoolfellow knew that the previous three or five or seven people had said exactly the same thing.

But he felt once more the weight of difference and of his responsibilities, and the faint tremble in his hands made him hold his writing kit more firmly.

The fifteenth person, his cousin Flion, said, "What an outfit that is, Cousin Kip! Here to impress everyone, are you?"

"How nice to see you, Flion," Cliopher replied, smiling.

"And your hat! What a thing that is. It looks like it came out of an old painting. Very fancy."

"Thank you. How is everyone?"

At least it wasn't the Council of Princes, he thought, and kept his expression pleasant through a long recitation of the woes of each of Flion's nearer relations.

After Flion continued on his errand to the bookmakers, Vinyë came up beside Cliopher and took his arm as they navigated a route through the crammed pathway between wharves and the businesses and cafés along the Saloa Lagoon. "Is that how everyone's been reacting, Kip?"

He smiled more genuinely at her obvious perturbation. "Oh, it's to be expected."

"*Did* you expect it?"

One of Vinyë's oldest friends came out from one of the hotels, saw them, blinked, turned their direction, greeted Vinyë affectionately, and said to Kip: "What an extraordinary outfit you have on, Kip! I nearly didn't recognize you. Come to town to impress everyone, have you?"

Vinyë's hand tightened on his arm. Cliopher didn't dare look at her face for fear he'd start laughing. He smiled at her friend. "You're looking magnificent yourself, Alora. Anything special on today for you?"

She looked self-consciously down at herself, then beamed at him. "I'm on my way to a birthday party, as it happens—and I really should go before I'm entirely late! Vinyë, I'll see you next week for lunch? Kip—" She gave him one lingering once-over, then shook her head. "That *is* a wonderful outfit. Nice to see you."

She strode briskly off in the direction of the sea temple. Cliopher chuckled slightly and answered his sister's question. "I suppose I'm always a little surprised at how frankly they tell me what they think. Disapproval is generally much more subtly expressed at court.—What? You look very dismayed."

"I didn't think ..."

"There's the café," Toucan said abruptly.

"And there's someone whose outfit puts Kip's to shame. Who in the world can that be?" Ghilly said softly, indicating a dark-skinned man in a white tunic and hooded silver mantle of exquisite simplicity who was approaching the café from the opposite direction to theirs, and who halted on seeing them.

"I appreciate the fact that you immediately recognize that his outfit is significantly nicer than mine. That is the Sun-on-Earth. Who appears to be here somewhat unofficially, so do not go into the full obeisance. Bow deeply.

Do not speak until he speaks to you."

"There's no reason for him to speak to us, surely?" Ghilly said in what almost amounted to a squeak.

Cliopher gave her a look and went forward the few steps necessary to reach the new prescribed distance, at which point he went down to one knee, was gestured up, and smoothly rose again.

"Kip," his Radiancy said, giving him a once-over almost as appreciative and simultaneously disapproving as any of his relations'. Unlike them he said nothing about it. "I am pleased to encounter you today."

"My lord?"

His Radiancy raised an eyebrow at him. Cliopher braced himself. First, however, came the pleasantries. His Radiancy glanced at the grouping behind him. Cliopher shifted over slightly to not be in the way, and so he could see both his Radiancy and his friends at the same time. "Saya Vinyë, Captain Quintus, it is a pleasure to see you again."

They curtsied and bowed. Quintus tried not to look panicked.

"Sayo Vawen. Your nephew is considerably more formally dressed than you, my lord chancellor."

Cliopher felt a modicum of relief—and more amusement—to discover the source of the disapproval. "I discovered a matter of some concern at the local Department of the Common Weal, my lord, and wished to deal with it immediately."

"Your efficiency is greatly to be commended."

He controlled his desire to laugh. "Thank you, my lord."

His Radiancy looked past Gaudy. "If my memory does not mislead me, these are the friends of your youth whom I met before. Toucan, I believe, and you would be Ghilly, and you are Bertie, sir, of whom Kip has spoken to me often."

They bowed, faces half-dismayed with astonishment. His Radiancy was about to continue speaking when the café's owner came bustling out to see if the pair of well—even grandly—even magnificently—dressed people standing outside his door might want some refreshments.

He poured this out in a single long sentence before realizing that he knew them. "Why, it's Cousin Kip!" he said. "In the flesh—and in splendid clothes. Is this a friend of yours? Would you like some coffee?"

"I am and I would," said his Radiancy easily. "Whatever you recommend."

"A long black, please, Erno," Cliopher said.

"You're here for the stuff up at the palace, I guess?"

"Yes," Cliopher replied. His Radiancy's eyebrow had gone up again.

"It sounds like it'll be quite the shindig. My mother's singing at it with Uncle Haido."

Cliopher smiled with genuine enthusiasm. "Are they? That's wonderful. I shall look forward to hearing them."

Erno gave the two of them another lingering glance, then turned to the party behind for their orders. Varro and Zerafin, his Radiancy's two guards, dressed identically to Cliopher's in their lesser panoply, stood four paces back, alert and aware of their surroundings. Cliopher focused on his Radiancy.

"It is practice," his Radiancy said meditatively, watching Erno bustle back into the building. "For when I go on my quest."

"Mm," said Cliopher.

"Regarding your zealous attention to provincial departments: is it serious enough for the case to be coming up before me?"

"I would greatly appreciate it, my lord, as one of my cousins was the Director."

His Radiancy chuckled. "In that case, we shall certainly make every effort to hear his case. The poor man will otherwise be doomed to the most exquisitely and punctiliously correct legal trial in Zuni history. We are to stay an extra week or so in the Vangavaye-ve. Will that be time enough?"

"I have sent for the auditors, my lord."

"Very good."

Erno came back out with a tray containing the first coffees. He offered it to his Radiancy, who looked at it as if he had never before in his life seen a tray with multiple options. Finally he chose Cliopher's long black, leaving a foamy café au lait for him. "This is excellent coffee," his Radiancy said after an experimental sip. "Where do the beans come from?"

Erno looked back over his shoulder. "Uh, I think these are from Ginlai's plantation over on South Epalo, uh, sir."

His Radiancy looked blandly at Cliopher. "Princess Oriana has informed me that the Vangavaye-ve does not produce coffee beans of more than average quality."

Cliopher spoke carefully. "The Princess was raised in Jilkano, my lord, and it is quite natural she prefers the flavours of her youth."

"The Princess spoke to me of your encounter last night."

"Is that so, my lord?"

His Radiancy sipped his coffee, looking out at the brilliant water of the lagoon and a flock of white pelicans perched on a row of pilings to which a number of small brightly-coloured craft were moored. "What do you think of Lord Balo?"

Cliopher spoke even more carefully. "I do not believe that youth and inexperience are necessarily disastrous, so long as they are balanced by good sense, intelligence, thoughtful advisors, and a strong desire to do as well as possible."

His Radiancy met his eyes, mirth bubbling in his own, and smiled slightly. "I see we are, as so often, of one mind." He went on in a brisker tone, as if on a different subject: "I met your kinswoman Aya inDovo Delanis and her husband Jiano as I came down here. I understand you invited them to the ceremony?"

He felt a jumble of emotions that Aya and Jiano, of all his friends and family, were the ones to make the effort to come. "Yes, my lord."

"They are staying at the Young Malo, if I heard the name correctly. They are seriously considering a change of habitation. It appears Aya would like to do some research for new books. I believe Jiano would appreciate your advice on his direction."

"I would be delighted," Cliopher said honestly.

His Radiancy swallowed the rest of his coffee and handed the cup to him. "The purification rituals will begin at dawn tomorrow. Come to my rooms by a quarter-hour to sunrise."

"Very good, my lord."

His Radiancy smiled at his friends, and appeared to be about to depart when yet another cousin, accompanied by a woman he didn't know, arrived. "Look, it's Kip!" Lenora cried, beaming at everyone as if she had personally conjured him up. "Kip, this is my friend Haila—Haila, my cousin Kip, the one who's in service in Solaara. I don't think you've met? He hasn't been back in ages. Haila's in my troupe, Kip."

"How nice to meet you!" Haila said, smiling brightly. "I've heard ever so much about you, Kip. That's a super outfit. Is it a costume for something?"

Cliopher tried not to laugh, but the blank expression on his Radiancy's face made it hard to keep his composure. "How do you do, Haila," he said, feeling bubbles of laughter rising up. How *absurd* the whole day had been.

"You're here for the thing at the palace, aren't you?" Lenora said conversationally. She hadn't been one of the relatives Cliopher had felt the need to invite personally, but he was glad, nevertheless, to see her. "We're going to be performing—before the Lord Emperor, no less! Can you imagine the honour? Everyone has been going around in a rush looking for costumes."

"We're going to be late for the dress rehearsal if we don't hurry," Haila said on this reminder.

"Oh, too true. Well, hopefully we'll see you tomorrow, Kip!"

Cliopher opened his mouth and then shut it again when Lenora and Haila hurried off, laughing merrily and chattering now about the rehearsal for their acrobatic troupe.

"There is still time for a parade," his Radiancy said, and then laughed when Cliopher just looked at him. "No? I do love a good parade."

"My lord, I will be delighted to arrange one for you on any occasion you please."

"Except this one?" His Radiancy laughed again. "I'll stop teasing you, Kip. I'm sure you wish to spend the rest of the day with your friends. Unless you are on your way to depopulate any other departments?"

"I am given to understand most of them are already closed."

His Radiancy's eyes glinted, and Cliopher nearly lost his composure. He managed to straighten his face. "Just so, my lord."

His Radiancy resumed his blandest expression. "While I am thinking of it, do you know of a bookstore near here? Aya did not have a copy of her newest book to hand, and I wish to read it."

Cliopher looked around at Bertie, who cleared his throat and said, "There's one a few streets over, my lord, next to the Pelican."

Before Bertie could launch into the rather complicated sequence of directions to reach the Pelican from where they were standing, Cliopher said, "Perhaps Gaudy might direct you on the way, my lord?"

His Radiancy smiled again. Rhodin, obviously realizing what Cliopher had—that it was unlikely in the highest that the Sun-on-Earth would have any money—murmured something to Gaudy, who nodded and murmured something back. "That will do nicely. Give my regards to your mother, Kip. Until the morning."

Cliopher bowed, hastily followed by everyone else. Gaudy, swallowing nervously, was gestured to walk next to his Radiancy, and led him down the quay towards the next cross canal and the bridge into the old quarter. "Gaudy had money, Rhodin?"

"He says he knows the bookstore owner if his Radiancy decides to buy half the store."

Cliopher smiled. "Excellent." Erno came back out to collect their cups and accept payment from Falbert, who frowned at Cliopher when he made a token protest. "Very well, thank you, Bertie. Erno, I need to keep this cup—"

"Really? Why?"

Cliopher looked at it doubtfully, then handed it to Koloi, who saluted. "It has to be ritually destroyed … My lord has certain ceremonial requirements. Now—I had best go to the Young Malo and see Aya and Jiano. I imagine they'll have a few questions to ask me."

"Oh, just one or two," Rhodin said, chuckling. "Namely, did his Radiancy actually ask them what they think he did—and what does that mean."

"Hush, now," Cliopher said. "Let us wait to see whether Jiano is willing or not."

"What will you do if he's not?"

He sighed. "Go to the contingency plan, I suppose. What about the rest of you? Do you want to come? You'll like Aya and Jiano—she's a novelist from the Western Ring, and he's, ah, active in community politics on Lesuia Island."

"Wait—this is Aya inDovo, who wrote *The Case of the Silver Bell?*" Ghilly asked, eyes brightening. "Certainly we'll come. I had no idea you knew her! How do you?"

"She claimed kinship with me that time I went with my lord holidaying near their village a few years ago. Then they came to Solaara as Speakers for Lesuia and the Outer Ring to speak out against that fish farm. Jiano was wonderfully eloquent—oh, I do hope he's willing to take on …" Cliopher trailed off, reminding himself that they were still very much in public.

"I suppose that means we're not allowed to ask what on earth you're talking about?" Ghilly said as they turned onto a quieter street and were able to walk abreast.

Cliopher was surprised that she had to ask, but before he could quite formulate his response they had arrived at the Young Malo and were being hailed by Aya, who had been sitting on the covered balcony facing over the street.

"Oh, Cliopher!" she cried, waving down urgently at him. "I am so pleased to see you! Please say you'll come up? I'll be right down."

She disappeared back into the house and shortly pattered down the stairs to greet him with enthusiasm underlain with deep anxiety. "*Hani*, I am so very glad to see you. Jiano has gone for a walk to clear his head, we just had a visit from your lord, and—"

"Let us discuss it inside," he said firmly.

"Oh—oh, of course!—but you were out with your friends?"

Cliopher introduced his party and said, "Perhaps we can come inside and talk it over? We also just encountered my lord, and he asked me to discuss his invitation with you."

"Did he?" Bertie said, in tones of mock puzzlement.

Cliopher gave him a quelling glance as they made their way up the stairs to the pleasant room Aya and Jiano were staying in. Aya asked them if they wanted any refreshments, but Cliopher explained they had just had coffee.

"Just as well, as the facilities here are shite. I suppose that will change—if I understood your lord correctly. Did he really—Cliopher, did he *really* mean it?"

"He did."

Aya sat down, then jumped up again to open the louvres. "I thought he must have. Jiano thinks—well, he's conflicted. It's such an honour—and an opportunity—and I think he would be excellent at it—but he thinks—well, he's never taken anything from his father's people, and doesn't like that that's the reason. Also, he's a bastard—doesn't that matter?"

Cliopher made a weighing gesture with his hand. "It does—or it can—but then again, it doesn't always. Bloodlines matter a great deal to the princes, I think more than legitimacy in this case."

"It's stupid. His father is not why he'd be good at the job."

"I know. That is why his Radiancy asked him. Now, Aya, before he returns, tell me truly: do you support this idea? Will you support him? I cannot pretend it will not be a seriously difficult position to take on and do a good job of—which is why we thought of him, of course."

"Aha!" she said, and laughed, all her tension suddenly easing. "I *knew* you must be behind it somewhere. If you're in favour of it, then I have no qualms."

"Really?" Cliopher said, valiantly endeavouring not to laugh since she appeared to be serious.

"I think that if the Sun-on-Earth trusts your judgment, it behoves us to follow his lead. Oh—that must be Jiano—I'll tell him you're here."

She darted back out to the stairs before Cliopher could say anything. He shrugged and smiled ruefully at his friends. "It is the sort of invitation that disturbs one's equilibrium."

"Are *all* your conversations this elliptical?" Bernie asked. "I feel as if I'm trying to figure out what the power structure of a pre-historic society is based on three fragmented pots and a stone knife."

Cliopher stared at him. "Whatever do you mean?"

"This is like last night with the princess," Ghilly put in.

"Yes!" Toucan said. "Will you enlighten us?"

Cliopher opened his mouth, but the door opened then on Jiano and Aya. He rose to greet Jiano, who clasped his arms in the Astandalan greeting and then said, with distracted air and distressed accents: "You can't really think I should become the Prince of the Vangavaye-ve, do you?"

CHAPTER SIXTY-SEVEN

BERTIE MADE A CHOKING NOISE. Cliopher gave him another quelling glance. "Come now, if you can't behave yourselves you'll have to wait outside. This is my sister Vinyë, Jiano, my cousin Quintus, and three of my oldest friends, Bertie, Toucan, and Ghilly. Jiano of Lesuia Island—and if he chooses, soon to be Prince of the Vangavaye-ve."

Unless—oh, *unless*—

And Cliopher's mind jumped to those secret yearnings, so close to possible now, of how the government of the world *could* work. Jiano was a communist, a Wide Sea Islander, a *wontok*: if ever there was a chance to break the princely system entirely this was it.

Jiano looked as if Bertie's reaction was more what he had expected.

Cliopher smiled at him, dizzy with the possibilities. "Of course I think you ought to take up the position. I cannot pretend it will be a very *easy* job, because Princess Oriana has proven herself to be minimally effective at her responsibilities and there will be a lot to do to make up for it, but I think it is something you will do very well at."

"I've never run anything bigger than our island council! How can you imagine I can run a bloody court?"

"His Radiancy usually prevents things from descending into bloodshed."

Jiano frowned at him hard. "You are both making a joke and totally serious, aren't you? But his Radiancy is going away—he told us that he was leaving you in charge when he goes. He assured me that if I—oh this is absurd even to say it—he said that if I agreed to take it on while he was away, he would be pleased and *you* would be delighted—and if I wanted to abdicate again when he came back, he would accept my resignation."

Cliopher answered the central thought. "I would be delighted to have someone I like and respect representing the Vangavaye-ve and sitting on the Council of Princes."

And wasn't *that* an understatement!

"But I don't know anything about governing!"

"Cliopher does," Aya said, glancing at him and then taking her husband's hand in her own. "Jiano, my love, surely if you ask—Cliopher has been running the *world* for years. I'm sure he knows more about ruling than practically anyone else."

"Well, I do know how to run a government. Although I do not myself *rule*, I have observed the princes for quite some time and can certainly give you my advice, if you would like it."

Rhodin made a soft snort and shook his head. Cliopher frowned at him. "I will gladly make the time to teach you the necessary nuances of court and relevant legislation. You will not find it difficult to be a better provincial authority than Princess Oriana."

Jiano laughed. "I know more about the Outer Ring, that's for sure. But Gorjo City—what will people think? I'm an Outer Ring tribesman!" He gestured at his outfit, which was that of, indeed, an Outer Ring tribesman dressed up for a trip to the city, with bright feathers in his hair, a layered multi-coloured grass skirt much adorned with shells, and several rows of very elaborate and very beautiful shell and bone efela necklaces.

Cliopher leaned forward intently. "Jiano, you were your village Speaker at a young age. Of all on Lesuia Island, you were the one willing to organize councils to speak about the fish farm and the other problems you felt the Princess was ignoring—and when she ignored the voices of the Outer Ring, of all the people in this province you were the one willing to make the journey to Solaara and present your case before his Radiancy and the Council of Princes. You performed magnificently. You are thoughtful, eloquent, persuasive, sufficiently charismatic, and you have Aya—" he smiled at her— "to keep you in reasonable time."

"But I am a communist!" Jiano wailed. "How can I abandon all my principles and become a *prince* based on the fact that I am the bastard son of an aristocrat?"

Cliopher's heart leapt. This was the kind of negotiation he was best at. "Do you stand by your principles?"

"I beg your pardon?"

"Do you believe in your philosophy?"

Jiano sat up straight, his eyes beginning to flash. "How *dare*—I am fully committed to my principles and believe they are the soundest foundation of good government."

"Are you? Prove it."

Aya made a noise as if she was swallowing a laugh. Cliopher glanced at her, then focused again on Jiano. Please, he thought, *please.*

"Here you are being granted the opportunity to put your principles into practice. Turn the Vangavaye-ve into a communist paradise—I invite you to make the effort! Come to Solaara and help me shape the new government. Argue with me and badger the Council of Princes into listening to you. Take up your throne and overthrow it for the betterment of all."

Jiano's eyes were wide with surprise. "You're the head of the government! Surely you shouldn't be advocating the dissolution of the principality!"

"I'm not advocating the dissolution of the Vangavaye-ve as an administrative district. But what do I care about the princes? I don't think it's the best possible form of government—and I am actively transforming it! His Radiancy has asked me to rewrite the structure of governance—come help me, Jiano! Help me show the rest of the world how it should be done!"

There was a pause. Aya smiled encouragingly at her husband. Cliopher felt a sharp pang of envy for the deep love and support, the casual way she held his hand, the fact that they were sitting there together to make the decision. He did not, however, glance at Ghilly. She had not chosen him—and he *had* chosen the life far away from Gorjo City.

Jiano sighed. "When do I have to decide by?"

"Ah," Cliopher said, a touch uncomfortably. "Today would be helpful."

"What? How can I possibly make this sort of decision in one day?"

"Will many days help?" Cliopher asked, reasonably he thought. "The problem is that his Radiancy has accepted Princess Oriana's resignation. I think what will happen is that during the regency ceremonies she will formally hand over her responsibilities, and they will be returned to you. Or whomever." He smiled wryly. "If you realize that you are incapable of swearing fealty to me, by the way, don't take the position."

Jiano made a face. "He wasn't joking when he said that you were his hands, was he?"

"It's one of my titles. I am the Hands of the Emperor."

"Who else would you ask? If I say no?"

"Please don't."

"That's not fair, Cliopher!" Aya said.

"I'm sorry to put pressure on you, but it's true. You are my choice. I have no good alternative, and if you say no I shall have to come up with someone this evening. It wouldn't really matter—it'll probably have to go to whoever is the next in the line after Lord Balo."

His Radiancy would probably not let him decentralize power to the extent of simply not appointing any successor to Princess Oriana at all, though Cliopher was fairly certain the Vangavaye-ve would be able to govern itself, as it had after the Fall, with very little difficulty. He did have some work still to do with the rest of the Council of Princes, of course.

"They—you—you would just skip over Lord Balo?"

"Lord Balo is incompetent, uninterested, foolish, and seriously lacking in political acumen. He gravely insulted me and mine last night, and did not even have the presence of mind to apologize when he discovered he had done so."

There was another little pause, then Jiano burst out, "I want to, but I can't help but thinking this is him *winning!*"

"Him being the Poz?" Cliopher said, picking his words with great care to shape the conversation. Surely Jiano would see how his bloodline gave him the door into the system, but that what he *did* with that opportunity was entirely up to him. Princess Oriana had played at being a princess; Jiano could be the most splendid and noteworthy prince the Vangavaye-ve had ever seen by taking the responsibility and transforming the position.

He smiled at the younger man, so full of the fire. The Delanis were a branch of the Nga family, whose dances were the Dances of Those Who Know the Way. Should he mention that? No; it would be best if Jiano came to that idea on his own. It would not take him long to learn how the ostentatiously courtly formalities of Cliopher's proclamations hid what was very essentially a commentary on the *Lays of the Wide Seas* in the practical form of a new government.

"Jiano, trust me, I cannot imagine any way in which your reign will be at all like your father's, unless you decide to go up on the Prince's Balcony and make rambling speeches in the third person while black-out drunk."

"I don't drink alcohol."

"A temperate communist from the Outer Ring, no less! Jiano, please, I have two years until I retire. At least figure out a way to get Vangavayen coffee beans traded as far as Solaara."

"Oh, in that case, Lord Mdang, I really must accept! I cannot have you faltering while his Radiancy is away due to inferior coffee. I could never live with myself."

CHAPTER SIXTY-EIGHT

"THIS HAS BEEN ONE OF the most enlightening days I have ever spent," Bertie said as they made their way out of the Young Malo and turned with one accord back towards their part of the city. "Thank you, Kip."

Cliopher glanced at him suspiciously. "Should I ask why?"

"You're the expert in unspoken conversations."

"Whereas you are a very forthright man, a quality I have always appreciated in you, Bertie. What do you mean?"

He didn't answer immediately, then spoke meditatively. "I think this is the problem. You used to be just as blunt."

Cliopher smiled ruefully. "Oh, I still say exactly what I think far too often."

"But your definition of 'blunt' has changed over the years," Ghilly said. "Don't you understand what Bertie means? For you, the conversations you've had—with the princess last night, with the Lord Emperor, with Aya and Jiano there—were clear and—and obvious. Weren't they?"

"Well, yes, but—"

"And when you lit into the department, we all thought you were jumping crazily to conclusions—but from half a paragraph in a letter and the signature, you were able to see that there were all those problems—and they were there, it was obvious you weren't just arbitrarily deciding—everything you said was grounded in fact and reality."

"Well, I would hardly—"

"And," she went on, "you probably think your letters are just as forthright and blunt as they used to be. But to us, reading them, they seem distant and opaque—or just bland courtesies and funny anecdotes. You've never presumed we would know all the people or places you write about, you always explain them—but you probably never thought that we wouldn't understand how *subtle* everything is, how much is unspoken but coded, expected to be understood from oblique hints."

He blinked at her. She went on, "You write, 'I have been very busy of late working on what must be done before the regency ceremonies commence', and expect us to understand—what? I'm guessing we should have realized you meant that you've been working ten- or twelve-hour days and are exhausted nearly to the point of physical collapse."

He almost laughed at the idea that it was a *twelve*-hour day that she thought long. "Ghilly ..."

"Kip, when you wrote to invite us to the regency ceremonies, you said, 'We have decided to conclude the regency ceremonies in the Vangavaye-ve. They are a spectacle well worth watching and I would be very pleased if you came to celebrate with me. You will get to see me in a particularly exciting outfit, at the least.'"

Cliopher had indeed thought that these were very clear invitations. He glanced uncertainly at Ghilly. "Wasn't that clear enough?"

"You might have explained that you are the central figure in the whole thing!"

"But you know I'm the Lord Chancellor."

"Nobody here has the slightest idea what it means for the Lord Emperor to set up someone as a viceroy. You have to *explain* these things, Kip. How else are we to know?"

"There are the official proclamations—"

"Why don't you *tell* us what you're doing?"

"Every time I've tried to tell you something you make fun of me for boasting."

"Oh," she said quietly, and there was a small pause.

They crossed a canal by means of a narrow bridge and turned into an even narrower alley on Ghilly's direction. They shortly debouched into a backwater lagoon Cliopher knew fairly well, though hitherto he'd always arrived from one of its other entrances. Not a dozen houses from the alley was the small, discreet store where he came to buy efela necklaces.

The proprietor was sitting on a bench outside, drinking something cool and watching a handful of little gulls bobbing on the lagoon in front of him. He glanced up as they approached; when he saw Cliopher he smiled broadly and stood to greet them.

"Sayo Kip! It's been a few years since you last graced my shop! I was half-afraid you'd taken your custom elsewhere, then I heard the news and realized how busy you must be. Congratulations!"

"Oh, thank you, Mardo," Cliopher replied, much taken aback.

"Please, come in—I have an efela I've been saving for you." He cast a curious regard across the others, lingering on Toucan and Rhodin. Rhodin made sense, as a *velio*, but Toucan?

Before Cliopher could marshal a question or a comment on that minor incongruity he found himself ushered into the store. The bell over the door jingled as his friends followed him, with what was clearly more than minor curiosity. Rhodin planted himself beside the door, though he was looking as much at the room as at the people.

The store was well worth the scrutiny. It was small, crowded with the half-dozen of them, the walls hung with woven mats and tapa cloth. Their colours were calm beiges and tans, their patterns subtle but complex and superbly made. They were well worth examining, but really were there as a backdrop for the many *efela* necklaces arrayed on them.

A row of waist-high cabinets lined the room, their drawers containing (as Cliopher knew from previous visits) many of the raw materials for the *efela*. Hundreds of types of shells, beads of bone and glass and coral, gemstones, pearls from many sources, feathers and seedpods, coiled lines made from everything from ahalo silk to sisal.

And on the walls, *efela* of every traditional style and status. Cliopher cast an eye across those closest to him, knowing that the further back in the room, the higher the status represented. He well remembered the day he had come in and asked to see one of the *efela* on the side wall for the first time.

Mardo bustled straight to the back wall where the central focal point held a princely necklace. Not that Princess Oriana would ever wear an efela. Jiano, on the other hand ... The merchant brought out a stepping-stool so he could lift it down from its hooks with great care, then beckoned Cliopher to come up to the display table in the centre of the room.

Cliopher slipped between Ghilly and Vinyë. He had the sense that the two women had given each other a meaningful look as he did so, but did not catch what the meaning was. He felt a brief stab of defiance. The fact that *they* chose to disregard his achievements outside the Ring didn't mean *he* had to, did it? He was sick and tired of pretending it didn't matter to him so as not to hurt their feelings. If his actions didn't match the picture they had built up of him ... well, was that entirely his fault? At court he sailed the route he had chosen regardless of everyone else's views of the matter, and so he had reached his destination.

He actually halted, hands on the edge of the display table, at that thought. He *had* reached his destination. Or very nearly. He was in sight of the

harbour, nearly at the dock. Two more years to go and the system of government he had imagined so long ago would finally be realized. The morning
his Radiancy had decided to make him Viceroy of Zunidh had been the first
sighting of the distant land after a lifetime at sea.

A cold shiver ran down his spine. He remembered too well that feeling,
the glory and the terror of it, when he had finally seen the Outer Ring after
those months, or years, or decades, or centuries, spent crossing the Wide Seas.
It had certainly been months between the last island and the Outer Ring,
months spent trusting that the stars and the sun and the traditional knowledge his Buru Tovo had given him would not let him down.

And so, a little later on, he had trusted the stars of his principles and the
guidance of the Sun-on-Earth and the traditional knowledge-turned-new
system of government to take him from the quiet foundational work of his
Radiancy's personal secretary to Viceroy of Zunidh.

Mardo spread out a length of imported silk in a sumptuous deep purple
and with ritual care laid out his chosen efela necklace. Cliopher was conscious of his friends' attention to both the necklace and his own reaction.
Toucan stood to his right; he was intent on the necklace, expression calculat-
ing. Of all their group, Toucan was the most traditional.

The efela consisted of a double loop of grand fultoni cowries separated
with white and gold pearls. The cowries were exceptionally well matched in
both colour and size, as were the pearls. Grand fultoni cowries were more
clearly marked than ordinary fultoni, the tan base a richer brown, the golden
ring a bit paler. They were nowhere near as brilliant as the gold-ringed amber, which reminded him that he kept forgetting to look up or ask what the
name of those were.

He smiled at the merchant, who seemed very pleased by their response.
"It's a beautiful efela, Mardo," he began.

"I have been keeping it for you," Mardo replied, gently straightening one
slight kink in the curve. "I feel a strong investment in your career's progress,
you know. Nothing like watching you gradually move from the front of the
store to the back over the years to make it clear what you've been doing with
yourself outside the Ring."

"Mm," he said, not quite wanting to catch anyone's eye. He was still
feeling far too defiant, unwilling to subordinate his own pride in his accomplishments to save his friends' face. He admired the efela a bit more, knowing
he would be taking it—it was indeed a perfectly appropriate marker for his
achievements over the past few years—knowing that Toucan, at least, and

probably Quintus, too, and Bertie for that matter—well—that they knew exactly what status this efela demonstrated. It had been displayed as the most valuable efela in the store, and it was.

"Thank you, Mardo," he said at last, not even pretending that he was unworthy of it. As Mardo smiled in satisfaction and began to roll the shells up in the silk, he added, "I had a question for you about an efela necklace I, ah, acquired out on the Eastern Ring when I was home last. The cowries were similar to these grand fultonis, but the base colour was a clear amber, and the gold ring much more—"

Mardo dropped the silk with suddenly clumsy hands. The efela made a soft ringing noise as a few shells hit the tabletop. "You—they—you—one moment."

Cliopher had not expected this response. He smiled at Ghilly's puzzled frown to indicate his own mystification. Toucan was frowning too, as was Bertie, while Quintus was staring at the grand fultoni efela with an expression hovering between smug satisfaction and total bemusement. It was an odd combination to see, though Cliopher was just about self-aware enough to admit he was feeling much the same at the moment.

The merchant had scurried into the back room, and now came out holding a small covered basket. It was of a very ancient design; Cliopher only knew enough to see that its central pattern was part of those used by the Walea family.

Mardo moved the fultoni cowrie efela away with nearly indifferent gestures and set the basket down in its place. He was breathing heavily, his hands trembling a little as he cradled the box between them. After a moment of silence he opened the lid. Nestled into a bed of cassowary down was a single gold-ringed amber cowrie.

"Yes," Cliopher said, "the efela is made of those."

"Plural?"

It took him a moment to grasp the question, since efela were always made with as many shells and beads as one could afford. He nodded solemnly. "Yes." Something more seemed necessary, so he added, a little bashfully—for this was a most respectable number for any efela—"Forty-nine."

Toucan emitted a low whistle. Mardo gaped at him. Cliopher was used to disconcerting people—the gods knew he did it often enough at court on purpose—but he had rarely done so with so very little intention. He wasn't sure what to do with the information that he had flabbergasted both the efela merchant and Toucan to this extent.

Mardo took a visibly deep breath through his nose. "My grandfather said ..." He shook his head to cut off the words, if not the thought. "What did you offer the, the one who gave it to you, that he gave you an efela of forty-nine sundrop cowries?"

"Is that what they're called?" Cliopher murmured, gazing at the one in the basket, hesitating to say the truth, here where people understood what it meant. The god of mystery had laughed, and Buru Tovo had laughed. He smiled self-deprecatingly, wanting to distance himself from the indisputable arrogance of the claim. "I might have said something about bringing a new fire from the House of the Sun."

"Might you have," Bertie muttered. Cliopher glanced sidelong at him, then back at the efela merchant, whose expression was more than a little awestruck.

Cliopher recognized the expression, of course; he had been his Radiancy's secretary far too long not to be able to identify all the many ways in which people expressed their awe at seeing the Sun-on-Earth. Mardo's slack jaw, dropped hands and shoulders, and slightly fixed stare was classic.

It was just that Cliopher was not sure he had ever seen that expression directed at *himself.*

He bowed his head, staring at the gold-ringed amber—the sundrop—cowrie in its nest of barbed cassowary down, not sure how to respond. At court there were forms to express awe and the respectful acceptance of it: he had seen his Radiancy use them often enough.

He *had* used them himself, he remembered now, in the first few weeks after the fire dance. None of the court or the secretariat had known what to make of a Lord Chancellor who not only could, but actually *did*, perform such a tribal ceremony right there in the throne room of the Palace of Stars. Their awe had been as much for his audacity as for the fire dance itself.

Mardo recollected himself with a great shudder that made the display table shake. Cliopher put out a hand to stabilize the grand fultoni efela. Mardo's hand moved a moment later, then dropped. "One thing," he said, and hastened to the back room again, every line of his back and the set of his shoulders proclaiming excitement.

Cliopher hazarded a mildly amused smile around to his friends, but received scowls and turned heads in return. He sighed, more loudly than he ought have, but could think of nothing to say that he had not already tried to say in a hundred different ways over the years. The defiance flickered in his breast, a young flame fanned by each snub.

Yes. That was what he felt: he felt *snubbed* by his family, for all their merry welcome.

This was why he had always come to the efela merchant alone, before. Mardo knew him in the context of what he was prepared to pay, in story and in coin, and had built up a picture of Cliopher in his mind's eye that was probably as fundamentally inaccurate as that of Cliopher's family, but at least did not leave Cliopher feeling that he had to hide and downplay every accomplishment.

He was not going to stand back, to hide, to downplay it all, not today. They had already seen that Mardo brought forth the grand fultoni efela; he had already had an afternoon of being carefully, kindly, cut down to size. Viceroy of Zunidh might not be an Islander title, a recognizable status in Islander terms, but—well—Cliopher had forced the good aristocrats of the world to witness an Islander dance not as an entertainment but as a solemn ceremony. He could make his family and friends witness a court ceremony for once.

Mardo returned with another ancient basket in his hands. This was larger, nearly a foot across, and as well made as the one holding the sundrop cowrie. Like that it showed Walea patterning. The Walea were Those who Held the Efela, and with the efela the knowledge of status and history and lineage that the shells and bones and beads displayed.

Cliopher was glad to see the merchant had more or less governed his face. Mardo's eyes were perhaps a little wild, his jaw a little set, his hands a little quivery. Cliopher's hands were trembling, too, though his expression had settled into his habitual court one, interested and unassuming.

Mardo spoke more to the basket than to him. "How close are you, then, with your fire?"

"I have entered in the Gates of the Sea. I see the harbour with the eyes of my body as well as the eyes of my heart." The formal words rose unbidden from deep within.

"You have always been one of the most traditional people to come here."

"I know the steps of my ancestors' dances."

"Yes," the merchant murmured. He put his thumbs to the lid of the basket, but did not yet lift it. "My father always thought you would be the one to earn this efela. He said that if you could hold yourself sane between the call of your island and the call of the sun over the sea you would bring a new song to the *Lays*."

It was Cliopher's turn to look down and away and bite his lip in embarrassment. Why was it so much easier to accept the courtly honours?

Oh, because he had years of playing those games, and because he had spent his childhood, his adolescence—hell, he still dreamed now—dreaming of doing something so glorious, so significant, so remarkable, that his people would feel compelled (no, not compelled: moved, honoured, *eager*) to add a new song to commemorate it. To be added to the *Lays* ... oh, that was to have his name made immortal.

Mardo said, "Every year, the pearl hunters of the Western Ring find three to five flame pearls amongst the rest. We, my family, the Walea, have a standing arrangement where we buy at least two. One of the two goes towards our tithe to the Lord Emperor. The other becomes part of the efela nai."

The merchant glanced around at the others, his gaze lingering first on Vinyë, then Toucan, then Rhodin. "Efela nai means 'the last efela'. If someone earns this one ..." He shrugged magnificently, taking a deep breath so his chest swelled. "Any further efela are gifts of the gods."

He opened the basket. Coiled inside, this time on a bed of ahalo silk threads—the iridescence was unmistakable—was a necklace of flame pearls. Each pearl was a deep ruddy gold marked with the brilliant white 'fire' that gave them their name.

"Each year we add one flame pearl to the efela nai. The learning of our family is that the one who comes for an efela after they have received one of the, ah, sundrop cowries is the one who has earned it."

He lifted the string of pearls. There were a lot more than Cliopher had expected, graded in size from smallest to largest to smallest again, in five ranks held in place by tortoiseshell clasps. Even amongst the Lord Emperor's regalia Cliopher had not seen quite such an array.

"The last person we gave the efela nai was Tuolayë of South Epalo," Mardo said, nodding at Toucan whose island that was. "She was a most gifted healer of animals and men. She received the sundrop cowries after she healed some ailment besetting the toll-keepers in the Gates of the Sea."

"Ey ana," Toucan breathed. "So my family stories say. There is an efela of three sundrop cowries and fifty-seven flame pearls that is an heirloom of my family. The efela's name is Tuolavenë."

Mardo inclined his head. "The efela nai are named in the songs." He turned back to Cliopher, who was standing, stunned, by a validation starker than he'd ever imagined. He did not want to be so set apart—

—But could he pretend to himself that he did not yearn for this? That he truly believed his achievements were unworthy of this?

Even *this*?

Forty-nine sundrop cowries had he been given, for the assertion that he would bring a new hearth-fire to the world. The beginning of the *Lays* told the coming of the first people and the bringing of the first hearth-fire, all the gifts of civilization from fire to law, to the Wide Seas. Dared he reach out his hand to accept *this*?

He couldn't resist any longer. He reached out to touch the efela, the pearls warm to his touch, smooth, shimmering, brilliant.

"Efela nai," he murmured, more to himself than the others. The last efela that he would ever come to buy; any others that might come to him would be bestowed as gifts or recognition.

"You do have efela ko, don't you?" Mardo asked, obviously wishing halfway through the sentence that he'd phrased it slightly differently.

Cliopher withdrew his hand from the efela nai and lifted the efela he always wore from beneath his robes. The dozen pearls and obsidian pendant were familiar and comforting under his fingers. There was no difference to the touch between pearl and flame pearl.

Someone grunted, but Mardo only nodded, pleased, and silently requested permission to look more closely. Cliopher lifted his chin as the merchant investigated with gentle fingers.

"Now ... if I may ask you ... how did you come by this efela?"

Rhodin was edging closer, evidently fascinated. Cliopher smiled at his aristocratic friend. "The efela ko is the first efela—the foundational one, you could say, the anchor."

He clasped the obsidian lightly. "My great-uncle, Buru Tovo of Loaloa, taught me; I was twelve that year. He had me make the efela ko myself."

"String the pearls and so on?" Rhodin asked.

Cliopher laughed. "No—well, yes, but that was the last step. I began with learning how to dive for the pearls. Not my favourite thing to do."

Oh, how hard the dream of following Buru Tovo had died.

"You like swimming."

"The molluscs that form the gold pearls are called nefalao. They're found along the edge of the Outer Ring reefs, in water between twenty and thirty feet deep. They're some sort of giant clam, about a yard across, with the most extraordinary blue eyes."

Rhodin blinked. "How do you bring them up from that deep? With nets?"

"You don't. You have to learn how to keep the nefalao from shutting and sealing themselves up, as they usually do in response to threats. Basically you have to stroke the shell in a certain way until it's calm, then you have to reach in and feel for a pearl without losing your hand."

"Or your arm, like Cousin Dola," Vinyë muttered.

"Or your arm," Cliopher agreed. He thought back to those diving lessons, the dim depths of water. Clear to many fathoms as it was, the nefalao were to be found hidden amongst the multitudes of corals and hosts of fish, in waters full of currents and cross-currents and the looming dark drop-off.

"So each pearl," Rhodin said slowly, eyes on the great efela nai, "is winkled out by hand by someone diving down ..."

"One in six or seven nefalao have a pearl of acceptable size. One in every thousand pearls might be marked with the flame."

"So these took you ... sixty or seventy dives?"

Cliopher laughed. "I wish! Try a hundred or more. Quite apart from finding the nefalao—each pearl hunter has his own section of reef, but it's still not easy to find the shells—then you find a pearl—and then to successfully bring the pearl to the surface is harder than you think. It's perilously easy to drop it along the way. And even then, once I had the pearl safely to shore, I had also to drill a hole for the line to string them. I shattered or otherwise ruined countless pearls and had to replace them."

And all the months he had persisted in learning the diving, for he had never been able to learn to love it, his Buru Tovo had sung him the *Lays* and taught him the ways of their ancestors and, one day when he had found Cliopher crying with frustration and grief that he was never going to be a pearl hunter, never going to take his place in his family that way, Buru Tovo had told him that there were more ways than one to find a flame pearl.

"What kind of drill did you use?" Mardo asked with professional curiosity.

"We were doing this the traditional way. A stone-tipped bow drill. Which I also had to make, for that matter, and repair, and start all over again when it turned out I'd not twisted sufficiently strong line ...That led to a whole long disquisition on making thread, and visits to the *fenà* to learn about cordage and thread so I wouldn't shame my lineage."

And no wonder he understood how a community was built, the many threads and lines and cords and cables that bound people together or apart. He might have consciously forgotten those lessons in the years he had done his best to assimilate, but the work he had been so committed to accomplishing was built on those foundations, anchored on the efela that never broke.

His hand went up to his efela again. "I did succeed in that, at any rate.

The thread binding the efela ko has never broken on me."

"I should think not," Mardo said, wide-eyed again, though Cliopher wasn't sure why in this case. "There's a chip or two out of the obsidian pendant ... ?"

"Shipwrecks," Cliopher replied succinctly, then relented at Mardo's expression. He still felt too defiant to look at Bertie or Vinyë and see theirs. "I've landed a time or two on atolls and needed to start at the beginning of things again."

"Have you ever had to sell one of the pearls?" Mardo asked intently.

"No, though there have been a few times when I came close."

He had been tempted, captured in the Grey Mountains; hungry in the coastal states; frightened by the pirates; bone-tired in the Central Massif of Jilkano.

He shook his head. "I suppose it was pride that kept me from selling any. That, and I really didn't want to have to replace any of the pearls. Diving was bad enough when I was twelve, and I knew after the first time that I was never going to be a pearl hunter as a profession. The thought of having to do it again gave eloquence to my tongue and courage to my heart."

Mardo regarded him gravely for long enough Cliopher nearly started to shift uncomfortably in response. He held himself still, however, thinking of the Council of Princes, of court tensions, of family arguments, of all the hundreds of ways he had hunted metaphorical pearls of great price so to avoid the literal search.

"One hundred and seventy-six flame pearls," Mardo said. "One hundred and seventy-six years since the last time the efela nai was given to anyone. What name will be given to this efela? What will we sing of you in the *Lays*?"

Cliopher took a deep breath, and then bowed solemnly, palm over fist. "When the lights went out in the House of the Sun it was I who re-lit the fire. I am Cliopher Mdang of Tahivoa. My island is Loaloa. My dances are *Aōteketētana*. I hold the fire that has been entrusted to me; I do not run from its burn."

"Forty-nine efe—sundrop cowries, and the city speaks only of your clothing and how once, long ago, it was hoped that you might bring glory back to the islands."

Cliopher smiled crookedly. "What shall I tell you? I cannot promise that you will live to see the return of the Paramount Chiefs, for that lies in the hands of the people and the gods. All I can say is that the flame that was given has not gone out, nor will it before I light a new fire."

"Ey ana," said Mardo, "the name of your fire will be a new song in the *Lays*."

★★★

WHEN THEY WENT OUTSIDE AGAIN, they walked for a few minutes in contemplative silence, Cliopher adjusting to the feel of the efela nai about his neck. Mardo had told him he had to wear it for the first day of its giving. He thought his friends were perhaps adjusting to the fact of the efela nai, having farther to go, perhaps, than he himself did. Though in point of fact his thoughts were carefully skirting any deeper consideration of its significance.

Vinyë said, "You're probably dressed down today, aren't you?"

Cliopher let out the breath he was holding in a kind of laughing sigh. "I might deliberately have dressed in one of my least fancy outfits this morning, yes."

They turned out of the back street into a small, leafy square around a central fresh-water pool filled with waterlilies. One of the houses facing them across the pool was faded and shabby-looking. Cliopher stopped as they came up to it. "That's a pity," he said, glad to start a new topic. "I always loved this house."

Bertie stopped to look at the facade. "It's not in too bad shape, all things considered, but it'd take a lot of money to fix it up again. I imagine they'll tear it down now the old lady's last relative is dead."

"Oh?"

"Yes, I heard about it a few weeks ago," he said. "I'm not sure who's inherited it—oh! There's your cousin—hoy, Melo! What can you tell us about this house?"

Melo was one of Cliopher's younger cousins. He had been crossing the square towards them and hastened forward. "Hiya Bertie, Vinyë, Ghilly, Quintus—Cousin Kip! That's a fantastic outfit."

Cliopher did not dare catch his sister's eye. "Thank you, Melo. Are you the agent for this house?"

"Yeah, much good as it'll do me. It's going to be a dreadful one to sell—I've just heard that it's been listed as of historic significance, since the architect was Onora, so it has to be sold to be renovated, not torn down." He frowned at the facade. "It's got good bones, but there's a lot of work to be done. The old lady who owned it hadn't done anything to it for about thirty years, and her heirs didn't even go in, best as I can tell."

Cliopher paused a moment, and then he said, "Can we see inside? I always loved this house. It used to have such beautiful window-boxes."

"I don't think window-boxes would make anyone buy it at the moment," Melo said dourly, but fished around in his pocket and pulled out a long brass key. "But certainly, if you want. Then I can pretend I've had a little bit of interest—though when my boss hears it's just my cousin Kip from Solaara in a fit of nostalgia, he'll be disappointed. Come on in—watch your head, the lintel's crooked."

He unlocked the door and ushered them into a crowded entry hall. "Someone at some point decided there needed to be a cupboard here and blocked off half the front hall. Onora's probably haunting him. As you can see, tired old painting, tired old woodwork, and a cracked floor. The back of the house is in a bit better condition."

He led them along, pointing at a couple of doorways and saying dismissively, "Store-rooms of one sort or another. The old lady was a pack-rat. It's taken us weeks to get most of the junk out, and there's still her collection of glass fishing floats to deal with. You'll see them upstairs."

The entry hall led into a set of broad rooms arranged around half the private courtyard and pool. "The other half of the courtyard was sold ages ago," Melo said, gesturing at the less distinguished buildings facing them. "This side has much the better view, though. Now, here's the kitchen—done up in the best Astandalan style, as you can see. The old lady was quite the stylist in her day—say, didn't you used to come ask her about Astandalas, Kip? I seem to remember hearing you did."

Cliopher was smiling at the memories conjured up by the room. "She used to give me tea and tell me about her time in the city," he said, going over to the bench where he had passed many happy hours. "She was mad as a hatter—she was a good practitioner of magic," he added to Rhodin, who was looking around the house with a degree of interest Cliopher found promising. "She'd gone to study at the Imperial College for a few years before coming home. She was always glad to talk to me about it ..."

"It's a good kitchen," Rhodin said, peering at the range. "Lots of countertops."

Melo grinned. "Are you a cook?"

"A dabbler, say."

"Then you'll appreciate this room," he said, going over to the next door and flinging it open to reveal a splendid pantry. The faint chill in the air proclaimed that the old lady's spells had not yet faded. "A cook's delight—or it would be, once cleaned up."

Rhodin made a face at the smell but went into the room to slide out drawers and racks and examine pegs and hooks and all sorts of intriguing little spaces. "Ingenious," he murmured, opening a cupboard door to reveal a dumb-waiter.

"The whole house is like this," Melo said. "Beautiful, ingenious, well-made, decades out of date, full of animal smells, shabby, and in dire need of repair. There are three large rooms and two suites on this floor, as well as the kitchen and the privy and a few nooks and crannies. The bath-house is that little building with the passionflower growing over it."

"Oh, what a delight," Vinyë said. "It's a miniature of the big house."

"One of Onora's specialties," Melo agreed. "I'm not sure what this room was for—I think it was possibly a dance studio at one point? The floor's reinforced, anyway, you can see it down in the undergirdings."

"Any problems with rising damp?" Cliopher asked, remembering Enya's comment about the building she was renovating.

"Cousin Kip, Gorjo City is built on water. There are always problems with rising damp. This house, the problem is that the old lady was a wizard and didn't like anyone else fiddling with her magic, but she couldn't keep it going at the end. It's stable now, but there will need to be some repairs and you'd need a really good wizard in to make sure everything's cleaned up and done proper. My boss brought in the staff wizard, who took one look at it and said the house was lovely but he'd be cursed if he tried to mess with it. Here's the staircase—outdoors, but there's a good awning over it, and the rain comes from in front of the house most of the time, anyway."

He clattered away upstairs. Rhodin was still looking at the spacious dance studio, so Cliopher let the others go up after Melo while he waited.

"What do you think?" he asked.

"I think it's just about big enough for practicing," Rhodin said, smiling. "Oh, do you mean the magic? I completely agree—but fortunately we happen to know a very good wizard who would be able to see to everything."

"Hélouzithe, hélouzanthe."

"Don't tell me you weren't thinking it."

"Oh, Kip!" his sister cried from upstairs. "Do come here!"

They climbed up the staircase, which was beautiful ironwork painted a pleasing clear blue. It was chipped in places and needed a few repairs to some of the more ornately curved prongs, but again had such an air of elegant homeliness that Cliopher found himself running an already-proprietary hand up the banister.

The view his sister had called him to see was that across the lagoon from the second floor. The upper floors projected across part of the courtyard to form a sheltered area down below and an airy sitting room reminiscent of the Kindraa Birdhouse in effect up above, but with an even more glorious vista.

Rhodin said, "Well now!" and promptly examined the deep window seats, the smoothly curving wood beams anchoring the wall, and the arched doorway that led into the dining room—the dumbwaiter here made a feature in a carved wall—and on the other side, three suites each containing a bedroom, a sitting room, a small office or reading room, and another small room or pair of rooms for children or clothing and other belongings.

"I like this style," Rhodin said. "I suppose it's meant for an extended family? You share the kitchen and main areas, but have your own private retreats. Very nice. There are three suites up here, and there were another two downstairs next to the studio ..."

"And then there's the glory of the house," Melo said grandly, opening another door to show a recessed staircase. "Come up here."

They followed him up obediently. The staircase was a narrow spiral and rather dark, which made the effect of the upper room all the more dramatic when they arrived.

The upper floor consisted of a large round room with a high ceiling and high windows. They had wide eaves and some sort of cooling system in place, so the room was filled with sunlight and fresh air and not at all hot. And hanging along the steam-bent beam that encircled the room were hundreds of glass floats twinkling and catching the light.

"Oh!" said Cliopher appreciatively.

"Oh indeed," said cousin Melo. "It's splendid, isn't it? Then you see that the birds have gotten in, and the floor is terribly scuffed, and the magic here is rather concentrated—I gather it was the old lady's workroom until she got too stiff to climb the stairs. But with a lot of work and a lot of money this house could be truly wonderful. And someone to deal with all the magic in the floats."

"How much are they asking for it, Melo?" Vinyë asked curiously, touching one of the glass floats. It knocked gently against its neighbour and sent up a tuneful chime.

"Three hundred and fifty thousand," Melo said glumly. "It's worth that for the location, of course, but it'll cost whoever buys it at least that over again to fix it up—and it'll all have to be done in accordance with those new laws on preserving historic buildings. I don't see why they needed to put all those rules in place."

"They were tearing down the old city of New Dair to build the most hideously ugly modern factories," Cliopher said abstractedly, walking to the other side of the room to see that there was a balcony encircling the tower. There were no other tall buildings nearby—no doubt another attraction to a wizard—and the views were of Mama Ituri on one side, the Son and the sky ship dock next over, then the city to the northern part of the Outer Ring, and finally the lagoon and the Bay of the Waters a darker blue behind it.

"What, so everyone has to go through all those hoops because of some idiots in New Dair?"

Out of the corner of his eye Cliopher saw Falbert was exchanging a meaningful glance with Toucan. "It seemed like a good idea to protect historically significant buildings for future generations."

"Of course it is, it's just that …" Melo laughed. "It's just when I'm stuck trying to sell an old lady's half-derelict pride and joy that it bugs me. Well, what do you say, Cousin Kip? Want to spend all your savings fixing it up so you can retire here?"

Cliopher turned to Rhodin, who was grinning. "What do you think?"

"I think that when you first broached the idea, you mentioned this house as being your ideal, and we all agreed that it sounded lovely—though probably we would have said that regardless of what it actually looked like, you were so excited about the mere thought."

"Tush!" Cliopher looked around at all the hanging glass spheres, still tinkling gently. "There's a studio with a reinforced floor for you and Ludvic to practice in, a kitchen for you, and all sorts of nooks and crannies for Conju to organize—I just want a room of my own—and then there's this room, which would be ideal for—"

Rhodin burst out laughing. "You cannot be serious!"

"You never know."

"Cliopher—Kip—he would never—you cannot even begin to think—"

"I think he would like it," Cliopher said firmly, "but even if I am wrong, I would prefer to have the place there to be rejected than not to offer it."

Rhodin breathed in sharply. "You do know him better than anyone else."

Cliopher shrugged, then turned back to Melo, was staring open-mouthed at him. "Well, Cousin Melo," he said pleasantly. "*May* I take your half-derelict building of historic significance off your hands for you? I am in fact looking for somewhere to retire to with some friends of mine from Solaara, and I have always loved this house."

"They must pay you well," Melo ventured.

"I'm happy with my wages. Do you think you could get the paperwork for me now? I should have time to go to the bank before it closes—unless they also keep island time?"

"Depends on the bank," Ghilly said.

"It's the Imperial Bank." At his sister's surprised look—for their family had always used the Island Cooperative—he added, "They're the only one with branches in both Solaara and here."

"I think they're open till four," Quintus said, going up to one of the windows. "Look, you can see my ship from here!"

"Are you serious, Kip? You really want to buy it?" Melo said.

Cliopher tried to suppress the little flare of annoyance that pricked him. "Yes," he said, with only a slight edge. "Though as I am going to be extremely busy with work for the rest of my time here, it would be much easier to get the paperwork dealt with today."

Melo gave him another astonished stare, then slowly, with many backwards looks and stops, proceeded towards the stairs.

Cliopher had a mild inspiration. "Perhaps you could leave us here to make a few notes about things that will have to be done? That way I can set them in train before I go."

"I'll be right back!" Melo said with sudden alacrity, and bounded off.

Ghilly laughed. "You've thrown him for a loop. Most people don't make decisions about houses anywhere near so quickly. Of course, most people have to consult the bank first."

"I don't make that much money," Cliopher replied, smiling, "but I also have few expenses, so my savings are quite adequate. What, Rhodin?"

"I'm just laughing at your 'few expenses', Kip. You must pay yourself well nowadays."

"I am paid ten percent more than Commander Omo, which is ten percent more than you, Rhodin."

Rhodin blinked at him. "There's no way you are maintaining a household of fifteen on that salary—let alone your clothes! That outfit alone would cost a quarter of your year's wages. The world appreciates your budgeting skills, but that's impossible."

Cliopher glanced at his sister, who was trying to maintain a blank face, and failing. "If I paid directly for my court costumes and household, I would have to have a yearly income in the region of seven hundred thousand valiants—which is considerably higher than I think seemly. Moreover, since the household and the costumes are requirements of my position, I decided that it would be far better for the money to attach to the position rather than the person. That way, if there is a Lord Chancellor to follow me, he or she does not need to be a great plutocrat in order to qualify. There is also accountability to the Treasury for how it is spent. It comes out of the Pomp and Circumstances line."

"Does his Radiancy know how little you're being paid?"

"His Radiancy and I have discussed it," Cliopher said loftily. "I set the salaries of the public service, so no one else was involved besides the Treasurer."

"That really doesn't seem—it's not as if I'm unhappy with my salary—"

"I am glad to hear it."

"—But neither Ludvic nor I work nearly so hard as you. You regularly work sixteen hours a day! Don't pretend you don't, I've seen your schedule."

"Things need to be done. And I do delegate, Rhodin—"

"It's just that your job hasn't exactly petered away while you've been taking up all of his Radiancy's work outside the magic—and you've been doing that review of the whole government—"

"And when his Radiancy leaves on his quest, we shall see how well the preparations we have been putting into place work. Come now, Rhodin, let us look at this house with proprietary eyes and see what needs to be fixed. I may not have Quintus' personal fortune—" and he grinned at his cousin, who looked nonplussed at this sudden address— "But I do think I have enough for some proper renovations."

"His Radiancy would give you the house if you asked him."

"His Radiancy would probably give me an island if I asked him, but that doesn't mean I'm going to."

Cliopher pulled out the small writing tablet and stylus from his writing kit and looked thoughtfully around the room. "I like these glass floats, don't you?"

"It sounds as if you think *he* would like them."

"Are you wizard enough to deal with the magic in them? Besides, he's going to need somewhere to put his books and fabric collection."

Rhodin looked at him. "What fabric collection?"

Cliopher scribbled notes about the floats and about the need for the windows to be cleaned, the walls washed, the trim polished, some of the woodwork fixed. "His private study is quite a bit smaller than this room, but as it is rather ... full ... I think—"

"I think you're edging rather far over the line, Cliopher."

Cliopher wrote, *Paint the stairwell white,* and raised his eyebrows over his writing kit at Rhodin. "I am not going to be the person who says, 'The four senior members of your household are planning on setting up a house in Gorjo City, but you're not invited.'"

"What if he wants to set up a house somewhere else?"

He shrugged. "What if the Moon comes down and asks him to be her lover again?"

He looked down at his tablet as he wrote, *Have the roof checked*, then looked up to see that the whole party was staring at him in befuddlement. He sighed. "What is it now?"

"You didn't sound as if that was a rhetorical question," Ghilly said.

"It wasn't," Cliopher said. "If none of you have anything useful to add up here, let's go back downstairs and contemplate the rooms down there. When we were on holiday on Lesuia that time, there happened to be a lunar eclipse. The islanders had a festival involving asking the Moon to grant their petitions. When it came to be his Radiancy's turn, she, er, replied in person."

Rhodin gave a great cackle of laughter as he followed him down the stairs. At the bottom, however, Bertie was scowling under his fierce eyebrows at him. Cliopher sighed again. "What is it, Bertie?"

"Leaving aside the question of the Moon Lady—"

"Albeit diverting—"

Ghilly snorted appreciatively. Falbert said, "Kip, you're … are you serious about retiring here?"

Cliopher made several notes about the more obvious problems in the main sitting room. "I may be less blunt than I used to be, but I do still tend to say what I mean. When I say, *I would like you to come*, I mean that I would like you to come. When I say, *I will be retiring in two years*, I mean that I will be retiring in two years. I do other people the courtesy of believing that they mean what they say, which is occasionally a mistake, but does have the effect of cutting through most of the folly of bureaucratic and courtly manoeuvring."

He glanced at Rhodin. "And when someone tells me that he would rather strangle himself with a curtain sash than spend the remainder of his life in a palace, I believe him!"

There was a brief pause, then Falbert said: "I've just realized you are talking about the Glorious One."

Cliopher opened his mouth, thought better of it, and walked through into the dining room, then into the suites.

He came to a halt in the farthest from the sitting room, at the great louvred-glass doors facing the square. He stood there, looking out at the water lilies in the central pool, watching people walk across. No one moving very fast, walking instead in the slow purposeless amble that was somehow emblematic of Gorjo City.

His hands were shaking again. He set down his writing kit on the display ledge running around half the room. Clenching his fists didn't really help, for he could feel the shivers running inwardly, the creaking anticipation and strain of the magic. It was hard to remember what it felt like without the stretched-string tautness. Even without the regency ceremonies it had been years since he had been fully relaxed.

Probably not since the last time he had been to the Vangavaye-ve, he thought, that trip that had changed everything. Not since he had been made the Lord Chancellor.

He took long slow deep breaths, as someone had shown him long ago—who was it, now? Not even a friend; just one of the other minor functionaries in the lower secretariat. A North Voonran mystic who had ended up working in the same department as Cliopher for a few months. He had seen Cliopher's focus, watched him with a sort of mysterious smile for a while, and one evening, when they were working late, he had come up to Cliopher and told him, with alarming intensity of gaze, that the spirits had spoken to him and instructed him to teach Cliopher the first stage of the mysteries.

To no avail had Cliopher refused, and finally he had acceded to the pressure, and learned the breathing ritual, and forgotten it for decades.

He breathed in, out, eyes on the wavelets in the lily pool. In, out, the white flowers each of them a blossom of joy. In, out, the gentle warm wind a herald of joy. In, out, the brilliant sunlight the flame of joy. In, out, the friendly shade the soft embrace of joy. In, out, his heart beating the heartbeat of joy. In, out, his lungs the bellows of the gods.

After a while, he felt his shoulders relax, his fists unclench, his muscles quivering as each let go the strain.

After a while, he felt ready to smile again at his family. He picked up his writing kit, turned, and saw them standing there in the doorway.

"Oh," he said, a little blankly.

Vinyë walked up to him, looked searchingly into his face, and then, while he was still not quite sure what she intended, she wriggled into his arms and wrapped hers around him.

They held each other for a long while. Cliopher tried not to weep, but his eyes were wet when she released him. He wiped his face, embarrassed, but laughing at the same time, for this was his family, his closest friends—bar the one he could not name—and they loved him.

His sister took his writing kit from him. He made an involuntary noise of protest. She laughed and handed it back to him. "No? I can't carry it?"

"You carry your cello yourself."

She stroked the worn, smooth wood of the case, still richly ruddy-golden, the grain beautiful under the nicks and dents. "And this is your instrument as much as the cello is mine? Where did it come from? You've had it a long time."

He turned it over in his hands so it was sitting right in the crook of his arm. "His Radiancy gave it to me on the first anniversary of my time as his secretary."

"A princely gift."

He smiled. "I'm the only secretary he's had who lasted a full year."

Ghilly smiled quizzically at him. "What, ever?"

"Eldo is just about there, but otherwise, yes." He took a deep breath. "I'm sorry that I have been touchy. I have been under a great deal of strain and I have found it—I—"

He stopped, took another deep breath. (In, out, the sea the incoming tide of joy.)

"I just wanted one person—I did not ask to be made Lord Chancellor, I did not ask to be made Viceroy. It is an incredible amount of work—I don't know if I can even begin to explain—and I don't mind—it has to be done—and I am good at it—but I suppose I wanted one of you to say you were proud of me … Every time I come home I am treated as if I'm a cross between a criminal who's been in jail, a long-term convalescent, and an exhibit in a travelling show. Sometimes you just ignore the fact that I live away, and other times …"

Ghilly looked at him. "Other times every single person you meet decides the most important thing is to make sure your head isn't swollen like a king coconut by your splendid new clothing—since no one realizes that you are, *in fact*, the second-most-important person in the world."

He smiled at the old familiar phrase. "You know, they don't say that in Solaara."

"What do they say?"

Rhodin cleared his throat. "Instead of that? 'Too big for his hat'. About Kip? That no doubt it's too much to expect a nobody from the Islands to understand the finer points of courtly display."

"I hope Jiano continues to wear Outer Ring finery." Cliopher did not want to think about the sudden shift in power in the Vangavaye-ve, however. He looked around the room, and smiled as he pulled out his pen and notebook from his writing kit again. "I do miss carrying this. I was firmly informed that it is below my dignity to carry it myself—but having sent Gaudy off with his Radiancy, I think I will enjoy the opportunity to do so."

Ghilly said, "Because Gaudy complains? Or his Radiancy?"

"Gaudy has the *honour* of carrying it—his Radiancy—well! His Radiancy takes a remarkably keen interest in my wardrobe. He and Féonie—she makes my costumes—have planned something special for this week. I live in some dread of what they've concocted. It will probably involve foamwork and ahalo cloth. The gods know what else. I did ask for some Islander patterns."

"It's very beautiful," Rhodin said.

"What, you've seen it?"

"His Radiancy was showing it off the other day."

Cliopher digested this for a moment, then shook his head in amusement. "If it gives him pleasure ... Shall we go down to the kitchen? I imagine there will be more notes to be made down there."

Falbert tugged his writing tablet out of his grip so he could peer at it, then scowled. "This is all in scribal shorthand."

"Of course it is," Ghilly said, smiling at Cliopher and holding the door for him to exit. "What else would you expect, Bertie?"

"I've just never seen his formal hand."

Cliopher thought of those boxes and boxes of correspondence in Bertie's office, and then a few small somethings his friends had said suddenly rose to mind, and he said, abruptly, as they returned to the upper sitting room: "What do you mean, no one realized that I'm the second-most-powerful person in the world?"

Everyone stopped to stare at him. Ghilly said, "Well, you didn't exactly explain in your letters, you know, Kip."

A few more small comments fell into place around him, almost forming a pattern. He said carefully, "Did you not understand the official proclamations?"

"What official proclamations?" Ghilly exchanged a sharp glance with Toucan. "From our counterparts in the mundial ministries, do you mean? They just make announcements about new grants and regulations and so on."

"I mean ..." He cleared his throat, not at all sure he wanted to verbalize what he was starting to suspect. "I mean, the official proclamations from the

Private Offices each quarter about what's going on with the mundial government as a whole. The last one would have been about his Radiancy's quest. The one before that about the Viceroyship."

"Um, I don't think those reached here."

Cliopher fumbled with his writing kit. "I think I have the final drafts of the last six or so in here ..."

He opened the latch, rifled through the papers, grateful for the little enchantment that let him keep more in there than seemed possible. Focused on that rather than the rising anger and disbelief that Princess Oriana had so thoroughly failed in her duties—had she truly just not made the announcements?—and shame that he had missed so crucial a piece of information—had he truly never understood his family didn't know—and a strange emotion behind that anger and disbelief that he could not yet identify, except that it was embroiled in his family.

He found the folder of final versions of the proclamations he drafted so carefully. Writing them, he always imagined his family being the ones to read them; imagined them standing outside the town hall listening to some official from the princess' court reading out the proclamation; tried always to live up to their imagined responses, which were often very harsh and sarcastic, perhaps increasingly so as the years went on and the letters he did receive ignored the vast majority of what he was doing, what he had accomplished, what he *was*.

Bertie gently took the folder from his hands and opened it to reveal the drafts. They were written in the common script so that any ambiguities in the Chancery hand could be resolved before publication. They often had a few notes from Kiri giving him notification of when they would be published and when his final notes were due to her.

Bertie read the proclamation about the Viceroyship out loud, his voice faltering in a couple of places. Looking at his face, at all their faces, Cliopher realized how totally wrong he had been about all those imagined responses.

"Oh, Kip," Vinyë whispered, "and no one said *anything*!"

Cliopher sat down in the window-seat, heedless of the dust, and—while his long-held views of his family disintegrated inside him—laughed and laughed and laughed.

CHAPTER SIXTY-NINE

HE RECOVERED HIS POISE EVENTUALLY, tucking away his anger at Princess Oriana for when he could do some good with it, but looked up to find that his friends were now disturbed and shocked and dismayed in their turn.

"Oh Kip, oh Kip, oh Kip," Vinyë said, turning over the proclamation about the Viceroyship. "And we all just—just—and you didn't say *anything!*"

Toucan was frowning at the proclamation about the creation of a Charter of Rights and Freedoms—an idea Cliopher had learned from his embassy to Ysthar and which he had (with some effort) managed to persuade the princes to accept in principle, and which he was making the central core of his new system of governance. Toucan said, "You really thought my response to this was to *ignore* it?"

Ghilly was looking at something he didn't immediately recognize from his position. Her eyes were shuttered, angry; possibly at him (and what he had assumed of them), possibly at the situation. "You never ... you always ... you thought we just ignored all of this?"

She reached into her bilum and pulled out the letters she had read to him yesterday—his invitation to her and Toucan to come to the ceremonies.

How much effort he had put into them to make it seem as if he was not boasting, to make them light and unofficial and to show by that very lack of formality how very much his friends meant to him.

She set the papers next to each other: the official proclamation with all its grandeur and pomp, and the little casual invitation he had intended as a demonstration that he was, despite it all, *their* Kip.

How bitterly he had resented their lack of response he could see now that it was lifting.

"You thought we had read this," she said flatly, pointing to the proclamation. "And so you sent us *this*—" pointing to the invitation—"and very carefully did not belabour the point about how important it was, how immense an honour it was for us to be invited, how much it meant to you that you organized the entire sequence of ceremonies so the final installation would happen here where we could all come."

Toucan was still reading through the proclamations. "You really thought we just ignored these? That we cared so little for the outer world that we never asked you about them? That we cared so little about you? That all we could think to say was local gossip?"

Bertie said, voice a deep rumble, "And yet you kept writing. And coming."

Cliopher looked at him. "Well, sometimes I appreciate not having to talk politics. And ..." His heart was singing, he felt so light, so—so relieved—he smiled brilliantly at them, as all those years of ruefulness fell away, as he could assign the blame of all that insularity he had resented so much to the right person. "It seemed of a piece with how you always react. I admit I've found your insularity baffling, but you've never asked me very much about the outside world."

"You never want to *tell* us much about the outside world," Ghilly said sharply.

"Every time I've tried to tell you something you take it as me drifting farther away from you."

"Whereas it appears—" Bertie sighed gustily. "It appears that you thought we knew all the official news and therefore didn't usually repeat it in your letters, and when we mentioned nothing of the official news but could only speak of the bits and pieces you did tell us, you read that as us being un-interested in the outer world, and so in response you wrote still less about anything of substance."

"Whereas for you ...?"

Toucan said, "Whereas for us we scour your letters for any news. Do you have any idea how often we get asked, 'Oh, have you heard from Kip Mdang recently? Any news from Solaara? What's going on in the world?'"

Ghilly and Bertie both rolled their eyes and laughed, at what was ob-viously something that had happened frequently enough to be funny, then tiresome, then astonishing, then funny again, and now had settled into a beloved sort of joke.

Cliopher felt his understanding of the Vangavaye-ve shifting, coming into a new pattern. "Why didn't you *ask* me?"

Bertie snorted. "Ask you what?"

"Anything! Why is it that every time I do try to say something you squash it? Why do you think I don't talk about my life—you've never expressed an

interest in it! I always feel that you think it's inappropriate or somehow—"
He tried to come up with the word. "Like it's rude. Uncouth. As if me men-
tioning the rest of the world, what I do, is distasteful. I always feel that if I talk
about anything other than what's happening in the Vangavaye-ve or the life
you wish I'd led that I'm hurting your feelings."

They looked at him. Ghilly said, voice stifled, "And you didn't want to
hurt our feelings."

He clasped his hands against the trembling. "No. Of course not."

Vinyë said, "You were so cool about Gaudy ..."

"Every letter you wrote to me was *come home, come home, come home.* How
could I possibly show how happy I was to have Gaudy want to follow me?"

"He wrote—when he first went into your department, I mean—he
wrote to say how your deputy gave them a little talk about working for you."

"Oh?" Cliopher wondered what Kiri had said.

"Gaudy said she said that the most important things to know about you
were that you were the most efficient man in the Service and probably the
smartest and that your holidays were sacrosanct. That no matter what else
was happening, you never let it interfere with your going home. That you'd
refused all sorts of appointments because they would keep you away."

Cliopher smiled wryly. "Ambassadorial appointments. Embassies are all
right—they're only for a few months at a time. Ambassadors go for years."

Quintus said, "You were asked to be an ambassador?"

"Oh, his Radiancy has offered me several appointments—Ysthar, Colhélhé, Voonra, Alinor several times." He considered a moment. "I wanted to
go to Alinor—I thought I'd be able to see if Basil—if I could find any news of
Basil—but that was when you were so ill that time, Vinyë, and I couldn't ..."

"You never said ..." She halted the instinctive protest, met his gaze soberly. "We never asked."

He smiled forgivingly. "Will you forgive me for thinking you astonishingly insular? I never have understood how you could be so—so—so uninterested!"

"Because we weren't, in fact," Ghilly said sadly, leafing through the proclamations again.

"Your holidays are sacrosanct?" Bertie said.

Cliopher smiled at him. "Well, the ones home are. The little holidays I
get—a few days here or there around festivals—they often get swallowed up
in things."

"You don't often write about your holidays," Bertie said, ignoring this, following one of his own trains of thought. "You write about going to the Liaau for hiking, but those always sound like going up to the Reserve, not *away*."

"It's usually an overnight trip to the Liaau, because dawn and sunset there are magnificent. Otherwise, I come here, and ever since my lord granted me use of the sky ship, it's not as if there's much to say about the travelling portion. As you have mocked me for I do usually work then! And for the rest of my holidays I am here, which you know about, so naturally I don't write."

"All of them? All of your holidays, I mean."

Cliopher raised his eyebrows at him. "Yes. Every holiday longer than a week I have put towards coming home. Where else would I go? And if I don't leave the Palace, the holidays usually disappear in unexpected urgent tasks. Which you saw, Vinyë, when you came to visit …"

"Every holiday?" Vinyë said slowly. "You have come home for *every* holiday? Since when?"

"Since the Fall," he said simply. "It was too far from Astandalas, so I went to see Basil instead. That was only a week's journey, back then."

"Every holiday you have ever had you have come home for."

"Last night, when you got muddled answering about when you were going home …" Ghilly said. "We thought you were just a little drunk, but …"

Cliopher did not fully comprehend what she meant (for he had, after all, been more than a little drunk), but Rhodin said diffidently, "I have never heard Cliopher refer to anywhere but the Vangavaye-ve as home. Never."

"Well, of course not," he said. "I am a Wide Sea Islander. You know where you are by where you have come from."

"But you *left*," Vinyë said.

"Are we not descended from people who crossed and re-crossed the Wide Seas looking for new islands? And have I not always come back?"

"But—" Vinyë stopped, frowning.

They all looked at each other. Rhodin was smiling slightly. The guard stood a little apart, holding his spear, watching, as he watched so many other interactions without participating. He had seen Cliopher in all the various developments of his professional life … and as his friend, also in his personal life. Rhodin had sat there asking questions when he had told Buru Tovo and his Radiancy of his journey across the Wide Seas. On that occasion Cliopher had not been able to express the reception he had found when he walked up the familiar streets and canals of the city with the *efani* shell in his hand.

He wanted something to anchor his stories. He looked around aimlessly, at the empty room, half-imagining it full of his own belongings, his few treasures. Then he remembered whose house it had been, and he said, "Come down with me."

He led them back into the kitchen. It was still a cheerful and beautiful room, though it was lacking all the details of life, of living, that had been on display when he had last been in it. He took a breath. How often had he wanted them to give him the space, the encouragement, the time, the attention? He could not squander it when it finally came.

"I used to help Saya Dorn—the old woman who lived here, Rhodin—carry parcels back from the market, that kind of thing. One day the rain came just as we were finishing, so she invited me in for tea while we waited for the storm to pass. That was when I found out she had been to Astandalas."

He ran his hand on the curved wooden back of the bench along the wall where he had spent so many eager hours sitting. "I was thirteen or fourteen, I think, when we first started talking about her travels. I just liked hearing the stories—I was always interested in how they did things in other places, like Bertie always was interested in how people used to do things in the past. The idea of Astandalas, the Golden City, the city of the Emperors—it was magical. But it never really occurred to me to go there, or to try to go there. I don't think anyone ever thought of going."

He went over to the tiny door that hid Saya Dorn's shrine. He opened it and found what he expected, the little board painted with a copy of the first state portrait of the Emperor Artorin Damara. He extracted it carefully.

"I was twenty-one when his Radiancy came to the throne. I remember coming to visit Saya Dorn not long after we heard the news. She had just received a parcel from a friend in Astandalas, which included this portrait."

He showed it to Rhodin, who said, "That's a copy of the portrait in his study."

Cliopher smiled at Bertie and Ghilly. "I sat facing the original for many, many years." He looked down at the picture, which was a fairly good copy. In it his Radiancy looked young—so young—and regal, magnificent, not quite human.

"The first time I saw this picture I felt—" He stopped, considered his words. "I felt a sudden impulse, almost as if someone had called my name. I knew from that moment that my life was somehow connected to the new Emperor's, that whatever I did, I was being ... summoned, I guess, to his service." He brushed his fingers lightly across the painted image, thinking of holding his Radiancy through the protection of the swath of violet cloth, thinking of sitting next to him on the sandbar, the breakwater, the table in his own apartments, nearly equal.

"I don't quite recall how I came to think of the Service as my way to fulfil that vocation. I suppose I'd thought of public service already. I was finishing my studies and was starting to look for work as an accountant. I had learned I was never going to make it as a pearl hunter!"

"What did you study?" Rhodin asked.

"History and statistics. I asked around, and eventually persuaded someone at the Imperial Consul's office to send off for the set books and arrange for the exams. It took months for everything to come, and with it an incredibly patronizing letter from the Regional Director of Western Zunidh, who informed me that I was the only applicant from the entire region of the Wide Seas."

"The only one?"

"Apparently there was one other person the third year I applied, but she didn't get in, either, and didn't keep trying. I did. I annoyed the Regional Director—I still have her letter somewhere—"

"It sounds as if it still makes you annoyed."

"Well—" Cliopher laughed ruefully. "I suppose I have a very different philosophy of bureaucratic service. I think it is much better to have as wide a range of people involved in government as possible. What does someone from an upper-middle-class family in New Dair know about conditions in far northwestern Mgunai?"

"Fortunately you are in the position to make a difference in that regard."

"To a certain degree of resistance from the old bureaucratic families. Anyway, I kept annoying the Regional Director, for of course the law did require her to provide me with the facilities to take the exams—but she had to send someone out to Gorjo City specially to monitor me—and then I kept failing."

Rhodin shook his head in bemusement. "That fact still astonishes me. You are easily the greatest public servant I have ever encountered, and it took you five tries to pass the exams?"

"Part of the problem was that there are expectations encoded into the exams—and those expectations, biases you could say, were set by people in Astandalas the Golden for people like them, also in Astandalas the Golden, or in the central provinces at best. There were all sorts of assumptions that were never explained in the set books—also written in the central provinces—because as far as they knew, they were perfectly obvious. Cultural biases."

He sighed. "I failed on the Etiquette sections not because I messed up the ones that were explicitly defined, but because there were all sorts of underlying ideas that I had never come across. The Vangavaye-ve is a society where elders, especially elder women, are always to be deferred to. The assumption that it is the father who is the head of the household tripped me up several times in a row. One of the questions was something about who had precedence in a complicated scenario involving a widowed duchess and the new duke and his duchess, who was herself a princess from some other region—I don't remember all the details. But of course, here the widowed duchess, as the eldest woman, would take precedence regardless of social rank. Not in Astandalas."

"Ah," said Rhodin. "But eventually you did pass."

"That was a surprise to everyone," Bertie said.

Cliopher grimaced at the memory. "I was so worried about what everyone would say."

"For passing?"

"You have to understand, Rhodin, the Vangavaye-ve was not like one of the central provinces. There was no one else from the Vangavaye-ve in the entirety of the Imperial Service when I got in. I found out later there was an admiral from Jilkano."

Rhodin blinked at him. "How many are there in the Service now?"

"From here? Two, Gaudy and me. Other *wontok*, Wide Sea Islanders? Captain Diogen and a handful of his crew in the sky ship fleet, and there are three naval officers and about a dozen crew members, and four or five others from the Islands taken as a whole."

Ghilly shuddered. Cliopher smiled, a little puzzled; she said, "I hadn't realized how alone you were. Are."

"I do have friends," he replied, though that was not the same. It occurred to him, not for the first time, that his generally avuncular attitude to those under him in the Service might be a result of his longing for the wide-spreading family he had left behind. He turned back to Rhodin.

"So when I got in, I was in a position much like Zaoul of the Tkinele, the first one of my people, of my country, of my entire province of the Empire—which was the whole of the Wide Seas, including what's now Jilkano and Nijan—to come to anyone's attention. We're not cannibals here, but we might as well have been as far as anyone knew what a Wide Sea Islander would be like."

"What did you think Astandalas would be like?"

Cliopher sank down against the table, looking at the icon he held. "I thought it would be gloriously beautiful, majestic, full of people. I thought it would be splendid."

"And did you find it so?"

He paused a moment, for he had fought so hard to go that he had never admitted to anyone (except once to his Radiancy, and yesterday to Aunt Oura) just how hard it had been. Then he smiled ruefully.

"It took me six months of travel to get there. Four months across the Wide Seas to Kavanor, another month and a half across eastern Kavanduru to Redtown, two weeks from Redtown across the Border to Ysthar and eventually to Astandalas. I had never gone past the Outer Ring before I set out on the trading ship.

"By the time I reached the city I was exhausted by novelty and the total estrangement—Rhodin, you have seen what Gorjo City is like! I cannot walk down the street without meeting someone I know. If anything happens here, chances are more than good that some relation is within shouting distance. I had never been anywhere where I was a stranger and all were strangers to me. The eagerness to get there kept me through the journey, but when I finally got there and encountered the disinterest and corruption of the Palace Service ...

"I had fought so hard and for so long to get there that I could not admit ..." He smiled at his friends, his family. "I wrote about all the wonderful things I saw, which were true, and the things I was learning, which were also true, and tried my best to hide how lonely and difficult it was. I was certainly not willing to admit that I had been wrong, that they were all right, that my place was here."

He made a gesture around the room, the city beyond its walls, the family and friends who had told him to come home in every letter. None of them said anything. After a moment he went on:

"I did not dislike my actual work, but the people—his Radiancy had inherited a deeply corrupt government, and although he was making reforms, he had begun with the court and army, and the changes had not yet trickled down into the secretariat. It was full of petty martinets and bullies, bribery and cronyism were rampant, and since I had no patrons, no family, no money, no name—since I was, in short, no one—I was treated accordingly."

Rhodin frowned, knowing better than the others what that meant. Vinyë said hotly, "You're not *no one!*"

Cliopher smiled. "No. I am Cliopher Mdang of Tahivoa, a Wide Sea

Islander, a descendant of the Wayfinders, whom the Astandalans called the Seafarers. Until quite recently, that meant nothing to anyone in power."

"And that is why his Radiancy gave you a title," Toucan said, jerking a little in realization.

Cliopher inclined his head. "Yes. Back then ... All I wanted was to serve the Emperor and help the Empire to be a better place, and in Astandalas the Golden I saw the—the disgusting underbelly of all the glory. My first year I spent reading the reports that came in from the provincial secretariat of the Ministry of Health and Illness. I was supposed to synthesize them and see what patterns there might be, which I did, even after I discovered that my superior was just stacking them in a pile in his office."

"What, literally stacking them?" Ghilly said.

"Yes. He called me and another new secretary in one day for the six-monthly review and showed me the stacks we had made. Mine was about four feet taller than the other secretary's."

"What did he do then?"

"He promoted the other secretary. Then he told me to take my stack and shorten it."

"And you did." It was not a question, not from Ghilly.

"I did. I read all my reports and saw how my writing had improved over the six months, and I looked for patterns, and I found them—researched how agricultural practices affect nutritional content of food and how that in turn affects health—researched air quality, effects of Schooled magic on newly conquered populations versus established provinces, anything I could think of."

"All those letters," Toucan murmured. He'd been studying law at the time, and he and Cliopher had begun the long correspondence comparing the ancient Islander practices with Astandalan forms of governance and discussing—in letters that Cliopher had taken very seriously, and Toucan, it seemed, had always thought purely hypothetical—how one might create a new form of government built from the Islander but applicable to the many cultures and requirements of the wider Empire.

Both of them would have to go back over their letters, Cliopher thought, to see how they had managed to write across each other all those years. He feared it was his own fault; he habitually wrote in hypotheticals, often humorous ones, so that no one could accuse him—should his letters go astray—of conspiracy to overthrow the government.

"I condensed all that stack into a document, and took it into my superior, who laughed in my face that I had not just thrown out the reports. Later on I discovered he had passed off my report as his own. He was given a major promotion and a minor title on its basis, but because I was not enough of a bootlicker he did not take me with him."

"Oh, Kip," Vinyë murmured.

Cliopher smiled at her. "But at least I did learn all that—and when I was transferred to the Ministry of Trade after that, I was able to take what I had learned and—well, I still wasn't very good at fawning sycophancy."

"You're still not," Rhodin pointed out.

"True. Fortunately his Radiancy does not demand it of me."

"I am interested in seeing how you react during the next two years."

Cliopher made a face and returned to the older, cooler discomfort. "I had learned to keep my mouth shut—most of the time—and so I did not make quite so many people quite so angry in the Ministry of Trade. I did keep getting passed around from sub-department to sub-department, however, as no one much liked the fact that I was far more efficient and interested in the work than they were. The Department of the Common Weal under Cousin Hillen has nothing on the Astandalan Secretariat. But eventually I did land in a department whose director was almost as, er, idealistic as me, and I began to feel that I was going to be able to do something worth doing."

"I remember you writing about that," Bertie said, brows jutting out fiercely as he considered. Cliopher had a sudden memory of the much younger Bertie waxing passionate in argument with him, eyebrows moving dramatically as he threw his whole body into the debate—and he thought that if Bertie had held the enthusiastically responding Kip of those arguments in his heart all these years, it was perhaps no wonder that he found polished and politic Cliopher Lord Mdang flat and empty and disappointing.

If he had not seen or heard the proclamations, he would not know what Cliopher's light allusions to the many battles fought in the halls and chambers of the Palace meant.

Cliopher was humbled at the realization that Bertie had never ceased encouraging him to not give in, to keep fighting the good fight, to keep holding the fire. Cliopher had never quite given up on his friendship with Bertie, the hope that they could again be what they once were to each other—but neither had Bertie given up on Cliopher. Kip.

"About the same time I started to make a few friends, and Basil and Dimiter came to visit, and I was happier than I had been since I left home. Then my director had some sort of accident and broke her back, and was replaced by a horrible bully who took an immediate and virulent dislike to me. Mind you, it was reciprocal. I put my head down and tried my best not to make trouble, but I have never been able to keep silent about things I care about, and ... well ... after a few months under the new director, I started to think that perhaps I had made my point and that it was time to figure out how to go home."

Rhodin nodded slowly. "I can see that. Did you feel you had fulfilled your vocation?"

"I had forgotten about my vocation. I was just being stubborn."

Ghilly tried to muffle a laugh, but Bertie made a great harrumphing noise of agreement. Cliopher grinned at him. "I do see it, you know. At that point—I had never seen the Emperor except at one of the open courts, and that was from such a distance I could not see anything but a gleaming golden figure on the throne."

Such a difference from how he saw him now: Tor with his absurdly over-stuffed private study, the Sun-on-Earth to whom the Moon listened, Lord Artorin enjoying Dora's babbling and Eidora's song, the friend with a secret name whom Cliopher dared imagine might come home to the Vangavaye-ve with him.

"I felt as if there was so very much wrong with Astandalas, and there was no way—I was trying so hard to make my small part better, but—I kept thinking about how the Province of the Wide Seas had never come up in my reports on health problems. It did come up very occasionally in the Trade reports, though all of Zunidh was subsumed under the Damaran holdings and the Wide Seas produced nothing except pearls, foamwork, ahalo cloth, and a couple of things from Jilkano that anyone was trading outside the province. But those did come up, sometimes, and I thought of Aunt Leonora working away at the foamwork, and our cousins diving for pearls, and it made me feel that maybe we were part of the Empire, and perhaps that I should go home and find another path to live."

"You sound as if you had given up."

Cliopher looked at Rhodin. "I had. Inside myself. I felt I had tried, and failed, to make a difference in the wider Empire. Then the person I thought was becoming a friend decided to drop me, and one evening when I was sitting planning my route home and trying to pretend that I had not wanted to go to any of the parties, anyway, there came the Fall."

Rhodin looked down.

Cliopher looked down, too, at the icon in his hands. He spoke quietly.

"Every person in my department but me was lost. Every person in my wing of the Palace but for three of us was lost. I woke up after the Fall and could not tell, at first, if I were dreaming or awake. The first time I opened the door of my room the halls were all completely dark—"

His voice faltered as the memories, which he kept quite firmly suppressed, rose up. "The second time it was daylight, but all the normal magic was gone, and it was dead quiet. I went out towards the cafeterias, through empty halls, through a palace that looked exactly as it had, but felt completely alien.

"I got to the cafeterias and there were a handful of other people there, all as scared and confused as I was. We eventually decided that we were not all dreaming, that some terrible calamity had happened. One of the survivors was a cook in the kitchens, and he made food for us. I was the only person who knew how to light a fire without magic, because Buru Tovo had shown me that, too, when he took me off to Loaloa after my father died. That was the first, and for a while the only, useful thing I did."

"You lit the first fire in the Palace after the Fall," Rhodin said. "And kept it going after."

Cliopher smiled wryly at this echo of his proud words to Lord Lior, the last time he had so thoroughly lost his temper. The rumours of that argument had run the Palace round three times before sunset.

"After we had eaten we felt braver, and I volunteered to go to the central block and see whether I could find any news. I went with another person, a page, who knew where to expect to find people. All through the Palace it was the same: everything looking right, and nothing feeling it. And empty, empty, empty. We went to the throne room, and … it was before they laid the Emperor there. Most of those who survived the Fall were in there, I think. Perhaps five or six hundred people, out of a Palace that usually houses five thousand."

"Five *thousand* people live in the Palace?" Ghilly said, at the same time as Vinyë said, "Five *hundred*?"

"I was there," Rhodin said thoughtfully. "But of course I didn't know you then."

"Nor I you. I'm sure I just thought of you as one of the young nobles of the court, if I saw you at all. And yes, five thousand people live in the Palace—well, at the moment there are three thousand seven hundred and twenty-three permanent residents, and then another eight hundred or so transients at any given time, and there are perhaps four hundred more rooms that are available for special congresses or the like. More during court and fewer in the spur weeks."

"I like how you know exactly how many people live there now."

"One of my duties is to oversee the Palace budget."

"I hadn't realized how few people survived in the Palace," Toucan said. "I had always thought that—I don't know—I suppose I thought it was just people in the city."

Rhodin said, "It was the Silverheart festival, and most people were down in the city at various parties, including one hosted by the Prince of Katharmoon that was supposed to be the crowning bash of the season, and which was attended by pretty much every noble in the Palace apart from a handful, such as myself, who couldn't go."

"The Princess Indrogan was one of those who had not, I gather because she personally disliked the Prince of Katharmoon. She was in the throne room, trying to organize people to find out what people knew. I liked the fact that she was doing something, so I went up to her and started to help, and, well, one thing led to another and when the Princess started putting together the new government, she hired me as one of her junior secretaries."

"That was when you wrote me that letter," Bertie said. "The one we were reading yesterday."

He shook his head. "No. That one came much later, the day the Emperor awoke. I did write to you—I wrote to you all—I wrote letter after letter. And every time I could I would scour the Palace, Solaara, the villages roundabout, and see if anyone was going west. No one ever was, so I started sending them with people who were going anywhere, asked them to pass it along to the next traveller they met. They just disappeared, those letters."

"Except for that one that had all the additions," Vinyë said. "The first—the only—letter we got from you after the Fall."

"That was the first one I wrote. Perhaps there was some good magic in the air when I wrote it, although at the time it seemed more of a curse. It kept coming back to me. A week later, three weeks later, four months, five years. And all the time as I waited for it to come back, or for you to write back to me, I worked on the reports of the state of affairs."

He swallowed, remembering that period. "We eventually figured out we were on Zunidh, in Solaara. Lady Jivane had not been in the Palace during the Fall, she had been home visiting her family. She came to the source of the magical disruption, found the Palace and the sleeping Emperor, took control, and set Princess Indrogan to the slow restoration of government. My job as the under-secretary was to read and condense the reports that started to trickle in from the rest of the world."

"You sound as if it was difficult."

"The people around Solaara rallied around the Palace, and there were stores of food in the lower levels that had come with it. We weren't starving. Lady Jivane was not the greatest of magi, but she was able to keep the worst of the effects from us. A good portion of the Guard had been in the Palace, so we were not faced with unrest and violence. But what I was reading ... Kavanor, all of Eastern Kavanduru, had fallen into the sea. Southern Dair was in the middle of a famine and had dissolved into anarchy. Northern Dair had been mostly destroyed by a volcanic eruption and country-wide lava flows. Western Dair was in the grips of a drought. Mgunai was flooding. Jilkano had been swamped by a tsunami. And from further west—nothing. Nothing. Every day I went to my desk, hoping, fearing, for something from the Vangavaye-ve. But there was nothing from west of Jilkano, or east of Amboloyo. From all the Wide Seas there was complete silence."

He swallowed again, had to pause while he regained control of his voice. Looked once around his friends, his family, could not sustain eye contact.

"I knew Eastern Kavanduru had fallen into the sea. I read the reports. And after a time, I read the reports that the natural and magical disasters had turned into anarchy, warfare, plague, famine. The only parts of the world that were not fully anarchical were the immediate area around Solaara—but not the Fens, nor the Grey Mountains—western Kavanduru, which has become Old Damara, and Xiputl. Order and good government were held there by the wills of Princess Anastasiya in Xiputl and the Grand Duchess of Damara and by Lady Jivane.

"I wrote letters that disappeared into the silence. I asked everyone who came to Solaara from anywhere if they had heard anything of the Wide Seas. I heard a few rumours of storms and monsters, but nothing certain. One of the reports from Jilkano said that anyone who went west disappeared. They had not even heard from Nijan, but they reckoned the tsunami would have swamped them, too.

"That one letter came back. Time was mixed up from the Fall, and I had no idea—reports came of strange jumps in time, people saying that it had been years in one place, months in another, barely minutes in a third. Everyone thought I was crazy, and I suppose I was, but I—I had no idea—so many people lost everything and everyone in the Fall—Rhodin, you did— Conju did—the thought that my family might have survived tormented me with hope. I kept thinking, what if there was famine, war, disaster—what if Mama Ituri had erupted—what if the gods threw the Outer Ring into the sea—what if, what if, what if."

"Kip," said Vinyë, but he shook his head to stay her while he said his piece.

"And then, one strange day, the Lord Emperor awoke. Everyone rejoiced, though we knew that there was still a vast amount of work to do to restore order—but we had hope at last, hope that we could restore order, that we were not just waiting to die. We started to prepare full reports for the Lord Emperor, and I was even busier for a while.

"Practically everyone in Solaara knew me as the crazy man trying to get news of the Vangavaye-ve. This didn't help my career any, but it did mean that when Captain Figar made it past the fens and asked the Emperor leave to go west, she was told by numerous people that I had a letter for her. I did; I had that original letter, and I had one I had written to Bertie about the waking of the Emperor—that was the one you read yesterday, Bertie."

"How many letters did you write?" Ghilly asked.

Cliopher laughed wearily. "I have no idea. Dozens. I lost count somewhere above fifty. Every week ... not that I found someone willing to take them every week, but whenever I did I had letters for him. And apart from that one that kept returning ... silence. Still no news of the Vangavaye-ve, still no news of the Wide Seas. Captain Figar was from Jilkano, but her family had come to the Vangavaye-ve for a visit just before the Fall, and she wanted to find them."

He paused, rubbing his thumb down the edge of the icon. It was easier to say it this time. He had told Buru Tovo ... and he had danced the fire ... and he had claimed this house for himself. "I should have gone with her. But I was very busy with what seemed important work, and Princess Indrogan did not want me to go, and I was frightened ... frightened of losing my position, frightened of what I might find, frightened of the silence. I was weak. I let myself be persuaded to stay. It is the greatest regret of my life."

"Kip—"

He smiled with difficulty at Vinyë. "As soon as I saw her sail head off down the Dwahaii I regretted not going with her. I counted out the days, weeks, months it would take her to get there ... the days, weeks, months for someone who wanted to come back ... and ... silence. Nothing. I was not even sure if she had made it past the fens. But the letter did not come back, and did not come back, and did not come back, and ... and finally one day I could bear the silence no longer, and I went to Princess Indrogan and resigned."

"You resigned?" Ghilly said, her voice sharp.

Cliopher did not look at her. He kept his eyes on the icon. He spoke softly, mildly, as if he were in the Council of Princes. "Of course I resigned. I was coming home, after all. You know what happened next."

"You've never told us your side of it, Kip," said Vinyë, reaching out to lay her hands on his. He looked at her for a long moment, and finally, finally, she said: "Please, tell us your story."

"It is a long tale of the sea," he murmured, causing Toucan to say, "And here we thought you'd abandoned all the old ways."

"You've never asked me about that, either," Cliopher replied, then relented. "It ebbs and flows sometimes, how much I have wanted, how much I have been able, to keep the old ways. But ever since I became Lord Chancellor I have made sure to keep the dances."

And Toucan said, "Will you tell us why?"

CHAPTER SEVENTY

HE LOOKED AT HIS SISTER. "I left Solaara. I went south through the Plains, across the Grey Mountains. I walked to the port of Csiven. I found people sailing to the Yenga—at Do Alouak I transferred onto another ship, pirates, who took me to the coast of Jilkano. I walked across Jilkano to the City of Emeralds. I persuaded a merchant from Nijan to sail with me to Zangoraville. And in Zangoraville under the guidance of a *wontok* who had studied the old ways I built a boat and sailed across the Wide Seas. And when I arrived you never asked me how I got here."

"Kip …"

"Grandmother was on her death-bed. Everyone, including me, was much taken up by that, by the ceremonies and the grieving and everything that went with it. And afterwards …"

Bertie made his harrumphing noise again. "You told us the news from half the world, and we didn't realize that it was because you'd pushed yourself through it all. We assumed it was all gleaned from other travellers."

"No, I was the first conduit of news from Solaara to the Wide Seas after the Fall." Cliopher shook his head. "And after all that journey, when I arrived in Gorjo City—ready for any disaster—I found—I found it exactly the way I remembered it. I was ready for anything, I thought, except …"

He sighed, looking out the kitchen window at the courtyard.

"I walked up from the docks, going home, and I kept seeing people I knew—and ducking away from them. I didn't know what to say. I saw you, Quintus, and hid in a doorway. I think I got all the way home before I spoke to anyone. It was so surreal … *nothing* was different. Nothing. It wasn't like the Palace, which looked right but felt wrong. It wasn't like all those places I'd gone through, smashed like eggshells, the people trying to rebuild. It was … the same. But I was different."

"You hid in a doorway rather than talk to me?" Quintus said in astonishment.

"I have to admit I'm glad you didn't actually see me. I've wondered for years if you were just being polite about it."

"Kip, you must know that I could never be that polite."

He was not sure he wanted to describe that first homecoming, but he looked at them, and he said, slowly, feeling out the thought as he said it. "Coming home was so much more difficult than I thought it would be. You barely realized that Astandalas had fallen, and apart from the fact that no traders were coming or going, life had not changed. The trade goods had almost always been luxuries, anyway, and not ones you really went for. You had my one letter, and what news Captain Figar had brought. And then … me. And I had changed."

"As we made sure to point out," Ghilly said in a low voice. "Just as everyone today has been sure to point out that you have fancy clothing on. Just in case you hadn't noticed."

"I was self-aware enough to realize that hiding from Quintus was not exactly my normal behaviour, but I had also just spent quite a long time travelling alone and in occasionally hostile places, so at the time I rationalized it, saying to myself that once I was accustomed to everyone again it wouldn't be a problem. And I suppose that was right. I've never actively hidden from anyone since then."

"Despite occasional provocation," Quintus said.

Cliopher smiled. "There have certainly been occasions I was strongly tempted. That first time … it took me a long time to work up the nerve to go to the door. I was so afraid …"

"Afraid of what?" Vinyë asked.

He looked at her soberly. "I think I was much more badly hurt by the Fall than I realized. I should have gone to a priest or a shaman for help. But I didn't see it—"

"And we had no idea how bad it had been for you. We didn't see it, either. We should have seen that you were … injured, hurt in your soul. But all we saw was that you had come home with what we thought were all those city ways."

"I had never felt so much of an Islander as I did coming home that time. I had sailed across the Wide Seas using the fire dance and the *Lays* as my guide! … Every letter you wrote to me in Astandalas you said, *Come home. Give up on this nonsense and come home. It's not too late for you to get a good position here—come home. Come home.* And when at last I did …"

He found he was not, after all, able to speak the depths. They were silent while he struggled with finding words. He gripped the icon with shaking hands. "We went out one day, Ghilly, you and I, to climb Mama Ituri's Son. We got to the top of the mountain and we sat there looking out over the Bay of the Waters to the Outer Ring, and ..."

He did not say, *And I asked you to marry me, and you said no.*

He said, "You told me I was too ambitious to be happy in Gorjo City, that I had set out after foreign stars, that I would never be able to be satisfied. That you—" he made a gesture to encompass more than just her— "That you, that none of you, that you did not deserve to always come second."

He swallowed. "I had come so far, with one thought in my mind. All I wanted was to know you were alive. I was prepared for the Vangavaye-ve to be in disarray like everywhere else, and I thought, I have been working with those seeking to restore order to the world, I can contribute something. I can help. Even if my family were—"

He faltered on saying the thought. "Even if the worst had happened, I would be able to do something, I thought, something useful. I had learned things worth knowing in Astandalas, in Solaara, on my journey home. I thought there would be a place."

There was a long silence. He could feel tears burning in his eyes. He looked at the icon, the smiling regal face of his lord, divinely serene and benevolent. Icon of a god whose heart was human, whose mind was still his own.

"Instead I—everywhere I turned I was rejected. No one wanted more than the surface of what was going on. No one wanted to hear any of my stories. No one wanted me to be as I was then. They wanted the Kip they remembered, who was smart and happy and full of ideas and enthusiasm. The one who was *whole*.

"Everywhere I went I met with rebuffs. Do you wonder why I've never talked about this? No one asked me what that journey was like. I said, 'The rest of the world has dissolved into anarchy and disaster,' and you said, 'Oh, how sad,' and never thought what that actually *meant*, what it had been like to go through it. You knew I was alive, from the letter Captain Figar brought for me, and I supposed that you didn't care more than that."

"Kip ..."

"Vinyë, do you remember when Mama Ituri exploded and killed Princess Aluria and her court?" He gestured towards the mountain, the scar of the lava flow through the jungle.

"That was awful," she said, frowning at the memory. "So much destruction and death."

"That was one mountain. One village. One party. And you didn't even know any of them! It took you years to stop writing about it to me as this terrible disaster—and to stop complaining about how cold and unemotional I had been in responding to it. My lord sent me to the Vangavaye-ve to restore order so that I could see with my own eyes that you were fine, because he knew how deeply concerned I was."

Concerned. Such a dry word. A courtly word.

"You *were* fine, and so my responsibility was to make sure the government was working even in the absence of the Princess and her court, and then to go find the next in line and inform her of her ascendancy. When I came after the Fall, the whole world was like that. Everywhere. Except here."

She met his gaze, then looked down, troubled.

It was hard to go on. "I had every intention of staying here when I came back after the Fall. It never even occurred to me that I might go back to Solaara. And if there hadn't been a pile of things all happening at the same time, I wouldn't have. If that ship hadn't narrowly avoided shipwreck and made it inside the Ring, and if I hadn't met the captain in Solaara, and if she hadn't offered me a berth because I had more recent knowledge of the Wide Seas—if I hadn't felt so comprehensively *alone*—all that time in Astandalas, in Solaara, I had consoled myself with the thought that I had a family, I had friends, who loved me—"

"We did! We *do* ..."

He smiled tremulously at Ghilly. "I know you did. Do. I knew it then, too, but I also knew—or thought I did—because you had all told me as much, that I no longer fit in. All those letters begging me to come home, and when I did, I was told over and over again that I was not the Kip you remembered, whom you wanted, who I was supposed to be. What was I supposed to do? Stay and be miserable, and have nothing to do? Or go and be miserable, and at least hope I could do something useful, help others. But I wouldn't have gone if that ship hadn't come."

"But it did."

"It did."

He was quiet for a moment, looking at the icon, thinking of his Radiancy. Somewhere inside of him was a truth he had never acknowledged, struggling to come out. Finally he said, very quietly, "I'm glad it did."

"You are?" said Vinyë, her voice troubled, but not as upset as Cliopher would have expected.

He glanced up at her, then down at his hands again. "I ... I am. I told my lord, a while ago, that I thought you had never forgiven me for leaving. None of you—especially not Mama. She sang the *Lament of Ani* when I left ... do you think that has not echoed in my heart all these years? But my lord said, in response, he asked me if I had ever forgiven myself."

He made himself look up, meet their eyes: Vinyë, Ghilly, Toucan, Bertie, Quintus, Rhodin. "I never have. I always ask myself what is wrong with me, that I am not content—that I have never been content—with the things I love most. Why is my heart called in two directions?

"When he asked me if I would take on what became the Lord Chancellorship, if I had said no he would have let me retire. He would not keep me if I did not want to stay. You ... I ..."

He stopped, took a few deep breaths, tried again. "If I had stayed then, when I came home after the Fall, when I felt rejected, I ... I think I would have lost myself for good. I don't think I would be sitting here today. I think I would have spiralled into ... I don't know. I am not given to lashing out. Probably I would have done something self-destructive and stupid."

"Oh, no, Kip," said Ghilly.

Cliopher said, "Ghilly, you made the right decision that day. I always thought it was the right one for you. It took me longer to accept that it was the right one for me, too." He smiled at Toucan, who was looking stunned. "I wasn't the person who had left to go to Astandalas, full of dreams and fire to change the world. I had come back changed, in ways I understood and ways I never did. Still don't.

"If I had stayed then I would have hated myself for giving up. I have always been proud of the fact that I have never compromised my principles. I suppose letting people mispronounce my name probably looks like compromise, but to be honest that has never seemed a very important thing. What does it matter what people call me when they are giving me the ability to shape the government of the world? But if I had stayed then I would have thought I was doing the right thing. All the externalities were right, were what I wanted ... but all the interior was wrong."

"We didn't see," Vinyë said. "We didn't ask."

"And I didn't tell you. I didn't show you. I didn't demand you ask me. You're right to be angry that I didn't—right to be angry that I never called you on being insular or for being so snooty about my accomplishments in the rest of the world—right to be angry that I have never said, *listen to me*. But I didn't want to be that person! I have worked so hard to govern my temper, control my tongue, to listen to people. I don't want to be the person who was so obnoxious and rude and mean. I didn't *like* that about myself."

"But we didn't want you to extinguish the fire!" Ghilly said.

Vinyë nodded. "You're so bloody *attentive*. You come home and sit and listen and smile and listen and we all just *wait* for you to say something— *anything*—of what you're thinking, and then you say something practical and useful and impervious and we—and we are disappointed. You never stand up for yourself. You never share."

Cliopher stared at her. "What?"

Vinyë took one of his hands in hers, leaving him to hold the icon in the other. "Kip, we don't want you to be mean, but we miss the wit, the energy, the fire. Everyone hates seeing *you* so *diligent*."

Cliopher blinked. Rhodin smothered a laugh. Finally Cliopher said, "But I like hearing all the family news and local gossip. I like sitting there with the aunts and uncles. I like feeling part of the family. I like the fact that no one is asking me to solve all their most urgent crises. It's so restful. I love the fact I can come home and be part of something good, that doesn't need me to fix things, or change them, or devise some sort of clever way to undo the knots of mismanagement and misgovernment and stupidity."

He sighed. "Although that was probably foolish of me, to think that nothing of the sort was going on here. I missed Hillen's corruption, and I missed Princess Oriana's ... folly. I thought she was only incompetent, not that she was actively working against good government. I'm sorry for that. I should have caught it—and I would have, if I hadn't been so caught up in my emotions. I catch it other places! Notwithstanding Cousin Louya's allegations, I am not actually bad at my job." He smiled. "I'm very good at it, actually."

They were staring at him with mixed expressions. He did not know how to keep going, what else to say. Had he cleared away enough of the old fears, the old hurts? Was this what it felt like, to be purified in heart as he had been in body and magic and spirit by the rituals?

Quintus said, "If what it takes is simply to ask, will you please tell us how you went from being here after the Fall to being his Radiancy's right hand man?"

Cliopher smiled slowly. "If you're sure you want to know? No. I know. That ship came. The captain had been sent by the Emperor to circumnavigate the world and report back. She had one of my letters, which she'd carried safely halfway around the world for me. She'd gone east from Solaara, along the Xiputl Arm to Amboloyo, through the New Sea where eastern Kavanduru had been destroyed, island-hopping to the Vangavaye-ve. So I went back with her, back across the Wide Seas, to Nijan and the City of Emeralds, and then down around the Cape of Snows at the bottom of Southern Dair and back up the coast to the Dwahaii and at last, back to Solaara."

"That was quite the sail," Quintus said.

"I suppose it was, but I was so unhappy that—I didn't care, you know. All the way out I had been guided by my heart, and going back ... the heart had gone out of me. If we'd gone down in a storm I would have just ... Well, we didn't go down. We made it back to Solaara. I wrote up my reports for the captain to present to her superiors, and I went to Princess Indrogan.

"She had been made the Minister in Chief—basically my position now—and she was a busy woman. She remembered her promise, but she didn't—I had missed all the good positions, and she did not appreciate that I had gone against her will to leave. She was willing to put in a word for me with the Master of Offices, but nothing more. And I ..." He sighed again. "I was deeply unhappy, and although I wanted to bury myself in work, I was—I was reckless and simply didn't care the way I needed to to make it out of the lower secretariat.

"I have never been good at toadying, but in that period I was fundamentally incapable of even being moderately politic. The Master of Offices did not much like Princess Indrogan. She was too powerful for him to refuse her request for him to find me a place—but I was nobody. I don't think he disliked me personally, or at least not more than he disliked everybody, but he deliberately set me up to fail so that the Princess would lose face. I was no help—I knew what was happening, but I didn't care. I think at some level I felt unworthy of success. I would say to myself that if I was so ambitious, I should do this or that to get ahead—but I hated—I just couldn't do it."

Ghilly said, "I had no idea you had taken my words so to heart."

He looked at her. "Did you not?"

She flushed slightly. Toucan frowned at him and took her hand in his. Cliopher said carefully, "You were right, though not, perhaps, in the way you intended. I did leave, that first time. I was so sure of my vocation, so sure of myself, so sure that going to Astandalas was what I should do. And even though that first time home was both the best and the worst time of my life—for you were alive—but—but I *did* go back to Solaara. I didn't fight your words and prove them wrong. I left again instead. I could have stayed to make my life here—but I did not."

They looked at each other for a few moments, the others very quiet. And who knew, Cliopher thought, whether by staying he would have won her hand (for it had been several years after that before she had written to tell him that she and Toucan had started seeing each other)—and whether he would have been happy, in the end, to stay, to marry, to have children, to have some sort of job that he would now have retired from, to have the life that everyone had wanted him to have.

The world would have been different if he had chosen that path.

And he could not quite help but think that if he had stayed, that one day he would have gone out swimming and not come back.

"I went back," he said quietly. "And I am glad I did, though at first it seemed like the worst mistake of my life. The Master of Offices decided to use me to destroy Princess Indrogan's reputation, and I played right into his hands by being unable to keep my mouth shut. Finally the Princess told me that she would give me one more chance before washing her hands of me, and in retaliation the Master of Offices assigned me to trial as his Radiancy's secretary."

He looked down at the icon, shifted its position so he could rub the smooth edge of the writing kit below it. "It was a very great honour, but that was not why I was being sent to the Imperial Apartments, and I knew it. I had been in the Service long enough by that point to know that the position of his Radiancy's secretary was considered the most onerous and most difficult of any. He himself was persnickety, particular, exceptionally demanding, the work was of the highest importance, and to crown it all he was a living god and there were so many rules of etiquette and religion surrounding him that more than one of his former secretaries had been executed for breaking the capital ones. He had gone through eight secretaries in the six months before I was assigned to him. I was terrified."

Vinyë said, "But he doesn't seem …"

Cliopher laughed outright at her puzzled expression. "Not now, no. But back then—remember, I had only seen him on a handful of occasions, all of them of the very highest degree of formality and ceremony. I had never been within a hundred feet of the Presence. I had failed to succeed in any of *my* last eight positions, and my patron was about to drop me. I had failed the Etiquette portion of the exams five times. I got everyone's back up by making inopportune jokes or being too intense or too angry or too self-righteous. Or too smart. Sometimes that was the problem. I wasn't very good at hiding the fact that I was more intelligent than most of my superiors."

Rhodin snorted. "You do know people call you the smartest man in the Palace?"

"Fools." Cliopher shook his head. "The Palace is designed to show off the Emperor. Every single element in it has the purpose of showing the might, the majesty, the authority, the greatness, the power, the divinity of the Sun-on-Earth. When you come to the Imperial Apartments there are seven anterooms, each of them more sumptuous and impressively appointed than the last, each of them with facing pairs of stern guards in full panoply. Don't snort again, Rhodin, I know you spend a great deal of time making sure you look appropriately fierce."

"Parno is going to have fun," Bertie said.

"He is, I expect. That first time I entered the Apartments I was shaking with fear—and awe. Terrified as I was, knowing as I did that I was expected to fail, I was still very much alive to the honour—and I remember I kept thinking, as I walked through those anterooms, I kept thinking that even if this was it, at least I would go home having once personally served the Lord Emperor. And at the time it all seemed worth it.

"I arrived at last in the Lord's Study, and there in person was the Sun-on-Earth. I made my bows—I had stayed up half the night practicing—and was told to set up my pens and things at the secretary's desk. I did, trying not to show how relieved I was that I had managed to get through the obeisances safely—"

Ghilly said, "Was that a real concern?"

"The secretary two before me had been fired before making it to the desk."

"*Very* persnickety."

"Knowing his Radiancy as I do now, I would imagine something else had happened to annoy him, but at the time all anyone in the Service had heard was that his Radiancy had rejected him during his obeisances."

"I can see where the terror comes in," Toucan said.

"So there I was, sitting at the secretary's desk, and we started in on the day's work. After an hour or so I started to calm down, and a while after that, when I realized I did know what I was doing—I was—I'm not sure how to phrase it, but—I was still expecting that I would do something wrong, and be sent packing, and that I would be going home for good—and at the same time I felt this, this rightness of being there. I felt oddly calm, and for the first time, almost, since I had left home the first time, I felt happy about what I was doing."

"Oh, Kip," Vinyë said, her voice breaking.

Cliopher said hastily, "I wasn't miserable the whole time. But I wasn't happy, either. Until that moment, when I sat there facing the Sun-on-Earth and taking down his words—his words! I was ten feet away—"

"On average," Rhodin said.

Cliopher laughed. "True. His Radiancy paces when he dictates," he added to the others.

"And you were happy."

"I was. It took me a while to realize that I was, which sounds … anyway, I sat there thinking about how amazing this was, that I was there, in that room, scribing the words of the Emperor of Astandalas. Then I started to—it wasn't that my mind was wandering, but I wanted to savour the experience. I very consciously tried to impress on my mind everything, the sound of his voice, the scents in the room, the feel of the air, the beauty of his garments. Then we were interrupted by one of the household staff bringing refreshments for his Radiancy, and he bade them bring me something, and I thought my heart would burst with wonder."

"That was unusual in those days," Rhodin said. "He must have liked you from the beginning."

"I had no idea. I thanked him—and realized afterwards that I had not responded properly according to the ceremonies, I had just said thank you the way one does. By the time I realized that, however, it was too long afterwards to recover, and I sat there thinking that I really was awful at courtly etiquette."

"What happened then?" Ghilly asked. "For obviously you did impress him."

He smiled down at the icon. "We went back to work. At the end of the day, as I was gathering up my papers, his Radiancy said something—I wish I could remember his exact words, but I don't. Whatever he said, though, was a perfect set-up for a joke, and I … I was feeling so happy, and so happy that I felt happy, if that makes sense, that I didn't stop to think, I just said the joke. Which was a good joke, but, er, not really one I should have been making to the Sun-on-Earth."

"And what did he do?"

"He capped it. Just flung the joke back at me—you remember how we used to have those punning matches, Bertie? Like that. It was magnificent—and so unexpected—I responded naturally. I laughed, and I looked him right in the eyes and I said, 'Oh, splendid!'"

He stopped, remembering the shock of the lion's gaze, the shock *in* the lion's gaze, the shock of magic and broken taboos and happiness shrivelling up under pure horror.

"And then?" Ghilly asked.

"And then I made the full formal obeisance and went home and I wrote a letter to Basil, and I put all my things in order, and I waited for the summons to the Executioners' Block to come. I stayed up all night, trying to pray, and I thought of seeing that portrait of the Emperor ..."

He looked down at his hands. "This portrait. This very one. Here, in this room. I remembered my sense of vocation, that somehow my fate was entwined with Emperor Artorin's. I sat there that night and thought that indeed it was, that my fate was to die for the impertinence of making a joke to the Emperor and then crowning impropriety with sacrilege and petty treason."

"But clearly that didn't happen."

Cliopher found a smile tugging at his mouth as he lifted his gaze from the icon to Ghilly's frown. "No, it didn't. After one of the longest nights of my life I went in the morning to the Master of Offices, who was exceptionally sour and bad-tempered. Not because I was disgraced—but because I wasn't. The message had come down from the Tower that his Radiancy wished me to continue as his secretary. So I went, very humble and subdued, grateful almost to the point of being able to fawn for his clemency. It didn't occur to me until many years later that he had appointed me because of that incident, not in spite of it."

Bertie harrumphed. "Which he had, obviously. It must have been as great a surprise to him that you would say that to him as it was to you."

"He told me once that I was the first person after his ascendancy who looked at him as if he were a human being." Cliopher saw Rhodin's flicker of amused outrage, and he shook himself. "And here I am, wandering into areas I shouldn't really be talking about."

Rhodin said, "I do not believe that anyone would ever think for a moment that you feel anything but the greatest love and respect for his Radiancy."

Cliopher decided to ignore that topic. He smiled at his family, his friends, who all looked troubled. "Thank you for listening to me."

"You've held all that inside you for so long," Vinyë said.

He reached out and took her hand. "I feel much relieved for having spoken. I have been going through these ceremonial purifications, and perhaps before the regency ceremonies finish this week I needed to cleanse my heart, as well. Vinyë, I know you love me, and I know you know I love you. I have never doubted that. Even when I felt rejected I did not feel *abandoned*. I knew that if I came back again I would face all the teasing and comments again— but I also knew that my room was waiting for me."

She smiled wanly at him. Rhodin said, "Are you sure you want to buy a house?"

Cliopher turned to him. "Don't you start, Rhodin. Yes. I want a place that is my own. Which is not much of a Vangavayen idea, but it's true. And to be honest, I have lived away for my entire adult life. When I come home for a visit, I am not—I am not working here, I am not doing anything but visiting my family and my friends. I am not trying to build a new life. So it doesn't much matter that in my mother's house I take up my old position, as the youngest child of the matriarch, the one who's perhaps a little strange and has odd ideas and dresses a little peculiarly ... Come to think of it, I'm basically our generation's Uncle Odo."

Vinyë said hotly, "Kip!"

But Ghilly and Bertie were laughing, and Toucan was having a very suspicious coughing fit. Rhodin said, "I can see why you perhaps do not, er, relish being a junior member of a household."

"A *very* junior member," Cliopher agreed, grinning. "I haven't done any of the things that increase one's status. I'm not married, I don't have any children, I don't actually have any sort of respectable adult position. Even the fire dance was done in Solaara."

"But you're the—"

"Oh, but that doesn't matter in the context of my social status *here*. As I'm sure you've gathered from today's interactions. I am not dressed appropriately for that."

Rhodin said, "I will never understand the happily middle-class."

"This is an Islander thing," Bertie said, and when Rhodin looked quizzically at him, began to explain the societal structure of the Vangavaye-ve from an anthropological perspective.

Cliopher carefully cleaned out the interior of the shrine, which was dusty, and put the icon back in. He closed the door and stood back to find Ghilly beside him.

"Do you worship him?" she asked curiously.

He glanced sidelong at her. "It would certainly be considered blasphemous for me to say I don't."

"But Kip ..."

He smiled, but was saved from answering by the reappearance of his cousin Melo with the paperwork.

CHAPTER SEVENTY-ONE

THE FIRST THING MELO DID was to anxiously question Cliopher about his intentions. "Are you sure, Kip? You're not just buying this to help me out, are you? I don't want you to feel obligated."

Cliopher looked at him for a moment, touched. "Thank you for worrying about that, Melo, but you don't need to. On my last visit home I had already decided to start looking for a house the next time I was back, but things have been so busy in Solaara I haven't had the opportunity for a holiday until now. Then here you are, agent for a house I have always loved! It is quite fortuitous."

"Well, if you're sure …"

"I am. May I have the documents?"

"Do you want me to go through them with you? I know this is your first house purchase, I can explain the law—"

Rhodin made a convulsive noise and hastily turned away to look out the window. Melo looked uncertainly after him. "Is he all right?"

"Yes," Cliopher said firmly, taking the papers. "I think I should be fine understanding the documents, but if I have any questions after I've read them I will certainly ask you."

"You don't really need to read them if you don't want to."

Cliopher had moved around the kitchen table to the bench, where he set his writing kit next to the papers. He seated himself and then, realizing his cousin was serious, smiled with some amusement. "Melo, I have only ever signed my name to a piece of paper without reading it carefully once, and I literally started a war. Trust me, I want to read them."

He took out his pen and applied himself to the task. Most of the phrasing was drawn from the old Astandalan Law Code, with only a few regional variations, all of which were quite clear to him. He read through the papers with his usual quick thoroughness, thinking briefly as he turned over a page that if there was one thing he knew how to do, this was it.

There was nothing in them of concern, Melo being as honest as Cliopher had always found him. He signed his name with a flourish at the various places indicated, then looked up at his party, who were watching him. "Toucan, Ghilly, and Bertie, will you be my witnesses, please?"

"Of course," Ghilly said, coming over, then when he presented her with the pen made a mock recoil. "What, may I use your pen? The honour!"

"It is," he said imperturbably, then spoiled the effect by grinning at her. "I'm sure you won't destroy the nib by the act of signing your name."

"Are you going to hold me in less respect if I do not myself read through all the paperwork?"

"Of course not. First of all, your signature is to witness the fact that I have read all the paperwork and signed it freely, and second—"

"And second," said Rhodin, who had governed himself, "everyone else relies on Kip to have read the paperwork thoroughly so they don't have to, so you might as well do so, too."

Toucan signed his name below Ghilly's and handed the pen to Bertie, who harrumphed, signed his name, and said: "I gave you this pen."

"So you did," said Cliopher, smiling at him, then transferred his attention to Melo. "Shall we go to the bank now? Then this can go be filed properly."

Melo riffled through the papers to make sure he had signed all the relevant points. "Oh, Kip," he said, frowning, "you've signed this with 'Cliopher'."

"Well, yes," said Cliopher. "That is, in fact, my name."

"Can you add 'Kip'? Otherwise it might not seem quite legitimate."

Rhodin turned hastily towards the window again.

Melo looked at him even more doubtfully. "Are you sure he's all right?"

Cliopher could not quite help himself. As he took the papers and readied his pen again, he said, "Possibly he is reflecting on the fact that my signature has been sufficient to legitimize intermundial treaties. Nevertheless, of course."

He signed *Kip* more extravagantly, for it was only in his letters home that he ever wrote that as his name.

★★★

AS THEY EXITED THE HOUSE and started off towards the central financial district, Toucan came up beside him. "What legal training do you have, Kip?"

"Nothing very formal, I'm afraid. I picked up a great deal of knowledge simply by being his Radiancy's secretary, and then at one point I decided I needed to be a bit more systematic about it. I don't know if you've ever heard of Judge Otaki?"

"Have I! He wrote half a dozen books about Astandalan law and the developments since the Fall, including the best introductory textbooks."

Cliopher reflected again on how blind he had been to assume—to *presume*—their insularity. He smiled apologetically. "We knew each other through work, got along fairly well, and one day when I was talking to him about how I wanted to understand the law code better, he offered to tutor me if I was willing to be his guinea-pig for his books."

"What, so you're 'The Student' in his texts?"

"I'm one of them, anyway. We started at the beginning of the Code and worked our way through it. I used to read as much as I could, and then we would meet once a week for a few hours and talk about it according to his principles."

"The legal students frequently complain that 'The Student' is much too smart to be a real person."

Cliopher smirked. "It makes a difference when one is coming at a topic out of definite need—and you know, I spend a huge amount of time reading and summarizing and synthesizing and writing reports. If I'd launched into it when I was twenty, I daresay I would have found it a lot more difficult, too. As it was, I was able to hang a great deal of the Code onto decisions I had seen his Radiancy make. I knew from experience how nuanced the law is—I had seen his Radiancy research and contemplate and discuss the most complex problems in the context of some legal crux or other."

"I'm really disappointed I didn't know that you were the model for 'The Student'," Toucan said. "How many missed opportunities ..."

"Don't tease him," Ghilly said.

"It wasn't teasing *him* I was thinking of."

Cliopher, finding himself happy, laughed. "You can tease me whenever you want, Toucan, you know that."

"I am going to be jealous that you studied law under Judge Otaki. Do you always walk this fast?"

"I beg your pardon?"

Toucan gestured behind them, where the others were already several yards distant.

Cliopher remembered his earlier thought about the ambling pace of the passersby. "I suppose that even without my clothes, that would mark me out, wouldn't it?"

His friend grinned. "You always did walk faster than the norm, but you are practically running now."

"He always has so much to do," Rhodin said, "he must walk quickly between appointments, usually while telling other people what they need to do next. Everyone in the Palace knows he has passed by the wake of slightly stunned people heading off on various tasks."

"Rhodin!"

Everyone laughed, because Cliopher was flushing. He forced himself to walk at Toucan's casual saunter, and found himself immediately fretting about making it to the bank before it closed.

"Cousin Haro works at the Imperial Bank," Quintus said, coming up on Cliopher's other side.

"I beg your pardon?"

"You seem concerned that we'll get there on time. Haro will be there and will stay late if we need him to."

"That would not be very courteous."

Rhodin said, "There is also the point that you could summon the manager—or indeed the owner—of the bank at any time of the day or night, and he would come."

"That would be even less courteous."

"Much more courtly, however."

Cliopher made a face, but he had caught the fact that Quintus had said *if we need him*. He felt a sudden surge of internal warmth. "Let's hope we don't need to presume on Cousin Haro. He might not like it."

"It's not as if you presume on your relations very often," Quintus said. "Not often enough, I might even say."

"I don't like it very much when people presume on me."

"But yet every time we have asked you to come here for something important, you have come."

"That's different."

"Is it? How?"

"You're my family. Of course I come when I can. It's different—you don't ask me to use my influence to do things."

Quintus chuckled, slightly wryly. "That's a combination of you exceedingly firmly rejecting the very idea the first time Cousin Louya tried to get you to support one of her mad starts, and you not telling us that you *are* a man of influence."

Cliopher wasn't quite sure what to say to this. Rhodin, walking behind his shoulder where he had learned not to look backwards too often at him, said after a moment, "I am still a little confused about how you understand your rank, Kip. I know what it is in Solaara—but here?"

"It's not rank here, it's status. My *rank* is part of the official hierarchy, depending from the favour and graciousness of his Radiancy. In that regard I am Cliopher Lord Mdang, Lord Chancellor of Zunidh, soon to be Viceroy, etc. My *status* within my family, however, comes from my place here. And here I am Kip, youngest child and only son of my mother. I have not married, I have no children, and I have no position *here* apart from being the unmarried son with strange ideas who left. I have not properly become part of the nexus of adult society in the Vangavaye-ve."

The fire dance in Solaara seemed to have had no effect, anyway, despite Buru Tovo's comments about their ancestors' practices.

"Surely it's not a total disaster not to marry. What of the ones who are not so inclined?"

"It's the combination of all three things. Quintus isn't married, nor does he have any children—" Cliopher cast a sidelong glance at his cousin, who was smiling slightly, and amended it to, "That I know of, anyway. He does have a position here: he is the captain of a ship, he has a place in society here. If I were married, even to a foreigner—if I had children, even if I were not married—if I lived here, in short, it would not be a problem. Not that it's really a problem," he added, eyeing the approaching bank.

"No?" enquired Rhodin.

"I made my peace with the situation many years ago. It is one of the many small casualties of choosing to live away."

"Will it be difficult to find a place here?"

"I imagine it will be easier to have a quiet retirement here than it would be in Solaara, where everyone would expect me to solve their most egregious and complicated problems for them. Everyone here will be preoccupied determining exactly how cracked I am as a result of my years away, and settling me accordingly into the status they think I have earned, and it will likely never occur to them to ask me advice on any subject whatsoever, even, or perhaps especially, the ones I am the world's expert on."

Rhodin snorted, but Toucan and Quintus both gave him speculative glances, and Toucan said hesitantly, "What subjects are those?"

"Oh, let me not vaunt," Cliopher said lightly, "but if you want to know how to make a government work, I am your man. Here is the bank, and fortunately for Cousin Haro's likely desire to go home at a reasonable hour, we appear to have made it in good time. Do you know what Haro's position is, Quintus?"

"He's one of the tellers, I believe," Quintus replied. "I deal with this bank every now and again for commercial transactions. They got a new manager recently, a *velio*. I haven't met him yet, but I hear he's a real pain in the neck to deal with."

As *velio* encompassed everyone from outside the Ring, whether an Isolate Islander or a Dairen city-dweller or an outworlder, Cliopher was more mildly curious than concerned. They entered the hall of the bank, which was in the old Imperial style and therefore portentous as a minor temple and better appointed. There was only one other customer, a portly middle-aged woman leaning on the counter and gossiping with one of the tellers.

"And in response Inder said—"

But whatever Inder had said went unspoken, for she had caught sight of Cliopher and his party, and both she and all three tellers focused, apparently riveted, on them.

Cliopher felt himself responding as he usually did to potentially hostile encounters, straightening physically and mentally shifting towards a mild courtesy that often appeared weak to people who had not met him before.

Cousin Haro was the third of the tellers. He stood up and hastened around the end of the counter, smiling in astonishment. "Cousin Kip! I heard some rumours you were in town with the Lord Emperor's entourage, but I didn't expect to see you down here!" He grasped Cliopher's arms with apparently genuine pleasure. "How wonderful to see you. Did you come in just to say hello? We're nearly done for the day."

"Oh," Cliopher said, blinking away internal amusement that Haro had not mentioned his clothing. "I have some banking to do."

"What, really?" Haro laughed and led him back towards the counter. "I didn't realize you had any accounts with us. What can I do for you?"

"I may need to speak to the manager, actually, as some of what I want to do involves transferring money from my accounts in Solaara here."

"Say no more!" Haro glanced at the other tellers and the gossiping woman, who were still watching. He shrugged and spoke slightly more quietly. "The new manager is a foreigner, Kip, and more stuck up than my brother."

Hillen was Haro's half-brother. "Oh? Where is he from?"

Haro rolled his eyes. "A *proper* city, with *proper* employees, with *proper* manners."

"Ah."

"I'll go get him for you," Haro added, and before Cliopher could say anything, darted off across the foyer to a gilded doorway.

"What are we reckoning?" Rhodin murmured. "At least a five?"

Cliopher grinned at him, then governed his face hastily as Haro re-emerged with a short, slightly cadaverous man wearing gold spectacles, a round hat, and a Western Dairen-style outfit of long tunic and wide trousers.

He assessed the man carefully, planning his best approach. That he was from Western Dair made a considerable difference, for to the manager Cliopher's clothing, accent, and bearing would tell quite a different story than it did to his relatives and compatriots.

Rhodin, no doubt, was assessing him for possible physical threat. Cliopher did not know what the guard saw, but he saw a popinjay with an elevated sense of his own importance and a tendency to try to bully his underlings.

He also saw a man he recognized as having been a minor player in the great banking fiasco of Csiven. He couldn't quite recall the man's name, but he saw very clearly the moment when the man recognized him.

Five feet from where Cliopher stood the manager halted, his face greying with fear. As Cliopher gathered himself for what would surely be a very uncomfortable interview, the manager swallowed visibly, washed his hands convulsively, and then threw himself down onto his knees.

It was a Western Dairen custom for a supplicant to kiss the feet of the patron. Cliopher waited with what he hoped was an impassive expression as the manager—Ekwebatana, that was his name, like the ancient lawgiver—launched into a speech as grovelling, sycophantic, and downright embarrassing as his posture.

Cliopher let him get out his first great rush of words, then shifted the position of his hands to indicate he wished to speak. Ekwebatana cut himself off in the middle of a sentence, gulping.

"Sayo Ekwebatana," he said with cool courtesy, "I am not here in any official capacity, but to do some private banking. Will you oblige me with your assistance?"

"Anything, of course, anything, your excellency," said the manager, getting awkwardly back up to his feet but keeping his posture as deferential as possible.

Cliopher did not much want to go into the manager's office. He weighed the gossip that would not doubt start circulating as soon as he exited the room, and decided he would prefer it if people knew he was buying a house, for that just might increase his familial status as the manager's obsequiousness would not.

"Thank you. I have an account here, but the majority of my holdings are in your partner bank in Solaara. I am buying a property here in Gorjo City and would like to set up an account for necessary repairs and management. You will have to request a transfer of funds in order to fulfil this."

"That will in no way whatsoever be a problem, your excellency," Ekwebatana assured him.

"I am glad to hear it." Cliopher walked over to the counter, where he set down Melo's documents. He glanced at his cousin. "To whom should I transfer the money?"

Melo was staring at Ekwebatana, and started. "Er, my boss is Deno Kindraa. The company's got an account here, I think?"

"Yes," Haro said. He also was staring at Ekwebatana. "Uh, shall I get the account information, sir?"

Ekwebatana gazed piteously at Cliopher, who buried any hint of a smile deep down. "Thank you, Cousin Haro. Regarding the other matter, Sayo Ekwebatana, I will send one of my secretaries in the coming week with the name of the person I have chosen to manage my new property. Before the funds are transferred from Solaara, will it be a difficulty to advance any monies as may be required by my agent over and above those remaining in this account? I assure you my holdings in Solaara are sufficient to the task, and will provide what surety you require."

Ekwebatana swallowed convulsively some more. "Your excellency, the world knows the value of your assurances."

Cliopher regarded him silently. The great banking fiasco of Csiven had involved a remarkable scheme for selling a wide variety of properties that did not exist, all on the assurances of smooth-speaking men. Sayo Ekwebatana started to wring his hands again. After a moment, Cliopher went on. "Nevertheless, I am certain your bank has some protocols in place for providing such surety, Sayo Ekwebatana."

"Your excellency, your word opens the Imperial Treasury. I would never presume—"

"This is a personal transaction, Sayo Ekwebatana. What are the protocols?"

The manager had started to sweat. "I believe the requirement is a signed contract stipulating the terms of the advance, with a promise of surety signed by a citizen of the community in good standing. But your excellency, I would never presume to ask such of you—I would never wish to insult your honour—your excellency is known to be a man of the very highest righteousness—you are the head of the government, sir!"

Cousin Haro, who had caught Cliopher's eye, was silently pulling papers from a drawer below the counter.

"His Serene and Radiant Holiness the Lord Emperor is the head of the government," Cliopher said mildly. "I am his chief minister, his Lord Chancellor, and shortly to be his Viceroy. It is my pleasure and my honour to fulfil the protocols that I put in place precisely to prevent the abuse of privilege. You do remember, I am sure, Sayo Ekwebatana, the relevant articles in the policies developed after the banking fiasco in Csiven."

Cliopher turned to the counter. "Thank you, Haro. These are the documents for the transfer of title for the property."

Cousin Haro accepted them. "These are the forms for a loan or an advance on transferring accounts, your excellency. If you will fill out the sums you require, I will look over the property sale."

There was no irony or amusement or even hesitation in Cousin Haro's address. Cliopher said, "Thank you," and read through the forms.

They were simple, with spaces for the terms and the names of the party and responsible citizen in good standing for the surety. Cliopher thought for a moment, then put 150,000 valiants in the sum required. That was a lot of money—two thirds of his own yearly income, in fact (or the cost, he thought in some amusement, of one of his grander official costumes)—but houses were expensive, and renovating them especially so. He signed his name, putting *Kip Mdang of Tahivoa* in parentheses after *Cliopher Lord Mdang*, then turned to consider his party.

"I'll be your surety," Quintus said, stepping forward before he could decide whom to ask. "Where do I sign?"

"Thank you, Quintus."

"My great pleasure, your excellency."

There was irony, and humour, in Quintus' voice, but he signed his name decisively. Cousin Haro took the form back, read it over, stamped it, and then passed the document to the manager, who was still sweating nervously.

"As I mentioned," Cliopher said, watching Ekwebatana sign his name without reading the documents. "I will send someone down with a letter of attorney naming my agent in this matter. You will recognize my seal, I expect."

"Yes, your excellency."

He turned back to Cousin Haro as a thought struck him. "I should also like to withdraw a sum from my account in cash."

Cousin Haro did not blink. "Do you happen to know the number of your account, your excellency?"

Cliopher opened his writing kit and withdrew his bank book, which he probably ought to have handed over before. His cousin took it with a perfectly straight face, though there was a glint of humour in his eyes, and opened it to the last used page.

"What sum would you like to withdraw, your excellency?"

"Five hundred, please. Twenty-five in coins, the rest in bills."

Haro nodded without comment, writing both the cash transaction and the house purchase neatly and quickly at the end of the book. He stamped the page with the bank's seal, turned to his drawers and counted out the money.

Cliopher then realized he did not have any pockets or a wallet with him, but, keeping his face as impassive as he could, he set the paper bills inside his bank book and the coins in a section of the writing kit.

Before he could thank his cousin, Sayo Ekwebatana launched in with, "Is there *anything* else we can do for you today, your excellency?"

"Thank you, Sayo Ekwebatana, that will be all."

"It was my very great honour to serve you, your excellency."

Sayo Ekwebatana showed definite inclination to kiss his feet again, so Cliopher stepped back, smiled at Cousin Haro, and said, "I expect you wish to close your bank for the day. Thank you for your assistance, Sayo Ekwebatana, Cousin Haro."

★★★

"WHAT ON EARTH DID YOU do to that poor man?" Ghilly asked as soon as the door closed behind them.

"I didn't do anything to him," Cliopher protested. "Or not to him personally. He was involved in a banking scandal in Csiven a few years ago."

"He kissed your feet."

"That's a Western Dairen custom."

"The only other time I've ever seen someone tremble with fear like that was when I was staying with my great-aunt in the Outer Ring and one of the villagers was called before the shaman."

"I think I'd call him a seven," Rhodin said meditatively.

Cliopher fought down the urge to wipe his hands down his robes. "Perhaps even a seven and a half. On the scale of grovelling sycophancy," he added to his friends.

"It gets worse than that?" Vinyë asked.

"Oh, yes. Not usually to me, but there have been a few occasions ..." An unpleasant thought struck him. "Do you think they'll be more frequent now, Rhodin?"

"When his Radiancy leaves on his quest, you will be the highest-ranking man in the world."

"Bah," said Cliopher, and made his steps slow down again.

CHAPTER SEVENTY-TWO

"IF COUSIN HARO WERE IN my employ," Cliopher said, "I would promote him."

Falbert, who appeared to have suddenly thought of a destination, had taken the lead. Melo had murmured something about his boss and disappeared down a side street with his paperwork. Quintus was again walking beside Cliopher, and looked speculatively at him. "Indeed? What makes you say that?"

"He was competent, thorough, quick without being hasty, polite, and aware of conversational subtleties and power dynamics. How long has he been working there?"

"Not quite three months, I think," Vinyë said from his other side, tucking her arm into his. "He was sick most of last year."

"Only three months? Then I would definitely promote him. He's wasted on that job."

"I've been looking for a secretary-manager," Quintus said. "Do you think—?"

"I would certainly trial him."

"That wouldn't have occurred to me. He was always such a flibberti-gibbet. Do you remember the time he tried to raise pigeons in his mother's laundry tower?"

"I recall the time you decided to take a canoe, by yourself, across the Bay of the Waters."

"Kip, that's not fair!"

"It's probably not fair to see Haro only in the light of what he did when he was twelve."

"Point. It amazes me how you notice things about people."

"Well, that is my job. Noticing things." They walked a bit further, and a thought struck him. "If you are seriously interested in trialling him, Quintus, I would do so quite soon. Ekwebatana is the sort of person who will take his humiliation out on his underlings, and of course his brother ..."

"He humiliated himself," Ghilly said, dropping back. "You didn't do anything. You were very polite, in fact, when he started kissing your feet and fawning all over you."

"Nevertheless."

"How many people do you have under you?"

Rhodin made a noise behind him. Cliopher shrugged. "There are fifteen people in my household, then my department—the Private Offices—has about forty people in it. The entire Service is approximately two thousand in the Palace, five hundred and seventy thousand across the world."

Ghilly looked at him for a long moment, walking into a lamp-post as a result. She caught herself, laughing, and while they paused to make sure she hadn't hurt herself, looked past Cliopher. "Speaking of, there's your cousin coming along behind us now."

They all swung around to see Cousin Haro. He walked at what Cliopher considered a normal pace, not the gentle saunter. He was looking quite downcast, too, but brightened when he saw them waiting for him.

"Cousin Haro," Cliopher said, greeting him again. "Will you join us? I'm not sure where we're going, but you can come along. Bertie seems to have an idea."

Haro looked quite flattered by this invitation. Cliopher realized he'd rarely been invited to tag along with their group of cousins. They had all done their best to avoid Hillen, which had unfortunately meant Haro got short shrift.

"Thank you, Cousin Kip—or—"

"Please don't use a title if I'm not doing anything official."

Haro laughed, expression easing. "That did my heart good, though Ekwebatana—never mind. It was a treat to see how you managed him."

Quintus cleared his throat. "Kip was just telling us that he reckons you're wasted in that job."

Haro looked stricken, as if the compliment was utterly foreign and incomprehensible, no source of delight or pleasure. He swallowed. "Oh ... thank you ... Kip, you shouldn't decide on the basis of ten minutes of ..."

"Of observing you at work?" Cliopher supplied when he trailed off. "One major element of my job is observing how people work and making decisions based on those observations. I have been known to make mistakes, though rarely enough that I am quite confident in stating that you have more to offer than being a bank teller under a snobbish popinjay."

"Oh ... thank you ... Kip, but ... I really don't have that many skills besides being good at numbers—Mama always says that I'm no good at anything else, and I'm afraid that she's right. I'm not like Hillen, you know. Not good at sports, or, or anything."

Cliopher felt a sudden surge of anger against Aunt Hilda, and a surge of the same avuncular sentiment that he felt with the younger members of the Service. Haro was not that much younger than he was, but was so retiring he seemed so. He said firmly, "Haro, you are nothing like Hillen, and much do all of us rejoice in the fact!"

"But Mama—"

"Earlier this afternoon I went down to the Department of the Common Weal and closed it because of incompetence and criminal activity. In ten minutes I had more than enough evidence to have Hillen arrested on charges of embezzlement, misrepresentation of the law, and bribery."

Haro stopped walking and stared at him. "You ... you arrested Hillen?"

"Ser Rhodin did, but I gave the order."

"Actually arrested? But that's won—" His voice dropped, and he looked down at the ground. "He'll get out of it, though, won't he? I mean, he always does."

Cliopher stepped forward, forcing Haro to look him in the face. "He will go before his Radiancy. I assure you, he will face the consequences of his actions."

Haro looked at him for a long moment before the pinched and anxious expression started to ease. After a while a smile started to emerge. "And the world knows the value of your assurances. Cousin Kip, do you know, Ekwebatana gets some sort of broadsheet delivered. He leaves them in the staff room—he was very condescending about giving us the opportunity to read some *proper news*—but I thought I would read them—and, well, you're mentioned all the time. *Lord Mdang has opened the Department of the Common Weal to entries for the newest Indrogan Estates Competition. In a recent press conference, the Lord Chancellor announced the expansion of the new lighting system to the northern cities of Amboloyo.* That sort of thing."

"Is that the *Csiven Flyer*? Their caricaturist is very talented."

Haro smiled shyly. "The most recent one has a picture."

"I can see why you were not quite as flabbergasted at Ekwebatana calling me *your excellency* as your brother was when I made him."

"Having gone into his department in an official capacity?"

Bertie huffed back to them. "What are you all doing lallygagging back here?"

"Talking to Haro," Cliopher replied. "Where are you taking us, Bertie?"

"I thought we could go to the Pelican for a drink. The afternoon is wearing on. Are you coming?"

"A delightful idea! Then I can pay Farlo back for whatever Gaudy couldn't."

★★★

GAUDY WAS HOVERING OUTSIDE THE bookstore, telling people it was currently closed. He brightened when they approached.

"My lord is still within?"

"Yes, sir."

Cliopher rarely paid attention to what Gaudy called him, except here where the accustomed formality was just slightly jarring. He glanced around, but Vinyë had been accosted by someone near the bridge and was speaking energetically about something. "I'll get us tables," Bertie said, and disappeared into the Pelican with Quintus and Haro.

Cliopher shrugged and went inside the bookstore. He found Pikabe and Ato just inside the door watching his Radiancy's progress about the store and Farlo awkwardly attempting to keep himself out of the way.

"Ah," said his Radiancy, looking over, when the doorbell chimed softly. "My lord Mdang and his friends."

Cliopher genuflected, rose easily at the nearly-imperceptible gesture. Behind him he was aware of the less-practiced obeisances of his friends. "My lord."

His Radiancy was holding a book open in his hand. He glanced down at it, then back up at him. "Something in your bearing suggests you have something to tell me, Cliopher."

Cliopher walked into the middle of the room. He glanced at Farlo, who was not one of the great gossips. He composed himself, then said in as neutral a voice as possible: "To my great regret, I must inform you, my lord, that I have recently discovered that the Princess Oriana was neglecting to disseminate the official proclamations from the Privy Office."

They had worked together for so long, and so intimately, that Cliopher did not have to say anything else to explain all the ramifications, personal, public, political, of that statement. He did not have to belabour his own failure to catch it: the embarrassment that it was—of all places!—the Vangavaye-ve where it had happened (the sure and shameful knowledge that it was *because* it was the Vangavaye-ve that it had been able to happen); what it said about Cliopher's relations with his family, his friends, his home.

His Radiancy looked down at the book in his hand again. He spoke meditatively, "What was the approximate growth in *falao* production in the past year?"

Cliopher blinked. "They were down slightly from their ten-year average, which was fourteen percent year-over-year, so somewhere between ten and twelve percent."

"And could you give me an estimate of the Vangavaye-ve's gross inter-provincial sales?"

"That was also slightly down ... somewhere between nineteen and twenty million valiants, my lord."

"What is your understanding of the *ahalo* cloth sales?"

"They have increased by something slightly over forty percent over the past eighteen months." He smiled a little ruefully. "Most of which is attributable to my court costumes, my lord."

"Eleven and a half, nineteen point eight, and forty-three. It would be tedious if you were infallible, my lord Mdang," his Radiancy said imperturbably, setting the book face-down. "When we adjudge the appropriate recompense to the Princess for her service to the Vangavaye-ve we will certainly bear your tidings in mind. We shall discuss other appropriate measures once the regency ceremonies are completed. In the meantime, perhaps you will send to your department for copies of the proclamations you believe were, ah, misplaced, and see that they are published appropriately."

"Very good, my lord," said Cliopher, relaxing slightly.

"I enjoy very much the fact that in this city one runs into acquaintances very frequently," his Radiancy added. "Perhaps we shall encounter each other another time this evening, my lord Mdang, though do not look for me. I am enjoying my day off. Ato, carry those." He nodded regally at Farlo, who flung himself down onto his face, smiled at the hasty courtesies performed by Cliopher's party, and swept out. Ato picked up a parcel on the small table by the door and followed him out.

Ghilly walked over to the book his Radiancy had set down. She flipped through the pages, then grinned at him. "*The Yearbook of Economic Activity in the Province of the Vangavaye-ve,*" she said. "Shall I quiz you some more?"

"If you insist," he said, but turned to Farlo. "I'm sure my lord was interested in more than just whatever was in that parcel."

Farlo snorted. "Gaudy said you'd pay. Himself said to send the rest up to the palace. I'll finish wrapping them."

He went to his table in the back. Cliopher started to follow, but was almost immediately distracted by a beautiful illustrated edition of *The Lays of the Wide Seas*, displayed in a prominent position in the middle of the store. "Oh," he said, opening it to relish the woodblock prints of birds and sea creatures and a splendid old ship. "Oh, this is magnificent. Oh, how wonderful."

He looked up to find Ghilly and Toucan smiling, and Gaudy and Farlo both grinning ear-to-ear. "What?"

"Your lord took one look at that book and said 'Oh, Kip will love this'."

Cliopher felt himself flushing with pleasure. He rallied himself. "How much do I owe you, Farlo?"

"Three hundred and thirty-five valiants. Your lord bought out half of Aya inDovo's books, plus a few others. Including that one, so don't go spoiling it."

He opened his writing kit and drew out the bills. "Here you are, then. May I have a receipt, please?"

Farlo gave him a look, then started to rummage around in his desk at the back of the store. "Look around while I write it up for you. Do you need all the titles?"

"No, just the sum, please." Cliopher wandered around, picking up books as titles or authors caught his eye. He got quite immersed in one, and looked up to see Gaudy and Farlo grinning at him again. "What is it?"

Farlo said, "You and your lord have remarkably similar tastes."

Cliopher felt as sheepish as Gaudy looked. "We have spent a long time working together," he murmured, setting down the volume of poetry and taking the receipt Farlo held out to him. "Thank you."

"I'll walk you out," Farlo said, carrying a box out with them. He set it down outside the door, then took a pole from its socket next to the door and used the hook on the end to catch the top of the window shutters.

Farlo slid the first one shut. Cliopher watched as he went methodically down the front of his store, then his gaze wandered to the street. A thin stream of people were entering the Pelican next door, and the general number of passersby was increasing. The bookstore looked across the canal to a theatre and was close to the back door of the opera house.

There were more restaurants each direction, and he was fairly certain another theatre was around the corner, not to mention the great hotels on the next canal over, which opened up to the lagoon.

"Why are you closing now, Farlo?"

Farlo grunted as he bolted the last shutter in place. "Because it's past four. Why?"

Cliopher thought better of it. "I was merely curious."

Farlo looked at him, frowned, and said: "It's more than that. Come now, Kip, I recognize that look in your eye. You have some sort of idea, don't you?"

Gaudy put his hand to his face and Rhodin, pretending to be on guard, turned to look at the canal. Cliopher smiled sheepishly again. "It's just that you're in the entertainment district, next to a number of popular restaurants and a good pub, on one of the major thoroughfares for people going home from the financial district, and just around the corner from the main hotels on the Lagoon."

"Yes, and?"

He gestured at the people wandering by. "You could have custom till midnight, if you were open. Good custom, too, the sort of people who go out to restaurants and the theatre, stay in the grand hotels, and, if they live in Gorjo City, generally work during the day."

Farlo looked at him and frowned again.

"In Solaara, there's a very good bookstore near the Palace that's open during ordinary business hours, and a slightly less good one that's open late. If I want a specific book, I can send someone to the first one—but if I want to just look around, I pretty much always go to the other one, because I usually can't get away from the Palace until the evening. You can imagine which one I spend more money at."

Farlo frowned at him some more. "You get going before you have any more strange ideas."

Cliopher felt he had done his best, so he bent to pick up the box. Gaudy immediately said, "*I'll* carry that, Uncle Kip!" so Cliopher contented himself with his old, familiar writing kit.

★★★

THE PELICAN WAS BUILT IN an old Astandalan style, with lots of latticework grilles and sinuous plant-shaped copper fixtures. Cliopher looked apprecia- tively up at the lazily turning fans, which were designed to look like hibiscus blossoms, and ambled after his party to where Bertie had brought together tables in a cozy nook overlooking the canal.

"We thought you'd gotten lost," he said, moving over so Cliopher could sit next to him. Quintus and Haro were deep in conversation in the corner, Haro looking doubtful and tentatively eager by turns.

"My lord was still there and I wanted to tell him about the proclama- tions. I don't think I've ever been in here before."

"Really? It's just around the corner from where Toucan's office was, and not too bad for the museum, so we used to come here all the time after work."

Cliopher was not quite surprised at the sharp pang of regret that assailed him. But he had his Radiancy—Conju, Ludvic, Rhodin—he smiled. "I shall look forward to exploring the pubs of Gorjo City with you two years from now."

The waiter—the young son of another cousin—came by, was greeted by everyone, was gently teased by Vinyë for having successfully auditioned for the dancers' chorus at the Opera House, and when he had taken all their orders, Ghilly said, "How definite are you about your retirement? It sounded a bit more vague earlier, but I am getting the impression that you have a set date in mind."

"What with buying a house and all," Bertie muttered.

"I am not quite at the counting-down of days, but that's only because it's not yet set when his Radiancy's Jubilee celebrations will finish and his successor will take power. The celebrations will begin on Emperor Day, however, so some time shortly after that. Probably around the beginning of the Lord's New Year—the Singing of the Waters."

"And just like that you'll step down?"

"Yes. I am very much a part of his Radiancy's regime."

"From what I've been reading, you basically are his Radiancy's regime," Cousin Haro said, emerging from his discussion with Quintus and pulling out a folded broadsheet from his bilum. He unfolded it on the table where the rest of them could look at it. It was upside down to Cliopher, but he recognized the general lay-out of the *Csiven Flyer*.

"What have you got there?" Ghilly asked, twisting around so she could see it. "This is one of the broadsheets you mentioned?"

"Yes, and it—"

Falbert sneaked an interior page to share with Vinyë. "Oho, here we are: *Debate Held at the City Hall This Week*—is this just the *Ring o'News* for, er, Csiven?"

"More or less, except that Csiven has a population of three and a half million people and all of the provinces of Dair and Jilkano read the *Flyer*."

"What was the debate on?" Toucan asked curiously.

Bertie read silently a moment, then laughed uproariously. "'The Legal Scholars' Debating Society met with the Young Argumentatives'—a wonderful name!—'for their annual moot this week. Their topic of debate was whether Lord Mdang has too much influence in Zuni politics.' You will be pleased to know that 'The debate was concluded in favour of the Young Argumentatives, who were defending the contrary, when it was pointed out that the only reason the debate was legal was because of the Lord Chancellor's sustained efforts in encouraging the growth of democratic processes, including public debates on state policy.'"

"Was that illegal before?" Toucan asked. "No, don't answer that, Kip, it was a joke."

Ghilly found another article. "Here's one to interest us all: *The Viceroy: an Introduction to the Position and the Personage.* Oh, Kip, are you a personage as well as a person?"

"Apparently so. Here are the drinks."

"I get the feeling you're going to want yours," Bertie said, eyebrows working suggestively.

"It's been that kind of day."

Ghilly shook the paper to gather their attention. "Shall I start with the position or the personage?"

"Definitely the personage."

She grinned at her husband and settled herself. "'Cliopher Lord Mdang was born in Gorjo City, the exotic floating capital of that wonder of the Nine Worlds, the Vangavaye-ve.' Oh, this is promising already. I hadn't realized we were considered so exotic. 'His background is the professional middle class, no doubt a contributing factor in Lord Mdang's notable interest in improving the plight of the lower classes of the world.'"

"There are worse things to be interested in."

"Thank you, Bertie."

"'Lord Mdang joined the Imperial Bureaucratic Service in the seventh year of the Glorious and Illustrious One's reign as Emperor of Astandalas, working until the Fall in the Lower Secretariat, primarily in the Ministries of Health and Trade.'"

Toucan said, "Don't try to clarify, Kip. Do go on, Ghilly."

"'After the Fall, Lord Mdang took on the position of Princess Indrogan's secretary and was instrumental in the restoration of order and government during the Dark Years. Soon after the Glorious and Illustrious One's assumption of the Lordship of Zunidh, Lord Mdang was appointed to the position of the Glorious and Illustrious One's personal secretary, a position he held until his appointment as Lord Chancellor.

"During his time as the Glorious and Illustrious One's personal secretary, he became Secretary in Chief of the Offices of the Lords of State, head of the Imperial Bureaucratic Service, and soon became known as The Hands of the Emperor—"

"Is that an official title?" Vinyë asked.

"Yes," Cliopher said, inured by this point to explaining things he'd thought they'd all known years previously. "You'll see at the viceroyship ceremonies."

Ghilly cleared her throat. "'The Hands of the Emperor, most trusted advisor and assistant of the Glorious and Illustrious One. He is particularly lauded for his work as Chair of the Littleridge Treaty negotiations, the development of the sea train, the restoration of the post system, and the creation of the Indrogan Estates. We in Csiven need only look at the Serpentine Park and the thriving community of Loa to appreciate Lord Mdang's great contributions to the health and wellbeing of the people of Zunidh.'"

"Loa is the name they gave the first of the Indrogan Estates," Cliopher murmured, and discovered he had finished his drink when the waiter came by and asked him if he wanted another.

"'Three years ago the Glorious and Illustrious One announced the elevation of his secretary to the position of Lord Chancellor of Zunidh. Since that time Lord Mdang has become responsible for overseeing the legislative and executive arms of the mundial government to permit the Glorious and Illustrious One to focus on the magical requirements of the prospective change in government.'

"Oh—there's an addendum: 'Editor's Note: As one who was born in the slums of Eano and was twelve years old when the move to Loa took place, I have every reason to be personally grateful to Lord Mdang for his tireless work on behalf of the poorest citizens of our world and wish to take this opportunity to thank him for the opportunities he gave me among many.' What a nice thing to say."

"What a nice thing to do," Vinyë said, reaching across the table to clasp Cliopher's hand.

"He wrote me a letter once, years ago," Cliopher said, "after he founded the *Csiven Flyer*. I'd bought a basket from him, when he was a little boy. He'd told me how he wanted to change his life. He wrote to tell me he had."

"What does it say about the position, Ghilly?"

Ghilly turned back to the broadsheet. "Here we go: 'The Position of Viceroy is a modification of the ceremonies of regency performed by the lords magi before the Emperor of Astandalas. In this case, the Glorious and

Illustrious One expects to spend some months travelling, and will not be able to fulfil his usual duties and responsibilities of governance during that period. Lord Mdang is not a wizard, but in all other regards is to be understood as Lord of Zunidh during the Glorious and Illustrious One's absence.'"

Everyone looked hard at Cliopher. He bore their scrutiny as best he could, but finally mumbled, "The Mother Superior of the Mountains is going to be looking after any magical problems."

"As if that's what we're thinking," Bertie said, eyebrows beetling. "And yesterday I said—I think I see why you were nonplussed by us having no idea what your position is."

"I think I'm going to see if I can get this delivered," Vinyë said. "Does it say anything further about our Kip?"

Ghilly looked down at the paper, read a moment, and smiled. "There's one further note: 'We expect our gentle readers will appreciate knowing the appropriate etiquette if they should happen to encounter the new Viceroy, as Lord Mdang is known for his unexpected appearances in unlikely places. The correct form of address remains *your excellency*, and is to be accompanied by a second-degree genuflection.'"

"You could call your memoirs that," Rhodin said. "*Unexpected Appearances in Unlikely Places*."

Quintus shook his head and turned over the pages of the broadsheet before him. "Such as the public room of the Pelican. You *are* mentioned in all sorts of places, Kip. We really must see about getting—oh!"

The exclamation was because he had come to the editorial cartoon. He stared at it for a moment then laughed until tears started. "Oh, Kip, Kip—"

"Let me see that," Ghilly said, tugging it out from under his hand. She smoothed the page before her, then let her breath out in a soundless whistle. "My goodness ..."

Cliopher looked warily at the cartoon.

A small child sat on the ground, wailing extravagantly. A recognizable image of himself dressed in a nearly accurate version of Outer Ring finery was leaning down over her, frowning solicitously, asking 'Whatever is wrong?' Over his shoulder was a huge basket of vaguely Wide Sea Islander design, in which he held a comically oversized globe of the world. Half-pushed away by the basket stood the Prince of Amboloyo, looking angry.

"Oh dear," he said, attention riveting on the prince. "Prince Rufus is not going to be happy with this."

His sister cried, "Kip!" and took the page from him. "That's all you have to say about this, that Prince Rufus isn't going to be happy? Who is he, any-way? Obviously not someone the artist thinks you pay much attention to."

Cliopher smiled reluctantly at this. "Prince Rufus is the Prince of Am-boloyo. He is the most powerful of the princes, the most ambitious, and, er, my major political adversary. Sometimes I think we were put in the world to be the banes of each other's existence."

"Kip!"

"Why are you wearing Outer Ring finery?" Ghilly asked, snickering at the depiction.

"Possibly because Jiano and Aya came as Speakers against the fish farm, they came in full Outer Ring finery, and mentioned, as one does, that they were my kinsfolk ..."

"Or?"

He sighed. "Or because when Buru Tovo came to see me, he insisted I dance *Aōteketētana* in full finery, which I did in the middle of open court."

They were staring at him again. Toucan was the first to speak. "You did the greater fire dance?"

"You *had* full finery there?" Vinyë added.

"You know how Buru Tovo is. He didn't think what I had was sufficient, so I had to go catch parrots and things—all I could be grateful for was that he decided his Radiancy's gracious offer to let me have pearls out of the Im-perial Treasury was better than going diving for them in the Azilint! Azilinti pearls are a hundred feet down and I'm not that good of a swimmer."

They all stared at him some more. Toucan said, "That explains a few things I've heard my grandfather say ... Nothing bad," he added hastily. "Just he's said a few things, when the subject comes up, that when the time comes there's someone to be the *tanà* after Lazo Mdang."

Cliopher clasped trembling hands around his glass, knowing that the tremor was not, this time, from the magic.

"May I ask what the *tanà* is?" Rhodin asked. "I did not fully compre-hend."

Toucan's steady gaze didn't waver from Cliopher's face. "The *tanà* is the person who speaks sense; who knows the things that are important to know; who knows what to say when the hard questions are asked. The *tanà* is not the chief or even the paramount chief; but when the *tanà* speaks the chiefs listen."

"That is entirely Cliopher," Rhodin said. "I can well imagine that Prin-cess Oriana had no idea such a person exists."

"She knows that my uncle Lazo exists," said Cliopher, "because I told the entire Council of Princes that she could do whatever the hell she liked but touch him and she'd regret it. Jiano was there," he added reflectively; "he will understand these things better."

Rhodin chuckled. "He will certainly not find it difficult in the least to listen to you."

Cliopher had no good retort to that. He glanced up; sighed again. "And speak of the man, here he comes." He waved resignedly at Jiano, who was weaving through the crowd around the main bar towards their table.

"You are remarkably easy to follow," Jiano remarked. "As soon as I started to get out 'Kip Mdang' all sorts of people pointed the way, usually with a complete description of your outfit. It is quite extraordinary. Up to a house you've just bought, down to a bank where you completely upended everyone when the manager kissed your feet, over here …"

"What can I do for you, Jiano?" Cliopher asked, folding his hands and resolutely not looking at the cartoon.

"Well, I was thinking that it's really the *title* that I don't like. Do you think I could be called the Paramount Chief of the Vangavaye-ve instead? I still don't agree with the idea, but at least that's a proper Islander title, not this foolish aristocratic nonsense."

Cliopher's heart leapt. *Yes, yes, yes!* he wanted to cry: let us indeed begin openly dissolving princely authority, let us indeed make it clear that the Wide Sea Islanders joined the Empire as equals, let us *indeed* make good the promise Cliopher had made to the god of mysteries. He smiled moderately, too aware of the need to approach the nefalao circumspectly if one wished to winkle out its pearl.

"I don't have the authority to change princely titles, but I will certainly broach the matter with his Radiancy."

"Thank you. I had another—oh, I don't know that I'll be staying, I am interrupting—"

"Please have a drink if you wish."

"Thank you. A rum and ginger, then, please. What are you drinking, Cliopher? I feel I should get you something, as I keep interrupting your time with your friends and family to ask you work questions."

"That clearly happens all the time," Vinyë said, moving over to let Jiano sit beside her and showing him the cartoon. "We were just admiring this Csiven artist's view of him."

Jiano crowed with laughter. "Isn't that you to a tittle! Who's the angry little man behind you?"

"The Prince of Amboloyo."

"He doesn't look a happy man."

"He often doesn't," Cliopher said, then shook his head at himself. "I really ought not prejudice you against him, Jiano."

"This sounds intriguing."

"Kip just told us that Prince Rufus is the bane of his existence."

"We have nearly completely opposite political philosophies."

"So I guess I will also be making him quite, quite angry?" Jiano examined the picture more closely. "I am the crying child—at what stage, I wonder, do I turn into the prince you're ignoring?"

"You'll have to work hard for that," Rhodin said. "It's taken decades of sustained vitriol for Prince Rufus."

Cliopher looked up at where the guard stood next to the door. He wanted to tell Rhodin to sit down, but knew he would refuse. And justly so, he thought glumly. "The Prince of Amboloyo is ambitious," he said to Jiano. "He finds it irksome that I have consistently blocked his efforts to expand his influence. He is already the wealthiest and most powerful of the princes. He wanted to be the Lord Chancellor."

"He wants the ear of his Radiancy," Rhodin said.

"Indeed."

Jiano looked at the cartoon. "Instead of which, he sees *you* ..."

"A nobody from the Islands with radical views."

"And clearly the Glorious One's *friend*."

Cliopher shifted to take a sip from his drink, uncomfortable with Jiano's insight. Rhodin caught his eye and said meaningfully, "Kip is his Radiancy's closest friend."

"Hélouzithe, hélouzanth."

"Says the man who was planning out rooms in the house he has just bought for his friend. Says the man who is the only person ever to have been alone in a room with his Radiancy."

"Rhodin!"

"It's true," he said imperturbably.

"What do you mean?" Ghilly asked, looking from Rhodin to Cliopher and down at the cartoon, frowning. Cliopher felt the urge to rip the thing up.

"I mean that his Radiancy is accompanied at all times by his personal honour guards, except that he has a private study in his apartments which is his alone. No one else has ever gone in there, with or without him, except on one occasion, when Kip did."

"What did you talk about?"

"It was a private conversation," he said shortly. "Rhodin perhaps exaggerates."

"There's no blasphemy in pointing out the truth. It is blindingly obvious. When you want to share some news, it is to him you look—and when he wishes to talk, it is with you."

"We have worked together for many years."

"When you made an overture of real friendship beyond your duty, he responded with elevating your rank as close to his own as possible so that you can be friends."

"Have you finished your drink again?" Ghilly asked sympathetically. "Do you want another one?"

"I would like some food. Is the Pelican's any good?"

"I'd rather go to Loko's, over by the museum," Vinyë said. "If no one minds?"

"That's an excellent idea," Toucan said, and waved at the waiter. "No, Kip, don't even try. This is *my* treat."

CHAPTER SEVENTY-THREE

THE MUSEUM WAS ONLY A few minutes' walk away, but before they had even crossed the bridge they managed to encounter five people who recognized Cliopher and wanted to express their opinions of his outfit. He bore their comments better than earlier, feeling that he had the silent—and occasionally vocal—support of his sister and his friends.

On the bridge itself they encountered a pale-skinned woman dressed as an Alinorel Scholar. She looked lost, so lost that Cliopher could not help himself and asked: "Do you need assistance, domina?"

She smiled in blatant relief at him. "Oh, thank you, sir, I'm afraid I've gotten entirely turned around. I am trying to get back to the Dolphin Hotel?"

"Come along with us," Bertie said, with a dramatic wriggle of his eyebrows at Cliopher, who was abruptly reminded of the cartoon. "We're headed in that direction ourselves."

"Thank you!" She smiled generally at their group before her glance arrested on Jiano.

He was eyeing her with almost equal wonder. She caught that she was staring first, and blushed brilliant pink. "Oh, I'm sorry for staring, sir!"

"I was, too," he replied genially. "You look just like the picture of the Alinorel Scholar in the *Atlas of Imperial Peoples!*"

"And you look just like the picture of the Wide Sea Islander! I had no idea—either that people really do wear feathers and shells like that, or that you had the book here, too!"

"We're not total barbarians, even in the Vangavaye-ve."

"You're not at all barbarians! My goodness, I don't think I've ever been to a city quite as beautiful as this one, or as well—let me think, what's the best word? Well-appointed, that's it. It's far more congenial than Boloyo. Everything you could possibly want is here—and far more beautiful than you could reasonably expect it to be. No wonder it's a wonder of the Nine Worlds."

"I suppose the city's not too bad, but you should see the Outer Ring," Jiano said. "What brings you here?"

"Me? I came for the Viceroy's induction. I'm a Scholar of Astandalan history, and I have always been terribly disappointed to have come of age as a scholar after the Fall. When we heard the Imperial Archives had been opened, I applied for a sabbatical to come, and then Lady Rusticiana invited me to come with her to visit her sister—and then when we got to Amboloyo we discovered that the Lord Emperor had appointed Lord Mdang as his Viceroy!"

"It's Mdang," said Vinyë, emphasizing the hard nasal a.

"Oh, is it? Thank you! There seems to be some confusion as to the proper pronunciation, odd though that is. Did he suddenly change it, I wonder? Or perhaps people are making the effort now that he's to be Viceroy."

She paused for a breath as they passed between two buildings to come out on the boardwalk alongside the Lagoon. "Just look at this place," she said, marvelling openly. "Every turn is a more beautiful vista. The buildings! The natural surroundings! And everyone looks so happy. Of course, if my town was home to a commoner risen by sheer brilliance to be Viceroy to the Last Emperor, I'd be pretty happy, too. I'm hoping I can interview Lord Mdang, assuming he has any spare time in his schedule. One of my colleagues was the Alinorel ambassador to Zunidh before he came to Morrowlea, and he said that he'd never met any government official who worked half as hard or anywhere near as effectively as Cliopher Mdang."

"Oh?" asked Quintus, encouragingly. Cliopher was just too far behind to kick his cousin, though he did contemplate it.

"Of course, if I were running a government while simultaneously trying to reform it, I suppose I wouldn't have any time, either. Ben, my colleague, told me he's not the sort of person you notice in a crowd, which is amazing when you look at what he's accomplished."

She paused a moment, apparently to contemplate both the lagoon and Cliopher's accomplishments. He did not quite manage to form words to interrupt her.

"Indeed?" Quintus said, even more encouragingly.

"There's a line in *Aurora*, about 'the unassuming magnificence of the common and ordinary good'. I think he, the poet, Fitzroy Angursell that is, was making a play on the different meanings of common and ordinary—and the nature of the good—well, it's Fitzroy Angursell's masterpiece, of course he was making plays on meaning—but that's what I keep thinking of when I look at Lord Mdang's career. I'm going to write a *book* about him."

Someone—it might have been Cliopher himself—hastily swallowed back an astounded splutter. Nothing on earth could have stopped the grins on his friends' faces, not even the suddenly-faltering expression on the Alinorel Scholar's.

"Oh my, I completely forgot," she said. "You probably know him—" She groaned, taking in their expressions. "You're probably related to him—" She glanced searchingly around the group, passed twice over Cliopher, latched onto Rhodin, and finally returned to him. Her face went an immediate bright red. "Or, of course, you could *be* him. Oh, oh my. Your excellency!"

She went down into the second-degree genuflection.

"Please get up, domina," Cliopher replied. "And do not be embarrassed."

"Oh, it's too late for that, your excellency. This is why I'm at Morrowlea, not Tara—I'd never be able to manage the formalities. Please do forgive me." She groaned again. "Oh dear, and I quoted Fitzroy Angursell at you! Of all people!"

"I am deeply honoured," he replied, very gravely.

"It can be a mixed honour, but that passage is particularly—oh dear, I shouldn't be talking about it, should I? Actually, I should probably just stop talking altogether."

"Does that resolution often help?" Cliopher asked.

She glanced suspiciously at him, cheeks still hotly flushed, then she laughed merrily. "Oh, practically never! Ben did say you had a wonderful sense of humour."

"I'm glad he remembers me so well, Domina—what is your name?"

"Oh, I am awful at this—I'm Estella Finhoulte, professor of Astandalan history at the University of Morrowlea—I started in ceremonial practices but over the past few years I have been shifting my focus to developments in Astandalan power structures after the Fall. Which *you* are the expert on! Your excellency ..."

She trailed off with a vague query in her tone, as if she was testing out where in the sentence to include the honorific.

"Here's the Dolphin," Cliopher said, with a small amount of relief that turned into total disbelief when an exiting party resolved themselves into Prince Rufus and his family.

They stared at each other for a moment, then Prince Rufus said, "Lord Mdang," and sank easily into the genuflection.

Cliopher had spent hours with the Master of Ceremonies learning the new behaviours expected of him with his elevation. Although he was not quite the Viceroy, Prince Rufus had already performed the rituals of fealty and subordination and clearly intended to fulfill all the modes of etiquette now required. Feeling self-conscious and slightly ridiculous, Cliopher made the gesture of acknowledgement and a turn to the lesser degree of formality which he had otherwise only ever seen from his Radiancy to himself.

Prince Rufus responded as elegantly as Lord Lior could wish, then he and Cliopher stared at each other for a few seconds more. Prince Rufus cleared his throat meaningfully and made an abortive gesture towards his party.

Cliopher just barely managed not to say 'oh!', like Domina Finhoulte. Instead he folded his hands in his sleeves, smiled politely, and said, "Good afternoon, your Highness."

"Will you—that is, may I present my party, your excellency?"

He felt unjustly pleased at the slight misstep. "Please."

Prince Rufus swelled slightly.

"My wife, Lady Felicia," he announced, expression pugnacious as if he expected Cliopher to contest this. "Her sister, Lady Rusticiana, Chancellor of the University of Morrowlea on Alinor. My eldest son, Rufinus, my second son, Paulus, and my third son, Eldo." He looked at Domina Finhoulte. "Domina Finhoulte is Lady Rusticiana's companion, but I see you have already met her."

"Lord Mdang was kind enough to give me directions here," Domina Finhoulte broke in before faltering under the look Prince Rufus gave her; though she did bravely essay the 'ang'.

Cliopher decided it was time to take control of the conversation. "I am delighted to meet your elder sons, Prince Rufus, as of course I am well acquainted with Lord Eldo. It is a pleasure to see you again, Lady Felicia, and you as well, Lady Rusticiana."

They murmured polite responses and eyed his party with curiosity, focusing especially on the gloriously dressed Jiano. Prince Rufus was frowning at Jiano with a more reflective suspiciousness.

Cliopher turned to his friends and family to draw them forward a few steps. "Prince Rufus, ladies and gentlemen: my kinsman by marriage, Jiano sayo Delanis, sometime Speaker of Lesuia Island in the Outer Ring. My sister Vinyë el Vawen saya Mdang, director of the Gorjo City Symphony Orchestra; my cousin Quintus, Captain of the merchant ship *Gold Pearl*; Falbert sayo Kindraa, formerly director of the museum here; Ghillian saya

Poyë of the Ministry of Agriculture; her husband Toucan sayo Nevan of the Provincial Department of Justice; my cousin Haro sayo Mdang; and most of you are already acquainted with my secretary, my nephew Gaudenius sayo Vawen."

The Vangavayen party essayed nods and half-bows, matched by somewhat bemused polite curtseys and bows from the Amboloyans.

Prince Rufus cleared his throat again. "I recall Sayo Jiano's visit to Solaara and his presentation before the Council of Princes. I was very favourably impressed."

"You are most kind," Jiano said, folding his hands and bowing slightly over them.

Cliopher could see that the Prince of Amboloyo had guessed that Jiano was the Princess' likely replacement, but before he could marshal his thoughts as to what was the best response if he asked about it outright, Prince Rufus went on in an entirely different tack.

"This is my first visit to the Vangavaye-ve, and I must say I am very surprised. Very agreeably surprised."

He nodded several times, grasped the edge of his mantle with his right hand, and thrust his left foot out so he was leaning forward slightly. Cliopher recognized the indications that the prince was about to embark on an oration, so he did not try to respond. Instead he balanced his own weight so he was comfortable. Out of the corner of his eye he saw his aunt Malania approach their group. She was gestured aside by Vinyë, who whispered something in her ear. Aunt Malania broke into a delighted grin and shuffled forward to stand within earshot.

Prince Rufus thrust out his chest like a pouter pigeon.

"From Princess Oriana's comments about her province, I had expected to find a place of outstanding natural beauty blighted by poverty and a lazy, ill-favoured, unmotivated, and unmannerly populace."

Rarely had Cliopher been so tempted to abuse his position. He settled for lifting his eyebrows in deliberate imitation of his Radiancy.

Prince Rufus gestured around with the hand that was not grasping his mantle. "Instead I find this—this jewel of a city. It is clean, it is orderly, it has every amenity one could desire—many, I notice, ones that *my* province has only just begun to implement. The people may be informal but they are very friendly, and they are clearly busy about their own affairs and nosy about everyone else's."

He made a tight little grimace. "It is evident to me how your character is shaped by your home. You are often lamentably informal and always exces-sively nosy but no one could justly accuse you of being *rude*."

He actually paused there, so Cliopher, somewhat bemused, murmured, "Thank you."

The Prince rocked a little on his feet. "Just after we arrived, while we were still adjusting to the surprise of finding the city so much better than expected, Princess Oriana took me aside to complain about you. She said you had ideas far above your station and yet you refused to behave with the noble decorum you ought. The woman has no logic. And she expected me to agree with her."

It was clear from his voice that this was the worse characteristic. Cliopher suppressed a smile, and was glad overall that Prince Rufus went on, warming up now into full oratorical mode.

"Princess Oriana, I said, you are a fool, and a fool five times over. I ex-pected to find your province destitute from your extravagance and lacking in all the basic necessities of civilized life because of your ignorance in the art of ruling, your improvidence, and your total lack of respect for your people. The only reason it is not is because Cliopher Mdang has made sure that your inadequacies harm only yourself."

Cliopher realized his mouth had dropped open. He closed it hastily.

"Look at your city! I said. When were the lights installed?—You can't answer, because you're an idiot who pays attention to nothing more compli-cated than your wardrobe, and even there Cliopher Mdang is better dressed than you."

A muffled snicker behind him reminded him that he was not in the Palace, not in one of the endless committee rooms where he and Prince Rufus had sparred over the years, but standing in front of a busy hotel, on a busy street, with the prince speaking as loudly as if he were haranguing his own populace.

Prince Rufus pointed accusingly at the lamppost beside him. "These lights have clearly been here for several years at least, and they were only invented seven years ago. They were only put into Boloyo city last year, and we haven't finished installing them into the northern cities. Yet here they are already an accepted part of the city, here in this complete backwater of the world—or what everyone thinks is a complete backwater, I said to that twit, because you are incapable of doing your job, but which isn't because Clio-pher Mdang does it for you! I'm sure you can't tell me when the sea train got here—but I remember that Cliopher Mdang made sure that the Western

Line's terminus was here, not Nijan as everyone else thought was quite far enough.

"Well," Cliopher tried, to no response whatsoever from the prince, though he saw Bertie's eyes narrow and Ghilly wince slightly.

"—You want me to agree with you that he is a blight and a burden to the world's government? Now, of all times, when I have sworn fealty to him as Viceroy—when even Princess Anastasiya swore fealty to him, and nearly broke her face trying to smile doing it?—now, when he has been appointed to the highest possible office in the world?—now, when I have just spent ten minutes detailing the merest outline of his contributions to your province, let alone the rest of the world?"

Prince Rufus had found *ten minutes* worth of things to detail? Cliopher bit the insides of his cheeks to keep from losing his straight face. The day just kept getting more and more surreal. He missed some of what the prince was saying, his attention flicking between Rufus' extraordinary words ("You are a complete idiot, madam, I said ..."), the expressions on the faces of Cliopher's friends and family, and the inner voice that commented dryly that Prince Rufus was saying all these compliments very carefully *after* Cliopher was sixteen-seventeenths of the way to being formally inducted as Viceroy of Zunidh.

Prince Rufus had nearly as ferocious a grimace as Bertie did, for although his eyebrows were less bushy their bright colouring combined with his brilliant grey and slightly protuberant eyes to add great emphasis.

"Now," he said, moderating his volume slightly, the better to raise it up again as he went onward with his speech, "the gods know that I have often disagreed with you, Lord Mdang. I have thought your policies disingenuous, dangerously naïve, impractical, and with all the hallmarks of the most dangerously seductive forms of utopian idealism. I have thought you willing to destroy all tradition and rightful order in your zeal to transform the world according to your principles. I think you stubborn, opportunistic, and a zealot for your causes. You are always ready to give advice to anyone and everyone from a beggar child to the Sun-on-Earth himself. You are an infuriating and relentless busybody."

Cliopher could *feel* the smirks of his friends behind him.

"When I asked Princess Oriana about the city lights, she said that she didn't know when they were put in, but she did remember you presenting the idea to the Council of Princes, because you had 'so many facts and figures and arguments and things'. I told her that you always have evidence to back up your arguments, because you are a man of reason and idealistic though you are, you are not *stupid*—and she asked me why I disagreed with you all the time if I thought you so smart."

Behind Prince Rufus Lady Rusticiana was trying to hide a smirk. Lady Felicia had courtly imperturbability down to a fine art, as was undoubtedly necessary with Prince Rufus for a husband, but she was holding her sister's arm in a tendon-straining grip.

"This is possibly the only intelligent thing that woman has ever said in my hearing. My lady wife pointed out to me that I have expressed admiration for your sheer bloody-minded singleness of purpose before. I have never known you to drop a project once you have decided it should happen. I have seen you stand against the world to push one of your innovations through, and seen the world turn around and embrace the innovation as if it were inevitable, and ignore your role in it entirely. I have forced you to modify your projects, forced you to make compromises on elements, forced you to improve them to answer criticisms, but I have never forced you to abandon one."

"Indeed," murmured Cliopher, rather amused, watching carefully as Prince Rufus switched which leg held his weight, adjusted the drape of his mantle slightly, and launched into an extraordinarily lengthy account of the responses to the annual stipend in Amboloyo, all of which Cliopher had read in report form.

After he had finally exhausted that topic, Prince Rufus switched his legs again and cleared his throat. "I still think you're an infuriating and relentless busybody, Lord Mdang, but I will also say that I think you are an excellent, indeed the only, choice for Viceroy. I look forward very much to arguing your ideas for the reformation of government into their best possible form over the coming year.

"I also hope that Princes Oriana's successor," and his gaze wandered to Jiano and stayed there, "should there be one, is astute enough to recognize the value of your advice and your contributions to this province's happy condition. Without your care and oversight the Princess would have drained its treasury three times over to pay for her wardrobe, and that the Vangavaye-ve has all the most recent and best improvements to public life is clearly due entirely to your efforts."

After a moment Cliopher realized he had said all he intended. He cleared his own throat. "Thank you for your, er, kind words, Prince Rufus."

The prince nodded in satisfaction and gave him a glimmer of a smile. "Don't think this means I won't be arguing with you in future, your excellency! Some of your ideas need a lot of bashing before they come into shape."

Cliopher's thoughts flashed to the book of insults he had compiled from all the things Prince Rufus had called him over the years. It took some effort and a lifetime of court training, but he managed to incline his head graciously without breaking into immoderate peals of laughter.

"I couldn't wish for anything else, your highness."

★★★

"THAT WILL MAKE YOUR LIFE much easier," Cliopher said to Jiano after they had rounded the corner and were out of earshot of the Amboloyan party. "That Prince Rufus likes you, I mean."

Jiano looked at him in disbelief. "Out of that entire rant, you managed to pick out the idea that he likes me as being most important?"

"I am still in total shock that Prince Rufus actually talked to one of his miners," Rhodin pronounced when Cliopher couldn't quite respond. "I didn't think he'd ever spoken to someone below the rank of earl—well, apart from you, Cliopher—"

"A fact that has always irritated him in the past."

"He's the one who was being pushed aside in that cartoon, yes?" Toucan said. "Just to be clear."

"He's the one who called me the scum that rises to the top of a boiling pot," Cliopher said. "Who has described me publicly as the Lord Emperor's pet monkey. Who has stated in open court that it is my sincere wish to deliberately incite the collapse of civilization into primitive barbarism. Who has declared that I would rather dissolve all the bonds of social discourse rather than admit I was wrong. That is literally the first time he has ever suggested I might have had even the inklings of a reasonable idea. Being an infuriating and relentless busybody is a major rise in his estimation."

"I like the picture he painted of you," Aunt Malania said, stepping forward to link her arm in his. "It reminds me of your father. Give me your arm, Kip, and tell me what advice you have for me."

"I don't actually—"

"Interfere with people's lives?" Falbert said, shoulders shaking as what turned out to be a guffaw worked its way out. "Kip, my dear Kip, in twenty-four hours—"

"Fourteen of which you spent asleep,"Vinyë put in.

"In ten hours, then, you have managed to fulfil my son's greatest dream, served that wretched Hillen his comeuppance at last—"

"Saved Cousin Melo's job by buying his problem house—"

"Made me feel moderately enthusiastic about taking over for Princess Oriana—"

"Given Cousin Haro the best character reference of his life and told me to hire him, which I will no doubt shortly discover is the best decision I have ever made—"

"Told Farlo how to substantially improve his business—"

"And dispensed good humour and unfailing politeness to every pass-er-by who felt the need to criticize your outfit."

"Oh, and directions and forgiveness to a random Alinorel Scholar who wants to write a book about your career."

Cliopher took a deep breath, willed his blushes to subside, and smiled at his aunt. "Well, maybe I do like giving suggestions, Aunt Malania. What are you up to?

CHAPTER SEVENTY-FOUR

LOKO'S TURNED OUT TO BE a hole-in-the-wall place selling fried fish sandwiches. Rhodin's eyes lit when he saw this, making Cliopher grin. "We'll find seats by the water, shall we?" he said as they collected orders.

"As you wish," Bertie rumbled, and struck off down one of the side canals.

"Which way are you taking us, Bertie?" Vinyë asked. "Not to the park?"

"Down by the marina is something I want Kip to see."

Cliopher resigned himself to having to wait a little longer to eat, and found himself eager for the surprise. A new sculpture, he guessed, as they cut down another narrow passage and came out at a boardwalk leading to the university marina.

And there, directly in front of them, half a dozen or so people were working on a boat the spitting image of the one he'd sailed across the Wide Seas.

"Oh!" he said, which was about the best he could come up with when they'd gone a few steps closer and he could begin to wonder if it was in fact the *same* boat.

Bertie grinned at him and waved at the people on the boat, several of whom had stopped to watch their approach. "Hola! Can we come look, Cora?"

"Sure thing." Bertie's ex-wife swung herself down onto the dock so she could greet them. "Toucan and Ghilly I know, and Quintus, of course. And— Kip Mdang! I haven't seen you in an age. I see the rumours of your new clothing did not do justice to the reality."

Cliopher smiled at her. and introduced the others. It had been a long time since he and Cora had last spoken, though they corresponded intermittently. He had always felt slightly guilty over much preferring her to Bertie's current wife, though then again, it was quite clear from their few interactions that Irela did not like him so well as Cora had, either. "It's good to see you, Cora. I presume you're still at the museum, then?"

"Is that an invitation to explain? You can eat, you know, while I'm talking. Well, a few months ago I discovered this old boat moored behind the Toka warehouses. Much to my surprise, it was a modern build of a very old design. I asked around, and no one had any idea whose boat it was or why it had been left there. It was in pretty bad shape, so we've been restoring it as best we can. It's hard," she added, looking fondly at the vessel. "It's not in any of the usual styles, and was obviously well-used—"

"That's a euphemism," one of the students muttered.

"—So the question becomes whether we restore it to what it was originally, or what it was when it arrived here, which must have been rather battered."

"It went through any number of typhoons," Cliopher said, finishing his sandwich and walking forward so he could lay his hand on the prow. "It's so small ... I always remembered it as being bigger ..."

"You went across the Wide Seas in this?" said Rhodin.

Cliopher smiled, but could not take his attention from the boat, every familiar scar in the wood, every poor attempt at decorative carving. "I'm not a very mechanically minded person, I'm afraid, and the person who was giving me directions on how to build it had never actually built one herself, either."

"I'm sorry," said Rhodin, who seemed to be the only one able to find his voice in response to this. "You went through typhoons in *this*?"

It was not much more than a dozen feet long, the two masts barely taller. He walked down the length, to where the various students at work had all stopped to watch him, turned around and walked back. "It seemed larger at the time."

He stopped again at the prow, next to Cora and Bertie. "The *Tui-tanata*, I called her."

Jiano said, "The *Song of the Home Fire*. That is a very Mdang name for a boat."

Cliopher nodded. "Thank you, Bertie. I am glad to see her again. We spent a long time together crossing the Wide Seas."

They all stared at him, and he spared a moment to imagine how it might look to an outside observer, him standing there in all his high court clothing, looking as foreign as anything, claiming that this exceptionally Islander battered old boat was his.

Cora said, "Please—please—Kip, this is yours? You built her? You sailed her? Where? *From* where? By *yourself*?"

"And can you explain how we're supposed to rig these sails?" one of the students said, jumping down with a rope in hand. "All the old books say it should be done on the triangle, but none of us can figure out what that means."

"Didn't you ask someone who holds the *Aōtekelēlona*? Toucan could have told you. The Nevans are Those Who Tie the Sails."

The student gaped at him. "We—we never thought—aren't the dances just—dances?"

Cliopher took the rope from him, regarded the jump up to the deck, looked down at his clothes, and handed the rope back to the still-gaping student. Then he took off the fine blue silk of his over-robe, and the fine bronze silk of the layer beneath, and then the white linen tunic underneath that, and finally he stood there in the undyed linen trousers that were the foundational undergarments of a Solaaran outfit and looked more or less like what half the people working on the boat were wearing.

All these layers he handed to his Aunt Malania, who said faintly, "Don't you get hot wearing all this?"

"The silk's very light," he said, enjoying the air on his back. He kicked off his sandals, rolled up the cuffs of his trousers so they didn't flap, took the rope back from the student, and swung himself onto the boat with a feeling of incredible satisfaction. The efela nai flapped unexpectedly against his collarbone and he suddenly recalled that along with his accustomed, relatively modest efela ko he now also wore five ranks of flame pearls.

Well, such was life. They could do with discovering there were secrets under every surface, decorative or not.

He spoke to all the students as he investigated what they'd done so far with the rigging. "The dances and the songs are our history and our patrimony. They teach us where we have come from and how we can reach where we aim to go. What is your name? Your island? Your dance?"

"Toro," the first student replied, stuttering a little. "I'm from Atikani on Ina'a. Our dances are … *Aōtehēhupa*."

"Are you Gēnang, then, or one of the branch families?"

"Gēnang, sir," said Toro. "My mother is Fara."

"I remember her," said Cliopher, undoing a knot and pulling out one of the other ropes. "She was in a class with me at university. She would have taught you the old songs."

"Yes, sir."

He considered the sail, shook his head, and let go of the ropes so he could undo it completely. "And so, Toro Gēnang of Atikani, whose island is

Ina'a and whose dances are *Aōtehēhupa*, your songs teach you the ways of the forest, of cutting trees and curing them, of knowing which wood is best for burning and which for building and which for making tapa cloth and so on. Do you not sing the *Lays*? They tell you the order of the ships that came to the Vangavaye-ve when our ancestors came here, the families upon them, the islands they chose, the skills each keep in the dances."

"I, yes, sir, yes, they do, but ..."

Cliopher laid out the ropes, chose the one that went along the long edge of the sail, and wove it through the woven grommets. "If for some reason I wanted to make a new kona'a drum, I would not go down to the lumber-yard to ask for a log, nor would I go off into the jungle to find a tree myself."

He took the second rope and tied it along the second edge's series of grommets in the pattern that came back to his hands so long as he did not think too hard about it. "I would instead go find one of the Gēnang—probably Fara, since I do know her—and I would ask her who holds *Aōtekehēhupa*. Once I knew the name, I would beg an audience of the *hupà*, and I would request his or her assistance in finding the right tree for my kona'a drum."

He threaded the third rope through the bottom edge in its sequence, then tied the sliding knot that permitted a single sailor to raise and lower the sail. "Similarly, if I found myself needing to know how to tie a sail of a traditional boat, I would ask one of the Nevan family who holds *Aōtekelēlona*." He turned to tie off the long rope and found no spar on which to do so. "There should be a pole here."

One of the other students offered him a long smooth piece of wood. "We weren't sure what to do with it. It was in two pieces, but we guessed it was supposed to be one."

"Hold this." Cliopher exchanged the rope for the pole and knelt to examine the place where it should go. After a moment he laughed. "Ah, I remember the problem. What are you using for leverage?"

They handed him a metal driver. He smiled, and glanced up at Cora. "I used metal tools to build it. I came to Nijan after the Fall and could find no way to get across the Wide Seas. They had lost their ocean-going ships in a tsunami and no one would take a small craft past the reef, into the storms. There was an old scholar there." He looked at Toro. "She was Nga. Do you know what dances the Nga hold?"

Toro visibly panicked. Cliopher dismissed him as useless—at least in the present circumstances—and turned expectantly to the student who had handed him the pole, ignoring a grinning Jiano (who was, after all, of a branch family of the Nga).

"*The Nga read the sea and the stars and the sky ...*" the student quoted. "They're the direction-finders?"

Cliopher nodded, using the driver to pry apart the pieces of the rudder. "She was from Lobau in the Isolates originally, but her family had moved to Nijan many years before. She held the dances, though, the *Aōtekevēvana*, and in the same way my great-uncle, Buru Tovo, taught me much of the ways of the ancestors, her grandmother had taught her. They were carpenters in her family, as mine are musicians, and like you, Cora, she had studied the old ways of the ships. She was the one who told me what to do."

He took the pieces apart and rearranged the middle one so it was the reverse of the position it had held. He grimaced apologetically at the students. "My carving skills, as you can see, are minimal. Every time I capsized I had to rebuild this section, and I frequently put the middle piece in the wrong way up. This way round, you see, it all slots together and is held in place by the pole." He slid the pole in, stood up, took the rope back, and tied it off on the pole. "There. Now, the other sail."

They had not put that one in the wrong way, so it took him less time to rig it. As he moved about the ship, looking at the way they had repaired things, he felt the water under him, the air on his back, the sound of the birds, the feel of the sky. He furled the larger sail. "The wind will pick up later, eh, Bertie?" he asked.

Bertie grunted.

"Kindraa are Those Who Know the Wind," said Cora, watching him with a marvelling expression on her face. "This is remarkable. We didn't think of Lobauven styles ... We assumed it was someone from the Ring."

"True enough," Cliopher said, checking the lashing on the outrigger. "As I said, I used metal tools in Nijan, but we were caught by a typhoon in the first month and lost most of the heavy items." He paused a moment. "I lost Saya Ng to that storm, too. Buru Tovo said she died valiantly, guiding a fire-tender across the Wide Seas, but it was very hard."

"Where did you end up?" Quintus asked.

"I never figured out the name of that first island. It was one of that smattering of uninhabited atolls very far south. I saw the aurora australis for the first time from it." He sat down athwart the prow to check the other end of the outrigger and smiled ruefully. "I was there for a long time while I fixed the boat using shell tools."

Quintus said, "If you didn't know where you were, how did you know where to go?"

"Ah, Quintus, you know that it's not where you are that matters, but where you came from and where you're going."

"Doesn't help much if you get blown off-course by a typhoon!"

"True." Cliopher drummed his heels against the hull, enjoying the still-so-familiar sound. He had spent uncountable hours sitting there, watching the sea, watching the sky, singing the *Lays*, drawing the dances over and over again in his mind's eye.

"*Ealoa'a te huwēa, kinava'a te vawēa, enadoa'a o nai gēlavaye-ve,*" he quoted, then glanced at the baffled Rhodin and expanded with the Shaian translation: "'Tell me not the stars, tell me not the winds, for I am the one who found the last island'."

He couldn't decide if it sounded more or less vainglorious in Shaian than in the old Islander tongue.

He looked at his aunt, holding the superlative cloth in her hands, bronze like her skin, blue like the sky, white like the clouds and the birds and the spray of the sea. She was staring at him as if she'd never seen him before. Jiano stood beside her in his Eastern Ring finery, young and strong and fearless and, just now, thoughtful.

Cliopher said, "I have never forgotten where I am from or where I am going. When I lost my way I held to what I had learned from those who went before me, alongside me, behind me. When my boat capsized in the second typhoon and each one that came after I held on until I came to land. I found clam shells and coconuts and relit the fire. I rebuilt my boat through the work of my hands. I sang the *Lays* and I danced *Aōteketētana* until they showed me the way home."

They were all speechless: students, friends, his sister, his aunt.

Jiano said, "You named your boat well: more than that you spoke the words properly. It is rare to find one of the city able to distinguish *Tua-tanata* from *Tui*."

"Except that one is wrong and one is right," Cliopher retorted immediately, wincing at the solecism of *Tua*.

Jiano grinned. "Yes, but still, you are from Tahivoa."

"My island is Loaloa, and my great-uncle taught me well." Cliopher smiled ruefully to soften his sharp tongue. "I was fluent in my youth, but that was a fair while ago now. Though I have tried to keep it fresh by reading—there are a surprising number of texts in Islander in the Imperial Archives.

Once I got used to the spelling conventions and how the texts were classified I found much of interest."

"There are *written* accounts in the old tongue?" Bertie interjected urgently.

"Yes! Did I never write to you about this? There was a scribe with Aurelius Magnus who took down a great deal of Elonoa'a's conversation and stories, in Shaian lettering but using our language. I keep meaning to go back to the Archives—I spent a lot of time at one point doing a comparison between the *Lays* and the Shaian accounts of the meeting of the Emperor and the last Paramount Chief. Then when I did the fire dance in the throne room the patterns matched the inlaid map of the Wide Seas. I've been wanting to find out if there are records of who designed it, for that can't be coincidence, but I haven't had enough ... what?"

They were all staring at him again. At length Jiano said, "I am not sure where to begin asking questions! Do I begin with the fire dance—the written *Lays*—that I am now beginning to suspect you are somehow making me beg you to let me do what you wholeheartedly want me to do—"

"Oh, we are going to have fun with the court," Cliopher murmured.

"—That you are versed enough in the *Lays* to quote Tinyë in language, or that you sailed across the Wide Seas in a boat of your own making?"

Cliopher raised his eyebrows at the younger man, rejoicing inwardly at the prospect before him. This was the thin edge of a wedge that was about to split open what remained of the Astandalan hierarchy like a felled log.

And oh, the ship they would build out of those split pieces! What voyage of discovery and creation awaited her new captain?

Rhodin said, "I begin to understand what you meant when you told Lord Lior you didn't care a whit about which way the wind blows."

"Did I say that?" Cliopher asked innocently, furling the sail he'd left up and tying it down.

Gaudy said, "You said, 'I don't care two shakes of a stick for the direction the wind blows'."

"Gaudy!" said his mother, as everyone else looked at Cliopher in amusement and slight scandal.

"From their reaction, the fact that the rumour mill of the Palace had you swearing at the Master of Ceremonies was perfectly in keeping with what you *meant*. What does it mean? Obviously it's a euphemism?"

Cliopher made a vague gesture at the pole he was holding. "It doesn't mean this sort of stick." Everyone laughed. He grinned at his sister, who looked slightly appalled, and jumped down to take his clothes back from his aunt. "I'd lost my temper, I'm afraid, and wasn't too keen on courtly conventions."

"Are you ever keen on courtly conventions?" Rhodin asked.

"Well, pretending I'm playing their games hides the fact that I have systematically stripped the majority of them of their power," Cliopher said, putting on the linen tunic. "People who choose appearance over substance tend to end up with a whole lot of nothing. I used to choose substance over appearance, and found that left me with a whole lot of knowledge and no way to change opinion."

He put on the bronze robe, and then the blue one, and stood there, looking, he knew, like the second-highest-ranked person in the world on holiday, and smiled at his stunned family. He stepped into his sandals. "Appearance and substance, now, that's the trick."

He realized the efela nai was still on the outside of his robes and moved to tuck it back under. The eager student said, "Those ... those are flame pearls ... how do you get those?" He seemed to realize how impudent the question was, for he put a hand up to hide his mortification. "Er, I'm sorry, sir."

Cliopher smiled at his honest repentance, and considered what he should say. What story did he want spreading around Gorjo City about that efela? He touched the five ranks of pearls and gently hid them from sight. "By making an exceptionally foolish promise to the Son of Laughter."

"There's surely more to it than that ..." Cora said sceptically.

"Mardo Walea gave them to him," Toucan said quietly.

Cora's expression cleared. "The Walea Hold the Efela. Mardo's never wrong about what people have earned." She glanced again at Cliopher, and awe stole onto her face. She breathed, "What on earth did you risk that you received *that* for succeeding?"

Cliopher exchanged a wry glance with Rhodin. "I believe the standard penalty is being strung up by one's toes, flayed alive, disembowled, quartered by four wild horses, and finally having one's remnants scattered across the Solamen Fens for the fen spirits and crocodiles to feed upon."

Rhodin made a demurring noise. "You would probably merely have been invited to commit suicide."

"If I had failed and fallen from favour that severely? Rhodin, you know that I would have been made an example."

"An example of what?" Vinyë asked, eyes wide with horror at Cliopher's account—or perhaps at his matter-of-fact recounting.

"I am a reformer of the government," Cliopher said plainly. "I have ensured that each step of my reformations have been fully known and approved before they were implemented. If I had not ... there is a line between reformation and rebellion. Usually it is quite clear where the line is drawn, which side is licit and which is not. Sometimes, however ... I have kept myself always to the side of the law, to legitimate reform. That is why I have the efela nai. If not ... the law treats those who commit blasphemy, treason, and conspiracy to overthrow the government harshly."

"But you have the efela nai," Vinyë said.

Cliopher's hand lifted to touch it, the bumps beneath the layers of silk in the colours of Zunidh, the Islander heritage won by his work far away on the other side of the world. "Yes, I do," he said.

"Even in Solaara they surely will respect the flame pearls," Ghilly said.

Rhodin chuckled. "Oh, Kip has taught the court to respect the Islanders. They respected *him* all along, even those who hate him, but now they respect his culture, too. The fire dance did that."

"I think you underestimate the respect people have for the hinterland cultures," Cliopher said, honestly and a little tiredly.

"I think you underestimate the number of people who grew up with stories of Aurelius Magnus and the Seafarer King. When his Radiancy said that the fire dance of the Seafarers was legendary, he wasn't exaggerating. No one ever thought they would *see* it! And even if we had not all grown up hearing how the Seafarer King won the respect of Aurelius Magnus by it, how could anyone not be impressed by seeing someone dance for a whole hour over burning coals? You may have grown up seeing respected administrators and statesmen dance over fire, but we didn't."

"I've only seen the fire dance once," said Vinyë, "and that was when I was six or seven, before Uncle Lazo hurt his knee."

"We don't dance over the fire," Toucan said. "I hold *Aōtekelēlona*, which is a dance of ropes and knots. The Mdangs hold the fire, and so they dance it."

"No one's done the greater fire dance since Tovo inDaina," Jiano said.

"Didn't he explain he'd come to Solaara and told me to?" Cliopher asked in exasperation. He turned to his sister. "Didn't Gaudy write to tell you?"

"Gaudy wrote to say Buru Tovo had come and that you'd done a dance, but he didn't name it."

"He was probably waiting for you to claim it yourself," Toucan added wisely.

Cliopher muttered a few of Rhodin's curses in a low mumble. That was exactly what his great-uncle would do. "Well, I did," he said, and gestured down at his sandals. "One of many things I apparently have not been clear enough in articulating."

"Leave the subtleties for court," Bertie rumbled.

Rhodin snorted. "Not that you need subtlety. A hundred and seventy-six flame pearls? Only the Emperor has such wealth to display. We understand, I assure you, what it means that you are Viceroy."

Unlike his family, who were just now learning what that meant; a matter almost more discomfiting than Cliopher's initial irritation and hurt that they hadn't seemed to care.

"Will you show us how to sail the boat?" asked the student with the pole eagerly. "We're nearly finished with the restorations, aren't we, Cora?"

Cliopher looked at him. "What is your name? Your island? Your dances?"

He looked completely thrilled to be asked. "I am Faro Repa of Hanivoa. My island is East Epalo. My dances are *Aōtekēkuna*."

"The weavers," Cliopher said, smiling at him. "Were you working on the sails?"

"Yes!" He grinned at Cora. "First time I've ever used some of the things my granny taught me at the university."

"You never do know when they'll come in handy," Cliopher replied, and was startled by the look of stunned comprehension on his nephew's face. "What is it, Gaudy?"

"That's why you gave me the efela necklace and the obsidian knife, isn't it?"

"One of the reasons. As Buru Tovo has not infrequently said to me, thinking first, questions later."

He glanced at the students. "Well, Faro, I'm afraid I will be fully occupied tomorrow, and it is starting to look as if I will be spending next week engaged in rearranging the governance structure of the Vangavaye-ve, but I will do my best to find a couple of free hours to come down and show you something worth knowing."

CHAPTER SEVENTY-FIVE

THEY ALL CAME BACK TO his mother's house. Cousin Haro joked nervously that he wanted to ask if he could spend the night; Vinyë assured him gravely they would find him a place. Jiano managed to wait until Aunt Malania had finished teasing him before launching into questions about the sixteen princes.

He and Cliopher were deep in a discussion of the uneasy balance of power persisting between the various Dairen provinces when they arrived at the front door. Vinyë invited Jiano to come in, assuring him that Aya would undoubtedly be able to follow their trail across the city.

"You are making a splash, aren't you?" Jiano said, chuckling.

In the upstairs sitting room they found Cliopher's mother and Aunt Oura and a number of their siblings, apparently having something approaching a family council. The reason for this was evident in the presence of Aunt Hilda, who sat in stony-faced rigidity. His mother looked very seriously at Cliopher when they entered and raised her eyebrows in silent query.

Cliopher saw that Vinyë made a motion as if to shield him from Aunt Hilda, but he put his hand on her arm. "It's fine," he said quietly, and walked forward between his suddenly-silent friends to greet his mother. After he had done so he turned to his aunt.

"Aunt Hilda," he said, inclining his head politely.

She rose to her feet. She was a tall woman, as tall as Vinyë, and towered over him. "How dare you show your face before me? You have ruined my life, my reputation, my standing."

He spared a moment's admiration for her rhetorical command. "Aunt Hilda, it was not I who was breaking the law."

"How dare you, boy? You arrested my son like a common criminal! *My* son! The son of Gore Baljan! You—you—who do you think you are, arresting my son?"

"I am, among other things, the Lord Chancellor of Zunidh. Your son—"

"You are a disgrace to your mother and your family."

He restrained his temper with a strong effort, reminding himself that they didn't, in fact, *know*. "Am I to understand you think I would have anyone arrested if I did not have the evidence? Or am I just to suppose that you think the fact that Hillen is related to me is sufficient reason to break the law and ignore serious criminal activity?"

She spluttered out, "He's a good boy!"

"He is a bully and a wrongdoer on many legal and moral grounds."

"You just don't like him because he's stronger and more successful and better looking than you. I'm sure you've been waiting your whole life for the opportunity to take him down."

Cliopher stared at her with genuine astonishment. "Aunt Hilda, Hillen's existence barely crosses my thoughts between one year and the next."

"You—you—you are a disgrace!"

"So you have said," he replied, and although he should have been calming down—every interaction, every morsel of training, every idea of courtesy said he should have been calming down—he found his temper was still roaring and his self-control slipping.

He took a deep breath, willing himself not to snap.

She said, "You will go and withdraw your trumped-up charges and you will apologize to Hillen for so grievously insulting him. And then—"

She took a step forward as if to strike him with her hand.

Cliopher fixed her with a glare so fierce that she stopped as if she'd walked into a wall. He spoke softly. "I do not know what you taught your son, Aunt Hilda, but my mother did not teach me to break my promises."

Someone behind him said, "Kip," but he held up his hand without turning around.

"No. I am not going to let it go. Aunt Hilda, you insult me grievously, you insult your sister my mother, and you insult your own character and intelligence. How dare you suggest that I break my solemn oaths? How—"

"Oh yes, you think you're such a big man now! Fine feathers do not make a bird-of-paradise out of a carrion crow. You embarrass your whole family—"

"I am the *Hands of the Emperor*."

The sound of his own voice raised into a shout shocked him. He took several long, unsteady breaths. Every aunt, uncle, cousin, friend was silent. His mother beside him was blank-faced with dismay.

He held Aunt Hilda's eyes with his own, but he spoke to his whole family.

"I stand before you as your sister's son, your nephew whom you have known since birth, who as a young man conceived the strange idea to go to Astandalas to serve the Emperor, and who struggled many years to be able to do so. You have seen me come and go over the years, and in your minds I have stayed that young man, eager, idealistic, stubborn under the joking, still somewhat an object of mirth.

"That is to a great extent my own doing. At first, there was nothing much to vaunt. Later, when there was, I discovered that in leaving I had ensured that my place here stayed as it was when I left, and it was almost impossible for you to credit seriously the idea that out there in the wider world I might have done something worthy of pride. Still later, as I attained higher and higher positions, I found it extremely difficult to convey to you what I did, what I do, in a way that did not sound vain and empty boasting.

"I told you my titles, and expected, I suppose, that you would ask about them—ask me, ask travellers, ask traders, ask someone at the Princess' court. But you did not, and I did not pursue the matter. It did not seem important to me. Here in the Vangavaye-ve I am a Mdang of Gorjo City, the son of Eidora, in our family the slightly odd one who left."

He took another careful breath. Still no one moved, no one spoke, whoever had called him out before to stop held his peace.

"I am still idealistic and stubborn. I am still eager, though somewhat weary at the moment. I am still slightly odd. I do not object to being the object of familial mirth. It is part of being in our family. We gossip, we tease, we help out when needed.

"Fifteen of the seventeen cousins I encountered today mocked me for my clothing, for dressing far too well for my status here, for being a crow wearing the plumage of a bird-of-paradise. Any one of them, should I ask, would drop what he or she was doing to come to my assistance.

"None of them asked me why I was dressed so well. They said, 'Did you dress up to impress us, Kip? To show off?' If I had wished to impress my family, evidently I did a poor showing of it. But with each question, each repeated comment, they had their own answer, had they but known it. If any of them actually understood my position, they would not have been indicating, in their own various ways, that I was trying too hard, that I was nowhere near as grand as my clothing.

"Perhaps I am vain, boastful, full of myself, for wanting you to recognize me, recognize my accomplishments—"

—Recognize the fact that he stood there the just recipient of an efela of one hundred and seventy-six flame pearls—

And on the thought that his Buru Tovo had not told anyone that Clio-pher had danced *Aōteketētana* because he was, most likely, waiting for Clio-pher to claim his place in his family himself, he lifted his head in the defiance he had felt too much today and reached up and withdrew the efela nai and said, "Recognize the fact that Mardo Walea gave me the efela nai today for good reason."

The silence took on an added depth, almost a crystalline quality to it, as half the people in the room held their breath and almost everyone jostled so they could see the efela nai with their own eyes. Cliopher looked around, met their gazes solemnly, seriously, intently.

"The thing is, I also stand before you as the Secretary in Chief of the Imperial Bureaucratic Service, the Lord Chancellor of Zunidh, very soon now to be Viceroy. I am the Hands of the Emperor. I am second in authority to the Sun-on-Earth. I run the mundial government for him."

He paused for a moment, letting that sink in.

"I rank above the chiefs. I rank above the paramount chiefs. I rank above the noble titles of Astandalan days. I rank above the princes. I rank above the priest-wizards. I rank above the commander of the armed forces. I may be—I *am*—a small and not particularly significant member of the Mdang family of Gorjo City. Elsewhere I am a man of high status."

Someone behind him grunted. Cliopher kept his eyes on Aunt Hilda, who he could see was vibrating with fury, but he held her with the force of his will, with every rhetorical trick he had learned.

"I have accepted the fealty of sixteen of the seventeen princes of Zunidh and promised to deal with them justly and fairly. The reason I am here now is for the seventeenth.

"Do you suggest I should go to them and say, 'I have spent my entire career fighting against the rule of privilege and cronyism, I have stood up again and again against bribery, corruption, false dealings, bad faith—I have argued for changes in the law to make legal processes fairer and more just to all, I have done my level best to see that a prince and a peasant have the same rights and the same justice before the law—but now that it is my own cousin facing these charges, I will drop all my fine rhetoric and all my splen-did arguments for honesty, transparency, and justice and instead let him get away with *admitted criminal activity*'?"

"My son would never—"

"Never admit, or never do? Aunt Hilda, Hillen has done both."

"You lie!"

He stepped forward, voice dropping with intensity, transfixing her with his stare. "There is no one in this world who can say I have lied to them, Aunt Hilda, and you are not the exception. There are more than forty witnesses to my treatment of my cousin Hillen and to his responses. Some of them are in this room, but if you prefer to deal with those who are not my friends, I am sure you will be able to find them. I do not break my word. I honour the sacred oaths I have sworn before my lord and his people.

"When my lord asked me to be his Viceroy I swore to him that I would see his world safe and govern it in his absence with justice and fairness to the best of my abilities. You are not asking me to go against my training for some ancient unwritten blood requirement—you are asking me to break the laws I myself helped to write simply because you do not wish to face the consequences of your son's action. To my mind that is by far the worse disgrace and dishonour."

"Oh, yes," she sneered, "you would do anything for your own ambition. You will sacrifice every decency, every family sentiment, every common good—"

"*Enough.*"

Cliopher knew that voice and that tone. He spun around to see his Radiancy framed in the doorway behind him, Ludvic and Oginu on either side. Cliopher met the lion gaze for one moment, then dropped down to his knees.

He rose again at the familiar gesture and stood aside as his Radiancy walked forward to stare down at the prostrate Aunt Hilda.

"We expect," his Radiancy said, in the level voice he used when he was very angry, "that only Kip, and Kip alone, knows what sacrifices he has made, and to what end. We will say only that we have never had any reason to doubt his loyalty, his service, his love, his devotion to his family, or his staunch upholding of the law. He has already spoken to us regarding the potential conflict of interest involved in this case and has asked to recuse himself from being its judge. While we have no doubt whatsoever that he would try his cousin fairly, we have agreed with his request. Your pleas for clemency are noted and will be remembered during the trial."

That was a mixed promise, Cliopher well knew, and could see that Aunt Hilda also realized. She muttered something into the floor that sounded like choked gratitude.

"As you undoubtedly have other things to be doing this afternoon than castigating our most loyal and beloved servant, you may now depart our presence."

Even Aunt Hilda did not dare stand against the expressed will of the Sun-on-Earth. She got gracelessly to her feet and scuttled out the room sideways to avoid turning her back on the Presence. His Radiancy watched her go, then nodded at Commander Omo, who shut the door and returned to his position.

His Radiancy turned to Cliopher, smiled briefly, then walked over to Eidora. She stood from her chair and began the obeisance, only to be halted by his gesture.

"Saya Eidora, I offer you apologies for dismissing your sister from your house."

At the use of the informal singular, the entire room seemed to relax and catch its collective breath. Cliopher himself felt some of the tension lift from his shoulders at the unexpected apology.

His mother sighed. "Glorious One, I am the one who should be apologizing for permitting her to continue to spew her poison. I was so surprised to hear Kip lose his temper that I'm afraid I did not know how to interrupt."

His Radiancy looked across the room and held Cliopher's gaze in his own. "It is a rare occasion indeed."

Cliopher looked down, ashamed at his loss of control.

His Radiancy said, "When a man discovers that his secretary has ideas, he has two options: to suppress him, and thereby hope to stifle the ideas, or to encourage him. I chose the latter course, and as a result have had the great pleasure and even greater good fortune of witnessing the development and coming to maturity of perhaps the finest statesman in recorded history."

"My lord," Cliopher said, in an embarrassed half-whisper.

His Radiancy smiled but kept his attention on Eidora, who was frowning, but as at an idea that almost but did not quite make sense. "Your son's modesty, madam, is as endearing as it is somewhat baffling. Cliopher, what is the purpose of government?"

"To steward the resources of all for the benefit of all," he replied automatically to the sudden sharp question, the response one he had laboured over for so many nights trying to discern the right way forward.

"A forthright answer, one I know you have thought long on," his Radiancy said. "But unlike many theorists of political activity, a definition you have striven most effectively to put into practice."

"My lord, I have done my best, but I could hardly claim to be ..."

He could not even get out the words his Radiancy had just said. He shifted position awkwardly, and saw Haro standing beside Quintus. Haro was staring at his Radiancy in open marvel and worship, but Cliopher thought suddenly of how difficult Haro had found his praise, how he had rejected any positive comments. He frowned. Was that how he himself reacted?

His Radiancy said, "When I became Emperor of Astandalas three-quarters of Ysthar was a frozen wasteland inhabited by exiles and primitives—a word I do not use lightly—their magic and their dignity taken for the glory of the Vale of Astandalas and the power of Schooled Magic. The poorest inhabitants of the Empire lived in the direst poverty, dying of starvation, illness, violence, magical ailments, vermin, while those above them lived in ostentatious luxury.

"The Empire was built on the blood of slaves, on the subjugation of conquered peoples, on stolen magic, and on the predication that the peace and prosperity enjoyed by most was worth the suffering of many, so long as it was done out of sight and preferably outside the boundaries of the Empire altogether. The government I inherited was dysfunctional; the court venal; the army, the wizards, and the priesthood corrupt. Despite the power and skill of the wizards, the Empire was so vast and its systems so broken that famines in the midst of plenty were common, pestilences were frequent, and violence broke out heartbreakingly often."

He paused a moment to let this sink in.

"You here in the Vangavaye-ve had very little direct experience of any of this. You entered the young Empire voluntarily; you were joined to the nascent Schooled magic by Aurelius Magnus, who was the greatest of the Shaian magi and who blessed these islands with peace and prosperity. You have paid the cost in insularity, both for good and for ill. Few have left, far fewer than one might expect from a place founded by the great voyagers of the Wide Seas. Very rarely, however, one is born to wander."

He paused again. Cliopher was looking at Quintus when he realized that everyone else was looking at him. Bertie winked when he caught his eye.

His Radiancy said: "I have accomplished many things as Lord of Zunidh, but it is my belief that when history judges me against the greater sweep of time, my greatest achievement will be said to be appointing Cliopher Mdang to a position of authority. I will say that the gradual diminishment of natural disasters is a result of my magic workings. The rest, however, I will give to his credit."

Cliopher's family made a soft noise of astonishment, like a soft hiss, a murmuration, like wind through pandanus leaves. His Radiancy smiled slightly.

"I began giving your Kip—*our* Kip—real authority near the middle of the Littleridge Treaty negotiations. Four wars were in barely-effective cease-fire for the negotiations, and three more provinces seemed set to break out into violence. Southern Dair was experiencing record flooding, Mgunai was in a drought, and famine soon brought pestilence with it. The weather changes were exacerbated by a sudden eruption of a magical problem, which required my immediate attention. I sent Cliopher in my place for one set of negotiations. He asked me what I wished him to accomplish during the period I expected to be fully absorbed in my magic working. Peace, I said. Peace."

He paused there, the room his, waiting with bated breath to hear his words.

"Peace, I said, expecting none. Two weeks later Kip requested an audience and handed me the draft of an agreement between the warring parties. That agreement became the foundation for the Littleridge Treaty, and those wars have never recurred.

"Having discovered I had a diplomatic genius in my excellent but unassuming secretary, I set to finding out what else he might do, given the chance."

His Radiancy paused for several heartbeats. Everyone looked from the Sun-on-Earth to Cliopher and back. Cliopher's hands were cold.

"We stand now in a world where there is no dire poverty; where the last war had three casualties, two of them in an accident; where the last great pestilence was Woodlark. Our cities are lit, our roads are safe, a child can accidentally get on the sea train in Csiven and end up safe and sound at a stranger's home in the City of Emeralds. Everyone has access to food, to money, to education, to housing, to medicine, to work. Natural disasters might still strike, but they will not be the cause of famine, for each province has food, seeds, and medicine stockpiled."

His Radiancy raised his eyebrows at Cliopher. "Princess Oriana could not answer this question, but I am sure you can. Where are the stores for the Vangavaye-ve?"

Cliopher found it was easiest just to look at his Radiancy. "The disasters most likely to strike the Vangavaye-ve are a volcanic eruption or a major typhoon, my lord. The stores are therefore split, some in a facility in Looenna, the majority on the Isolate Islands, and a third stockpile on Tortoise Island to the north. The Isolates belong to a different geological plate and should not be triggered if Mama Ituri were to erupt."

"I could go on," his Radiancy said, with emphasis. "Your Kip's brilliance lies in his combination of a superb attention to details with his grasp of systems. Few understand how individual and personal ills can be the result of systemic failures; fewer still have the vision to see how the systems might be overhauled to work towards good instead.

"Your Kip is the most gifted public servant I have ever had the pleasure of working with, and certainly a statesman unequalled by anyone living. When he stands before his ancestors he will be able to hold his head high. It should be the same amongst his living family. Do not fret that he has left you behind, for he never has. I knew your names long before I ever stepped foot in the Vangavaye-ve; and I know the philosophies of your *Lays* as well as any *velio* might."

Cliopher looked into the lion gaze. He knew his lord's expressions. He knew all the delicate shadings of truth and double meanings. He also kept thinking in the back of his mind about Haro. He did not want to be like Haro; he did not have Aunt Hilda for his mother, did not have Hillen as his brother.

He said, "Thank you, my lord."

"You are entirely welcome," his Radiancy replied. "Now, I did not come only to give you encomia, delighted though I am to do so. Jiano, I wish to speak with you. Have you made your decision?"

Jiano started. "Yes, Glorious One. That is, yes, I have made my decision, and also my answer is yes. Though I was wondering—" He stopped and bit his lip, glancing at Cliopher.

"Yes?"

"I was wondering if the title might be changed to 'Paramount Chief'?"

His Radiancy raised his eyebrows. "What did my Viceroy say?"

"That he did not have the authority to change princely titles."

His Radiancy looked at Cliopher, who said, "I think it is an excellent idea, my lord. It is even possible that the Prince of Amboloyo will support it."

"Come," his Radiancy said to Jiano. "We shall discuss this further. A quarter-hour before dawn, Kip. I shall leave you now to your family. Saya Eidora, good evening."

Ludvic had already opened the door. His Radiancy swept out, Jiano behind him, and disappeared down the stairs. Cliopher looked around the room at his visibly dumbfounded family. They were all staring at him. He opened his mouth several times but could not come up with anything to say.

And then Zemius came bounding up the stairs and cried, joyously, "Is it true Cousin Kip just bought a house?"

CHAPTER SEVENTY-SIX

THE HOUSE, UNSURPRISINGLY, PROVED A far easier topic of conversation.

In the course of being exhaustively interrogated on all the problems with Saya Dorn's old home, Cliopher managed to edge himself away from the centre of the room and to the side nearest Bertie. Three feet away he was caught up by Zemius, who wanted to tell him he had come up with one further refinement about his Radiancy's journey.

"That's wonderful, Zem, and thank you," Cliopher said patiently, wondering where his writing kit had gotten to. He looked around but was unable to see Gaudy. He did catch Leona's eye, who grinned and came over. "Do you need something, Uncle Kip?"

"I'll get my notes," Zemius promised, and thundered off towards his rooms.

"Thank you," Cliopher said to his niece, and then a thought took hold of him. "Leona, would you like a job?"

"For *you*?"

"Don't sound so scandalized," he said, laughing.

"I would be honoured, Uncle Kip!"

"Wait until you hear what it is. You have gathered, I would suppose, that I have acquired a house, and that it needs some renovations."

"Just a few, it sounds like."

"Would you like to be my agent in charge of them? I have made some notes about things I could see need to be done, but you would have to do a full assessment of the building, hire people to fix it, oversee their work, that kind of thing. I've put aside a sum for it to be done, and we could work out a fair wage for you."

"I'd do the work just for the experience!" She said, eyes suddenly brilliant. "Oh, Uncle Kip, would you really like me to? You really think I could do it? You'd really let me do it?"

"Why not?"

"What do you mean? I'm only twenty-one, I don't have any experience, I'm still in school ..."

"Studying to be an architect. And you must gather the experience somehow. But you should not sell your time short, Leona. It is a precious thing."

She glanced at him speculatively. "You don't have very much time, do you, Uncle Kip?"

"I have the same amount everyone is given, twenty-four hours in a day. It's what we use it for that matters."

Leona bit her lip, looking puzzled and a bit challenged. Cliopher smiled at her, feeling more avuncular than ever. He was prepared to expound further on the topic, which was one he had thought about, when Vinyë suddenly pushed through the crowd and grabbed him firmly by arm.

"Vinyë!" he protested, laughing, as his sister dragged him back across the room. "What is it?"

She planted him before their mother and Aunt Oura. Aunts Malania, Leonora, and Moula stood in a cluster to one side, with Uncles Lazo, Galenius, and his own namesake, Cliopher, on the other. They were all frowning severely.

Cliopher stared at them as the room slowly quieted. After a moment he realized he had gone once more into his battle position, back straight, head high, expression mild, hands relaxed, abdomen firm, weight balanced. His aunts and uncles regarded him seriously. Vinyë's forehead was furrowed.

He felt he was probably supposed to apologize for shouting at Aunt Hilda, but as he did not feel sorry in the least, he could not bring himself to. Instead he waited, amused in a way to be on the other side of the judges.

"How can you bear it?" Vinyë cried suddenly, thrusting herself away from his arm with the force of her emotion. "How can you just stand there *smiling* at us?"

Cliopher looked at her. "I beg your pardon?"

She gestured at the room of surprised relatives. "You're doing what you always do. You're letting us—oh, how can you bear it?—you're just standing there letting us ask you about your *house!* How *can* you?"

He was nonplussed. "It's what you want to talk about," he said finally, when it became evident everyone was waiting for him to speak. Still no one responded. He smiled placatingly. "And I am fairly excited about the prospect of owning a house."

"The Lord Emperor just declared you the greatest statesman in history!"

He blinked at her, not sure where she was going with this. "I am honoured by his praise."

"Is that all you're going to say about it?"

"What else is there to say?" he replied, amused, and turned to Zemius, who had just come back in with a dossier of papers. "Thank you, Zemius, I will be sure to pass these on to his Radiancy. How is your new book coming along? I think you said in your last letter that you were nearly done the first half?"

Zemius' response was forestalled by Aunt Oura saying, "Kip!"

He turned. "Aunt Oura?"

"Vinyë is perfectly correct. You are doing what you always do, which is let us turn the conversation away from your accomplishments to minor activities of various family members."

"I would hardly call Zemius' efforts *minor*," Cliopher said.

"Much as I love and respect my son's studies, it is not the same thing at all as being honoured as *the greatest statesman in recorded history* by the Emperor of Astandalas!"

"No, really, did the Glorious One call you that, Kip?"

Quintus, coming to stand next to Uncle Lazo, said, "I would go so far as to say you *encourage* us to turn the conversation away from your accomplishments."

Cliopher considered, and rejected, a number of responses. He did know, after all, what Vinyë and his aunt meant; and he could see the frowns and nods and muttered comments of his gathered relatives.

He straightened his back again, lifted his head, and ensured his voice stayed unemotional and calm, without defensiveness, just the quiet authority that had served him well through all the tumults of his professional life.

"I am unclear as to what response you would prefer from me." He gestured around the room. "I do not understand how I would be anything but the most intolerable coxcomb if I insisted on keeping the conversation circling about me."

Aunt Oura said, "You do not like being the centre of attention, even when you ought to be."

"I am standing before the tribunal. Aunt Oura, what would you have me do?"

"Telling us what your position *is* would be a good first step."

He realized that this was going to be a long conversation, and he settled himself into a better position on his feet, as for listening to Prince Rufus' oration. But perhaps it was time … if he did not speak forth now, he might never have his family's attention again.

"Aunt Oura, my position is no secret. You, and most of the people in this room, were present when his Radiancy made me his Lord Chancellor. You were invited in person by the Sun-on-Earth to come to Solaara, where you saw me at work during a major crisis. Some of you work in provincial departments of mundial ministries; all of you have dealt with them at one time or another. We all know relatives or friends who work in the princess' palace, or who trade across the Wide Seas. Perhaps I have been wrong in assuming that if you were interested in what it means for me to be Lord Chancellor, you would have asked."

He looked from aunt to aunt, uncle to uncle, cousin to cousin to friend, none of whom were smiling, except for Quintus, whose mouth was quirked. "In letters and when I have come home, you have asked me what I have been doing. I have told you. Not perhaps at the greatest length, or with great detail—"

"Or with any detail," Bertie rumbled, causing several to nod.

Cliopher lifted his chin slightly. "No? It is difficult to know how much to describe, when no questions are asked. When I came home to tell you that I had been made Secretary in Chief of the Offices of the Lords of State, you told me about how cousin so-and-so had just had a baby. Well, babies are important, and I was pleased to talk about it, and tried not to be upset you asked *nothing* about what my new position meant."

Aunt Oura said, "Kip—"

He made a gesture of resignation. "When I told you that I had started a new ministry, you told me cousin so-and-so had just gotten married. Weddings are important, too. When I told you I had been sent on a diplomatic mission to Voonra, you told me about how cousin so-and-so had just gotten a new boat and the debate there was over what colour she was painting it."

He raised his eyebrows at his sister, who knew exactly whose boat he was referring to. "What was I supposed to say? That the fact I had just negotiated a treaty on another world was more interesting than someone's new boat? Clearly it wasn't, or you would not have changed the subject."

"But you didn't persist—" Aunt Malania, who had also been there for that conversation, protested.

"No, that occasion was the last straw as far as *persisting* went."

And how his younger self would have been struck dumb by that admission! But Cliopher had *persisted* in other areas of his life, far beyond what anyone else thought was reasonable.

"It was something that happened every time—Why would I try to tell you in great detail what I am doing? It is not something you have ever expressed a desire to know. I decided long ago that there was no point in being angry or hurt that you are who you are, that you are interested in what you are interested in."

He looked around the room again, gathering in their attention easily, looking at their familiar, loved, loving faces, their expressions ranging across most of the range of anger through embarrassment, with Rhodin standing blank-faced by the door. He'd be a poor diplomat if he left people in those moods.

"This is one of the things I have sacrificed," he said.

Quintus grunted. "Your family's respect?"

Cliopher smiled as numerous people made gestures of protest. "I like to think you do like and respect me for my character as well as—or, you know, instead of—my accomplishments. I'm not sure how to phrase this ... I think what I mean is that I have sacrificed your willingness to take me seriously. We were laughing earlier today about how I used to say that when I was in charge of the government, the first thing I would do was fix the post. Then, when I did come to be in charge of the government, the first thing I did was fix the postal system. When I came home afterwards, most of you laughed about how much improved it was, and joked about how I must be a big man in Solaara now."

He looked at Bertie and Toucan, who had been in that number. "You said something like, 'Are you in charge of the government now, then, Kip? We have the evidence laid before us!' And I said, 'Yes, certainly, aren't you impressed with the new uniforms?'—ready to explain the real details when the joking stopped ... but there was never any opportunity to talk about it seriously. Until now, that is. But really, this is enough. I am glad you all have a better idea of why I'm here, why I've been so busy over the past few years and haven't been able to visit, and why I'll continue to be rather busy over the next year or two."

"Rather busy?" Uncle Lazo said, somewhat faintly. Cliopher unfolded his hands out of his sleeves (when had he put them in there?) and nodded. His uncle said, "But surely you're exaggerating ... it's not as if we all routinely ignore the fact that you know things we don't about the wider world ... really, Kip—" He seemed about to add something else when the door opened and Cousin Clia strode in.

Since Cliopher was still standing in the middle of the room by himself, her gaze landed on him first. She stopped, hands on hips, to look him over critically. He reminded himself that she was the assessor for one of the ahalo cloth merchant cooperatives, and was wearing a red skirt of equally superb cut, if lesser materials. "Cousin Kip! You must be in town for that thing up at the palace?"

"Yes. How are—"

"That is a remarkable outfit. Is it what you'll be wearing for the shindig?"

"Thank you. No, I'll be wearing a court costume for that."

She looked him up and down once more, then nodded decisively. "Made by the same tailor? I shall look forward to seeing it. I'm singing with the chorus."

"I shall look forward to hearing you," he replied, truthfully enough.

"I've heard the most delicious rumour just now, that the Princess is abdicating!" She looked past him at the aunts and uncles and cousins. "Does anyone know anything about that? Quintus, you're always in the loop."

At the expression on Quintus' face Cliopher could take no more. He started laughing before he made it out of the room, though the loudest whoops came after he'd reached the hallway. He did not get far along, just sank down at the top of the stairs so he could try to muffle his mirth with his hands.

★★★

"YOUR FAMILY SEEM SOMEWHAT PERTURBED," Rhodin observed after a few minutes.

Cliopher wiped his streaming eyes with the edge of his under robe, which Féonie would undoubtedly chide him for. His throat felt a little raw from the exuberant laughter. He coughed. "Ah, well, it's not the first time, and I doubt it will be the last." He straightened his robes to fall over his legs, but did not get up. "I suppose I should go back in."

"I'd wait a few more minutes," Toucan said.

"Hours, even," Ghilly added. Cliopher twisted around so he could see her face. She smiled down at him. "We could all hear you laughing hysterically. Not that anyone blames you! But ..."

"But no one much likes their cherished view of the world—or of other people—to be contradicted. Oh, I know." Cliopher considered his dusty toes peeking out from his sandals. "Myself included. I am sorry I have been so retiring, especially of late."

"We are merely waiting for you to retire," Bertie said, harrumphing, and offered his hand.

Cliopher took it, surprised when Bertie drew him into a bear hug. They stood like that for a few moments. Cliopher withdrew at last, wishing he had a handkerchief and surprised when Toucan offered him one. He turned to blow his nose and recover his poise.

"So much for the perfect bureaucrat," he murmured, smiling weakly. "Thank you, Toucan."

"Glad to be of service. To the *tanà*." Toucan glanced over his shoulder. "Your aunt's gesturing at you."

Aunt Oura stood in the door, watching. "Kip, will you come back in, please?"

He wasn't quite sure what he should be bracing himself for. He followed her in, his friends crowding close behind him, and was drawn once more into the middle of the room. But not alone, not this time, not with Bertie and Toucan and Ghilly and Vinyë clustered around him.

Uncle Lazo's gaze travelled across them. "Kip, Malania has been telling us what she heard that prince from Amboloyo say about you."

Cliopher considered what to say, and settled for, "Indeed?"

Aunt Malania winked at him. "I was much struck by him saying that the Vangavaye-ve would be better off if we had no princess at all and instead let you continue to run things from Solaara."

"Well—"

"And then we were thinking," Uncle Lazo went on, glancing at Aunt Oura and Uncle Galenius for confirmation, "that there have been some issues with government in the last couple of years—which happens to be the same time when you have been so busy you couldn't come home for a visit and barely write."

"I do try—"

"To write?" Vinyë said, coming up to take his arm. "Kip, my dear, you never fail to write Mama and me. I think Uncle Lazo means that you haven't been writing long letters, nor as many to the rest of the cousins."

"I have been very busy," he said, and then he thought, *no*, and he turned to the room at large. "No. How many of you write more than four letters a week?"

They all looked at each other and then at him, and eight or nine people, including Quintus, put up their hands.

Cliopher said, "Not for work. Personal letters." Most of them took their hands down. A couple were looking puzzled, and he smiled, guessing they had figured out his point. He turned slowly around the room, meeting his family's diverse expressions. "How many of you write to me at least once a month?"

"Kip," said Vinyë.

"I know the answer," he said. "I don't think you do."

They looked around again, seeing, as he knew, that almost everyone had put their hands up again. Cliopher didn't try to count, but if he'd had to hazard an estimate, he would have said thirty to forty.

"Please don't mistake me," he said. "I love receiving your letters. I sit down in the evening and I read the ones that have come that day and I try … I truly do try to answer. I'm sorry that I do not have enough time to do them all justice."

Uncle Lazo said, frowning, "While that is an excellent point, Kip, and I thank you for making it clear that our expectations might be slightly unrealistic, that isn't the main point. What we want to know is: what in the Vangavaye-ve have you actually been responsible for?"

"And no fudging," Aunt Oura said firmly. "This is not the time for false modesty."

Cliopher's mind went totally blank.

At last he laughed softly. "I am trying to think how to describe my life's work," he said, trying to include them in the joke, that he whom they had always thought was jesting was now unable to speak the serious truth.

"He asked you what you have done for the Vangavaye-ve," said Aunt Oura.

Cliopher raised his eyebrows the way his Radiancy did. Aunt Oura frowned; Uncle Lazo went very still. Aunt Malania leaned forward to murmur something to him, her hand going to her throat as if to touch a necklace. Uncle Lazo's stillness turned, if anything, more intense, but he said nothing.

"I think I may be able to assist," Quintus said, clearing his throat loudly. He pushed away from the wall to stand next to Cliopher. He had a small pamphlet in his hand.

"I've just come back from Zangoraville—Yes?"

Cliopher turned to see who had come in now: a middle-aged man, unknown to him, wearing ordinary clothes for the Vangavaye-ve—drab linen trousers, a green linen shirt—and holding a folded waxed-wood writing tablet. He gazed wide-eyed around the gathering before settling on Cliopher.

"I'm, er, looking for Cliopher Mdang?" he asked nervously.

Cliopher was irresistibly reminded of Cousin Haro under trial by compliments, and found his interest piqued.

"Which one?" Uncle Cliopher asked, stepping forward despite the fact that his attention, like everyone else's, was flicking to Cliopher. Kip.

"Er, um, the one who's the, um, Viceroy of Zunidh."

"That is I," Cliopher said, fighting down a burble of laughter. "What can I do for you?"

"Er, um, there's nearly a riot at the palace, and everyone said you'd fix it."

Someone in the throng of his relatives snickered softly.

Of course there was nearly a riot at the palace. The Princess was on her way out in disgrace and her court of toadies, sycophants, and the odd dedicated administrator would be in a corresponding state of fear, dismay, and delight.

Cliopher closed his eyes very briefly, asking no one in particular for patience. This day was surely a gift of the Son of Laughter.

He breathed in through his nose, called upon his legendary (within the Service, at least) self-control, and slipped into his professional demeanour with a definite sensation of relief. "What's your name, sir?"

"Er, Falo Minaa."

"And why, Sayo Minaa, are you the one to come find me?"

It took a few increasingly focused questions before Cliopher managed to extract the necessary information out of Falo Minaa's stuttering replies. Eventually he determined that the man had had enough initiative, on seeing the increasing chaos, to ask the Solaaran party what should be done about the situation, and when they had referred him to Cliopher (a fact he was going to have to address later, but never mind that), it was his own idea to come searching in the city. That he'd started with the Mdang family house boded well for his logic under pressure.

"Very well," Cliopher said, when Falo Minaa had stammered his way to silence in replying to the last question. "Congratulations, Sayo Minaa: you have just been temporarily promoted to the position of Chamberlain; that is, chief of the palace administrative staff." He could not start handing out Islander titles, not before Jiano was properly inducted and made it clear how his government was going to work. "Do well and I'm sure you'll be recognized by the next prince."

"And, er, in the meantime?" Sayo Minaa said, perking up a little.

Cliopher blinked at him, recognizing belatedly that the man probably thought the interview had been an interrogation and one that had not gone well. The fact that he stuttered was a little unfortunate but hardly an indication of the man's skill or ability; and his answers had been good as far as they went.

"In the meantime," he said, "I expect you to calm the chaos. Give everyone tomorrow as a holiday; it ought to be one, really, anyway."

"Yes, sir."

"The main things to ensure are that no one messes with the paperwork or the treasury." Cliopher pondered a moment. "If Princess Oriana or any of her court attempts to remove her familiar treasures from the storehouse, or what she claims are such, you might remind her that as she has never seen fit to make use of the intellectual and personnel resources of her province, I have been obliged to assist her with her budgets for her entire tenure as Princess of the Vangavaye-ve. This means as a result that I know how much ought to be in her treasury within five hundred valiants, and that I shall hold her responsible for any discrepancies."

Sayo Minaa gaped at him for a moment, then scribbled something into his tablet, a fierce delight stealing over his features.

Cliopher turned, to find Gaudy already at his side, his writing kit in hand. Cliopher smiled at his nephew and took out one of the sheets of official paper for proclamations. He wrote a short letter of appointment, signed and sealed it, and handed it to Sayo Minaa. "There: sufficient authorization to act for the next week. I shall be thoroughly occupied the rest of today—" Assuming the day, did, in fact, end at some point—"and tomorrow as well. I trust you will be able to maintain the status quo."

"Shall I, er, put together some, um, reports, for the new, uh, prince?"

"That would be most helpful, Sayo Minaa."

He seemed to take this as a dismissal, for he made a peculiar sort of bow, halfway between the Islander style and what was probably intended to be a Jilkano court courtesy, and took himself out, clutching the furled scroll with his letter of appointment to himself.

Cliopher recollected that he stood in the midst of his family and not in some office of his department when Quintus cleared his throat.

"As I was saying before what I think we will all agree was a most illuminating interruption, I've recently come back from Zangoraville. My last few interactions with Kip—his letters, the time I went to Solaara with Aunt Eidora, the last time he was home—I realized I didn't really understand—basically I did what Kip earlier said he'd thought we'd done, or would have done if we were interested. I asked people what they knew of Cliopher Mdang, the Lord Chancellor."

He smiled slyly at Cliopher.

Of course, it would be Nijan.

"I discovered that everyone, practically everyone, in Nijan had thoughts about our Kip. I guess he acts as the arbitrator for all their disputes, since they don't like their duke—really don't like him. I'll tell you stories later. For now I'm going to read from this little booklet they were giving out. It's called *The Viceroy: An Introduction*. From what Kip said earlier today Princess Oriana was supposed to see something of the sort put out here, but obviously didn't."

He cleared his throat again. Cliopher had not read the booklet. He hoped Kiri had.

The list of projects implemented under Cliopher's auspices or with his determined patronage went on for some time. Whoever had put together the pamphlet appeared to have been heavily indoctrinated by the radical spirit of the Nijani police service, for he or she or they made no discrimination between small-scale grants and worldwide projects. They had also not discriminated according to time; some of the initiatives mentioned went back decades.

But because 'a grant for small farmers to buy their own land' was stated instead of 'policies to improve diversity and effectiveness of agricultural production,' as was more usually how he described it, his family heard all the activities, big and small, that affected them.

He had known at least three dozen little grants and bursaries he had created out of his family's pet projects. He knew of a score more that had been awarded to various among them, because they had written to tell him. He was not expecting the starts and murmurs of 'But I got that one'—'Didn't so-and-so do that?'—'I just applied for that'—to swell into a surge.

And it kept going.

In Solaara it had been nearly a thousand years since the Fall, though if pressed Cliopher could not focus his memory on the long stretches of time that in retrospect seemed nothing more than a year or two between holidays. But those years had been filled by activity if not by interior life, and far away in the Vangavaye-ve the fruits of his labours had been known.

Quintus read through to the end of the booklet, raising his voice over the murmurs. Somewhere in the middle Vinyë took his arm, and Bertie put his hand on his other shoulder.

The murmurs grew into conversation.

The doorbell clanked, causing everyone to look at each other.

"But Uncle Kip's here," Leona said after a moment. "He's the only one who usually rings."

"Surely other people use the doorbell?" Cliopher said, desperate for a change of topic.

Half the room laughed. "No, everyone else just comes inside and hollers," Vinyë said. "Go and see who it is, Leona. Last time Kip came home it was the Emperor of Astandalas!"

"Who didn't use the doorbell this time. I take your point."

Leona didn't shriek in surprise, so it was presumably neither the Red Company nor the Moon. It was, instead, Aya, who checked her step slightly on seeing how many people were in the room.

Cliopher greeted her in the Vangavayen style. "Aya! Are you looking for Jiano?"

She smiled brightly around the room, her glance stopping on Eidora. "I am, Cliopher, but I have clearly interrupted a … family occasion?"

"We are discussing my career. Everyone, this is Aya inDovo Delanis, our kinswoman from Loaloa. Aya, my mother, Eidora, my aunts Oura, Malania, Moula, and my uncles Cliopher, Galenius, and Lazo. The rest are miscellaneous Mdang cousins and friends." He rattled off their names, hoping no one expected Aya to learn them all immediately.

Aya bowed over her hands to the room, most deeply to Eidora. "I am so delighted to meet you! I'm not sure how I never had much to do with the Mdangs when I was in the Department of Finance, but I suppose I was preoccupied. It is wonderful to meet so many I have heard so much about."

"My lord wished to speak to Jiano, Aya," Cliopher said, "I imagine they will be some time."

"He's decided, then? Good."

"Please stay that we may come to know you," Eidora said. "We have not heard much of our family in the Western Ring for some time."

"I haven't been back to Loaloa for several months," Aya said, shrugging ruefully. "My husband and I live on Lesuia Island—or have done so. I suppose we will be moving to the palace now—Cliopher, how much time will he be expected to spend in Solaara?"

"The Council of Princes will be every six weeks." Alas. But he did have to keep a certain degree of accountability … and he wanted to ensure they were there, step by step, as he persuaded them to transform their powers. "There will not be full court while his Radiancy is away, so Jiano will not have to be there for that. There may be some other occasions depending on what is happening, what other committees he chooses to join …"

"That you persuade him to join, you mean?" She grinned; several cousins laughed. "We shall have to talk to you about putting together a council of advisors here. Do you have anyone you'd recommend?"

Cliopher choked. Over by the door Rhodin actually raised his hand to hide a pretend cough.

Aya swung around at the noise, then back to Cliopher. "That wasn't the right question, was it?"

Cliopher gestured around the room. "Aya, I am related to half of Gorjo City. It would be entirely incorrect of me to suggest specific names. I can tell you what sort of person I would recommend you look for, but specific people? No. Just—no."

Several people suppressed snickers. Aya grinned unrepentantly at him. "Fair enough. I shall just have to remember what you said about the names on that petition when we were in Solaara—oh!" She swung around to look at the uncles. "Did you say this is your uncle Lazo?"

"I am," Uncle Lazo said, with a puzzled air. "May I ask why?"

Aya bowed deeply over her hands. "When Jiano and I went to Solaara to present our case against that fish farm, we took Loo—er, Louya Mdang's petition, which I'm guessing pretty much all of you signed? I recall many of your names. When it came to the petition, the Lord Emperor noted that it had many people named Mdang on it, and asked Cliopher whether he was related to any of them." She grinned at Cliopher. "He said, all of them. One of the other princes asked Princess Oriana what she proposed doing to the people who had signed their names, and she said that she would remove them all from their positions."

"What?" cried Quintus.

"She also said that since Lord Mdang had been so insistent on the annual stipend, he surely would not be concerned at their survival. Then Cliopher got up to speak, and he said he was impressed the princess was so willing to give up on so many pleasures for her principles, and went through the list of names explaining what everyone did." She transferred her grin to Uncle Lazo, who was looking decidedly nonplussed. "And at the end, he said that the Vangavaye-ve would be just fine without trade, commerce, agriculture, the opera house, and the rest of the world, but not without your barber shop."

Uncle Lazo said, "And what was the response to that?"

Aya laughed. "He sat down, the Lord Emperor called the vote, and we won."

Everyone looked at Cliopher again. He shifted position uncomfortably, caught sight of Rhodin's smirk, cleared his throat. "Not all of the princes are so lacking in political acumen as Princess Oriana."

"Stop fudging, Kip," Aunt Oura said severely. "What do you mean?"

He smiled reluctantly. "None of you would listen to Princess Oriana's order to leave your jobs. I made sure they all knew that."

"And also that you would hardly support the princess against her people?" Quintus said.

Cliopher felt his smile broaden. "Well, there is that, too."

CHAPTER SEVENTY-SEVEN

THE PURIFICATION CEREMONIES WENT ON for most of the next day and left his Radiancy looking tired and Cliopher feeling as if he'd just spent the day wrangling with the Council of Princes. At the end of the last sequence, the two high priest-wizards who were conducting the rituals enveloped them in thick clouds of dense incense. By this point Cliopher was so enervated and emotionally numb that he could not raise the energy for more than a faint cough.

"Your attendants will have prepared the correct baths," one of the priest-wizards said. "After that the final stages of the ceremonies for the Viceroyship will complete the magical and ceremonial purification."

Which meant, Cliopher supposed, that his Radiancy could not yet touch anyone.

"Very good," said his Radiancy, and gestured at Cliopher to accompany him out of the room they'd been using for the ceremonies. It opened onto a covered corridor running along the outside of the building, open to the air on its outer side. He walked over to the side to turn his face to the lowering sun and feel for a moment the fresh air.

His Radiancy stood beside him. Cliopher only realized that he had tears running down his face when the gardens and buildings below him swam into a bright blur.

"Come," said his Radiancy. "Two hours from now you will forget this."

"I don't think I shall ever forget this," said Cliopher, but he managed a smile. He walked beside his Radiancy to the door leading up to the rooms they had been given. "Is there anything else I can do for you, my lord?" he asked when his Radiancy walked past his own door to stop at Cliopher's.

His Radiancy smiled. "I was involved in Féonie's creation of your costume for this evening, and I wished to see your reaction."

"I am sure it will be splendid," said Cliopher. The door opened (Havor,
looking full of importance), and he followed his Radiancy into the room.
These were designed much along the usual Gorjo City pattern, with a sitting
room, a bedroom, and two smaller rooms behind for family or attendants.

In the main room Féonie stood next to two clothing racks. Cliopher saw
a bright blur of bronze and blue and orange and then his eyes focused.

"Oh," he said, walking forward.

The costume was to usual Islander finery as his court costumes were to
his day-to-day wear. In this case it was not so much materials as quality of
construction that showed that difference. Cliopher could not have woven a
grass skirt with that level of detail, could not have dyed the pandanus leaves
with those subtle tints of bronze and orange and midnight, could not have
embroidered the thousands of tiny tortoiseshell cowries and even tinier gold
and ivory seed pearls into the patterns of the headdress.

He circled the clothing rack slowly, taking in every detail. Nothing was
disproportionate, nothing distorted, nothing missing. Every smallest element
of the design was correct, declaring his identity as a Mdang of Tahivoa in
Gorjo City, whose island was Loaloa, whose dances were *Aōteketētana*.

And every smallest stitch and perfectly placed feather or shell declared
his power, his authority, his rank, his status. The surmount of the headdress
rose out of the bands of cowries and pearls through bronze and black lyrebird
feathers to tiers of iridescent blue superb bird-of-paradise feathers crowned
with the two long tail-feathers of the Glorious Imperial bird-of-paradise, the
rarest of all, to be worn (like ahalo cloth) only by the very highest ranks. The
gold-eyed royal blue tips, more brilliantly coloured than a peacock, rose a full
six inches above the rest.

He had only ever seen the feathers in the Museum of Comparative Anthropology, as part of the regalia worn by the Paramount Chief Elonoa'a for
the joining of the Islanders to the Empire under Aurelius Magnus.

Cliopher realized he was crying again when he came round the front and
tried to look at his Radiancy. Féonie handed him a cloth and he wiped his
face. "I'm sorry, my lord," he said.

"Beauty is recognized in many ways," his Radiancy said. "We have our
answer, Féonie, do you not think?"

"Indeed, Glorious One," she replied. "Shall I remove the other costume?"

Cliopher blinked at her. "There's another costume?"

His Radiancy laughed. Cliopher turned, saw that his Radiancy was gesturing to the side, and recalled that there was a second clothing rack. It held a court costume made of ahalo cloth and foamwork and cloth-of-gold and enough jewellery to outfit an ambassadorial delegation.

"Oh," he said, and, feeling that was insufficient, added, "It's very lovely."

"We will be able to find another occasion for it," Féonie said, smiling indulgently at him, and made as if to take it away.

"Wait," said his Radiancy. "I have had an idea."

★★★

IN THE COURT COSTUME CLIOPHER felt exceedingly grand.

He stood at the bottom of the daïs in the main hall of the Vangavayen palace, as he had stood at his Radiancy's right hand for any number of occasions, and considered the fact that it was the first time he had ever actually been inside the room.

It was a lovely room, but had a faint air of disillusionment about it. He tried to figure out what made him think that, for there was nothing so obvious as disrepair. Eventually (for the initial ceremonies took some time to involve him) he determined it was because the ancient Islander patterns painted and carved on the walls had been hidden by banners and tapestries fashioned in the manner of the Jilkano principalities and the Solaaran court. There was none of the pride in local heritage that he had seen in other royal palaces.

Even in Amboloyo or Xiputl the royal palaces celebrated the arts and material wealth of the province. Ahalo cloth and foamwork were far too rare and expensive to use as hangings, and the golden pearls given as tithes usually were passed up to his Radiancy, but Princess Oriana had eschewed woven hangings or basketwork or paintings from the Vangavaye-ve.

He wondered how different it would be the next time he saw the room.

Down below the daïs the hall was filled with many small tables. He had no idea where they had come from or if that was Princess Oriana's usual manner of arranging her court. She was known for enjoying table games. Cliopher could imagine her enjoying presiding over a room full of beautifully garbed aristocrats playing sophisticated games with elegance and poise. The tables had centrepieces consisting of bowls of flowers and currently unlit candles.

He frowned at the candles, wondering who had decided to place them there and for what purpose. In some regions of the world that would have been a slight, suggesting the audience was not worthy of wasting light; here, however, lighting the candles might have been part of Jiano's intended ceremony.

He liked the fact that he knew nearly two-thirds of the people he could see, and was related to fully a quarter of them.

His Radiancy gave a short speech explaining that due to irreconcilable differences of philosophy between the Princess Oriana and his excellency Lord Mdang she was being relieved of her appointment as of that evening. While the room was still reacting to this, his Radiancy added blandly, "Due to her appalling inability to perform her duties to our satisfaction she will be facing us in court."

Even Cliopher blinked at that.

The remnants of the Vangavayen court—including the elderly Duke of the Isolate Islands, who sat next to the Prince of Amboloyo and appeared more amused than concerned about his own position—sat to either side of the room near the daïs. Cliopher's heart sang as he saw that in the central table sat his mother, his sister, his great-uncle, and his closest friends. Aya and Jiano's places had been taken by Conju and Rhodin, who was not on duty that evening for reasons that Cliopher presumed had to do with him spending the previous two days following along behind him.

His Radiancy called Princess Oriana. She walked up the long aisle leading from the opposite end of the hall to his Radiancy's throne. She was dressed for the last time in ahalo cloth and her court costume, her makeup impeccable. Her posture was rigid, her face a mask behind the powders and paint. Her eyes glittered; when Cliopher moved to stand before the throne to fulfil his office he nearly lost his breath at the hatred in them.

But she knelt at his feet and presented him with the physical emblem of her rule, an okana shell cast in solid gold. He cupped his hands below hers, taking the weight of the gold himself, and kept his face very calm. She stared past him at his Radiancy as if he wasn't there.

Behind him his Radiancy spoke sonorously, the rolling syllables of the formal renunciation of office.

He thought of the hours he had spent each year going over her budgets. The hours taken from other work to go over the reports from the Vanga-vaye-ve. All the times he had told her to sign a paper giving him the authority to implement one of his new projects in her name, since he had so quickly found they would simply not get done if he left them to her. (And why, he wondered, had he ever thought she would follow through with making all those proclamations of what he, and not she, was doing? She could not take credit for the things he publicly announced were his initiatives.)

The okana shell was very heavy. He had only ever seen the real shell a handful of times, for they were very rare, as rare in their way as *efani*. His Buru Tovo had shown him one, teaching him the song of the okana, the story of the paramount chiefs of the old days before the coming of the princes. The real shell was delicate pink and gold and brown, like someone's cupped hands.

The ceremony washed over him like waves of the sea. He held his hands steady, even when Princess Oriana started to push down against him. He would not drop the symbol of the Vangavaye-ve.

He did not have any words to say. He stood as the Hands of the Emperor, conduit for the magic of unbinding, and when at last Princess Oriana said her final words of submission and snapped her hands away from his he did not drop the gold okana.

She spared the time for one final hateful glare as she rose from her knees.

He kept his face perfectly unemotional. It was easy, with all that magic and the armour of formal ceremony raised up about him. And it was easy, for he could find it in his heart to pity her, squanderer of so many gifts as she was.

He did spare a thought for how likely it was that she would work (perhaps with the former Duke of Nijan, her kinsman) to unseat him, perhaps try to have him disgraced or even assassinated.

Rhodin and Ludvic would keep him safe, he thought, and hard on the heels of that thought two of the Imperial Guard came out from their positions along the wall to escort the former princess away.

Cliopher did not watch her go. His role was to stand there, the Hands of the Emperor, conduit for the ceremonies. He kept his attention down the length of the hall, to the far door where Jiano stood waiting for the signal to approach.

His Radiancy said, "Jiano Delanis of Ikialo village of the island of Lesuia, approach."

There was a quiet murmur through the hall, among those who had not yet heard who would be Princess Oriana's replacement, Cliopher surmised. They did not know that usually there would be heralds and trumpeters and a host of other attendants and officials to mediate between Lord Emperor and prince-elect. His Radiancy had told him that since the planned ceremonies would already be considerably extended to accommodate the stripping of Princess Oriana and appointment of Jiano he had decided to streamline what he could.

Cliopher had not said that he wished that all court ceremonies could be so streamlined, but knew that his Radiancy had seen it in his face.

He watched Jiano walk down the axis of the hall, back straight, chin up, eyes on his Radiancy. He was dressed in his full Eastern Ring finery, knee-length grass skirt and feather-and-shell headdress, armbands adorned with fresh greenery, face and torso painted yellow and blue and white in his family designs. Cliopher's heart sang for the rightness of it.

Jiano bowed in the Vangavayen style to his Radiancy, hand over fist, before performing the court obeisance. At his Radiancy's gesture he rose, climbed the steps to the lower daïs where Cliopher stood, and knelt before Cliopher.

"Jiano of Lesuia, we offer you our province of the Vangavaye-ve to govern under us to the best of your ability. Do you accept this responsibility?"

Cliopher offered him the okana.

"I do." Jiano lifted his hands and cupped them firmly around Cliopher's. His grip was firm, his arms steady, despite the sudden weight of the solid gold shell. Cliopher hoped he kept all trace of relief off his face, but the shell must have weighed three or four pounds, and he was starting to feel the long holding of it.

He smiled inwardly as his Radiancy began the invocations, the reverse of the unbindings he had just performed. These were punctuated by Jiano's responses, which he gave in a clear and confident voice.

His hands and Jiano's were much the same colour, Jiano's perhaps a trace darker. Cliopher had performed this office for—what was it, now?—all of the provinces except for Xiputl and Old Damara. Those had kept the same rulers since the Fall, Princess Anastasiya and the Grand Duchess. Each of the other provinces had changed princes at least once since Cliopher had become the Hands of the Emperor. He had performed it when Oriana had become Princess of the Vangavaye-ve, in fact, but that ceremony had taken place, like all the others, in Solaara.

It felt so much *righter* for it to happen here, in the royal palace of the Vangavaye-ve, with his Radiancy on the throne that was placed there out of symbolic necessity (for this was the first time his Radiancy had ever sat in it for a formal office). Cliopher stood there while words and magic and ritual washed in waves over and through him, and revised his idea of how provincial governors should be appointed in the new order that would come into existence so soon now.

And finally Jiano finished the ceremony, and was announced by his Radiancy as Our Well-Loved Deputy in this Our Province of the Vangavaye-ve, the Paramount Chief Jiano Delanis.

Jiano rose easily. Cliopher turned so that the audience could see the transfer of power as Jiano took the okana from his hands. Jiano walked to the edge of the daïs and lifted the shell up, as was traditional, and then he turned and made his new degree of obeisance to his Radiancy, as was also traditional. He then bowed over his hands to Cliopher, which wasn't, but Cliopher appreciated this variation in the usual order, since the full greeting of the new Paramount Chief to the Lord Chancellor would be superseded by the oath-taking that was about to follow.

And then Cliopher bowed to his Radiancy and walked off the daïs and out through the side door into the hall outside. Behind him he heard his Radiancy announce that before the ceremonies appointing the Viceroy commenced, Paramount Chief Jiano wished to address his people.

Cliopher did not wait to hear how Jiano began, though he was curious. He walked briskly down the corridors that led parallel to the hall until he came to the room where Féonie and Franzel waited to assist him with changing into his traditional finery. Jiano had agreed (said his Radiancy; Cliopher had been preoccupied with the bathing as required by the priest-wizards and had not spoken to him) to occupy sufficient time for Cliopher to change his clothes and make his way to the main door of the hall. He would also indicate when it was time for Cliopher to enter by some form of an invitation.

Féonie helped him remove the gossamer layers of ahalo cloth and foamwork, which took more time than putting them on had required. Cliopher tried not to hurry, not wishing to damage the superlative garments and knowing just how much work went into those fabrics. "There," he said, when he was down to his linen under-trousers. And then he looked at the grass skirt and at Féonie.

"Sir?" she said, with a wicked twinkle.

"I'm old enough to be your father," he said. "Turn around, will you?"

She giggled but did so. He stripped off the trousers, handed them to Franzel, and stepped into the grass skirt. "All right," he said, when a fruitless moment had made it clear that the inner fastenings of the skirt were not the ones he knew. "How do I fasten it?"

"Here, sir," she said, and with deft hands tied several knots. "Does that feel secure, sir?"

He had to stifle something approaching a giggle of his own. It would not do to begin making innuendoes with Féonie (who was, indeed, at least half his age). Besides, if he started laughing he might not be able to stop.

She fixed the headdress with several long pins woven into his hair. "It will not come off of its own, sir," she said solemnly when she had inserted the last. "If you need to remove it for some reason, here are the ends."

She guided his hand to the pin heads. "They are blue pearls, sir, so you will be able to see them in a mirror."

"Is there a mirror?" he asked, starting to look around but stopping when she lightly struck the side of his head.

"Hold still, sir! The mirror in a moment."

He held still while she adjusted something to her satisfaction. Finally she nodded. "Very good, sir. Now, Franzel, the necklaces."

"The necklaces?"

Cliopher held his breath as Franzel presented him with a tray on which were three efela necklaces. The *efani* shell, strung on a simple knotted cord with the five gold pearls on either side. The sundrop cowries, forty-nine of them, long enough for three loops. And third, a new necklace, made of polished coral the colour of fire.

"Your great-uncle said these were the necklaces," Féonie said. "The *efani*, the *efevoa*, and the *efetana*." She pronounced the words carefully.

Cliopher touched the *efetana* with a trembling hand. "These are for fire dance," he said.

But they were more than that. They showed that his Buru Tovo had judged him worthy of being *tanà*.

And *efevoa*? Like *efani*, that was a name he knew, a story he knew, but had not known what the shells so named looked like. They were the gift of Vou'a, the god of mystery, whom Jiano would call Iki. To wear the three necklaces together suggested that Cliopher had been marked by the Mother of Islands, and by the Son of Laughter, and was bound to both by the thread of the gift of fire brought back after great travels from the House of the Sun.

No wonder Mardo had looked so stunned.

He removed the efela nai—for once superseded!—but left the efela ko. However far he had come, whatever he might have accomplished, he had not forgotten his island or his name or whence he came.

He hung the efela around his neck one after the other. First the *efani*, the white and blue shell centred on his chest. Then the *efevoa*, three loops joined by a single gold clasp that Féonie did for him. And finally the *efetana*, made from a coral only to be found in the most dangerous waters off the outer edge of Pau'lo'en'lai, the island of the ancestors, where it fell into the open ocean on the outer side of the Ring.

"Now for the mirror," said Féonie, touching the *efani* so it hung perfectly. Franzel held the mirror for him so he could see himself.

Cliopher caught his breath. He had thought he looked an Islander when he had dressed for the fire dance, but on that occasion his heart had been full of defiance and challenge and the urgent need to prove himself. He had looked good for someone who spent his days indoors reading and writing reports. He had not looked like someone who could sail across the Wide Seas in a boat of his own making.

He straightened his shoulders. He had not liked his flabby middle and his weak arms, revealed so clearly by the Islander finery in that dance. He had asked Ludvic (thinking the Commander less of an embarrassing person to ask than Rhodin) for exercises he might do to strengthen his upper body. He had done them without really attending to any of the changes in his body that had come as a result.

He had noticed that his reflection in court costume looked increasingly magnificent, but had assumed this all to do with Féonie's increasing skill as a tailor and his own increasing status.

He had thought, two days ago, that he had crossed some invisible line into old age.

But in that superlative version of his customary finery, he realized that what he looked like was the *tanà*, the Tender of the Fire, the advisor to chiefs and paramount chiefs—and emperors.

"Thank you," he said. "It looks magnificent."

"You make it easy," said Féonie, smiling, and he laughed at her flattery; but he knew also that it wasn't entirely untrue.

★★★

HE WALKED TO THE MAIN door of the hall. Varro and Zerafin in full Imperial panoply stood there. They saluted with parade-ground perfection and then, since no one else was in sight, grinned at him. "You look splendid," whispered Varro. Zerafin nodded; Cliopher was astonished to realize the young man had tears in his eyes.

"What is it?" he asked softly.

Zerafin swallowed hard. "My mother is from the Isolates, sir," he said. "I never thought to see someone wear Islander finery for such a high court ceremony."

That nearly made Cliopher start to weep himself. He broke convention sufficiently to take the young guard's arms and perform the Islander greeting.

"Thank you, Zerafin, for saying that. I never thought, when I joined the Service, that I would ever be able to claim my culture this way."

"You make the world proud," said Varro, and saluted again. "Shall we open the door, sir?"

"Quietly," said Cliopher, when he felt he was ready. "I will stand here until Jiano gives the signal."

He hoped Jiano was not standing there waiting for him; he couldn't hear anything like a speech, and, thinking about it, realized he had not heard anything at all since he had left the hall.

He discovered the reason for this as soon as Zerafin and Varro opened the two leaves of the door for him. Cliopher stood just at the threshold, waiting his invitation.

Jiano was walking up and down the hall, snaking around each table, his feet snapping on the floor the only sound. He was holding what looked like a carved ebony stick in the air, silently displaying it to each group of people.

As he turned around one of the last tables, Cliopher saw the stick clearly. It was ebony, and was very intricately if simply carved, in smooth bands of wood curving in spirals around a hollow core. As soon as he realized what he was looking at, he knew what it was, though he had only seen representations of it before. It was a ngali staff.

There would be twelve spirals, one for each of the original ships of the Wayfinders who had crossed the Wide Seas to come to the Vangavaye-ve. The ngali staff was the symbol of the families who traced their lineage back to those ships. Like the okana shell, it had been part of the original regalia of the Vangavaye-ve when the last of the true Paramount Chiefs had allied with Aurelius Magnus.

If Jiano did nothing else as the Paramount Chief, Cliopher thought—if he turned out to be as ineffectual and vainglorious as Princess Oriana—this was more than any prince of the Vangavaye-ve had ever done to show that he spoke for the people. And of course, since Jiano had chosen to spend the day since he had agreed to become the Paramount Chief looking for a ngali staff, his action indicated that he was going to take all those fine oaths he had just sworn to guide and govern and respect his people very seriously indeed.

Jiano finished his circuit of the room by going around the table where Eidora sat with Vinyë and Bertie and Irela, Ghilly and Toucan and Quintus, Rhodin and Conju and Buru Tovo. Cliopher watched him remount the daïs and girded himself for the invitation, and the ceremony, that would come next.

Jiano bowed to his Radiancy, who inclined his head solemnly, and then turned to face the hall. He looked down the long axis at Cliopher, who felt his heart begin to beat faster with anticipation.

And then Jiano struck down with the staff onto the wooden daïs, which boomed, and as everyone stared in astonishment at him, he lifted his voice and cried,

"*I sing the Wide Seas.*"

CHAPTER SEVENTY-EIGHT

CLIOPHER LIFTED HIS FOOT TO step across the threshold and then he hesitated, thought again, and placed his feet back on the outside.

He could see heads turning as people asked their neighbours how they should respond.

Jiano thudded down the ngali staff again. For the second time he cried, "I sing the Wide Seas!"

He would not get very far restructuring the government of the Vangavaye-ve as a radical communist, Cliopher thought in amusement, if he could not persuade his people to respond to the ancient demand.

For a third time Jiano struck the staff and cried, "I sing the Wide Seas!"

And this time, out of the dimmer recess of the hall, someone lifted up her voice in the ancient reply.

"*O Ani o Vou'a o Vangavaye-ve ea Eana Loa!*"

Cliopher let out a breath he had not realized he was holding. Few knew more than a handful of words in the old Islander tongue, even out along the Ring; but every Islander born knew the opening the *Lays of the Wide Seas.*

We come in our ships to the gift of Ani and Vou'a, to the Vangavaye-ve.

And every Islander born knew what happened next.

Cliopher had not witnessed the Singing of the Waters since he had left for Astandalas, as the great annual festival fell at the same time as the most important of the court sessions in the Palace. But he had learned the whole cycle of *Lays* from his great-uncle, and he had sung them over and over again on his voyage across the Wide Seas, and he read or sang them to himself each year when the time came for the festival, renewing his own sense of self and community no matter how far he was from home.

O Ani o Vou'a o Vangavaye-ve ea Eana Loa ...

There was a breathless moment, and then Bertie raised his rough, powerful baritone. "I sing the ship *Huaketētē*. I am Kindraa, and I sing for Those Who Know the Wind."

"I sing the ship *Aio-aiatē*," came the voice of Cliopher's uncle on his father's side. "I am Varga, and I sing for Those Who Touch the Water."

"I sing the ship *Lovau'en'ai*," came Ghilly's thin voice, loud and proud if not beautiful. "I am Poyë, and I sing for Those Who Carry the Seeds."

The elderly Duke of the Isolates, whose mother had been an Islander, lifted a beautiful voice to sing, "I sing the ship *Huai'a-ve*. I am Ela, and I sing for Those Who Went Farthest."

And so it went, ship by ship, until eleven of the ships of the original settlers and the core families descended from them were sung out.

Cliopher realized he was holding his breath again, this time in wonder, as half the room lifted their voice to cry the name of the twelfth: "I sing the ship *Ouvaye-ve*. I am Mdang, and I sing for Those Who Hold the Fire."

There was an undercurrent of laughter in the sheer number of those singing for the Mdang family, but it quickly transformed into polyphony as the descendants of the twelve ships sang out the next passages of the *Lays*.

Cliopher stood there listening in astonishment, facing Jiano down the long axis of the hall, his Radiancy a glowing golden figure on the throne above all the rest.

These songs were as familiar to each member of his family, each Islander in the room, as they were to him. These passages were sung at least once a year, at the Singing of the Waters, when the young men and women raced outrigger canoes across the lagoons and the families strove to out-sing, out-dance, and out-feast each other. The polyphony was partly traditional and partly spontaneous, each singer riffing on the ancient melodies. Some percussionist from Vinyë's orchestra in the corner started to play accompanying drums, another lifted a deep horn in place of the traditional conch, and the deep familiar pattern of wave over wave filled the room.

Buru Tovo had told Cliopher stories of the great sea-going ships setting out to see what was behind the sunrise. They had come (so said the *Lays*) from a land no longer to be found, which had lain between the Isolates and Amboloyo. Some stories said they had sailed from another world altogether to find the Wide Seas of Zunidh; others that the land had fallen in some cataclysm forgotten long before the coming of the Empire and its scribes.

Wherever exactly they had first come from, they had brought with them their wealth in knowledge and adventure, and sought new islands and new homes, singing the songs of their people all the way. They had crossed first to the north, then turned back again at Nijan across the southern ocean to find at last the Vangavaye-ve.

Cliopher half-recognized a number of voices and knew that some of his cousins had left the part of *Ouvaye-ve* to shore up the thinner representations of the other ships. He stood there, listening to the tale of the crossing, listening to the catalogue of the families and the names of their dances. Jiano took up the part of the *mafa*, singing each bridge between the *Lays* before the audience-become-participants sang the fuller narrative.

Jiano sang:

> *Over the Wide Seas we sailed*
> *Learning the ways of the winds*
> *Speaking to the waves*
> *Learning the ways of the birds*
> *Speaking to the sky*
> *Learning the ways of the Islands*
> *Speaking to the land*

And someone—it might be Uncle Haido or Aunt Malania, lead singers at the Opera, or it might be someone with an untrained but enthusiastic voice, or it might be some cousin or friend or minor aristocrat of Princess Oriana's court who had never before declared his knowledge of the *Lays*—would respond with the name of the islands or the winds or the waves that the Wayfinders had found, and others in the room, in trios or quartets or great floor-shaking masses, would sing forth the replies.

> *Over the Wide Seas we sailed*
> *Ai! In our ships which we built with our own hands*

> *Over the Wide seas we sailed*
> > *—The names of our ships are our families*
> > *—The names of our families hold our ships*

> *We sing the Aio-aiatē, fair as a leaping dolphin*
> > *—We the Varga*
> > *—We who Touch the Water*
> > *—By our hands in the water*
> > *—We feel the shape of the water*
> > > *—We know the ways of the water*

> *Over the Wide Seas we sailed*
> *Ai! In our ships which we built with our own hands*

Over the Wide Seas we sailed
Learning the ways of the winds

Ai! We sing the name of the winds of the Wide Seas
—The winds the come in the morning
    —E'ta the wind of the morning sun
    —Out of the east she called us
      —We the Kindra
—We Who Know the Wind
      —By the shape of the invisible
      —We learn the shape of the unknown
—We know the ways of the winds

Ai! We sing forth the way to the morning and the evening
Learning the ways of the winds

And so the song went, voice over voice, wave over wave. Cliopher stood listening, half-vocalizing the words, half-hearing his Buru Tovo's voice (gruff but true) singing the *Lays* over and over again, some days not saying anything else but the *Lays*, until Cliopher went to sleep with the songs of his ancestors in his ears and woke to the songs of the islands they had come to know so deeply.

And still his Buru had sung the *Lays*, over and over again, until Cliopher was able to reply to any question suddenly thrown at him with a line or a passage or a phrase from the cycle of songs.

He stood there at the threshold of the hall, at the edge of his community, feeling the song rise up out of the deep core of his being.

Ai! We sing the Islands of the Wide Seas
The coming of the ships across the sea
What we found there on the other side of the morning

Ai! What we found when we were
called by the wind of the morning
When the wind of the evening filled our sails
And sent us to find the Mother of the Islands
The singer of the first song

Jiano guided them to sing the whole of the first sequence of the *Lays*, the coming of the ships to the Vangavaye-ve and the settlement of the Ring. When they had sung the naming of the islands and the first villages, he slowly lowered the ngali staff to indicate that they would not be going immediately into the second sequence.

The hall slowly fell silent as each voice in the polyphonic chorus finished her part. When Jiano finished the last line the room was silent, but with a quality of silence totally different from those it had earlier held. This silence was alive with expectation and attention, each person focused on Jiano at the foot of the throne of the Sun-in-Glory.

In the moments of the silence as everyone waited eagerly for what Jiano would choose to do next, Cliopher thought very clearly that this was true government.

Jiano bent his head over the ebony staff. A slight sheen of sweat on his torso was the only indication that he might be nervous or exhilarated from leading an extended choral celebration of the culture and history of his people.

Cliopher had no idea how long the first of the *Lays* had taken. There were no bells here to mark the hours and divide up the day. There was the song, and the singing, and the feast that would come in its time, and that was all that mattered.

Jiano lifted his head. He lifted the staff, and made a wide sweeping gesture to encompass the room. Then he took a breath, and Cliopher prepared himself for the shift from the traditional to the court ceremonies that would come next with the fealty rituals.

Satisfied he held the room, Jiano looked down the axis straight at Cliopher. He held Cliopher's eyes long enough that the audience turned in their seats to see what he was looking at. Cliopher braced himself for the murmurs, the attention, the looks, and hoped he had not forgotten everything Lord Lior had so thoroughly instructed him in.

Jiano pointed the staff at him. Cliopher took a deep breath.

"Who is this that comes out of the sunrise?"

Cliopher's heart turned over with an incredibly painful thump.

The response was quicker this time, as everyone but him had been waiting for the next sequence of the *Lays* to begin.

> —*Who is this whose ship comes across the Wide Seas*
> —*Who is this?*
> —*Who is this that comes out of the sunrise?*

Cliopher knew this. He and his cousin Basil had run around play-acting it out. In those games Cliopher had always been the Paramount Chief,

Elonoa'a.

> *Who is this that comes out of the sunrise?*
> *—Who is this?*
> *Who is this whose ship comes across the Wide Seas?*
> *—Who is this that comes?*
> *Who is this that comes from the house of the sun?*

He held Jiano's eyes. And then, the motion coming from his childhood, he raised his hands in the open-palmed gesture that tradition said was that made by Aurelius Magnus, the Emperor of Astandalas, when he beseeched Elonoa'a's permission to land.

> *—Let him approach*
> *—O let this stranger from the sun approach*
> *—We would have news of the other side of the sunrise*
> *—O let him come*

Cliopher swallowed. He did not properly know the dances that went with the part. He had never studied any of the dances but those of his family; he had never thought himself a good enough dancer, nor had he felt much of a need to display himself like a cock bird-of-paradise. He had not been a solo singer, either, content to be part of the chorus.

He took a deep breath.

Jiano sang, "Come, then, stranger, and be welcome."

Cliopher stepped across the threshold of the hall. He was very conscious of the wooden floor against his bare feet, the bobbing of the two Glorious Imperial tail feathers in his headdress, the sound of the leaves of his skirt, the brush of his thighs against each other, the scents of all those people not wearing courtly perfume.

Every instinct in him called for him to dance.

He and his cousin Basil had played at Aurelius Magnus and Elonoa'a, had played at this dance. His feet went into the forgotten steps, the music calling him; when he would have faltered, unsure of how next to move, he found a sequence from the fire dance starting, and so he danced from island to island across the room, the choral questioning rising up around him like a cloud of butterflies.

> *Who is this that comes out of the sunrise?*
> *Who is this whose ship comes across the Wide Seas?*

—Who is this?
—Who is this that comes?
Who is this that comes out of the sunrise?

Cliopher followed the route taken first by Princess Oriana and then by Jiano. They had come with silent witness; he came with a cloud of song.

At the foot of the stairs he bowed over his hands to Jiano, who in this moment represented the government. Jiano made the gesture of welcome. Cliopher climbed the stairs and stood before him as his equal, as Aurelius Magnus had stood before Elonoa'a.

The questions, and their answers, were traditional, sung sometimes by Jiano alone, sometimes by the whole chorus or any part thereof that felt like participating.

—Who is this that comes out of the sunrise?

Cliopher could not remember the last time he had sung in public. He hoped he would not disgrace his family. "I come in the name of the Sun."

—Ai! He claims the name of the Sun.
—And why have you come?

"I come seeking those who know their way."

—Ai! He has heard of our songs.
—You have come yourself from the sunrise.
—Why do you need our songs?
—What way have you lost that we know?

Cliopher found he did know the right gestures. He was making them half-unconsciously; like rigging his boat (his little Tui-tanata!), they came so long as he did not think about them. "I wish to know ways that I do not myself know."

—Ai! He comes with true questions.
—Where shall we guide him?
—What song does he know?
—What does he bring?

His voice nearly broke as he sang the words that Aurelius Magnus had sung. "I bring the wide world."

—Ai! We know the Wide Seas.

"I bring good laws."

—Ai! We know the ways of the sea and the sky.

"I bring new songs."

—Ai! Our songs are the songs of the mother of music.

"I bring a new fire."

His voice did break on that line. Jiano waited—the whole room waited—while he swallowed down what were almost tears, until his jaw firmed and he was able once more to form words. He sang the line again. "I bring a new fire."

—Ah, came the softer response to his words. *He offers a new fire?*

Cliopher waited while the chorus repeated and parsed out the offerings of Aurelius Magnus to the Vangavaye-ve and, eventually, decided they were good. He realized at one point that he was clenching his teeth in dread that the chorus would decide against him.

Was that the power of the music, he wondered, or the fact that everyone singing knew that the questions were more than traditional? That on this occasion, as perhaps never so explicitly in all the years the exchange was performed in the Singing of the Waters, this was a true renewal of the vows between Vangavaye-ve and Emperor?

That on this occasion, as never before, the person who stood in the place of the Emperor in this traditional performance, was in the wider world one who sought to bring good laws and new songs and a new fire; and even more, one who officially *did* stand in the place of the Emperor?

He was the Hands of the Emperor.

This was his family asking him these questions.

Finally the chorus decided that they wished to know more of the one offering these things to them. They sang their questions of identity again, this time not the general *who is this out of the sunrise* but *who are you?*

> *—What is your name?*
>> *—In whose name do you come?*
> *—What is your island?*
>> *—In whose ship did you come?*

—What are your dances?
    —In whose steps did you learn?

The song went on, spiralling up and down, call-and-response like in the kotua challenges at the end of the sugar-cane harvest, like the challenges from boat to boat in the festivals, like the songs that must once have been sung from ship to ship on sunny days or to keep heart in storms across the Wide Seas.

And finally it spiralled down again to one voice, to Jiano lifting the staff and singing, *What is your name?*

In the usual run of the festival the performer would be wearing a mask and would claim the name of the Emperor.

Cliopher turned to the hall—for it was not Jiano who was asking these questions, and if Jiano wished to indicate by every means possible that he spoke for and of and from his people, Cliopher was not the one to insist otherwise. He lifted his hands and made the gesture that indicated he wore no mask for the dance and spoke in his own right.

He took a deep breath and waited. Like Jiano calling the opening line of the *Lays* and waiting for the response, Cliopher made that gesture and that turn and waited.

He waited.

He waited.

Out of the hall he heard the superb tenor of his uncle Haido sound forth: *What is your name?*

His own voice sounded harsh next to it. "I am Cliopher Mdang of Ta-hivoa."

From another corner of the hall, a dozen voices lifted up: *In whose name do you come?*

"I come in the name of the Emperor over the sea."

Aunt Malania asked the next: *What is your island?*

"My island is Loaloa."

He did not recognize the next voice, a deep bass: *In whose ship did you come?*

Cliopher took a breath. He had crossed the Wide Seas in every possible form of transportation. Only one was significant. "I came in a ship of my own hand's building."

It was customary to go on to the next question; but it was a far older custom to ask the name of a ship when someone claimed to have built one according to the ancient tradition.

He did not know the voice that rang out, a loud and pure alto: *What is the name of your ship?*

"The name of my ship is *Tui-tanata*."

He was so glad that Cora had found it still moored where he had left it behind the warehouses and had decided to restore it. Standing there with the *Lays* filling the air like a thunderstorm around him, he could not imagine how he could ever have simply walked away from it.

> —*Ah! The name of his ship is the Tui-tanata.*
> > —*The Song of the Home Fire*
> > —*The Song of the Home Fire*

> —*Ah! The name of his ship is the Tui-tanata*
> > —*He is Mdang*
> > —*He is one who Holds the Fire*
> > —*Does he hold the fire?*

The spontaneous chorus stabbed him. He found his hand lifted involuntarily to the *efetana* necklace. Jiano, who was standing now beside him, looked at his hand at the movement. His eyes widened slightly as he took in the necklaces Cliopher wore. The *efani*, the *efevoa*, and the *efetana*. Three necklaces of the greatest significance.

> —*What are your dances?*

The question spun out from the single voice who asked it to the full chorus of the room. Cliopher waited, knowing he was shaking, until the chorus narrowed, and narrowed again, and finally returned to the first single voice.

> —*What are your dances?*

"My dances are *Aōteketētana*."

He could feel the surprise in the room when he claimed the greater dances. But he did know those dances. He had danced them from necessity, and when he had been asked, and now he claimed them as his own.

The same single voice lifted up: —*In whose steps did you learn?*

He made the wide gesture of humility. "In the steps of Tovo inDaina of Loaloa did I learn the dances."

> —*Ah! He claims the greater dances*
> > —*The dances of Those Who Hold the Fire*
> > —*The dances of Those Who Tend the Fire*

—His teacher's name is known
   —His teacher's name is respected
   —His teacher is tana-tai

—Ah! He is one Who Holds the Fire
   —Does he hold the fire?

Cliopher waited. He had heard challenge-songs before, knew some of the famous ones that were part of the *Lays*, but he had never before sung one himself—let alone one on his own behalf. He knew he was trembling, was far more anxious than Jiano before him.

Jiano walked in a circle around him, the ngali staff uplifted. Cliopher turned in place to match his motion, for a moment seeing his Radiancy look down on him from the throne. That steadied him, that reminder that he stood where he stood for good reason: that this was his own choice, but not only his own choice.

Jiano turned to the hall. "Ah! He sings wisely, this one who comes from the sunrise."

In some challenge-songs that would be the end, but Cliopher knew that it was not, could not be. He had made the claims, but he had not proven them.

With a curious sense of relief he recognized his Uncle Lazo's voice: *What tokens do you show us?*

Cliopher turned again to face the room. He started with the third and most recent of the necklaces, lifting it away from his neck so the light caught it. "I show you the *efetana*."

—From whose hand did it come?

"It was given to me by the hand of Tovo inDaina of Loaloa."

—Ah! He bears the efetana
   —He has danced Aōteketētana

—He offers the token of the tanà
   —The tana-tai has given him the efetana

—He is one Who Holds the Fire
   —He holds the fire

He took another breath and lifted the gold-ringed amber cowries. "I show you the *efevoa*."

It took a moment before Uncle Lazo responded, a little shakily, with: *From whose hand did it come?*

"From the hand of the god of mystery, from the hand of the Son of Laughter was it given to me."

The chorus said, rather than sang, *Ah!* and then paused while everyone looked at each other. Finally Aunt Malania raised her voice and sang until others took up the answers.

> —*Ah! He bears the efevoa*
> > —*He has met the Son of Laughter*
> > > —*He offers the token of Vou'a*

> —*The Son of Laughter has given him efevoa*
> > —*The sign of one who has dived deep*
> > > —*He has spoken with the gods*

He let go of the *efevoa* and lifted up the single shell on it knotted cord. "I show you the *efani*."

The wait for the response was even longer this time before Uncle Haido raised his voice. *From whose hand did it come?*

"From the sea, from the Gates of the Sea in the morning, was it given to me."

> —*Ah! He bears the efani*
> > —*The tear of Ani*

> —*The Mother of Islands has wept for him*
> > —*The Mother of Music has touched him*

> —*The sign of one who has travelled far*
> > —*He has been beloved of the sea*

Cliopher waited, heart thundering, as the three choral responses were repeated, the voices separating and blending as if they held his words up to the sky to look through them. He could not easily see expressions, but he could see the way people kept looking at his mother and at him.

The singing grew quieter and quieter but did not quite fall into silence as it modulated keys to move from the challenge to the offering of alliance and friendship between the Islands and Astandalas.

The expression of surprise that rose and fell like a great wind passing through palms made Cliopher turn to face Jiano. The Paramount Chief had set aside the ebony staff—Aya stood at the edge of the daïs, Cliopher saw in a split second—so that he could hold the okana shell in both hands.

This was not the heavy gold replica Cliopher had given him earlier. This was a real shell; and it held within its hollow a single flaring ember.

"Ai!" he exclaimed, surprised out of all courtliness.

Jiano smiled slightly. He made a slow turn around Cliopher, holding the shell up so that the ember was visible, displaying it to the assembly.

Cliopher watched carefully. With this they were back in the familiar sequence of the *Lays*.

Or—not quite. Jiano began: *This stranger from the sunrise—*

The chorus was supposed to respond *He is become a friend.*

They sang:

> *He is no stranger*
> >   *—He holds Aōteketētana*
> >   *—He has the gifts of the Mother of Islands*
> >   *—He has the gifts of the Son of Laughter*
>
> *He is a son of our islands*
> >   *—He sits at the feet of the Sun*
>
> *He brings us the wide world*
> >   *—He brings us good laws*
>
> *He brings us new songs*
> >   *—He brings us a new fire*
> *He sails our ships with us*

Jiano paused, presumably to gather his thoughts to shift with this new course. Cliopher, waiting to see how he would respond, saw that the ember was starting to go out, and all thoughts of ceremonial decorum went out of his head as the first and most fundamental lesson his Buru Tovo had taught him rose to the forefront.

He tore out a few of the perfectly dyed and arranged strands of his grass skirt, spat on them, and took the two steps necessary to reach the okana shell and carefully feed the ember.

"You're getting a bit ahead of yourself," said Jiano, grinning.

Cliopher said, "You don't have to give me the okana, Paramount Chief, but you must know that once you have begun you must not allow the ember to go out before you have lit a new fire."

Jiano turned to the hall. "Thus speaks the *tanà*!" Laughter rippled through the room. Cliopher flushed and stepped back into his position.

"What say you, people of the Vangavaye-ve? Do we trust this man with our fire?"

The song of alliance was one of the traditional set-pieces. Cliopher had never heard it sound finer; or perhaps it was that the moment Jiano set the okana shell with its smouldering ember into his hands all the hovering magic and tension of the past six months snapped into place.

With the song still cascading around him he turned from Jiano, made one full circle with the shell held up, and then at last he turned his back on his family so that he could look up the remaining steps to the throne.

He did not need to be a wizard himself to know that that ceremony had fulfilled all the requirements of ritual and magic for the swearing of fealty between Paramount Chief and Viceroy. The shell in his hand, the air on his back, the magic singing around him, all told him that the songs were true.

As the song faded away into silence he knelt, the shell held as carefully in his hands as if he held the true reality of the Vangavaye-ve and not just its representation.

The room thrummed with the expectancy of magic.

His Radiancy spoke the great question: "Cliopher Mdang, what do you offer us?"

Cliopher took a deep breath. His voice had to be clear enough to be heard to the back of the room though he faced the wrong direction for it.

"Lord of Rising Stars, I offer you in my hands the Vangavaye-ve."

"Cliopher Mdang, what is the Vangavaye-ve?"

"Lord of Rising Stars, the Vangavaye-ve is the home of my heart, the land of my birth, the anchorage of my soul."

That was not something he had said for the other sixteen provinces. His Radiancy gave no indication of the deviation from the ritual.

"Cliopher Mdang, what is the Vangavaye-ve?"

"Lord of Rising Stars, the Vangavaye-ve is the seventeenth of the provinces of Zunidh. You have given me this province with the other provinces to keep and to guard, to govern and to love."

"Cliopher Mdang, arise."

Cliopher rose.

Someone far away was ringing chimes, high-pitched and tuneful. Cliopher's eyes were focused on his Radiancy's face, on his Radiancy's brilliant gold eyes. There was no danger, he knew, not today, not with the magic in him, around him, behind him, before him.

They had gone through this ceremony. He knew what he was supposed to do. He had never—no one had ever—stepped above the lower daïs.

"Cliopher Mdang, approach."

He obeyed. He walked the five paces to the bottom of the three steps leading to the upper daïs on which the throne was placed. He paused a moment, while the chimes shimmered and someone started a trumpet fanfare.

"Cliopher Mdang, draw near."

Cliopher climbed up the three steps and sank down to his knees at the foot of the throne.

There was a complete silence now in the hall, the horns silent, the chimes silent, everything silent but for the pattering of Cliopher's pulse and the sound of his Radiancy's steady breathing.

His Radiancy looked straight in his eyes. "Cliopher Mdang, offer us your hands."

Cliopher was far from fear, far from the taboos. His gaze was held in golden brilliance. He reached forward—up—and around his trembling hands closed the beautiful long fingers of his beloved lord.

"Cliopher Mdang, we name you our Viceroy of Zunidh."

He heard the words. They were imprinted, he was sure, on his heart. Nothing had ever been so real as the words—except for the hands clasping his.

His Radiancy's hands were warm and dry. It was something else that was burning, pouring in a huge rush through him and into him and from him.

Fire in his eyes and in his hands and in his heart.

And through it all, behind it all, in it all, love, and amusement, and trust, and the singing of a soul crying out an affirmation to the gods.

In his heart echoing love, amusement, trust.

He felt the world standing around him in his Radiancy's mind, felt the magic of a world turned to listen to its master's voice, accepting his magic-blind self as worthy regent. He felt himself in his Radiancy's regard, the one solid rock in a tumultuous sea of responsibilities. The rock: vivid, strong, certain, sure.

Beloved came the assurance.

Good humour, running as a burbling current always through their interactions, the small interactions of friendship that took loyalty of vassal to lord and lord to vassal to some height beyond them as song was beyond speech.

And in and around and through the golden splendour of the Sun-on-

Earth, the hope that had been lost for so long now coming so close to fruition: the hope of the inner man, whose name was even so still shielded from him, that he might at last, at last, come out from behind that brilliant façade—or no, it was no façade—it was no mask—he was the Radiancy and he was the inner man, and dislocation between the two was so sharp and so wrong that Cliopher turned his hands so that instead of his being clasped by his Radiancy's his were on the outside.

His Radiancy caught the okana shell.

Cliopher gripped hard, as if through force he could create telepathy.

"I will not fail you."

He spoke the words aloud. He was not a wizard or a wild mage, though his heart was open as a shell on the beach.

His Radiancy smiled. The sun rose in Cliopher's eyes, but they were strong enough.

After a small silence, his Radiancy spoke very quietly. "Are you ready to go on?"

Cliopher considered, then nodded.

Without removing his hands or his eyes from his, his Radiancy lifted his voice. "Witness this, you people of the Vangavaye-ve. Cliopher Mdang of Tahivoa, whose island is Loaloa, whose dances are *Aōteketētana*, whose ancestral ship is the *Ouvaye-ve*, is our chosen Viceroy. Cliopher Mdang, Viceroy of Zunidh, make your declaration."

The Master of Ceremonies had given him numerous lessons on which titles he should use to address his Radiancy at this moment, but in the face of things they flew out of his mind, and Cliopher spoke the ones he had always loved best.

"Lord of Rising Stars, Sun-on-Earth, Last Emperor of Astandalas, Lord of Zunidh, I, Cliopher Mdang of Tahivoa of the Vangavaye-ve, do swear upon my soul and my heart and my life that I will keep this world of yours safe while you are absent and return it hale to you when you are come home."

His Radiancy released his gaze so he could look over Cliopher's head to the crowd gathered beyond.

"People of the Vangavaye-ve, you are his excellency's chosen witnesses. Witness this his oath: on his soul and his heart and his life he will protect and cherish this world of Zunidh for you and for us."

The tinkling chimes were starting again, very softly, as soft as the burbling humour running through the magic in their still-clasped hands.

And down in the hall Cliopher's mother started to sing the song of homecoming.

CHAPTER SEVENTY-NINE

CLIOPHER KNELT WHERE HE WAS, the tears streaming down his face, his hands in his Radiancy's, the ember flaring softly in the shell cupped between them.

Eidora had been called the finest soprano in the Ring. The last time she had sung in public had been when Cliopher left for Astandalas and she had sung the *Lament of Ani*.

He crouched there, at the feet of the Sun-on-Earth, as the great song of joy filled the hall.

> *O he returns*
> *Over the sea I see the sail*
> *O he returns*
>
> *My son who left for the morning*
> *My son who left to see the other side of the morning*
> *My son who left*

His mother's voice was true and glorious as ever. He had her heard sing before his Radiancy, in intimate chamber pieces, old folk songs, a few of the court pieces that had made their way to the Vangavaye-ve.

He could not turn. He knelt there, his hands trembling in his Radiancy's, as her voice soared up.

> *The sail comes over the horizon*
> *The ship that went to find the other side of the sky*
> *The ship that sailed to the country of the sun*

O he returns
Over the sea I see the sail
O my son returns

If the *Lament* was considered the first song, the *Tui-na*, the Song of Homecoming, was the one that had taught the people of the Wide Seas the gift of community. Vou'a, the god of mystery, raised up the first of the islands to show to Ani that her son Vonou'a was not lost in the underworld, and there on the most beautiful threshold between one world and another, between the sea and the land and the sky, she had sung first the *Lament* and then the *Tui-na*.

My son who left for the morning
My son who left to see the other side of the morning
My son who left
O he returns

And with each recurring passage, it was said, Ani in her joy had called up the islands to give him places to rest on his way home.

At the end of the song his Radiancy squeezed his hands gently.

Cliopher looked up and met the lion eyes through blurry vision. All he could see was gold and shadow and the pale hangings behind his Radiancy's head: white and black and gold, the colours of Astandalas.

In their hands the ember in the shell of the Vangavaye-ve, the ember of the sacred fire that must not be permitted to go out before a new fire was lit.

Cliopher took a deep breath. He slid his hands back around his Radiancy's so that he now cupped the shell. Very carefully he lifted himself back to his feet and backed down the stairs. At the bottom of the upper daïs he bowed over the shell, and at his Radiancy's nod turned to face the hall again.

Jiano stood to one side of the stairs down to the floor. The room was dim in its lower reaches, still striped with gold and orange and pink where the windows let in the sunset. The air was replete with wonder and admiration and, he dared think, approval.

He walked slowly and ceremoniously to the top of the stairs. He could feel the tears drying on his face.

This was his family. They all knew exactly how important that song was.

And this was the Vangavaye-ve. It was the court-trained part of him that thought that showing such deep emotion was improper. Islander culture did not think it shameful to show strong emotions. It was, in fact, considered the mark of a strong soul, one to be admired, when beauty or love or grief could call forth such powerful response.

The hall was as electric and alive with attention as it had been for Jiano. It was a very odd feeling to be its focus. Cliopher was not certain he would have relished it if he had not known and loved so many of those thus attentive. As it was, he had consciously to decide to step forward, to speak forth, and not return to his usual position beside the throne, the silent and impersonal Hands of the Emperor.

He had not prepared a speech. There had always been the opportunity for one, but he had thought he would be standing between Princess Oriana and his Radiancy, the audience very much spectators beyond her, their numbers perhaps greatly swelled by his family but not … not this. They were not merely spectators now, the people in the room. They had not been since they had answered the opening call of the *Lays* and in full-throated response claimed the ancient rights and responsibilities of the people before their Paramount Chief.

A lifetime in the court had taught him to keep his expressions muted, his emotions to himself, his passions channelled into his work and not his words.

He did not think he could sing. His voice was too thick with emotion. He had trained, over the past years as Lord Chancellor, in how to speak clearly and distinctly in a large room.

He said, "There is a story I have heard of three brothers, the sons of Vonou'a. One left to see what he could see on the other side of the horizon. One left to find his heart's desire. And one left to sit at the feet of the Sun and learn what he could."

The words were those that had been spoken to him by the seller of shells of Lesuia, who might have been Vou'a, according to his great-uncle and according to the old stories of the god of mysteries, who was something of a trickster. They fell into the hall as sparks falling from a fire down to the sand.

He held the shell up with its ember flaring in the dimming hall. He turned from side to side, following the pattern Jiano had set, and finished where he could look from his Radiancy to his family. "I went to sit at the feet of the Sun."

Ah, came a soft whisper from many voices.

"I went to sit at the feet of the Sun," he repeated. "I went to learn what I might learn, and from the house of the Sun I have brought home the fire."

He stepped carefully down the stairs. He walked to the table where his immediate family sat. Vinyë was staring at him. Ghilly met his gaze with the wondering speculative expression he knew so well, and then she reached to the centrepiece and lifted the unlit candle.

He bowed solemnly to her before taking the candle in his right hand. He touched its wick to the ember and blew softly until it lit.

When the candle was burning strongly he held it out. Bertie took it from him, with an expression almost as quizzical and wondering as Ghilly's. Cliopher smiled at him and returned at a ceremonious pace to the stairs and thence to the daïs. He displayed the okana shell and its ember once more to his Radiancy before turning again to the hall.

He saw first that Bertie had extended the candle to the next table over, and Quintus had used it to light theirs, and was even now reaching out to the next table over from him.

Cliopher used his free hand to touch the sundrop cowries, the *efevoa*. "When I stood in a market-place on Lesuia, out along the Eastern Ring in a village named for the Son of Laughter, I met a seller of shells. He asked me who I was: my name, my island, my dances. I answered him as I have answered you. I am Cliopher Mdang of Tahivoa. My island is Loaloa. My dances are *Aōteketētana*. He spoke next of the three brothers, the sons of Vonou'a."

He focused intently on the room, the soft movements and sounds as lit candle reached to unlit in a wave of wavering light.

"I thought of myself, of my cousins Basil and Dimiter who were close as brothers to me—and to some of you. Dimiter went to see what he could see, and perished looking for a land where no other human had ever walked before him. Basil went to find his heart's desire, and I do not know what became of him and his beloved wife in the years since the Fall of Astandalas. And I went to sit at the feet of the Sun, that I might bring home the fire."

The lit candles rippled. The pinpoints of light spread into a galaxy, as if Cliopher looked down from the high daïs of the throne room of the Palace of Stars over the sea of stars set into the jewelled floor.

From the sky ships across the Wide Seas the archipelagos were scattered too wide to see all at once, but he held them in his mind, in the pattern of the fire dance, in the maps intrepid cartographers had drawn, and he thought that perhaps to the Sun and the Moon looking down the islands of the world looked like the tables in the hall before him.

"The one who gave me these shells, the *efevoa*, whom my great-uncle the *tana-tai* named the Son of Laughter and the god of mysteries: he asked me what fire it was I would bring home."

He held up the okana shell again, the ember still flaring in its little nest of damp pandanus leaves. "I told him I would bring home the hearth-fire of a new life for the world."

There was a murmur of response to that from the people watching him, from his family and his friends who were the only ones whose opinions of himself he truly cared about.

"It will not, perhaps, seem very new to you, in the way that this ember, this shell, does not seem new to you. And yet." He looked at the shell in his hands, the shell the colour of his hands, light and fragile and so much more beautiful than the heavy gold replica Princess Oriana had given him.

"And yet, this shell is the new iteration of an ancient custom long since fallen into disuse. Princess Oriana presented the Sun-on-Earth, through me in my role as his Hands, with the gold replica of the okana shell that has been used as the Astandalan symbol of the Wide Seas and the Vangavaye-ve. Through me the Sun-on-Earth returned the gold okana to Jiano as the new Paramount Chief as a symbol of the authority which is being granted to him."

He took a deep breath. "I stand before you now not only the Hands of the Emperor, but as the Viceroy of Zunidh. In the swearing of fealty the Paramount Chief called forth the Singing of the Waters and presented me with the symbol of the Vangavaye-ve as he understands it: this okana shell and the ember that was lit from a fire that has been burning since our ancestors came out of the sunrise to find the home of music and the Mother of Islands."

Cliopher displayed the shell. He could see faces now, in the candlelight, all the intent, wondering, and yes, approving faces of his family.

"In the stories the fire of civilization, the laws and the *Lays*, was brought by the son of Vonou'a from the house of the Sun. It is the property of a fire that it can light another fire without itself being diminished. From fire to fire, from ship to ship, from family to family, the flame of the Sun has been tended and guarded by each *tanà*, each One Who Tends the Fire, until it comes to me in the shell that was used to represent the alliance of Elonoa'a, the last of our Paramount Chiefs, with Aurelius Magnus, the first of our Emperors.

"And so I return it to you, this fire that is the fire you know, but which has passed from your hands to those of our new Paramount Chief, and from his to mine, and mine to the Last Emperor's, and from the Last Emperor to me, and from me once more back to you."

Cliopher gestured ritually at the lit candles filling the hall below him.

"I am Cliopher Mdang of Tahivoa. My island is Loaloa. My dances are *Aōteketētana*. When I went to sit at the feet of the Sun—" He gestured at his Radiancy— "I took with me the songs and the dances of my family, my people, my home. The fire the son of Vonou'a brought here was the hearth fire of civilization, the laws and the *Lays* with which our ancestors build a community stretching over ten thousand years and the whole width of the Wide Seas.

"I took our fire back to the house of the Sun. I found the house cold, its hearth–fire nearly extinguished. I have built a new fire on the embers of the old. It may not seem altogether different to you, as I do not seem altogether different to you. I am the one who left, come home again with long stories of the sea to share with you.

"So the fire that I bring home is familiar: but like the light that shines now through this hall, it has travelled far and been shaped by many hands and many needs and lit many other hearths along the way."

He glanced down at the table where his mother sat, and his Buru Tovo beside her. His mother met his glance, her eyes brilliant with tears but her face brilliant with pride. His great-uncle was grinning.

Cliopher could not think why at first, and then he recalled the very ancient and little-practiced way that one was supposed to conclude the high ceremony of lighting a new hearth fire.

He hesitated.

But he had not come this far to stop here. If he claimed the fire ...

He took a deep breath. "The new fire is lit. The old fire does not go out in its lighting. We honour the fire that has been passed down to us, hand over hand through the years, each day a new fire, each day an old one. We honour our ancestors who brought us the fire and kept it safe for us. The new fire now is lit. Let the old fire return to the sea and the sky and the heart of the one who holds its dances. I am Mdang. I hold the fire: I do not run from its burn."

And since they did not stand by the sea or on the edge of a cliff and Cliopher had claimed in every possible way the *Aōteketētana*, he picked up the coal between the fingers and thumb of his right hand and before he could think too much about how his right hand and his tongue were the tools of his trade, he put the coal in his mouth and ate it.

Into a shocked and impressed silence Jiano struck down the ngali staff. "The fire is lit. Let the feast begin."

★★★

HIS FAMILY WERE ALREADY GATHERED by the time he extricated himself from the noble party on the daïs and made it to his rooms. He paused in the doorway to drink in the sight of them gathered there to celebrate with him.

They fell silent as they noticed his arrival. Face after face turned to smile at him. He might have felt uncomfortable with their regard on other occasions, might have felt embarrassed, but tonight he was exalted with magic and ritual and song.

"Thank you," he said simply. "Thank you for coming, for witnessing, for being here with me tonight, for giving me a splendid spontaneous rendition of the Singing of the Waters."

"Are you going to give us a speech?" Bertie called out from the back of the room. He lifted up a bottle of rum. "Or do you want a drink?"

Cliopher grinned. "Do you want a speech? I burned my tongue on that coal, so I think I'd prefer a drink. I should probably get changed."

Several people groaned. "Don't be absurd, Kip," Aunt Malania said, "we're still in our costumes, and we all want to ogle yours."

He looked down at the efela necklaces and the superlatively woven skirt. "It is lovely, isn't it?"

"Stop admiring yourself and come sit down so we can," Vinyë said, patting the space between her and Ghilly on the sofa. Someone passed him a drink and he sipped it with a sensation of utter contentment.

"You look transformed," Ghilly said.

"I feel high as a kite," he said, laughing easily. "All the potential magic of the past six months has suddenly——" He made a coming-together motion with his hands, nearly splashing his drink. "Oh, I'd better not spill dark rum all over this."

"Are you going to wear it again? Or just hang it on your wall to admire?"

"Shall I wear it to the Jubilee ceremonies when his Radiancy and I retire, do you think?"

Vinyë laughed. He laughed again, and they fell into easy conversation, jokes and debates swirling around the room, people breaking out into snatches of song.

He was so deeply euphoric that he did not notice his Radiancy's entry. He recognized his rich laugh rising above the other noises in the room. Pikabe and Ato were on duty by the door; Ludvic was talking with Quintus, Rhodin was deep in conversation with Enya. Conju could not have been far, he was sure, and his Radiancy—his heart almost broke with overflowing emotion—his Radiancy was happy.

Dora was not far away, and took advantage of his Radiancy's outburst of laughter to come up to him. "Hallo again, Lord Artorin," she said. "Can I come talk to you for a bit?"

"I would be very pleased, Sayina Dora," his Radiancy said, smiling brilliantly. "You've grown a great deal since I saw you last."

"Yes," she replied soberly. "Lord Artorin, Cousin Kip touched your hands."

"So he did. He has been—we both have been—undergoing many rituals and ceremonies to permit that to happen."

She looked at him very seriously. "Did it feel very strange? I have been thinking, it must be strange for you to touch someone, as it would be strange for us not to."

His Radiancy looked down at his hands for a moment, then across at Cliopher. He smiled again. "Yes, it was, but in a good way."

Dora nodded. "I don't quite understand why you had to do that. Was it a play?"

"Something like that. More like a temple ceremony."

"Did you get married? It looked like you got married."

There was a pause. His Radiancy looked at Cliopher, who must have appeared totally stunned given how heartily his Radiancy then started to laugh. "No, Sayina Dora, though the vows were as solemn and important as for a wedding. Let me explain."

He started to do so, with many gestures and many interpolated questions from Dora, who did not want to let the idea that it had been a kind of wedding go so easily. Cliopher decided there was no indication he had to worry about it and fell back into conversation with Bertie, who had replaced Vinyë beside him on the couch. Out of the corner of his eye he saw Dora get drawn away by Zemius and his Radiancy start speaking to Ghilly and her brother, who was an astronomer.

He and Bertie were reminiscing about studying for exams when his Radiancy's voice cut once more through the clamour.

"Cliopher!"

He looked up immediately. "My lord?"

"Can you find me five hundred thousand valiants?"

"Of course, my lord. When would you like them for?"

His Radiancy looked at him. "What if I said immediately?"

"The provincial treasury should have at least that much to hand, my lord," he said, wondering if he would be able to get up from the couch without falling over.

"Don't you wish to know what I want it for?"

Cliopher regretted the third—or was it the fourth?—rum cocktail Bertie had given him. He tried to focus his thoughts. "As you wish, my lord. There are sufficient funds in the discretionary account for any whim, but if it is for a purpose that falls under an established ministry project …"

"There you are," his Radiancy said to Ghilly's brother. "I'm sure Kip will be able to tell you if building a new telescope falls under a whim of mine or some other more serious activity."

Cliopher leaned back against the couch and said aloud, "I wonder if there's any coffee anywhere."

"Coffee *and* food," said Enya, appearing from nowhere with a plate containing lotus buns. "Also one of your staff wants to know if you want your oboe."

"I've been practicing," Cliopher said to no one in particular. "Not very often, but it's something."

"I'll take that as a yes," Enya said, and disappeared again.

He lost track of his Radiancy again, except that the music started in more earnest. Other people had brought instruments, and even those who were not very musical could sing the choruses of the old songs.

At one point Cliopher heard the plinking cascades of his Radiancy's harp, and felt his heart overflowing again with gratitude, that his family could make his Radiancy so happy, that he was so happy, that his Radiancy was happy, that his family was happy, that they were playing all sorts of things including all his favourites, that his efforts to make time for his oboe meant that he could keep up.

The last notes of one song led so naturally into one of Fitzroy Angursell's banned songs that he started to play it, realizing several incriminating bars in that only one other person was playing along.

He lowered the oboe and met the lion eyes as his Radiancy's fingers stilled on his harp. The room was full of the suppressed sounds of a large number of people trying very hard not to laugh.

Then his Radiancy said, "I am really not supposed to know those songs, but since my fingers have already betrayed me—" He shrugged and tossed back the sleeves of his court costume. "I feel it is a wasted day if I have not managed to discompose Kip at least once. Come, my friends, we shall announce an amnesty on Fitzroy Angursell's music tonight, and let us make merry in honour of the great statesman with the music of the great outlaw. There is something delicious about the whole idea."

And he set his hands to his harp and launched straight into the introduction to *Aurora*, which had been banned throughout five worlds on pain of death, and was regarded by pretty well everyone, including Cliopher, as the greatest work of poetry to come out of the Empire of Astandalas.

CHAPTER EIGHTY

ONE WEEK BEFORE HIS RADIANCY was due to leave he summoned Cliopher to his apartments. Once there, he drew him into his private study.

"I have been thinking," his Radiancy said, gesturing Cliopher down to the only available seat. The room was, if anything, even more spectacularly untidy than on Cliopher's one previous visit. His Radiancy had clearly been searching through the flotsam and jetsam of a long life to find what he considered necessities for his journey.

Cliopher had to admit he was deeply curious about just what, exactly, his Radiancy considered *necessary*, but this, alas, did not seem quite the right moment to ask.

"I have been making a bag like the one Fitzroy Angursell famously had—bigger on the inside than the outside—I do not wish to carry all the luggage Conju thinks I need to take."

"A wise decision," Cliopher said, with an internal sigh of relief that he would not have to keep acting as the buffer between Conju's anxieties and his Radiancy's. On this one matter, at least. He didn't even want to begin imagining what his Radiancy considered *too much* luggage.

"I have also been thinking—Kip—I don't—I don't know how to greet people."

Cliopher blinked at him. "I beg your pardon, my lord?"

His Radiancy made a gesture eloquent of frustration. "I watched you in the Vangavaye-ve, greeting your friends, your family, strangers. You were not bowing all the time—you clasped shoulders, embraced, hugged, kissed, touched foreheads, bowed over your hands—I have not—Kip, I haven't touched anyone! I don't know *how*."

Cliopher realized that it was the frustration, the embarrassment, the human uncertainty that had prompted his Radiancy to invite him within the private study. He took a deep breath. There was one week remaining in the

879

rituals, but even so … even so, he told himself firmly, he had undergone all the ceremonies of purification that he might touch his Radiancy's hands in the regency ceremonies.

"Here, my lord," he said, getting up and opening his arms slightly. "I will show you."

★★★

THE NIGHT BEFORE HIS RADIANCY left there was the official end of court and transfer of authority. His Radiancy made a speech, Cliopher replied with all the proper phrases the Master of Ceremonies had told him to say, and it was overall cold and important and boring and glitteringly magnificent and five hours long, as most court banquets were.

At noon of the appointed day his Radiancy performed the spell that would draw him to his successor. All the Palace bells rang, in the cascades Cliopher remembered from the day the Last Emperor awoke after the Fall. This time he was the non-wizard witness to the spell casting, watching intently as his Radiancy performed the casting of the yarrow and hammered the bells.

The spell snapped into place with a thrum that resonated in Cliopher's bones. It went on for some time, the great palace bells beside him picking up the note at a level just barely audible.

His Radiancy stepped with great care out of his circle. He scuffed the line of ochre and herbs with his foot to break it, observing as he did that the sensation of bare skin against floor was almost totally foreign.

Finally Cliopher could wait no longer. "And the spell, my lord?"

"It is cast. Oh, do you mean is there someone in the Palace? I have a strong sense that I must travel, and none that I must stay."

He sounded more doubtful than relieved. Cliopher looked at his lord, at the uncertainty on his face. He stood looking at his sandals as if they would bite him or jump magically onto his feet or disappear.

Cliopher went up to him and when his Radiancy turned his attention, slowly and cautiously grasped his arms in the Astandalan greeting.

"My lord," he said, "Tor."

"Kip … I am worried. What if I can't …"

His voice was very low. Cliopher waited, giving him the space to form the words. After a prolonged silence he said, still very quietly, "What if I am no longer anything more than the Last Emperor?"

Cliopher took a breath, then drew his Radiancy over to the bell-ringer's padded seat, away from the spell-circle and the Schooled magic his Radiancy did not like to perform. The guards were down at the bottom of the stairs, and after the thunderous cascade the bells would be silent until the first hour was struck.

"My lord," he said, "Tor. Last night I had a dream."

His Radiancy looked sidelong at him and said nothing.

Cliopher took his hand. His Radiancy's was warm and damp from his exertions. Cliopher said, "In my dream I came to the Moon's country looking for you. I was with other people, people I do not know, though Domina Black was there, and a pale-skinned man with hair the colour of crystallized honey."

"Blond," his Radiancy said, as if with an effort. "That colouring is called blond."

"Oh yes. I had forgotten the word."

His Radiancy mustered up a smile. His hand in Cliopher's trembled. "You, forgetful? Go on."

"We came to the Moon's country, and we found you in company with the Moon. She was gloating, exultant that you had come to her, that you were now hers. We—Domina Black, the blond man, and I, and the others who were there—we said you were not there of your own will, that she had enchanted you somehow, that you belonged with us. Perhaps the people—they were all different races—represented the peoples of your empire."

Cliopher had a pretty good idea of who the people were, although in his mind all but the two speakers had faded into indefinite outlines. He said, "The Moon was annoyed with us. Domina Black and the blond man were very insistent that she release you, and at last she said that if you chose to come, she would not stop you. Domina Black pushed the Moon until she swore by the River of Stars to release you if you asked."

"Even the gods can be forsworn, but they will not break their oaths on the River of Stars. They, too, are bound by fate."

"He went up to you first, the blond man. You were there, reclining on a divan like a Central eating couch, but you were not present in the room with us, as if you were drugged or enchanted or asleep and dreaming. The blond man went up to you and he called your name—"

"What name did he call?" his Radiancy said intently, sitting forward. His hand clutched Cliopher's tightly; he could feel his Radiancy's pulse increasing.

"In my dream I knew your true name." Cliopher stopped, rephrased himself carefully. "That is, my lord, in my dream I knew the name you named yourself. The blond man called your name, and in my dream I knew it for that name, your heart's name, but I do not now waking remember it."

His Radiancy closed his eyes and turned his head, pressed his lips together tightly. After a moment he looked again at Cliopher, his eyes brilliant with tears. "Go on."

"He called your name, and you roused, and we all rejoiced. He said, 'Come along, my friend—' But he used your name—'it's time to go. We have adventures waiting.' You smiled at him and said, 'Certainly, certainly, but first I must finish my dream,' and you sank back into the enchanted stupor.

"The blond man was very angry, but you did not rouse again for his words, just fluttered your hand and went back to your dreams. Domina Black went forward next, and she called your name, your true name, and spoke to you of many things—in my dream I understood some of them, but they are fading now—stories and poetry of old, songs she wanted you to sing. You roused a little for her, as you had for the blond man, but again you just smiled and said you would come after a while, when you were ready, and then once more you drifted away from us, even deeper into sleep.

"The Moon gloated and said that she had granted you unstinted pleasure and divine idleness, and nothing we mortals could offer you could compare. And that was when I—when I stepped forward. In my dream I was very angry, even angrier than Domina Black and the blond man, for they were calling your inward heart and the Moon was keeping you from hearing them. In my dream I knew more," he said, frowning as he tried to collect the fragments before they dissolved, though the dream stood sharp in his mind.

"I was angry. I strode forward and I said to the Moon, 'You shall not have him. Sloth and pleasure will destroy him. You offer him a false image of the good, a false reflection of his heart's desire. You may bedazzle him for a short time, but he will not stay with you of his own will.'

"She said, 'You are a fool, little man. What are you to come to my country? What poetry, what songs, what fire do you have in your heart? You do not understand me, and you cannot understand him. His love for what I offer him is greater than you can possibly begin to imagine.'

"I said, 'His love is as deep and as broad and as beautiful as the Wide Seas, but his honour is the bed of the ocean. His songs are as numerous as the birds of the air, but his honour is the wind that lifts their wings. His heart is as brilliant as the Moon in her glory, but he is the Sun-on-Earth, and his honour is greater. And I am a Wide Sea Islander of Zunidh, and I know my way by the fire and the songs and the poetry of my ancestors.'"

His Radiancy's hand gripped his so tightly Cliopher felt his circulation might be cut off. "What then? What happened then?"

"Then I knelt by your side and I asked you a question about the Nijani police service."

His Radiancy choked out a laugh. "You didn't!"

"I did, my lord, I swear to you. In my dream I knelt there and asked you a question. You roused, but not smiling as you had for Domina Black or the blond man, you roused frowning, and tried to turn away from answering. But I did not let you, I kept talking, I kept asking you for details, I kept pushing—"

"I am familiar with that habit."

Cliopher ducked his head, smiling ruefully. "Sometimes I must pin you down, my lord, when you do not wish to continue on a topic."

"And in your dream …"

"And in my dream I did so. You kept trying to return to your dreams, and I kept spinning out more and more complex problems out of the Nijani police service, and finally you threw off the blanket over your legs and you jumped up and you thundered at me that you had given me full authority and by the River of Stars I should take it, and stop *pestering* you about things I knew very well were my job."

"And then? What then?"

"You stood there, shouting at me, then looked around and saw Domina Black and the others, and frowned in puzzlement to see them there with me, and you looked around again and saw that we were not in the Palace, and you said: 'What is the meaning of this?'"

His Radiancy frowned even more intently. "What did you reply? What were the words, Kip? This is very important."

Cliopher took a breath. "I said, in my dream I said, 'My lord—' and then I said your true name, your inner name—'my friend, this is a moment of choice. The Moon offers you immortality and eternal youth and divine pleasure.' You frowned at me, and looked uncertainly back across to the Moon, and then I said, 'I offer you the Nijani police service and the Prince of Southern Dair's costumes, Jiano's attempts to overthrow his own throne, the Palace of Stars waiting for your return, and a world wanting to say thank you before you give them someone new to love.'

"The Moon said, 'Don't be absurd! What can those things mean to him?'

"And I said, 'They mean the common and ordinary good of duty honourably fulfilled, of love occasionally accompanied by quarrels, of friendships that will not fail, of a home filled with laughter and music and family.'

"She said, 'What are those things to the Lord of Rising Stars?'"

"And you said, 'Everything,' and came with us."

★★★

FROM THE BELL TOWER HIS Radiancy went back to his apartments and changed his clothing into a plain linen tunic and ordinary sandals. The ritual requirements permitted him to carry one small bag and to have one outer garment. Lady Ylette had fashioned a sweeping mantle, something like the Amboloyan garment but apparently from a different part of the Empire, in a splendid scarlet silk.

"Are you not worried about standing out too much?" Cliopher asked as she and Conju draped it lovingly around his Radiancy.

They were in his public study. His Radiancy glanced up at the portrait of himself on the wall in all his Imperial finery. He ran his hands down the silk, making a fine susurrus. He wore only his signet ring of his usual jewellery, and the bag he carried was a plain leather thing that looked much like a physician's workbag.

"No one is going to expect me," he said at last. He glanced once more around the room. His gaze stayed on the tapestry map, on the gems representing the cities of his Empire, the great embroidered continents of five worlds, and his eyes lit with a quiet anticipation.

Cliopher said no more. Conju was weeping, Ludvic and Rhodin very stern, Ylette scowling furiously. She stayed behind as the rest of them made their way through the service hallways to one of the back doors of the Palace, rarely used by anyone but lower servants.

"I have never been this way before," his Radiancy said as they left the central block to walk down the length of the Voonran wing. "There are so many things I have not done."

Conju wiped his eyes. Cliopher swallowed hard. His Radiancy did not look at them, had his eyes forward, gazing eagerly at each new portion of the hall.

They came at last to the exit. Cliopher had arranged with the Mistress of the Lower Staff that no one was to use it this afternoon. The hallway terminated at the door, which was painted blue and had a small round window at head level.

Ludvic said, "Shall I open the door for you, my lord?"

His Radiancy said, "I must cross the threshold alone." He turned to Conju first and with gentle, almost hesitant movements, reached forward and clasped his upper arms. "Be at ease, Conju. I am not so delicate as you fear, and you have prepared my belongings well."

"Oh my lord, I will miss you!"

His Radiancy swallowed. "And I you. But this is something I must do myself."

"I know, my lord," Conju whispered. His Radiancy released him and turned to Rhodin, who saluted gravely.

"Be well, Rhodin. I have listened carefully to your directions for how to choose places to eat. I will enjoy telling you of them when I return."

Rhodin saluted again, eyes brilliant but motions crisp and perfect as ever.

His Radiancy turned to Ludvic, whose arms still bore the golden scars and always would. Ludvic also saluted, then dropped his hand when his Radiancy reached for it. "Ludvic, you have guided and guarded me from the beginning of my reign as Lord of Zunidh till now, as we come to its end. Keep as good a guard over Cliopher for me, that I may rest easy knowing he is safe."

"I will, my lord."

At last he turned to Cliopher, who stood closest to the door. His Radiancy regarded him solemnly for a moment, then walked forward to embrace him.

"I know you will keep Zunidh safe and sound for me," his Radiancy said, leaning forward until his forehead touched Cliopher's in the Islander greeting. "Do not neglect yourself in so doing. I want you to have many years to enjoy your family and your friends in peace and good health afterwards."

Cliopher bit his lip until the lump in his throat subsided. "Thank you, my lord."

His Radiancy took his bag from Conju and slung it over his shoulder. Conju fussed a moment with the fall of the mantle, then stepped back, tears running silently down his face. His Radiancy set his hand to the handle on the door and opened it. He stood still a moment, looking out at the narrow path curving through the gardens towards the city, the sun burning copper-gold in the west over the Grey Mountains and the sea still gleaming to the east, the Moon just rising. He looked back at Cliopher.

"No final words, Kip?"

Cliopher felt a great rush of endearment welling up. "Have fun."

And his Radiancy laughed as he set his face to the sun and stepped alone across the threshold of his Palace for the first time.

EPILOGUE

THE SUM OF ALL THINGS

EPILOGUE

CLIOPHER LOOKED UP FROM HIS novel to see Gorjo City blazing like a fire opal below him.

He put the book down and watched.

The entirety of the Eastern Ring was washed in sunset, pink and orange and yellow, waterfalls cascading fire. The Bay of the Waters looked like the sheets of molten gold Cliopher had seen in the refineries of Amboloyo, the evening flights of birds gilt froth. Gorjo City itself added pinpoints of human-made light to the brilliant tints of the sunset.

The ship moved in wide spirals as it descended towards the Spire leaping up like an ivory spear. The air rising against his face was warm and cool by turns as the ship dropped nearly imperceptibly between the layers of the winds. When it was cool it was scented with the wild clarity of the air above the Wide Seas; when it was warm it was redolent of flowers whose Islander names teased at his memory but whose images came readily to mind. Scarlet, white, orange, pink, purple as the shadows cast by the Western Ring across the Bay.

And down they went, and down, in circles so that they could take in the sunset itself, spread across the west with gestures broad enough to paint half the world, and the effect of the sunset on the Vangavaye-ve as the sun moved behind the encircling islands.

The ship heeled, slowed, heeled again. The sailors in the rigging called to one other. The sound of the air changed as they shifted the angle of the sails against the wind.

There was one perfect view down of the lights of the city coming on star-like across the darkening waters. Then the ship curved away, and Cliopher's view was once again to the Outer Ring and the stars sprinkling across the pale blue and pink sky.

He took several deep breaths, and then turned smiling to Ludvic, who sat beside him.

★★★

CAPTAIN DIOGEN WALKED CLIOPHER AND Ludvic to the gangway across to the Spire. Cliopher looked at the rope and slat bridge and felt the memory of fear stir, but not the fear itself. He was glad, and nearly missed what the captain was saying. "Oh, yes, of course," he said vaguely. "The first hour after dawn."

"That's when we leave," Captain Diogen said. "You're always so punctual, m'lud, but in this instance ..."

"I'll pay attention," Ludvic said, even as Cliopher, eyes on the city, started across the gangway. "We'll be back in time."

"I think I understand how his Radiancy felt when we came here on holiday," Cliopher said as they went past the Light Minders' office and an official came out of the other one to see who they were. "Feeling truant. Oh, good evening, Cousin Cedric," he said to the officer, who stopped to gawp at him.

"Kip!—er, your excellency, that is. I thought you weren't coming?"

"It was a bit last-minute," Cliopher said, adjusting the fall of his upper garment. He'd left the heavy middle layer in his cabin on the ship, after a discussion with Ludvic about whether it was better to be absurdly overdressed or excessively underdressed had made him start laughing at the thought of his family's general sentiments about his clothing; but he could not go down to a party in Captain Diogen's extra trousers and nothing else. "We'll be leaving again in the morning, I'm afraid. I'm just hoping I don't miss all the party at Enya's new restaurant."

"They were starting at sundown, so I doubt it," Cedric replied. "I'll be down later—I was just finishing up some paperwork, but I guess I'll have a bit more to do for your ship. Hola, Captain!" he added, then smiled at Cliopher. "Everyone will be so thrilled to see you, Kip. I'm glad you could come."

Cliopher was still smiling as they made their way down the tight spirals of the stair. He found himself moving lightly, not feeling the creaks he had on other occasions. "I'm so happy to be here," he confessed to Ludvic, gesturing through a window at the lights around them. "I feel lighter."

"Losing that robe must help," Ludvic replied. "It must weigh fifteen pounds."

★★★

ENYA'S NEW RESTAURANT WAS LOCATED in a prime position, right on the waterfront with a splendid view back towards the brilliantly-lit palace. Cliopher paused a moment at the door to take in the sight, familiar but yet not.

Jiano had made changes to the illuminations, so that the palace's beauty was highlighted. Lights glimmered in the park around it, and he wondered if Jiano had made them open to the public.

After a moment he turned in the door, where he was immediately stopped by a very grand personage who appeared to be the door-warden.

"The restaurant," this man said pompously, "is hosting a private event. Do you have an invitation?"

His voice suggested that this was inconceivable. Cliopher had, of course, received a written invitation; equally *of course* he had left it with the rest of his things in his room at the Grand Hotel in Zangoraville. "Well," he began, smiling apologetically, "I'm afraid I left my card at home. However, I'm—"

"It doesn't matter *who* you are," the man said even more pompously. "Only those with invitations are being admitted."

Cliopher stared at him a moment, nonplussed. "Really? That seems unlike Enya. I'm her cousin—"

"A *velio?*" the man made a magnificent snort.

Beside him he could feel Ludvic vibrating, though whether with suppressed laughter or indignation he wasn't sure. Cliopher gave up on the direct approach as the door-warden snubbed him (even more magnificently) in order to take the invitation cards of several people whom he didn't know. He tried to see if there was anyone he knew in hailing distance, but the door-warden moved his body to block the doorway.

"I cannot believe I came all this way only to be snubbed at the door," Cliopher murmured to Ludvic. "If worse comes to worst, when Cedric comes down he can vouch for me—everyone else will already be inside, I expect."

"Is there another way in?"

"Almost certainly, but I don't know this building, I'm afraid. Do you think we—"

But whether Ludvic would have recommended a spot of housebreaking, Cliopher did not know, for just then Quintus came loping up to the door-warden, who started to fawn.

"Quintus!" Cliopher called before his cousin could disappear, hastening forward.

Quintus stopped and stared at him for a disconcertingly long moment, then actually genuflected.

Cliopher felt his jaw drop and hastily closed it. "Quintus, you really don't have to do that. Will you vouch for me to the door-warden? I'm afraid I came in great haste and neglected to bring my invitation with me, and he's refusing to let me in."

"There are all sorts of *velioi* here now," the door-warden muttered darkly, though it was clear he was shaken by Quintus' courtesy. "You don't know what they're about."

Quintus grinned at him. "Hoby, despite his clothing, haircut, accent, and general demeanour, this is actually my infamous Cousin Kip, who was nearly the first person Enya asked to come to this event."

"They look like they stole costumes out of a play," the door-warden said, even more darkly.

Cliopher looked at Quintus, who was grinning, then at Ludvic, whose face was unreadable. "I think that's a first for me. I don't generally have that actor's charisma."

Quintus laughed. The door-warden scowled, but opened the door for them. A wall of sound came out to meet them.

It had been a long time since he had been a participant in such a crowd. Cliopher hesitated on the edge of the throng, looking for those he knew—which was, admittedly, many of them—thinking with some amusement how unexpectedly accustomed he had become to being the observer or the observed in such a gathering. Outside the throng, in any case. Ludvic stood behind him, solid and comforting. Quintus had plunged in without waiting, presumably assuming that Cliopher would plunge in equally easily.

After a moment he got a sense of the movements of this particular gathering, how people were eddying to and from three different points deeper in. One would be the food, and another the drinks, and the third was likely either Enya herself or the elders, who would be seated in a place of honour. There seemed to be more people with food on the left, and drinks on the right, so he made for the centre.

"We'll see if we can find my mother," Cliopher said to Ludvic, who nodded as if this was perfectly reasonable.

He found the food first. Or rather, one plate of it, but since this contained Enya's superlative crab cakes he made no bones about taking two from the waiter, who said, "What a splendid outfit that is, Cousin Kip! Did you just get here?"

"Thank you, and yes," Cliopher replied, not at all sure who this was but presuming it was someone's son, grown since their last encounter. There was no time for any further conversation, for a knot of people on his other side turned, saw the crab cakes, and descended en masse on the waiter. He smiled at Ludvic, who had shaken his head at the offer of a crab cake, and began proceeding along his original path as best he could. Snatches of conversation and laughter washed over him, and the many scents of food and perfume and drinks and bodies, all so much more homely than similar events at the Palace.

He found a more-or-less quiet corner next to a pillar to eat the crab cakes and survey this portion of the crowd. He had yet to find anyone he deeply wanted to have a conversation with, though had caught glimpses of any number of more distant relatives. But where had Quintus gotten to? Or Vinyë, or Galen, or Bertie, or anyone?

"This seems to be quite the event," said a familiar voice, seemingly in his ear. Cliopher turned, smiling, only to see that Bertie was standing on the other side of the pillar talking to Enya.

"Yes, I am very pleased," Enya replied. "I think everyone came."

"Everyone in the city, it looks like!"

She laughed. "Well, everyone except Kip, alas. I got a letter from him yesterday apologizing that he couldn't make it after all."

"He's a very busy man," said Bertie. "But I know he was trying hard to get home for this."

"I always wonder what he's eating, way off on the other side of the world," Enya said thoughtfully.

Cliopher decided he had eavesdropped long enough; any longer and he was likely to hear something he'd prefer not to have. "Very rarely anything as good as these truly excellent crab cakes," he said, stepping forward to catch their attention and capture Enya in an embrace. "Congratulations, my dear," he added to her. "This seems well on its way to being a triumph."

"Kip," she said, holding his hand as if she couldn't quite believe he was there. "We were just—I just got your letter saying you weren't going to make it!"

"Tease," rumbled Bertie.

Cliopher laughed. "No, I really didn't think I could. I am playing truant!"

"What's this I hear?" said Vinyë, turning around to join their conversation. "Surely it can't be the sound of my brother's laugh? Kip!"

"That sentence seems to have gone in the wrong direction," he said, embracing her. "Oh, Vinyë, it's lovely to see you."

She held him out at arm's length. "Whereas you, my dear, look magnificent in every sense of the word."

He flushed, seeing Ludvic (Ludvic!) suppress a smile. "I was limited in my clothing choices."

"No! I don't believe it."

"I had jealously guarded this week clear in my schedule so I could come," he explained. "I arranged to hold court in Nijan, to cut the journey time, but that was a mistake as they'd had the most dreadful series of crimes they wanted me to judge. These are my robes of judgment—well, two-thirds of them. I had very reluctantly decided I had to stay and was in the middle of the court case when the chief plaintiff's lawyer tripped and broke his leg."

"Oh dear," said Vinyë.

"Was it foul play?" asked Bertie.

Cliopher shrugged. "I adjourned the court for three days so they could start looking into it. When we came out of the court, that is, Ludvic and Pikabe and I, we walked along the crest of the hill towards the place where I was staying. As we came past the bottom of the Spire Captain Diogen came out and asked if I were coming after all. I asked him if there was enough time to get here for this, Enya, and he said that if we left within the next ten minutes we could. And so … I did!"

They all stared at him. His sister cleared her throat. "*You* just got on and left?"

"I'm feeling very proud of myself," he said, grinning. "I did. That's why Gaudy's not here—I didn't have enough time for anything but to send Pikabe to the hotel to tell everyone where I'd gone. Ludvic and I climbed up the Spire and got on the ship and Captain Diogen set sail, and we promptly realized we hadn't brought any clothing or things to work on or anything. I had to borrow Captain Diogen's spare trousers."

"And his books," Ludvic rumbled. "There's a drink."

"I didn't even bring my writing kit," he said, claiming one of the cocktails a passing waiter presented him with. "Thank you. Did you have one, Vinyë? Anyhow, I read three of Aya's novels, one right after another, and slept for most of the day, and I do indeed feel quite magnificent."

"You sound as if you've just gone off marauding with the Red Company."

He laughed at his sister. "That'll have to wait until after I've retired, I expect. Anyhow, I left the main part of this costume on the ship—overdressed is one thing, in the full regalia of judgment is quite another. I'll have to go back in the morning, I'm afraid, so don't go off to bed without saying good-bye later."

"This is not a night where anyone is going to be going off to bed," Enya said, with great satisfaction, and cried a pleased greeting to a friend who'd caught her eye.

***

HE SPOKE WITH BERTIE AND Vinyë for a few minutes next to the pillar before Quintus found them. Then Galen came sweeping by with a bottle of wine, and in talking to him Cliopher was swirled from party to party until he ended up once more beside Enya, who was talking now to two pale-skinned Amboloyans.

"Cousin Kip, this is Fina and Tara. They're the ones with the vineyard on Looenna. Oh—yes, Maura, I'm coming!" and with a smile she swept out into the crowd.

Cliopher smiled at Fina and Tara. Tara was staring at him in astonishment. At first he presumed that this was for his presence at that party, or possibly his costume, but then she cried, "I don't believe it! Are you truly the infamous Cousin Kip?"

Quintus had also described him to the door-warden as *infamous*. Cliopher wondered what, exactly, had happened to occasion this. Surely it wasn't only that they now had all the proper official proclamations? "Yes," he said. "Dare I ask why I'm infamous?"

Tara blushed. Fina patted her fondly on the arm and answered. "We were beginning to think 'Cousin Kip' was a prank the wider Mdang family was playing on us. Every time we ask someone a question, they answer, 'Oh, Cousin Kip'—or so-and-so's Cousin Kip—'would know the answer to that'. But whenever we ask about you directly, they just say to write to you and then sigh and give us the answer themselves. So we started to think he didn't really exist." She laughed. "I do apologize. It's lovely to meet you at last."

"Likewise," he said, and then, curiously. "Didn't anyone tell you I don't live here?"

"They pointed out a house they said was yours," Tara said.

"And a boat," added Fina. "A very Islander boat."

Cliopher laughed, hard enough that the tears started in his eyes. "I'm sorry," he gasped presently. "I ... I'm not sure what to say. What sort of questions were you asking? Did you have any that weren't answered?"

They looked at each other. "I think we just had one about a trading partnership we were wondering about forming. We wanted to work with some friends of ours from back home in Amboloyo and some cousins of theirs who live on Alinor. No one's been able to give us a straight answer about how we even begin with that."

"I can, at least, help with that," he said, turning automatically for his writing kit and then feeling slightly foolish when he realized that only Ludvic stood with him. He masked his movement by greeting a random cousin and taking a drink. "Right. The proper procedure is to write to the relevant mundial department. In this case, you could write to either Interprovincial or Intermundial Trade."

Fina nodded earnestly. "Of course, there is a ministry for intermundial trade. I'd forgotten."

"They're not very big."

Tara frowned. "Do we need—I don't know. Do we need to write to any-one specifically? Will our letter actually get anywhere?"

Cliopher had spent a considerable amount of time and effort refining this particular sequence of events and procedures. He explained what usually hap-pened in such a case, finishing up with, "To save myself half an hour of time and you approximately six months of waiting, please send your query directly to the Offices of the Lords of State, and I will deal with it as soon as possible."

Tara and Fina stared at him. "Um, who *are* you?"

He grinned as he caught sight of Clia making her way through the crowds towards him with Toucan pressed behind her. "Everyone's Cousin Kip. Hullo, Clia. You look splendid."

"And you look utterly magnificent!" She reached out a gentle hand to touch the fabric of the sweeping over-mantle. "I don't think I've ever actu-ally seen someone wearing ahalo cloth before. I remember that bolt coming through. Such a subtle pinkish-bronze."

"It's like an okana shell," Cliopher replied.

She picked up the trailing end with its heavy fringe of pearls. "I was try-ing to see how it was staying put draped over your shoulder like that, but now I can see it's because it's dripping with thousands of pearls."

"One thousand four hundred and seventy-two," he replied, amused at the Amboloyans' continuing bemusement and knowing he should explain what he did at some point. "One for each of the laws in the Criminal Code."

"And how many of those are you personally responsible for?" Toucan asked.

"Forty-three."

Toucan laughed and clasped his hands in the old greeting. "Oh, I've missed you, Kip. I didn't think you were coming?"

Cliopher explained about how he was playing truant. Toucan laughed until he snorted wine out his nose. Clia had not been attending to his words, but still examining what she could easily reach of his costume. Finally she said, "I'm so glad to see you wearing it, Kip. You look magnificent."

"Thank you. I've been exercising more, which helps, but you must know most of the credit goes to my costumier—and to you and your cooperative, you know. You must be working hard?"

She laughed. "No, it's a quiet season—as you should know! No one's ordering new court clothes with the Last Emperor away."

"Yes, but surely you're starting to stockpile in readiness for the Jubilee celebrations and the new Lady?"

"It'll be a lady?" Toucan asked intently. "Have you heard from your lord?"

Cliopher smiled, but did not have a chance to explain the one letter he'd so far received from his Radiancy (and which had been largely an account of how appreciative his Radiancy was in Cliopher's foresight in arranging funds to be available to him at various banks on Alinor, Voonra, and Colhélhé; which made Cliopher rather suspicious as to what his Radiancy was actually doing) before he was interrupted by a bell ringing loudly.

The chattering crowds fell silent and turned to face a point not too distant from where they stood. Jiano leaped up onto some sort of platform, looking young and virile and very much an Islander chieftain. He grinned at everyone, then caught sight of Cliopher through the crowd and started to laugh.

"Ah!" he said. "It's time for the formal opening of this restaurant. It was going to be my great honour and privilege to perform the ceremony, but I have just seen through the throngs a much more appropriate personage to do the honours." He beckoned at Cliopher, who sighed, smiled, and made his way, Ludvic behind him, to the platform.

It was an actual stage, he was relieved to see (and not simply a table, as he had at first thought), with stairs. He climbed up and stood a little self-consciously beside Jiano.

"This is a man who needs very little introduction," Jiano announced, "but for those few people in this room who are neither related to him nor his close friends, let me do so. Around here he is generally known as one of the many Mdangs' famous Cousin Kip, but in the rest of the world he is much better known as his excellency Cliopher Lord Mdang, the Viceroy of Zunidh. Lord Mdang!"

There was an actual wave of applause. Cliopher looked at Jiano, who did not look apologetic in the least as he jumped off the platform, and then turned to the room, where he could see the two Amboloyans looking completely stunned.

"Thank you, Paramount Chief," he replied, and settled himself into his formal role. "It is indeed a pleasure, an honour, and a privilege to be standing here and invited to perform the ceremony of opening. I have done so for many places in the world, and stood beside my lord, the Last Emperor, for many more, but this is the first time I have done so in the Vangavaye-ve."

There was another round of applause. Cliopher wondered who was starting it; he thought it might have been Bertie, who was grinning wickedly up at him.

"Usually before such a ceremony I, or one of my secretaries, would do some research into the background of what is being opened. In this case I did not do so, though I'm sure that if I had I would have learned something worth knowing about my cousin Enya."

He paused and searched the crowd until he could see her, standing not far from the bottom of the platform and looking torn between delight and embarrassment at all the attention.

"As I travelled here I remembered an occasion from when she was very young. We were taken out to a restaurant for a meal—it was the first time she had ever been to one. I enjoyed it, but what I recall most clearly is how fascinated Enya was with the whole idea of the place."

He smiled at her. "Before we left she declared to us all that one day she would have a restaurant of her own. Everyone teased her about it. Enya said that it would be in the most beautiful place in all the world, that it would serve the best food in all the world, and that she would be the chef and our cousin Galen would do all the rest of the work."

A ripple of laughter went through the room. Cliopher gestured around. "It would be hard to find a more beautiful location than a place with a view across the harbour to the palace and the university and the lit gardens of Gorjo City of the Vangavaye-ve."

There was a murmur of agreement, as people turned to take in the view through the glass windows running along half the wall.

Cliopher nodded. "As for the cooking: Enya, I have eaten at the table of the Last Emperor of Astandalas. Moreover, he has eaten at yours. I am partial: you cook the foods I like best. But his Radiancy has spoken of what you made him months and years after the meal, and I can tell you that few indeed are the dishes that he requests twice."

Enya had lifted her hand to her mouth. Galen slung his arm around her shoulders and hugged her tightly.

Cliopher raised his glass. "Not everyone achieves their dreams—let alone the dreams they thought up when they were six-year-olds learning about the wider world around them for the first time. Enya, I salute you. And in the name of the Sun-on-Earth ..." He moved smoothly into the formal ceremony, which tied all the little magics of the building into those of the wider world.

When he stepped down off the platform it was to find his Uncle Lazo waiting for him. Cliopher bowed over his hands.

Uncle Lazo tilted his head to regard him. Cliopher waited patiently, knowing he had the whole night to talk to everyone, knowing that everyone knew he was here now and would not leave without coming to greet him.

Finally his uncle smiled and took his arm. "Come sit with me, Kip. I have some questions for you."

Cliopher had never before been invited to sit with the uncles—let alone beside his Uncle Lazo. "Oh?"

Uncle Lazo, of course, knew exactly what he was thinking. He grinned. "Yes. I want you to tell me about this fire you've lit to change the world."

And Cliopher, walking by his side through the crowd who watched him with curious and proud and pleased (and amazed) eyes, took a deep breath, and with a singing heart began to explain the principles of the Great Plan, which he had developed from those fundamental teachings of the proper relations between people and communities he had long ago been taught from the *Lays*.

AUTHOR'S NOTE

The Hands of the Emperor is a standalone novel set within a wider sequence of books about the Nine Worlds. Currently available are several short stories and novellas about the Red Company (including *In the Company of Gentlemen, The Tower at the Edge of the World,* and stories of the Sisters Avramapul, *The Bride of the Blue Wind* and *The Warrior of the Third Veil*).

There is also another standalone novel about the Lord of Ysthar and the end of the Great Game Aurieleteer, *Till Human Voices Wake Us,* and the Greenwing & Dart series of mysteries and comic misadventures set on Alinor (*Stargazy Pie, Bee Sting Cake*, and *Whiskeyjack* are currently available, with *Blackcurrant Fool* coming next). Keen-eyed readers might spot a couple of cross-over characters between *The Hands of the Emperor* and the Greenwing & Dart books.

CPSIA information can be obtained
at www.ICGtesting.com
Printed in the USA
LVHW041534020723
751376LV00009B/43/J